THE
CHILDREN
OF
THE SKY

BOOKS BY VERNOR VINGE

ZONES OF THOUGHT SERIES

*A Fire Upon the Deep**
*A Deepness in the Sky**
*The Children of the Sky**

*Tatja Grimm's World**
*The Witling**
*The Peace War**
*Marooned in Realtime**
True Names . . . and Other Dangers (collection)
Threats . . . and Other Promises (collection)

Across Realtime
comprising:
The Peace War
"The Ungoverned"
Marooned in Realtime

*True Names and the Opening of the Cyberspace Frontier**
*The Collected Stories of Vernor Vinge**
*Rainbows End**

*Available from Tor Books

THE
CHILDREN
OF
THE SKY

VERNOR VINGE

TOR®

A TOM DOHERTY ASSOCIATES BOOK

NEW YORK

THE CHILDREN OF THE SKY

Edited by James Frenkel

Map by Ellisa Mitchell

A Tor Book
Published by Tom Doherty Associates, LLC
175 Fifth Avenue
New York, NY 10010

www.tor-forge.com

Tor® is a registered trademark of Tom Doherty Associates, LLC.

Library of Congress Cataloging-in-Publication Data

Vinge, Vernor.
    The children of the sky/Vernor Vinge.—1st ed.
        p. cm.
    "A Tom Doherty Associates book."
    ISBN 978-0-312-87562-6 (hardback)
    1. Life on other planets—Fiction.   I. Title.
    PS3572.I534C47 2011
    813'54—dc22

                                2011024210

First Edition: October 2011

Printed in the United States of America

0   9   8   7   6   5   4   3   2   1

To Carol D. Ward and Joan D. Vinge

ACKNOWLEDGMENTS

I am grateful for the advice and help of:

David Brin, John Carroll, Cyndi Chie, Howard L. Davidson, Robert Fleming, Mike Gannis, Cherie Kushner, Keith Mayers, Sara Baase Mayers, Tom Munnecke, Diana Osborn, and Mary Q. Smith.

I am very grateful to my editor, James Frenkel, for all the time he has put into this book. Jim and Tor Books have been very patient with me in the long process of creating *The Children of the Sky*. (I know I said that about my last novel—but this one was about four times as much work.)

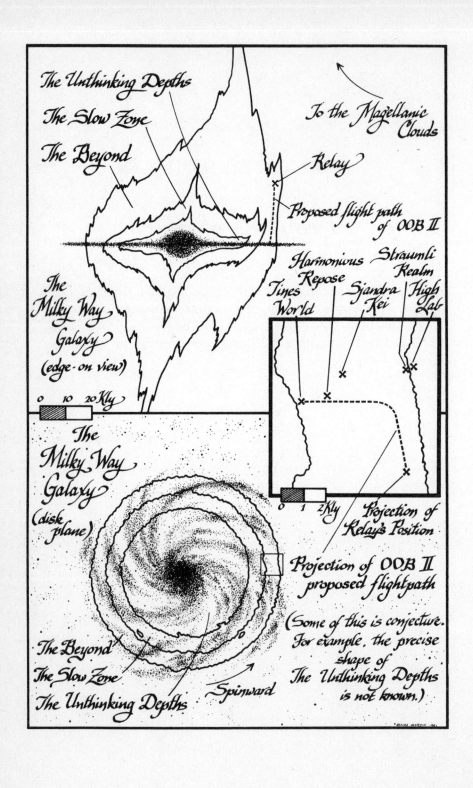

The Unthinking Depths

The Slow Zone

The Beyond

To the Magellanic Clouds

Relay

Proposed flight path of OOB II

The Milky Way Galaxy (edge-on view)

0   10   20 Kly

Harmonious Repose

Straumli Realm

Tines World

Sjandra Kei

High Lab

The Milky Way Galaxy (disk plane)

0   1   2 Kly

Projection of Relay's Position

The Beyond
The Slow Zone
The Unthinking Depths

Spinward

Projection of OOB II proposed flight path

(Some of this is conjecture. For example, the precise shape of The Unthinking Depths is not known.)

Two years after the
Battle on Starship Hill

CHAPTER 00

How do you get the attention of the richest businessperson in the world?

Vendacious had spent all his well-remembered life sucking up to royalty. He had never dreamed he would fall so low as to need a common merchant, but here he was with his only remaining servant, trying to find a street address in East Home's factory district.

This latest street was even narrower than the one they had left. Surely the world's richest would never come here!

The alley had heavy doors set on either side. At the moment, all were closed, but the place must be a crowded madness at shift change. There were posters every few feet, but these were not the advertisements they had seen elsewhere. These were demands and announcements: WASH ALL PAWS BEFORE WORK, NO ADVANCE WAGES, EMPLOYMENT APPLICATIONS AHEAD. This last sign pointed toward a wide pair of doors at the end of the alley. It was all marvelously pompous and silly. And yet . . . as he walked along, Vendacious took a long look at the crenellations above him. Surely that was plaster over wood. But if it was real stone, then this was a fortified castle hidden right in the middle of East Home commercialism.

Vendacious held back, waved at his servant to proceed. Chitiratifor advanced along the alley, singing praise for his dear master. He had not quite reached the wide doors when they swung open and a hugely numerous pack emerged. It was nine or ten and it spread across their way like a sentry line. Vendacious suppressed the urge to look up at the battlements for signs of archers.

The huge pack looked at them stupidly for a moment, then spoke in loud and officious chords. "Employment work you want? Can you read?"

Chitiratifor stopped singing introductory flourishes, and replied, "Of course we can read, but we're not here for—"

The gatekeeper pack spoke right over Chitiratifor's words: "No matter. I have application forms here." Two of it trotted down the steps with scraps of paper held in their jaws. "I will explain it all to you and then you sign. Tycoon pay good. Give good housing. And one day off every tenday."

Chitiratifor bristled. "See here, my good pack. We are not seeking employment. My lord"—he gestured respectfully at Vendacious—"has come to tell the Great Tycoon of new products and opportunities."

"Paw prints to suffice if you cannot write—" The other interrupted its own speech as Chitiratifor's words finally penetrated. "Not wanting to apply for work?" It looked at them for moment, took in Chitiratifor's flashy outfit. "Yes, you are not dressed for this doorway. I should have noticed." It thought for a second. "You are in wrong place. Business visitors must visit to the Business Center. You go back five blocks and then onto the Concourse of the Great Tycoon. Wait. I get you a map." The creature didn't move, but Vendacious realized the pack was even more numerous than he had thought, extending back out of sight into the building; these Easterners tolerated the most grotesque perversions.

Chitiratifor shuffled back in Vendacious' direction, and the nearest of him hissed, "That's a two-mile walk just to get to the other side of this frigging building!"

Vendacious nodded and walked around his servant, confronting the gate-keeper directly. "We've come all the way from the West Coast to help Tycoon. We demand a courteous response, not petty delays!"

The nearest members of the gatekeeper stepped back timidly. Up close, Vendacious could hear that this was no military pack. Except at dinner parties, it probably never had killed a single living thing. In fact, the creature was so naive that it didn't really recognize the deadly anger confronting it. After a moment, it reformed its line, and said "Nevertheless, sir, I must follow my orders. Business visitors use the business entrance."

Chitiratifor was hissing murder; Vendacious waved him quiet. But Vendacious really didn't want to walk around to the official entrance—and that wasn't just a matter of convenience. He now realized that finding this entrance was a lucky accident. Woodcarver's spies were unlikely this far from home, but the fewer people who could draw a connection between Tycoon and Vendacious, the better.

He backed off courteously, out of the gatekeeper's space. This entrance would be fine if he could just talk to someone with a mind. "Perhaps your orders do not apply to me."

The gatekeeper pondered the possibility for almost five seconds. "But I think they do apply," it finally said.

"Well then, while we wait for the map, perhaps you could pass on an enquiry to someone who deals with difficult problems." There were several lures Vendacious could dangle: "Tell your supervisor that his visitors bear news about the invasion from outer space."

"The what from where?"

"We have eyewitness information about the *humans*—" that provoked more blank looks. "Damn it, fellow, this is about the mantis monsters!"

Mention of the mantis monsters did not produce the gatekeeper's supervisor; the fivesome who came out to see them was far higher in the chain of command than that! "Remasritlfeer" asked a few sharp questions and then waved for them to follow him. In a matter of minutes, they were past the gatekeeper and walking down carpeted corridors. Looking around, Vendacious had to hide his smiles. The interior design was a perfection of bad taste and mismatched wealth, proof of the foolishness of the newly rich. Their guide was a very different matter. Remasritlfeer was mostly slender, but there were scars on his snouts and flanks, and you could see the lines of hard muscle beneath his fur. His eyes were mostly pale yellow and not especially friendly.

It was a long walk, but their guide had very little to say. Finally, the corridor ended at a member-wide door, more like the entrance to an animal den than the office of the world's richest commoner.

Remasritlfeer opened the door and stuck a head in. "I have the outlanders, your eminence," he said

A voice came from within: "That should be 'my lord'. Today, I think 'my lord' sounds better."

"Yes, my lord." But the four of Remasritlfeer who were still in the corridor rolled their heads in exasperation.

"Well then, let's not waste my time. Have them all come in. There's plenty of room."

As Vendacious filed through the narrow doorway, he was looking in all directions without appearing to be especially interested. Gas mantle lamps were ranked near the ceiling. Vendacious thought he saw parts of a bodyguard on perches above that. Yes, the room was large, but it was crowded with—what? not the bejeweled knickknacks of the hallway. Here there were gears and gadgets and large tilted easels covered with half-finished drawings. The walls were bookcases rising so high that perches on ropes and pulleys were needed to reach the top shelves. One of Vendacious stood less than a yard from the nearest books. No great literature here. Most of the books were accounting ledgers. The ones further up looked like bound volumes of legal statutes.

The unseen speaker continued, "Come forward where I can see you all! Why in hell couldn't you use the business visitor entrance? I didn't build that throne room for nothing." This last was querulous muttering.

Vendacious percolated through the jumble. Two of him came out from under a large drawing easel. The rest reached the central area a second later. He suffered a moment of confusion as Chitiratifor shuffled himself out of the way, and then he got his first glimpse of the Great Tycoon:

The pack was an ill-assorted eightsome. Vendacious had to count him twice, since the smaller members were moving around so much. At the core were four middle-aged adults. They had no noble or martial aspect whatsoever. Two of them wore the kind of green-tinted visors affected by accountants everywhere. The other two had been turning the pages of a ledger. Pretty clearly he had been counting his money or cutting expenses, or whatever it was that businesscritters did.

Tycoon cast irritated looks at Vendacious and Chitiratifor. "You claim to know about the mantis monsters. This better be good. I know lots about the mantises, so I advise against lies." He pointed a snout at Vendacious, waving him closer.

Treat him like royalty. Vendacious belly-crawled two of himself closer to Tycoon. Now he had the attention of all Tycoon's members. The four small ones, puppies under two years old, had stopped their pell-mell orbiting of the accountancy four. Two hung back with the four, while two came within a couple feet of Vendacious. These pups were integrated parts of Tycoon's personality—just barely, and when they felt like it. Their mindsounds were unseemly loud. Vendacious had to force himself not to shrink back.

After a moment or two of impolite poking, Tycoon said, "So, how would you know about the mantis monsters?"

"I witnessed their starship *Oobii* descend from the sky." Vendacious used the human name of their ship. The sounds were flat and simple, alien. "I saw its lightning weapon bring down a great empire in a single afternoon."

Tycoon was nodding. Most East Coast packs took this version of Woodcarver's victory to be a fantasy. Evidently, Tycoon was not one of those. "You're saying nothing new here, fellow—though few packs know the name of the flying ship."

"I know far more than that, my lord. I speak the mantis language. I know their secrets and their plans." And he had one of their *datasets* in his right third pannier, though he had no intention of revealing that advantage.

"Oh really?" Tycoon's smile was sharp and incredulous, even unto his puppies. "Who then are you?"

An honest answer to that question had to come sooner or later, fatal though it might be. "My lord, my name is Vendacious. I was—"

Tycoon's heads jerked up. "Remasritlfeer!"

"My lord!" The deadly little fivesome was clustered around the only exit.

"Cancel my appointments. No more visitors today, of any sort. Have Saliminophon take care of the shift change."

"Yes, my lord!"

Tycoon's older four set their ledger aside and all of him looked at Vendacious. "Be assured that this claim will be verified, sir. Discreetly but definitively verified." But you could see Tycoon's enthusiasm, the *will* to believe; for now, the puppies were in control. "You were Woodcarver's spymaster, convicted of treason."

Vendacious raised his heads. "All true, my lord. And I am proud of my 'treason.' Woodcarver has allied with the mantis queen and her maggots."

"Maggots?" Tycoon's eyes were wide.

"Yes, my lord. 'Mantis' and 'maggot' refer to different aspects of the same creatures, *humans* as they call themselves. 'Mantis' is the appropriate term for the adult. After all, it is a two-legged creature, sneaky and vicious, but also solitary."

"*Real* mantises are insects, only about so tall." One of the puppies yawned wide, indicating less than two inches.

"The mantises from the sky can be five feet at the shoulder."

"I knew that," said Tycoon. "But the maggots? They are the younglings of the grown monsters?"

"Indeed so." Vendacious moved his two forward members confidingly close to the other pack. "And here is something you may not know. It makes the analogy nigh perfect. The actual invasion from the sky began almost a year before the Battle on Starship Hill."

"Before Woodcarver marched north?"

"Yes. A much smaller craft landed secretly, thirty-five tendays earlier. And do you know what was aboard? My lord, that first lander was filled with maggot eggsacks!"

"So that will be the real invasion," said Tycoon. "Just as insect maggots burst from their eggsacks and overrun the neighborhood, these humans will overrun the entire world—"

Chitiratifor popped in with, "They will devour us all!"

Vendacious gave his servant a stern look. "Chitiratifor takes the analogy too far. At present, the maggots are young. There is only one adult, the mantis queen, Ravna. But consider, in just the two years since Ravna and *Oobii* arrived, she has taken control of Woodcarver's Domain and expanded it across all the realms of the Northwest."

Two of Tycoon's older members tapped idly at an addition device, flicking small beads back and forth. A bean counter indeed. "And how do the mantises—this one Ravna mantis—manage such control? Are they loud? Can they swamp another's mindsounds with their own?"

This sounded like a testing question. "Not at all, my lord. Just like insects, the humans make no sounds when they think. None whatsoever. They might as well be walking corpses." Vendacious paused. "My lord, I don't mean to understate the threat, but if we work together we can prevail against these creatures. Humans are stupid! It shouldn't be surprising since they are singletons. I estimate that the smartest of them aren't much more clever than a mismatched foursome."

"Really! Even the Ravna?"

"Yes! They can't do the simplest arithmetic, what any street haggler can do. Their memory for sounds—even the speech sounds they can hear—is almost nonexistent. Like insect mantises, their way of life is parasitic and thieving."

All eight of Tycoon sat very still. Vendacious could hear the edges of his mind, a mix of calculation, wonder, and uncertainty.

"It doesn't make sense," Tycoon finally said. "From my own investigations, I already know some of what you say. But the mantises are superlative inventors. I've tested their exploding black powder. I've heard of the catapults powered by that powder. And they have other inventions I can't yet reproduce. They can *fly*! Their *Oobii* may now be crashed to earth, but they have a smaller flyer, barely the size of a boat. Last year it was seen by reliable packs just north of town."

Vendacious and Chitiratifor traded a glance. *That* was bad news. Aloud, Vendacious said, "Your point is well taken, my lord, but there is no paradox. The mantis folk simply stole the things that give them their advantage. I have . . . sources . . . that prove they've been doing that for a very long time. Finally, their victims tired of them and chased them out of their original place in the sky. Much of what they have, they do not understand and cannot re-create.

Those devices will eventually wear out. The *antigravity* flier you mention is an example. Furthermore, the creatures have stolen—and are continuing to steal— our *own* inventions. For instance, that exploding black powder you mentioned? It might well have been invented by some creative pack, perhaps the same one who truly invented the *cannon* catapults."

Tycoon didn't reply immediately; he looked stunned. Ever since Vendacious had heard of Tycoon, he'd suspected that this pack had a special secret, some- thing that could make him a faithful supporter of Vendacious' cause. That was still just a theory, but—

Finally, Tycoon found his voice: "I wondered. . . . The blasting powder and the catapults . . . I remember . . ." He drifted off for a moment, splitting into the old and the young. The puppies scrabbled around, whining like some forlorn fragment. Then Tycoon gathered himself together. "I, I was once an inventor."

Vendacious waved at the mechanisms that filled the room. "I can see that you still are, my lord."

Tycoon didn't seem to hear. "But then I split up. My fission sibling eventu- ally left for the West Coast. He had so many ideas. Do you suppose—?"

Yes! But aloud, Vendacious was much more cautious: "I still have my sources, sir. Perhaps I can help with that question, too."

CHAPTER 01

So many impossible things. Ravna is dreaming. She knows that, but there is no waking. She can only watch and absorb and choke on horror. The Blight's fleet hangs all around her, ships clustered here and there like bugs stuck in slime. Originally, the fleet was a hundred fifty starships, and clouds of drones. The drones have been cannibalized. Many ships are gone, some cannibalized. Where it serves the Blight, crews have been cannibalized, too, or simply cast out. Her dreaming eyes can see hundreds of corpses, humans, dirokimes, even skrodeless riders.

The Blight's prey is almost thirty lightyears away, an ordinary solar sys- tem . . . where Ravna and the Children have fled. And that is part of the reason this vision must be a dream. Thirty lightyears is impossibly far in this part of the universe, where nothing goes faster than light. There is *no way* she can know what is happening in the enemy fleet.

The fleet floats in death, but is not dead itself. Look closer at the clustered ships. Things move. Construction proceeds. The fleet was once the hand of a living god; now it exists to resurrect that god. Even trapped here, in this encyst- ment of pain, it plans and builds, second on second, year on year, working as hard as its living crews can be driven. If necessary, it can do this for centuries, breeding more crew to replace natural losses. This program will eventually produce ramscoop vessels. They will be the best that can exist Down Here, capable of reaching near-lightspeed.

Now perhaps none of that effort is necessary, for the Blight can see Ravna as she sees it, and the encysted god is saying to her: *Rules change. I am coming. I am coming. And much sooner than you think.*

Ravna woke with a start, gasping for breath.

She was lying on the floor, her right arm painfully bent. *I must have fallen. What a terrible dream.* She struggled back into her chair. She wasn't in her cabin aboard the *Out of Band II*. The automation aboard *Oobii* would have turned the floor soft before she ever hit it. She looked around, trying to orient herself, but all she could remember was the dream.

She ran her hand across the side of her chair. It was wood, local Tinish manufacture, as was the table. But the walls had a greenish cast, gently curving into the equally greenish floor. She was inside the Children's landing craft, under Woodcarver's new castle. That took long enough to recognize! She leaned her head into her hands, and let the cabin spin around to a stop. When her dizziness had passed, she sat back and tried to think. Except for the last few minutes, everything seemed reasonable:

She had come down to the catacombs to inspect the Children's caskets. This part of the castle spanned a range of technology from the pre-gunpowder to fallen transcendence, the walls carved with chisels and mallets, the light provided by lamps from *Oobii*. Two years ago, the coldsleep containers had been removed from the Straumer Lander and laid out with enough space between them to dissipate the waste heat of the refrigeration.

Half the caskets were empty now, their passengers awakened. That included almost all the oldest Children. Nowadays, the kids lived in or near the new castle; some were in school classes here. If she listened carefully, she could hear occasional shrieks of laughter mixed with the gobble of Tinish packs.

So why did I enter the Lander? Oh yes. She'd spent a only few minutes outside, looking through the casket windows at the faces of little ones who still slept, who waited unknowing for there to be enough grownup caregivers. Most of those revivals would be routine, but some of the caskets tested as borderline defective. How could she save the kids in those withered caskets? *That* had been the reason for today's visit, to review the results on Timor Ristling, her first attempt with the withered caskets.

The Lander was originally Top-of-the-Beyond technology. Much of that could not function down here in the Slow Zone; she'd never been able to transfer the Lander's maintenance records to the stable technology of her own ship. She *had* to come onboard to access those records. Her gaze slid uneasily around the Lander's freight cabin. Too much had happened in this green-walled room. The Lander wasn't just Top of the Beyond. It had been at the High Lab, in the Low Transcend, and it had been . . . modified. If she looked up she would see some of that, the fungus hanging from the ceiling. The magical Countermeasure. Nowadays, it seemed to be as dead as a dusty cobweb, but Countermeasure had dimmed the sun, and killed her dearest love, and maybe saved the galaxy. The remains of the fungus bothered even the Straumer Children.

This was not a surprising place to have a really bad dream.

But now she remembered what she had been doing just before the crazy dream overtook her. The last two days had been a nonstop guilt trip, with far too little sleep. It was clear that she had screwed up Timor's chances. Not deliberately, not through incompetence. *But I did pick him for the first damaged-casket revival.* The problem wasn't the boy's twisted leg, it wasn't the fact that he might not be quite as brilliant as the other children. The problem was that in the tendays since his revival, Timor had not grown.

Ravna Bergsndot was thousands of lightyears from reliable advice. *Oobii* and this strange Lander were all she had. She remembered pounding on the data for almost an hour, combining Timor's casket records with *Oobii*'s latest medical tests, and finally understanding what had gone wrong. No one and no machine Down Here could have known that ahead of time. In cold, cruel truth, Timor had turned out to be a very valuable . . . experiment.

When she'd finally realized that, Ravna had put her head in her arms, too tired to look for any more technical fixes and raging against the possibility that she had become a player with other people's lives.

So then I just fell asleep and had the nightmare? She stared at the greenish bulkheads. She had been very tired, and totally beaten down. Ravna sighed. She often had nightmares about the Blighter fleet, though this was the most bizarre yet. A tip of the hat then to the subconscious mind; it had dug up something that could distract her from Timor, if only briefly.

She disconnected her tiara interface from the Lander, and climbed down from the freight cabin. Three years ago, when Sjana and Arne Olsndot had brought the Children here, this ground had been open meadow. She stood for a moment by the spidery pylons, looking round the cool, dry catacombs. Imagine a spacecraft with a castle built over it. Only in the Slow Zone.

She would have to come back here again and again until all the Children were revived—but she was grateful to be done with this place for today. Up two flights of stairs and she would be in the castle yard, in the summer sunlight. There would be the Children just leaving class, playing with each other and with their Tinish friends. If she stayed to chat, she would likely be in the new castle all afternoon. It might be the sunny evening before she had to be back in her cabin aboard the *Oobii*. As she started up the steps, she could imagine feeling light-hearted. She would take some time off, just to play with the Children. Somehow she would make things right for Timor.

She was still in the dark of the stairs when she remembered something else about the dream. She paused, steadying herself with a hand against the cool stonework. The mind in the fleet had said, "Rules change." Yes, if the Zone shifted and faster-than-light transport became possible again—well, the Blight could arrive very soon indeed. It was a possibility she obsessed upon both awake and in her dreams. She had zonographs aboard the *Oobii* that monitored the relevant physical laws, had done so since the Battle on Starship Hill. There had never been an alarm.

Still leaning against the wall, Ravna queried *Out of Band II*, requesting a window on the zonograph. The graphic came up, a stupidly self-formatted plot. Yes, there was the usual noise. Then she noticed the scaling. That couldn't be right! She slewed her gaze back five hundred seconds, and saw that the trace had spiked. For almost ten milliseconds, Zone physics had shot above the probe's calibration, so high it might have been Transcendent. Then she noticed the pulsing red border. It was the Zone alarm she had so carefully set—the alarm she should have received at the instant of the spike. Impossible, impossible. This had to be some sort of screw-up. She rummaged in diagnostics, horror rising. Yes, there had been a screw-up: she had only enabled the Zone alarm for when she was local to *Oobii*. Why hadn't ship logic caught that stupid error? She knew the answer to that question. She'd explained it to the Children dozens of time. The kids could not understand that when you scrape your knee, it might be your own fault. *We're living in the Slow Zone. We have virtually no automation, and what we have is painfully simple, devoid of common sense.* Down Here, if you wanted something done right, you had to provide the good judgment yourself. The kids didn't like that answer. Where they came from, it was a far more alien idea than it was even for Ravna Bergsndot.

She glared at the displays that hung in the dark all around her. This was clearly a Zone alarm, but it could be a *false* alarm. It had to be! The spike had been so brief, less than ten probe samples. An instrumental transient. Yes. She turned and continued up the stairs, still searching back and forth along the timeline's trace, looking for evidence of an innocuous explanation. There were a number of system diagnostics she could run.

She thought about this for five more steps, making a turn from one flight of stairs to the next. Up ahead she could see a square of daylight.

Since the Battle on Starship Hill, the Zone physics had been as solid as a mountain's roots . . . but that was a comparison with fatal consequence. Earthquakes happen. Foreshocks happened. What she was seeing could be a tiny, sudden slip in the foundation of the local universe. She looked at the times on the Zone trace. The spike occurred about when she took her odd little nap down in the Children's Lander. So then. For almost one hundredth of a second, maybe *c* had not been the ultimate speed, and the Lander could have known the current state of the Blighter fleet. For almost one hundredth of a second, Countermeasure could have functioned.

And her dream was simply *news*.

Even so, she still didn't know how much time they had left. It might be just hours. But if it were years, or decades—then every moment must be made to count. Somehow.

"Hei, Ravna!" came a childish shout from across the yard, in the direction of the school. They would be around her in a moment.

I can't do this. She half turned, retreating toward the stairway. Nightmares can be the truth. It wasn't just villains who had to make the hard decisions.

CHAPTER 02

There was no school on the last day of every ten. Sometimes that made the end of the tenday terribly boring to Timor Ristling. Other times, Belle would show him some dank corner of the New Castle, or Ravna Bergsndot would take him across the straits to Hidden Island.

Today was turning into the most entertaining kind of day, one where the other kids let him come along on their projects.

"You'll be the lookout, Timor," Gannon had told him. Gannon Jorkenrud had organized the expedition, and specifically invited Timor, even though it meant they had to carry him part of the way down from Starship Hill. Gannon and the others even helped Timor across the boulder field at the base of the cliffs. Sea birds skirled all about.

The kids were right down on the seashore now, the cliffs towering behind them. It was strange to be at eye level with the water. The froth of the waves seemed to merge with the sea haze above, misting over the buildings of Hidden Island just a couple of kilometers away. Here you could see what was beneath the cliffs. You could see how "low tide" had pulled back the water, leaving this field of slick rocks, a jumble of giants. There wasn't a single dry place; all this was underwater when the tide was highest.

Belle pattered along beside and around Timor, grumbling as she often did. "This dirty water is going to smudge my pelts." Belle was all white. This was quite rare among Tines—though one of her, the old male, might have had black patches when he was younger.

"You didn't have to come, crapheads," said Gannon. He and Belle didn't get along.

Belle gave a hiss and a laugh at the same time. "Try and keep me away. I haven't been to a good shipwreck in years. How did you figure it was going to come ashore here?"

"We're humans. We've got our ways."

Some of the other kids laughed. They were strung out, walking down a narrow path between the rocks. One of them said, "Actually, Nevil saw it on *Oobii*'s surveillance monitors when he was studying shipside. Ravna and the packs know about the wreck, but they haven't seen the latest updates."

"Yeah! Woodcarver's packs are probably down at Cliffside harbor. We'll be first where stuff really happens."

Walking down here, they still couldn't see the wreck, just the water crashing on the rocks. Ahead, a swarm of seabirds towered over one particular spot. Timor felt an odd twinge of nostalgia. It still happened, when there was something about this world that reminded him of before. Those birds were so alien, but at the same time, their clustering was just like construction swarms back home.

The water surged ankle deep now, soaking through Timor's leather shoes, gripping like icy hands. "Wait up, guys!"

"See, I told you walking in this was bad." That was Belle, dancing around in discomfort.

Gannon looked back. "What is it now? . . ." Then he shrugged. "Okay, this is where we put you up on a rock."

Gannon and some of the other kids came back and boosted Timor to a ledge on the nearest monster boulder. Belle climbed two of herself over the remaining three, and reached the same cleft in the rock.

"You can make it to the top from there, can't you?" said Gannon.

Timor twisted around, trying to see beyond the slick curve of stone. He really didn't like to say he couldn't do something. "Yeah, I can."

"Okay. We're gonna go on ahead. Heh. We'll make friends with the shipwrecked doggies. You crawl on up to the top of this rock. If you see Woodcarver's packs coming or Ravna Bergsndot, then have your pack give us a shout. Got it?"

"Yup."

Gannon and the others continued on their way. Timor watched them for a moment, but only Øvin Verring turned to give him a little wave. Well, these kids had gotten older than him; he shouldn't be surprised they didn't include him in much. On the other hand, he was the lookout.

He slid along the ledge toward some obvious handholds. Below him, Belle was poking around to find a way up for her bottom three. Oops, there was a pair of sea birds perched above him. He remembered the lectures about birds and nests. "Nests" were a little like autoform crèches except without the safety overrides; those birds might come down and peck at him if they thought he was after their replicates.

Fortunately, the birds contented themselves with loud cackling, then one after the other they took off for the swarm that hovered over the water's edge. He noticed that that was in the same direction the kids had been walking. Hei! He was almost at the top of the rock! He maneuvered carefully across the slippery black stone, doing his best to avoid the bird poop.

One of Belle's heads poked up from the edge of the rock. "How about a little help here?"

"Sorry." He lay flat on the rock and reached down to the first one's forelegs. That was her one male, Ihm. By the time Timor had him pulled up, Belle was able to help him with the rest of herself. She clambered to the middle of the rock and sat on her feet, complaining all the while about her frozen paws. He turned awkwardly around and finally got a glimpse of the wreck. The raft was mostly still in the straits, but sliding meter by meter toward the rocks.

Three of Belle hunkered down, listening. The others sat tall on either side of Timor. He guessed those two were watching the wreck. In most ways, Tinish vision was worse than humans', but if they chose to spread out, they had much better depth perception.

Belle said, "Can you hear the timbers breaking on the rocks?" And of course Tinish *hearing* was lightyears better than the naked human ear.

"Maybe." Timor looked at the front of the raft. Okay, rocks would break wood, right? Especially if the rocks didn't have avoidance systems. And nothing had avoidance on this world. He saw how the timbers had split down the middle. The two halves of the vehicle were sloping separately. Surely that could not be part of its design.

He squinted, trying to make out the details. The raft was piled high with barrels. And now he saw that there were *lots* of Tines, though they wore brownish rags and were mostly hunkered down between the barrels. Occasionally four or five of them stood together and tried to do something with the rigging. Yes, they were trying desperately to keep their craft off the rocks.

"They're in trouble," he said.

Belle made a hooting sound, a Tinish laugh. "Of course they're in trouble. Can't you hear the ones in the water, screaming?"

Now that she mentioned it, he could see heads here and there in the water. "This is terrible. Shouldn't someone be trying to help?" Timor was quite sure that Gannon and the other kids weren't capable of providing much help.

He felt Belle shrug. "If they hadn't been swept so far north, or if they had come at high tide, there'd be no problem."

"But shouldn't we help those packs in the water?"

One of Belle's heads looked in his direction. "What packs? These are Tropicals. The individual members are probably as smart as any northern singleton, but they just don't make packs except by accident. Look at that raft! Junk made by mindless Tines. Sometimes the idiots get swept away from their jungles and the ocean brings them up here. I say the more of them that die along the way, the better." She grumbled on the way she often did, gossiping and complaining at the same time: "Our own war veterans are bad enough, broken up bits of people. But at least we keep them decently out of sight. These rabble coming in now have no call on us. They'll be idling around town, soiling the alleys, dumbhead singletons and trios. Mangy, smelly, mindless thieves and beggars . . ."

The rest made even less sense. Belle was one of those packs who spoke almost perfect Samnorsk, but sometimes part of her would rattle on even after her main attention was elsewhere. Timor noticed that the pack was intensely focused on the wreck, her long necks twitching back and forth. She had been even more eager than Timor when Gannon Jorkenrud had invited them to come along. He followed the center of her gaze. There were barrels bobbing in the foaming surf.

"So if the Tropicals are such problem, why are you interested in the wreck?"

"That's the thing, boy. These shipwrecks have been going on since time out of mind; I remember legends of them. Every few years, a crowd of Tropical singletons gets washed ashore. They're always a problem, the ones who live. But the rafts usually have valuable junk on board, stuff we normally don't see, since the Tropics are so filled with disease and choirs that no pack can survive there."

She paused. "Hei, some of the barrels are on the rocks. I can hear them breaking up." Two of her scrambled to the edge of the rock. Her oldest hung back, watching to keep them all oriented. "Okay, Timor, you stay here. I'm going down to have a look." Her two youngest were already sliding and scrambling down, risking cuts and sprains in their eagerness.

"But wait!" shouted Timor. "We're supposed to stand watch."

"I can do that close up," she said. "You stay up here." Her two youngest were out of sight now, hidden by the edge of the boulder. Two others were helping old Ihm to negotiate the slippery rocks. She emitted a Tinish chord that Timor recognized as evasive mumbling. "You be the overall lookout, okay? Remember, Gannon is depending on you."

"But—"

All of Belle was out of sight now. Of course, she could still hear him, but she could be pretty good at ignoring him too.

Timor settled back on the middle of his rock. This *was* a good lookout position, though with Belle gone, it would be just his voice to shout directions. As best he could see in the sea haze, there were no rescue boats coming across the straits from Hidden Island. Cliffside harbor to the south was much closer, but the marina was a forest of unmoving spars and masts. It really was up to Gannon and the other kids to help the shipwrecked Tines.

He looked back to where the sea met the rocks. Here and there, he could see Belle's members. She had worked her way through several narrow passages and was almost into the foam. She moved carefully, trying to keep her paws out of the icy water; nevertheless she was within a few meters of Tropicals who had fallen overboard. Could she help them? Tines were wonderfully good swimmers; Ravna said that the Tines had evolved from sea mammals. But watching Belle, Timor guessed that the arctic waters were too cold for them.

Nevertheless, Belle had two of herself partway into the surf. The others were tugging at the cloaks of the furthest out, keeping them from being swept away. Maybe she could rescue a member or two. Then he noticed that she was desperately reaching for a wooden barrel that was jammed between half-submerged rocks. Some kind of green fabric peeked out of breaks in the container.

"Oh, Belle," Timor said to himself. He moved to the south side of his rock, trying to get a better view. There! Gannon and the others had finally reached the water. He could see most of them now. There were also a couple of packs with them, but Gannon's pals didn't have much to do with Tines. These packs looked pretty uncomfortable, huddling close among themselves and complaining loudly enough that Timor could hear them from fifty meters way. The Children didn't look comfortable either. Their pants were soaked; Øvin and the others were visibly shivering. Gannon had climbed onto a little terrace, was waving to the others to follow him.

A big part of the raft was barely ten meters from the kids. It bobbed out and in, sometimes getting so close to the terrace that Timor feared it would ram the Children. This piece of raft had remnants of sails flying from broken-looking masts. Timor hadn't taken any sailing classes; those were only for the older kids, the ones who wanted to be explorers and diplomats. But these masts and sails weren't the tidy, regular things he saw in the Hidden Island harbor or at Cliffside. Unless these parts were regenerating—and the Tines had no such technology—this raft system was totally out of control. It probably had been ever since it ran into some storm.

Belle continued to ignore everything except her barrel of treasure, but Gannon and the other kids were shouting to the mob on the raft. The two packs on the shore were shouting too. Timor couldn't understand any of it, but the noise *from* the Tropicals was loud. It didn't sound much like Interpack. Maybe it was some other Tinish language, or just frightened screeching.

Timor couldn't imagine what the kids could do to help. He looked again in the direction of Cliffside harbor. Hei! Something was moving along the curve of rocky beach. It looked like four or five packs hauling carts. And way high above them—the antigravity skiff! It didn't matter that it wasn't a human design and that it constantly teetered like a falling leaf. It was a little bit of home.

The agrav descended along the cliffs, cautiously tipping around the updrafts. It was coming down well ahead of the approaching packs, but still short of Timor's position. For a moment, Timor wondered why Pilgrim—the only possible pilot—hadn't brought it closer. Then the skiff tipped over, scraping the rocks with its canopy. It flipped again and landed with a crash. It crashed a lot lately. Fortunately the hull was stronger than wood and harder than rock. The top hatch popped open and after a second a human head appeared. No surprise, it was Johanna Olsndot; she was almost always the passenger.

Timor turned back to give a shout to Gannon and the others. Help had arrived!

Gannon Jorkenrud was teetering near the edge of his rocky terrace. The big piece of raft had grounded just out of reach. Øvin Verring and some of the kids were hanging back, but Gannon and others were throwing things at the raft. They were shouting, or laughing, and throwing again and again. *They were throwing stones at the Tropicals.*

Timor stood up and shouted, "Hei, you guys! Stop that!" No doubt his words were lost in the wind, but his windmilling arms caught their attention. Gannon gave him a wave, perhaps thinking Timor was warning of discovery. The stone throwers backed away from the edge of the water. Timor slipped on the rock, landing hard in one of the puddles that pocked the surface.

So he'd probably earned Gannon's good will. That had been awfully important to him, but it seemed kind of ugly now.

———

The Year Two shipwreck was the first since the Children had come to Tines World. Johanna Olsndot was just sixteen, yet she managed to establish her Bad Girl reputation in the aftermath of the wreck—a remarkable achievement considering that other kids misbehaved for years without getting so labeled.

Pilgrim Wickllrrackscar had heard there was a shipwreck, and the two of them had flown down to help out. Certainly that was not Bad Girl behavior. They bounced to ground well ahead of Woodcarver's shore patrol. Johanna was out the hatch and running toward the wreckage even before Pilgrim had the agrav locked down. Behind her, the flyer rose briefly back into the air, and fell again. She paid that scant attention. The Tropicals' raft had already broken on the rocks.

She saw that other rescuers were already here, an unlikely crowd of Children led by Gannon Jorkenrud. And—well, by damn!—they were throwing rocks at the drowning Tines! Johanna skirted the boulders, splashing through the icy water of the Inner Straits, shouting and swearing at Gannon's gang.

The group had already retreated from their position on the rocks. They were busy disappearing in the direction of the cliff path. All of them were younger than Johanna and none quite as tall. Besides, Johanna was the one with the reputation for temper and she was the only Child who had actually fought in the Battle on Starship Hill.

Johanna took one long look around the blocky talus, searching for any other wrongdoers. There, one more Child, very small. It was Timor Ristling, awkwardly scrambling down from a rock, helped by Belle Ornrikakihm. Now there was a sneaky pack of beasties. Then Timor and Belle were out of sight, too, and the thought flitted from her mind. Pilgrim had come down from the agrav. All five of him was trying to drag her out of the ankle-deep water.

"Hei, what's the problem?" protested Johanna. "The water's still enough." It was bone-chilling cold, but here behind the rocks, the sea was tamed into a gently swirling pond.

Pilgrim led her along the gravel, a meter or so back from the water. "It's not all that shallow. There are holes and dropoffs. You get confident, walk about, and things can get very bad, very fast." For a death-defying pilgrim he could be a wuss. But to be honest . . . just four or five meters from where they were standing, there was already white foam spinning up from the water. Standing at the level of the sea, the surface of the water was almost indistinct, the churn of sea mist transforming the daylight into murk.

The shore patrol had arrived. The five packs were already working with ropes to slide the biggest parts of the raft away from the grinding rocks.

Out on the wreckage, dozens of Tines were perched on piles of junk. These were the first Tropicals Johanna had ever seen. They were every bit as strange as the locals claimed. The foreigners didn't cluster into packs. They were like a mob of singletons, doing whatever they pleased. Some of them cooperated to pull on the ropes thrown to them; others cowered in terror. She looked across the misty water. Here and there, she saw a head, or a single Tine lying across a bit of broken timber. Dozens of the creatures had been swept overboard.

Johanna reached out to the nearest of Pilgrim. It was Scarbutt, still the largest of the pack. "Look there! Those ones in the water are going to drown! We should go after them first."

Pilgrim gave a general nod of agreement. "Not sure that can be helped."

"Hei, it sure as hell can be helped!" Johanna pointed at the coils of rescue rope that the shore patrol packs had brought. "Grab those ropes! Get the shore patrol to do the important stuff first!"

Pilgrim was normally a very forward fellow. Now he hung back for a second, then ran along behind the shore patrol packs, gobbling loudly. Even after three

years of listening to Interpack, Johanna found the language mostly unintelligible. The words got stacked up in chords, some them too high pitched to hear.
By the time you got the sounds separated out, you were trying to make sense of
the next chord. Just now, Pilgrim was shouting some kind of demand. The
sounds of "Woodcarver" popped up several times. Okay, so he was invoking
higher authority.

Two of the shore patrol packs left their posts and helped Pilgrim drag un-
used loops of rope away from the rocks. More packs were running toward them
from Cliffside harbor. These didn't look like shore patrol. Most of them avoided
Johanna and Pilgrim. Like the rest, they seemed mostly interested in the raft.
Well, there were more lives at stake there, but the ones who needed immediate
help were out *in* the water. In all, only three packs—counting Pilgrim—
were now working to save them. Over and over again, the packs would whirl
about, tossing floater-tipped ropes out into the sea. The struggling singletons
leaped from the water, desperately reaching. They looked almost like seamals
when they moved like that. In warmer, quieter water they would have been
quite safe. Here, the rescue ropes were essential; when a singleton managed to
snatch a throw, it was quickly dragged into a stretch of flat pebbly beach.
Johanna and the others managed to save a dozen of the swimmers, but there
had been at least thirty heads out there before. The others must have been lost
to the cold or been swept further north.

Meantime, the rest of the packs had dragged in what remained of the raft.
The Tropicals on board came streaming off as the shore patrol and local citizens climbed on the junk heaps and began rooting around. Johanna belatedly
realized that the main purpose of the "rescue" was to get at the wreck's cargo.

There were no more survivors visible in the straits. Except for Pilgrim, the
packs who had been helping with the rescue tosses had joined the other salvage
maniacs. Along the flat stretch of beach, the surviving Tropicals were clumped
together in shivering groups. The smallest of those was at least twenty Tines.
These weren't packs; they were just singletons hunkered together for warmth.

Johanna walked to the edge of the crowd, listening for Interpack speech.
There was nothing that she recognized. After all, there were no real packs
here. She could feel an occasional buzzing sensation, though; these creatures
were not silent in the range that the packs called mindsound—about forty to
two hundred fifty kilohertz.

Pilgrim was pacing her progress, but staying fifteen meters or more away
from the nearest of the Tropicals. "You're not too popular right now," he said.

"Me?" replied Johanna, keeping her eyes on the strange mob. Scarcely any
of them had clothing, but their pelts were just as mangy as the stories had
claimed. Some of the creatures were almost hairless except down near their
paws. "We saved these fellows."

"Oh, they aren't the ones you're unpopular with," said Pilgrim. Johanna
drifted a little nearer the mob. Now there were dozens of heads following her,
jaws snapping nervously. Pilgrim continued, "Hei, I didn't say the Tropicals
like you either! I'll wager that none of them realize you helped save them."

Necks lunged in her direction, and one or two of the critters tumbled down from atop the others. For a moment, she thought this was an attack, but when the Tines reached the ground, they just looked startled. Johanna backed away a step or two. "Yes, I see what you mean. These are like battle fragments. They're scared and mindless." And they could go into attack mode if something spooked them.

"That's about right," said Pilgrim. "But keep in mind that these fellows are not the remains of packs. Most likely they have never been part of a coherent pack. Their mindsound is just a pointless choir."

Johanna continued along the edge of the mob. There was a certain distance the crowd seemed comfortable with. If she got inside that, they would begin to come at her. Pilgrim was right. These weren't like war casualties. Battle fragments she had known longed to be part of coherent packs. They would react with friendliness toward Pilgrim, trying to entice him close. If they had known humans before they were damaged, they would be quite friendly to her. "So what's going to happen to them?" she said.

"Ah well, that's why you're a bit unpopular with the shore patrol. You know we get a shipwreck like this every few years. The cargo is mostly junk, not the sort of things you'd find if serious trade were intended."

Johanna looked across the misty beach. There really weren't enough shore patrol packs to contain the rescuees. The Tropicals wobbled around weakly and most seemed intimidated by the coherent packs, but there was a steady trickle of mangy seafarers who took advantage of the gaps in the shore patrol cordon and ran off along the beach. When a pack pursued, *then* there was a concerted rush by five or ten of the other refugees. Not everyone could be corralled and brought back. She looked at Pilgrim, "So the patrol would prefer that more of them had drowned?"

Pilgrim cocked a couple of heads at Johanna. "Just so." He might be consort to a Queen of the Realm, but he was not the least bit diplomatic. "Woodcarver has enough trouble with local fragments. These will just be trouble."

Inside herself, Johanna felt something colder than the water. The packs' treatment of fragments was her most unfavorite thing about Tines World. "So what happens to them, then? If anyone tries to force them back into the sea—" Her voice rose, along with her temper. Ravna Bergsndot would not put up with that, Johanna was sure. Not if Johanna got to her in time. She turned and began walking quickly back to the agrav flier.

All of Pilgrim turned about and trotted along beside her. "No, don't worry about that happening. In fact, Woodcarver has a longstanding decree that any survivors be allowed the run of Cliffside village. These patrol packs are waiting for reinforcements, to chivvy the mob into town."

About a third of the seafarers had already disappeared, trotting off as singletons and duos. They might do better than the fragments Johanna was used to. Frags of coherent packs were generally anxious mental cripples; many starved to death even if they were basically healthy. Elderly singletons, the castoffs, lasted only a short time. Johanna didn't slow down. An idea was percolating up. . . .

"You're planning something crazy, aren't you?" said Pilgrim. Sometimes he claimed he stayed with her because in a year she did as many weird things as he would see in ten anywhere else. Pilgrim really was a pilgrim, so that was an extreme claim indeed. His memories went back centuries, hazing off into unreliable history and myth. Few packs had traveled their world so much, or seen so much. The price of the adventuring was that Pilgrim was more a surviving point of view than an enduring mind. It was Johanna's great good fortune that that point of view was currently embodied in someone whose attitudes were so basically decent. Of all the Tines in the world, Pilgrim and Scriber had been the first she'd known. That bit of luck had saved her. Ultimately, it had saved all the remaining Children.

"You're not going to tell me your plan, eh?" said Pilgrim. "But I bet you want me to fly you someplace." That was not a difficult thing to guess, considering that Johanna was still walking toward the flier, which was parked—crashed—at the base of a cliff so steep and smooth that no pack or unaided human could hope to climb it.

Pilgrim ran around in front of her, now leading the way. "Okay, then. But keep in mind. The Tropicals can't live here very well. The packs they make are loose, even when they try to form them."

"So you've lived in the Tropical Choir?" That was something that Pilgrim had never quite claimed.

Pilgrim hesitated. "Well, for a time I lived on the fringes—you know, in the Tropical collectives. The true Choir of the deep jungles would be very quickly fatal for a coherent pack. Can you imagine being surround by such mobs, no one caring to keep a decent distance? Thought is impossible . . . though I suppose if the stories of nonstop orgies are true, it might be a happy way to dissolve oneself. No, I just meant that these shipwrecks have happened before. We'll have a year or two of nuisance, far more singletons wandering around than normal old age and accidents would account for—more even than after the war with Steel and Flenser. But eventually the problem will take care of itself."

"I'll bet." They were walking between house-sized boulders now, scrambling over lesser rocks that had fallen in between. This was not the safest place to promenade. All those rocks had come from somewhere above them. Sometimes after a spring thaw you'd see the rocky avalanches adding to the talus. At the moment, that was just a passing thought in the back of Johanna's mind, another reason to fly away from here. "So after a year or two, these poor animals are mostly dead and Woodcarver's folk have solved the problem?"

"Oh no, nothing like that. Or almost nothing like that. Over the centuries, Woodcarver and her people learned that if they waited till a good chill autumn and a surface current that was mainly southerly, you could get rid of most of the survivors in an almost friendly way: just repair their rafts or make new ones. After all, it's not that hard to make junkwork like that out of the flotsam that is always rolling in."

"You mean the surviving Tropicals can just be led aboard and put out to sea?"

"Not quite, though sometimes that's enough. What the Old Woodcarver learned was that the Tropicals are like jaybirds. They like shiny things. They like firemakers—which doesn't make sense since those go bad so fast in humid weather. They like all sorts of silly things. And long ago, folks around here figured what those things were. So pile the trinkets up on the rafts. Put some food aboard—and if the tide is right you can coax the remaining Tropicals aboard. Then just push them out into the southerly stream. Hei, problem solved!"

Johanna reached for the smooth silvery metal of the agrav flier. Her touch caused the side hatch to flip upwards, and a ramp to slide out. The craft had been designed for wheeled creatures. Entrance was easy for the likes of humans or Tines. She climbed aboard and settled into her usual slot (which was not so well designed for the human form).

Pilgrim came scrambling over the rocks, and one after another padded up the ramp. "It's not as if they are whole people, Johanna. You know that."

"You of all people don't really believe that, do you, Pilgrim?"

The fivesome was busy seating himself all around the flight cabin. The agrav's user interface might have been flexible in the Beyond, but down here in the Slow Zone, it defaulted to the form most fit for its original owners. Those had been Skroderiders. There might not be a single one alive on the whole planet. Too bad, since that default user interface had the flight controls scattered around the periphery of the cabin. Maybe a human crew could have flown the agrav—if that crew had trained their whole lives for the instabilities of the flight system. A pack, on the other hand, if it were as practiced and crazy as Pilgrim, could fly the thing, but just barely.

As the door closed and Pilgrim busied himself resetting the boat's agrav fabric, part of him looked around at her, considering her last question. He made his human voice a little bit sad sounding, "No, they're more than animals, Johanna. My love Woodcarver might say that they're also *less*, but you know I don't believe that. I've been in pieces often enough myself." He pushed at one of the dozens of control holes set in the console. The agrav lifted up on the left side, then on the right. They slid sideways, smacking into the cliff face. He corrected, and the boat sagged left, coasting away from the cliff but bouncing against the largest of the rocks below. By then Pilgrim had the rhythm, and the boat fluttered upward, only occasionally scraping the cliff. Two years ago, after it became apparent that someone like Pilgrim was needed to fly the boat, Pilgrim had made a hobby of scaring the pee out of his passengers. Partly that was pilgrim humor and partly it was to give him an excuse to fly wherever he pleased. Johanna had been on to his game even if Ravna was fooled. She had called him out on the issue, and she was pretty sure that nowadays when the boat behaved insanely it wasn't Pilgrim messing around. The problem was that the agrav fabric was weakening and becoming less rational. More and more, the best performing parts of the fabric were salvage from *Oobii*. Pilgrim was forced to constantly relearn the boat's flight characteristics. He didn't have time for his old hoaxing around.

The skiff slid down five meters, but well away from the cliff. It was twenty meters above the rocks now, with enough clearance all around so that its wobbling was not a concern. This was really not a bad takeoff at all.

As they drifted generally upward, most of Pilgrim turned to look at her. "I forgot to ask. Where is it you want to go?"

"We're going to get these sailors a decent home," Johanna replied.

———

Woodcarver's Fragmentarium was perched in the lower walls of the Margrum Valley, not far above Cliffside harbor, where the Tropicals were being herded. Pilgrim's flight path was more or less straight toward the Fragmentarium. That is, it wobbled in all directions, but the *average* was straight. At higher altitudes he could have risked supersonic speeds, but for short little hops like this, a running pack might outpace him.

Though the boat looked like silver metal from the outside, Pilgrim kept the hull transparent for those within. The view remained surprisingly bad. The scavenged agrav fabric was stubbornly opaque, a patchwork of russet scraps. In some places the repair work was so extensive that it looked like a Tinish muffling quilt sewn together by a crazypack. It was that pattern of obstacles that determined Johanna's favorite perch. Her seat really wasn't a seat—she had to lean forward to clear the ceiling—and the safety harness was *ad hoc*. On the other hand, she had a good view straight down.

They were just passing over the Children she had seen down by the shipwreck. Five boys and two girls. From this altitude she could recognize every one. Yeah, these were the ones. Johanna shook her head, muttering to herself. "You see that?" she said to Pilgrim.

"Of course I see." Pilgrim had three snouts pressed close to one clear spot or another. He had no trouble seeing in multiple directions. "What's to see?"

"The Children. They were throwing stones at drowning Tines." She checked off the names in her mind, vowing to remember. "Øvin Verring. I never dreamed he would do something like that." Øvin had been exactly her age. They'd been evenly matched at school, and friends in a non-romantic way.

The skiff performed a tooth-rattling dip and bounce. Johanna had learned to keep her tongue from between her teeth when she rode this gadget. Nowadays she barely noticed the acrobatics, except when they were close to hard objects.

Pilgrim recovered control; he didn't seem to notice the bouncing either. "To be honest, Jo, I don't think Verring was throwing stones. He was hanging back."

"So? He should have stopped the others . . ." They passed over another Child, this one smaller, falling behind the others. A fivesome was walking with the boy. It was one of only three packs that seemed mixed up with these delinquents. "See? Even little Timor Ristling was down there messing around. He was acting as lookout for the others!" Timor was a cripple now. He had been healthy enough at the High Lab, but even then she had pitied him. He'd been about her brother's age, but he came from a family of low-level integrators, far beneath the brilliant scientists and archeologists who were reanimating the old archive. The closest analogy on Tines World would be to say Timor's folks were janitors, sweeping up the glittering trash that more gifted folks left behind. The boy had never done well in his school classes; he just didn't have a mind for technological thinking. You'd think all that bad fortune would make him more kindly disposed to those poor souls on the shipwreck. Hmm. "I'll bet it's that pack he's hanging out with." The pale fivesome was clustered around him. Belle Ornrikakihm was a grifting wannabe politician out of Woodcarver's pre-human empire. It was a shame she'd gotten her claws into Timor. The boy deserved a better Best Friend, but he was old enough to refuse mentoring.

Their agrav skiff had pulled ahead of the cluster of humans. She could see back now, almost into the faces of the kids at the front. Yeah, there was Gannon Jorkenrud, waving and joking to his pals. *Jerkwad.* Back at the High Lab, Gannon had been one year older than Johanna. He'd skipped grades, had been at the point of graduating from their little school. Gannon was a flaming genius, even more talented than Jo's little brother. At age fourteen, Gannon was as much a master of *anguille borkning* as any of the research staff. Everybody agreed that someday he would be the best *borkner* in all Straumli Realm. Down Here, Jerkwad's talent was good for nothing.

The agrav wobbled higher, flying a little faster. Below them were more shore patrol packs and ordinary citizens, walking north from Cliffside village, probably headed for the shipwreck. There were even a few humans. One of them was running.

"Hei, that's Nevil down there," Johanna said.

"He was throwing rocks?" Pilgrim sounded surprised.

"No, no, he's coming from Cliffside." Nevil Storherte was the oldest of the Children. Certainly he was the most sensible. At the High Lab, Johanna had had such a crush on him, but necessarily from a distance. He probably didn't even know she existed back then. She'd been barely a teenager and he'd been almost ready to graduate. A year or two more and he might have been one of the Straumer researchers. His parents had been the Lab's chief administrators, and Nevil—even when so young—had had a natural aptitude for diplomacy.

Somehow he had learned that Gannon and the others were coming down here. He hadn't been in time to stop them, but she could see that he wasn't running to be first to the shipwreck. He had turned inland, heading for the cluster of Children. As he approached he slowed to a walk, waving to Gannon and the others, no doubt giving them a proper chewing out. She leaned down further, trying for a clear view. The sea mists had been driven inland and the kids were almost out of sight, but she could see that Nevil had stopped all the miscreants and was even waiting for Timor and Belle to catch up. He looked up and waved to her. *Thanks, Nevil.* She wouldn't have to feel bad that she hadn't hung around herself.

Johanna leaned back and looked out the south-facing side of the flier. Though they were half hidden by sea mists, she could see Cliffside village and its little harbor, right down at the mouth of the Margrum River. The agrav climbed into a cloudless day of late summer, and she could see forever. The "U" of the glacier-carved Margrum Valley stretched inland, green lowlands rising to stony bluffs and the patches of high snow that lasted all the way through the summer. Historically, the Margrum had separated Flenser's domain from Woodcarver's. The Battle on Starship Hill had changed all that.

Woodcarver's Fragmentarium was ahead, just above the mists. The Fragmentarium had started out as a temporary war hospital, Woodcarver's effort to honor the packs who'd suffered in support of her. The place had grown into something much more. Pilgrim claimed there had never been such a thing in this part of the world before. Certainly, there were plenty of packs who still did not understand its purpose.

The buildings sat on a small tableland in the side of the valley. Fences followed along the edge of the flat space, taller than any Tinish farmer would ever build. The buildings within were crammed together, leaving as much open space as possible for exercise and play. Woodcarver joked that it was actually to give enough space for Pilgrim to make a safe landing. Considering how often Johanna and Pilgrim came here, that was a good thing.

As they came fluttering downwards, she noticed that among the Tines drifting around the exercise yard there were some who looked suspiciously mangy. How had they gotten past the fence? She realized that she might not be the first person bringing word of the shipwreck. She began revising her sales pitch accordingly.

CHAPTER 03

Usually, Johanna was mobbed by whatever singletons were out in the exercise area. Today a few of the more articulate called out to her, but most of the patients seemed more interested in the Tropical visitors. None of the place's keepers—the broodkenners—were in evidence.

Johanna and Pilgrim left the exercise field and walked past buildings that Ravna Bergsndot called the "old folks' home." Pack members rarely lived longer than forty years. These buildings housed Tines that were too aged to live and work with their packs. The rest of theirselves would visit, in some cases stay for days at a time, especially if the old ones had been some special intellectual or emotional part of the pack. For Johanna, it was the saddest part of the Fragmentarium, since without decent technology none of these fragments would get any better. The rest of theirselves would visit more and more rarely, eventually incorporating younger members, and not coming at all.

Here and there a head raised to watch her. Some of the visiting packs—the ones who valued their old selves enough to be united—honked greetings and even whole sentences of Samnorsk. There were grateful folk here, but all in all it was too much like the dark ages of human prehistory, *like what we Children ourselves must face Down Here.*

The broodkenners' office was at the upslope end of the encampment, beyond the exercise field and the barracks for able-bodied fragments. There was one more shortcut they could take, but Johanna and Pilgrim stayed well away from the war criminals' compound. *That* was an institution that many Tinish kingdoms supported, though usually it was a public pillory where partially executed enemies of the state could be put on display. Woodcarver had never been such a sadist. Pilgrim often assured Jo that the Children were fortunate to have fallen in with the kindliest despot in the world. Since Flenser was rehabilitated and Vendacious had escaped, there was only one war criminal left in the Domain, and that was Flenser's monster, Lord Steel. The original Steel had been cut down to three members. His remnant had a prison cell with its own little exercise yard. She hadn't seen that fragment in two years. She knew her brother came here occasionally to talk to the threesome, but then Jefri and Amdi had personal issues with Steel. She hoped the visits were not meant to taunt the creature. Steel was thoroughly mad, surviving in a weird tug of war between Woodcarver's caution and Flenser's demand that the remnant not be destroyed. Today she heard shrieks of rage coming from the prison compound, demands to be released. The Remnant Steel knew something was going on, and apparently there was no keeper to let it out into its exercise yard.

"So where are the broodkenners?" said Johanna. Not even Carenfret was around, and she was obsessively dutiful.

"Harmony's here. I can hear him talking." Pilgrim jabbed a snout toward the admin office.

"He's here?" Damn. Harmony was the chief broodkenner, a pack of the old school and a real jerk. Now she could hear Tinish gobbling ahead. It was loud enough; she'd mistaken it for the usual random shouting that came from the patients' barracks. Yes, the pack was talking on the telephone. That was probably a good thing, since Harmony's judgment could only benefit from outside advice. She lifted the high bar on an inner gate and let herself and Pilgrim through. The admin building was actually a dorm for the overnight broodkenners, most often Carenfret. It was big enough for two or three packs, but right now there seemed to be just the one voice within. The front door was open. She bent low and awkwardly waddled indoors, preceded and followed by Pilgrim.

Harmony was way in the back, in his official office. That wasn't as large as Harmony would probably like, but it was the room with the telephone, and the Chief Broodkenner had claimed it his first day on the job. Johanna was pleased that no one had ever told him how easy it would be to wire the phone into a different room. She wasn't the only one who thought ill of this pack.

Harmony was just racking the phone when Pilgrim and Johanna stuck heads into his room. "Well, well," he said, sounding cordial. "Here is the source of so many of my problems." He gestured at the floor in front of his desk. "Do please have a seat, Johanna."

Jo settled herself on the floor. Now she had to look up to see Harmony's heads. Well, it beat standing stooped over to avoid the ceiling beams. Pilgrim settled himself in the hall, with just one head poked around the door. He could participate in the discussion without his mindsound interfering too much.

Johanna had put together a little speech, but this phone call might change things. "So," she said, winging it, "you've heard about the shipwreck."

"Of course. I just finished discussing the matter with the Tinish Queen Herself."

"Oh." *So what did Woodcarver say?* Harmony looked too self-satisfied for it to be anything good. "There are almost two hundred surviving Tropicals, sir. Pilgrim tells me that's substantially more than in the average South Sea wreck."

Harmony gave an irritated little ripple of his heads. "Yes. I understand you are largely responsible for this problem."

"Well, I helped too," Pilgrim put in cheerily.

Harmony waved a dismissive snout at Pilgrim. The Chief Broodkenner always tried to ignore Pilgrim. The two packs were about as different as packs could be, one as tightly held as a human's clenched fist, the other so loose that sometimes it seemed to dissolve into lesser parts. Unfortunately for Harmony, Pilgrim was the queen's consort, had been for more than two years. Part of the queen herself was now from Pilgrim. Harmony was far too cautious to say anything reportable against him. All his heads turned back in Johanna's direction: "No doubt you're wondering where my assistants are this afternoon." He meant the other broodkenners, most of whom were very nice people.

"Well, yes."

"You're the reason for their absence. That's what I was just discussing with the Queen. It's bad enough that you've transformed this shipwreck from a commonplace opportunity into a serious inconvenience. But it's inexcusable that you directed them to come here for refuge."

"*What?* I did no such thing."

Pilgrim said. "Hei, I was there, Broodkenner. Of course, Johanna did no such thing. I doubt if any of the Tropicals knows a word of Samnorsk."

Harmony all came to his feet, his various members adjusting the trim red jackets of his uniform. Two of him came partway over his desk, gesturing emphatically at Johanna. "Forgive me then. This is simply what I would expect of you. It's what my assistants thought too. Every one them is downhill from the broodkennery right now, holding off the onslaught of Tropical riffraff. We all speculated just who put the creatures up to this."

Johanna crossed her arms and leaned forward. She knew that the main body of the mob was still on the beach being herded toward Cliffside village by the shore patrol. There couldn't be more than thirty or forty who had slipped free—and those would be wandering across the hillsides. As for the idea that *she* had suggested the Tropicals come here: well, bunk. Harmony had done this sort of thing to her in the past, making wild accusations that turned out to be exactly what she was about to suggest. This time she refused to be disarmed. "Sir, if your staff thought I directed the Tropicals here, maybe that's because it's a good idea. The Tropicals are creatures just like your own members, just like the singletons whom we help here at the Fragmentarium."

"Here at the broodkennery," Harmony corrected. Broodkenning was an essential part of Tinish civilization, a cross between marriage counsellor, animal breeder, and reconstructive surgeon. Johanna respected most broodkenners, even hardclawed ones who couldn't stand the sight of her. It took real skill to properly recommend which puppies should go with which packs or whether a whole new pack should be made. It took even greater talent to create well-functioning packs from adult singletons and duos. Some of the local broodkenners were geniuses at their craft. Harmony Redjackets wasn't one of them. He was an East Coast expert who had somehow flimflammed Woodcarver when she was in the dumps for having lost two of her oldest members. The redjackets of the East took a harsher attitude toward individual members than most packs out here. In a way, they were like the Old Flenserists—though she would never suggest that straight out to Woodcarver.

"That's the fundamental problem with your meddling," continued Harmony. "Your notion of fragments as patients. I can understand it. It's based on the fundamental human weakness. You simply can't help it."

Johanna almost interrupted with a sneering comment. *If we Children weren't lost in this pre-tech wilderness, we could replace any part of our bodies, and easier than you, Mr. Harmony, can imagine.* Unfortunately, that might tend to support Harmony's main point. At a loss for a cutting response, Johanna let the other's argument roll on.

"We packs can *choose* what we are. We can live beyond our members of the moment and always be the best that can be."

At least Pilgrim had a reply: "I've been around long enough to know that's not always true."

"Loose pack that you are," said Harmony.

"Ah, true. But a loose pack who has the ear of the Queen. So tell me, Harmony, you're just going to turn away the mob that came ashore this morning?"

"Yes." The redjackets was smiling.

"There's more of them than usual," said Pilgrim. "As a Choir, they're a loud nuisance. As singletons and duos they'll soon be drifting around our towns, making an even bigger nuisance of themselves. Neither villagers nor merchants will approve. And I know Woodcarver would not approve killing them."

Harmony was still grinning. "That would not be such a problem if you two had only let nature take its course with the superfluous ones." He shrugged. "No one is talking about killing the survivors. I'm quite aware that eventually the remnants will sail away with what trinket garbage we provide. Woodcarver has told me that it happens every few decades." He gave a pointed and unanimous look in Pilgrim's direction. "You are not the only one with the ear of the Queen." He waved at the telephone. "Marvelous instrument, this. Certainly the best toy you two-legs have brought to civilization."

Damn, fumed Johanna. *I could have called both Woodcarver and Ravna during the flight up here. Instead I just wasted my time fuming.*

But Harmony was still talking. "The Queen and I agreed it would be absurd to cram more bodies into the Royal Broodkennery. Without extensive enlargement, there is simply not enough room. More important, housing a Choir of Tropicals is quite the opposite of the purpose of this institution." He paused, as if inviting Johanna or Pilgrim to object. "But you need not worry about them burdening the alleys and markets of Newcastle town or Hidden Island. I've suggested an alternate option to Her Majesty, and she has enthusiastically blessed it. The Tropicals will be guided to a new enclave, built specially for them."

"A *second* Fragmentarium?" asked Pilgrim.

"Not at all. This will be at the south edge of Starship Hill, far from all the places where such creatures can make trouble. It will need no staff, since it's for containment, not treatment."

"So, a prison camp?"

"No. An embassy! The Tropicals' Embassy. Sometimes absurdity is the best solution." Honking laughter backed up Harmony's words. Tines could do that, provide their own audio accompaniment. Mostly it was cute, but then there was Harmony Redjackets. "Of course, there will be some fences needed, and in the early days guarding the exterior will be good practice for all those soldier packs the Queen keeps on payroll. But the compound will include a little farmland, enough for hardicore grass and a yam garden. We all know that Tropicals don't like meat."

Johanna glared back at the pack. Tines were omnivores, but they all loved meat. The only vegetarians among them were the very poor. Harmony had definitely won the argument if that was all the comeback she had. She glanced at Pilgrim. "Well, then," she finally replied, "I suppose that's a solution."

In fact," said Pilgrim, "it might even be a good solution, depending on the details. You have to realize, this situation could go on for several years. I'm not sure that—"

"And that," interrupted Harmony, "is, thank goodness, not my problem. You can take your concerns about the future to the Queen, as I'm sure you will continue to do."

"Um, yes," Pilgrim replied.

Behind her, Johanna could feel one of Pilgrim pulling gently at her waistband, telling her it was time for an orderly retreat. Pilgrim was afraid she would try to get the last word. He knew her too well. Okay, this time she would prove Pilgrim wrong. She came to her feet, careful not to crack her head on the ceiling. "Well then, Sir Harmony. Thank you so much for solving this problem in such a timely and, um, graceful way." *See, I can be diplomatic.* She bent a little more, but it wasn't a bow; she was just trying to back out of the office.

Harmony made a little "don't go yet" gesture. "You know, I had an excellent chat with Her Majesty. I think that she and I have come to think very much alike on issues of probity and public health. After all, broodkenning is one of the foundations of a happy nation. I think we in the East understand that much better than most people here. The reaction against Flenser's excesses was bad enough. You humans have added your own confused ethics to the mess." ·

"Yes, I'm sure," said Johanna, waving a gesture she was fairly certain Harmony would not recognize. She really had to get away from this guy.

Unfortunately, Harmony was the kind who liked to rub it in. Or maybe he thought that the time to press ahead is when you've already scored some points. "You should understand, Johanna, that your crazy influence on the Royal Broodkennery is coming to an end. We simply don't have the resources for your notion of a Fragmentarium."

That got her attention. "You're giving up on the war veterans, the accident victims?" She took a step back in Harmony's direction, pulling against Pilgrim's jaws.

Harmony seemed oblivious to her tone. "No, not that. The Queen is quite explicit. Though the odds are against success, and merges of adult fragments are often ineffectual packs, even so we owe the veterans our best efforts. It's the foolishness that has to go. Pack *members* get old, they get incurably ill, and they die. I'm sorry, I have to say it. Despite all your wishful thinking, members die. It's not our job at the broodkennery to prolong that process—and we simply do not have the resources to do so."

"But the old ones die in any case, Harmony. Why should you care that their last year or two is pleasant?"

The redjackets shrugged. "That's why, when I first came to this job, I thought your foolish ideas were harmless. But have you noticed? Your unhealthful approach has just encouraged normal packs to linger over their dying parts. We have more and more of these sick and unproductive parts here. They aren't getting any better. We agree, they never will get better. But they are filling up our floorspace, taking away from the cases—including those adult singletons you so seem to love—that we could save. Someone has to make the hard decisions. There needs to be a thinning."

Pilgrim stuck a head back into the room. "You may have trouble justifying your 'hard decisions' to soft-hearted western packs who want to carry on with their oldest members."

Harmony steepled a couple of his heads judiciously. "It will ultimately be the choice of the packs involved. We'll simply tell them our assessment of their weaknesses and point out that we no longer have the resources to care for their morbid members. They'll be free to let us deal with them—or they can take that responsibility themselves, as decent packs have always done." Traditionally, that meant that when a member could no longer keep up with normal hunting, well, it would fall behind. In fact, "to fall behind" was the Interpack euphemism for member death.

"And the ones you take care of, how do you kill them, hmm?" Johanna took another step back into the room, far enough that Harmony finally understood the threat.

Two of him surged forward, blustering, but the others were staring up at her a little nervously. "Th-there are traditional ways, not at all painful or distressing. You poor two-legs, trapped in a single mortal body, I can't expect you to understand our point of view." Now all of him seemed to have recovered courage. Five pairs of toothy jaws were waggling around in front of her.

Behind her, all of Pilgrim had grabbed her pants and the bottom of her jacket. No more subtlety; he was doing his best to drag her from the room. His voice was diplomatic, belying the effort: "Well, thank you for the advance notice, dear Harmony."

The redjackets gave a gracious wave. "My pleasure—though it was the Queen's suggestion that I inform you."

"I'll thank her myself," said Pilgrim, "the next time we're together."

There were implications in Pilgrim's words that should give the chief broodkenner pause. For packs, "being together" could mean literally "being of one mind." It was certainly a stronger retort than anything Johanna could think of. She let her toothy friend lead her away.

Jo didn't speak until they were out of the building, beyond even Tinish earshot. "I hope you meant what you said, Pilgrim. About talking to Woodcarver."

"Oh yes indeedy. Harmony takes his redjackets much too seriously. His kind is the worst thing about the East Coast." But Pilgrim sounded more amused than enraged.

"He's a monstrous sonsabitches," said Johanna.

Pilgrim was looking around at the multistoried barracks that stood on both sides of the path. From here, you couldn't even see the exercise field and the valley beyond. "This place has really gotten overcrowded, you know," he said.

———

The rest of the afternoon was spent in something unusual: a screaming argument with Pilgrim. Fortunately for her hearing, it was Johanna who did all the screaming. How could her best friend in the world be so lukewarm about the murders planned at the Fragmentarium? By sundown, Johanna was convinced that he was taking her case to Woodcarver just to keep Jo mellow. Pilgrim was certainly doing his best to avoid arguing the issues with her. He really *didn't* understand why thinning the old members was murder. And he didn't want Johanna to come along to talk to the Queen.

"It's an intimate thing, Johanna. You know, sex and mindtalk." He waggled his heads salaciously.

Normally that excuse worked. She certainly had no place in a Tinish love affair—but tonight she suspected Pilgrim thought that Jo and her weird human notions would just cause trouble. "Okay, then," she said. "You do your thing with Woodcarver. But make her understand! This redjackets crap is just as bad as the Old Flenser."

"Oh, I will, I promise. I'll do my very best." The fivesome danced around nervously, then finally chased himself out the door. Coward.

She should follow him up to the New Castle, maybe talk to Woodcarver herself. Pilgrim just didn't have the proper fire.

Fortunately, some shred of common sense remained, and Jo stayed inside until Pilgrim was well gone. She could give Ravna Bergsndot a call. Along with Woodcarver, Ravna was Queen of the Realm. Ravna might not take her title seriously, but she was the most powerful person in the world. She could tell Woodcarver what to do about this, and by the Powers Above, her word would rule. Yeah, the trouble was that Ravna was too much of a compromiser. She would compromise about anything, as long as it didn't get in the way of fighting the Blight.

Johanna stepped out into the twilight and took a few deep breaths. The northwest still held sunset colors, but elsewhere the sky was darkening blue, with stars already visible in the east. She cursed this world often enough, but summer was mostly a beautiful time. You could forget how deadly a natural world could be. You could even sometimes forget what you had lost. This little cabin that she shared with Pilgrim was an upper-class residence by the standards of the locals. If Ravna's plans for heating water with the starship's beam gun could be implemented, houses like this would be more comfortable than any old Tinish castle.

Maybe she should walk up to Newcastle town. That was where most of the Children lived, and all of the toddlers. Her brother might be up there. No, Jef and Amdi were in the north woods this tenday, learning to be scouts. But there were other Children she could talk to. Nevil? He was probably still down in Cliffside village. He'd be perfect to talk to; he'd understand. Too bad the phone lines hadn't been strung that far, or else she'd call him for sure.

Johanna walked downhill, away from the New Castle and the town that surrounded it. There really was no one to talk to tonight. Maybe that was best; she was so bloody angry. Packs could be lovable, nicer than most humans. But even the nicest of them didn't really see their members as persons. She walked a little faster, letting the old frustration grow. Today had brought a lot of that to a head, and she wasn't going to let it go. In the past, she had seen members die; they were people, even if she could never convince the packs of that.

Well, if talking could not make a difference, maybe there were actions that would. She let that thought rattle around in her mind for a few moments, imagining what she could do if she had some of the powers that every Straumer— even every Straumer child—had had before they fell Down Here. Ravna's starship, that was nothing compared to a few merge toys and braemsjers. She'd raise the fragments to mindfulness, give them tools that would wipe the smug expression from packs like Harmony.

It really felt good to imagine such a turn of fortune. And it would have all been possible, not dreaming at all, before they were cast down from the Top of the Beyond. Before everything had gone so terribly wrong at the High Lab.

She looked around, realized she'd walked more than a kilometer. She'd reached the edge of the Margrum Valley. The moon had risen, showing the far side of the valley afloat above an evening fog. The path—its official name was the Queen's Road—became a bit twisty, zigzagging back and forth as it descended the north wall of the valley. During the day, there would be plenty of wagon traffic here, the kherhog handlers arguing about their right of way.

While she was imagining impossible revenge, her feet had carried her halfway back to the Fragmentarium. Maybe her feet were smarter than her head. Harmony complained about not having floorspace, and Woodcarver agreed. Well, there were ways of making floorspace. There were ways of making everyone look up and listen! Her pace picked up. Now both head and feet were cooperating—what a Tinish thing to say—as she realized how much change she could make all by herself. Somewhere in the back of her mind a little voice was saying that what she could do might be worse than not doing anything at all. But for the moment that voice was easy to ignore.

She came around the last turn before the Fragmentarium. The top of the cloud layer had just submerged the buildings, so all she could see were a few dim lights, probably from the old-members barracks. Admin would be hidden around on the other side of the compound. The Queens's Road continued on its winding path down to Cliffside village, but the turnoff to the Fragmentarium was just another fifty meters or so. She walked forward, into the fog.

"Hei, Johanna." The voice came from a little way ahead.

Jo gave a squeak of surprise, her mind cycling through variations on fight, flight, or make friendly social conversation. She peered into the mist. Aha. Friendly conversation was in order. It was a pack of four. No, five if you counted the puppy in a pannier.

"Hello," Johanna said. "Do I know you?"

The four adult members brought their heads together. Even a meter or two of fog was enough to soak mindsound into silence; the pack was trying to think clearly. After a moment the voice replied: "Not understand, Johanna. Sorry."

Jo made little sweep of her hand. Most packs seemed to take that motion to be like the Tinish head gesture for "That's okay." Of course, it might be too dark for the pack to see.

After a moment, they all continued along the path. As usual the fog was playing little tricks with sound. There was a buzzing sound that might have been some beat frequency of mindsounds. Or maybe it was just humming nervously. "I, *hmmm*," it said—trying to think of the Samnorsk words? "I . . . am," there was a Tinish chord that might have been familiar, "I . . . work . . . New Castle, *um* . . . work stone."

"You're a mason at the New Castle?"

"Yes! Right word. Right word."

Before the humans came, before the Children's Academy, stonemason work was a fairly high-standing tech profession; it was still quite respectable. They walked together in silence, divided by a difficult language barrier. Now she realized that they were not alone; there was a pack pacing along behind them, and maybe another behind that. Certainly Mr. Stonemason had heard them, so it seemed more mysterious than sinister to Johanna.

"Turn. I turn . . . here," said the stonemason. They were at the turnoff to the Fragmentarium. Johanna followed the pack down the flagstoned path. They passed a wick lamp and she got a look at the other two packs. One was just a threesome. The other was four but two of its members were scarcely more than puppies. So, mystery explained.

As they came near the old-members barracks, the other two packs both started gobbling. Various voices responded from within, and the packs were both racing off toward the building. The stonemason stayed with Johanna. As they came near the entrance, it spoke again: "You don't remember me, but except for my puppy, I was with you and Pham Nuwen when you entered the New Castle. You know, the day Pham made the sun go dark."

Johanna turned to the pack, struck by its sudden fluency. An old, balding member had limped out of the shadows. The stonemason had flowed around it, and now all heads were pressed close together. The pack must have been one of Woodcarver's guards at the Battle on Starship Hill.

Jo smiled. She didn't remember this particular pack, but—"I do remember the day. You were outside? You actually saw the sun go out?" Almost any technology could overawe a pre-tech civilization such as on Tines World, but what Pham had done, twisting the laws of nature across hundreds of lightyears . . . that was something that awed even the Children. It was no surprise that the act had sucked up all the output of the sun.

The five—even the little puppy—were nodding agreement. "A thousand years from now, it may only be a myth in the mind of the pack of me, but it will be the greatest myth of all. When I looked up at the dark of the sun, I felt the Pack of Packs."

The stonemason, now including the halt member who lived in the Fragmentarium, was silent for a moment. Then it gave a shiver. "It's too cold out here for some of me. Why don't you come inside? There are several whole packs tonight. They don't speak Samnorsk, but I can translate for them."

Johanna started to follow the other into the hall, but then she realized that most of the critters within were not reunited. They really were falling behind. If she stayed more than a minute or two she would start blabbing about what Harmony had in mind . . . and too many would understand. She stopped at the door, and waved the stonemason through. "I'll come here another night," she said.

The pack hesitated a moment. "Okay, then, but you should know. I'm grateful to you. Part of me is very sick, but with her I am much more clever. I can plan better. Every night I come here, and I work better the next day. It's partly the planning I do when I'm smart. It's partly what my new puppy learns from my old part. Rich people do this all the time." All the heads looked up at Johanna. "I think that's part of how they stay rich. Thank you for suggesting this place to Queen Woodcarver."

Johanna bobbed her head. "You're welcome." Her words came out strangled. She turned and walked stiffly away, into the dark. *Damn, damn, damn.*

She wandered in the mists for some minutes, long enough for the guilt to boil back into rage. She needed a proper act of creative revenge against Harmony and all of his traditionalist ilk. Something that would kick even Woodcarver in the teeth if she couldn't see sense.

Eventually she ran into the high fence that surrounded the exercise yard and the able-bodied barracks. She walked along the barrier, trailing her fingers against the wooden slats. So Harmony figured there wasn't enough *room.* Yeah, it was crowded. Helping one's old members was more popular than anyone had predicted. No doubt Harmony was also complaining about the various resources consumed too. *That* would make more of a difference to Woodcarver. But Woodcarver was rich. If she wasn't rich enough, Ravna could kick in some of *Oobii*'s tech rents. This world was so poor, so stupid. In the High Beyond, caring for individual sophonts was one of the smallest costs of operations, handled invisibly for the most part. Wealth went for other things. . . .

She almost tripped over the creature that was digging under the fence. The Tine pulled its head and paws out of the dirt. Its jaws snapped shut just where Jo's face had been before she startled back—but there was no further attack. The critter had no backup; it was a singleton. No, wait. There were a couple others, lurking about in the misty moonlight. They were all Tropicals. Glares were exchanged, but then the mangy critters backed down. The three wandered off—and in different directions. You'd *never* see a pack casually lose itself like that. How many of these troublemakers were lurking around the Fragmentarium? The notion of bundling the Tropicals off to a separate camp wasn't completely stupid.

Jo continued toward the entrance to the able-bodied barracks. There was plenty of noise from inside the building. Outside, on her side of the fence, she saw occasional shadows move, heard an occasional howl. Harmony must still have his broodkenners playing dogcatcher all over the valley; she was here all by herself. The thought was not frightening, quite the opposite. The Tropicals weren't especially friendly, but they also seemed to be total scatterbrains. And the fragments in the barracks ahead were Johanna's friends—at least to the limits of their intelligence.

In fact . . . being alone here, she was in a position to get that proper revenge she'd been thinking of. She walked faster, purpose informing her direction. The idea was crazy, but it would create plenty of the precious "room" that Harmony was complaining about. It would show that sonsabitches and Woodcarver, too, that the fragments weren't to be pushed around.

The racket from within the barracks was really loud. Johanna came up here a lot, and in the wintertime her visits were necessarily after dark—but she had never heard this much angry gobbling. Of course, these frags were never as civil as whole packs. They had the moods and whimsies of hundreds of separate animals. Most in this barracks were big and healthy, and desperate to be part of whole packs. That was why the fence and the barred gate were necessary. Most of the time, most of the frags were a little bit frightened of escape— even at the same time they yearned to run out into the wide world and find some likely pack. Over the last two years, Jo had made such matchmaking her business. Carenfret actually called Johanna the "littlest kenner." Johanna could walk right into the barracks and chat with singletons and duos who knew a little Samnorsk. Even when speech wasn't possible, the frags enjoyed having something as smart as a pack that they could come near to, that they could pretend with. Any number of times, she had started new packs by pairing duos or getting a singleton together with a duo. At least as often, she had chatted up damaged packs on Hidden Island, or Newcastle town, or Cliffside, and persuaded them that she had an ideal completion for them.

It was that sort of effort, both by her and the decent broodkenners, that made the escape attempts very half-hearted.

Tonight sounded very different.

The wick lamp mounted over the gate showed dozens of fragments milling around just inside the entrance. More were coming by the second, pushing and shoving against the fence.

As she came into view (or hearing, which perhaps was more important for Tines) there were the usual calls of "Hei, Johanna!" "Hei, Johanna!" Those shouts were drowned out by angry gobbling, by howling and yapping that almost sounded like the baying of dogs.

The more articulate actually made sense. The occasional Samnorsk matched what Interpack she could understand: "Let us out. We want to be free!"

Now she saw what might be the explanation for all the incautious wanderlust: the Tropicals that had sneaked *inside* the fence. She could spot only a couple, but they were in the loudest clusters. Apparently, their attitude had tipped the overall consensus.

She'd never seen so many fragments simultaneously eager to break out. Besides banging the fence, some were digging at the foundations of the barrier. Right at the entrance, a knot of singletons had piled up, trying to reach over the top. If they had been a coordinated pack, wearing jackets with paw straps, they could have boosted some of themselves out. As it was, the pyramid would reach about two meters fifty and then fall back on itself.

"Hei, Johanna! Help us." The voice came from those piling against the entrance.

"Cheepers!" said Johanna. She recognized the white splash of fur on the back of its head. This was the most fluent of the Samnorsk speakers; sometimes he actually made sense. The poor guy would have been a big plus to almost any pack, but he was from one of Steel's recycled monster packs. He had memories that eventually repelled whomever he was intimate with. Cheepers himself was gentle and friendly, and as smart as a singleton can be, which made his situation that much sadder to Jo. She went to one knee so she could look at the singleton eye to eye, through the tiny gaps in the fence. "What's up, Cheepers?"

"Get us out, get us out!"

Johanna rocked back. How could she explain? Nuance was rarely a singleton's strong point. "I—" she started to make some excuse and then thought, *Well, why not?* Slowly, she stood up. Yes, she really could have revenge. And it would end the crowding, and it would give Cheepers and his friends what they wanted.

She looked at the gate. It was barred on the outside, but with a simple timber and clasp. It was almost two meters off the ground. An escaped singleton couldn't reach the bar. She was vaguely aware of the three Tropicals on her side of the fence, watching her. No doubt they were too scatterbrained to figure out the mechanism, but any coherent pack on this side of the fence could have opened the gate easily, just by climbing up on itself. Johanna could open it most easily of all.

Jo stepped forward, already gloating about imagined consequences. She reached for the gate bar, then hesitated. Consequences, consequences. There was a reason these poor creatures had been brought here. Where else could they go? In the towns of the Domain, a very few might find new minds, but the rest would be cuffed about, some killed, some enslaved. There was a reason for having the Fragmentarium. She herself had fought to make Woodcarver's wartime field hospital into this institution. Releasing the patients would be vengeance mainly on these patients themselves. She glanced to her left, at Cheepers bouncing up and down, urging her on. If they hadn't been all whipped up tonight, these frags would mostly shrink from escape.

Johanna stepped back from the gate. No, there were some things too loony even for her, even in a rage. *But I could have, and the look on Harmony would have been—*

Something came streaking in from her left, knocking her off her feet. All three Tropicals bounded past. They clambered over each other even as she scrambled to her feet. Maybe they had seen what she was going to do, maybe they were that smart by themselves. In any case, the top one eased its snout under the bar and flipped it loose. The pressure from within swung the gate open, knocking the three's pyramid in all directions. The crowd within stampeded through, some of them knocking Johanna down again, most flowing smoothly around her. Some even said "Hei" on their way past.

Johanna curled forward, protecting her face behind her knees and arms.

Finally the thundering herd had passed. Their shouts and caroling echoed back from the hills as they chased themselves both south and north along the Queen's Road.

Jo got back on her feet. The damp ground had been trampled into mud. The open gate hung at an angle. She saw a half dozen figures near the entrance.

"Guys?" Johanna walked toward the remaining Tines. It wouldn't be surprising if the departure had left some injured behind.

Even close up, she didn't see any blood. None of the Tines were limping, except the one she called Dirty Henrik, and he'd had a bad forepaw ever since the rest of his pack got squished in a rock fall. No, these six just couldn't decide whether they were staying or going. They milled in and out of the entrance, making nervous noises as they looked out into the dark.

Jo stood by the gate for a moment, feeling just as uncertain as the remaining Tines, and thinking through her reasoning of moments before—before the Tropicals had put everyone on the other side of the question. Finally she said, "You gotta make up your minds, guys, cuz I'm gonna close this gate."

None of them understood Samnorsk, but when she put her hands on the gate and began to push it shut, they seemed to get the message. All but Dirty Henrik quickly slipped inside. Henrik remained half in and half out, his nose twitching as he smelled the night air. His pack had been a lumberjack; maybe he could do all right in the outside. Dirty Henrik wobbled back and forth, then realized the gate was still closing on him. He gave a little squeak and retreated within.

Jo had to force the gate upwards to overcome the bent hinge, and then it was shut. She left the lock bar on the ground. Hell, if he wanted to badly enough, Henrik could probably push his way out.

And now . . . Johanna stood in silence for a moment, trying to make sense of what had happened and decide how she should feel about it. Finally she shook her head and started up the steps that led to the admin building. She had some phone calls to make.

The other Children called the events of that night "Jo's great jailbreak." Some of them thought it was all very funny. The consequences? Maybe they were as bad as Johanna had imagined, though not quite so obvious and visible. For the next year or so, the back alleys and garbage dumps of villages all around had a surplus of singletons and duos, aimless beggars who importuned and incompetently burgled and robbed. A few came back to the Fragmentarium. A very few found refuge in the new Tropical "embassy," though the Tropicals seemed much less happy to have recruits than they were to raise hell with the local singletons.

The majority of the runaways simply disappeared into the awesome wilderness. Pilgrim thought that more than a few of the disappeared had survived and made packs of themselves. "I can tell you from personal experience," he told Jo some tendays later, when he caught her crying, "when times get really tough, you'll patch up with parts you could never imagine sharing even a single thought with. Hei, look at me." That turned her sobs into a hiccupping laugh; she knew what he meant better than most humans. Nevertheless, she was sure that the wide, deep silence of the northern forests had swallowed the lives of most of the runaways.

And consequences for Johanna Olsndot herself? Leave aside her most idiot classmates who thought it was all a joke. Her little brother seemed to regard the incident with uneasy awe. She was the sister who corrected *his* foolishness. In his view, this situation upset the natural order.

Woodcarver actually stopped talking to Jo for a time. Her Majesty knew the odds against singletons in the wild. She had allowed the Fragmentarium from the same good will that she extended to her war veterans—and Harmony's plans had been an attempt to make room for those healthy singletons to remain in safety. More, she knew that the escape was a slap not just at Harmony Redjackets but at Woodcarver herself.

Maybe it was because of good words from Pilgrim to Woodcarver, but the Fragmentarium remained open. Indeed, one happy consequence was exactly as Johanna had imagined: now there was plenty of room in the institution. Woodcarver did not move to boot the old members out of the place. Mr. Stonemason and the others had a place for their elderly parts, even doomed as they were. That crowding problem was postponed for a while—and Harmony looked like the ineffectual, pompous assholes that he was!

Any time in the first days after the Breakout, Johanna could easily have proclaimed her innocence. After all, the evidence against her was circumstantial, with Harmony the loudest proclaimer of her guilt. The only eyewitnesses were very confused singletons, and some of them apparently thought she *had* been the one to throw the gate open. She almost told Pilgrim the truth—except that she soon guessed that he already knew. Johanna came even closer to telling Ravna Bergsndot. It hurt to think that Ravna saw her as just a stupid little teenager; the poor lady had to deal with too many of those already. But the days passed, and Johanna's reputation grew and solidified. Yeah, she was very glad she hadn't done what people thought she had. But hell, it had happened—and in the future, maybe people like Harmony would think twice before they crossed the Mad Bad Girl of Starship Hill.

Three years after the
Battle on Starship Hill

CHAPTER 04

Remasritlfeer had been working for the Great Tycoon for more than two years. This was a constant source of surprise to Remasritlfeer, who had never taken kindly to fools, even ones as rich as Tycoon. The two years had been one crackbrained mission after another, some more dangerous and exciting than the explorer in Remasritlfeer would have ever dreamed. And maybe that was why he continued to work for the madpack.

This latest piece of insanity might finally bring an end to their relationship. Exploring the Tropics! The assignment was more dangerous, more insane—literally insane—than anything Tycoon had demanded before. But truthfully, the first few days had been magnificent: Remasritlfeer had totally survived and in two ways he'd matched or exceeded the triumph of any explorer in the history of the world.

Unfortunately, that was four tendays ago. Tycoon just didn't know when to give up. Glory had degenerated into deadly tedium, tenday after tenday of failures.

"There has to come an end to it, you know." The words expressed Remasritlfeer's heartfelt opinion, but they were spoken by his passenger on this flight. This *final* trip, if there was any mercy in the world. Chitiratifor was a well-dressed sixsome who barely fit in the balloon's passenger platform. The *Sea Breeze*'s gondola was a cramped place where every pound had to be accounted for. The insulation round the passenger platform was so thin that Chitiratifor's anxiety was painfully loud. Remasritlfeer could see claws and jaws here and there through the partition. His passenger was gouging the frame of the gondola with all his strength. There were retching sounds, some of his members barfing into the muddy water below.

Remasritlfeer waggled a semaphore at Tycoon's sailing fleet below. They paid out the tether a bit faster, let the sea breeze blow the *Sea Breeze* steadily toward the swampy inland. This had been the routine twice a tenday since the beginning of this horrid exercise. All through the predawn, Tycoon's support vessels would puff away, mixing iron filings with various corrosive poisons, filling the gas bag of the *Sea Breeze* or its alternate. Then, as the morning wind picked up, Remasritlfeer would lift off, sailing through the air like no one in history, like no one in the world (if you didn't count the Sky Maggots).

"We'll be over land in a matter of minutes now, sir," he said cheerfully to Chitiratifor.

Chitiratifor made some more mouth noise. Then he said, "This has to look good, you know. My master says that Tycoon is still claiming the Tropics will make him rich beyond the dreams of all packs past. If we are not convincing today, he'll be sailing around down here forever, pissing away our treasure."

Our treasure? Chitiratifor and his master Vendacious were a presumptuous pair. They had some reason. They had provided critical fixes that made Tycoon's inventions—including these balloons—workable. Remasritlfeer could sense their contempt. They figured they could use Tycoon; it seriously upset them when the Boss could not be swayed.

It was too bad that in this particular case Chitiratifor and Vendacious were absolutely right. Remasritlfeer looked inland. The weather had been perfect so far, but there were high clouds ranked to the north. If those clouds marched south, this afternoon could get exciting. At the moment, they simply blocked the far view, the jungle basin that fed the River Fell. Even on the clearest days, one pack's eyes could not see the all of that. The Fell stretched northward to beyond the horizon. Its fringes were a vast network of great rivers descending from smaller and smaller ones, ultimately from mountain streams at the edge of arctic cold. Those lands had their own mysteries and threats. They were the scene of endless deadly stories and many of Remasritlfeer's own explorations— but they could not compare to the Lower Fell, to the mystery and the threat of the ground below him now. Their balloon wasn't more than a thousand feet up. Details were lost in the humid mist—except when he looked almost straight down. There was the muddy water, the occasional swamp grass. It was hard to tell just where the outflow of the Fell ended. Normal ships ran aground on barely submerged mudflats that extended more than a hundred miles out. The color of the shallows and their smell had given the Fell its name before any pack set eyes on the river mouth itself. You needed rafts or special-built ships to get as close as Tycoon's fleet. *And I am even closer yet!* thought Remasritlfeer. It was a rare privilege, one that he would treasure—after he was far away from here. As for now, well, he'd seen cesspools in East Home with much the same appearance as the murk below, and the smell was like nothing he had ever experienced, a mix of rot and body odor and exotic plants.

The *Sea Breeze* moved steadily northwards, not much faster than a pack might walk. The wind and the tether combined to keep them at altitude, sparing them the awful death that had claimed all previous explorers—and incidentally keeping them out of the heat and damp of the tropical jungle. The grass below had taken on its tree form. The trunks might still be below water, but yard by yard, as the balloon drifted north, those trunks became thicker, holding more silt from the Fell. "Most of what we're seeing now stays above sea level except during storms and the highest tides," said Remasritlfeer.

More of Chitiratifor's snouts were visible now. The pack was peering down. "How far still to go?" he said.

"We just have to move a little eastwards." Remasritlfeer had been watching the ground, and Tycoon's ships, and the payout of the tether. You could be sure Tycoon was watching back. If Tycoon had stayed back in East Home, they all could have abandoned this foolishness by now. Directly below, he recognized a pattern of trees that he had used on the last few flights; he signalled for the ship to stop the payout and move eastward. The *Sea Breeze* bounced gently against the limit of the tether. The ground below slid sideways. Remasritlfeer took on the manner of a tour guide: "And now you'll see the lost city of legend, the Great Choir of the Tropics." Maybe it was a city. There were hundreds of Tines wherever he looked. As the balloon took them across higher ground, they could see more. Thousands of Tines. More. Perhaps as many as legend claimed. And nowhere was there even one coherent pack, just the simple mindlessness of the vast crowd. The sound . . . the sound was tolerable. The *Sea Breeze* was several hundred feet up, too high for mindsound to reach. What Tinish sounds did reach the gondola were in the range of normal Interpack speech. Some of it might be language, but the chords that sounded from thousands of tympana were smeared of any meaning they might have had. It was an eerie dirge of ecstasy.

And it squashed Chitiratifor's arrogance. Remasritlfeer could feel the gondola shift as the fat sixsome huddled in on himself. There was fascinated horror in his voice: "So many. So close. It . . . really is a Choir."

"Yup," Remasritlfeer said cheerfully, though he had been similarly affected the first few times he'd been here.

"But how do they eat? How can they sleep?" *In endless debauchery* went unsaid, but Remasritlfeer could almost hear the thought.

"We don't know the details, but if we go lower—"

"*No!* Don't do that!"

Remasritlfeer grinned to himself and continued. "If we go lower you'd see that these creatures look half starved. And yet there are buildings. See?" He made a pointing sound. Indeed, there were mud structures visible, some reduced to worn foundations peeking out from below later structures, and those submerged beneath still later mounds. No coherent pack would ever make such random things, barely recognizable as artificial constructions.

In places, the generations of mud structures were piled five or six deep, a chaotic mixture of midden and pyramid and multistory hovel. There must be holes and crannies within; you could see Tines entering and emerging. Remasritlfeer recognized the neighborhood from previous flights. There were patterns, as if some fragment of conscious planning had worked for a few days and then been swept away by noise or some other plan. In a couple of tendays, all the landmarks would be changed again.

"Another hundred feet will do it," he said, and signalled to Tycoon's ship to drop anchor. Actually, navigating the tethered balloon was rarely this precise. Today's sea breeze was as smooth as fine silk. "Coming up on the Great Trading Plaza."

There was some shifting around on the passenger platform above him, Chitiratifor screwing up his courage to poke additional snouts over the railing. Then an unbelieving, "You call *that* a plaza?"

"Well, that's Tycoon's term for it." More objectively, it was an open patch of mud, fifty feet across; Tycoon had a peddler's talent for using words to redefine reality. For several moments, Remasritlfeer was too busy for chitchat. He reached over the edge of the gondola to cast a mooring line downward. At the same time he shouted a big *halloo* to the Tines below. Of course, there were always watchers down there, though sometimes they seemed to forget the point of this exercise. Today, the response was almost immediate. Three Tines ran toward the center of the open space. They came from widely different points and were clearly singletons. Only when they got within a few feet of each other was there any sort of coordinated activity. Then they scrambled around clumsily, snapping at the rope that Remasritlfeer dangled down to them. Finally, two stood steady and third scrambled up and got the rope. Then all three got jaws on it and dragged the cord round and round a mud pillar.

Chitiratifor did not seem encouraged by this show of local cooperation. "Now we're trapped, are we? They could just pull us down."

"Yup, but they don't try that so much anymore. When they do, we just drop the rope and fly away home."

"Oh. Of course." Chitiratifor said nothing for a moment, but his mindsound was intense. "Well then, let's proceed. We have a failure to observe, and I want some details for my devastating report to our employers."

"As you say." Remasritlfeer was at least as anxious as anyone to dump Tycoon's Tropical fiasco, but he didn't feel like agreeing with the likes of this rag-eared thug. "One moment while I prepare the trade." Remasritlfeer ducked down to the bottom of the gondola, opened the drop door. Their cargo was in a bannerwood kettle hung just below. It didn't look like any water had slopped over during the balloon's ascent.

"Are you guys ready?" Remasritlfeer focused his words into the kettle.

"Yessir!" "Righto." "Let's go!" . . . The words coming back were all piled up, the response of dozens—perhaps all—of the creatures in the kettle.

Remasritlfeer ladled a dozen of the wriggling cuttlefish into a trade basket. Their huge eyes looked up at him. Their dozens of tentacles waved at him. In all the jabbering, he did not hear a particle of fear. He stuck a snout down to just above the rippling surface of the basket. The cuttlefish were very crowded in the small space, but that was the least of the problems they would soon face. "Okay, guys. You know the plan." He ignored the tiny cries of enthusiastic agreement. "You talk to the folk below—"

"Y-ye-yes, yes, y-yes! We ask them for safe landing for you. More trade. Harbor rights. Yes, yes! Yes!" The chords piled up in a tinkling mass, the speech of a dozen little creatures, each with voracious memories, each smarter than any singleton—but so scatterbrained that Remasritlfeer could not decide how smart they really were.

"Okay then!" Remasritlfeer gave up on his attempt at guidance. "Good luck!" He latched the trade basket's rope to the mooring line and paid out the cord.

"B-b-b-bye, g'bye!" The tinkling of chords came from both the basket and from the crowd in the bannerwood kettle, comrades calling to one another. Way beyond the tiny basket, the muddy space below was still empty of all but a few Tines. That was normally a good sign.

Chitiratifor's voice came from above: "So why not send down the whole kettle of fish?"

"Tycoon wants to see how this goes, then maybe send down a few more with different instructions."

Chitiratifor was silent for a moment, perhaps watching the trade basket as it swayed down and down along the mooring line. "Your boss is freaking insane. You know that, don't you?"

Remasritlfeer made no reply, and Chitiratifor continued, "See, Tycoon is a self-made patchwork. Half of him is a skinflint accountant. But the other half is four mad puppies the accountant picked just for their crazy imaginations. That might be a good idea, if the miser was the dominant half. But this miser is driven by the lunatic four. So do you know the reason he's mucking around here?"

Remasritlfeer couldn't resist showing that he understood something of the matter. "Because he counted the snouts?"

"What?—Yes! The accountant in him estimated the number of Tines in the Tropics."

"It could be more than one hundred million."

"Right. Then his lunatic four realized that dwarfed any other market in the world!"

"Well," said Remasritlfeer, "Tycoon is always on the lookout for new markets, the larger the better." In fact, new markets were Tycoon's greatest obsession, the driver of almost everything he did.

Two of Remasritlfeer continued to watch the descent of the cuttlefish. Their multiple monologues were still clearly audible. The basket would touch down in just a couple of minutes.

Angry talk continued to come from the passenger platform: "Tycoon has lots of stupid ideas, including the notion of getting power by selling things. But this time . . . so what if the Tropics has—what crazy number did you say? The point is, those millions are *animals*, a mob. Unless we could kill them all and exploit the land, the Tropics are worthless. I'm telling you, in confidence of course, my boss is getting tired of this tropical adventure. It's bleeding from our essential strengths, the technological advances that Vendacious is providing, the factory base at East Home. This foolishness has to stop, now!"

"Hmm, I hope your boss has not been this emphatic with *my* boss. Tycoon doesn't react . . . favorably . . . to being ordered around."

"Oh, don't worry. Vendacious is much more the diplomat than I am. I'm just an honest worker, much like yourself, um, sharing my doubts and irritations about our betters." Remasritlfeer himself was far from being a diplomat, but he could tell when someone was feeling him out. He almost blasted back, telling the six assholes above him where he could stuff Vendacious and his treacherous plans. *No. Be cool.*

After another moment of silence, Chitiratifor changed the subject. "The talking cuttlefish have almost reached the ground."

"Yup." In fact, the cuttlefish in the bannerwood kettle were chirping their interest, too. Apparently they could hear their siblings far below.

"Your boss told my boss that this would be the definitive test. If it fails, we can all go home. I count that as very good news—and yet, who but a madpack would bet on speech-mimicking cuttlefish?"

That was a reasonable question, and unfortunately Remasritlfeer didn't have any answer that would not make Tycoon look like an idiot. "Well, they're not really cuttlefish."

"They look delightful. I love cuttlefish."

"If you took a taste of their water, you wouldn't be interested in eating these. Their flesh is nearly inedible." Remasritlfeer had never eaten one of the strange wrigglers, but the South Seas packs who fished the atolls in the far west had learned of the creatures' intelligence and foul taste almost at the same time. It was Tycoon's collecting of fantastic rumors that had sent Remasritlfeer halfway around the world to visit those islands, talk to the natives, and bring back a colony of the strange animals. What had seemed as absurd as the present adventure had ended up being the most exciting time of Remasritlfeer's life. "And these little critters really can talk."

"But it's nonsense, like the words of a singleton."

"No, they're smarter than that." *Maybe.* "They're so intelligent that Tycoon has conceived the test we do today."

"Yes, his secret plan. I don't care what it is, as long as this is the last try. . . ." Chitiratifor was silent for a moment, presumably watching the trade basket descend the last few feet to the muddy ground. Others were watching. Intently. At the edges of the open space, where the unending mobs swirled and eddied, there were heads turning, thousands of eyes watching the *Sea Breeze* and the little package that was descending from it. It had taken tendays of dangerous balloon flights—and some truly expensive jewels—to establish this small open space and the erratically obeyed rules for these exchanges.

"Okay, tell me!" Chitiratifor's curiosity had won out. "What in heaven's name are you doing with these fish?"

"My boss's brilliant plan?" Remasritlfeer kept all doubt and sarcasm out of his voice. "Tell me, Chitiratifor, do you realize where we are?"

Chitiratifor emitted a hiss. "We're stuck just above the heart of the packs-be-damned largest Choir in the world!"

"Precisely. No explorer has ever come so close. Tycoon's fleet is anchored two thousand feet offshore. That is the closest of all explorations. Over the ages, who knows how many explorers have attempted to reach the heart of the Tropics from the North, either on foot or sailing the River Fell. There's pestilence and strange beasties on that approach—but those are survivable. I've survived them. And yet the explorers who go further south all disappear, or return in pieces, near mindless but for the stories that have made the Tropics legend. And now, you and I are here, just a thousand feet from the center of it all."

"Your point being?" Chitiratifor tried to make the question sound lofty and impatient, but there was a quaver in his words. Maybe the guy had finally gotten a good view of the creatures below, the unceasing roil of the mob around the clearing. Given the heat, it was no surprise that the creatures wore only random trinkets and splotches of paint. But clothing aside, most of them could never be mistaken for Northern Tines. Tropicals' pelts were thin. Many had puffs of fur near their paws but were almost hairless on their sides and bellies. There were so many Tines that even up here you could hear some mindsound. That vast chorus was truly the most unnerving thing about this place, and probably what had put Chitiratifor into his near-panic.

Now most of Remasritlfeer's gaze was on the trade basket below. By protocol, the three Tines should not touch it until the rope went slack, but he was taking things slow and easy. He interrupted their descent and took a very careful look with two of his heads gazing down from opposite sides of the gondola. It looked like the basket was twenty feet up. It was time for touchdown. And then . . . Remasritlfeer had no idea what would happen then.

"My point? . . . Um, can you imagine what it would be like to be down on the ground here?"

"Madness," said Chitiratifor, and it was hard to tell if that was his answer, or his reaction to the question. Then: "A coherent pack down there, surrounded by the unending millions of the Choir? The mind would disintegrate in seconds. It would be like a lump of coal tossed into a vat of molten iron."

"Yes, that's what it would be like if you or I were dropped into the Choir, but look: The result of our previous trading is that we have a clear space down below. There are just three Tines in that space, the rope handlers. The nearest parts of the mob are almost thirty feet away. The situation would be uncomfortable and you'd have to keep an absolute grip on your mind, but a pack could survive down there."

Chitiratifor emitted a dismissive tone that warbled into the sound of fear. "I can hear the pressure all around. That open space is a tiny bubble of sanity in the middle of hell. The Choir doesn't tolerate foreign elements. If you were on the ground, that precious open space would disappear in an instant."

"But no one really knows, right? If Tycoon can get packs safely on the ground, this tedious trading process might be speeded up."

"Oh. But that's a theory you could easily test. Just drop a pack"—Chitiratifor hesitated, choosing his words with care—"just find a condemned criminal, give it the offer of freedom if only it will descend to this clearing and have a chat with the delightful Tines we see below."

"Unfortunately, we don't have any condemned prisoners to help us out. Tycoon thinks that these talking cuttlefish might be the next best thing. . . ." The reasoning sounded very thin even to Remasritlfeer. That was Tycoon for you: he had lots of ideas, but most of them were absurd. The only people the Tycoon had convinced in this case were the cuttlefish themselves, who seemed endlessly eager to talk to new strangers. You had to wonder how creatures like that survived in the world; tasting bad was surely not a sufficient defense.

Chitiratifor forced a chuckle. "This is the brilliant solution Tycoon has been hinting at? And you'll honestly report what happens?"

Remasritlfeer ignored the patronizing tone. "Of course," he said.

"Well then, let's land these fish!" Chitiratifor honked laughter.

Okay, little friends. I wish you well. From a thousand feet up, the last few feet were always tricky, but Remasritlfeer had had plenty of practice. The little guys would come to no harm from the Choir's mindsound; the cuttlefish minds were as silent as the dead. The real question was how the Choir would react to the presence of non-Choir talkers. The parts of him that were watching the edge of the open space could see a strange kind of tension spreading out through the mob. Remasritlfeer had seen this sort of thing before. The Choir was not a co-herent mind, and yet small parts of it clearly thought to one another, and those mindsounds percolated for hundreds of feet, creating patterns of attention that were wider than he had ever seen except in sentry lines.

"The Choir's mindsound," came Chitiratifor's voice, filled with overtones of awe. "It's getting louder!" Chitiratifor was shifting around on the passenger platform, beside himself with fear. He was causing the entire gondola to bounce and sway.

Remasritlfeer hissed, "Get ahold of yourselves, fellow!" But in fact, the mindsound of the Choir did seem louder, a mix of lust and rage and pleasure and intense interest, a rising madness. If all those Tines below could think together . . . well then maybe they could focus this high. And destroy them even aboard the *Sea Breeze*. Then he realized that although the mindsounds were louder and more unified, something else had changed. Almost all low-frequency sounds had ceased. Gone were the moaning and fragments of Inter-pack language that had been a ceaseless churn from the mob. It was so quiet in the low sounds that he could hear the sigh of the River Fell as it swept past the mudbanks and grass trees of the delta.

Even the cuttlefish—both here in the kettle and down below in the trade basket—had ceased their tinkling chatter. It was as if the entire world had taken a moment to watch and see what would happen.

Remasritlfeer's wide-spaced eyes told him that the trade basket must be on the ground. At the same time, the cord he'd been paying out went slack in his jaws. Yes, touchdown!

Now as clear as tiny bells, he could hear the cuttlefish chattering at the three Tines who stood by the landing spot. They were saying exactly the sales pitch that Tycoon had worked out for them, exactly what Remasritlfeer himself would have said if *he* had the courage to land in the middle of this hell (though Remasritlfeer would have spoken with a single voice rather than the dozen spouting from the little cuttlefish).

The three Tines by the basket didn't immediately react. The eerie, low-sound silence continued a moment more. Then there came a spike of mindsound that near froze Remasritlfeer's hearts, anger so loud it seemed to come from his own mind. From all directions, the myriad Tines broke the fragile protocol Remas-ritlfeer had worked so long to construct, rushing inwards upon the trade basket.

The lash of anger numbed Remasritlfeer's mind, but he saw and remem-bered what happened next: The mob surged in like some monstrous wave, five and ten Tines deep. They came in from all directions, the open space vanishing in less than two seconds. Somewhere under the mob was the trade basket. Myriad voices screamed. The frenzy lasted almost a minute, so that for a time the attackers were piling up on themselves. Finally the mob retreated, leaving something like the agreed-upon open space. By some miracle, the *Sea Breeze*'s tiedown line remained in place, but the trade basket was reduced to splinters.

"What happened? Where are they now? What happened?" came the voices of the rest of the cuttlefish in their bannerwood kettle.

"I . . . I'm sorry, guys." The trading space was almost restored, those who remained in the space were limping back toward their fellows. He could see no signs of cuttlefish in the churned-up mud.

Chitiratifor gave out a satisfied laugh. "An excellent test. It's exactly as I predicted. Okay, fellow. It's time to drop the tiedown line and get ourselves back to sanity."

Four hours later, Remasritlfeer, the surviving cuttlefish, and Chitiratifor were safely back on Tycoon's steamship. Three of those hours had been spent fighting through the worst afternoon storm Remasritlfeer had seen so far. Even now, the wind was lashing across the deck of the *Pack of Packs*, making the balloon recovery job almost impossible. *Hell, the landing crew had better cut it loose before the lightning finally set its remaining lift gas afire.*

Remasritlfeer had his heads down, pushing the bannerwood kettle across the deck toward shelter. The rain had long ago soaked him; it was amazing he could think at all.

The cuttlefish were still complaining: "Why-why-why didn't you let us try again? again?"

"You shut up!" Remasritlfeer hissed back. Multiple tries had been part of Tycoon's orders. Before the storm came up, at least four of Remasritlfeer would have sacrificed the rest of these suicidal maniacs; the fifth of him had some weird maternal sympathy for the cuttlefish. Between that and the storm and Chitiratifor, they had not done quite all Tycoon planned. Leaving early had probably saved all their lives.

He tied down the kettle and sprinkled the water with fish food. Behind him, he could see most of Chitiratifor clustered at the railing, barfing into the sea. Far beyond the railing the swamplands of the coast were a dark shadow behind the rain. These last few tendays, Remasritlfeer had accomplished more than any explorer in the history of the Tropics, but now he knew he would never stand on the ground there. No pack would, not and live to tell the tale.

Remasritlfeer shook himself. Now to get cleaned up, dried off. There remained the toughest job of the day—to convince Tycoon that no matter how big the market, no matter how great the desire, there were some dreams that were just *not* going to come true.

*Ten years after the
Battle on Starship Hill*

CHAPTER 05

Woodcarver's Domain stretched along the continent's northwest coast. The Domain's northern part, the lands around Starship Hill, had been taken in the conquest of Flenser's empire. That was two hundred kilometers north of the arctic circle. Tines World was a mellow and beautiful place, very much what Old Earth had been for humankind's first civilization. Of course "mellow and beautiful" were relative terms. The arctic winters, even on the coast with its warming ocean stream, were frightful things. The islands were lost in the ice, the snow piled deep, and night was unending, usually so stormy that you couldn't even see the stars.

The summers, however . . . Ravna Bergsndot had not imagined there could be such contrast in a natural place. The snow mostly went away, or hid in the higher hills and the glaciers above them. This year there had been plenty of spring rain, and bright green spread across the forests and heather and farmers' fields, across all the world below the tree line. And today, today was beautiful beyond that. The rains had ended, and the sky was clean, with only a few chunky white clouds hanging beyond the seaward islands. Here, on a clear day in summer, the sun was above the horizon for the dayaround. At noon, it climbed almost halfway up the sky and the rest of the day was like an endless afternoon.

It was warm! It was even *hot!*

More by luck than anything else, Ravna and Johanna chose this day for a visit to the markets on the South End of Hidden Island. They'd taken the funicular down from Starship Hill and then the ferry across the fifteen-hundred-meter inner channel that separated Flenser's old capital from the mainland. Now they were walking down wide, cobbled streets, just enjoying the sun and the light and the warmth.

Most of the town packs had taken off their jackets and leggings. A work gang of three packs was in a line along one side of the street, digging up the gutter drainage. On a task as simple as ditch digging, the three packs could work with a kind of superpack coordination, the dirt being hoisted from ground to shovel, into buckets and then away, in perfect synchrony.

These weren't the slaves of the time of Flenser and Steel. When Ravna and Johanna came strolling along, the super-pack seemed to notice and for a moment resumed its three coherent identities, shouting greetings with human

voices. Ravna recognized the one in the middle as Flenser-Tyrathect's city
planner.

Johanna chatted with the two who didn't speak very good Samnorsk. Ravna
had a few words with the city planner, learning what these repairs were all
about, answering the pack's question about the tools that had been promised
for more than a year. "It's the power supplies we're having trouble with, of
course. But you'll see them in time to help with the snow."

And then the two humans continued on, toward Hidden Island's very own
high street. "Johanna, I think this may be the most beautiful day we've ever
had." Beyond low roof lines, the inland hills stood tall. The New Castle on
Starship Hill might have been something out of a fairy tale, and downslope
from the castle, the hull of *Oobii* sparkled greenfly bright.

The younger woman was smiling. "It's a winner, all right."

Packs walked past them in both directions, avoiding each other as much as
they could. Wagons and kherhog traffic were banned in this part of town, leaving just enough room for the packs. There were even a few humans up ahead,
the oldest of the refugee children, now adults and working in local businesses.
For a moment, Ravna could almost imagine . . . "It's almost like something
back in civilization."

Johanna was still smiling, but now her look was puzzled. "The High Lab
was nothing like this." From what Ravna knew, the High Lab had been a grid
of barracks on the airless planet of a red dwarf star. "And before that," Johanna
continued, "well, we were mostly on Straum. That was cities and parks. This?
I'm more used to it now than anywhere else, but how does it remind you of
civilization?"

Ravna had her own opinion of Straumer civilization; she'd had ten years of
practice in keeping that opinion to herself. So all she said was, "Some are little
things, some are big. There are both humans and aliens here; outside of civilization, that can rarely happen. The streets are clean and quaintly wide. I know
the packs need the extra space, but . . . this place looks almost like some historical city park on a multi-settled world. I can pretend the technology is just
hidden away, perhaps in those little shops we're visiting today. This could be at
Sjandra Kei, kind of a happy tourist trap."

"Well, that's fine then, because I've come to shop for a birthday present!"

Ravna nodded. "Then we have a constructive purpose for this trip." The
Children took their "birthday" parties seriously. However arguable the calen-
dar dates, birthdays gave them a bridge to their past. She hesitated. "So whose
birthday are we talking about?"

"Who do you think?" There was something about Jo's look that made the
answer obvious.

"Nevil?"

"Yup. He's out of town today, checking out trade prospects on the East
Streamsdell. Nevil has such a wonderful way with humans; I know he'd like to
be just as good with Tines. In any case, we can get him a present without his
ever knowing."

Ravna laughed. She had been so patient with these two, but Jo was twenty-four, and Nevil would be twenty-six as of this birthday. They were the most perfect couple she could imagine among the older Children. "So, what are you thinking to get him?"

"Something princely and charming, of course." Actually Johanna had several ideas. It turned out she had been down here more often than Ravna, and she'd quizzed both Woodcarver and Pilgrim about the things that might be available from far parts of the world. Hidden Island was not the imperial capital the Old Flenser had planned, but it had come to be the heart of Woodcarver's Domain—and this side of the Long Lakes, it was the place to go for exotica.

So the two of them visited one after another of the high street shops, as well as the summer markets that occupied the cobblestone plazas. Johanna had a list, not just from Woodcarver and Pilgrim, but also from her friends Rejna and Giske—themselves already married—and partly from Nevil himself. Johanna bought some mosaic fabric that showed landscapes that could be separately viewed by each of the wearer's members.

"This is not really very human," said Ravna.

"Ah, but Nevil might like the pointillist staining. It reminds me of Ur-digital."

In another shop, they looked at semiprecious gems set in statuary of gold and brass. Ravna was technically royalty, but there were no free gifts, nor even requests to be "officially sponsored" by the co-Queen of the Domain. For a medieval ruler, Woodcarver was something of an economic innovator.

"You could have something made special, maybe out of the mosaic cloth."

"Yeah!" said Johanna. They turned down Wee Alley. At the back was Larsndot, Needles & Co. The store was a two-story affair, now extended out on tent poles into the street. Wenda Larsndot Jr. was on her knees, pinning velvet around a customer's new puppies.

"Hei, Johanna! Hei, Ravna!" The seven-year-old was full of cheer, but she didn't get up. "Can't talk now. The slavedrivers are riding me hard." Then she chirped something at her customer, some kind of reassurance.

"But you'll be at school tomorrow, right?" said Ravna.

The little girl—oldest of all the second generation—rolled her eyes. "Yup, yup. This is my day off. I like tailoring better'n multiplication. Dad's over there. Mummy's in back." Those would be Ben and Wenda Larsndot, Junior's chief "slavedrivers."

Ben was even busier than Junior. The place was so crowded that—for packs—it must be mind-numbingly noisy. Was it beautiful days like this that brought on a buying frenzy?

They gave Ben a wave and walked through the tent toward the back. Larsndot, Needles & Co. had Tinish employees. In fact, "Needles" was a mostly young sixsome who had been the original owner. Needles had done quite well by the partnership, for tailoring was one of the "problematical professions." If standing close to another pack is mind-numbing, then there are only a few things that packs could easily do at such close quarters—chiefly, make war, make love, or just generally blank out. Humans were ideal for close-up work. Each human was as smart as a pack, and each could work mindfully even right next to the customer. It was the perfect combination—though Ravna was afraid the Larsndots had gone too far. Fitting in, being needed by the locals, that was terribly important. At the same time, the humans should be building a tech civilization, not measuring cloth to fit.

Today there was far more business than the humans could help with. The company's three Tinish tailors sat on thickly padded platforms. On the floor, each of the customers had a single tailor member doing its best with fitting. To human eyes, the process was comical. The isolated members were decked out in flamboyant uniforms studded with big-handled needles, and tailor's measuring tapes looped from spools on their collars. They were not quite mindless— the rest of their packs were up on the pallets, peeking down, trying to maintain contact without numbing the customers. The groundside members had a lot of practice and significant guidance from above—but physically they were not much more adept than dogs. The lips at the tip of their jaws could squeeze like a pair of weak fingers. Their paws and claws were what you'd expect of dumb animals, though the creatures often wore tools or metal claws—hence the human name for the race: Tines.

These tailors had plenty of experience. Their groundside parts could pull measuring tape from their shoulder spools, could pass it to the customer. With spoken directions from the tailor above, the customer—if not too befuddled by having a foreign snout in its midst—could hold tape properly while the tailor marked the measurement. In other circumstances the customer held the draped fabric and the tailor's groundside member grabbed a pinhandle in its jaws and carefully inserted it.

Ravna and Johanna passed through an older section of the building that had *not* been built with humans in mind. They bent low to clear the ceiling and walked awkwardly down a short hallway toward the sewing room. Indoors, in a Tinish building, the whiff of packs was overpowering. Ravna had dealt with many races in the High Beyond—but with good air control. Here there were no such amenities.

She heard Wenda Sr.'s laughter right ahead. Wenda Sr. handled most of the business management, except for the accounting. Like most of the refugees, she was no good at manual arithmetic.

"Hei Johanna! Ravna!" Wenda was standing by one of the sewing tables. Those were lined up below high windows of smoky glass. Sunlight fell on the work tables. Larsndot, Needles & Co. had three seamsters; right now all were busy. Wenda moved back and forth, adjusting the measures, rolling in additional bolts of cloth, some of it the precious *Oobii* weave, the last functional output of the starship's reality graphics display.

Wenda's younger child, Sika, was sitting on the table beside her, evidently "helping to supervise."

"Hei Wenda! I'm looking for advice." Johanna laid the mosaic cloth down on a display table. "I want to get something for Nevil. His birthday, you know. Would this look too silly on a human?"

"Sika, you stay put, okay?" said Wenda, Sr. For a wonder, the three-year-old did as requested. Whatever the Tinish seamster was doing fascinated her.

Wenda came over to their table, turning sideways to fit between the heavy wooden stools. She nodded respectfully at Ravna, then lifted Johanna's fabric sample, turning it in the sunlight. "Ah, this is the real Down Coast stuff, isn't it, Johanna?"

The two woman chattered about the fabric. Wenda had been sixteen when the kids escaped from the High Lab, and one of the first to be wakened. That made her as old as any of the refugees, as old as Nevil Storherte. She was twenty-six. Her face and her voice were happy, but there was gray in her hair, the beginnings of age in her face. Ravna had read human histories obsessively since their exile began. In a state of nature, untreated humans began to decline almost immediately upon reaching adulthood. Wenda had never complained, but more than most—certainly more than the boys her age—she bore the burden of living Down Here. And yet she was luckier than some. She was old enough that, before the escape, she had almost completed the usual prolongevity treatments. Most of her cohort would last a couple of centuries.

The youngest kids—and certainly the new generation—had not even begun their medical treatments before the escape. They would age quickly, probably not live more than a century. *They might not even last long enough for the new technologies to save them.* In that case, a return to coldsleep might be their only hope.

One of the seamsters came around the table. Four of it scrambled up on the stools, leaned over to look at the fabric from all directions. The pack was a mostly old fivesome. He understood some Samnorsk, but spoke in careful Inter-pack. The chords were largely unintelligible to Ravna, but she could tell the fellow was pleased to be chatting with Johanna. This guy was a veteran of Wood-carver's long march up the coast and the Battle on Starship Hill. Johanna had more Tinish friends than anyone Ravna knew, and among many she was a paramount hero. Maybe that was why Woodcarver had forgiven Jo for running amok back in Year Two.

In the end, Johanna and Wenda and the Tinish seamster came up with a bizarro cape and pants scheme that Wenda claimed would please both fashion and Nevil. It was the best evidence Ravna had ever seen for the absence of a universal esthetic.

". . . and I'll bring you those buckles," said Johanna.

"Fine, fine," Wenda was nodding. "Most important, what I need right away, are Nevil's fitting measurements."

"Right, I'll get them. But remember, this is a surprise. He knows there'll be a party, but—"

"Hah. Taking a tape measure to him will likely make him guess."

"I've got my ways!"

And that got both Wenda and Johanna laughing.

———

Back on the street, Johanna was still laughing. "Honest, Ravna, no double meaning." But when she stopped laughing, she was grinning like a loon.

The afternoon went on forever, the shadows turning and turning without ever lengthening into sunset. They stopped by a couple of silversmiths, but what Johanna wanted might have to be done one-off. Now they were at the north end of the high street. The warren of merchant tents was still as crowded as packs could tolerate, not more than a few meters separating one from another.

"Seems like more foreigners than ever," commented Ravna. It was partly a question. She could recognize East Home packs by their funny redjackets. Others were distinguished by their scattered posture or their scandalous flirtation. Getting all the details explained was just another reason why she liked to go on these walk-arounds with Johanna Olsndot.

Today Johanna wasn't quite the perfect tour guide: "I . . . yeah, I guess you're right." She looked around into the tented chaos. "I wasn't paying proper attention." She saw the smile on Ravna's face. "What?"

"You know, today you only stopped to chat with every fourth pack that we came across."

"Oh, I don't know everybody—wait, you mean I really haven't been up to my usual social standard? Well, huh." They walked on a few paces, out of the tented area. When Johanna looked at her again, the girl's smile was still there but perhaps it contained a touch of wonder. "You're right, I haven't been feeling the same lately. It's strange. Our lives I mean. Things were so tough for so long."

When Ravna Bergsndot was feeling most sorry for herself, she tried to imagine what life had been like for Johanna and her little brother. Like all the Children, these two were orphans, but their parents had made it all the way to the ground here. Johanna had witnessed their murder, and then the murder of half her classmates. At just thirteen Johanna had spent a year in this wilderness, often befriended, sometimes betrayed. But she and her little brother had still guided the *Oobii* through the battle on Starship Hill.

Some of the Children had accepted all this too readily, forgetting civilization. Some others couldn't make any accommodation with their fall from heaven. It was the ones like Jo that gave Ravna faith that—given time—they might survive the fate coming down upon them all.

They had left the merchants behind, were walking toward the part of town where in recent years public houses had been established. Johanna didn't seem to notice; she was still far away, smiling that small wondering smile. "Things were tough, and then we unmasked Vendacious and won against Lord Steel. And since then . . ." surprise rose in her voice ". . . why, now I'm generally having a great time. There's so much to do, with the Fragmentarium, with the Children's Academy, and—"

"You're wrapped up in making the new world," said Ravna.

"I know. But now things are even better. Ever since I started dating Nevil, lots of things are more fun. *Human*-type people seem much more interesting than before. Lately, Nevil and I have been even, um, closer. I want this birthday to be special for him, Ravna."

Hah! Ravna reached out, touched Johanna's arm. "So when . . ."

Johanna laughed. "Ah, Nevil is so traditional. I really think he's waiting for me to propose." She looked at Ravna, and now her smile was both merry and sneaky. "Don't you tell, Ravna, but after the birthday party, that's exactly what I'm going to do!"

"That's wonderful! What a wedding that will be!" They stopped and just grinned at each other. "You can be sure Woodcarver will invent new ceremonies for this," said Ravna.

"Yeah, she uses my reputation unmercifully."

"Good for her. In fact, this means even more to us than to the Tines. You and Nevil are so popular, he with the Children, you with the Tines. Maybe—" *Maybe this is the time.*

"What?"

Ravna drew Jo toward the middle of the street as they continued along their way—she didn't want to be snooped upon by passing packs. "Well, it's just that I am so tired of being co-Queen."

"Ravna! It's worked great for almost ten years now. Woodcarver herself suggested it. There's precedent in Tinish history and even in ours."

"Yes," said Ravna, "on Nyjora." In the Age of Princesses, there had been the Elder Princess and the Younger, the Techie. The Age of Princesses was the most recent rediscovery of civilization in any known human history—and that civilization was also the ancestor of Ravna's Sjandra Kei and therefore of Johanna's Straumli Realm.

The Straumers were not much for looking back, but Ravna had told them about the Age of Princesses. At the Academy, she used that history to make a bridge between humans and the Domain. Johanna smiled. "You should be glad to be co-Queen, Ravna. I bet you played at being one when *you* were a child."

Ravna hesitated, embarrassed to admit the truth. "Well maybe; I've discovered that the reality is . . . distracting. It was necessary to begin with, but you kids are established now. I need to concentrate on the external deadline. We only have a few centuries before some really bad guys blow into town." Ravna hadn't told the Children of her crazy dream, or the zonograph glitch. There had been no repeat, and the data was less than credible. Instead she worked harder and harder, and did her best not to seem like a madwoman.

Ravna looked away from Johanna. For a few steps, she just watched her own feet trudging along the cobblestones. "It could be less than centuries," she said. "The Blighters weren't left with any working ramscoops, but they could probably boost a few kilograms to near-lightspeed. Maybe, when they still had their pipeline to god, maybe they even figured out some way to nail us at light-speed. I need to spend all my time making sure we'll be ready."

Johanna didn't reply. Ravna was silent for a few more steps, then repeated her main point: "I just mean, I should be spending more time with *Oobii*. I'm a librarian, after all, and in a situation like this, any other use of me is a waste. I think it would best if maybe you and Nevil could lead, with Woodcarver."

Johanna stared at Ravna in shock. "Are you crazy?"

Ravna smiled. "We've both been accused of that at one time or another."

"Hah!" said Johanna. She put an arm across Ravna's shoulders. "If we're both crazy, it's in very different ways. Ravna, we *need* you—"

"Yes, I know. I'm den mother to all that's left of humanity!"

That old and whimsical complaint should have brought a smile to Johanna; instead her expression became positively fierce. "Ravna, you're the mother of all that's left here. Ten years ago we were kids and babies, and to the Tines we were weird animals. Without you to hold us together—to mother us along— most of us would have died in coldsleep, and the few who survived would be freaks in Tinish wilderness!"

". . . I, um, okay." *Time to regroup*: "I guess I did what had to be done. And now we must prepare for the future. I'm the only one of us trained to manage *Oobii*'s planning systems. That's where I need to spend all my time now. You and Nevil and Woodcarver should lead. I'm a *librarian*, not a leader."

"You're both! Librarians and archeologists have always been the ones to bring civilization back."

"This is different. We don't have any ruins to search. We have all the answers aboard the *Oobii*." Ravna raised her chin in the direction of Starship Hill. "You needed me to begin with, but now Children like you have grown up. My technical planning is needed more than ever, but . . . but I'm tired of being the leader."

"Your decisions are popular, Ravna."

"Some of them. Some of them not, or not for a year or five or ten." Some might seem obviously wrong for a century—and then suddenly, dreadfully *right*.

"I hadn't realized you felt so . . . alone. We all have *you*, so I guess we thought you see all of us the same." Johanna looked down at various bags of fabric samples and birthday trinkets. She gave a little laugh. "Okay, turn it all around. I've been so happy with Nevil. He's made life a bright place. I should think what it would be like without that, without anyone to share it all with. Do you think about Pham very much?"

"Sometimes." *Often*. "We had something fine, but there was too much else going on within him. What owned him was scary."

"Yeah." Johanna had met Pham Nuwen, just before the end. She had seen how scary scary could be. "There are one hundred and fifty of us, Ravna. We all love you—at least most of the time. Have you ever thought that there might be enough people now that you could find some one person you could—you could be with?"

Up the street, Ravna could see some Children. They were Johanna's age and older. They were just going into one of the pubs. Ravna gave a nod in their direction. "Are you serious?"

The girl gave an embarrassed smile. "Look, *I* found someone. I'm just saying, you think of us all as children. Think . . . well, you'll live longer than any of us."

"*Don't say that.* You're ageing now, but that's only for the present. Someday we'll have the resources to go back and rebuild a decent medical science. This is just temporary."

"Right. If you guide us there, we'll eventually have the technology. And eventually, there'll be tens of thousands of us. If you can't find Mister Right in that mob, there's something wrong with you!"

"I guess you're right."

"Of course I am!" said Johanna. "In the meantime, please remember how grateful we are, even when we complain. And Nevil and I will work harder to support you."

"I *want* debate."

"You know what I mean. It's your voice, up front, that makes the big difference for people like Wenda and Ben."

"Okay, I'll lay off you and Nevil, at least for now."

"Whew!" Johanna's look of relief was comic exaggeration, but behind it Ravna saw the real thing. "Oh, and Ravna? *Please* don't mention this to Nevil. It would just go to his head."

———

The tavern district was near the center of Hidden Island, just south of the Old Castle. In fact, the castle was not really old, though it pre-dated the Children's arrival by some decades. Flenser's castle had been a fearsome place, a legend across the continent. Flenser—the unreformed Flenser—had had extraordinary plans for the Tinish race. Before the humans arrived, this world had not even discovered gunpowder, and the printing press was the big new thing. From that, Flenser had been busy building both a totalitarian state and something like the scientific method. There were rumors that his monster packs still lurked in the Old Castle. Ravna knew that wasn't true, though Flenser-Tyrathect still did have his supporters, spies who shadowed Woodcarver's own secret agents.

The sun was sliding into the north, the shadows now extending all the way across the street.

The two women walked past the first of the public houses. "Been there just yesterday," Johanna said of it. "These days the customers are mostly herders from the mainland, celebrating the livestock drive.

Up ahead were the pubs more likely to attract merchants from the Long Lakes and spies from East Home. Those shops were full of gossip and questions and strangeness. She noticed the pack across the street; it looked a lot like the one that had been hanging around behind them in the market.

Johanna saw her glance. "Don't worry. That's Borodani, one of Woodcarver's guys. I recognize his low-sound ears." She gave the pack a wave, then laughed. "And you say this is really like a city of the Middle Beyond?"

"A little. I could fool myself for minutes at a time. Sjandra Kei had half a dozen major races, though nothing like packs. We humans were only the third most numerous. But we were popular. There were tourist towns that imitated olden human times—and they attracted at least two of the other races as much as us humans."

"So folks would promenade, right? We could almost imagine we're out looking for action in some high-priced dive?"

"You had such romances in Straumli Realm?"

"Well, yes. I was a precocious tot, you know. But you actually lived it, right?"

"Um, yes. A few times," as a shy college girl, before she graduated and shipped out to the Vrinimi Organization. At Vrinimi, the socializing had been exclusively nonhuman—at least till Pham came along.

"So are these taverns much like the bars you remember back in civilization?"

"Hmpf. Not too much. The 'bars' in Sjandra Kei were very crowded—choir-crowded, by Tinish standards. For the humans and some of the other races, it was a bit of a courtship thing. Here—"

"Here, every human has known every other since they were little, and there aren't enough of us all together to fill these public houses. Still, it's fun to imagine. For instance, this place up ahead."

That would be the Sign of the Mantis. The words were chiseled in Tinish runes below a one-meter-high carving of an odd insect that walked on two legs. Ravna had never seen the real thing, but she'd heard that the critters were a ubiquitous pest in downcoast towns. Of course, the largest of the real mantises were less than five centimeters tall. Whenever the story of the human landing was told, there was always the question of what the strange new aliens looked like. And since there were no videos to show around, just a pack talking to credulous listeners—also packs—the humans were often likened to "huge, *huge* mantises." The Sign of the Mantis sign—the wooden sign itself—had actually been imported from a bar in the Long Lakes. Here it was a great joke, since this particular pub was indeed a human favorite.

Music came from within.

"See? Just like a nightclub back in civilization?" said Johanna.

It was human music, human voices and the sounds of a dozen instruments—or one synth. Inside, there would be no synth, no instruments and maybe not even any singing humans. The words were some children's rhyme, and the music . . . not quite a child's melody. A single pack was probably the source of all the sounds. No doubt it was embellishing on something from *Oobii*. Human culture was being re-created from the ground up on the Tines World, from machine memories and the distortions of a race of medieval pack critters.

A set of neatly painted wooden stairs wrapped back and forth up to the overhang of the main floor. Johanna bounced up the shallow steps with Ravna just behind. They were about halfway to the entrance when the door above opened and a group of teenaged humans came out onto the top landing.

One of them leaned back into the bar and said something like. "Yeah, just think about that. It makes more sense than . . ."

Ravna had scooched out of the way when she saw the crowding above. These steps were intended to be one-way for a pack; they were just a bit wider than a single member. The boys hadn't seen her, but when they saw Johanna, suddenly their voices cut short. As they came down the steps, she heard one of them say, "It's your sister, Jef."

Johanna's voice sounded a little sharp. "Hei now, so what are you doing?"

The lead boy—it sounded like Gannon Jorkenrud—replied, "Just telling people the truth, little missy." Yes, that was Gannon. The boy saw Ravna and the sneer left his face. For a wonder, he actually looked *furtive*! He carefully edged past her without quite making eye contact.

The three boys who followed were younger, two seventeen, one nineteen, all fairly large pains in the neck. And today, all looked similarly sneaky, passing by her silently, then proceeding a little too quickly down the steps. Something else about them: they wore those short pants and silly low-cut shoes that had come into fashion at the beginning of the summer. Given a cool, rainy day, they'd have freezing shins and soaked feet.

Further up on the stairs, Johanna was saying, "So Jefri. What's up?" The words were lightly spoken, but Ravna saw that the girl had stepped into the middle of the stairway. And there indeed, at the top of the stairs, were Jefri and Amdi. Both human and pack were a study in unhappy surprise. The pack—Amdiranifani—was the more obviously upset; even Ravna could see it in his aspect. Jefri was a bit smoother. "Hei, Sis. Hei, Ravna. Been a while."

Amdi came down the stairs, butted one head softly against Johanna and two more against Ravna. "It's good to see you!" said the pack, using its little-boy voice. Amdiranifani was an eightsome, about as numerous as a clear-thinking pack could be. When Ravna had first met him, he'd been entirely puppies. They were so small you could carry half of him in your arms, while the other half tumbled around your ankles, asking questions and showing off. He and little Jefri had been so close that some Tines thought of them as a single pack, and gave them the name Amdijefri. No packs called them that anymore. Now, each of Amdi's members had grown to be large and a little overweight. At first glance, he was physically intimidating. At second glance and after casual conversation, you'd realize Amdi was too shy to menace anybody. And at third glance—if you really got to know him or if he wanted to show off—you'd realize that Amdi was about the smartest creature you could ever meet Down Here.

Ravna patted the nearest head, and smiled at the pack and then at Jefri. "Yes, it is good to see you."

"And about time," Johanna inserted, not buying her brother's casual manner.

Ravna waved a kind of "it's okay" at Johanna. Civility had been in very short supply from Jefri; she had no desire for a return to his rebellious years.

Johanna didn't seem to notice. "So, Brother?"

There was a shadow of a glower from the boy. "So. You know. I've been the whole spring downcoast with Meri Lyssndot's team, surveying the special metals that *Oobii* thought—"

"I *know* that, Jef. And I know you've been screwing Meri and every other girl you can lay your hands on. But you've been back how many days and not a word from you?"

Now the glower was on full. "Lay off, Jo. You don't own me."

"I'm your sister! I . . ." Indignation choked off her words.

Ravna noticed that Amdi had snuck back and seemed to be trying to hide behind Jefri. She cast about for something that might deflect the oncoming debacle. Things had been going so well with Jefri this past year. *Ah:* "It's okay, Jefri. I've seen the survey report. Good work." Or maybe that was laying it on too thick. "I'm more interested in what was going on with those three . . ." She waved down the stairs. *Should I call them your friends? I hope they're not.* "What was this 'truth' that Gannon was talking about?"

"Um, nothing."

"Yup, nothing," said Amdi, nodding all his heads.

"Well then." Ravna came up the stairs. Jefri was nineteen, an adult by the human standards of Sjandra Kei and Straumli Realm. It didn't matter any more that Jef had been the nicest child, brave and well-meaning. It shouldn't matter that in later years he was often the most rebellious of the pimply mob. Thank goodness that Johanna had pointed Nevil at him. Where even Johanna had not managed to talk sense into him, the level-headed, diplomatic Nevil had succeeded. With any luck, his current problem was just a temporary backsliding. "We just want to see how people are doing," said Ravna. She waved at the entrance just beyond Jefri and Amdi. "The three of us can talk another time if you want."

Jefri dithered a second, and then her mild words seemed to bring him around. "That's okay. Let's talk. The whole thing is, um, a bit strange." He turned and held the pub's door open for Ravna and his sister.

Inside the pub it was *warm*, a reminder that even the summer-day shadows could be cold. There was the smell of smoke and spice and the usual pack body odor. Jefri eased past Jo and Ravna, leading them along a low, narrow corridor, where the smoke was even thicker. Health and fire-safety regulations were still in this world's future.

Ravna just followed along silently, bemused by the crazy carvings that lined the walls—Tines' ideas about what life in the Beyond had been like—and wondering at the changes that even ten years had made in her Children. Funny.

She had always thought of Johanna as being tall, even when she was only thirteen. But that was Johanna's personality. Even now, Johanna was only one meter seventy, scarcely taller than Ravna. And Jefri? He had always seemed so small to her. He *had* been short, when Pham had landed and saved him from Lord Steel. She remembered the little orphan raising his arms to her. But now she noticed how much he had to scrunch down to clear the ceiling. The guy was nearly two meters tall when he stood straight.

The music was loudest straight ahead. There was a flickering colored light that must be one of those crazy mood candelabras. Jefri stepped through the opening, Ravna and Johanna and Amdi right behind.

The Mantis tavern had a vaulted ceiling, and space for padded alcoves all around the upper walls. Today, the clientele was mainly human. There were two or three packs up in the lofts, but the bartender pack was the only one on the main floor. All the music was—no surprise—coming from the bartender.

"Back so soon?" someone shouted at Amdi and Jefri. Then they caught sight of Ravna and Johanna, and there was nervous laughter. "Wow, we can't talk treason for more than five minutes and the secret police show up."

"I ran into them on the steps," said Jefri.

"Just shows you should use the *exit* stairs, like decent folk do." That was Heida Øysler. She was still laughing about her secret police crack. Some of the others seemed a bit pained by it, but then Heida's sense of humor was her greatest enemy. At least here there were none of the closed expressions Ravna had seen on the stairs. Heida pulled over extra chairs and waved them to sit down.

As they did so, the bartender's roving member was already bringing out more beer. Ravna glanced around the table, taking in just who was here. Ten kids—*no*. Ten adults. Jefri and Heida might be the youngest here. None of these were parents yet, though there was one recently married couple.

Johanna snagged a beer. She raised it to Heida in a mock salute. "So now that the secret police are here, consider yourselves under interrogation. What are you miscreants up to?"

"Oh, the usual mayhem." But then Heida was out of clever responses. That could be a blessing. When Heida babbled, things could get marvelously embarrassing. There had been that mock adultery claim about Tami and Wilm—which then turned out to be essentially true. "We were just, you know, speculating about the Disaster Study Group."

"Ah." Johanna settled her beer back on the table.

"What's that?" said Ravna. "It sounds terribly official. And I thought I was into all the terribly official things around here."

"Well, that's only because—" began Heida, but one of the other girls, Elspa Latterby, stepped on her wit:

"It's just three big words covering up a lot of wishful thinking." No one else said anything. After a moment, Elspa shrugged and continued, "You see, Ma'am—"

"Please, Elspa, call me Ravna." *Oops, I always say that, and some, like Elspa, always forget.*

"Sure, Ravna. Y'see, the thing is, well, you and the Tines have done your best to stand in for our parents. I know how much Woodcarver and Flenser-Tyrathect have spent on our academy. And now we're doing our best to make something of ourselves—in this world. Some of us, the very youngest, are quite happy." A smile flickered on her face. "My little sister has Beasly and human playmates. She has me—and she doesn't remember our folks very well. To Geri, this seems like a wonderful place."

Ravna nodded. "But for the older ones, life here is just the epilogue to a holocaust, right?" Certainly, that was often how Ravna saw it.

Elspa nodded, "It's wrongheaded maybe. But there it is. Not all us feel this way, but we remember our parents, and civilization. It's not surprising that some of us feel just a little bitter to have lost so much. Disasters have that effect even when no one living is responsible."

Jefri hadn't bothered with a human chair. He had set himself on one of the high perches normally used by the Tines. From there he looked down gloomily. "So it's not surprising such people might call themselves the Disaster Study Group," he said.

Ravna gave them all a smile. "I guess we've all been members of that club at one time or another—all of us who seriously look at the recent history."

Now that the bartender's member had retreated, Amdi had surfaced all around the two tables, a head here, a head there, some of him perched on the high stools. He liked to watch from all directions—and there were enough of him to do a good job of it. The two on the stools cocked their heads, but his voice seemed to come from everywhere. "So then it's a little bit like me and some of Lord Steel's other experiments. A lot of killing went into our making. I came out very well, maybe, but others are still a mess. Sometimes we get together and just moan and groan about how we've been abused. But it's not like we can do anything about it."

Elspa nodded. "You're right, Amdi, but at least you have a specific monster to dump the hate on."

"Well," said Ravna, "we have the Blight. It was monstrous beyond the mind of any in the Beyond. We know that in the end, fighting that evil killed your parents and Straumli Realm, and indirectly killed Sjandra Kei. Stopping the Blight destroyed civilization in much of the galaxy."

They were shaking their heads. One of the boys, Øvin Verring, said, "We can't know all that."

"Okay, we can't be sure of that last; the destruction was so vast that it destroyed our ability to measure it. But—"

"No, I mean there's very little we can know of any of it. Look. Our parents were scientists. They were doing research in the Low Transcend, a dangerous place. They were playing with the unknown."

You got it, kiddo, thought Ravna.

"But millions of other races have done that," Øvin continued. "It's the most common way that new Powers are born. My father figured that Straum itself would eventually colonize some vacated brown dwarf system in the Low Transcend, that we would transcend. He said we Straumers have always had an outward reach, we are risk takers." Øvin must have noticed the look coming into Ravna's face. He hurried on: "And then something went terribly wrong. *That* has also happened to thousands of races. Expeditions like our High Lab sometimes get consumed by what lives Up There, or are simply destroyed. Sometimes, the originating star system is destroyed, too. But what happened to us—what has forced us Down Here—that just doesn't square with what we personally know about the situation."

"I—" Ravna began, then hesitated. *How can I say this? Your parents were greedy and careless and exceptionally unlucky.* She loved these kids—well, most of them, and she would do almost anything to protect all of them—but when she looked at them, sometimes all she could think of was the destruction their parents' greed had brought down. She glanced at Johanna. *Help me.*

As often happened when the going got tough, Johanna came through: "I have a little more personal memory than most of us, Øvin. I remember my parents preparing our escape. The High Lab was no ordinary attempt at Transcendence. We had an abandoned archive. We were doing archeology on the Powers themselves."

"I know that, Johanna," Øvin said, a little sharply.

"So the archive woke. My parents knew there was the possibility that we were being led around by the nose. Okay, I guess all the grownups knew that. But in the end, my folks realized that the risks were much greater than was obvious. We had dug up something that could be a threat to the Powers Themselves."

"They *told* you that?"

"Not at the time. In fact, I'm not sure quite how Daddy and Mom pulled off the preparations. There were originally three hundred of us Children. Somehow, coldsleep units were smuggled out of medical storage, put aboard the container ship. Somehow we were all checked out of our classes—you all remember that."

Heads nodded.

"If a Power were coming awake, surely it would have noticed what your parents were up to."

"I—" Johanna hesitated. "You're right. They should have been caught. There must have been others working with them to set up our escape."

"I didn't notice anything," said Heida.

"No," said someone else.

"Me neither," said Øvin. "Remember how we were living, the temporary pressurized habs, the lack of privacy? I could tell my folks were getting edgy—okay, frightened—but there wasn't room to do things on the sly. It seems reasonable—and this is one of the Disaster Study Group's points—that our escape was just a move in Something's game."

Ravna said, "We talked about Countermeasure at the Academy, Øvin. You children did get special help. Ultimately, Countermeasure—" *with Pham and Old One*—"was what stopped the Blight."

"Yes, Ma'am," said Øvin. "But all this illustrates how little we know about the good guys and the bad guys. We're stuck Down Here. We older kids feel that we have lost everything. But the official history could just as well have the good guys and the bad guys switched."

"Huh? Who is peddling such crap?" Ravna couldn't help herself; the words just popped out. So much for gracious leadership.

Øvin seemed to shrink back on himself. "It's not anybody in particular."

"Oh? What about those three I passed on the stairs?"

Jefri shifted on his high stool. "You ran into me on the stairs, too, Ravna. Those three are just gossips. You might as well be blaming all of us."

"If it's 'just everybody' then where did a name like Disaster Study Group come from? Somebody must be behind this, and I want to—"

A hand pressed lightly on Ravna's sleeve. Johanna held the touch for an instant, long enough to shut down her spew of angry words. Then the girl said, "Something like this doubting has always been around."

"You mean doubts about the Blighter threat?"

Johanna nodded. "Yes, in varying degrees. You yourself have doubts on that, I know. For instance, now that the Blighter fleet has been stopped by Countermeasure, will it have any further interest in harming Tines World?"

"We have no choice but to believe that what remains wants to destroy us." *My dream—*

"Okay, but even then there's the question of just how deadly they can be. The fleet is thirty lightyears out, probably not capable of travelling more than a lightyear per century. We have millennia to prepare, even if they do wish us ill."

"Parts of the fleet could be faster."

"So we have 'only' a few centuries. Tech civilizations have been built in less."

Ravna rolled her eyes. "They've been *re*built in less. And we may not have that much time. Maybe the fleet can build small ramscoops. Maybe the Zones will slip again—" She took a breath and proceeded a little more calmly: "The point is, the point of everything we're teaching in the Academy is, we have to get ready as fast as we possibly can. We must make sacrifices."

A little boy's voice spoke from all around them. Amdi. "I think that's what the Disaster Study Group disputes. They deny that the Blight was ever a threat to humans or Tines. And if it is, they say, Countermeasure made it so."

Silence. Even the background music from the bartender had faded away. Apparently Ravna was the last to realize the monstrous issue under discussion. Finally she said, softly, "You can't mean that, Amdi."

An expression rippled across Amdi: embarrassed contrition. Each of his members was fourteen years old, each an adult animal, but his mind was younger than any pack she knew. For all his genius, Amdi was a shy and child-like creature.

Across the table, Jefri patted one of Amdi comfortingly. "Of course he doesn't mean *he* believes it, Ravna. But he's telling you the truth. The DSG starts from the position that we can't know exactly what happened at the High Lab and how we managed to escape. Reasoning from what we *do* know, they argue that we could have the good and the bad reversed. In which case, Countermeasure's actions of ten years ago were a galactic-scale atrocity—and there are no terrible monsters bearing down on us."

"Do *you* believe that?"

Jefri raised his hands in exasperation. ". . . No. Of course not! I'm just spelling out what some people are too, ah, diplomatic to say. And before you ask, I wager none of us here believe it, either. But among the kids as a whole—"

"Especially some of the older ones," said Øvin.

"—it's a very attractive way of looking at things." Jefri glowered at her for a moment, challenging. "It's attractive because it means that what our parents created was not a monstrous 'blight.' Our parents were not silly fools. And it's also attractive because it means that the sacrifices we're making now are . . . unnecessary."

Ravna struggled to keep her voice steady: "What sacrifices in particular? Learning low-tech programming? Learning manual arithmetic?"

Heida chipped in with, "Oh, part of it is just having other people tell us what to do!"

These kids probably didn't even know the names of pre-tech consensus-building methods. Skipping that stage had just been one of the simplifications Ravna had chosen. She had hoped that trust and affection and common goals would suffice until they had more tech and more people.

"Getting bossed around may be part of it," said Øvin, "but for some, the medical situation is a bigger issue." He looked directly at Ravna. "The years pass and you rule and you still look young, just as young as Johanna does now."

"Øvin! I'm thirty-five years old." That was human-standard thirty-megasecond years, the same as Straumers used. "It should be no surprise I look young. Back in Sjandra Kei, I'd still be a very junior specialist."

"Yes, and a thousand years from now, you'll still look that young. All of us—even the older children—will be dead in a few hundred years. Some of us already look decayed—you know, losing our hair like we've suffered rad damage. Getting fat. The youngest of us have scarcely had any prolongevity treatment. And our children will die like flies, decades before us."

Ravna thought of Wenda Larsndot's graying hair. *But that doesn't mean I'm wrong!* "Look, Øvin. We'll get the medical research ramped up eventually. It just doesn't make sense to put it first. I can show you the progress charts that *Oobii* generates. Effective medicine has a million gotchas. Which cure is going to be hard—and hard for which child—that's something we can't know ahead of time. A crash medical program would just be a morass of delay. We've got at least twenty coldsleep caskets that are still in working order. I'm sure we can generate the consumables for them eventually. If necessary, we can freeze anyone who gets mortally old. No one need die."

Øvin Verring raised his hand. "I understand, ma'am. I think all of us here do—even Screwfloss, Benky, and Catchip—who are so quietly listening in." There was some embarrassed shifting around in the tavern's lofts. From across the room, the bartender said, "Heh, this is all between you two-legs."

Heida couldn't resist: "You packs just don't die properly!"

Øvin gave a little smile but waved for Heida to pipe down. "Nevertheless, you see the attraction of the Disaster Study Group. They deny that our parents messed up. They deny that there's a need for sacrifice. We refugees can't really know what happened or who was to blame in getting us Down Here. The extremists—and I don't think any of *us* have knowingly talked to such; the extremists are always referred to at third hand—they say since *we* know the goodness of our own parents, then the right bet is that the Blight is no monster at all, and all this preparation and sacrifice may be in service to . . . well, maybe to something evil."

Johanna gave her head a sharp little shake. "Huh? Øvin, that logic is a jumble."

"Maybe that's why we can't find anyone who says it for themselves, Jo."

Ravna listened to the back and forth. *What can I say to this that I haven't said before?* But she could not keep silent: "When these deniers say 'we can't really know,' that is a lie. *I* know. I was at Relay, working for Vrinimi Org. The Blight was doing evil almost half a year before *Oobii* took flight. It spread out from your High Lab, probably within a few hours of your escape. It took over the Top of the Beyond. I could read about it in the news. With Vrinimi's resources I could follow the destruction in detail, the Blight killing whomever it pleased. The thing took over Straumli Realm. It destroyed Relay. It chased Pham and me and the Skroderiders down here, and the wake of that pursuit killed Sjandra Kei and most of the humans in the Beyond." These were things she had told them again and again and again. "The defense against the Blight wasn't undertaken until we arrived here. Yes, what Pham and Countermeasure did was horrendous—more so than we can measure. Countermeasure did strand us. But it stopped the Blight and it left us with a chance. Those are *facts* that are being denied. They are not something beyond knowing. I was *there*."

And all around the table, these Children now grown up were nodding respectfully.

CHAPTER 06

Ravna had plenty of time to think about that terrible surprise at the Sign of the Mantis. More accurately, she couldn't think about anything else. Everything she'd ever said or done looked different now that she imagined it through the eyes of the Deniers.

In the beginning, the Children had all lived in the New Castle on Starship Hill, just a hundred meters from the academy. The youngest ones still lived there with older siblings or Best Friend packs. Most of the others—grown and with the beginnings of families—lived on Hidden Island or in the string of houses south of the New Castle.

But Ravna still lived aboard the starship *Out of Band II*—thirty thousand tonnes of unflyable junk, but with technology from the stars.

She must seem crazed and remote, hunkered down aboard the supreme power in this world.

But I have to be here! For the *Oobii* had a small library, and Ravna was a librarian. The tiny onboard archive comprised the technological tricks of myriads Slow Zone races. Humankind on Earth had taken four thousand years to go from the smelting of iron to interstellar travel. That had been more or less a random walk. In the wars and catastrophes that followed, humans were like most races. They had blown themselves back to the medieval many times, and sometimes to the Neolithic, and, on a few worlds, even to extinction. But—at least where humankind survived at all—the way back to technology had been no random walk. Once the archeologists dug up the libraries, renaissance was a matter of a few centuries. With *Oobii*, she could cut that recovery time down to less than a century. *To thirty years, if bad luck will just stay out of my way!*

That afternoon, at the Sign of the Mantis, bad luck showed it had been around all the time. *How could this have blindsided me?* Ravna asked herself that question again and again. The Children had always been full of questions. Many times over the years, she and the Tines had told them the story of the Battle on Starship Hill, and the history before. They all had walked around Murder Meadows, seen how the land looked when Lord Steel had killed half the Children. But they had only Ravna's words about other half of the battle, how Pham had stopped the Blighter fleet and the price that had been paid. The Children had always had lots of questions about that, and about what had happened to their parents at the beginning of the disaster. The Children had gone from a world with families and friends, to waking up surrounded by Tines and a single human adult. All they had was her word about what had made that happen. Foolish Ravna, she had thought that that would be enough.

Now the Children had more than doubts. Now they had something called the Disaster Study Group.

Just hours after the Sign of the Mantis, she and Johanna and Jefri (and Amdi of course) had another chat. These were the first two kids Ravna had met Down Here. Ten years ago, they had shared a terrible few hours. Ever since, Ravna had felt they had a special relationship—even when Jefri hit his teenage years and seemed lost to all reason.

Now Johanna was livid about the Disaster Study Group—but even more angry with Jefri, since he hadn't told her of the group's latest lies.

Jefri had flared right back at her. "You want to go on a witch hunt, Jo? You want to flush out everyone who believes some part of the DSG claims? That would be just about everybody, you know." He paused, his glance flickering doubtfully in Ravna's direction. "I don't mean the worst of it, Ravna. We know you and Pham were good guys."

Ravna had nodded, trying to look calm. "I know. I can see how natural some of the doubting is." Yeah she could see, with brilliant hindsight. "I just wish I had known before."

Johanna bowed her head. "I'm sorry I never talked to you about this. The DSG says some despicable things, but both Nevil and I thought it was so nuts it would just die away. Now, the whole thing seems much more organized." She cast a look at Jefri. They were back on the *Oobii*'s bridge, a good place for very small, very private meetings. Amdi was out of sight, hiding around under the furniture. "You and Amdi obviously knew that the DSG has turned a whole lot more nasty."

Jefri started to snap back, then gave a reluctant nod. In fact, Ravna suddenly realized, he looked ashamed. Jefri had the same stubbornness as his sister; he just frittered it away on aimless frustration. Their parents were the closest thing to heroes in the sorry High Lab mess. They had worked miracles to get the kids here. When Jefri finally spoke, his voice was soft. "Yeah. But like Øvin said, the worst of the claims are just third-hand . . . repeated by foolish people like Gannon Jorkenrud."

Johanna shook her head. "Why do you still hang out with that loser?"

"Hei! Gannon was my friend at the Lab, okay? I could talk to him about things even the teachers didn't understand. Maybe now he *is* a loser, but . . ."

Johanna's angry expression shifted to frank worry. "This is too much, Jef. Suddenly DSG seems like a real threat."

Jefri shrugged. "I don't know, Jo. The latest stuff just sort of popped up, one or two people on Meri's expedition, then more when I got back here. And even if there is a conspiracy, putting pressure on the likes of Gannon is only going to make the Executive Council look thuggish—and Gannon might just start accusing people he's got it in for. He's got a mean streak."

Ravna nodded. "How about this, Jefri: Maybe this is complaining based on legitimate issues—issues I *do* intend to address, by the way. But maybe this is the doing of a clique of older Children planning some kind of mayhem and exaggerating the real issues for their own ends. *You* are in a position to find out which is which. Everybody knows, um, that you—"

Jefri's glance flickered at Johanna, and the boy grinned. He'd always had a nice smile. "Don't be shy," he said. "Everyone knows I've been a bloody ass-hole. Still am sometimes. Part of my refugee angst, y'know."

"In any case," said Ravna, "people seem quite happy to confide in you. If you act sympathetic toward this evil nonsense, and if there really is a Denier conspiracy, I'll bet they will approach you more directly. Is this a role that, ah, you'd—"

"You mean, will I find out which of my friends might be behind this and rat them out?" There was no venom in his words, but Jefri didn't look happy. For-tunately, Johanna remained quiet, keeping to herself any sisterly harangues. Finally, he shook his head. "Yeah. I'll do it. I still don't think there is any real conspiracy, but if there is, I'll find it."

Ravna realized she had been holding her breath. "Thank you, Jefri." If the ones like Jefri Olsndot were on her side, then this was something she could get through.

Johanna was smiling, looking a bit relieved herself. She started to say something to her brother, then wisely left well enough alone. Instead she looked around the table. "Hei, Amdi! You got all this? Any problems?"

Silence, and not a head in sight. That was the trouble with Amdi. Some-times he got distracted with the math problems that forever flitted around in his heads, and was lost to daydreams beyond the imagination of all but an Archi-medes or a Nakamore. Sometimes—especially in recent years—he simply fell asleep.

"Amdi?"

"Yup, yup." Amdi's little boy voice drifted up from carpet level. He sounded wan, or a little sleepy. "Jefri and I are still a team."

Ravna's chat with Jo and Jef and Amdi had been only the first of several private conversations. Since Pilgrim was out of town, her next stop was Woodcarver.

Ravna's co-Queen had ruled much of the Northwest for more than three centuries. None of her individual members were that old, of course, but she had been very careful about keeping herself together, and the pack had clear memories going back to a time when she had been a simple artist in a cabin by the sea. For Woodcarver, empire had grown out of that art, the goal to build and mold and carve. Woodcarver was a true medieval lord. Given that she was also a decent (if occasionally bloody-minded) sort, her presence and position of au-thority were miraculous good fortune for Ravna and the refugees.

Nowadays, the co-Queens shared Starship Hill, Ravna in her starship *Oobii* and Woodcarver in the New Castle, the Dome of the Children's Lander.

Walking toward the castle gate, Ravna was always struck by the balance of symbolic powers that she and Woodcarver had achieved. Ravna had the tech-nology, but she lived lower on the hill. Then a bit higher—between them—there was the Academy for Humans and Their packs (or packs and Their Humans), where everyone raced to learn what the future required of them. And finally, at the top, was Woodcarver in the New Castle. Deep beneath the dome of the castle were odd scraps of technology that had come down with the Children. There were the coldsleep caskets, and the Lander with its remnant automation. There was the spot in the Lander where Pham Nuwen had died, and a slime of silica-ceous mold that had once been Countermeasure itself.

Today, Ravna pursued the upper corridors, sunlit from dozens of narrow window slots. But the caskets, the mold, and her terrible dream—they were still near in her mind.

———

Ravna talked to Woodcarver in the Thrones Room. In the beginning, New Castle had been scarcely more than a shell, Lord Steel's trap for Pham and Ravna. Woodcarver had filled in the interior spaces, completing the place. The Thrones Room was the most visible addition, a huge, tiered hall. On audience days, all the Children could fit in here, along with a number of packs.

Today it was empty but for one pack and one human. As the guards closed the doors behind her, Ravna started down the long carpet toward the thrones and the altar. Out of the shadows on either side of her, Woodcarver emerged, accompanying her on the walk.

Ravna nodded at the pack; the co-Queens had always observed a careful informality. "So I imagine your bartender-agent has already told you about the charming surprise I encountered at the Sign of the Mantis."

Woodcarver gave a gentle laugh. Over the years she had experimented with various human voices and mannerisms, watching how humans reacted. When she spoke, her Samnorsk was completely fluent, and she seemed perfectly human—even when Ravna was looking right at the seven strange creatures who together were her co-Queen. "The bartender?" said Woodcarver. "Screw-floss? He's a Flenser whackjob. My guy was one of the customers up in the loft; he told me all about it, including what Gannon Jorkenrud had to say before you arrived."

I wouldn't have guessed about Screwfloss. Weird human words were unac-countably popular as taken names among the local packs; Flenser's minions were fond of the more satanic variations.

Her co-Queen waved for Ravna to take a seat. Between grand audiences, Woodcarver treated this room like a private den. Up around the altar, she had fur-trimmed benches and disorganized piles of blankets. There was a strong Tinish scent from the well-used furniture, and a litter of drinks and half-gnawed bones. Woodcarver was one of the few with her own radio link to the oracle that was *Oobii*; her "altar" had a very practical significance.

Ravna plunked herself down on the nearest human-style chair. "How could we miss something this big, Woodcarver? This 'Disaster Study Group' operat-ing right under our noses?"

Woodcarver settled herself around the altar, some of her on perches near Ravna. She gave a rippling shrug. "It's purely a human affair."

"We've always known there are reasonable disagreements about what's left of the Blighter fleet," said Ravna, "but I never realized how that was being tied into our rotten medical situation. And I never guessed that the Children might doubt the cause of the disaster that had dumped them here."

Woodcarver was silent for a moment. There was something embarrassed in her aspect. Ravna's look swept across the pack in an encompassing glare. "What? You knew about this?"

She made a waffling gesture. "Some of it. You know that even Johanna has been exposed to some of these stories."

"Yes! And I can't believe that neither of you have brought this up in Council!"

"Grm. I just heard rumors rumbling in the background. A good leader hears more than she acts upon. If you can't use spies, you should go out and mingle more with your Children. As long as you're the remote wizard on the starship, you'll have unwelcome surprises."

Ravna resisted the temptation to put her face in her hands and start bawling. *But I'm not a leader!* "Look, Woodcarver. I'm very worried about this. Leave aside the 'surprise' aspect. Leave aside the unpleasant fact that this must mean a lot of my kids despise me. Don't you see a threat in *organized* disaffection?"

The co-Queen hunched down slightly, the equivalent of a pensive frown. "Sorry. I thought you had run into this before, Ravna. Yes, I do get reports from Best Friend packs: What Øvin Verring and company told you is true. This is all rumors, exaggerated by the telling. I haven't found any hard core of believers—though, hmhmm, that may be because the hard core is among the humans without close Tinish friends."

". . . Yes." That point raised a world of possibility. "Had you even heard of a 'Disaster Study Group'?"

"Not until Gannon started making noises about it."

"And the really extreme claims, that the Blight is not evil, that Pham was the bad guy—I'll wager that is something new, too."

Woodcarver was silent a moment. "Yes. That's also new, though there have been weaker versions." Then she added, almost defensively, "But among Tines, rumors can be impossible to track, especially when there is Interpack sex. Transient personalities pop up with notions that would not have been imagined otherwise. Afterwards there is no one to point to."

That bit of Tinish insight forced a chuckle from Ravna. "We humans also talk about rumors taking on a life of their own, but it sounds like Tines have the real thing."

"You think there are conspirators?"

Ravna nodded. "I'm afraid there may be. On this world, you qualify as a modern ruler, but your notion of 'spies everywhere,' well, it's—"

"Hmpf. I know, by civilized standards, my surveillance is pitifully weak." Woodcarver jabbed a nose in the direction of the radio altar, her private pipeline to *Oobii*'s archive. In the winter, she used a treadmill to keep it charged. In the summer, she had the sunlight from this hall's high windows. Either way, Woodcarver practically camped around her radio, studying indiscriminately.

Woodcarver wasn't the only pack with a spy apparatus. Ravna tried to put the question diplomatically: "This is a case where any information would be welcome. Could you perhaps consult with Flenser-Tyrathect—"

"No!" said Woodcarver, making jaw-snapping sounds. She'd never stopped suspecting that Flenser was plotting a takeover. After a moment she continued, "What we really need are a couple of dozen wireless cameras. Cams and networks, that's the foundation of surveillance ubiquity." She sounded like she'd been studying some very old text. "Since we don't have proper networks yet, I'll settle for more spy eyes."

Ravna shook her head. "We only have a dozen loose cameras, total." Of course, much of *Oobii* could act as cameras and displays. Unfortunately, when you took a crowbar and pried pieces off those programmable walls—well, you sacrificed a lot of functionality. The twelve cameras they did have were low-tech backups. Ravna recognized the irritated expression spreading across Woodcarver. "Come the day that we can fabricate digital electronics, all this will change, Woodcarver."

"Yes. Come the day." The pack whistled a dirge-like tune. She had three of the cameras herself, but apparently she wasn't volunteering them. Instead: "You know that my illustrious science advisor is squatting on nine cameras?" Scrupilo was doing his best to create networks even though he lacked distributed computation. He had the cameras transmitting from his labs back to the planning logic aboard the *Oobii*. That trick had actually speeded up materials evaluation tenfold. Any time they could use the starship's power or logic, they had a win. Those labs were the biggest success story of the last few years.

"Okay," said Ravna. "I'd be willing to give up part of Scrupilo's testing system for a tenday or two. I really want to find out if there is an organized conspiracy behind these Denier lies."

"Then let's see which cameras I can grab." Three of Woodcarver hopped onto perches around her radio altar. She warbled something that was neither pack talk nor Samnorsk. Woodcarver had used *Oobii*'s customizer to make sound substitutes for the usual visual interface. For the pack, the result was almost as convenient as Ravna's "tiara," the fragile head-up display Ravna was normally afraid to wear in the casual everyday.

Woodcarver listened to the *wheeps* and *beeps* coming back from *Oobii*. "Ah, that Scrupilo. *Oobii* says my dear science advisor has been using the cams for more than your product development. Hmm. You ever hear of 'mass-energy conversion drip'?"

"No. . . . It sounds dangerous."

"Oh, it is." Woodcarver warbled some more, probably "looking up" definitions. "Without adequate process control, the 'drip' normally turns into something called a 'conversion torrent.' That's destroyed more than one civilization. Fortunately for most histories, it's very difficult to create before you know the danger of it." She queried some more. "Oh good. That was last tenday. Scrupilo dropped the project, took the path of sanity for once. What he's doing now looks like the materials research he's supposed to be doing." There was pause, then a human-sounding chuckle. "Scrupilo will throw a personal riot when we take those cameras from him. It will be fun to see." The science advisor was another of Woodcarver's offspring packs. They had turned out to be Woodcarver's own dangerous experiments.

Ravna was doing her best to think sneaky: "I bet we can keep the diversion a secret. Two or three of them could officially 'break.'" Very few of the locals understood what was durable and what was not. Over the years, she had broken all but one of her head-up displays, but the low-tech cams could probably survive a twenty-meter fall. "Scrupilo won't have to disguise his outrage, just the details of the affair."

"I *like* that!" Woodcarver gave a rippling grin, and one of her on a high perch gave Ravna a pat on the head. She spoke some notes to *Oobii*. "Okay, let's take three cameras. We should think on where and how to best use them."

"I want this done quickly. The word is out that I've been tipped off. If someone's behind this, then wouldn't they move now, to keep us off balance?"

"Just so."

Three cameras scarcely made a surveillance system, no matter how cleverly they were placed. Ravna decided to ask directly about the others. "What about the three that you're already using to spy on Flenser? It's humans who are the greatest threat just now."

"No. Those stay in place. If there really *is* a conspiracy here, then I'd bet a champion conspirator is behind it, not one of your naive Children. Flenser is as devious as any creature alive." And Old Flenser had been another of Woodcarver's offspring packs, the deadliest—if not the most malevolent—of her attempts at creating genius.

"But this is the reformed Flenser. Only two of his pack are still from you."

Woodcarver sounded a loud sniff. "So? Old Flenser chose the other three . . ."

"It's been ten years."

"We get along. The three cameras I've hidden down in Old Castle, they give me reason to . . . well, 'trust' is not the right word . . . to tolerate him."

Ravna smiled. "You're always complaining that he knows where you're watching him."

"Um. I *suspect* he knows. Always suspect him, Ravna. Then you won't be disappointed. Maybe . . . if I can get my people into the castle, we could move the cameras around. I've been wanting to do that anyway. Flenser must remain at the top of the suspects list. I don't want those cameras diverted to anything less likely."

"Very well." The Original Flenser had been a scary beast, combining extremes of human history. Ravna would have been as paranoid about Flenser as Woodcarver was if she didn't have her own special source of information. *That* source was one the very few secrets that she'd never told anyone, not even Johanna. She wasn't going to reveal it now just to pry three cameras away from her co-Queen.

One of Woodcarver bumped up against Ravna's chair and set its paw on her arm. "You're disappointed?"

"I'm sorry. Yes, a little. We've freed up three cameras. Surely there are more targets."

"And I'll look at Flenser still more carefully than before."

Ravna couldn't respond to that, not without revealing her own source of information.

"Look, Ravna. In addition to the cameras, I'll bring in some of my agents from the outlands. We'll get to the bottom of this."

Woodcarver was really trying to be cooperative. More than any pack except Scrupilo, she seemed to understand what drove Ravna.

The human reached out to pat the nearest of Woodcarver. This was Sht— hei, that's what the name sounded like to human ears. Member names were normally little more then broodkenner tags, mostly meaningless even to Tines. Little Sht was just a few tendays old, a necessary addition in the careful balancing of youth and old age that was a coherent pack. This baby was so young that it had only basic sensory sharing with the rest of Woodcarver. Beyond that, all Ravna knew was that the puppy was not the biological get of any in Woodcarver or Pilgrim. In dealing with Tines, puppies were often a problem, especially if a pack's lifegrooming was careless. Woodcarver had done much better with her own soul than with her offspring packs; she had maintained a steady purpose for nearly six hundred years. Ravna shouldn't have to worry. She petted the small creature's fine dense pelt and felt comforted. Hei, if there was a change it might be like the congenial evolution that Woodcarver had engineered for herself in the past.

CHAPTER 07

Scrupilo was beside himself. "This is an outrage!" The six of him crowded together, two members climbing up on the shoulder straps of the others to get their muzzles closer to Ravna's face. "They were stolen. This is treachery, and I will not stand for it!"

Ravna had arrived at the North End quarries a few minutes earlier. Looking down from the edge of the carven stone walls, things had seemed relatively quiet, no blast banners or fire-in-the-hole beeping. This seemed like a good time for a nice chat with the science advisor.

As she'd started down the open stairs, she had waved to the humans who were helping with the work. They cheerily waved back, so maybe Scrupilo wasn't too angry. She was still halfway up the rock face, when she heard the science advisor's outraged shouting. By the time she arrived at the laboratory entrance, two of his assistants had come racing out, passing her with scarcely a how-de-do.

Now she faced the madpack in his own office. She hadn't dreamed that Scrupilo would be so angered. For that matter, she'd never had any pack get in her face so abruptly. She backed toward the open doorway, raising her hands at the snapping jaws.

"It's just temporary, Scrupilo! You'll get the cameras back soon enough." At least she hoped so. If they had to keep those cams from Scrupilo's use for very long, large sections of her own research program would get jammed.

The good news was that Scrupilo did not bite her face off. The bad news was that the pack continued to lunge around—and he wasn't speaking Samnorsk anymore. The chords she could hear were loud and jagged, probably cursing. Then abruptly Scrup's oldest member, the white-headed one, hesitated. In half a second, the surprised silence spread across the pack, like some comedian's exaggerated double take. "Cameras?" His volume dropped by some decibels. "You mean the three video cameras that officially failed earlier today when Woodcarver's goons came and took them away?"

"Y-yes." Hopefully the world beyond Scrupilo's office had not made sense of this exchange, state secrets being betrayed in a temper tantrum.

Scrupilo climbed down from himself. For a moment he just circled around, glaring. Scrupilo could be an officious twit. On the other hand, he was a genius and a true engineer. As long as you could keep him pointed in the right direction, and keep him from getting too jealous of the perks of others, he was a treasure.

"Honest, Scrupilo," Ravna continued in a soft voice. "This is an emergency. We'll get those cams back to you as soon as possible. I know—at least as well as you—how important they are."

The Science Advisor continued his angry pacing, but now his voice was level. "I don't doubt that. It was the only reason I went along with the confiscation and the cover story I'm supposed to tell everyone." Jaws snapped a couple of times, but not in her direction. "But I fear we are talking at cross-purposes. The video cams were lawfully confiscated by Your Highnesses and with some explanation. So then, you and Woodcarver had nothing to do with the disappearance of the *radio cloaks?*"

"What? No!" The cloaks would have been practically useless for surveillance, and wearing them was dangerous to boot. "Scrupilo, that was never our plan."

"Then I was right. There is treachery afoot."

"How could the cloaks disappear? You keep them in your private vaults, right?"

"I took them out of the vault after the Queen's agents made off with my cameras. I had this idea for using the cloaks . . . a clever idea really, a way I might wear them without getting killed in the process. Y'see, maybe if only part of me wore them, and off-the-shoulder, then—" Scrupilo shook himself free of geekish distraction. "Never mind. The point is, I had the cloaks laid out in the experiment factory, ready for use. I was still afume about Woodcarver's confiscation, and there were way too many other distractions this morning. Let's see . . ." Scrupilo brought all his heads together for a moment, the very picture of Tinish concentration.

"Yes. You know how the experiment factory is set up." Long rows of simple wood benches. Hundreds of experiment trays, each a simple combination of reagents, all designed by the planning programs on the *Oobii* as the ship matched the reality of Tinish resources with the archival data that it possessed. Some of the rooms would go for hours without any pack or human presence— and then the starship automation would issue a flurry of wireless requests to the scheduling receivers in the dispatch room. Scrupilo's helpers would sweep through, removing some experiments entirely, shifting some to new stations, placing some under cameras for *Oobii*'s direct observation.

"I was alone with the radio cloaks, quite distracted by my new idea." Scrupilo's heads all look up. "Yes! Those clowns from the Tropical madhouse showed up."

"They came in among the experiments?"

"No. That used to happen, but nowadays we keep them in the visitor area. Heh. I've fobbed them off with junk like unconnected landline telephones. . . . Anyway, I had to go out and chat with their 'Ambassador.'" Scrupilo jostled together. "I'll bet that's it! I was out of the room for almost fifteen minutes. I wish we didn't have to be nice to that guy. Do we really need gallite that much? Never mind, I know the answer.

"Anyway, today they were louder and more numerous than usual, the whole gang painted up like the loose things they are." Some of Scrupilo was already edging toward the door, outpacing the conscious stream of his surmise. "The scum. While they distracted my people, one of them must have swiped the cloaks!

"Damn! C'mon, milady!" And the rest of him was out the door, White Head bringing up the rear. The pack clattered down the outside stairs, shouting chords of alarm in all directions.

Ravna would have had a hard time keeping up with some packs, but White Head had arthritis, and Scrupilo was not running completely amok. The pack wouldn't leave him behind.

Scrupilo was also shouting in Samnorsk, "Stop the Tropicals! Stop the Tropicals!" The guards at the top of the exit stairs had already lowered the gates.

As Ravna and Scrupilo ran across the quarry terrace, Scrupilo muttered a constant stream of Samnorsk. The profanity was a bizarre combination of translations of pack cursing and Samnorsk naughty words: "Get of bitches! I should have realized it was the fuckall Tropicals. I was just too damned pissed about the cameras. I thought you and Woodcarver were dumping on me again."

Shouts came from ahead: "We got them!" The packs and humans in the quarry were not armed, but they had formed a barrier around . . . somebody.

Scrupilo wriggled through the crowd of mindsounds, Ravna close behind. Ambassador Godsgift and its gang were still in the quarry. They had been inspecting the most spectacular part of the laboratory, where much of the dull planning and experimentation finally led to miracles.

There was an open space between the crowd and the suspected thieves.

Godsgift and his people were backed up against Scrupilo's flying machine, the *Eyes Above*. This was not an antigravity craft, but something weirder, at least to Ravna's mind: a propeller and basket hung from a pointy balloon.

Scrupilo spent a moment pacing back and forth in front of the crowd, gobbling in Tinish. Ravna couldn't really understand, not without *Oobii* analysis. He seemed to be asking everybody to cut the high-sound screaming. In cold dry air—say, like here, today—such sounds could carry a number of meters, and if every pack went into a tizzy at the same time, things could get very confusing for them.

Ravna took a few steps in the direction of the Tropicals, then thought better of it. These Tines looked frightened and edgy, eyes wide. They stood close among themselves, pressed hard back against the airboat's crew basket. The self-styled "Ambassador" was the only clearly-defined group, but there was sharp steel visible on more than one forepaw. These fellows might be loosely minded but they had been in the North long enough to pick up many Northern habits.

Scrupilo shouted in Samnorsk and Tinish. The Samnorsk was: "Anybody see what these scum were up to?" Part of him was looking at the airboat, and it suddenly occurred to Ravna that the Tropicals might actually have been moments from flying away!

A human fifteen-year-old, Del Ronsndot, stepped forward. "I—I was just showing them around the *Eyes Above*. I thought they were allowed."

"It's okay, Del," said Ravna. Such tours were standard policy.

"Did they ask to see the airboat?" said Scrupilo.

"Oh, yes, sir. All the visitors like to see it. Once we get some practice, maybe we could even give them rides." His eyes slid across to the Tropicals, and he seemed to realize that perhaps such generosity would be postponed.

"Did they ask to let any of their packs aboard?"

There was a loud chord or two from the Tropical side of the confrontation, and then a human voice: "Ah, Master Scrupilo, if you suspect evildoing you should talk to me directly." The ambassador stepped forward. It had taken the name "Godsgift," and today it was huge. Some of it dated from the founding of the Embassy, and it was often fluent. Just as often, it behaved more like a club for singletons who liked to swagger and pose. It wore mismatched jackets, some quite elegant. It was hard not to smile at the buffoon. Right now . . . well, there was something deadly in its gaze. *Think back, Ravna. Remember the butterflies in jackboots?* She'd seen enough aliens to know how misleading physical appearance could be.

Scrupilo was still too angry to be cautious. He sent two of himself forward, crowding the Ambassador's personal space. "Fair enough, Mister Ambassador. What have you done with my radio cloaks?" The two snapped their jaws in Godsgift's direction, and though the adversaries were still three meters apart, the gesture was very much like one human poking a finger into the chest of another.

Godsgift was not impressed. "Ha. I've heard of those cloaks. Surely they can find themselves?" It pointed a snout in the direction of Starship Hill. "I haven't seen your precious cloaks since that amusing demonstration you gave at Springtime's Last Sunset." He spread into an aside. "What wonderful holidays you Northerners have. For us, the springtime is just more rain—"

"*Be quiet!*" Scrupilo turned a head toward his assistants, both human and Tinish. "Bring me some soldiers with long pikes. We're putting these thieves to the question."

The Tropicals surged toward Scrupilo, steel glittering on their claws. They would lose any battle, but Scrupilo's two forward members would likely get their throats slashed.

Ravna stepped forward and raised her arms in the way that most packs seemed to find intimidating. "*Wait!*" she shouted, as loud as she was able. "No one's going to be put to the question. We'll either respect your embassy or boot you out of the Domain."

Scrupilo settled back, gobbling to himself.

The Ambassador had edged away from the mob, no doubt to keep a clear mind. Now he gave a little warble, and the others relaxed a fraction. Godsgift bobbed heads in Ravna's direction. "Ah, so blunt and yet—how do I say?—so full of the common sense. I am grateful, Your Highness. I came today expecting a happy and friendly tour. At least it will not become a bloodbath."

"Don't count on it," Scrupilo muttered back.

Ravna lowered her arms and leaned forward so her eyes were more at the level of Godsgift's. "Our radio cloaks went missing just in the last hour, Mr. Ambassador. So, how interested are you in maintaining your embassy here? Will you and your people submit to a search?" She waved at Godsgift's mob and their suspiciously numerous panniers.

The Ambassador's heads flipped up, probably a dismissive gesture. "Perhaps the question should be, how much does your Domain value continued trade with the Tropics?"

In the past, the trade with the Tropics had been an almost unrecognized silent barter, where bid and response were spread across years of occasional shipwrecks. The "Tropical Embassy" had begun as a charity for shipwrecked singletons, a joke of an embassy. Now the joke had a life of its own and—maybe—some influence in the South.

Ravna crossed her arms and gave the ambassador a look. It was amazing the effect the soundless stare of a two-legs could have on some packs.

Whatever the reason, the ambassador gave a shrug. "Oh, very well. We, of course, have nothing to hide."

Ravna gave an inward sigh of relief. *Now to find who really did the thieving.* She turned to the crowd behind her. A couple of dozen humans stood nearby, looming tall over the packs. And one at the back—

"Hei, Nevil! How long have you been here?"

Johanna's fiancé trotted forward, a couple of his friends close behind. "Just got here. I was at the top of the quarry when I saw everybody go berserk." Nevil stopped beside her. He was still breathing heavily. "I heard the last part though. You want these fellows searched?"

Scrupilo was nodding. "Yes. You humans can get in close without upsetting our delicate guests." He jabbed sarcastically in the direction of the Tropicals, but his gesture lacked spirit. "I was so sure it was them," he grumbled to himself.

Nevil squatted down so he could speak more privately. No human could direct *sotto voce* mutterings as well as a pack. Ravna leaned closer. "Godsgift did give in a bit easily," said Nevil. "Are you sure you have all his entourage here?"

Scrupilo's eyes widened. He poked a head up and gave the Tropicals a long look. "They're so hard to count." He did a double take. "God's Choir, Nevil, do you think they split off an extra pack?"

Ravna looked at the visitors. The Tropicals always seemed a bit strange, with their patchy fur, body paint, and mismatched clothing. Now that they weren't jammed against the airship, they had separated into something like packs, mostly foursomes. If they had come in with extra members, then split to make an additional pack. . . . It was the sort of playing with souls that would have left Domain packs dazed and disoriented.

Scrupilo looked back and forth at the Tropicals. "I don't know how many came in, but . . . look at that body paint. Don't you think there are gaps within those two fellows at the end? These *are* Tropicals. There's no end to their perversions."

Godsgift might be hearing every word. In any case, it was becoming restive: "I say, Your Highness. We've agreed to be searched. Be about the indignity, if you please!"

"Just a moment more, Mr. Ambassador." Ravna dropped back into her head-to-heads with Nevil and Scrupilo. "I have no idea, Scrupilo. Those paint jobs mean less to me than anyone." *I wish Pilgrim were here.* Pilgrim would know just what the Tropicals could do with themselves.

Nevil turned, waved one of his friends forward. Then he continued, whispering. "Actually, Bili saw something weird when we were up on top of the quarry."

Bili Yngva dropped to his knees beside them and nodded. "Yeah. There was a fivesome skulking around the quarry hoists. Its panniers were *stuffed*. When I tried to get a closer look, the critters took off for the boat landings. And the strangest thing—I think there were blue smudges on its pelt, like these fellows' body paint, but rubbed off."

Scrupilo let out a hoot of triumph. "I knew it!" Then he dithered. In a second more, orders would be flying in all directions.

Nevil stood up, gave Ravna a look. "Your Highness?"

Yes, Ravna abruptly realized, *it's time to act the co-Queen.* She put a restraining hand on one of Scrupilo's heads. "Please bear with me, Mr. Science Advisor." Then she stood and turned to the crowd, which itself was milling uncertainly about. "People! *People!*" Well, that worked in the classroom. And goodness, it got everyone's attention here, too! "We're going ahead with the property search the Ambassador just agreed to. Scrupilo will advise, but I want

humans to do the close-in." *Who?* She was suddenly even more grateful that
Nevil had shown up. He was on good terms with all the kids, and was a born
leader. "Nevil Storherte will supervise."

She said, in an aside to Nevil: "Is Johanna close by?"

"Sorry, she's on the mainland this afternoon."

"Okay, check out our visitors."

Nevil nodded, and began to gather a proper crew. Ravna glanced at Godsgift. "We'll have you out of here very soon, Mr. Ambassador."

The Tropical leader smiled broadly. "Excellent." Quite evidently, it had no
worries about its guilt being proven here.

Scrupilo was dancing with frustration. His gobbling chords broke into a
hissed Samnorsk whisper. "This is all *useless*! I should phone the boat moorage, put out an island-wide alarm, and contact *Oobii*."

They also needed some aerial surveillance. . . . She looked up at the airboat that had been the backdrop for this confrontation. "Is the *Eyes Above* fly-
able?" She pointed at the aircraft. "And does it have a radio on board?"

"What? No radio, but the motor is charged . . . hmm, grmm! Yes!" He
started shouting to his ground crews, chords and Samnorsk all mixed together,
in various loudnesses and different directions. What she could understand
was: "Phone Woodcarver!", "Nevil, move your investigation away from the *Eyes
Above*! I have use for it." And a whisper for her ears: "The craft is fully prepped.
I wonder if Mr. Crapheads knew that." He ran to the wicker basket as two of
his helpers approached from the other side. They were fiddling with a row of
gas valves, arguing with Scrupilo about details.

Nevil's people and the Tropicals had moved twenty meters off. The suspects
were grudgingly removing their panniers and jackets. Huh, the intricate body
painting covered much of their bare skin. Some of the Tropicals were watching
the airboat curiously, but they didn't seem the least disconcerted by Scrupilo's
activity.

One of Scrup's assistants came rushing out with the lab's loose radio. The
nearest of Scrupilo grabbed the box and passed it to himself, up the gangplank.
Then he hesitated, looking around as though he had forgotten something critical. "Oh, if only Johanna were here. This will go better with a combo crew."
That is, a pack and a human. "Nevil!" he shouted.

Ravna put a foot on the gangplank. "That's okay, I can help you as well was
anybody here." That was probably true; she'd been up with Scrupilo a number
of times. Besides, she didn't want to stay here and second-guess Nevil.

Nevil Storherte had started back in their direction. For a second, Ravna
thought he was going to object. The boy—no, the man; he was only eight years
younger than she—was always going on about her indispensable role in high
planning. This time, he seem to realize that he already had a job and that seconds counted. He hesitated, then gave her a little wave. "Okay. Good hunting."

She waved back, then shooed the rest of Scrupilo up the ramp, into the airboat's narrow basket.

For once, Scrupilo was not arguing. He scrambled aboard, all the while shouting to his ground crew. The basket did its usual disconcerting wobble as Ravna climbed across into the chair at the stern. She wasn't quite tied down when the ground crew cut the tethers and the balloon drew them firmly skywards.

This was almost like agrav—but steadier then Pilgrim's flier. The ground simply fell away. Looking over the edge of the basket, she could see all the Tropicals' gear laid out. No way that an entire set of radio cloaks could be hidden in that.

Scrupilo powered up the boat's propeller and turned the rudder. They were over the dark ponds that filled the old mining pits and covered the lab's tanks of stabilized hydrogen. The placid waters reflected the towering walls of the quarry. If she leaned further out, she'd be able to see the reflection of the airboat.

. . . But not just now. Ravna tied onto a safety harness and began crawling around the aft end of the basket. There were a number of equipment cabinets, mostly waterproofed wicker, with latches that could be released by hands or paws or jaws. She opened one after another, glancing in each: a heliograph (not enough radios to go around), maps, two telescopes. It suddenly occurred to her that there was something to check before anything else. She set the spyglasses down and turned to the stern cover.

"Highness," Scrupilo shouted to her. She looked out, saw that they had cleared the top of the quarry. "Please handle the driving. I'm best with the telescopes." Then he noticed that Ravna was trying to pull up the stern ballast cover. "Highness? The telescopes, please . . . What are you *doing?*"

"It just occurred to me—what if they stuffed the cloaks in the ballast tanks?"

"Uck." The pack thought a second, no doubt imagining how this chase could wreck what they were trying to recover. It was a long shot, but—"I'll check the bow and mid tanks." A pair at a time, Scrupilo's members released the various controls they had jaws on and poked around in the water tanks that were set along the length of the hull. The main rudder slid free and the propeller slowed till you could see its three blades. The *Eyes Above* slowly turned in the nearly still afternoon air, now pointing toward the outer islands, now at the north channel, now at Starship Hill. They were high enough that she could see the dome of the New Castle.

"There's nothing in these tanks but water," he said returning to his controls.

"Same back here."

"Very well then. Time is wasting." He angled both horizontal and vertical rudders and spun up the screw. *Eyes Above*'s stern gently bobbed upwards, and the airboat angled down, turning toward the island's North End boat landings. "Can you circle us around the North End while I take a look?"

"Yes." Flying was easy in air this placid. The backseat controls included two jaw levers by her chair and another pair set far enough forward that she could use them as foot pedals. Together they provided control of the rudders and propeller. It wasn't as simple as a point-and-move interface, but Ravna had practiced.

Scrupilo hauled the two telescopes forward. The eyepieces were curved masks that could be rotated to fit either side of a member's head. Midway down each barrel was a clasp suitable for the usual shoulder strap on Tinish jackets. In a matter of seconds, he had the scopes mounted on two of himself, and two of his other members were looking around for things to spy on. "Okay. Take us a little north. . . . Hah. Except for my construction barge, the moorage is almost deserted."

The North End moorage had been mostly taken over by Scrupilo's *serious* aircraft project, the creation of a rigid airship. The superstructure of the *Eyes Above 2* was already evident in the spars and ribs rising from the construction barge. When completed, in another half year or so, the *EA2* would be more than two hundred meters long, capable of transporting a dozen packs across the continent nonstop.

Most of Scrupilo was maneuvering the two telescopes like binoculars, sweeping across the piers and boat shelters. The rest of him lay together in the bottom of the basket, as if asleep. More likely, they were busy with the others, bringing all that two of them were seeing into a single, analyzed vision.

Scrupilo was humming to himself; at least the chords meant nothing to Ravna. "Ha! I see the pitter-patter of wet paws along the quay. See the gap in the moorage? Some pack was down here recently, departing in one of the single-hulled day fishers. So we know what to look for!" The two telescope bearers stood down. The others spread out to the ballast dumps. "Let's get upstairs quickly, Your Highness!" He dumped some water. One way or another, they were going up.

Ravna angled them northwest, across the outer straits. The channel islands were numerous, forested, and largely uninhabited. If the thief made it there he could probably get away.

Scrupilo glanced at the gear-driven clock he kept on White Head's jacket. "Take us to Ridgeline, that's the only place the thief could have reached in this direction." He was on his telescopes again, scanning the open water, all the way to where sea mist hung round the furthest islands. "Hmm, a couple of twin-hulls, nothing like our fellow."

They drove along for a few seconds, the propeller pushing them along at about five meters per second. The wicker basket was a cold, shadowed place, but at least the air stream was diverted by the basket's bow cowling.

Ravna locked down the rudders and rummaged around for the radio that Scrupilo had brought aboard. These radios were one of the stranger of *Oobii*'s reinventions. Of course, the device had no onboard processors; it was totally analog, indiscriminately spewing across the entire radio spectrum. No matter. The starship monitored all aspects of the space around it.

"Ship. Can you see where I am?" Ravna asked into the microphone.

"Ravna. Yes," acknowledged a pleasant male voice, *something like Pham's voice perhaps*. But there wasn't a bit of mind behind this voice. *Oobii*'s automation was simply the best computation that could run in the Slow Zone. By now she was almost used to the interface, and it was the best she could do when she wasn't wearing the data tiara.

She described the problem situation in terms the starship could work with. "And watch for radio lights near my location."

"Watching," *Oobii* replied.

"What transmissions do you see, out to, ah, four thousand meters?"

"I see a number of—"

"Ignore the North End lab."

"—I see one, your current transmission."

"Do you see any radio light from Ridgeline Island?"

"The radio frequency energy from Ridgeline Island appears to be normal scattering."

"Okay," said Ravna. "Ongoing: report on artificial radio light seen within, um"—Here she really needed a better interface. She settled for something short and crude.—"everything within ten thousand meters of the north end of Hidden Island."

"Done and ongoing. Do you want the reports streamed now?"

Ravna thought a second. "No. Report anomalies and forwarded transmissions." There were several radios that might legitimately be in use at this end of the Domain. They were part of the clunky forwarding operation that *Oobii* managed.

"Very good," replied *Oobii*. "I see nothing unusual at this time."

"You know, Your Highness, praps you should let me manage the radio interface." Scrup was almost as clever with voice comms as Woodcarver.

"No, keep your attention on the ground."

Scrupilo grumped around the basket. Their path had taken them in a low sweep of Ridgeline's shore, giving his telescopes a view beneath the tall evergreens. "There's nothing down there, no marks in the sand, and this is about the only place they could have reached land by now. The thief is either holed up on Hidden Island or he's on the inland channel, heading for the mainland. And now we'll never catch up! We are useless."

Scrupilo was like that, getting all frustrated and then giving up for a while. But Ravna was just getting interested in the problem. Given both the *Eyes Above* and the *Oobii*, there were some possibilities. She chatted with *Oobii*. It reported a mainland-trending windstream about five hundred meters up and a few hundred meters south. They dumped a little ballast. She brought the rudders around and drove the propeller as fast as its little electric motor could go. The airboat angled upwards, Ravna steering according to directions from the starship. It was fun as long as she didn't dwell on the fact that she was reduced to being a mere servomechanism for her starship's very dumb automation.

They climbed their invisible staircase, turning through 180 degrees as they went. Scrupilo looked out in all directions, then concentrated his attention on the Inner Channel, between the mainland and Hidden Island. Every few seconds he'd comment on the new areas he could see. "Still no sign of . . . But

wow, the ground speed! Milady, your maneuver is worthy of Johanna herself!"
The starship reported that the *Eyes Above* was driving along at almost twenty
meters per second. "And I can see the whole of the mainland shore. Mark my
words, we'll catch this thief!"

They drilled along, airspeed no greater than before, but the North End
lab passed below them and they were already cruising southward along the
Inner Channel. *Oobii* reported no new radio emissions. Of course, it had been
a long shot that the thief would try to *wear* the radio cloaks. To the Tines, the
devices were almost religious icons. Wear them, and you'd most likely fry
your mind—but if that didn't happen then you were transformed into a godlike pack who could stride the world with kilometers between one's pack
members! Somebody like Godsgift might be arrogant enough to wear the
cloaks in the middle of trying to steal them, but that was probably not true of
his minions.

She looked out at the cliffs of the mainland, the shoulders that Starship
Hill rested upon. If somehow the thief got ashore, it would be hiding in the evergreens that grew in the steepness. *Oobii* said there would be a summer rain
shower in another few hours. Under cover of that, the thief might make it to
whatever rendezvous the Tropicals had planned. She looked at the froth of dying spring leaves that floated in the evergreens' crowns. In most places, the
ground was hidden. *Oobii* had no line of sight on these cliffs. Even so . . . she
gave the starship another call.

Scrupilo's attention was on his telescopes; apparently he didn't notice what
Ravna was saying to the Starship. He pointed a snout downwards. "There are
Woodcarver's troops coming down to the mainland shore! We should tell them
that I've covered the shore north of us. Forward a call to them, Your Highness."

Then her science advisor noticed that she wasn't making the call. "Your
Highness!"

"Just a moment, Scrupilo. We may be able to detect the cloaks, even if they're
not turned on."

"But we need to make that call to Woodcarver!" Even his telescope members were looking around at her. Then he gave a start and began to sniff at his fur.
"Wow! Did you feel that, Your Highness? Like a tiny electric shock, but through
all my members, all at once."

Ravna hadn't felt a thing; maybe that was because she didn't have six fur-
covered bodies. However, she had an explanation. "*Oobii* just hit us with a very
bright pulse. Even if the cloaks are turned off and around a corner, they might
give back an echo."

"Ah!" One good thing about Scrupilo, he really admired clever surprises.
"Well, in that case, I'm pleased to be your personal radio pulse sensor."

Ravna grinned back and put through a call to her starship.

Oobii replied, "Except for known radios, no device echoes detected."

Scrupilo stuck out his snouts from both sides of the basket and took a naked
eye look at the passing scene. "I say we radio pulse every so often. No way this

Tropical would guess your clever trick, Highness. Sooner or later he'll move where *Oobii* can detect him."

Ravna set up a surveillance plan with *Oobii*, got some more winds-aloft advice, and also forwarded Scrupilo's observations through *Oobii* to Woodcarver. They continued southwards, climbing another hundred meters. They were almost even with the long row of telephone poles that marched off to the south along the Queen's Road.

The *Eyes Above* wasn't making good time anymore, but it was well ahead of Woodcarver's search parties. Just a few hundred meters to her left, paralleling the telephone poles, were the "town houses" of older Children and wealthy packs. They might be her most visible achievement of the last ten years. Ravna didn't know whether to laugh or cry about that. The half-timbered houses were large, each big enough for a married couple, a young child or children on the way, and one or two pack friends. *Oobii* was able to keep the buildings warm by shining a very low-power beam gun on the hot water towers that stood next to each house. So the town houses were comfortably warm all year round, with hot and cold running water and indoor plumbing. A large part of *Oobii*'s tech rent had gone into paying for the Children's town houses. The second-generation kids thought they were heavenly. Their parents regarded the houses as a small step up from purgatory.

"Ha. I felt another pulse," said Scrupilo. Ravna called the ship. Still no joy.

"We're almost to Cliffside harbor, Scrupilo. I think that's beyond where the thief could have come." In any case, the straits between Hidden Island and the mainland was far busier than the polluted water at North End. There seemed little hope of spotting a suspicious boat here.

". . . Yes. I suppose we should turn around and"—Scrupilo had raised his telescopes, pointing them at the highlands ahead.—"but not just yet! The Tropicals may have outsmarted themselves. Something strange is going on near their madhouse. Can you fly there, quietly?"

The embassy compound was just south of the town houses, a fenced-in collection of ramshackle sheds perched on the edge of the Margrum Valley. "I'll check." She gave *Oobii* a quick call, then turned back to Scrupilo. "In that direction, we have a southbound breeze all the way to the ground." She ran the propeller for another thirty seconds, long enough to put them on a path that would take them past the compound. They were just a few dozen meters above the heather now. She cut the motor, and they coasting along with the breeze, surrounded by eerie silence. "How's that?"

None of Scrupilo looked up from his intent surveillance. "Excellent. The bastards are up to something. They're in a crowd off to the northwest of the compound."

"What, they're playing with their snow sleighs again?" There'd been heavy snowfall last winter, and the Tropicals had become enamored of large sleighs. Typical of the mob's long-term planning, they had begged and worked to buy a number of sleighs—getting possession just in time for the spring mud.

"No!" said Scrupilo. "These fellows are by the fence, near the telephone trunk line. I wonder how close we can get before they see us."

Ravna glanced behind her. The northering sun was peeking under the curve of the balloon. "We're coming at them from out of the sun." Ahead, she couldn't actually see their shadow on the ground, but there was a bright spot, a glory shine, in the heather beyond the compound, marking just where their shadow must be. The roundish light had almost reached the edge of the valley. She vented a little hydrogen. As the *Eyes Above* sank, the bright spot moved into the compound.

"Brilliant, Milady! Can you keep us in the sun all the way down?"

"I think so." When the spot of backscatter brightness drifted beyond the compound, Ravna vented a little more hydrogen. Goodness, this was like having a guide program! She felt a small thrill at finding something so convenient built into the raw nature of the world.

They were about 500 meters from the compound, and losing attitude. Ravna had to push up from her seat to see over the basket's bow. The *Eyes Above*'s shadow was clearly visible now, surrounded by just a halo of back-shine. She vented a bit more gas, brought the shadow to just beyond the Tropicals.

There were a bunch of them down there, standing at the edge of the Queen's Road, right where it passed closest to the embassy. This crowd plus the ones at the lab would add up to most of the embassy's total population, though the count was always vague. A number of Tropicals returned south when their wrecks finally slid back to sea. Others had probably been involved in Fragmentarium breakouts over the years.

Ravna could see their ragged jackets and leggings, the body paint on their exposed heads and tympana. There were probably twenty packs' worth, all tangled together. Yup, an orgy in the making.

Now less than two hundred meters away, none of them looked up to see the *Eyes Above*. Ravna vented a little more hydrogen, keeping their shadow just out of the packs' eyes.

Scrupilo had no need for his telescopes now. Five of him had heads stuck over the rim of the basket, staring down. He wriggled his White Head member back to Ravna. "*Sst*," whispered White Head. "I can *hear* them!"

A few seconds passed—and now Ravna could hear them too. The sounds were clear in the wider silence, growing louder as the *Eyes Above* swept closer, the gobble and hiss of Tinish excitement. The chords were otherwise nonsense to her, but then she could understand very little of the local language, even when the packs were trying their best to be clear.

Scrupilo was not so limited. His White Head reached its nose close to Ravna's face, where its fore-tympanum could whisper even more quietly. "You hear what they're saying? The get of bitches already know about the theft! That's solid proof they're behind it. No way any of their party could be back from the lab this fast!"

Now the *Eyes Above* was coasting over them. There was no more point in careful navigation. Ravna left her pilot's chair and leaned over the edge of the basket. They would pass dead even with the compound's twisted tower. Directly below, not more than forty meters away, was the mob of Tropicals. These guys did look excited. Then there was a gap in the crowd and she saw the telephone resting on the ground. A thin wire hung down from the nearest telephone pole.

"Oh," said Scrupilo. Well, that explained their excitement, and why they were standing here by the road. Memo: never give half a solution to these critters.

Just then, someone finally noticed the *Eyes Above.* Heads turned up all across the crowd, and the Tines started running around, making a racket that seemed impossibly loud coming from dog-sized bodies.

Scrupilo blasted back, and Ravna just hunched down and stuck her fingers in her ears. The battle of the noisemakers continued for several seconds, getting louder on both sides. Were the Tropicals running along beneath them? She was afraid to look and get a direct face full of that tormenting sound.

The *Eyes Above* slid out over the Margrum Valley. Behind them, Ravna could see the Tropicals ranged along the edge of the drop, still hopping up and down in apparent outrage. It was like human fist-shaking.

Scrupilo huffed indignantly: "Mindless prattlers! All they can talk about is how we've abused their ambassador, and how they have every right to splice into our phone lines. . . . Deceit! Deceit! Deceit!" This last, he chanted in time to the chords he was directing toward the enemy.

Ravna dropped some ballast and kicked on the propeller, bringing the *Eyes Above* into a long climbing turn that headed back north over the inner channel. By the Powers, it was amazing the range at which Scrupilo and the Tropicals could keep up their long-distance shouting match.

CHAPTER 08

Days passed. The affair of the stolen radio cloaks was not resolved. The search of the ambassador's party at Scrupilo's lab turned up nothing. Eventually, the lab and North End and all the accessible anchorages in the near islands and mainside were searched—without success. Ravna marvelled at the elegant way Godsgift managed Tropical indignation. The fellow hadn't always been so smart. During the last eight years, the thing they called Ambassador had mixed and matched itself. Now he had almost-credible excuses for why his people spliced into the land line: they had expected a phone call from the ambassador to a nearby Domain house. When that homeowner brought no message to the embassy compound, the Tropicals became afraid for their ambassador's safety and so undertook the splice (rather expertly done, on their very first try) and began raising hell up and down the phone line. Normally, *Oobii*'s routing advice made the system quite usable—but that depended on users honoring that advice.

At the same time he was complaining and excusing himself, Godsgift refused to allow any search of the embassy compound. Woodcarver responded with a siege. This lasted about a tenday—and ended when Godsgift accepted a year of free telephone access in return for his granting permission to search the building.

Of course, nothing was found in the Embassy search.

The oscillation between sneaky and clownish was both effective and suspicious. Scrupilo and Nevil lobbied for booting the Tropicals out of the Domain, strategic materials be damned. Johanna thought the Tropicals had never been mentally together enough for serious theft. Woodcarver figured they were being used by Flenser (natch!) or maybe by the long-missing Vendacious. Flenser denied everything.

Meantime Ravna concentrated on *her* main problem. She was doing her best to remove the dissatisfactions that gave support to the Disaster Study Group. She had to make changes, reforms. Unfortunately, even the simplest of the projects could have hidden gotchas. Take the idea of giving the Children more access to *Oobii*. Ultimately, that might slow the research program slightly, but that was a price she'd have to pay. Ravna had no trouble clearing the ship's main cargo deck. It opened directly at ground level now, and what gear remained could be safely stored in the New Castle. It was even less of a problem—a simple request to the ship's automation—to turn the inner walls into displays. Now the vaulting space of the cargo hold was a warm meeting hall. The Children were eager to decorate the space.

Soon, the inside of the cargo bay was a crude imitation of various places they remembered from before their world fell apart. There was actually an elected committee (democracy rearing its head) for deciding the ambiance of the tenday. The kids and their Best Friend packs showed up in crowds. Since they were effectively inside the starship, *Oobii* could manipulate the acoustics so packs could sit within a couple of meters without interfering with one another's mindsounds. That was something magical and new for most packs, and it brought the place even greater popularity.

So the New Meeting Place was an overwhelming success, with unintended side effects that were themselves a benefit. Right? Not quite. There was a serious gotcha. It first showed up as Ravna was clearing out the cargo hold. When the carts carrying the gear from the hold (much of it Beyonder arcana that might someday be very useful) arrived at the New Castle, Woodcarver's guards had blocked the cargo for nearly half a day. Woodcarver was Downcoast, Ravna was told, without radio relay—and she hadn't left clear word about where the cargo should be stored, or if it should be accepted at all! *What admin idiocy!* Ravna had thought. This was the sort of thing that Scrupilo occasionally pulled, but Woodcarver's castle chamberlains were normally more sensible. Besides, she had checked out the undercastle space around the Children's Lander; there was plenty of room.

Woodcarver had legal say at the castle, just as Ravna was the boss aboard the *Oobii*. It was part of their co-Queendom arrangement, but Ravna had never before been denied use of the catacombs. And Woodcarver had known of Ravna's plans for the cargo hold.

In the end, Ravna got the gear stowed away, but in the days that followed—and for the first time in the ten years that the two had worked together—she felt a distance and a frostiness between herself and Woodcarver.

Ravna asked Pilgrim about the problem. As both the Queen's consort and a parent of some of her recent members, he should have some insight!

"Woodcarver was too shy to say anything about it, Ravna."

"Huh?" Ravna replied, remembering Woodcarver's directness in the past. "Why would Woodcarver be shy about complaining to me?"

"Um, I think because she knows she's wrong to be pissed at you."

"Y-you two have discussed this?"

"Yup. Basically, she thinks this new meeting place upsets the balance of reputations between the two of you." He tapped a couple of noses together and looked a little embarrassed. "I know, that's—well, childish is the word a human might use. I would have warned you, except I was sure that Woodcarver recognized her foolishness in the matter. She's not usually like this, but she doesn't have that new puppy entirely in step with the rest of her." He brightened. "I'll talk to her. The three of us could get together and—"

"No. I'll talk to her myself. I should have taken more time explaining the idea to her in the beginning. The New Meeting Place doesn't replace the Thrones Room. It's just a informal place where everyone can get closer to the world we're trying to build."

So Ravna made an appointment with her co-Queen, in the Thrones Room atop Starship Hill. Even that was a change. Up till now, she'd felt welcome to drop in almost without notice.

She talked to Woodcarver for some time, pointing out what a smash hit the New Meeting Place had become, how it was bringing both the Children and their packs to understanding and eager participation in what Ravna and Woodcarver were trying to accomplish.

"It's working better than I ever dreamed, Woodcarver. There are packs unrelated to the Children—some of them traditionalists from Woodcarver City—who've come to the New Meeting Place. Ultimately, it could be a kind of diplomatic center."

Most of Woodcarver was curled up around her radio. She nodded courteously at Ravna's enthusiastic description. "Rather like a capitol, then?"

"Yes—I mean, *no*, not a center of power. Woodcarver, packs and Children have always had data access at the ship." Ravna managed a weak laugh. "That's why so many Tines are great experts on everything human and Beyonder! The New Meeting Place just makes that access easier."

Woodcarver's heads gave a gentle shake. "But your starship *is* the center of power, no matter what you or I might say. When I look out from New Castle's parapets, I see the telephone mainlines all leading to your starship."

"But we're using *Oobii* for switching and access logic."

Woodcarver's voice rolled on: "And, invisibly, your starship manages radio access and relay—without it, our little radios would be a short-range muddle."

"That's only until we get past torsion antennas." Actually, Ravna was hoping Tines World would not have to detour through the era of analog frequency management. Central management should work fine until the Tines had digital signal processing.

"And we Tines have developed almost none of the energy schemes we see described in your archives. Your ship's beam gun warms our water and our homes."

Ravna raised her hands. "Without *Oobii*'s shortcuts it would be decades before we had anything like these services."

Woodcarver said, "I know that. But nowadays, when I look out and see *Oobii* with its beam gun so artfully positioned to cover the heartland of the Domain . . ."

Ravna sat in shocked silence. After the Battle on Starship Hill, Woodcarver had chosen Flenser's Old Castle as her seat of office, and Ravna had moved *Oobii* down to Hidden Island. In that first year, the queen had come to realize that however hastily it was built, the New Castle up on Starship Hill was the proper center for a great empire. She had moved herself up here, and asked Ravna to follow, putting *Oobii* back on the hill, guardian of all Woodcarver could see. Moving *Oobii* had not been easy; Ravna could not imagine that the ship would ever fly again. And now . . . ?

Woodcarver exchanged looks with herself. Conflicted? "I'm sorry. I know, I asked for *Oobii*'s help. I know you have removed the beam gun's amplifier stage. I would never regard your stewardship of *Oobii* as a threat. It's just that lately I'm seeing the risks with new insight.

"Our dependence on your ship for all things makes it a single point of failure—I think that's your technical term for it—which of course I learned from texts in *Oobii*'s archive. Isn't it unwise to bet everything on the proper operation of a single part?"

For Ravna, the answer to that question had always been obvious. Ravna had a deadline. It might be less than a century away. She bowed her head. "I understand. But haven't we discussed all this before? I thought we were agreed. We're using *Oobii* to support Scrupilo's research and move us as fast as possible."

Woodcarver sighed. "Yes. In any case, we are too far down this path to change."

Thank the Powers! Ravna suddenly realized that a disaster had been avoided. This was so much worse than what Pilgrim had said. "W-Woodcarver, if on balance you regard *Oobii*'s meeting place as a negative thing, just tell me clearly, and I'll take it down."

"No, I accept your reasoning, Ravna. I'm content with your new meeting place."

"*Our* New Meeting Place, Woodcarver. Thank you." Ravna cast around for some different topic of conversation. "S-so how are the border inspections going?" Since the cloaks' disappearance, Woodcarver had attempted to enforce something like nation-state control on the various mountain passes leading over the Icefangs.

Woodcarver bobbed her heads in a smile. "All in place, and rather faster than I had thought possible." She shrugged. "No matter. In this case, the real threat is not foreigners. I'm confident the cloaks never left the Domain."

"Oh, right. Flenser."

"You mean the *reformed* Flenser," Woodcarver said archly. "Reformed or not, I know Flenser has always coveted the radio cloaks. They feed his messianic urges."

"You could kick him off the Council."

"I've thought of taking action against him. I don't think you realize how clever he is. For a fact, I think he's as clever as before his four were assassinated. Tyrathect, 'the humble school teacher,' was well chosen. And he still has plenty of political connections on Hidden Island and to the north. He's too subtle to catch, and too powerful to ease aside."

"But there's no evidence he had anything to do with the theft."

"There is a certain amount of indirect evidence. Pilgrim has noticed. Scrupilo would have noticed, if he weren't so focused on the Tropicals. . . . Not many thieves could have escaped your pursuit, Ravna. You showed again the remarkable usefulness of *Oobii*."

"Oh?"

"I got the details from Scrupilo, more than he said to the Council. You used all sorts of tricks that the Tropicals could never have guessed. No one who wasn't deeply involved with *Oobii* technology could have slipped past your search. Scrupilo might have managed it. Maybe I could have—after a lot of research. And then there's Flenser, who over the years has wangled who knows what out of *Oobii*—and who I still suspect stole Oliphaunt."

Ravna opened her mouth to protest, then decided that she had already challenged Woodcarver's paranoia too much today. In fact, whoever had stolen the Oliphaunt dataset had an oracle that in some ways was as significant as *Oobii*. Possession would make almost any sneaky plan feasible. And Woodcarver had absolute faith in her smartest offspring's continuing villainy. *I should be grateful*, thought Ravna. *Better that Woodcarver obsess about Flenser than about the New Meeting Place.*

When Ravna came back down the hill from the New Castle, it was an hour or two before midnight. The heather was in twilight. An occasional star was visible in the southern sky; there was the orbiting hulk of the freight device that had carried the Children's Lander here.

The darkness and the clear sky together brought a deep chill that mostly hid during the summer. By the time Ravna reached *Oobii*, the breeze had picked up, driving like icy needles through her locally made sweater. The Children called such clothing "unspeakably dumb"; in any case, the fabric had no ability to average temperatures.

The lights from *Oobii*'s cargo bay—the New Meeting Place—splashed warm and welcoming out upon the hillside. Ravna stood in the outer fringes of the light and looked in. Even now, there were packs and Children within. They were probably just playing games, but even so, the sight comforted her. Woodcarver would eventually love this place.

But just now Ravna didn't want to talk to anyone. She passed the light, continued on around the ship. Since the theft of the cloaks, local security had been a big topic at council meetings. Nevil, with Scrupilo in loud support, and Johanna soberly nodding, thought that any number of other terrible things might happen now, including smash-and-grab attacks. That sounded foolish to Ravna, but in fact, they didn't know who they were up against. Maybe the added surveillance cams would help. Maybe they needed more guards. *We'll get all the evils of a nation state before we get the tech we need.*

In any case, nothing could go wrong so close to her ship's watchful eyes. She stepped near the hull, and *Oobii* quietly opened a hatch for her. She walked inside and let the ship take her up to her rooms by the bridge. She changed out of the heavy sweater and pants, into her shipboard clothes. Just doing that reminded her again of her special perks. Very soon she must move out of these digs. That had become a personal imperative, even though she hadn't yet spoken of it to anyone. Living outside of *Oobii* would slow her work, but now she realized that staying aboard might be even more destructive.

Meantime, tonight, she had more than enough work to do, and it required all the tech that her starship bridge could provide:

What was Flenser-Tyrathect up to? Woodcarver had such strong suspicions about the pack. In fact, Ravna knew that some minor part of those suspicions was correct. The wily (reformed) monster had indeed figured out that Woodcarver had bugged his sanctums. But the reason Ravna knew that was also the reason she knew Flenser wasn't behind the current mysteries.

She hunkered down in her favorite-style chair and called up *Oobii*'s surveillance suite—the High Beyond system that she had kept hidden from everyone.

The *Out of Band II* had been designed for operations at the Bottom of the Beyond and even in the Slow Zone (where they were now marooned). But the ship had been *built* in the Middle Beyond, where technology tapdanced at the edge of intelligibility. Almost none of the ship's highest functions worked Down Here. Certainly, no ship could fly faster than light Down Here. And the antigravity was slowly dying. The natural-language translators were laughably incompetent. Even where local physics allowed a phenomenon, the ship's software was often incapable of exploiting it. That was why a lot of *Oobii*'s design involved Very Dumb Solutions to classic problems.

Nevertheless, there were surprises. In the days after Pham died, after the Battle on Starship Hill, Ravna had taken inventory of what remained. Here and there amidst the wreckage, she found advanced devices that more or less still functioned. With one exception, she'd revealed these to Johanna and then to Woodcarver, and—after it was founded—to the Executive Council. Ravna had kept her mouth shut about the surveillance suite; she and the Children were trapped on a world of medieval strangers. The only other galactic on the planet was the Skroderider Greenstalk, and she was too soon gone. *Oh, Greenstalk, how I miss you.* The thought still popped up, for Greenstalk had been with her through all the most desperate times in space.

So at the beginning Ravna had kept some secrets. It was now years too late to reveal this one. In the Beyond, "cameras" were more than what early tech civilizations imagined. Cameras could be a coat of paint, or critters that looked like insects, or even a bacterial infection. Delivery of the information to the observer could be even stranger, a diffuse cloud of perturbations—acoustic, visual, thermal—that took enormous processing to reconstruct.

One such hardware system had survived Countermeasure's surge. Even more miraculous, *Oobii* could still reconstruct the output. Early on, Ravna had to decide just who to target with that special surveillance. It had not been a difficult choice. The Old Flenser had created a strange culture that was both cruel and fiendishly inventive. Flenser had seemed every bit as dangerous as Woodcarver claimed.

And so one day during the early years, Ravna had infected Flenser-Tyrathect's members with the surveillance system. The infestation was physically harmless, and the devices could not replicate, but there were more than enough devices to cover the pack, hopefully for as long as she needed them.

Over the years, Ravna had often wished—but never with the desperate frustration of one who has made a profound mistake—that she could infect somebody else with the surveillance system. But the "reformed" Flenser *had* been the greatest unknown, potentially the greatest threat, and Ravna's camera had revealed to her that whatever strange thing Flenser-Tyrathect might be, it was *not* working against Woodcarver or Ravna or their plans for the Domain. That certainty had more than once brought Ravna to the verge of revealing her methods to Woodcarver. Now, after the misunderstanding about the New Meeting Place, Ravna wondered if she could ever dare tell her.

Woodcarver's latest suspicions about Flenser and the radio cloaks made perfect sense—if one didn't know about Ravna's special surveillance. The ship was constantly monitoring the Flenser data, keeping a record of the reconstructed images and watching for specified alarm conditions. Ravna had reviewed that record very carefully in the days immediately after the theft of the radio cloaks, and the reformed Flenser had seemed just as darkly innocent as ever. What more could she do?

I wonder what the pack is up to right now, tonight? A frivolous thought perhaps, since "real time" views from the system were a strange and scattered thing. Nevertheless, Ravna made the request. Several seconds passed. Range was the great weakness of this system. Beyond the local area, reception became extremely ambiguous. Fortunately, Flenser had been out of the area only a few times in ten years—a very *good* consequence of Woodcarver's strict hold on the fellow. The reports from the infestation were forwarded in unsynchronized driblets across the nearly random locations of devices that previously had been shed from the pack's members. Sufficient data to build one picture might take a thousand seconds—and then less than one second for the next image.

Sometimes important adjustments would show up later and *Oobii* would revise the image stream in really strange ways.

Tonight, reception was poor, but as *Oobii*'s signal-processing software struggled with clues, the pictures gradually became clearer, more colorful, brighter. There were a few moments of motion and then the stream froze again. Ravna fiddled with the parameters.

Flenser was somewhere in the sub-basements of the Old Castle. He went there two or three times a year. Several years ago, Ravna had concluded that Flenser did indeed know where Woodcarver's spy cameras were located. That was a scary conclusion, but then she realized that most of these trips "downstairs" were just part of Flenser's hobby of enraging his pack parent.

There were exceptions; Flenser had some things he really didn't want Woodcarver to know about. For instance, Woodcarver had forbidden Flenser to try to rehabilitate *his* creation, Steel. In that, Woodcarver had reneged on her peace treaty with Flenser. It was the only such incident Ravna knew of. The remains of Lord Steel were allowed to live, but as a slobbering, slashing threesome. The madpack had been kept in isolation, at the veterans' fragmentarium.

For a time, it had looked like Flenser might restart the war over Woodcarver's broken promise. Instead, he used the issue to win a number of concessions—including repossession of the Old Castle. But Ravna knew that the wily Flenser had not given up on Steel. In the early years, Flenser had often come down to these sub-basements to meet with Carenfret, a broodkenner at the Fragmentarium. That pack was unquestionably loyal to Woodcarver, and probably opposed to every one of the Old Flenser's horrific experiments. Flenser and Carenfret had been conspiring all right, but only to persuade Woodcarver to make Steel whole. Maybe they would have succeeded eventually. Unfortunately, Steel's problem was a torment from within; the poor wretch had fought itself to death, rendering the conspirators' plans moot.

Ravna was certain that Woodcarver would not see things so forgivingly. Meeting down in the Old Castle catacombs was itself the stuff of treason. The chambers were steeped in horror. Woodcarver had once attempted an inventory of the place. Her packs had found at least five levels, with many fallen tunnels still unsurveyed.

In recent years, the catacombs had become much too intriguing to the Children. When they got to be ten or eleven years old, they just had to take a crack at exploring "Flenser's Caves of Death." If you counted natural erosion and rock falls, there were plenty of entrances, a new one discovered every few years. Sooner or later, some kid was going to fall down a hole and get killed. That and the onshore cliffs had been Ravna's biggest day-to-day worries, until this Denier cult thing.

In tonight's expedition, most of Flenser was carrying solar cell lamps. The light was scarcely brighter than tar torches, but it didn't consume oxygen or make smoke. Ravna recognized the low-ceilinged cavern Flenser was passing through. Some kids had gotten lost here just last year. It was—she hoped—the most grisly place they would ever see. She remembered how it stank, even after all the years. The dark floor was punctuated with stone plugs that looked like small manhole covers. In the view *Oobii* synthesized from Flenser's various heads, she could see the hexagonal pattern of dozens—hundreds—of covers stretching off into the darkness.

The picture stream froze. *Oobii* was waiting for signal or—more likely—had fallen behind in its analysis. Ravna didn't rush it. She wanted the high-resolution video, and if it took a while for the clues to dribble in and be interpreted, that was fine. In fact, this sequence seemed usable. Sometimes, no matter how long she waited, all she could get was ambiguity.

So she stared idly at the still picture. There was a missing "manhole cover" just to the right of one picture. *That* was what had scared her when the kids went exploring. In the dark, you could fall into one of those open holes and break your neck. She idly merged the views from several of Flenser's members. The synthesis gave her a view into the hole. The bottom was lost in shadow, but she knew each hole was about two meters deep, ending in a sewage sump. If *Oobii* was not interpolating from past experience, this particular hole was not empty.

She could see bones and desiccated flesh. *Yech.* No doubt about it, Old Flenser had been a monster. These holes were a combination of dungeon and rack. Flenser—and later Steel—would split a prisoner into its component members, sticking each of them into a separate hole. There, they could be fed and watered, physically tortured or simply left to go mad in the mindless closeness. Flenser called the process "recycling," since once the individual members went mad or catatonic, they could be reassembled into "custom-designed" packs, the parts mixed and matched with those of other prisoners. A few of the recycled packs still wandered about the Domain. Most were sad, lobotomized freaks; a few were twitchy psychopaths. Recycling was Flenser's grisliest, *stupidest* achievement.

Finally, the video stream came unstuck, and the various viewpoints moved past the ghastly hole. A tiny window by Ravna's hand showed a diagram of how the various members were positioned and which field of view was being shown in the main display. As usual, Flenser's crippled member was rolling along near the front. Its white-tipped ears showed at one point or another in most of the other views. White-Tips was the limiting factor in the Flenser-Tyrathect's mobility. The critter had a crushed pelvis. It lay, swaddled in blankets, in a wheelbarrow-like contraption that the others pushed or pulled.

In recent years, White Tips' eyesight had fogged over. The creature was getting old, and cataract cures were decades in the future. So the White Tips' view showed what was ahead first, but even more hazily than most of *Oobii*'s reconstructions. Still, there was *something* in the way of the pack. Ravna switched back to a synthesis from all the members. There was another pack, just at the edge of the lamplight. It was Amdi!

Where was Jefri? Ravna looked carefully in all the windows. Nothing more could be seen in the shadows. She rolled back a few seconds, and did some

pattern analysis. . . . No, there was no sign of Jef. She stifled the impulse to
raise the humaniform probability and reanalyze.

Amdi hunkered down as the lamplight spread across him. White Tips'
wheelbarrow was rolled forward amazingly close, and the rest of Flenser-
Tyrathect spread out, forming a semi-circle around Amdiranifani.

The video stream froze again; a diagnostic window showed that this delay
was related to Flenser's hearing. Till now, the sounds coming across the link
hadn't received much analysis. Ravna had heard the click of Flenser's nails on
the stone, the creak of the wheelbarrow, but Flenser's mindsounds—ultrasonics
from 40 up to 250kHz—were mostly ignored. Patterns that indicated startlement or anger would be reported, but constructing a detailed thought stream
would have been impossible for the *Oobii* even in the Beyond.

Now *Oobii* heard the chords and gobble-hiss of Interpack speech.

After a moment more, video and synchronized sound continued, with
Oobii's best guess at translation appearing below the main window.

Flenser-Tyrathect:
    You have my [time | curiosity],
    [little one | little ones].
    Why did you want this meeting?

Amdiranifani:
    I [?] very sad. I [?] [?] scared.
    What [?] me [?] [?]

Ravna replayed the audio a couple of times. By combining *Oobii*'s guesses
with her own knowledge, she could often make sense of Tinish. Amdi's last
statement was pretty clearly: "What will become of me?"

But now Amdi switched to Samnorsk: "Could we please speak in human,
Mr. Tyrathect? It's the language I like best. My problems are hard to say right
in Tinish."

"Of course, my dear boy. Samnorsk will be fine." Flenser's human voice
had its usual cordial tone, the manner of a clever sadist.

Surely Amdi recognized the mockery in Flenser's tone? After all, the eightsome had known Flenser-Tyrathect since the final days of the Flenserist regime.
But now the eight huddled together and edged forward a few centimeters, almost
crawling on their bellies. "I'm so afraid. There are so many things to be sad about.
Maybe if there weren't so many, I could cope and not just be a silly self-pitier."

Flenser-Tyrathect's chuckle was gentle. "Ah. Poor Amdiranifani. You are
enjoying the gift of genius. When ordinary people are confronted with multiple
tragedies, the pain scarcely increases. They simply can't feel the extra burdens. But you have a greater capacity for suffering. Even so—"

The diagnostic window showed serious relay problems. Some of the forwarding devices were probably riding with the evening glowbugs up on the

surface; maybe those insects were thinning as the night air cooled. Several seconds passed. *Oobii*'s guesses were not converging. Finally a little red flag appeared, indicating that clarity was unattainable with the data being received. *Sigh.* Ravna raised the level of acceptable uncertainty, and waved for the programs to proceed. Sometimes this surveillance reminded her too much of pre-tech fairy tales: She was a sorceress hunched over her crystal ball, doing her best to scry truth from uncertain auguries.

After a moment, *Oobii* generated its best guess: The displays jigged back a second or two and restarted. Flenser was saying: "Even so, my boy. What problems are troubling you?"

Amdi moved a little closer. "You made Steel and Steel made me."

Gentle laughter. "Of course. I made Steel, and mainly from my own members. But Steel assembled you from the new-born puppies of geniuses that he purchased, stole, and murdered for—from all across the continent. You are among the rarest of packs, born all at once, all of puppies. Like a two-legs."

"Yes, like a human." *Oobii*'s imagery showed tears in Amdi's eyes. "And now dying like a human, even though humans don't begin to get old while they're still children."

"Ah," said Flenser. Ravna noticed that the one with the white tipped ears had tilted its wheelbarrow forward and extended its neck toward Amdi. *Wow.* The overlapping mindsounds should be loud enough to be emotionally confusing to both packs. But Flenser's voice—*as represented by the surveillance program, always keep that in mind*—was as cool as ever: "Haven't we discussed this before? Unanimous ageing is a tragedy, but your members are still only fourteen years old. Your bad times are easily twenty years in the future, when my grand schemes will finally—"

Amdi's interruption didn't quite fit: "I loved Mr. Steel. Of course, I didn't know he was a monster."

Flenser shrugged. "That's how I made him. My mistake, I'm afraid."

"I know. But you made up for that!" Amdi hesitated, his voice coming more quietly. "And now there's Jefri's problem. You. . . ."

Ravna's head came up. *What about Jefri?* But Amdi didn't finish the sentence.

After a moment, Flenser said, "Yes, I'm doing what I can about that. Now what *new* problem has ambushed you?"

Amdi was making human crying sounds, the sounds of a small lost child. "I've learned that two of me are Great Plains short-timers."

Ravna had to think for a second. Great Plains short-timers? That was a racial group. They didn't look different from most other Tines, though they tended to congenital heart disease. Short-timers rarely lived more than twenty years.

In the other windows, Ravna could see Flenser's heads bobbing. "Those two of you have chest pains?"

"Yes. And eyesight problems."

"Oh my," said Flenser. "Short-timers. That *is* a problem. I'll check—" The audio faltered, perhaps *Oobii* grappling with some exceptionally great ambiguity. "I'll check Steel's records, but I fear you may be right. It's a well-known tradeoff among broodkenners: the Great Plains short-timers often have excellent geometrical imaginations. Still and all, it's not unanimous ageing."

Amdiranifani was shivering. "When those two of me die—I won't be me anymore."

"Every pack faces that, my boy. Unless we get killed all at once, change is what life is all about."

"For *you*, maybe! For ordinary packs. But I came into the world all at once, with nothing before. Mr. Steel struck a balance when he brought me together. If I lose two, if I lose even *one*, I'll—"

"Woodcarver's broodkenners can find some kind of match. Or you may find that six is as large as your mind can comfortably be." Flenser's tone was overtly sympathetic, but—quite consistent with his usual manner—somehow dismissive at the same time.

"No, please! If I lose any one of my eight, I will fall apart like an arch without a keystone. I beg you, Mr. Tyrathect. You made Mr. Steel. You made the Disaster Study Group. You made Jefri betray everyone. In all that monstering, can't there be some good miracles?"

Ravna watched, numb, making no move to pause the stream or look at the log window. Now that the scene had surpassed all bounds of credibility, it played on with scarcely a hiccup. Amdi wasn't talking anymore; there was just the sound of human weeping. That sort of made sense. The eightsome had crumpled into a posture of abject despair. The Reformed Flenser wasn't saying anything either, but what *Oobii* was showing in the displays was incredible: All five of Flenser-Tyrathect edged closer to Amdi. The two that had been the original Flenser pushed White Tips and its wheelbarrow forward. Some of them were less than a meter from Amdi's nearest members. That was almost as unbelievable as anything else. Flenser-Tyrathect was notorious for his fastidious, standoffish behavior. Normal packs, friendly ones, would often send one or two of their number into the space between for a brief exchange of mindsounds. It was like a human social embrace or a light kiss. Flenser-Tyrathect was *never* so familiar. He was always the pack at the far end of the table, or hunched behind the thickest acoustic quilts.

In this increasingly fantastic video, White Tips had reached forward to cuddle two of Amdi against its neck. Several of the other were almost as close. To a naive human it might look like one crowd of animals giving comfort to another. Between Tinish packs it would be profound intimacy.

And any resemblance to what is really happening is purely coincidental! Ravna angrily flicked all the views into nothingness.

Ravna sat for a long time, staring into the gentle warm darkness of her study. She had pushed the analysis much too far. *Oobii*'s attempt to make sense out of nearly pure noise was madness. And yet . . . the proper nouns could scarcely have been introduced by the software without some reason. She knew she was damned to return and return to this scene, to try to tease apart software glitches from signal noise from underlying revelation. Maybe she could get something out of it by starting with external truths—for instance, the fact that Jefri was no traitor.

She went back over the data, only now she wasn't looking at the lying video. Instead she went down to the surveillance program's logs. As she suspected, the transmission conditions tonight had been poor to rotten. And yet, it had been almost this bad before and she had still received sensible results. She waved the network logs away and moved up to the program's analysis. These were probability trees showing the options considered and how those options related to one another. The crisp video Ravna had been watching was simply the most probable interpretation coming out of that jungle of second-guessing. For instance, Amdi had almost certainly asserted that some particular person was behind the Disaster Study Group. She found that node of the analysis, expanded it; reasons and probabilities appeared. Yeah, and Flenser had been named as that person simply because of context and something about Amdi's posture. Similarly, Amdi had probably said that "someone" had betrayed "something"—but the software had generated the particular nouns from a long list of suspects.

It was amazing that Jefri had even made it onto that list, much less coming out at the top. So what logic had put him there? She drilled down through the program's reasoning, into depths she had never visited. As suspected, the "why I chose 'this' over 'that'" led to a combinatorial explosion. She could spend centuries studying this—and get nowhere.

Ravna leaned back in her chair, turning her head this way and that, trying to get the stress out her neck. *What am I missing?* Of course, the program could simply be broken. *Oobii*'s emergency automation was specially designed to run in the Slow Zone, but the surveillance program was a bit of purely Beyonder software, not on the ship's Usables manifest. It just happened to work Down Here.

Surely, if something serious happened, there would be warnings? Ravna looked idly through the application's error logs. The high-priority messages were just what she expected: "Proceeding with Inadequate Data, blah blah blah." She dipped down into low-priority advisory messages. No surprise. Just for this evening's session, there were literally billions of those. She sorted them a couple of different ways and spent some quality time browsing the results. . . .

Ravna froze in her chair, staring at the monster she found lurking:

```
442741542471.74351920 Advisory Notice Only:
                    Flenser sensor count summary: 140269471
442741542481.74351935 Advisory Notice Only:
                    Flenser sensor count summary: 140269369
442741542491.74354327 Advisory Notice Only:
                    Flenser sensor count summary: 140269373
442741542501.75439121 Advisory Notice Only:
                    Flenser sensor count summary: 140269313
```

442741542511.75439144 Advisory Notice Only:
                        Flenser sensor count summary: 140269265
442741542521.74351947 Advisory Notice Only:
                        Flenser sensor count summary: 140269215
                ...29980242 lines omitted

"Explain!" her voice sound strangled even to her own ears.

A window popped up, defining the relevant fields, pointing to the provenance of these notices, pointing to analysis of the sensor devices on each of Flenser-Tyrathect's members.

The short of it was that these notices said precisely what she thought they said. In all of the Flenser pack, there remained fewer than one hundred and fifty million sensors. The original infestation had numbered in the low trillions and even that had been barely sufficient. If the infestation had fallen to the low hundred millions then . . . then her surveillance was a self-deceiving joke!

How long has this been going on? She waved up a curve fitter and asked for the best three models of the failure history. It gave back three of course, but the first was near certain: from day one of her surveillance, almost ten years ago, her little spies had been steadily failing, a smooth decay with a half-life of less than a year. In the Beyond the sensor infestation would have been good for a century. For that matter, the supporting software would have been smart enough to tell her if she was using junk. *No wonder these gadgets aren't on the Usables Manifest.* Her desperate cleverness had turned around and bitten her on the nose.

Ravna curled up in her chair, miserable. Tonight was just a microcosm of her life over the last few tendays. *But if I review past surveillance, knowing how bogus it really is, maybe I can see how far my trust of Flenser should still extend.* She opened her eyes, wiped away her tears, and looked at the inexorable decay curve glowing in the air before her. It had been years since the surveillance had had even a trillion sensors. During all those years the failure notifications had been piling up, but at invisibly low priority levels. Meantime, the higher layers of the spy program had continued supplying Ravna with—face it—*fantasy*. She might never have noticed, if the real threats had not become so numerous that the fantasy began to spout flagrant lies.

If I decide the past surveillance was bogus too—I'll have to tell Woodcarver about this. Yeah, and destroy whatever trust still remains between us.

For some moments, her attention was lost in bleak contemplation. Had she ever messed up this badly before? No. Had things ever looked darker? . . . Well, watching the Battle on Starship Hill, that had been scarier. Losing Pham a few hours later, that had been sadder. But for despair, there had been nothing worse since the destruction of her home civilization at Sjandra Kei.

I got through that. Pham had been there for her.

Ravna opened her eyes. It was just past midnight. The outside windows looked upon a dark landscape; they were that far into the autumn.

There was something she must do, irrational though it might be. She hadn't done it in more than a year. Neither the Children nor the Tines would understand, and she had no desire to encourage superstition. But if ever there was a time, this was the time to go visit Pham.

CHAPTER 09

Cemeteries were ghastly places. There had been a few such memorials at Sjandra Kei. People in the Beyond died, eventually. The death rate was comparable to the half-lives of the underlying civilizations, which mostly migrated up and up and—if they were not supremely stupid, like the greedy fools of Straumli Realm—eventually transformed themselves into Powers.

Enormous cemeteries existed among sedentary civilizations, where the weight of the past grew larger than any present time. Ravna remembered seeing something similar in the terranes of Harmonious Repose: the cemetery had gradually transformed the terrane into a mausoleum with incidental living tenants.

The cemetery on Starship Hill had been Ravna's idea, come to her when she suddenly realized why cemeteries played such an important part in the stories of the Age of Princesses. She had picked the spot before the town grew up around the New Castle. The two hectare plot stretched across a curving slope of heather, with a view extending from the northwest islands all the way to *Oobii* in the south. In another ten years, the place might be surrounded by Newcastle town. There was no room allotted for cemetery expansion. *And if I have my way,* thought Ravna, *this terrible place will never need to become larger.*

The Children came up here sometimes, but in the warmth of day. The youngest didn't understand about cemeteries. The oldest didn't want to understand, but they didn't want to forget their friends, either.

Ravna mostly came after dark, and when *she* felt the darkest. By that measure, tonight was most definitely the time for a visit. She walked along the main path, her shoes crunching the frost-stiffened moss. Night in the arctic autumn, even here near the channel currents, ranged from cold to deathly frigid. Tonight was relatively mellow. The clouds had come in around sunset, stacking deeper and deeper over the land, trapping the day's warmth. The hillside breeze had dropped to nothing more than a faint, chill breath. *Oobii* said there would be rain a little later, but for now the sky was dark and dry and there was clear air down to the waters of the inner channel. Here and there, she could see lights on the north end of Hidden Island. Very close by, there were occasional glows of lavender. Glowbugs. The tiny insects put on a big show only two or three nights a year, and usually earlier in the autumn than this. As she walked on, there were more of the lavender glints. The occasional glimmer was not enough to light her way . . . but they were welcome.

Rows of graves lay on either side of the cemetery's main path. Each place was marked by a headstone carved with a name and a star. The design was modeled after something she'd found in *Oobii*'s classical human archive. The little four-pointed stars were an early religious symbol, perhaps the most common in human histories, though she was not clear on the details. There were 151 graves in these four rows, almost all the inhabitants of the cemetery. One hundred and fifty-one Children, from less than a year old to sixteen, all murdered on the same summertime night, burned to death as they lay in coldsleep. The heather south of town was called Murder Meadows, but the actual killing field lay beneath the center of the New Castle, the central chamber where the Children's Lander still sat upon charred moss.

Ravna had known none of those Children. They had died before she even knew they existed. Her pace slowed. There could have been more dead Children here; many of the surviving coldsleep coffins had suffered fire damage. Reviving Timor had taught her what she could safely do. Only a few of the original kids still slept in their caskets under the castle, along with the four miscarriages from the new generation, and two accidents; someday she would wake them all. Someday she would fix Timor, too.

Strange as it might seem, there were also a few Tines buried in the cemetery. Originally, that had been just twelve packs who had fully died in the Battle on Starship Hill. In recent years, Johanna's Fragmentarium for Old Members had begun to change that—much to the chagrin of redjacket factions.

There was a thirteenth pack, buried just before Pham's place: six little markers, each with the glyph of its one member, then a bigger one that marked the group: Ja-que-ram-a-phan and then the pack's taken name, Scriber. Scriber was another whom Ravna had never met, but she knew his story from both Pilgrim and Johanna: Scriber, the gallant, foolish inventor who had persuaded Pilgrim to befriend Johanna, the pack that Johanna had reviled, and who had been murdered for his efforts. Ravna knew that Jo had her own midnight trips up here, too.

Just ten years, and so many people to remember. Sjana and Arne Olsndot. Skroderider Blueshell. Amdi was one of the few packs who came up here regularly—always with Jefri, of course.

Ravna had reached the huge glacial boulder that marked the end of the path. Pham's stone made a shoulder in the hill, protecting the children's graves from the north winds. But tonight, the air was almost still. The glowbugs didn't need to hide in the heather. In fact, they were thickest in the air around Pham's grave, so many that their pulsing was in sync. Every few seconds, there was a silent surge of lavender that washed around her like a welcoming tide. She had seen them in such numbers only once before. That had also been around Pham's grave. It must be the flowers that she had planted here, now grown high. Ravna and the Children had put flowers round their classmates' graves, but they had never taken quite so well as here. That was strange, considering Pham's northern exposure.

Ravna turned off the end of the path, walking around to a special spot at the side of the rock. Funny thing about religion. At the Top of the Beyond, religion was the scary, practical matter of creating and dealing with gods. Down here in the Slow Zone, where humankind had been born . . . Down Here, religion was a naturally grown hodgepodge, mostly the slave of local evolutionary biology.

Still, it's amusing how quickly our weakness makes us embrace these old ways.

It was dead dark between the slow pulses of lavender light, but Ravna knew exactly where she stood. She reached out and set her palm on a familiar stretch of smooth granite. It was so *cold* . . . and then after a long moment, her body heat warmed it. Pham Nuwen had been a little like that. Quite possibly, he had never existed but for the year or so that she knew him. Quite possibly, the Power that created Pham had made him as a joke, stocked with bogus memories of an heroic past. Whatever the truth, in the end Pham had made of himself a real hero. Sometimes when she came up here, it was to pray *for* Pham. Not tonight. Tonight was one of the despairing nights. Worse, tonight there was an objective reason for despair. But Pham had overcome worse.

She silently leaned against the rock for a time.

And then she heard footsteps crunching on the main path. She turned away from Pham's stone, suddenly very glad that she hadn't been sobbing. She wiped her face and slipped the hood of her jacket a little forward.

The approaching figure blocked an occasional light from up in New Castle town. She thought for a moment that this was Jefri Olsndot. Then the glowbugs pulsed together, a lavender haze that swept out around her and revealed the other. Not Jefri. Nevil Storherte was not quite Jefri's height, and in all frankness, he was not as pretty-boy handsome.

"Nevil!"

"Ravna? I—I didn't mean to surprise you."

"That's okay." She didn't know whether to be embarrassed or just pleased to see a sympathetic face suddenly pop out of the void. "Whatever are you doing up here?"

Nevil's hands were fumbling nervously with each other. He glanced over her head at the huge boulder. Then the light dimmed and there was just his voice. "I lost my best friends on Murder Meadows. Leda and Josj. I should care about all my classmates, but they were special. . . . I come up sometimes to, you know, to see them."

Sometimes Ravna had to tell herself that the Children weren't all children anymore. Sometimes they told her that themselves.

"I understand, Nevil. When things get bad, I like to come up here, too."

"Things are going badly? I know there's lots to worry about, but your idea with the ship's cargo bay has been a wonder."

Of course, he wouldn't know about Woodcarver's anger, much less about the terrible screw-up with her own special surveillance of Flenser.

Nevil's voice continued, puzzled. "You shouldn't keep to yourself if there are problems, Ravna. That's what we have the Executive Council for."

"I know. But I'm afraid that on this . . ." *I've messed up so badly that certain Council members are the last people I can talk to.* The glowbugs pulsed again and she saw Nevil's intelligent, questioning gaze. Since Johanna and Nevil had been together—which was also since Nevil had been on the Council—she had rarely chatted with the fellow except when the two young people were together. Somewhere deep down she'd been afraid that Johanna might take the interest wrong. Tonight, that thought almost made her laugh. *My problems are so much worse than all I used to worry about.* "There are things that can't really be brought up in the full Council."

She couldn't see his face now. Would he condemn her for plotting out of the Council's sight? But his voice was sympathetic. "I think I understand. It's a very hard job you have. I can wait to hear—"

"That's not what I meant. Do you have a minute, Nevil? I'd like to . . . I'd really like to get some advice."

"Why sure." A diffident laugh. "Though I'm not sure how much my advice is really worth."

Pulse of lights. It was as if they were suddenly standing in a field of lavender flowers, surely the most beautiful glowbug show she'd ever seen, so bright it lit the huge boulder almost to the top. Ravna scrambled up to a perch she had discovered years ago, and waved Nevil to a spot almost as comfortable. He nodded, clambered up in the dying light. The boy—the *man*—was sure-footed. He settled on the rock, half a meter down from her and almost a meter away. Good. Any crying on his shoulder would be safely metaphorical.

They sat silently for a moment. Then Nevil said, "It's about the Disaster Study Group, isn't it?"

"It *started* with the Disaster Study Group. That's where I first realized how totally I was messing up."

"That was my mess-up, and Johanna's. *We* should be your objective pipeline to what our people are—"

"Yeah, yeah, I know Johanna has beaten herself up about that. But the DSG was only the beginning." And then Ravna found herself letting go about the problems that had been weighing her down. It felt so *good*, and after a few minutes she realized this wasn't just because it gave her a chance to say what she had said to no one previously. In fact, Nevil actually had intelligent questions, and insights that came close to being workable advice. He understood instantly why Woodcarver was so upset about the converting the cargo bay into a meeting place.

"The New Meeting Place is the best thing that has happened in years, Ravna. But I can see what you're saying. The effect on Woodcarver is a negative, but that just makes it that much more important—not to retreat on the New Meeting Place—but to make it something that Woodcarver *wants* to buy into."

It was the sort of thing that Ravna had thought, but hearing him say the words was heartwarming. She caught a glimpse of his face as he finished the sentence. Nevil Storherte had always had a kind of brash diffidence, and now she realized what that contradiction amounted to. Nevil Storherte had *charisma*. Even untrained and unplanned, it fairly oozed from him.

"Your mother was the chief administrator at the High Lab, wasn't she?"

"Actually, it was my dad. Mom was the vice chief, or chief of vice when she was feeling mischievous."

Ravna had her low opinion of the Straumers' High Lab. At best it was good intentions gone cosmically wrong. But the Lab had been the pinnacle of the Straumer civilization. It had been mind-boggling hubris, but it had also enlisted the best and the brightest of their entire civilization. Very likely there had been other heroes besides the parents of Johanna and Jefri. "Your Dad must have been a management superstar." A more talented leader than anyone on this poor world.

Nevil gave an embarrassed laugh. "If you go by the selection process, he was. I remember how it dragged on through most of my grade school years, all the hoops my folks had to jump through. But Dad said it didn't matter, that there were so many geniuses at the Lab that 'administration' was more like herding cats. . . . You know? You had cats at Sjandra Kei, didn't you?"

Ravna smiled in the darkness. "Oh, yes. Cats go back a lot farther than Sjandra Kei."

Nevil Storherte might have only childhood recollections to go by, but he'd grown up among real leaders. And obviously, he had the magic touch himself. *And stupid me, all self-pitying, ignoring resources that were here all the time.* She took a deep breath and launched into something more than the shallow confidences of a minute before: "You know, Nevil, the most important thing in the world—maybe in this part of the Galaxy—is our raising a civilization here in time to face the Blighter fleet."

"I agree."

"But the DSG thing has made me realize how much our long-term goal distracted me from what's happening in the here and now. I fear I've screwed up so badly that we may lose the main game before it ever begins."

Silence, but then in a moment of pale light she saw that it was a thoughtful, attentive silence, and she continued: "Nevil, I'm trying to correct my mistakes, but what I've tried so far has had unhappy side-effects."

"Woodcarver's reaction to the New Meeting Place?"

"That's just one."

"Maybe I can help on that. I don't have a private channel to Woodcarver, but Johanna certainly does. And I'll bet my friends can think of changes to the New Meeting Place that will convince Woodcarver that it honors the whole of the Domain."

"Yes! That would be great." *Thank you.* "Let me fly the other changes by you. Most are a lot scarier to me than the New Meeting Place seemed." *Maybe you can show me which is dead wrong and which can somehow be made to work.* One by one she described her ideas for reforms, and for every one Nevil's reaction was like warm sunlight, sometimes agreeing, sometimes not, but always illuminating.

About instituting formal democracy: Nevil was in favor. "Yes, that's something we must do, and fairly soon now that so many of us are adults. But I think it's something that has to grow up naturally, not imposed from above."

"But the only traditions the Children—I mean you all—have experienced are embedded in heavy automation and large marketplaces. How can the idea come from within?"

Nevil chuckled. "Yeah, lots of nonsense can emerge too. But . . . I trust my classmates. They have good hearts. I'll talk this around. Maybe we can use the New Meeting Place to model how things were handled in the most successful of the Slow Zone democracies. And figure out how to do it without offending Woodcarver!"

About Ravna moving out of *Oobii*: Surprisingly, Nevil was almost as uneasy about this suggestion as she was. "We need you aboard *Oobii*, Ravna. Anybody who thinks about the question knows that you're the only person who knows how to use the planning tools there. If we're going to raise civilization before we die of old age, we need you there." He was silent for a moment. "On the other hand, you're right in fearing that this angers people who don't think things through—and it's an irritant for everyone sitting out in the cold. We Children were born into a comfortable civilization. Now that's been lost—except where we see it sitting, gleaming green on Starship Hill. So maybe it makes sense for you to move out for a while. But choose the time, some turning point where it gains the greatest good will. If you stay out, our highest priority will have to be getting you proper communications back with *Oobii*."

"Okay. So we should begin planning for just when to make the move. Can you—"

"Yes. I'll check around, but very quietly. I suggest you don't discuss this with others. I'll bet that it's the sort of thing that once suggested becomes a popular imperative."

And then there was the hardest, scariest item: the priority for medical research. And here, Nevil's reaction was the most surprising and comforting of all. "You mean shift resources from the general technology program, Ravna? In the long run, wouldn't that slow everything, including bioscience?"

Ravna nodded. "Y-yes. Basically, we need to build our own computers for process control and create the networks between them. Then all the rest of technology will take off; prolongevity will be easy. But in the meantime, you kids will age. Pre-technological ageing is just dying, withering, year by year. I can already see it in some of the oldest Children. *I* look younger than some of them. It's a little like the problem of my living the good life in *Oobii*—but it looks much uglier."

"I—" Nevil seemed to be struggling with himself. "Yeah, you're right. I've been doing okay, but then I probably have a naturally healthy body type. I think this is a very serious future problem. The good news is that among the kids I know well—which is most everybody—this is *not* currently a major source of complaint."

"Really? I had been so afraid—" *I've been seeing monsters everywhere since the DSG raised its ugly head.*

"I suggest you continue with your best long-term research plan. But think about having a general meeting soon, where you explain the changes and your development schedule."

"Okay." Ravna nodded. "Right. Right." These were her reforms, but with a big dose of constructive common sense. "We could do it in the New Meeting Place after you get it properly rebuilt."

"Yes. I should have something by early winter. Whenever after that you feel—"

"Good," she said. "The sooner the better." This was progress on almost all fronts. Somehow that brought her back to the debacle that had made this night so desolate. She hesitated for just a second. Her special surveillance of Flenser had always been the secret beyond telling. Now? Now she finally had someone to share it with.

"There's one other thing, Nevil." She explained about Flenser and her spy infestation.

He gave a low whistle. "I had no idea that Beyonder surveillance tech could work here."

"Well, it turns out that in the long run it was a disaster," she said, and then described the latest session, under Flenser's castle. She heard her voice rising. *This* part felt as bad as ever. "And confessing to Woodcarver on top of everything else—I just can't do it!"

The breeze had risen ever so slightly, and the glowbugs had fallen out of synch. Now they were only isolated spots of light. There was the occasional tap of raindrops on her hood, the beginnings of the shower *Oobii* had predicted.

Nevil was quiet for a long moment. Finally he said. "Yeah, that's a problem. But the surveillance itself—I think that was the right thing. Johanna has always been very suspicious of that pack. And from what you said, you got years of valid intel."

"Some *unknown* number of years."

"True. But my Dad used say that there's no way to be a successful leader without taking considered risks. And that means occasionally doing things that fail miserably. The point is to make what you can of the successes—then revisit the failures. When Woodcarver is happy about things, *then* come back to her with this."

Ravna looked up into darkness, got a couple big raindrops in the face for her trouble. She licked at the cold water and suddenly was laughing. "Meantime, the weather is telling us to adjourn this summit meeting."

She reached out to pat Nevil's shoulder, and his hand found hers. Surely both hands were chilled, but his was the warmer. It felt so comforting. "Thank you, Nevil," she said softly.

He held her hand for a second more. "It's just the support you deserve. We all need you." Then he withdrew his hand with an embarrassed laugh. "And you're right about the weather!" He stood and slid down from his perch on the rock, then shined a dim light on the rock to help her down. Thankfully, he did not give her a hand with the descent.

They trudged down the mossy path, keeping a good one meter fifty between them. The rain had increased to a downpour, and the breeze had become a driving wind. The glowbugs had surrendered the night, and she imagined that the path down to *Oobii* must already be flowing with mud. It was a dark and stormy night! And yet, and yet . . . Ravna felt more comfort and optimism than she had for a very long time.

CHAPTER 10

Autumn around Starship Hill was beginning to show its teeth. There was still about half a day of sunlight in every day, but most days were cloudy, with ocean squalls coming and coming, each a little colder than the last. The rain was slush, then it was slush and snow. The only uglier season was the endless mud of late Spring, but that held the promise of greenery and summer. Autumn's promise was different: the deadly cold of Arctic winter. Winter was a good time for one of Ravna's favorite projects. In the Northern Icefangs, the tendays of night were dry and clear and less than 185°K. A space-based civilization would count that as so near room temperature as to make no difference, but *Oobii* had dredged up some metamaterial studies from its archives of bypassed technologies: Given a hectare at those temperatures, you could carve out macroscopic logic and then use a laser interference scheme to fabricate micron-scale semiconductor parts. Their last three attempts had been tantalizing failures. Maybe this winter would be different. . . .

Of course, the project had been discussed in the Executive Council. Scrupilo was obsessed with the experiment, his Cold Valley lab. And though this third attempt was not a secret, Nevil suggested to Ravna that it was just as well not to make much of it to the Children at large. The ice experiments could be a game changer, moving the world to automation decades ahead of schedule, ending the worst of the kids' everyday discomforts. On the other hand, this was the third try and *Oobii* gave it only a modest chance of success.

Ravna obsessed right along with Scrupilo; discovering the Disaster Study Group had made the likelihood of a failure this winter all the more depressing. But now, since that evening with the glowbugs at Pham's grave, she could settle for knowing that things were on the right path. Every day that passed, Nevil brought some new insight, often things that could not have been brought up in Council, sometimes things she would *never* have thought of by herself. For Nevil was the perfect complement to Johanna. Before the *Oobii* landed, Johanna had been alone here, surrounded by the Tines. She had become their hero. She had close friends at the highest Tinish levels, and the lowest. The packs loved her for what she had done in combat and even for the crazy breakout she had fomented at the old Fragmentarium, which had started the private hospital movement. Ravna was constantly surprised at how many Tines claimed to know her personally—even packs that were not veterans.

But though Johanna had plenty of friends among the Children, she—and Jefri—were still somewhat apart from them; both had spent that terrible first year here alone. *Nevil*, on the other hand, was Ravna's perfect bridge to the Children. He was a born leader and had known every one of the kids back at the High Lab. Nevil had their pulse; he seemed to know every quirky reason for what they might like or resent or desire.

————

"How do you like the New Meeting Place?" asked Ravna.

"I love it!" Timor Ristling was fourteen years old now, but he still looked to be only six or seven. He walked with a limp and had a spastic tremor. Ravna was terribly afraid there were mental deficiencies, too; Timor was very good at manual arithmetic, but lagged behind in most other topics. It didn't help that his Tinish Best Friend was a bad-tempered foursome who regarded the boy as her sinecure. Belle Ornrikak was tagging along behind them, a calculating glint in her eyes.

But just now, Timor's unhappy history was nearly invisible. He held her hand, all but dragging Ravna along. His tremor could have been taken as part of his joyful excitement for what Nevil's design suggestions had made of the *Oobii*'s cargo bay.

The space was forty by thirty by twenty meters. Ravna and Pham had made good use of a tiny part of it in their journey here, smuggling themselves through customs at Harmonious Repose. Now the space was almost empty, its inland side resting at ground level. A half-timbered wall had been built across the cargo hatch, enough to keep out the weather.

Nevil had remodeled the interior, partly with local materials, partly by re- vising walls into explicit access points and game stations. He'd decorated every- thing in what he confessed was a poor imitation of the manner of Straum. Timor led Ravna across the gem-tiled floor, showing her wonder after wonder. "And see above?" The boy was staring up, wavering a little with his uncertain bal- ance. "It's the skyline round Straumli Main. I remember it from just before we left for the High Lab. I had friends in beginning school there." She knew he had been about four years old when he left Straumli Main, but somehow those memories had survived everything since.

"It's nice, Timor."

"No, it's *beautiful!* Thank you for building it for us."

"It wasn't just me," said Ravna. In fact, virtually none of the detail design had been her own. Most was from Nevil and his friends, but Nevil thought it best if for now she got as much credit as possible.

Belle slipped around Ravna to stand by Timor. The pack was mostly watch- ing the stations running hunter games, but she sounded bored: "I've heard this is nothing like the real Beyond; the Children will get tired of the gimmicks soon enough."

"No, we won't!" responded Timor, his voice getting a little loud. "I love it here, and there's more! I'll show you." He turned away, leaving Belle's gaze still caught with an addict's intensity on the game displays. Not until Ravna had walked past her did she recover and follow along.

Timor took them away from the game and sports floors and up a ramp. Here, the exciting noises of the gaming area were muted by *Oobii*'s active acoustics. Ten or twelve of the oldest Children were sitting around a projecting display space. Maybe this was a strategy game, or— Then she noticed Nevil standing a little back from the chairs. It looked as if he had just arrived, too. She started toward him, but Timor was plucking at her sleeve. "Do you see what they're doing?"

There were intricate models floating in the space between the chairs and the wall. Small windows hung by each of the kids. The models looked like some kind of network thing, but—she shook her head.

"Øvin can explain!" Timor drew her over to where Øvin Verring and Elspa Latterby were sitting together.

Øvin looked up at her appearance. There was a flash of surprise in his face, and perhaps nervousness. "Hello, Ravna!"

"Hei," said Elspa, and gave a little wave.

Ravna grinned at him. "So what are you all doing?" She looked around at the entire group. Except for Heida Øysler, these were some of the most serious of the Children. "Not a game?"

Elspa shook her head. "Ah, no. We're trying to learn to, um—"

Heida took over: "Ever wonder why we kids haven't pushed to use *Oobii*'s automation?"

"A little." In fact, most of the Children had resisted learning programming almost as much as they had more primitive skills.

"Two reasons," said Heida. "You seemed to want it for your projects—but just as important, this starship is as dumb as a rock."

"It's the best that can exist here, Heida."

"I like it a lot!" put in Timor.

Heida grinned. "Okay then, so it's not a dumb rock; it's more like one of those whatsits, a flaked stone arrowhead. The point is, it's worthless for—"

Øvin shook his head. "What Heida is trying to say in her own gracious way is . . ." He thought for a second, perhaps trying to come up with something less ungracious. ". . . is that now that we have access beyond our classes, maybe we should learn to change our ways and make the best use of *Oobii* that we can. So far we're visualizing the problem. That's usually the hard part. Let me show you."

He turned and glanced at the others. Each was suddenly busy with details on his or her own display. What Ravna could see looked like art programming, but performed in some incredibly roundabout way. Elspa Latterby looked up. "Yes, all clear. Go for it, Øvin."

The structure forming in the space between the kids didn't look like art. There were thousands of points of light, variously connected by colored lines.

Will someone please explain this to me? thought Ravna. It might be a network simulation, but there was no labelling. Ah, wait, she could almost guess at the power law on the connections. Maybe this was a—

Øvin was talking again: "This was hell to put together using *Oobii*'s interface, but we've visualized a whole-body map of the transduction network in a modern human. Well, it's what *Oobii* has on file, a racial average across Sjandra Kei. We Straumers can't be much different. Anyway—" He zoomed in on one cluster in the network. The rest of the complexity shifted to the sides, not exactly disappearing, but moving into the far distance. "This," Øvin continued, "covers part of the motor stability region."

Ravna nodded back, and tried to keep a smile pasted on her face. She was beginning to guess where all this was going. From the corner of her eye, she saw that Nevil was drifting around the outer edge of the group in Ravna's direction. *Help!*

Her smile must have been encouraging, for Øvin continued with his explanation: "This is really just a test case for a much larger class of problems— namely medicine in general. If we can learn enough of *Oobii*'s programming interface, we can get the ship to generate pathologies on the motor stability region and compare them with the symptoms it perceives in—"

"In *me*!" said Timor. The boy had settled down on the floor when Øvin began his demo, but now he struggled up to his knees, making sure that Ravna would notice. "They're going to cure what's wrong in *me*."

Øvin glanced down at the boy. "We're going to try, Timor. Everything's a crap shoot Down Here."

"I know." Timor sounded irritated by the obvious caveat.

After a second, Øvin looked back at Ravna. "Anyway, if—I mean, *as soon as*—we do all that, we'll have *Oobii* start generating treatment targets and running experiments." Suddenly, Øvin was more hesitant. He was looking at Ravna for some kind of approval. "We think we have something, Ravna. What do you think?"

Ravna stared at the network sim for a moment. That was so much easier than looking into Øvin Verring's eyes. These kids were very bright, the children of geniuses. The oldest ones, before their flight from the High Lab, had had a good Straumer education. Down Here? Down Here, the kids were relatively uneducated. Down Here, experiments didn't run themselves, there were intermediate steps required, infrastructure to create.

She looked back at Øvin Verring, saw that *he* saw through her attempt at mellowness. Her smile cracked apart, and she said, "Øvin. How can I say this? You—"

And then rescue miraculously arrived. Nevil. He patted Øvin on the shoulder and smiled comfortingly in Ravna's direction. "This will be okay, guys. Let me talk to Ravna."

The wannabe medical researchers seemed relieved—though not nearly as relieved as Ravna felt.

Ravna gave them all her best smile. "I'll get back to you." She looked down. "I promise, Timor."

"I know you will," said Timor.

Then she let Nevil spirit her away. Thank goodness. He must have some control on the New Meeting Place environment, since they hadn't gone five meters before she felt the sound quality shift and knew that even standing here in the middle of the floor, it was just the two of them who could hear each other. "Thanks, Nevil. That was awful. How did the kids come to try—"

Nevil made an angry gesture. "It was my fault. Damn. The Meeting Place has plenty of these Slow Zone games, but I figured the best of us would want to see how what we've learned in the Academy could be put to work here."

"I think we both wanted that. I *do* need planning help."

"Yeah, but I should have guessed that they'd zero in on the impractical. We both know how crazy it would be to get diverted into heavy bioscience at this stage."

Ravna turned so that only Nevil would see her unhappiness. "I've tried to explain this to Øvin before."

Nevil shook his head. "I know. Øvin . . . he can be a little unrealistic. He thinks this is as easy as improving harvest yields. You need to sit everybody down together and—"

"Right, my speech." More and more, that looked essential. "And the sooner the better." *Get everybody together, explain the problem and ask for their support.* "I could ask for formal procedures for handling medical emergencies, how we might use the remaining sleep caskets till we have proper medicine."

"Yes!"

"I should go back, tell Øvin and the others and try to explain." She looked over his shoulder at where the amateur *Oobii* managers were still clustered around their network simulation. Except for Timor, none of them were quite looking in her direction.

Nevil seemed to notice the indecision in her face. "If you want, I can explain to Øvin and the others. I mean, the general idea—and how you're still working out the details."

"Would you?" These all were Nevil's friends. He understood them in a way that Ravna never could. "Oh, thank you, Nevil."

He waved her away. "Don't worry. I'll take care of it."

Ravna stepped out of their bubble of audio privacy. As Nevil turned to go back to Øvin and the others, she gave them a little wave. Then she was off to the exit leading up the bridge. There was so much she had to get right for this speech, for making it something that everyone—including Woodcarver—could get behind.

A full tenday quickly passed. Outside, the snow now stayed on the ground, even on the streets of Hidden Island. There was more twilight and true night. The moon and the aurora were coming to dominate the sky.

Except for a trip with Scrupilo to Smeltertop and Cold Valley, Ravna spent most of her time indoors, on *Oobii*'s command deck. There was so much to do. Up north, the bottom of Cold Valley had been planed smooth. Scrupilo's packs were nearly done with carving a thousand square meter design; two of *Oobii*'s micro lasers were already on site. Come the truly cold weather, they planned on fabbing their first hundred-micron-scale components . . . ten thousand adder circuits. *Ta-dah! Really!* It was a silly goal, but a major proof of principle. The previous winter they hadn't quite reached that point when spring arrived.

Her work on the speech was coming along, hopefully a masterpiece of realistic optimism. Every day, Nevil came to her with way too many details of what they were doing with New Meeting Place. The speech and the New Meeting Place would work together. And she'd set the date for the speech. She was committed. It felt good!

There was only one full Executive Council meeting in that time; Woodcarver was in an ugly mood again. Scrupilo, too, was being a pain. He was the most politically ignorant fellow Ravna had ever met—an amazing thing considering his parentage. Even though he got most of Ravna's attention and most of *Oobii*'s support, he was still complaining about her lack of attention for the Cold Valley fab. He was right—if you ignored the political necessity of assuring support in the future. Nevertheless, she gave Scrupilo extra time and attention, letting Nevil handle more of the event details.

There were other reasons for not having more Council meetings. Ravna had reviewed the early years of her Flenser surveillance; she was still certain the camera infestation had been accurate for the first few years. That and the patent absurdities of the most recent session made it very foolish to get paranoid about Flenser. And yet she was still a bit uncomfortable about seeing him at a Council meeting.

And finally, Pilgrim and Johanna were out of town, on what Ravna considered a dangerous and unnecessary adventure. The two had taken the agrav flier and were snooping around East Home, five thousand kilometers away. That was beyond direct radio range, but they'd reset one of *Oobii*'s few remaining commsets to transmit in the five-to-twenty-megahertz range. They splattered their radio emissions off the sky and let the planet's ionosphere reflect them across the continent. On Starship Hill, *Oobii* was clever enough to pick out the signal even when the aurora hung its brightest curtains above the Domain—and to blast a much stronger response signal back to Johanna's commset.

The one full Council meeting had been mainly about that expedition:

"I'm glad we flew out here," came Pilgrim's voice. "The stories about Tycoon haven't been exaggerated. He really has started his own industrial revolution."

Flenser looked up from his accustomed place at the far end of the table. "Aha! Vendacious shows his claws!"

Woodcarver gave a little hiss, but didn't otherwise respond. In fact, East Home was the only place there had been sure sightings of the misbegotten Vendacious. That had been eight years ago, shortly before a series of major disappearances from Scrupilo's labs: printers, a telephone prototype, even one of the three printer interfaces. At the time, the thefts had been an even bigger scandal than the recent radio cloak theft, though two of the burglars had been caught—both former lieutenants of Vendacious. Since those thefts, Tycoon had been a steady source of "innovation."

"We've talked about this before," said Ravna. "Tycoon may regard himself as our rival, but any diffusion of technology will just speed up our overall progress. Keep in mind the main threat." *The Blighter fleet coming down upon us.*

Flenser eyed himself slyly—a packish smirk. "The main threat won't matter if you get the Domain murdered beforehand."

"That's why Jo and I are checking this out," said Pilgrim. "What we're seeing makes us think that over the years, Tycoon may have accomplished much more than he advertised. Now the true operation is too big to be disguised. I think Tycoon—or Vendacious—has spies high in the Domain."

Woodcarver raised heads at this. Two of her—three if you counted her puppy, little Sht—were glaring at Flenser.

"These are real technical innovations," said Johanna. "I think the leaks have to originate in the North End labs."

"What!" Scrupilo's interjection was an indignant squawk.

"Have you met this Tycoon fellow?" said Ravna.

"Not yet," said Pilgrim. "Even his factory managers rarely see him. He doesn't seem very involved in day-to-day operations."

"We're being very cautious about this," said Johanna. "And me, I'm staying completely out of sight."

"Good!" that was from both Ravna and Nevil, and very emphatic. There were things Johanna could do as a two-legs that gave the Pilgrim-Johanna team great advantages—that was Jo's argument, anyway. Ravna was far from convinced that it justified her presence on a spy mission.

"I wish you were back here," said Nevil.

"I'm fine, Nevil. Like I said, keeping a low profile."

A strange sound came over the radio link, probably a chord from Pilgrim. Ravna smiled, imagining the pack and the girl hunkered down by their commset. It would be early morning on the east coast now. She wondered just where they were hiding.

Flenser-Tyrathect was shaking his heads, grinning.

"What?" Ravna said to him.

The pack gave a shrug. "Isn't it obvious? There is no need for spies high in Scrupilo's organization. Who stole the Oliphaunt computer? I know *I* could use Oliphaunt to engineer all—"

Woodcarver's shriek would have been downright painful but for *Oobii's* sound damping. Three of her leaped partway onto the table, their claws clicking on the surface. "You confess to treason, do you now?" she said.

Flenser showed lots of teeth even as he replied: "Don't be an idiot. Ah, but I forgot, you're already the idiot who didn't kill Vendacious when you had the chance. You're already the idiot who let him escape and who still blames *me* for stealing Oliphaunt."

This brought another of Woodcarver onto the meeting table. There was a time when Ravna could have been the peacemaker in such confrontations. Now? Ravna fleetingly wondered if Woodcarver might take a swipe at her if she tried to intervene.

Nevil was braver, or faster, or perhaps just more foolish. As Woodcarver scrambled forward, he was already on his feet. "It's okay, Your Majesty!" He started to extend a hand toward her, then seemed to realize he was cajoling someone who was seriously not human. "Um, this is just one of those burdens of a wise ruler."

The stilted, medieval approach seemed to work. Woodcarver didn't retreat, but her forward surge subsided.

"Flenser has a point," said Johanna, sounding unperturbed, perhaps because the sounds of jaws and claws had not survived the low-quality radio transmission. "Tycoon may really be Vendacious plus Oliphaunt, but spies in Scrupilo's labs could also explain his success."

That satisfied all except Scrupilo: "I do *not* have spies in any of my labs!" But not surprisingly, he was perfectly happy to talk about technical fixes to such nonexistent espionage. Monitoring user access to *Oobii* was relatively easy. The problem was to correlate that with exactly what inventions were appearing elsewhere.

Nevil was looking more and more unhappy. "We have to get this nailed down. Surely there must be clues at the Tycoon end of this. You're due to leave East Home almost immediately, aren't you, Jo?"

"That was the plan." There was mumbled conversation between Johanna and Pilgrim, too scattered for *Oobii* to clean up. "Our equipment is in good shape and we have a safe hidey-hole outside of the city. We're good to stay a while if it will help, especially if you can feed us some clues to follow up on."

Nevil was clearly torn. Ravna could guess how much he'd been looking forward to Johanna's return.

"Do we have any clues to feed them?" Ravna asked.

Pilgrim said, "There's Scrupilo's lab logs. We could look for coincidences in detail."

Woodcarver—now back on her seats—had a different angle. "From what Johanna and Pilgrim say, Tycoon grows steadily more powerful. If they come back now, we may have hard time getting this close again."

"We should have a full-time gang of spies over there," said Flenser-Tyrathect.

Woodcarver shrugged agreement. The two were almost talking to each other.

In the end, that meeting was almost the sort of Exec Council meeting they should be having these days—except that now Johanna and Pilgrim would be absent for at least another twenty days.

———

Twenty days. Johanna and Pilgrim wouldn't be back till after Ravna's big speech. Since that night by Pham's grave, she had not had much chance to talk to Johanna. The younger woman had been off spying most of the time, and when she'd been back she'd been mainly with Nevil. Now Ravna would have virtually no chance to chat privately with her.

And Woodcarver seemed to be in a bigger snit than ever.

Ravna had written multiple drafts of her upcoming speech. There were so many issues to bring together. Some were joyously good news—how New Meeting Place could be used for increased participation, formal democracy. Some were hard truths—the Blighter threat that loomed in their future, the need to solve underlying technology problems before they took on prolongevity research. Some were proposals to make the hard truths more palatable. Without Woodcarver, now without Johanna and Pilgrim—it all came down to Ravna's own best judgment and Nevil's advice. Over and over, he showed her nuances that she would have missed on her own. For instance: "Arrange things so you can end the speech with the good news that gives realistic reasons to be optimistic about it all." And: "We can merge this speech with your idea for a Public Council, Ravna. My Dad used to say that responsible people can deal with bad news if they have some control over the hardships." So they would announce the meeting as occasion for her speech and as an opportunity for Children and Tines to feed back into the process. "I've talked to Woodcarver about this, Ravna. She thinks it will work." And that was one of the best pieces of news. Woodcarver was still avoiding Ravna, but she was at least indirectly part of the planning.

Nevil and company had figured how to make the New Meeting Place seem bigger, and he was showing her dozens of variations on how they might decorate the place. Finally she just offloaded all that onto him and concentrated on polishing her speech, doing her best to implement his final suggestions.

And then it was the day before the "grand meeting." Ravna was already thinking of the event in countdown terminology. They were at Meeting minus fifteen hours. She had a final chat with Nevil, going over what she would have to know about the physical setup of the New Meeting Place, rehearsing her presentation still again. "Don't worry if the speech doesn't come out one hundred percent perfect. I'll be out there. The Public Council makes it easy for me to stand up, ask a question that gets things back on track—and just as easy for all your friends to show support."

". . . You're right," said Ravna. "I'm just chewing on my own nervousness." Ravna glanced at the little clock window she'd been using to time her speech rehearsals. It also showed the countdown: 14:37:33 till show time. She and Nevil were up on the bridge, but they'd set the displays to make it look like her lectern in the New Meeting Place would be in . . . well, in 14:36:55. She looked across at Nevil. His face had a certain earnest nervousness of its own—and she decided he was mainly worried about her being so obviously worried. Johanna was so lucky to have this guy.

"Nevil, I want to thank you for everything. Without you, I would still be flailing."

He shook his head. "You can't do it all alone, Ravna. But what you are working toward is absolutely necessary. It's what the rest of us, all the Children, should be helping with. If we pull together, we can't lose."

That was something like the language in her speech, and suddenly Ravna realized that Nevil must really live those words, even as they had come to seem platitudes in her ears. *Too much rehearsing, that's for sure.*

She stood and walked carefully around the fake lectern, toward where the bridge entrance was tonight. She waved the door open and turned back toward him. "So I'll see you tomorrow then." She smiled. "In a bit less than 14:35:21."

Nevil stood. Maybe there was a little bit of relief in his smile. "That you will, my lady."

He stopped within arm's length from her. "Sleep well and don't worry," he said.

"Thanks, Nevil. G'night."

He smiled. "G'night." And then he was gone.

————

Of course, it was no surprise that sleep didn't come. In fact, Ravna didn't even head for bed immediately. *But I deserve a pat on the back for not doing another rehearsal.* She retreated from the platform and lectern and settled down with her usual analysis tools. Nowadays, *Oobii* ran elaborate threat detection software all the time—sometimes so intensively that it slowed Scrupilo's research programs. During the last tenday, Ravna had not kept up with the security monitoring as much as usual. That fact supported one of her Theories of Worry, namely that every worrywart has a natural Worry Max. When there are other concerns—such as preparing for this meeting—normal obsessions weaken.

Nevertheless, she settled down for a bit of distracting logfile-surfing. *Oobii* had a system of prioritized alarms, but—as past debacles had shown—there was always the possibility it would miscategorize things.

After some tedious time with the logs, she suddenly realized she wasn't nearly as obsessed with her speech. Ha! And there really wasn't all that much that was troublesome in *Oobii*'s logs either! . . . She browsed on, through lower priority results.

Here was something interesting in the "old threats" department: *Oobii* was still watching for any sign of the stolen radio cloaks. Those gadgets were nothing like the Beyonder commset that Pilgrim and Johanna were using, or even the voice-band radios Scrupilo built nowadays. The cloaks made an analog smear of the wearer's mindsounds across a big swath of the radio frequency spectrum. The resultant signal was fairly short range—and essentially impossible for *Oobii* to translate. Hate, fear, lust—those might be recognized, but mind reading was very much not possible.

The ship had heard none of that. And yet, *Oobii* had detected something very like cloak noise. By correlating with the changing footprint of the aurora, *Oobii* guessed the source was high in the Icefangs, about seventy kilometers to the east. The signal was sporadic and at its loudest scarcely more than a suspicious correlation. If this was a radio cloak, there was only one. It was even fainter than a cloak should be at that distance, and it was being worn for only a few minutes in every day.

Ravna played with the results for some minutes. There really wasn't enough signal to do much analysis. If she asked for more, she might get another taste of

Oobii's wishful thinking. *No thank you.* . . . But what conceivable use was *one* radio cloak? Without the rest of a Tinish soul wearing the others, a single cloak was the sound of one hand clapping.

She leaned back, imagining: a party of thieves sneaking out of the Domain, travelling through a steep-shouldered mountain pass. Those passes could be deadly, even in high summer. An avalanche could have killed them all. Or perhaps they'd been ambushed by ordinary bandits. One way or another, the cloaks were lost, all but one. The theory almost made sense. But this remnant cloak would need a wearer, and occasional light for power. So how about this: The cloaks were beautiful things, the solar cells as dark as velvet but with glints of gold. Maybe some primitive pack was wearing the remaining cloak as a trophy, totally ignorant of the magic it was making.

What sad irony. She made a note. She should bring up this with the Executive Council—better yet, take it to Woodcarver directly. It might get them talking again. In any case, they should send a search party to the location before winter came crashing down.

Now her countdown window said 13:25:14. She had frittered away an hour, not thinking about her speech once. *I really should review it some more, maybe do another rehearsal.* She had never been so nervous about talking to the kids. But in the past, it had always been one on one, to small groups; now she would be talking to them all. If she properly made the points that she and Nevil had worked so hard on, so many problems would be solved. *But if I mess up . . .*

CHAPTER 11

The morning was a dark and blustery thing, perhaps the last rainstorm of the year and autumn's chill goodbye. Ravna had the bridge's windows looking out on a panorama of the gloom, and she gave it all a kind of vague attention as she dressed. Down the hill toward the dropoff, there was a scudding fog, parting now and then for a gray-on-gray glimpse of the inner channel and Hidden Island. The rain came slanting in from the north. Ship's sensors showed it was liquid water, not hail, but it froze as it splashed across Starship Hill, turning the streets of the New Castle's town to ice.

She could see the Children and Tines of the Domain were coming south from Newcastle town and north along the Queen's Road. In the westward view, she could see others emerging from the fog at the top of the funicular. Ravna paused a second, zoomed in on those muffled figures, the clumped packs that accompanied them. They must have left Hidden Island almost an hour earlier— all to make it here on time for the beginning of Ravna's speech. *In just 00:25:43.*

At least they would be warm and comfortable once they got in their New Meeting Place.

The sight gave her pause. *Shouldn't I be dressed as plainly?* Not like this: She looked at herself front and back. Somehow the outfit had not seemed so much like a uniform when she and Nevil had decided on the design. Even though Woodcarver wasn't talking to her, she had relayed her desires through Nevil: The Queen intended to wear all her crowns and regalia and she expected that Ravna would show a formal aspect as well. *Okay.* The Children of the Sky could surely see through such material spin—but if Woodcarver didn't buy into the New Meeting Place as a kind of thrones room then her hostility might never melt.

Ravna looked at herself for a moment more. In fact, this style had an honorable history—even if she was only person in the world who really understood. Blysse herself had worn something like this when she went out to win the support of the archeologists and software engineers.

You look good. Hold onto that thought. She grabbed her hud/tiara and left the bridge.

00:03:51 till show time.

The passage from the command deck currently opened onto a space above the cargo bay's inner wall. Today that small place had the atmosphere of backstage at a classic live theater. For the moment, she was all alone. Ravna paced the length of the darkened space, not bothering to change the light level. On one side she had a window on her speech, especially the opening lines. *Don't botch the opening!* On the other side, she had some windows Nevil had set up looking into the New Meeting Place itself. These were very temporary views, fisheye perspectives that were really more limited than was reasonable. Or maybe that was appropriate. She could peek out like an old-time performer gauging the crowd.

All the seats that Ravna could see were filled. Nevil would be there, somewhere in the first rows. It was only Woodcarver and Ravna who were to come from within the ship. Nevil said that was Woodcarver's desire, more royal psychology apparently.

00:00:50. There was the faint metallic clatter of multiple tines on the floor behind her. Woodcarver. Ravna turned and bowed to her co-Queen. "Ready for the big day, Your Highness?" There was so much Ravna wanted to say to Woodcarver. *If this day goes right, perhaps you will listen to me again, and be my friend once more.*

Some of Woodcarver's heads bobbed. That was a smile, though in the semidarkness there seemed something strange in it. "Oh yes, though it's you who seem to have prepared the most." She jabbed a snout at the wall, presumably pointing at the meeting place beyond. "What an . . . extraordinary . . . place you have made for yourself."

"For us, Woodcarver. For us all."

00:00:00. Her tiara chimed unnecessarily in her ear. *Such precision. A minute or two more or less should make no difference.* But Ravna was terribly afraid that if she didn't move forward on a schedule, she might never get herself on stage. So she didn't try to say any more, but simply bowed for Woodcarver to proceed through the doors that were now opening wide.

Bright sunlight—totally artificial, of course—splashed down upon Woodcarver as the pack stepped through the doorway. The portal was as wide as a Tinish pack-level entrance. Woodcarver proceeded through, all abreast. For that matter, there was room for Ravna, too, but Nevil had learned that the co-Queen thought it best for her to appear and then Ravna separately.

So she waited till Woodcarver had cleared the opening and disappeared toward where her thrones waited on the left. For an instant, Ravna just hesitated, terrified. *This is what happens when you truly realize what a make-or-break situation you've created for yourself.* But it was time, and she had a schedule to keep. She stepped forward. Strangely, the traditional uniform gave her a kind of strength, and a purposeful stride.

As she stepped into the light, unseen trumpets blasted out a jaunty flourish. There was nothing Tinish about the music. It was the sort of honor that went to humans in old historicals. *Oh no!* That was Glitch Number 1. If there were to be any flourishes, they should have been for Woodcarver.

Ravna turned to the right, started toward her own throne. Then she remembered that she'd intended to turn and bow toward Woodcarver first. *Okay, that was Glitch Number 2, but a small one.* She had always known there would be glitches.

The stage was well above the level of the audience area. As Ravna walked across it, she looked out at the people and tried to give them a casual wave. It felt more like shaking a stick, but she heard friendly applause. Her eyes strayed upwards for a second and—my *goodness* what an enormous place this looked to be. She knew the precise dimensions of the latest build out, but Nevil and his friends had played clever little tricks with vision and perspective to make it seem even larger. Gone were the gaming nooks of days past. Today there were slender arches along the walls. They rose and rose into a ceiling so high that flying birds would not have been out of place. The fake sunlight spilled down through a crystal canopy. She recognized the style. This was rainforest architecture of the Middle Recovery on Nyjora. The Princesses had used building materials from the fallen ruins—hence the crystal skylight that would have been impossible for them otherwise. It was a scene that touched her heart, though it would mean nothing to most packs—and perhaps not much to Straumli children.

Fortunately, the speaker's platform and the lectern *were* just what she had been rehearsing with up on the bridge. Ravna's own queenly throne was just a few paces beyond the lectern, far closer to it than Woodcarver's thrones. There were no other seats on the stage. She'd hoped that the Executive Council would all be part of this, but Johanna and Pilgrim were still on the East Coast. Apparently Nevil hadn't been able to persuade Woodcarver to allow the others up here. Okay, so Woodcarver wanted governance to be simply the two Queens and the People.

Ravna hesitated at the steps ascending to her throne. The thing was a monster, two meters tall, not counting the steps, drenched in fake gems and precious metals and symbols that didn't mean much beyond certain human legends. *I really don't want to go up there.* Woodcarver can have the show, but—

Ravna glanced across the stage. What Woodcarver sat upon necessarily was different from Ravna's setup. The pack needed a separate perch for each member. Woodcarver's thrones were set at the same height as Ravna's, but the total area was no more than Ravna's single throne, and the individual perches were laid out in short straight rows, not at all the way a pack would arrange itself for forceful thought. This was Glitch Number 3 and far the most serious.

Belatedly, Ravna bowed toward Woodcarver. As she did so, it seemed like a great shadow moved across the wall behind the platform. It was . . . herself . . . her own image, towering across the ten meter expanse. Just staring up at it made Ravna a little dizzy. There was no place in the hall her image would not intimidate. And the camera must be a fixed tracker. Even when she looked back at Woodcarver, she could tell that the giantess on the wall was still herself, not her co-Queen.

This was when Nevil was to come on stage, introduce the two Queens and Ravna's own very special speech. But Nevil was not to be seen. *Surely Woodcarver will let him give his intros?*

She gave Woodcarver a second bow, at the same time searching for a private voice channel.

Then Woodcarver showed mercy. She shifted a bit awkwardly on her human-style thrones, bringing her heads closer to one another. When she spoke, her voice seemed to come from everywhere, conversational tones that sounded as if she were just a meter or two away. Hopefully, she sounded like that to everyone here. "Welcome all to the New Meeting Place. I hope this place will bring openness and power to those who deserve it."

Ravna's face was still the one on the giant display, but Woodcarver was sitting only a few meters away. Ravna could see that her dress was Tinish queenly, but not much different from the fur cloaks and half jackets that she normally wore. As for her expression—a pack's aspect lay mainly in the posture of its members: sitting on her thrones, Woodcarver seemed to have a sardonic expression. "So today, my co-Queen, Ravna, wishes to tell you what her rule may bring and what it will expect of you." Woodcarver extended a snout in Ravna's direction and waved her graciously toward the lectern.

For an instant, Ravna froze, thoroughly rattled. There were so many things, little and maybe not so little, that already had gone wrong. *This is not how it was supposed to be!* But she still had her speech and the ideas she had slaved over. And now she had the undivided attention of everyone she had hoped to reach. She turned and climbed the steps to the lectern. A window opened on the familiar, glowing words of her speech. For one moment, she ignored those words and simply looked out at her audience: one hundred and fifty humans, perhaps fifty packs. From her lectern, the main floor was almost three meters down. It spread into a misty, artificial distance. The seating was far plainer than anything on the stage, barely more than wooden benches and perches. Everywhere faces were looking up, and all—even most of the packs—were so familiar to her.

And there was Nevil, right in the first row! He was dressed in the same country-spun quilting as all the Children, and right now he looked cold and soaked and dripping—much like the rest, come in from this morning's rain.

But he'd been here after all, just hidden from her view by the lectern. Sitting right beside him was Timor Ristling, for once without his possessive Best Friend pack. The boy had an enormous smile on his face. He seemed totally taken by Ravna's image on the wall. Then he saw that she was looking at him and he started waving. Something going right at last. Ravna twitched her hand up to wave at them both and Nevil gave her back a wide grin of his own.

Now there was her speech to give. She slid the text window so that wherever she looked, the words were writ large and translucent across her view. If she had been Nevil or Woodcarver or Johanna, she could have ad libbed a new beginning to the talk, something that would mellow all the screw-ups, that would honor Woodcarver and maybe give everybody a good laugh. But she was Ravna Bergsndot and she knew that if she departed from her written speech she would be lost. It was her life raft.

This was where all the rehearsing would come to her rescue. She could looked through the misty words, speak them even as her gaze moved from face to face.

"Thank you, um, Woodcarver." *Hei, an ad lib!*

She essayed a sympathetic smile. "Thank you all for coming here this morning despite the weather." That wasn't really an ad lib, since *Oobii* had been confident of this morning's storm front.

"We humans have been here on the Tines World for a little more than ten years. The packs rescued us and became some of our best friends. But we must remember, both humans and packs, that our coming was part of a vast and tragic debacle." Here she made the proper gesture, dramatically pointing at the heavens beyond the crystal dome. "The evil that chased the humans to Tines World, still waits—even though diminished—in the near interstellar space." And Ravna went on to describe *Oobii*'s best estimate of the status of the Blighter fleet, thirty light years out. She didn't bring up the possibility of further Zone shifts; a real shift would be a game ender, and she had no hint of such beyond the weird glitch *Oobii* had reported years before. No, the story she told was pretty much what she'd been telling the Children from the day they came out of coldsleep. Nevil had told her that many of the kids had lost sight of that big picture. Telling them one more time, in this awesome setting, could make it clear why their present sacrifices were so necessary.

"In just twenty years, the first light from the Blighter fleet will arrive at Tines World. Will that by itself be a danger? Perhaps, though I have my doubts. But in the decades after *that*, it's possible that very small payloads, just milligrams, may arrive—all that the Blighters can accelerate to near-light speeds.

With sufficiently high technology, even such tiny payloads could conceivably harm Tines World." That was speculation from the nebulous end of *Oobii*'s weapons archive, extrapolating as best it could from their last information on the Blighters and the most exotic weapon systems that had ever been fielded in the Slow Zone.

"What's sure is that *if* the Blighters still wish us harm, then over the next century, certainly over the next thousand years, they can kill everyone in the world, *unless*—" here she paused dramatically just exactly as in all her rehearsals, and swept a steely look across her audience "—*unless* we, both humans and packs, quickly raise this world to the highest technology the Slow Zone can sustain. It's our best hope, perhaps our only hope. It is worth hard sacrifices."

As she spoke, she continued to look back and forth across her audience, occasionally sending a nod in the direction of her co-Queen. Ravna wasn't running any analysis tools, but she had the speech so well rehearsed that there was time to notice the listeners' reactions. Her eyes caught on those she most respected. Nevil—not really a good test case, but a comforting one—was nodding his head at the right times, even though this all was something he'd heard over and over again during the last few days. Others: Øvin Verring and Elspa Latterby, they were paying close attention, but every so often they would look at each other with a shake of their heads. The tailors, Ben and Wenda Larsndot, they were sitting far in the back with their kids. They had given up listening early on, were spending their time keeping their children quiet. They acted as though they had heard all this before. *Which they have, in a dozen dozen conversations with me over the years.* Some, the likes of Gannon Jorkenrud, were mugging her words.

I have to move on. If only she and Nevil could have foreseen this reaction when they were planning the speech—or if she were clever enough to amend it on the fly—she would skip forward with some clever segue and keep everyone's attention on the overall message.

The thought made her stumble on the words, almost lose her place. No. Her only hope was to plow ahead. These words might not sing, but she knew they made logical sense.

"So what is the greatest sacrifice that we must make for ultimate survival? It's a sacrifice I see each of us making every day. It's a very hard thing, though I want to convince you that the alternatives aren't really workable. That sacrifice is the relatively low priority that we're putting on biomedical products." *That* seemed to get everyone's attention. Even the packs perked up heads here and there.

Start with the bad news, build up to the good—but it was taking so long to get there! Okay, she was almost to her ideas for repairing more of the coldsleep caskets and creating an emergency medical committee. "For now we can treat only minor injuries. We have only basic epigenetic triggers. Ultimately, all that will change. In the meantime, how are we to deal with ageing? It's what our ancestors accepted for thousands of years . . ." Ravna never got to the "but."

"We are not your fucking ancestors!" It was Jefri Olsndot. He was halfway back in the crowd; she hadn't seen him before this moment. But now he was on his feet, enraged.

Jefri? Amdi was clustered all round him, his heads extended in an expression Ravna could not parse.

Jefri was shouting at the top of his lungs. "How dare you dictate to us, you so safe and smug? We refuse to die for you, Ravna! We—" he was still shouting and gesturing, but the sound was gone. *Oobii*'s acoustics had damped his voice.

Now Gannon Jorkenrud and another fellow were on their feet. "We will not die for you, Queenie! We will not die for—" and then their voices slipped away, too.

Then there were Tami Ansndot and others, all shouting yet silent. Ravna cast about for sound controls, but they were bundled in the meeting place's general automation. *I don't mean to shut people up!*

Her eyes focused back on the words of her speech. She had paragraphs to go! She felt a moment of helpless terror. Then she saw that, down in the first row, Nevil had come to his feet.

Thank goodness. She and Nevil had planned that he would speak later, when they went to Question and Answer. If only they could go to that now, and bail out of the nightmare her speech had become.

She gave him a jerk of her hand, urging him to come up to the lectern.

Nevil climbed the steps to the platform, but did not come around to take her place. In the audience, Jefri and the others were still standing, but they weren't shouting now. Instead there just a fretful murmur that seem to come from the crowd as a whole.

Nevil turned to them and raised his palms placatingly. After a moment, the protesters settled back on their benches. "This is *our* New Meeting Place, folks. It's what Ravna has built for us. We should use it to do what's right." The murmuring and angry sounds died away—naturally, as far as Ravna could see—and everyone was watching Nevil, giving his sensible words the attention they deserved.

Ravna looked over her shoulder at the monster display that loomed behind the stage. The camera was still locked on her. Maybe it would switch to Nevil if she moved away from the lectern. She stepped to one side, then descended from the platform. But even when she sat in one of the side seats, there was still her face up there, now frowning down upon them.

The audience could only see Nevil as a human-sized figure, standing beside the lectern. At least his voice was not damped:

"That's probably the most important thing about the New Meeting Place. It's where we refugees have our say and our vote." He looked to his left, toward Woodcarver.

Woodcarver gave him a civil nod or two, and her voice was downright conciliatory. "You're quite right, Nevil. It is more than time that the humans and the packs of the Domain have their say."

Nevil looked to his right, at Ravna. "And you, Ravna?"

"Yes, indeed! I—" but he had looked back at the audience, and Ravna let him run with his presentation. It was going better than her rehearsing.

"So then I suppose the question is, what to vote on?" He grinned, and there was even laughter from the crowd. "I think there might be a lot of separate things to vote on. For instance, it's important that when we are given the floor to speak, that our voices always be heard."

Agreement on that was loud and, happily, now unstifled.

"I think the most important issue is medical research. And that's not just to keep us looking young and beautiful." He flashed his smile again, then became very solemn. "You all know Timor Ristling." Nevil waved down toward the front row. Timor still sat there. When Nevil pointed at the child, the tracking camera finally woke up to its higher logic and suddenly Timor's image was towering on the wall behind the stage. This was not just a head and shoulders shot. The unhappy twistedness of his limbs was evident, and the faint tremor in his hands. The boy stared up at the giant image, then clapped in surprised glee.

Nevil smiled back at him, then looked out at the crowd. "How many of you remember Timor as he was back at the High Lab? I do, even though he was scarcely four years old. His mother and father maintained our legacy bootstrap logic—honorable work, and they did it well. They had every reason to believe their son would be just as steady." His voice fell. "But that was not to be. Instead, our situation here has nearly killed him." He paused and looked out again at his audience, and spoke with sober determination. "This is not a burden to be borne, not by Timor, not by anyone." The words brought a cheer.

In the tendays that followed, Ravna Bergsndot played this part of the meeting over and over in her mind, and marveled at the patchwork way the facts breached her preconceptions, and puzzlement yielded to understanding. She remembered standing, waving for Nevil's attention, trying to guide him back where she thought he'd been going, to talk about improved coldsleep facilities.

But Nevil had already moved on, riding the approval that seemed to come from all directions. "So yes, that is something we must surely vote on. But even that is only a symptom of the systematic problem we must cure. For whatever reason, there's been too much secrecy. The Executive Council should not be meeting in private. Perhaps there should be no Executive Council at all. I would give up my place on it."

Several in the audience had stood to speak. Nevil stopped and gestured, "Jefri?"

Jefri stood arms akimbo. His voice was angry, and he never quite looked at Ravna. Amdi had hunkered down around him with only a head visible here and there. "You want the one thing to vote on? It's not whether we have an Executive Council or whether you're on it, Nevil. The real question is whether we're going to have a megalomaniac nut case running us all into the ground!"

For a moment, there was true silence. For a moment, perhaps everyone was as shocked as Ravna. Then Gannon Jorkenrud was on his feet, shouting loud support for Jefri. But others were on their feet, too. Wenda Larsndot and Gannon Jorkenrud were suddenly in an angry shouting match.

Nevil raised his hands again. After some seconds the tumult died. Wenda angrily sat down and then so did Jorkenrud and the others. Nevil let the silence grow for a moment. Then he said, "It's clear we have much to discuss, more than we can vote on in this one meeting. We also have the day-to-day problems of maintaining the Domain. Perhaps there is a safe compromise. For everyday administration, we have a stable, proven resource." He turned and bowed to Woodcarver. "Madame, are you content to continue without the advice of an Executive Council? To administer in those noncontroversial issues of Domain affairs?"

Two of Woodcarver cast a look at Ravna. The others, including her puppy, were looking at Nevil and the audience. The co-Queen's aspect was one of sober attention. But Ravna had worked closely with Woodcarver for ten years. And right now, behind the solemn aspect, Ravna thought she detected amused satisfaction. None of that showed in her voice or words: "Quite content, Mister Storherte. Of course, I would still want everyone's advice."

"Of course," Nevil gave Woodcarver a nod that was almost a bow. And then he turned to Ravna. But he didn't have any similar request for her. Instead, his tone was comforting, conciliatory. "Ravna, we owe you so much. You supported Woodcarver in her war against Steel and the Old Flenser. We all remember your love in the early days of our exile, how you made it possible for Woodcarver and her packs to care for the youngest of us. Even now, we desperately need your expertise with *Oobii*'s archives." He hesitated, as if uncertain about how to continue. "But at the same time . . . we . . . we think you have become fixated on potential threats that are very far away. We think you have fallen into a kind of mental trap, where your losses and loneliness lead you into a"—he looked up at the magnificent fakery of the Age of Princesses architecture—"into a kind of personal fantasy." His gaze came back to her, compassionate and probing. And now, *finally*, Ravna fully understood. She could feel the eyes of all the Children and packs upon her. Some might hate her, as Jefri seemed to. But most simply saw the uniform she wore, and this imperial hall—and concluded that her grand plans were madness. She could almost see that conclusion spread in the five or ten seconds of Nevil's silence. Then his voice gently continued: "So that is why I think that that must be our vote here today: That we ask you to stand aside from administration for a time, that you continue to give us the value of your insights and your help with *Oobii*, but that you let Woodcarver and the votes of this New Meeting Place do the governing. Do you understand the vote I'm suggesting, Ravna?"

For the first time in several minutes, Ravna looked Nevil Storherte straight in the eye. He did not flinch. There was nothing but firm respect in the gaze he showed to her and the world. Ravna opened her mouth to shout denunciations back at him, . . . but she didn't have the words. Without a minute or two to think, only enraged babble would emerge. *But I could stop him.* Nevil Storherte might have his petty audio and scene control, everything she had given him to make the New Meeting Place, but Ravna still had overall master control of the starship *Out of Band II.* She could take control of this room, blow out the Age of Princesses lie and force everyone to listen to . . . the ravings of one now proven mad. She noticed that Woodcarver had tensed. *She* realized that at the level of raw force, Ravna held the whip hand.

But I'm not a mad woman. And so, when she spoke, Ravna said, "I understand, Nevil. I understand very well."

"Thank you, Ravna," Nevil's voice was full of compassion and relief.

Now Nevil was looking back at this audience. "And so I think we have something to vote for. A serious change that gives us all a hand in making a safe and healthy future. Is there debate before we vote?"

Actually there was, but not very much. Jorkenrud had his say, and then Jefri. *That* was more detailed and pointed and cutting than Jefri's shouted interruptions had been. Ravna almost started crying in the middle of it. As far as she could tell, Nevil was not using the *Oobii*'s acoustics to shut anyone up, but there were very few who had much to say in opposition, and they seemed a bit confused. All around them they had the evidence of Ravna's megalomania, and when she turned a bit to the side, she noticed that the camera was tracking her again. Her scowling glare was monstrous on the wall above.

When it came, the vote was no surprise. The mad woman was safely elevated to the status of technical advisor.

There were cheers, and then the Children were coming into the aisles and moving forward. Around Ravna there seemed to be a bubble of emptiness. Fortunately, the vast display no longer captured her face. Where Ravna sat, there seemed to be only shadows.

Nevil came down from the speaker's platform. The babble grew louder as folks moved in close to shake his hand. Nevil was grinning and waving. He reached down to lift Timor high into the air. "We're doing this for him! We're doing this for us!"

Then he set the boy down, and both were lost in a swirl of well-wishers. After a few seconds, Timor came out from the crush, ignored for the moment. He looked around and then ran awkwardly across the open floor, toward the shadows that hid Ravna.

Up close, she could see that Timor was crying. He looked lost and devastated, not suddenly saved as Nevil proclaimed. *He looks like I feel.*

She went to one knee to greet him. He threw his arms around her neck. His voice came in her ear, the tone wondering. "Ravna, Ravna. What happened?"

CHAPTER 12

For Ravna, the days that followed were strangely placid. She was told that Johanna and Pilgrim were en route back from the East Coast, but that no Executive Council meetings were planned. Woodcarver was not available. For the moment, the new "Technical Advisor to the Domain" had few responsibilities. She was asked to leave her apartment aboard the *Oobii*. That space would be used for the additional medical support that Nevil had promised. Apparently that involved upgrading the coldsleep gear, though Ravna wasn't clear on how that was to be accomplished.

Ravna was assigned one of the newest town houses on the Queen's Road. Bili Yngva showed her around the place and helped her move in. Bili was apparently Nevil's chief lieutenant. Bili was smiling and respectful. "Nevil wanted to show you this place, but I think he's discovered just how much work admin can be," he said, with a disarming grin. They were on the second floor of her new home. Like all the town houses, this had steam heating and indoor plumbing. These new ones had a second flush toilet on the upper floor.

The upper floor had both a front stairs and a back stairs. There was a living room with wide glass windows. The southwest exposures gave a grand view across the Inner Channel. "This is the first house with the new optical-grade glass sheeting. It's almost like having a real display, except that the view menu is a bit limited." He waved at the swirls of frost that encrusted the margins of the glass. "Don't worry about the ice, That'll go away once we connect the water. Your heater tower is already registered with *Oobii*."

Ravna nodded. Once the ship began heating her water, it wouldn't matter how much heat was leaking through those windows, except as it was used by *Oobii*'s sensors as thermostat feedback. Ah, the wonders of central heating and central computing.

After a moment, Bili seemed to realize she wasn't going to respond further. "Well, I should go down and help the guys get your baggage installed."

Yngva went downstairs, and she heard him shouting out the front door. In moments there was crashing and banging, the sounds of people doing battle with large objects. Ravna followed him downstairs, but Bili was firm in preventing her from helping out. In fact, the boxes were intimidating, not something that Tines or small humans could do much with. Bili had four helpers, some of the biggest older boys. They didn't have much to say to Ravna, though every once in a while, Gannon Jorkenrud cast a sneering smile in her direction.

There was so *much* furniture, crockery, curtains, clothing. None of it was really hers, not her stuff from *Oobii*. Aboard ship, she'd had a few souvenirs and everything else was ship recycles. What Bili's crew was bringing in was pack made, though much of it had benefited from *Oobii*'s technological contributions to the Domain.

The first floor rapidly filled with physical loot. Bili gave her a big grin, acknowledging the scale of the job. "Hei, I know it's crazy, but you need a lot of stuff to live well in primitive conditions. We'll get you helpers for the cooking and laundry."

Servants.

Ravna retreated to the top floor. She walked around the polished parquet floor, stopped at the window to examine the fittings. In the early years, many of the Children had had trouble with raw physicality, with systems so stupid that you had to understand them. She remembered how often the little ones were unnecessarily cold. In the early days, she'd had to remind the kids that they must consciously plan for their comfort. Down Here there was a harsher truth: even planning was not sufficient to avoid physical hardship.

Her new situation crippled her abilities with *Oobii*, yet it was far more luxurious than what most Children possessed. Nevil's maneuvering had not ended with his coup. Surely Bili understood all this, even as he smiled and indulged her.

There was noise on the stairs. Yngva's gang of movers had discovered the second floor. But it wasn't furniture that came up first. She turned to see an enormous roll of carpeting snaking up, one push-and-heave at a time. Yngva and Jorkenrud and the others finally got the thing across the center of the room. A pack carrying hammers came up the stairs after them. She recognized Screwfloss, sometime bartender and Flenser minion. And a carpet installer, too?

"Hei, Ravna, hei, hei," said Screwfloss, his heads bobbing at all the humans. He did some ostentatious measuring, then unrolled the carpet, four of him moving to the corners. One watched from the side. The pack edged the carpet into position. "Oops, not quite square." He tried again . . . and a third time, finally nailing it down with tacks lipped from one of his panniers. The margins were still not quite right, but no one said Screwfloss was an *expert* carpet installer. On the other hand, the carpet itself was magnificent. This wasn't one of those plain, durable items that came out of the weaving mills. She leaned down and felt the plush. This was an art weave, some classic Tinish scene. The multiple anamorphic images were a meaningless jumble to Ravna, but the piece looked extremely expensive, the work of thousands of hours of traditional Tinish labor.

Ravna stood and noticed that Bili seemed faintly impatient at all the adjustments.

"Heh! Looks great, doesn't it?" said Screwfloss; he was asking her, but two of him were slanting an impudent look at Bili.

"It's . . . beautiful," said Ravna.

"Good!" said Bili. "We want the Technical Advisor to be happy. Let's get the rest of the furniture up here."

"It looks like you've thought of everything, Bili, but—"

"Yes?" his smile became questioning.

"There's nothing . . . nothing to think with." That was how a Straumer would say it.

Bili nodded. "Oh yes, computation, data access, communication? We'll install the house telephone tomorrow, Ravna. But remember, this is all any of us have away from *Oobii*."

Gannon Jorkenrud made a little noise, and Ravna saw the smirk on his face. Bili's other guys were blank-faced. Bili Yngva was only one with a friendly smile pasted on his face. "Don't worry, Ravna, we're working on special access for you down in the New Meeting Place."

"There are things I really need to keep up with, Bili. If I'm to be Technical Advisor, I—"

Yngva raised his hands placatingly. "I know, I know! We really need your help. Working out the priorities of that is just about Nevil's most important job these days. He'll get back to you with the task list in just a few days. He's promised me." He glanced out the windows. It was late afternoon and the sun had already set. "We should finish up here, or you're going to be cold."

They were already trooping down the stairs. Only Screwfloss seemed to notice that Ravna was not following. She waved the pack to go ahead, and then it was gone, too. Down below, they were banging around again, but this sounded like plumbing. Were Bili and Gannon and the other boys really this handy? Or was the noise mainly Screwfloss?

She resisted the urge to go downstairs and check on them. Instead she walked across the room to the broad windows. The glass had seemed distortion free earlier, but now there were faint ripples . . . Oh. Warm air was already rising from the vents.

Ravna gazed out at the neighborhood. There were only a few other town houses visible in this direction, nothing to block the view. Beyond the darkening lands and black sea, the sky was now without color. She could see a handful of the brighter stars. Now that she was stuck on a single planet, the random position of a few bright stars told her of the seasons and the hours and . . . there, at the edge of a pair of stars settling toward the sea, she was looking at the most important place in all the heavens. It was a nondescript patch of sky, showing only a few faint stars on even the darkest, clearest nights.

Just thirty lightyears out were perhaps one hundred starships. It was the threat that had hung over her for ten years, informing every decision, forcing her to push and persuade and bully both Children and Tines to attempt the impossible: to prevail against the Blight.

Now? Those terrible decisions were no longer hers to make, and she felt the strangest feeling . . . of peace.

———

There was no word from Nevil the next day, or the next. A few of the Children visited her at her new house, but they didn't stay long. The older ones looked around at its glory and seemed to sense invisible walls.

The storms of the previous tenday had moved inland, blocking Johanna and Pilgrim's return. Their agrav was battened down hundreds kilometers to the east. Not all misfortune was Nevil's doing.

Ravna visited the *Out of Band II* every day. Bili Yngva had given her an interim access credential for the New Meeting Place. The cargo bay's one night of megalomaniac glory was past. Nevil had reverted the place to something like his original design. As Ravna had expected, the popularity of the primitive game stations had waned; what *Oobii* could create and display was pitifully weak compared to what the older Children remembered. Nowadays, the gamers were mainly packs and the youngest Children—and Timor. The boy was practically camped out by one of the stations, boring even the also-addicted Belle Ornrikak. Sometimes Timor didn't even notice Ravna, and when he did he was an unending firestorm of gaming esoterica. Ravna's only sympathizer was now distracted and ecstatically happy.

Other than Timor, the kids seemed reluctant to talk to her. Maybe when they saw her, they remembered only how she had seemed at that terrible meeting. So Ravna sat in the public area and puttered around with an interface, careful not to exceed the powers that came with Nevil's "interim access credential." That meant no sysadmin activity of course. The compute-and-search allowance was minimal, and some of the archives were not visible.

On her third visit, Wenda Larsndot came over and asked for help. "Needles is in love with the idea of mass production. So I've been trying to see what *Oobii* says. There's tonnes of stuff about numerical control tailoring, but I need something easy and low tech."

So Ravna gave her a tour of the hybrid planning tools that she'd built on top of the ship's archives. It was the sort of thing she'd pushed at the Children for years, even though it was awfully dull—at least by Straumer standards. There were millions of dead ends in such searches, and *Oobii* couldn't prune them all away. But solving *this* problem might be easy! In her mad race to head off the Blight, Ravna had chosen to skip over mechanical automation. . . . It turned out that most pretechnical civilizations invented mechanical readers for pattern-driven looms. So Wenda's real problem was simply to find one such that could easily fit the weaving equipment the Tines already had. Once Ravna had properly set up the Tinish constraints, it didn't take long. *Oobii* dredged up some insect race whose ancient history included a gadget for driving a near perfect match for a Tinish loom.

"Wow," said Wenda as she looked at the first-pass designs. "So now we can just hire a good artist, and turn out thousand-hour capes in less than a day!"

Ravna grinned back at her. "It still might not work. There are lots of small moving parts, and our weaving mills aren't exactly the same as this. *Oobii* is weak on doing final coordination." She waved at the design uncertainty flags that floated over the gears and cams. "You might have to ask Scrupilo to make a special purpose mill."

"Oh, we'll make this work." Wenda was already lost in consideration of the options and parts lists. Somehow it made her look twenty again.

Ravna glanced up and noticed that Edvi Verring and some still-younger kids were clustered about. Edvi gave her a nervous smile, "I was wondering, Ravna, we've been having some trouble with a game . . ."

––––––

It had been so long since she'd had time for this. And helping the Children with games was fun. These games didn't have the intransigence of reality. Ravna didn't need the good luck she'd had with Wenda. When something didn't work right, she could often just step back and tweak the game parameters. Sometimes, librarians—even with just an interim access credential—could have godlike powers.

"Ravna?" That was an adult voice, bringing her back from the depths of Edvi Verring's game craft.

She looked up and saw Bili Yngva standing beside her. *How long have I been playing around?* Wenda was still here, working on the weaving mill gadget.

"Sorry to bother you, Ravna, but—"

Then she noticed various mail flags. "Oops, I didn't notice."

"No problem. I just got word from Nevil. He'd like to chat with you, if you can drag yourself away from the important business here." He grinned at Wenda and the gamers.

About half of the New Meeting Place had been converted to offices. Yngva led her down tiny corridors. The construction was local timber and the lightweight plastic sheeting that *Oobii* could still extrude.

Ravna found herself lagging behind Bili. She could feel outrage thrusting up through her numbness. Sooner or later she and Nevil would have to talk, but she couldn't imagine how he could face her, what he could say. . . .

Bili looked back at where Ravna had slowed to a halt. "It's just a little further, Ravna."

. . . so why am I the one who can't face this meeting?

After a moment, Ravna nodded and followed along. Indeed, Nevil's office was just around the corner. It looked no different from the others except that the display function showed his name in businesslike Samnorsk script.

Inside, Nevil Storherte looked unchanged, as handsome and calm as ever. He was seated at a plain workplace, surrounded by plain gray walls. "Come in, come in," he said, waving Ravna to one of the chairs beyond his desk. He glanced at Bili. "This will be about ten minutes. Can you come back then?"

"Sure thing." Bili departed.

And for the first time since The Day, Nevil and Ravna were alone, face to face. Ravna folded her arms and gave Nevil a long stare. Words wouldn't quite come.

Nevil stared back mildly, and after a moment raised an eyebrow. "So you're looking for an explanation, an apology?"

"The truth, before all else." But she couldn't help the strangled way her words came out.

"Okay, the truth." Nevil looked away from her for a moment. "The truth is that you brought this on yourself, Ravna. In the early years, you did enormous good. You're still the most important human being in the world. That's why everyone let you run loose for so long, that and the fact that anyone who thinks about it knows how much we owe you. That's also what makes your . . . quirks . . . so tragic."

"You really don't believe in the Blight?"

Nevil shrugged irritably. "I believe that we're not in a position to know exactly what happened Up There. Our presence here is good evidence that a deadly accident happened at the High Lab. *Your* presence here, and what's visible in *Oobii*'s files—those are good evidence that your home worlds and probably mine have been destroyed. The silence across the sky is proof that some terrible catastrophe has been visited upon the Beyond. But your obsession with the 'Blight' goes beyond reasonable logic."

"What's left of their fleet is just thirty lightyears out, Nevil."

Storherte shook his head. "Thirty lightyears. Yes. Perhaps a hundred ships, moving at just a few kilometers per second on no coherent bearing and without ramscoop drives—all this by your own telling! Thousands of years from now, they may make planetfall, somewhere. When that eventually happens, whatever the facts behind all this uncertainty will be ancient history. Meantime—"

"That's all wishful thinking, Nevil. The—"

"No. I've heard all this from you before, Ravna. Over and over. It's your mantra, your excuse for hiding aboard this ship. The problem just got worse in the years since we older kids could take care of younger ones. You might still be in charge now, if you had not so totally lost touch with us."

Ravna stared for a moment, vaguely aware that her mouth was hanging open. "No one complained—"

"You never would have listened." He paused. "Understand me: I'm a moderate. We Children remember our parents, and we know they were not fools. The High Lab attracted the best minds of Straumli Realm. They would not have wakened a Great Evil. And yet, when we look at your ship's records, we see how you and Pham Nuwen brought disaster wherever you went. You admit Pham Nuwen was infested by some part of a Power. You call it Countermeasure and admit it destroyed civilizations for as far as our eyes can see. Some of us look at these facts and conclude that everything you say may be true—but with the values of good and evil reversed." He waved his hand dismissively. "I regard that position as extremism, as nutty as yours but not nearly as dangerous."

"Not . . . as . . . *dangerous?*"

"Ravna, you were running wild, diverting more and more resources into your obsession. You had to be stopped. So yes. I lied to you. And I told Woodcarver of *your* deceit. I set you up for a fall. But however brutal it seems to you, it was the gentlest way I could find to make the change. It removed you from authority, but it left you in a position to contribute." He was staring into her eyes, perhaps assessing, perhaps waiting for some response. When none came, he leaned forward and his voice was a little softer. "Ravna, we *need* you. You are beloved by all the younger ones. You were the only adult they had. On a coldly logical level, your importance is that you're the only surviving professional, and a librarian at that. Some of my friends are smart and cocky. All their lives they've lived with decent computation. They've solved lots of problems— but at the Top of the Beyond. Now they are beginning to realize their cluelessness. You are on a different level from all of them."

Nevil leaned back, watched her steadily for a moment. "Ravna, I don't care that you hate my guts, but I'm desperate for your cooperation. That's why I've tried to make your new quarters as comfortable as possible. That's why I've tried to minimize the humiliation you may feel. Even if you can't run the show anymore, I'm hoping you'll help. Our projects are mundane and practical, but they're essential for survival on this world."

Ravna gave a jerky nod. "And you expect this with the game-level access that Bili gave me today?"

Nevil gave her a smile. It was his first of the conversation, and perhaps more meaningful than all his friendliness of before the coup. "Sorry. That was all he has authority to pass out. I've discussed this with Woodcarver. She understands that you are best qualified to exploit what computational powers *Oobii* possesses. We'll get you an office like this so you won't have to waste time on frivolous distractions. We ask for two limitations: Your work should always leave other users with continuity of access. And second, Woodcarver—well frankly, me too—we don't want you taking control." He hesitated again. "You have some kind of bureaucratic authority over *Oobii*, right? Is that called 'system administration' on a machine this small?"

Ravna thought a moment. "Sysadmin is the usual term," she said. *And you have no idea what that means, do you, Nevil?* Once upon a time, Ravna had been equally ignorant. It was Pham Nuwen and the Skroderider Blueshell who had shown her what a very special, terrible thing it was to command a starship.

"Ah. Well, I want to thank you for staying within the access that Bili gave you this afternoon. It shows that Woodcarver's worst fears are groundless." He looked a little embarrassed, another first for this conversation. "Nevertheless, we ask that you transfer that authority now."

"To you."

"Yes. That would only make the facts fit the result of the general vote." When she didn't reply he said, "It's for the best, Ravna, and no more than what you accepted at the time of the meeting."

She thought back to the last minutes of that meeting, right before the vote. She remembered her rage, and even now felt it return. She had turned away from physical force then.

Ravna bowed her head. She would turn away from it now.

CHAPTER 13

The clear weather moved inland and a new storm front rolled onto the coast. So while the first big snow fell on Newcastle, Johanna and Pilgrim had a chance to lift off from their camp to the southeast. Ravna went to bed late that night, worrying that the two were making a big mistake. The wind across Starship Hill was rising. What if the two arrived and found a blizzard in progress? Much safer to wait things out on the ground, even if far away. Three years earlier, Pilgrim had been stuck in the wilds for five tendays while storms danced across takeoff and landing points with perfect synchronization. This time . . . well, she knew the two travelers had heard only bits and pieces of what had happened here. She prayed they wouldn't let their curiosity trump their good judgment.

The worry and the wind kept her awake for several hours. When she finally dozed off . . . she massively overslept. That had happened much too often since she'd moved to the town house. All her life she'd had convenient external re-minder services. Her body's natural system needed discipline that it had not yet learned.

In this case she was wakened by muffled pounding. She lay for a moment, trying to imagine what that could flag—then suddenly realized someone was banging on her front door. She skittered across the cold floor, out of her bed-room. Through the windows she had a glimpse of darkening overcast, snow piled deep on nearby homes, drowning the street below. The wind had died sometime during her sleep.

Ravna was halfway down the front stairs when the delicate lockbolt finally gave up its defense. The door crashed opened. Frigid air swept in around a figure in a heavy parka. "What damn cheap construction!" That was Johanna's voice, and as the figure advanced toward the stairs, it pulled back its hood. Yes, it was Johanna.

She advanced through the cloak room, pulling off her parka as she came. A pack of five entered the house behind her. Tines in the arctic winter had deep pelts, but even they wore heavy jackets in cold like this. Nevertheless, Ravna recognized Pilgrim. Two of him were inspecting the shattered lockbolt while two others quietly shut the door. The fifth was keeping an eye on Johanna.

The young woman threw her parka to the floor. "That *fucker!* That mother-less, shit-eating traitor! That—"

From there, Johanna's criticism became more pointed. There were words Ravna was a little surprised Johanna would know, though maybe in the Strau-mer dialect they were more mellow than Ravna thought.

At last there came a pause in the verbal hellstorm. "You're talking about Nevil, are you?"

Johanna glared at her for almost five seconds as she seemed to struggle for speech. Finally, she said, "In case you haven't guessed, the wedding is *off.*"

"Why don't we go upstairs and talk about it?"

They trekked up the wooden stairs, Ravna in the lead, Johanna thumping along behind her. Halfway, Ravna heard her muffled voice say something like, "Sorry about the dirty boots."

Pilgrim's voice came from further back: "We've talked to Nevil; I've had a hearts to hearts chat with Woodcarver."

Maybe I won't have to explain everything. Just the most embarrassing parts. "How long have you been back?"

"Five hours," said Pilgrim. "We took a navigational chance, and it paid off. A mere twelve hours hanging in the air and then the wind died to nothing and the snow stopped, and here we are!"

As they entered the second level, Ravna turned on the glow panels. Jo-hanna teetered at the edge of the carpet, then sagged down to sit with her back against the wall, her butt on the bare wood margin of the room. Pilgrim helped her take off her boots while he walked around the room, apparently admiring the carpet.

"We got only the most scattered fragments on our commset," he said. "We—"

"You got screwed, Ravna" said Johanna.

Ravna sighed. "I can't believe I was so naive."

Johanna shook her head. "You knew I trusted him enough to marry him."

Pilgrim's voice was comforting even if his words were not: "Nevil is a big surprise for all of us, a political genius. He accomplished so much with so little effort. And I truly think he—"

Jo interrupted him, "You should have been there, Ravna. He was so full of deeply felt straight talk. He would have lost some teeth if Yngva and Jerkwad hadn't been close by." She looked up at Ravna, and her face seemed to crumple. "I love, I *loved* him, Ravna! I can't believe Nevil is evil. I think he really b-believes he did the r-right thing." She leaned forward, sobbing.

———

Johanna had moved to the room's long sofa. Now she simply looked exhausted. Pilgrim's big, scarred one was sitting next to her, his head in her lap. The rest of Pilgrim was lying at the traditional viewing positions on the carpet. "I've got to find Jefri," Jo said. "Jef was so little when we left the High Lab. He was almost as talented as Jerkwad, but he didn't have any training. I never thought he even liked the place. How could he betray—"

"He's not the only Denier, Jo," said Ravna, remembering the angry voices denouncing her.

"Yeah. I never paid attention to the whiners. For that matter, since . . . since I've been on this world, Tines seem much better friends than humans." Her look got a little distant. "I thought Nevil was bringing me back from that." She glanced at Pilgrim. "You know, there's a more surprising idiot than any of us, and that's Woodcarver. I can see she'd be pissed when Nevil told her about your secret snooping on Flenser, but *Powers!*, why would she let Nevil lead her around like all the rest?"

A soft chuckle rose from Pilgrim. "Ah, dear Woodcarver. She wouldn't have been fooled if she weren't going through a change of life."

Jo was nodding. "I've been worried about her new puppy."

"Yes. Sht. Keeping Sht was a mistake. Not a big mistake. Woodcarver and her broodkenners are too experienced for that; normally this would only be an inconvenience. Now with little Sht onboard, our co-Queen is a bit more . . . vindictive than before." The four of Pilgrim on the carpet had been staring down into the weave of its design. Now they all looked up at Ravna. "I understand why you didn't tell Woodcarver about your spying on Flenser. But telling Nevil—"

"May be my biggest mistake of all?" said Ravna.

The pack nodded heads. "Nevil's revelation outraged Woodcarver far more than it would have pre-Sht. She rationalized this to me in some detail. She considers that she is using Nevil."

"I don't know," said Johanna. She idly petted the scarred one's head. "Back at the High Lab, Nevil was the most popular guy in school. I loved him even then—well, I had a crush on him. But he comes from a long line of leaders and politicians. His folks were the lab's directors, the best in Straumli Realm. Both naturally and by training, Nevil is a star."

"Yes, but my Woodcarver has had centuries to observe sneakiness and breed sneakiness into herself," said Pilgrim. A smile rippled. "Sharing puppies with her, I've inherited some of that myself." The four on the carpet hunkered down. For a moment an old-time human tune filled around the room, Pilgrim "humming" to himself. "Still, there's Sht's influence. Woodcarver honestly believes that Ravna has drifted into power madness."

Johanna straightened abruptly. "What?"

"Woodcarver studied the decorations in the New Meeting Place, and Ravna's words and dress."

"Which were all helpfully put together by Nevil, right?" Jo looked at Ravna, who nodded.

Pilgrim: "Oh, Woodcarver figured that out—but she says, even so, it was a valid reflection of Ravna's inclinations. She is really angry with you, Ravna. Sorry."

Ravna bowed her head. "Yeah . . . I've gotten too wrapped up in the Age of Princesses. Nevil didn't have to exaggerate much to make me look like a nutcase." *The Age of Princesses will never seem beautiful to me again.*

"Don't be that way, Ravna." Johanna eased the scarred one aside and came around the low table to hold her hand. "Nevil has outsmarted everybody." She sat on the carpet beside Ravna's chair, rested her head in their clasped hands. "Everybody. That's the biggest surprise, you know. So what if we Children have disagreements with you, or complain that you make mistakes? Most of the kids love you, Ravna."

"Yes, Nevil said something similar to me. He—"

"Okay then. I'll bet his biggest problem is keeping the Children from connecting that affection with their common sense." She paused for a long moment, staring at the floor.

"You finally noticed the carpet, eh?" said Pilgrim.

Johanna gave him a weak glare. "Yes." Her gaze swept along the windows, the carven knicknacks that Bili had set on the wall shelves. "This place is beautiful, Ravna. Nevil has set you up with swankier digs than Woodcarver's own inner rooms."

Pilgrim: "And I'll bet he wants Ravna to work in separate quarters, too."
Ravna nodded.

Johanna made a grumpy noise. "We already know he's a great manipulator." She came to her feet and walked to the windows. There was a break in the overcast way out at the horizon. Aurora light spilled through. After a moment she said. "You know what we need?"

"To finally get some sleep?" said Pilgrim, but Ravna noticed that his eyes were open and all watching Jo.

"True, but I'm thinking further ahead. If Nevil is a great politician, we just

have to be better. There must be whole sciences of sneaky. Ravna knows *Oobii*'s
archives. We're smart; we can learn." Johanna was looking at her expectantly,
and suddenly Ravna realized that the girl thought librarians must be experts at
everything.

"Johanna, I could set up a sneakiness research program, but—"

"Oh! You think Nevil knows enough about *Oobii* to track you on this?"

"Ah," said Ravna. "I didn't tell you what happened yesterday," They had
gotten sidetracked by the overwhelming unpleasantness that had come before.
"Nevil explained my new situation."

"Okay?" Suddenly Johanna looked wary.

Ravna described Nevil's "moderate" position, his plea for her help. "Then,
well, he said that since I had lost the vote and agreed to step down, it was only
right that I give him system administration authority over *Oobii*."

Pilgrim said, "Is that what it sounds like?"

"Ravna, you didn't!"

"I gave him the sysadmin authority, but—"

Johanna had covered her face with her hands. "So now he can see everything we do? He can block whatever archive access he wants? He can redocu-
ment records?"

"Not . . . exactly. I gave him what he literally asked for. I lucked out; if I'd
had to actively lie, I'm sure I would have botched it."

Johanna peeked from between her fingers. "So . . . what does sysadmin
mean?"

"Literally, bureaucratic control over the *Oobii*'s automation. The thing that
Nevil didn't understand is that *Oobii* is a *ship*. It must have a captain, and the
captain's command must exist independent of administration."

"Really? I don't think it was like that on Straumer vessels."

Ravna remembered back to the near-lethal conflict between Pham Nuwen
and the Skroderider Blueshell. "Maybe not, but it's the case for *Oobii*." *Straumli
Realm always cut corners*—but she didn't say that out loud. "The *Out of Band II*
has a n-partite memory system. Only a minority is accessible through sysadmin. If that deviates from the rest, then the person with Command Privilege
has a number of options."

Johanna had lowered her hands. A look of triumph was spreading across
her face. "And . . . *you* . . . have Command Privilege?"

Ravna nodded. "Pham set up a contingent transfer, just before he dropped
onto Starship Hill. It, it was one of the last things he did for me."

Pilgrim: "So you're like the *Goddess on the Bridge*!" The pack looked back
and forth at itself, embarrassed. "Sorry. That's one of your Sjandra adventure
novels."

Ravna remembered no such title, but that was no surprise. Most civilizations had more fiction than they did real history. In any case: "I'm deleting
such references from what Nevil and company can read."

"Command Privilege can do that?"

"Oh yes. The places he's likely to see, anyway. *Oobii* doesn't have the compute power to revise its entire archive. The point is, Nevil can go on about his business, messing and snooping—"

"But it's all in an invisible box!"

"Right. He shouldn't notice a thing, unless we have bad luck or we cause some external effect."

CHAPTER 14

A few days later, Ravna had her very own office aboard *Oobii* . . . and the opportunity to begin her research into sneakiness. *Oobii*'s archives were mostly about technology. Even so, "sneakiness" was far too broad a search concept. Normally in the Beyond, where interactions were almost always positive-sum, "sneakiness" was no more than knowing one's customer and driving a shrewd deal. It was exactly the peaceful pursuit of her old employers at the Vrinimi Organization. The winners got fabulously wealthy and the losers—well, they only got rich. At the other extreme, in the unhappiest corners of the Slow Zone, there were sometimes true negative-sum games. On those worlds, only a saint could believe in return business, and all advancement depended on diminishing others. Pham Nuwen's childhood had been in such a place—or so he had remembered.

Alas and thank goodness, neither extreme was appropriate here. The sneakiness Ravna was interested in was nonviolent maneuvering and politics, what had worked so well for Nevil. *Oobii*'s little social science archive covered hundreds of millions of years, in the Slow Zone and the Beyond, data from a million different races. The ship popped up a query classification template. She filled it out, leaving aside for now the pack nature of the Tines—group minds were so rare that it could easily skew the results. But the rest of the situation, including the presence of exiled spacer travelers, should get lots of matches. The present situation on Tines world was a marginally positive-sum game, teetering on the edge of a takeoff into enlightenment.

She glanced at her command window, which showed all the various snoopers that Nevil was running. Most of them were targeted on her, and all were clumsy, wasteful things. In any case, all they would see of Ravna was the agricultural research she had been assigned.

Then she fed her template into a syllabus generator, setting its priority very low. That was probably over-cautious, but if she pushed the system too hard, everything else would drag—one of those "external effects" she must be careful to avoid. So this dredging operation would take a while. She sat back for a minute or two, content to watch the process. Okay, *that* was not a good use of her time. She should be down in the New Meeting Place, talking to the Children, fighting fire with fire, innocently undermining Nevil's position.

Ravna waved away the displays and left her "private office." It was even bigger than Nevil's, but there was a large Keep Out sign splashed helpfully across the door. Of course, Nevil didn't have such a sign. On the other hand—as Pilgrim had pointed out—his office probably had a back entrance.

Jo and Pilgrim seemed to be enjoying every hour of this campaign. Ravna was not so naturally talented, but she was very happy that the two were now living at her town house. Thanks to Nevil's "generosity," there was more than enough room. Johanna had chortled at that irony.

Ravna walked out of the maze of office corridors and down the *ad hoc* wood stairs to the main floor, where Nevil had left the game stations. Nowadays, this area of the New Meeting Place was almost deserted. The remaining game addicts consisted of a few packs, and of course Timor and Belle. Strange. Timor wasn't at his usual station. She walked around the floor watching the games. Normally, when Timor wandered, it was to give long-winded advice to any gameplayer who did not shoo him away.

She turned, headed for the ramp to midlevel, where most of the programming stations were located. Those had gained popularity as the limitations of the games had become apparent. In earlier years, the kids had turned up their noses at Slow Zone programming. Now their vision of medical necessity had changed that. It made perfect sense for Children and Tines to gather and work with *Oobii* in a nearly civilized venue. Some of that was gaming, but most was research that forced them to deal with the available automation. *I should have created this place years ago.* But at the time, she had been too concerned with the colony's self-sufficiency and establishing the Children's Academy. She would have seen the New Meeting Place as frivolous.

There were plenty of human-sounding voices up ahead, including the polite insistence of Timor Ristling: "But I just want to ask you—"

"Not now, I'm trying to set up the day's projects." That sounded like Øvin Verring.

The top of the ramp was dark, just another place where the makeshift construction interfered with Nevil's lighting. Ravna hesitated there, watching the scene. Øvin was facing five or six of the oldest kids, the most intense of the medical researcher wannabes, essentially a group Nevil had whipped up for his coup.

Øvin was talking to the group even as he fiddled with the interface of the big display, which at the moment was just showing idle status. "What I wanted to show you all was the tutorial I found yesterday. We not only have to—"

"Øvin, I just want to ask you if—" interrupted Timor.

Øvin waved the boy away. "Not now, Timor." He continued to work at the interface. He was speaking again to the group: "*Oobii*'s automation is pitiful, but the tutorial I found claims to show how we can solve simple—"

Timor again said, "Øvin, I was wondering, could I—"

That got Timor a moment of Øvin's full attention. He glared at the boy and Ravna prepared to rush in. She didn't think Øvin Verring had ever been one of the kids who had been mean to Timor—but she was damned if he was going to start now.

"Look Timor! Give me a minute, huh? I just want to get this display to show folks the tutorial. Then you can ask me whatever you want."

Timor glanced at the display pedestal, as if noticing it for the first time. "Oh that. You need to—" He reached out, his fingers flicking across the maintenance interface, below where Øvin had been working. "It's just partly broken," he said, as if that was an explanation.

Øvin Verring stepped back as the expanding display image formed into what Ravna recognized as a programmer primer environment. Huh, Øvin had found one she hadn't seen, "Algorithms for Bottom Feeders." His audience was already sucking in notes and playing with the first lesson, "Constrained Search."

Øvin stared at it for second. "Oh! Yes, that's what—" he glanced down at Timor. "Okay then. What did you want to ask me?"

"Is it okay if I use that workstation? I mean, just for today." The boy waved across the room to the station that Belle Ornrikak was already lolling around, staking out the territory for Timor. It was the only station without an obvious user in residence.

Verring hesitated. "Um, sure. Go ahead."

Timor gave a whoop and hustled across the room to Belle.

Ravna let out her breath and strolled in as if she had just come up the ramp.

"Oh, hei, Ravna." Øvin came around his audience—which was now thoroughly distracted by the tutorial—and walked over to her. He made a small gesture in the direction of Timor and Belle. "Now that I seem to have lost my workstation . . . could we talk for a minute?"

"Sure."

Since Ravna's fall, Øvin had actually been friendly. Lately, most of the medical wannabes had seemed friendlier.

"As—as a kind of starter project, we want to refurbish more of the cold-sleep containers. But the in-casket manuals are useless, and so far we can't get *Oobii* to refine us a wish list—even though coldsleep is an ancient, simple technology."

Ah. This sounded like something from her speech—the part she hadn't gotten to say. So Nevil had put him up to this? She looked over at Øvin's team, all working hard to understand the tutorial.

Okay. "You're right about the manuals, Øvin. Down Here, they can't do repairs. On the other hand, *Oobii* does have an enormous amount of information about coldsleep implementations. If you could devise a search list that uses what you see in the casket manuals and properly feed that to *Oobii*. . . ."

"You'd really help? Even after . . . ?"

Ravna nodded. "One important decision you have to make is what level of medical risk you will tolerate." Her gaze drifted almost involuntarily to where Timor sat on the other side of the room.

"Oh." Then Øvin seemed to follow her gaze. "Oh! . . . I remember risk was one of the reasons you wanted to postpone this kind of work." He watched Timor Ristling for a few moments. Timor had set his workstation display to

large, perhaps so it would be easier for Belle to follow what he was doing. That
was wasted effort, since the foursome had curled up on the floor around his
chair, all eyes closed. At the moment, Timor was oblivious to this. He pounded
away enthusiastically. This was no ordinary game. It looked . . . much simpler.
Ravna could see simple dotmarkers making rows across a plane. Below that
was what looked like a synthetic machine language, three-letter abbreviations
and numerical operands.

"It looks like he's written a binary counter," Øvin said softly. "That's so sad.
The human mind should not be wasted on tasks so trivial." Øvin glanced back
at Ravna and seemed to think better of making a further comment.

She smiled. "You feel sorry for me, too, hei Øvin?"

"Actually, I was feeling sorry for *me* and . . ." he waved at his friends struggling away at the bottom feeder tutorial. "It's such a waste."

———

Even without the daylight, the northern winter still had its time markers. There
was bright twilight in the hours near noon. On clear nights, away from the twilight,
the aurora swept from horizon to horizon, shifting minute by minute. The moon
bobbed along the horizon in its tenday cycle. Winter storms came every third
or fourth day, some lasting hours, some continuing on with no letup through to
the next storm front. Many buildings were reduced to bizarre humps beneath the
snow, the smoothness broken only by streets that absolutely must be kept clear.

The lowest parts of *Oobii* were lapped by the snow. The rest, the arching
drive fronds, the curves of the hull—all that glittered green in whatever light
there was. The area around the main entrance was tramped down by the constant traffic.

Twice a tenday, Nevil held his public meetings in the New Meeting Place,
and every day the Children of Øvin's team and others were working in the ship,
honestly trying to master its automation. One group managed to revive the
freight device that had carried the Lander. Nevil had a big party after that—
and Ravna had to admit that the orbiter would improve things. It was close to
being a dead hulk, but still had enough life in it to act as a remote sensor and
radio relay.

The Executive Council no longer met, its members now keeping to their
separate factions. Scrupilo's Cold Valley lab had not been directly affected by
Nevil's coup, though that was mainly because the necessary simulations had
already been done and the experimental equipment was in place. Scrupilo was
clearly nervous about the future, but he continued to play along with Nevil and
Woodcarver, and radio relay through the orbiter had made the Cold Valley
setup much more convenient.

And tenday by tenday, Ravna and Johanna and Pilgrim pursued their little
conspiracy from the second floor of their town house.

"It's just a matter of time," said Johanna. "Nevil is losing support every day.
That's what Ravna's programs say. And that's what *I* see when I talk to Scrupilo
and Benky and the Larsndots." She looked around at Pilgrim, seemed to detect
insufficiently enthusiastic agreement. "So what's your problem?"

"Heh, someone has to balance your mood swings." Pilgrim was perched at various viewpoints of Ravna's grand carpet. Pilgrim loved that carpet. He said it was a Long Lakes masterpiece. Just now, three of his heads were resting on the plush, staring across its interleaved landscapes. "I agree with Ravna's projections, yes. I'm even more pleased that Ravna's able to counterspy on Nevil."

Ravna grinned. "Yes! Abusing Command Privilege is much more fun than I ever imagined."

"I'm also pleased with what an excellent politician one of my friends has turned out to be—not you, Johanna, you're still the Mad Bad Girl."

Johanna frowned. "We're gonna teach that bas—that fellow Nevil a proper lesson in, um, civic leadership. See? I can be suave."

Ravna said, "You can't mean that *I'm* the excellent politician! I haven't been able to do any of the clever maneuvers in *Oobii*'s guide. I'd trip on my tongue if I tried, and besides, Øvin Verring and the others are doing their best. I don't want to fool them."

Pilgrim nodded from all around the carpet. "Yes. And they know that. Since Nevil's coup, you've done your best for them, more than anything Nevil has done."

"They know it, too!" said Johanna.

Nevil had assigned some of the oldest kids to help with the research. These were his special friends, mostly top students at the High Lab. The effort had lasted scarcely a tenday. Nevil's friends had no concept of *Oobii*'s limitations. Gannon Jorkenrud had spent less than a day trying to "negotiate" with *Oobii*— that was the word Gannon himself used. He had almost punched Timor when the boy tried to give him advice about access methods. In the end, Gannon had departed in a towering rage.

Pilgrim was grinning. "You haven't played the little games, but you are playing the big one. The Children know you're their friend. More and more, they realize that your planning methods can *work*, but the shortcuts they've undertaken will *not*."

"Okay, then," said Johanna. "If you agree everything is going so well, what does worry you?"

"A couple of things. My dear Woodcarver has rejected me. No more hanky-panky." Some of the cheeriness had gone out of his voice.

"I'm sorry, Pilgrim," said Ravna, though even after ten years she wasn't quite clear about Interpack romance—there were so many *different* things it could be.

Pilgrim gave a little shrug. "Nothing lasts forever; we made good puppies for each other. But now—well, that little Sht is something else. Woodcarver is more suspicious and less forgiving than ever. If you really love another pack, if you have members from the other, sometimes secrets can leak across when you get intimate. It's hardly ever more than mood and attitude, but for now . . . well, there is only talk going on between us." His heads angled around toward Johanna. "But at least we *are* still talking."

Jo bowed her head, some of her aggressive optimism evaporating. "Yeah. I still haven't been able to pin down my little brother." Jefri and Amdi were at Smeltertop, about sixty kilometers to the north. That was the base camp for the Cold Valley lab, and also the lab's source of glass templates and high purity carbon. "They have a radio at Smeltertop, but it's very public." She looked at Ravna. "I'll bet he'll stay up there the whole winter; my guess is he's terribly, terribly ashamed."

Ravna gave a nod. Her sharpest, most painful memory of Nevil's coup was the moment when Jefri stood and denounced her. She looked around at Pilgrim, searching for something less uncomfortable to discuss: "What's the other thing bothering you?"

"Oh yes. That's the prospect of our inevitable success. You've focused *Oobii*'s political science research too purely. Politics is good; when it works properly, disagreements get solved without people beating each other up. But when a regime knows its days are numbered, there's always the chance it may use its position to change the rules and make the debate it is losing irrelevant."

Jo's chin came up with a little start. "You mean violence? Between the Children? We kids grew up together, Pilgrim. Nevil is a sneaky rat bastard, but I think he's doing what he thinks is right. At the bottom of it all, Nevil is not evil."

———

A tenday passed. There was another sea storm, followed by days when the moon skittered along beneath the aurora.

Ravna spent more than fifteen hours a day in the New Meeting Place and her little office. The various programming teams were improving, but it was the younger Children who did best with *Oobii*. Timor Ristling was the star. He could reach the depths of *Oobii*'s automation; he claimed that he could program without user development tools, though Ravna doubted that. Again and again it was Timor who patched together little fixes for the Children, or explained things in ways that made sense to them.

More Children came and talked to Ravna, some to apologize, some to give a friendly word. Some wanted her okay to demand another election.

Besides working with the kids, she had other . . . projects. There was her agriculture assignment; that ran in the space Nevil could see. *Oobii*'s genetic modification capability was extremely simple-minded, but it had been one of the ship's greatest success stories. The modified fodder crops brought in more tech rent than the rest of *Oobii*'s services combined. Tines of Woodcarver's Domain had prospered as hundreds of small farms—scarcely more than private game reserves—had merged into large ranches. Newcastle town itself could never have grown as it had without the livestock herds that were now possible.

But Nevil wanted a more direct payoff, some new and tasty food for humans. That was tricky, since *Oobii* didn't have the computational power to avoid ecological disasters with modified plants that were fully human-compatible. In the end, Ravna made a minor tweak in natural hardicore grass—well within natural selection bounds—and then enabled another of the epigenetic triggers that most humans had carried since their earliest stargoing civilizations. The Children who used the trigger would be able to eat and enjoy the new hardicore grass. The combination mod should be safe for both humans and Tines World, though Ravna wouldn't have done it she had still been in charge: every new human compatibility carried a small risk of making the user more susceptible to local diseases.

Eventually, her project was complete except for minor window-dressing. So now, when she was alone in her office, she had plenty of time to review her spy programs. These were not the high-tech magic she had used on Flenser—but at least they worked. Pham Nuwen was the sneakiest good person she had ever known, and a Slow Zone programmer to boot. During his most paranoid time aboard *Oobii*, Pham had set up an elaborate system of booby traps and internal security. That had contributed to the hellish atmosphere of that terrible time; undoing the traps had cured some of *Oobii*'s worst glitches. But now she found that the security programs gave her a kind of protection that she could have never managed by herself. Pham's last gift, unrecognized till now.

So Ravna could check directly on Pilgrim's fear of Nevilish villainy. Using Command Privilege and Pham's programs, she could see inside every one of Nevil's *Oobii* operations, could read every mail and every conversation. She could even see much of what was happening in the orbiter.

Yes, Nevil and Bili and their inner circle were getting desperate. They had stepped up their snooping, and even planted supporters in the groups who were going to demand new elections. But there was no talk of violence, just spin and nasty tricks. Both *Oobii*'s guide and Pilgrim were recommending that Ravna begin to talk compromise with Nevil's people, something mellow enough that no one would regard the outcome of the elections as unendurable disgrace.

It all kept Ravna shipside more and more, with her catching little naps and working all the way through till twilight of the next day. Up north, Scrupilo was ready to fabricate his adders! Unfortunately, that meant he needed new results from *Oobii*.

Ravna juggled that problem all through one night, hoping that the kids' programs would give the system some slack. She could have used her command privileges to invisibly override the Children's priority. But that might be noticed . . . and in any case, it would've felt like a betrayal. In the end, she let the Children's priority stand. Finally, she straggled out of the ship via the private corridors behind the cargo bay, too tired to talk to anyone in the New Meeting Place.

Outside, the brightest of the midday twilight had faded. To Tinish eyes, this might qualify as full night. To human vision, the landscape was gray on gray, lighter sweeps of the recent snowfall piled up around the arching spines of her starship, falling away to the darker grays of steep, naked rock, thence to snows that covered the sea ice far below.

Ravna trudged uphill toward Newcastle town. It was just beginning to snow, per *Oobii*'s predictions. But this was a soft, windless fall. It would be a big problem by the time it ended, but for now it just brought a nearly inaudible sighing to the air. She lit her handlamp and continued on. Earlier snows had narrowed the way, but there were only a few humans and fewer packs abroad.

She knew that until humans arrived, the winters in the Domain had brought life nearly to a halt. Even in recent years, with indoor light and heat, most businesses slowed in the dark and cold. But up ahead, in the heart of town, the Academy classes would be in session. Almost all the youngest Children, both first and second generation, would be there. *They* were the least affected by winter depression. The youngest humans had so much energy that if you gave them light and food and warmth, they got along fine. Before the New Meeting Place, the Academy had been the center of social life in winter. There would still be dozens of packs up there, dazzled by the warmth and the energy. She wondered if Nevil realized that the Academy still gave Ravna leverage.

Her lamp light reflected off sheets of snowflakes coming down ever more densely around her. She had reached the outskirts of Newcastle town. Ten years ago, this had been where she first set foot on Tines World. There had been no town here, and the castle was still being built. This ground had been a battlefield. Now it was a medieval city. No, not medieval. The buildings were stone and wood and wattle, but they had pipes climbing their walls, and hot water towers sticking high above the rooftops. No one threw garbage out the windows overlooking this street, and even at the height of summer, there was no sewage floating down the gutters. In building Newcastle town, Scrupilo had used *Oobii*'s design archives to plan his understreet sewer pipes—and *Oobii*'s beam gun to keep water flowing year-round. Such tiny changes had created a place that might be safer and friendlier than any other in the world.

. . . And just now, here on the Queen's Road, she was close to being lost! She could see only a meter or two, and her stupid handlamp was perhaps worse than useless. The new snow had already covered all but the deeper wheel tracks—and even her own footprints. Looking up, Ravna could see a blurry bluish glow: probably a light in a high window. Huh. In a rainstorm, even a blinding drencher in the middle of the night, she could have walked over to the nearest building and proceeded along with one hand on the wall, recognizing locations as she went. Here, this afternoon, the snow shoveled up from previous storms blocked her from touching anything familiar.

She proceeded, assuming that the main axis of the street was simply where it was easiest to walk. The occasional window lamps were her stars. There ought to be a fountain square every hundred meters or so.

"*Sssssss.*" The sound was barely louder than the sound of the falling snow, and matched its timbre precisely. Either her ears were playing tricks on her, or a pack was quietly trying to attract her attention. She drifted away from her guess about the road's center, toward the sound. There was a gap in the snow pile, a notch that would mark an alley or side street. She pointed her lamp onto the space.

The strange hissing stopped. At the center of her lamplight she saw a pack hunkered down in the snow. The creature gave her a little wave. "Screwfloss here." The voice was a whisper, and she suspected it was focused on her head alone, inaudible anywhere else. "I wonder if we might have a brief chat?"

Ravna stepped forward and took a good look at the pack. Yes, this was

Screwfloss; she recognized two of him by the white blazes running from muzzle to crown. "What do you want?" she said.

Screwfloss was backing away from her, angling his heads for her to follow. "Not so loud," he said. "One of Bili Yngva's boys is about, um"—his heads bobbed a measuring gesture—"about thirty meters behind you. I'd just as soon he doesn't know you took a detour." He was already sweeping snow over her tracks.

Oh! She hadn't realized anyone was following her; damn, the new Ravna should have assumed that was case. She brought her light down to a dim point, just enough to keep her footing and see the nearest of Screwfloss. The pack led her down the alley and around two turns. It moved all together with itself. Ravna knew that the snow damped mindsounds down to just a couple of meters; the pack would probably lose its mind if it didn't bunch up. Looking up, she saw no more bluish lights. This must be one of the windowless, single-pack-wide streets. They were ubiquitous down on Hidden Island; the new town had some, too.

"Okay," said Screwfloss. "This should be private enough. The human will just follow the main road. He could get to the castle before he ever figures out he lost you." The pack gave a crafty chuckle; this critter watched too much human drama. "It's just a little further, My boss is waiting to talk to you."

Ask him straight out: "Flenser, right?"

"That's supposed to be a secret." He sounded insulted.

A proper caution was finally catching up with her—now that she was deep into the windowless alley. She had decided *Oobii*'s later surveillance of Flenser was essentially noise—but this was much more of a test of her theories than was sensible. She trudged along after Screwfloss, but now she was watching for turnoffs. The snow was deep-piled and untrodden. In such fluffiness, maybe she could outrun him. Finally Screwfloss hesitated. "The Boss is a few meters on, my lady." In her dimmed lamp light she had the impression of his heads bowing her graciously forward.

There was no help for it, so: "Thank you, Screwfloss." She gave his nearest head a patronizing pat and strolled forward.

Shadows and flickering sheets of falling snow. So how could Flenser get to the top of Starship Hill unnoticed? This wasn't Hidden Island, with its old maze of secret passages.

She brightened her lamp and swept it quickly around her. She saw snow up to shoulder height and windowless, half-timbered walls above that. This was not a cul-de-sac. It was more like a T-intersection—and another pack sat in a clump beside one of the exits. It was a fivesome. One of the members was perched in a wheelbarrow.

Ravna walked up to the pack, and gave a shallow bow. "Flenser-Tyrathect," she said, using the full name. *A feeble attempt to remind you of your better three-fifths.*

As usual, the pack sounded sly and coy: "And greetings to you, Ravna Bergsndot. I had hoped for a private conversation, and now the elements have cooperated to make it even more so."

Ravna tried to sound nonchalant: "You can get the ship's weather predictions just like everyone else."

"Um, yes. Still, I didn't want to postpone this meeting much longer. Will you walk with me?" Snouts gestured toward the path behind him. "This alley intersects the Queen's Road a bit further on. With any luck, Nevil's boy spy will never even guess you strayed."

"Lead on, then."

Flenser came to his feet, and struggled to turn the wheelbarrow around. Ravna reached out to help. "No, no, I'm quite good at this." Flenser's voice might have been frosty; in any case, it lacked some of its slithery quality. Most of the pack was healthy, but navigating the wheelbarrow that held his maimed member—that raised in Ravna's imagination the vision of an elderly medieval human, hobbling through his last years. Many broodkenners would have advised the discarding of such a weakened member.

Then the pack was underway, a lurching progress, but still as fast as a slowly walking human. Somehow this cripple had popped up all undetected in the middle of a blizzard in the heart of Woodcarver's most secure city. Ravna couldn't resist: "How *did* you manage this, Flenser? I thought you were down on Hidden Island—"

She heard the characteristic sly laugh. "And I was, all tidily bundled up in the Old Castle, with Woodcarver's police watching the entrances three packs deep, and her secret cameras watching my 'innermost' haunts. Yes, I know about those cameras. Ha ha. And I know *Woodcarver* knows. But she can't see me when I'm in other rooms or down in the catacombs. I have ways out of my castle, and I still have a few truly loyal retainers. With the Inner Channel frozen, it was easy to sneak me across to the mainland."

Ravna knew that Flenser had used that trick in the past, to visit Steel's remnant on the mainland. She hadn't told Woodcarver, partly because the visits seemed innocent, and partly because it would have revealed Ravna's "magical" surveillance system. "So sneaking over the ice got you to the mainland. That's still six hundred meters down from where we're standing now. How did you get yourself up here all unseen?"

"I would have been noticed on the funicular, that's for sure." He gave her a sly look. "Who knows, Ravna? I'm a master of disguise; perhaps I came up separately." He let her chew on that for a moment. "But I'll let you in on the secret: call it evidence of my good faith." *Or evidence of the well-known vanity of all Woodcarver's creations.* "You see, while you and Woodcarver and Scrupilo were congratulating yourselves about Newcastle town's water and sewage system, *I* was more interested in the fault map that *Oobii* devised. Using that map, it was an easy matter—well, years of labor, actually, since doing it under Woodcarver's snouts was a nightmare—to dig a stairway. It's a narrow thing, almost as narrow as my member tunnels of old. You remember those?"

"Yes," Ravna said shortly. Amdi and nine-year-old Jefri had come close to being burned alive in something similar—though that had been on Steel's orders. "You couldn't get the wheelbarrow through one of those tunnels."

"True. On the stairs, I use a special sling for my White Tips"—the maimed one—"but even so, the climb is excruciating. Isn't that so, Screwfloss?"

"Yeah, Boss." The voice came from immediately behind her. She flinched and turned: Screwfloss was practically treading on her heels—which put him barely two meters behind Flenser. That was amazingly close for packs. Okay, the snowfall attenuated mindsounds considerably—but perhaps Screwfloss was one of the old White Jackets, a Flenser lord. Those had been trained to give up hunks of identity when their master demanded it.

Screwfloss continued. "I had to drag White Tips up 151 stairsteps. It will be worse going back down. We won't get home till after tomorrow noon twilight."

She turned back to Flenser and tried for nonchalance. "Okay, you've shared a real secret with me. What do you want?"

"Simply to help, my lady. It's as I've always told you and your co-Queen, from the very first day that you and she met the New Me."

"But you're not sharing this with Woodcarver?"

"Alas, she is so untrusting!" He paused, struggling to roll the little wheelbarrow through a shallow snow drift. "And now I fear we are dealing with a new Woodcarver. No, not something evil, but maybe something worse. Something *foolish.*" He layered a regretful chuckle over his words.

"Foolish? I'm sure Woodcarver knows that Nevil is trying to manipulate her."

"Of course," said Flenser. "And she thinks she is in control of the situation. She's dead wrong and—well, I'm here to rescue you both. I'm cleverer than Woodcarver ever was. And you—"

"I'm the utter fool who didn't see even the most obvious parts of all this conspiracy."

Flenser's wheelbarrow came to a halt. All of his members were staring up at her, and his voice was suddenly somber and uncoy. "No, Ravna. You're not a fool. You're an innocent, too pure of heart to live on this real world. Outside of damaged packs and saints, I've never seen that among my people. Tell me. Is this a feature of star-born culture? Are there places where such minds as yours can survive?"

I'm doing my best to change! Aloud she said, "You packs have your innocents. What about Tyrathect?"

"Heh. But she didn't survive as a mind, did she?" Flenser shrugged, looking back and forth at himself. "Tyrathect graduated to being an attitude, the bane of my otherwise happy life." He pointed a snout at his maimed member. That creature's rear was hidden in blankets, but its eyes were large and dark, and right now it was staring at Ravna. "If White Tips dies before the rest of me, things will suddenly become very interesting for the Domain." He gave a theatrical sigh. "In the meantime, I would find it quite amusing to be your special secret advisor. Please, I'm at your disposal."

They walked some paces in silence. *Powers!* There were consequences, good and bad, stretching in all directions. What if Woodcarver thought Ravna and Flenser were conspiring against her? What if Flenser was using Ravna just as Nevil had? There was that little threat analysis program she'd found the other day; it could probably list a hundred more possibilities. *I have to talk to Pilgrim and Jo.* Meantime, here and now, what was she going to say?

The wily pack just let her stew. . . .

"Okay, Flenser. Your advice would be welcome. Not that I feel any obligation in receiving it."

"Oh, of course, of course. And this first meeting was mainly to establish our trusting relationship. I have one major insight and few minor facts for you. You see, Nevil has made such a mess of you."

"That's an insight?"

"Even now you don't truly know. And Woodcarver, my overconfident parent, is equally ignorant. She thinks Nevil is just a simple-minded dilettante."

"You think he's more."

"In himself? Certainly not. But what you're both missing is that Nevil is the tool of persons much more clever than he is."

"Huh? I know the Children, and there's no one else in Nevil's league."

"I agree. Nevil's senior partners are Tines—and not in the Domain at all."

Flenser rolled on, leaving Ravna to stand for a moment in the falling snow. "Impossible!" she said, then trotted to catch up. "Most of the older Children don't have close contacts with packs. Nevil Storherte certainly doesn't." Nevil treated packs cordially enough, but she suspected he was as much a racist as all extreme Straumers, hell-bent on achieving their special form of Transcendence.

Flenser shrugged. "I didn't say they were his friends. They use him and he thinks he uses them. The combination is dangerous, especially if you and Woodcarver don't know about it."

Ravna slowed again, boggled by the possibilities—but there were things about the claim that didn't make sense.

Flenser wasn't slowing. He said something in Interpack. She couldn't pick apart the chords, except to understand that it was an interrogative. A second later there was a reply from ahead of them. "Ah," said Flenser, talking to her again. "I fear we'll have to cut this short. We're almost to the exit of this convenient alleyway—and you should be back on the road ahead of Nevil's spy. I'll get all the details to you soon." One of him came back to her and grasped her mitten in its jaws, drawing her forward.

"But, but . . ." All the minutes he had spent on build up and now he had no time for the details! That was Flenser for you! She dug in her heels. "Wait!" her whisper was almost a hiss. "This doesn't make any sense. An international Tinish conspiracy? Who is involved? And how could you know the details?"

Flenser didn't relax his hold on her mitten, but his voice came from all around her. "How do you think, my dear? The conspirators think I'm on their side." Two more of him came back and gently pushed her out onto the Queen's Road.

"Now, shoo." His last words faded into the sound of the falling snow.

CHAPTER 15

Johanna and Pilgrim both agreed that Flenser's news should be passed on to Woodcarver immediately. Pilgrim reported back the next evening: "I told her the claims Flenser made, leaving out the details of just where and how the meeting happened."

"Did she believe you?" asked Ravna.

"What is she going to do to Flenser?" asked Johanna.

Pilgrim gave a little laugh. "I don't think Flenser has any more to fear than before. At least, the Woodcarver of the moment is mellow. She told me she had always figured that Flenser was conspiring with Vendacious and/or Tycoon, and she's not surprised that they're doing their best to manipulate Nevil. She asked me to congratulate you, Ravna."

"For what?"

"'Tell that silly Ravna she's a step closer to understanding what a mischievous threat Flenser is.'" Pilgrim was suddenly speaking with Woodcarver's voice; it was more a playback than an imitation.

Ravna realized her mouth was hanging open. "So why would Flenser come to me with this story, now?"

Pilgrim shrugged. "Woodcarver thinks it's just Old Flenser sadism; after all, he didn't provide you with any details. Personally, I don't think Flenser-Tyrathect is truly sadistic. He just *wishes* he was."

Johanna waved away his point. "But if this is more than Flenser games, if Vendacious *is* playing with Nevil . . ."

The comment seemed to bring Pilgrim up short. He was quiet for a moment and then his voice was serious. "Okay. You're right. We need to squeeze some of those details out of Flenser."

Johanna's look was haunted. "We know Nevil is a self-convinced son of a bitch. But Vendacious is a monster. A soft little politician like Nevil wouldn't stand a chance with him. Maybe . . . maybe we should warn Nevil. There are games that are too deadly to play."

CHAPTER 16

"So what does this word 'crone' mean?" Belle pointed a snout at the page in Timor's storybook, *Fairy Tales of Old Nyjora*.

"Um, I don't know," Timor replied. His brow furrowed the way it did when he was puzzled. "We can look it up the next time we're over at *Oobii*." When she had first known this Child, such a question would have provoked a panic attack. Timor's eyes would get wide at the shock of realizing there was a question for which he didn't instantly have an answer. Such was the best evidence Belle had that these human creatures had once been something like all-knowing.

Nowadays, when confronted with a question, Timor would ask someone else or go to the public place on *Oobii* or devise the answer from materials at hand. Right now, the boy was paging back and forth through the storybook, his nimble human fingers flipping the pages. "Okay!" he said. "Here on page thirteen, the wise archeologist is talking about the lady who was called a 'crone' on page forty. He says she's a 'beldame.'"

"Belle means beautiful," said Belle. It was her taken name, one of the earliest any pack had chosen in the human language. That had been a bold move, even if it was right after she was kicked out of Woodcarver's cabinet, when her former name, "Wise-Royal-Advisor," became a mockery.

Timor squinched his mouth in a smile. "I know. Hei, and I remember from the story of the 'Princess and the Swamp Lilies'—'dame' is just a word for lady. So 'beldame' must mean 'beautiful lady.'"

"Hmm." Maybe she could become "Beldame" or "Beldame Crone." Those had possibilities for chords and trills. She played with the possibilities even as Timor returned to reading the story aloud. There was a time when Belle had really concentrated on learning from books such as these, the Two Queens' mass-printing project. Such books would surely give insights into Ravna Bergsndot's clever plans. That was before Ravna had been deposed.

And the stories in this particular book? If you discounted the ugly tropical background, and the necessary weirdness of humanity, they were very much like the folktales of Tinish realms. In her speeches, Ravna had talked about Nyjora again and again, claiming it was a model for what she was trying to do here. That had snared Belle's early interest in stories of Nyjora. But even though Timor liked this latest book, it had turned out to be frankly fictional. From eavesdropping on the older Children, Belle had gradually come to realize how stupid Ravna Bergsndot was. The history of Nyjora meant something deep to *her*, but to the Children it was as much a myth as this little book. If anybody had asked Belle (the Crone Belle Dame, that sounded even better), she could have told them that Ravna Bergsndot was headed for a fall. Which now had come.

One big difference between Ravna and Belle: Ravna still lived in what was nearly a palace. Belle had gradually figured out the politics behind that. There would come a time when Nevil Storherte could not continue to ignore Belle and her Timor—

"I'm sorry what crone turns out to mean," said Timor, closing the book and reaching around to hug her nearest shoulders. "Do you want to read another story tonight?"

Usually Belle paid more attention to what this Child was saying. But all any of her remembered was how Timor had looked around at her a few minutes ago, when she was deep into her little fugue. Timor could rattle on for hours about this and that even when he wasn't reading aloud. It wasn't natural—or at least it wasn't Tinish—how many different things he could talk about, all without making the tiniest mindsound. For a moment, she considered confessing her inattention. He seemed to guess at it occasionally. But no, she could sneak back later, when he was asleep, and find out what "crone" was all about. Maybe she should read the whole book tonight and be done with it. But then the next few evenings would be *really* boring.

Outside something big was banging along the street. It sounded like a six-kherhog team, pulling multiple wagons. It had to be something big to be heard through the noise-quilting that was built into the walls. There were high-pitched screeches and pings, as if the wagon wheels were throwing up pebbles against the walls of the houses. Their little house was at the south edge of town, right on Haulage Way. When it had first been built, Belle had thought Wood-carver had fallen into imperial madness: the way was so wide and so perfectly graded. Now, after she'd seen the freight that streamed along it, bound for Cliff-side harbor, Belle acknowledged (to herself) quite a different opinion.

She was half-minded to go outside and scream at the drovers. Instead she fell back on something more practical. "Timor, don't you think it's unfair that we live in this hovel?" Never mind that it had brightness and warmth at the click of a claw, even in the northern winter. Never mind that it was more comfortable than anything that royalty owned before the Sky Children came. It was the *comparison* with what some others had that made it poverty.

Timor stroked her shoulders, trying to comfort her. It was strange that he had actually been with her long enough that it really did comfort. She did her best to shrug away the thought. *He* should despise their situation even more than she did. It was Belle's great good fortune that she had her own personal human; it was her bad fortune that Timor Ristling was the most accepting and even-tempered and *reasonable* creature she had ever met:

"We could live in the general dorms, Belle, with the other kids and their Tinish friends. Or we could probably room with one of the new families. You know, like with the Larsndots, down on Hidden Island. I thought you wanted us to have our own place?"

If Timor had been one of the other counselors back when Belle was still "Wise-Royal-Advisor," she would have been *sure* that this was a devilishly clever counterattack. Instead, with Timor, she knew it was absolute innocence. Of course, Belle wanted to have private quarters! How else could she keep this Child for herself, keep him from falling in with human friends or even with some other pack? Timor had been her meal ticket for almost nine years now. If she lost her status as his official caregiver, she couldn't even afford to live in this house.

"No," she said and made the sound of a human sigh. "I just think you deserve better. You know I only think of what's best for you."

"Oh, Belle." Timor set the book down and wiggled back among the four of her. "If you really want a better place, I could complain to Ravna. I just don't like to do that."

Who cares about Ravna? thought Belle, but she didn't say that aloud. The Bergsndot human was out of power, at best a minor player. On the other hand,

Timor himself was becoming an important one, even if he didn't realize the fact. Down in the New Meeting Place, Belle often lay at his feet pretending to sleep while eavesdropping on the humans.

As far as Belle could tell, Timor's parents had had roughly the same social status as did offal collectors in the Domain. Timor had inherited their talents— and somehow those abilities were rare and precious down here. Nevil and his friends didn't like Timor. They didn't like his innocent opinions or the effect he had on the other Children. *One way or another, Timor is my lever!* The main thing was to pick the right time and issue to use against Nevil and his pals. She was already planting the seeds for that: "Maybe we could complain to Nevil, or that nice Bili Yngva."

The boy yawned. "I guess." He gave a little shiver. "I'm too tired to read any more now. I need to go to bed."

When Timor had been just a puppy of a Child, she had tucked him in every night. It had become an unnecessary ritual. But the boy was still as small as he had ever been. He hadn't grown like the other Children. And there were other problems. He weakened so easily, and he still needed a lot more sleep than any human or pack she had ever known. Even if he stayed loyal to her, she might still lose out.

She led and followed Timor up the stairs to the tiny sleeping loft. At the top was one of those wonderful little light switches. With a tap of a snout, there was a bluish glow from a ceramic square mounted on the wall.

"Huh, the light's kinda dim," she said.

"It's okay," said Timor. "But the room is colder than usual. I'll bet there's some problem with the steam pipes." That happened often enough. Their little house had been one of the first with a heating tower, hence it had one of the crummiest of the devices.

Tonight's cold was something substantive they could complain about. She checked the small glass windows. They were all shut tight, no trace of a breeze. The nearest street lamp was broken, so there wasn't much of a view either. They'd have a very nice list when they finally went complaining.

The rest of her was busy tucking Timor in. "We'll use extra blankets," she said. She topped them with a frayed green quilt, her only prize from the last real shipwreck. She had almost lost Timor's loyalty over that. He'd accused her of robbing from the dying. Hah! But who had been dying? Not a single pack. And what was left of the Tropical mob was sitting pretty now, in its semi-mindless way. Besides, no one ever came looking for goods lost in the sea.

She had used her old bone needles to make a quilt out of the green fabric, stuffing it with froghen down. It was a crude job, the stitching irregular; not a single member of herself had direct memory of sewing skills. After eight years, the stitches were coming loose, and the fabric was riddled with insect holes. Now it was Timor who insisted they keep the thing.

"Is that warm enough?" she asked.

"Yes, it'll be enough." He patted her nearest head.

"I'll just listen for a while then." This was part of the ritual too. One of

Belle scooched down to the end of the bed and sat on the covers. Another lay on the floor by the bed. The other two sat a few feet away, listening and watching. She flicked off the light. "G'night, Timor."

"G'night, Belle."

Now the room was really dark. On this winter night with the street lamp gone and the clouds she had noticed earlier, it was probably too dark even for Timor to see. On the other hand, she could hear everything in the room, and when she emitted squeaks up in the range of Tinish thought, she could hear the walls and the floor. With work she could have even made out the shape of Timor's face. And Timor's heart and lungs made so much noise that even without such effort she could make out his form under the covers.

Eight years ago, when Timor was just out of coldsleep, he had cried himself to sleep every night, cried for his lost parents, cried for things he couldn't explain. In those first years, Belle would sometimes sit two of herself on his bed, cuddling him. He hadn't cried in years now, and he said he was too old to cuddle, but he still liked her to lie in the dark and listen for a while.

She didn't mind. She'd always been a planner and a schemer. She'd never been fast at thinking on her feet, even when she'd been Belle Ornrikakihm and not Belle Ornrikak. With Ihm dead, she was down to four. A pack of four could be a clever person. More often it was dull and unimaginative. Sometimes, sitting here in the dark, slowly slowly creating strategy, she wondered if she was only fooling herself to think her plans were clever.

Timor was still awake and restless, but she could tell he really was tired. Funny how much she knew his mind even though his thoughts were silent. Sometimes even silent, he could be almost member useful: Without climbing, he could reach higher than some of her. His fingers could solve problems that her Tinish snouts would just fumble over. At the same time he was as smart as a whole pack, and like all the humans he had the strangest ideas.

A clever pack could see the power in those ideas.

If only I was a royal advisor once more. That damned Woodcarver had always favored Scrupilo and Vendacious, her own offspring packs. *If I had guessed that Vendacious was a traitor, I could have unmasked him and now* I *would be second in the realm.* Sigh. She was edging toward that waking nightmare, where she came more and more often: she might never climb back from the trap she had made for herself. She had not the cleverness, and with Ihm gone she had lost the last of herself who was fertile.

While Ihm was still alive, she had the possibility of trading puppies with some other pack. But she had not tried hard enough for a match, or maybe even when she was five, she still was not attractive. Now she was four barren old ugly females. Her schemes would never carry her so high that she would have the pick of a decent litter. In truth her choices were very few. She could go to the Fragmentarium, adopt some dregs. She could run away from herself. Or she could simply die off one by one, until she was nothing, as dead as poor Timor would someday be.

Timor still wasn't sleeping. This might be one of those rare nights when he stayed awake longer than Belle. Then she noticed that he was shivering. The room must be too cold for him, even with all the blankets. He hadn't complained, but then he rarely complained. This just proved that there was something seriously wrong with the house's features. Tomorrow she'd advance her schedule and stuff Timor's torment down the throat of Nevil Storherte. She and Timor would pry some really nice digs out of this outrage. . . .

But what if the cold made Timor really sick? He was so fragile, and he could die *all at once*. She'd be left with nothing.

Okay, something had to be done about this tonight. She could call in and complain—assuming the phones weren't broken too. She thought for a moment about how these homes were powered. The teachers at the Children's Academy had talked about that in mind-numbing detail, more than the four-sized Belle could properly remember. Hot water boils into steam, which can "do work." So a water pipe had been laid all along the Queen's Road, with an outlet at every house on nearby streets. The skyfolk magic was in the fact that they didn't need a thousand bonfires to keep the water from freezing—or to make it steam. The starship *Oobii* had limitless fire somewhere inside and it could deliver the heat of that fire to any point that was visible from its upper hatchway. (Think on *that*, enemies of the Domain! Belle had often wondered why Ravna and Woodcarver didn't make more of *Oobii*'s awesome deadly power. Back when she had still had Ihm, Belle had concluded that the only explanation for the humans' meekness must be that there was an upper limit on the rate that the heat could be pumped out. She no longer understood the reasoning, but she held the conclusion close in her remaining mind.) Anyway, all the homes near the Queen's Road had a view down upon *Oobii*. They should never lack for warmth, and the steam also powered the smaller magics like the lights. And the telephones?

She slipped off the end of Timor's bed and all of her headed quietly for the stairs. She was mostly on the steps when Timor's voice came to her, soft and half asleep. "You're a good person, Belle."

"Um, yes," she replied. "G'night." What did he mean by that?

Now back in the downstairs sitting room, she flicked on the light. The glow lamp came on, but it was so faint she could barely see it. The steam pressure must be near zero. She walked across the room, easily avoiding the knickknacks that she and Timor had collected. There were just too many books, too. She shuffled them out of the way, digging down to the telephone. It was made for both humans and Tines. A foursome could easily manage it. She was still smart enough to voice some righteous indignation on behalf of Timor Ristling. The poor Child could *die* with these terrible housing conditions! One way or another they were going to get the house they deserved. *Just don't waste your rage on the starship's call director.* The *Oobii* had a perfect imitation human voice (at least at low frequencies), but it was almost as dumb as a talky singleton. Once she had mistaken the telephone call director for a real human. She'd railed at it for five minutes, uselessly of course. No, she would just say she was Belle

Ornrikak, Best Friend to Timor Ristling, with an emergency call to, hmm, Nevil? In any case, save the rant for some real person.

She held down the base and raised the receiver to one of her low-sound ears. There was no wire tone, and none of the little clicks and sputters she had grown used to. She hissed an ultrasonic obscenity. So steam pressure really was necessary for telephone service! Belle stomped around the crowded little room, whacking at whatever was in claw range—but quietly, so it wouldn't disturb Timor. It would be hours before she could unload her wrath on the incompetents who were running things. A proper politician would use that time to sharpen its rhetoric, but she wasn't in the mood. And in fact . . . Belle opened all her mouths and waggled her heads. She could feel the bite of frost on her tongues. It really was getting cold. Without cloaks, even a pack would be uncomfortable.

She hunkered down and tried to think things out. Why would steam pressure go away? Well, because the water wasn't hot anymore! Maybe *Oobii* had screwed up; maybe it wasn't targeting the heaters in this area. Since she didn't hear anyone out in the street, complaining, the failure might be just affecting this one house. She could just go up the street and ask around. Maybe Timor could stay overnight at one of the houses that still had heat.

Belle sat in the dark for several minutes, painfully trying to figure the pros and cons of the scheme. Such an emergency move in the middle of the night would certainly prove how seriously Timor had been abused. But she was very afraid that someone like Ravna or Nevil might use it as an excuse to permanently move Timor in with others.

That thought should have vetoed any plan to get help from the neighbor Children. But now, where Belle was sitting nearest to the window, *she* was chilled. *All this strategy is worthless, if Timor dies.* The thought was strangely terrifying, even worse than the silence of mind she'd felt in Ihm's last days.

Belle stood up, pulled her cloaks tight around her bodies. As she filed out the house's back door, she was already plotting just how she should put the situation to the neighbors. They were Children, a married couple. She didn't remember their names. In fact, she had done her best to keep them out of Timor's way. Now she would have to be nicey-nice.

She latched the door behind her—and was immediately struck by the quality of the air. This cold might be deadly to an unprotected human, but it wasn't that bad for a winter night. The clouds blocked out any possibility of aurora or starlight or moonlight, but she could feel a thick fog all around her, the humidity bringing a profound silence to all the upper reaches of sound. There was also a new sound, a hissing, low-pitched and mechanical. She had a moment of prideful insight. Maybe *Oobii* was still sending its ray to the local heater—but there was some leak that was stealing steam before it could get in the house. *I might even be able to fix this!*

She walked around the side of their little house, trying to imagine just how a fix might be accomplished. Her negativity was complaining like it always did. She really didn't know anything about steam technology, much less leak-fixing.

But she could easily sound out the leak. Maybe she could just push a proper-sized rock into the hole.

So dark, so silent in the higher sounds. Except for the hiss of the leak there were no sounds but her own breathing and her paws on the ice. Without echo location she was reduced to feeling her away along like some dumb deaf human.

She slid down the gully on the north side of the house. The leak was just a yard or two ahead, almost at ground level. Right here there was faint illumination from a street lamp way up the street. It glinted off something stringy, hanging from the wall above her. It was the house telephone line. Cut.

She took a step or two more before the implications hit her. Then for a second she froze in terror. Living with all this sky magic made you forget the life and death things you learned in your earlier life. Fog masks mindsound. In olden days, fog was weather's arbitrary contribution to war and treachery. Now all that ambushers need do was puncture a steam pipe and they could have all the fog they wanted.

Belle quivered with the effort to see and hear. What could she do? Killers could be all around. But they hadn't acted. Maybe if she just ignored the silence they would let her be. Surely they didn't care about a worthless pack of four.

She turned, casually she hope it looked, though two of her started to turn in the wrong direction, straining to run off to the street below the house. As she returned to the back door, she played a human humming tune, sounds pitched low enough to pass through this fog. She strained for the echoes and at the same time listened way higher up for some telltale of Tinish thought. Now that she was searching, the clues all came together, the echoes of flesh and the faint skirling of mind. She could even see some silhouettes of heads against the dim white fields of the snows uphill. There was one pack nearby, though it might be as small as four. Perhaps one or two more packs lurked at the edge of the snow.

And still they didn't act. If she turned again, she could walk off into the street. They could get what they wanted.

And what was that? The intruders circled the back of the little house. Timor? They wanted Timor? Why, why, why? But now they had him alone, and all she need do was walk away.

Or she could scream so loud that everyone in the neighborhood would come running. Maybe would come running.

She dithered a second more, slow of thought as always. Then one overriding thought united her. *No one steals my Timor.*

She gave out a shriek so loud that it would have pierced the eardrums of any human standing nearby. "HELP HELP HELP," were the Samnorsk words. As the nearest pack charged her, she realized that it was *eight*. The noise of her scream echoed back at her revealing the shapes and gaits of the attacker. It had been ten years, but she recognized the villain! *Chitiratifor.* She would have screamed that name aloud, a single Tinish chord, but something flashed and

Orn dissolved in pain. Orn's head flew down on the rocks. The rest of her was surrounded, awash in blood and noise. Maybe she was two. One.

And could only think to scream, "TIMOR!"

———————

That night, Ravna was in her office aboard *Oobii* until very late. To Nevil and his snoop programs, she was working hard on her farm assignment. In fact, she was using *Oobii* to check everything she could imagine about Flenser's accusations. Even if Nevil had scams that didn't involve using *Oobii*, she still knew his comings and goings and could monitor all the electromagnetic noise in the area. If he was relaying through the orbiter, there would be correlations. She drummed idly on her desk, watching the analysis for blockages and search decision requests. It was annoying to have the power to grab more computing resources—and not dare to do so. Another hour, though, should be enough. She'd have results to show Jo and Pilgrim. They should be back from the Cold Valley lab this evening with the latest from Scrupilo's icy fab. Those results rated a big celebration. Instead, the three of them would probably spend the evening worrying about Flenser and Nevil.

A little flag popped up. "Guidance request: Widen relevance window to include local anomalies?" One of the older heating towers up on Starship Hill was failing—at least in *Oobii*'s infrared view. The first-built towers had never been very reliable, and she had told the ship to track their decline. So why was it bothering her now? She brought up an explanation: Okay, no physical danger, but this was going to leave people in the cold unless somebody took action. It was the sort of thing Nevil & Co. should be on top of. Maybe she could handle it, just tell Nevil that the warning message had somehow been misrouted to her. Another flag appeared, reporting telephone failures. Strange. Ravna couldn't imagine a connection between the two problems—

She heard shouting downstairs; usually the ship suppressed game station noise better than that. Moments later, someone was pounding on her office door. Her displays automatically cut over to the agriculture research she was supposed to be doing.

"Ravna, we need you!" Someone—it sounded like Heida Øysler—was slamming against the wall so hard that the wood fasteners were cracking.

"Ravna!" That *was* Heida, and even louder than usual.

It wasn't till hours later that she remembered the perfection of Tinish mimicry; this was Heida *or* some pack. In the here and now, she simply popped open the door.

It really was Heida. She grabbed Ravna's arm and dragged her into the hallway.

"You gotta help us. Right *now!*"

"What? What?" said Ravna as Heida pulled her toward the stairs.

"Geri Latterby, she's gone!" said Heida.

Down on the main floor now. The few kids present were clustered around someone bundled in outdoor clothing, sitting at one of the desks. Øvin Verring turned, saw Ravna. "You got her!"

Now Ravna recognized the seated figure. It was Elspa Latterby. The kids parted before Ravna, letting her near. The girl's head was bent forward. She had vomited all over the desk.

Ravna touched her shoulder. "Elspa?"

The girl looked up. The left side of her face was scraped and she was bleeding from near her eye. It looked like she had fallen on her face. "Geri . . . we were almost home. Bunch o' raggedy Tines jumped us. They took Geri. Beasly 'n' I chased 'em . . . I couldn't keep up."

Ravna brushed her hand gently across Elspa's hair. "We'll get her back, Elspa." She looked around at the angry, frightened faces. Run-ins with fragments were an occasional problem. There had even been a robbery three years ago. But an *abduction?* Okay then. "Lisl? You're our favorite medic. Please help Elspa."

The young woman had been hovering in the background, too shy to push her way forward. But Lisl Armin was one of the few who had really believed Ravna's rants about the importance of first aid. With Lisl, and *Oobii*'s diagnostics, Elspa should be okay. As for Geri, "Øvin, start phoning around. There should be an auto list at the top of Emergency Procedures. We can set up a search—"

"The landlines, they're down." Øvin was wall-eyed.

Of course. "You've radioed Woodcarver and Nevil?"

"Y-yes," he said, "Woodcarver is sending out the city troops. Nevil is—"

"Hei! Everybody!" It was Bili Yngva, standing at the outer entrance to the Meeting Place. He waved a radio at them. "I'm coordinating with Nevil. He's spotted the Tropicals; they're running south!"

The Children swarmed toward the exit.

————

You can't be two places at once. Ravna took a chance, and left the *Oobii* to accompany the Children.

Queen's Road ran parallel to the cliffs, gently descending toward the top of Margrum Climb. There were town houses along the road, their pole lamps bright circles of light. A trickle of Children joined their group, and soon they were overtaken by packs of Woodcarver's city troops.

The Children were full of rumors, stories of attacks all over town.

Bili and his radio had something closer to hard facts—but not very many of them. "Yes, there've been several attacks on Children and city packs," he said.

"Who?" that was the shout from several corners of the crowd.

"We don't know yet! Geri and Elspa, but Elspa is okay. Edvi Verring and his Best Friend."

Up ahead, Øvin Verring stumbled. Edvi was his cousin. Øvin twisted around and pushed his way close to Bili. "Are they okay?"

Bili lowered his voice. "We don't know, Øvin. Both Edvi and Geri are missing. Parts of Dumpster and Beasly are dead or missing."

"Sons of bitches!" said someone. "Best Friend" packs ranged from opportunists to groupies—to truly best friends, very much like Pilgrim. Ravna remembered Beasly and Dumpster. They had been ideal companions for the youngest.

"Look," Bili shouted. "All the witnesses agree the attackers were Tropical nutcases. We're on this. Nevil is almost down to the embassy." The same direction the rest of them—and the Tinish troops around them—were going.

They were leaving the area of newest construction. The last lamppost marked the south end of Ravna's own house. There were no lights in the windows, and the agrav was missing from its customary place behind the house.

Ravna stepped across the frozen ruts. "Let me borrow the radio for a moment, Bili."

Yngva stared down at the gadget clutched in his hand. "I have to keep in touch with Nevil."

She held out her hand. "Just for a moment."

The conversation had not slowed Bili down, but he looked around at the nearby Children. He was not as smooth as Nevil, but he could recognize an audience when he saw one. "Okay, but please keep it brief."

He handed the device to Ravna. It was one of Scrupilo's analog radios, not a proper commset. Not that it mattered much now; Ravna only had to get through to the ship. Fortunately, what had to be done was well within the authority Nevil had granted her:

She had *Oobii* ping all the existing radios, repeat back their locations. Yes, Nevil was already on the grounds of the Tropicals' Embassy. Woodcarver was on a wagon, driving down the inner road. She'd reach the embassy before Ravna. Scrupilo was at North End, trying to get airborne. Johanna and Pilgrim . . . their agrav was still aground at the Cold Valley lab. She punched a message through to it, ending with ". . . and we'll need some active search." She asked *Oobii* to relay all priority items.

"Please, Ravna. Nevil needs this radio for the rescue work and it's already low on charge."

As she handed it back, *Oobii*'s voice began babbling from the device. Bili listened for a second, then announced. "Everybody! More casualties. Belle Ornrikak is dead. The Tropicals grabbed Timor!"

Belle was the least known of the casualties. Half a year ago, Timor might have counted as the least of the human losses. Tonight . . . a groan went around the Children. Some of them started running, trying to keep up with the soldier packs who were steadily passing by. But the frozen, rutted ground was not kind to spindly two-legs who wanted to run. These kids were just causing a traffic jam. Ravna caught up, persuaded them to keep to a fast walking pace, at the edge of the road. Even Heida slowed down.

They were beyond most of the town houses now. Only a few of the kids carried lamps, but Ravna persuaded one squad of packs to stay with them. Their oil torches lit the way.

Tonight, that light was really needed, even by humans. The sky was completely dark, without aurora or moon or stars. She hadn't checked the weather earlier, but the cloud cover must be thick and complete. They walked on about a thousand meters. Bili reported—actually *Oobii* relayed—that there were no more casualties; all the other Children were accounted for. Jo and Pilgrim were airborne and coming south.

Now at the southern horizon, there might be a break in the clouds. There was light, shifting in much the same slow way as the aurora. The kids were pointing to it now, "Strange color!"

Heida climbed the drifts by the road, stood precariously at the crest for a moment. "That light. It's a fire!"

There was only one large structure this side of the Margrum dropoff: the Tropicals' embassy.

———

The fire had not been large. It looked like only one area near the top of the central tower had burned. In the troops' torchlight, it was hard to see much damage. The main gate was open. Two packs in military line formation guarded the entrance. Four reserve packs were visible in the shadows. Numerous ordinary packs and some Children were already here. They milled around, blocked by the troops from going further.

Ravna walked toward the gate, followed by Øvin and Heida and the others from *Oobii*.

Bili strode ahead, talking on the radio. "Right. Okay." He stopped just short of the guard line and waved everybody back. "I'm sorry guys, they're still gathering clues in there."

Ravna took a step or two more, till she was face to face with Yngva. "What about Timor and Geri and Edvi? They could be in there." The words just popped out; she really wasn't trying to make trouble.

Bili lowered his voice. "Help keep these people back, Ravna. Please. Be responsible."

"Let Ravna through, Mr. Yngva. The Queen asked especially to see her." It was a pack in the shadows, behind the guard line. One of Woodcarver's chamberlains.

Maybe Bili frowned, but the light was dim and the expression quickly passed. He waved her through, then turned to shout to the crowd: "Okay, Ravna is going to help us out here. She'd really appreciate it if you'd all give us some room to work, folks."

Ravna didn't stop to contradict him, but *I could learn to dislike Bili Yngva.*

The chamberlain and Gannon Jorkenrud guided Ravna back into the depths of the embassy. Both had lamps, and Jorkenrud was waving his light all around. His voice seemed both angry and triumphant. "We nailed the bastards." He had an axe—a bloody axe?—in his other hand.

This was the first time she'd been in the so-called "embassy." The sanctum was less and more than the stories. She saw random pieces of metal and polished stone, items chipped away from public buildings and turned into interior decorations. The walls were bare of acoustic quilting, scarred with holes that might mark recent removals. Trash lay in various depths. The ceilings were almost high enough for her to walk standing upright, but the paths through the trash weren't wide enough for pack privacy and there were no turnouts for packs to courteously pass. Here and there, through openings in the walls, she could see Woodcarver's troopers searching further corridors.

They passed doors that had been smashed in. Here the air was warm and humid, smelling of body odor and incense. The chamberlain led them up a round of stairs that circled the central tower. Gannon came right behind, still talking angrily about how "we done 'em good tonight."

The stairs ended at a door with a shattered lock. The chamberlain pulled the door open a crack, and a breeze swept past them into the room beyond. There was a gobble of Interpack between the chamberlain and some pack inside. Ravna thought she heard a chord that meant contradictorily "too crowded" and "come in." The chamberlain waved snouts at Gannon and Ravna. "You two go in, please. I'll stay out here." Some of him streamed down the steps, the members spreading themselves as far as they could think. The one at the bottom of the stairs could talk to the troops on main floor.

Ravna and Gannon stepped through. The draft slammed the door shut behind them.

She looked around, taking in the broken windows and the burned fabric hangings. Once upon a time—up until a few minutes ago?—the ceiling had been much lower, with hanging silken canopies. No doubt the place had been as swampy-warm as the rest of the embassy. Now it was cold and smelled of smoke. Woodcarver stood around a pile of rubbish that had tumbled from an armoire. Still-glowing embers smouldered near her feet, but all of her—even the puppy—was looking in Ravna's direction: "We'll find Geri/Edvi/Timor." She spoke the three names as a chord. "I promise, Ravna."

Nevil nodded. "We know who did this and we have a good idea where they are now." He wore the ship's remaining HUD tiara, but away from that, his face was sooty. Behind the tiara, his eyes were a little wide, the first time she had ever seen horror on his face. "The Tropicals must have been planning this for some tendays. They had perfect knowledge of the three kids' habits and their Best Friends." He kicked savagely at whatever was behind the papers, then recovered himself, brushing at his face with a faintly trembling hand. "I'm coordinating with Jo and Pilgrim. They have the agrav flying, looking for the kidnappers. Scrupilo says he'll have *Eyes Above* in the air in another hour or so."

Ravna walked across the room, looked down at what Nevil had kicked: a pack member. Two pack members. One lay in an enormous pool of blood. The other was stretched out, as though in mid-leap. Now both lay motionless, beyond any punishment. In life, they had been part of something that thought well of itself. Few of the Tropicals dressed so royally. She glanced around at Woodcarver.

"That's two of Godsgift," said the Queen.

"These were the only ones left when Gannon got here."

From behind Ravna, Jorkenrud said, "All the rest must have taken off at least an hour earlier. They took their sleighs, everything."

Nevil glanced at Gannon. "Gannon didn't know that at the time, but—I take full responsibility. I messed up. There was a chance the kids were here; we couldn't wait for Woodcarver—"

Gannon interrupted. "Look. I didn't do anything wrong. We busted in, chased what we thought was a whole pack up into the tower here. The critter said they had the kids, said he'd cut their throats. We could smell fire in here, so we busted in and he attacked. We just killed two of him—and then we realized that's all he was!"

Ravna turned to look at him. "And there were no Children either?" she said.

Gannon glared at her and visibly bit back some angry retort. "No, nobody."

She walked over to where Woodcarver was nosing around the corpses. Ravna had never liked Godsgift, but—"I really didn't know packs could do this sort of thing."

Woodcarver shrugged, but Ravna guessed she was trying to look unimpressed: the Puppy from Hell had a kind of dazed expression in its eyes. "Tropicals are crazy asses," said Woodcarver. She nosed at the one lying in a pool of blood. "I think this was the pack's verbal center; it was a fixed point in their recent swapping. And these two always paid more attention than the others to written materials."

Nevil looked surprised. "I didn't know that. Downstairs, there were several smaller fires—blubber oil tossed around and lit, though nothing spread far enough to bring the whole place down." He looked around at the charred papers. "Maybe at the last moment they realized there were secrets left behind."

Woodcarver's heads turned toward him. She said, "Together, these two might have been bright enough to decide what to burn first." She shook herself. "So Godsgift maimed himself to keep a secret."

———

A bit of good fortune: the cloud cover broke, and the next real storm was two days out to sea. Scrupilo's great airship was still ten days short of its maiden voyage, but Scrup managed to get his little electric airboat into the search, circling out to the limits of its motor charge. Air search beyond that depended on the agrav skiff and the very-low-resolution pictures from the orbiter. Woodcarver's Domain covered millions of hectares of snowfields, naked rock, and channel ice, but clues littered the bloody snows where Geri and Edvi and Timor had been taken, and not all the witnesses were dead. The best ground trackers searched all the nearby forest trails. Video from the orbiter guided them to the most likely places further out, where mountain farms were scarcely more than wilderness marked with property boundaries.

Meantime, Johanna and Pilgrim accomplished what no dirigible could: they shadowed the main party of fleeing Tropicals. They ghosted along within clouds and behind mountain walls, watching every move the Tropicals made. The mob had fled before any of the actual kidnappers could have made it to the embassy—but there might be a rendezvous. . . .

The main group mushed on along the East Forest Road, not pausing for any rendezvous. The embassy Tropicals had always looked so stupid, playing with their huge sleighs in the most inappropriate weather. Now for once, the weather and the terrain were ideal for a mad sleigh ride. When they got over High Knob Pass, they all hopped aboard and took a single long slalom, interrupted only by occasional overturnings and mayhem collisions. Even so, the next blizzard caught up with them as they came barrelling down upon the East Gate border garrison, their eight remaining sleighs crowded with all who had so far survived. They smashed through the Domain's border garrison on the East Gate, causing casualties but no total deaths.

In principle, the Tropicals were now beyond Domain jurisdiction. In fact, that was where their pursuers finally moved to stop them.

————

Within hours of the East Gate debacle, Johanna and Pilgrim were back with Ravna, up on the second floor of the town house. Outside, the blizzard was a roaring blow, white swirling just beyond the windows. Inside was snug and warm. On the table by the windows was the cargo Ravna had been waiting for from the Cold Valley, ten thousand adders fabricated on a fifty-centimeter disk of pressed carbon. These must still be delivered to Scrupilo for testing, but Jo and Pilgrim's mission up north had delivered the images for the next step: true processors and memory devices. If these adders tested out, the way was clear for what Ravna and Scrupilo had worked ten years to create.

The delivery should have been the joyous high point of Ravna's year. Instead, when Jo had presented her with the carbon black disk, Ravna had barely taken the time to tilt it in the light, to admire the nearly microscopic patterning. She would get the devices to Scrupilo soon enough; he would do his testing. Meantime, three of the youngest Children were gone. Three packs were mostly murdered.

Ravna sat with Jo and Pilgrim on that beautiful carpet, and felt as cold and miserable as if she'd been in the blizzard outside.

Maybe Johanna had been crying, but all that was left was the strain that showed on her face. "We would have let the Tropicals run right on into the wilderness, except that the storm had caught up with us." She had reported most of this by radio. She'd be saying it again tomorrow morning when all the Children got together at the New Meeting Place. She punched angrily at the big pillow she held on her lap. Pilgrim was stretched out around her, also looking tired and unperky.

"We rescued *no one*," Jo said. "We discovered *nothing*. The only good thing that came out of this was getting to work with Jefri. He handled the ground chase, and for the first time in years we really cooperated."

"Jefri is the best of all the humans at woodcraft," said Pilgrim. "He and Amdi came down from Smeltertop, watching all the way for signs of small escaping parties. They were just ahead of the main group of Tropicals when the storm hit."

"So between him and Woodcarver's troops, the Tropicals were boxed in?" said Ravna. She had followed the chase with most of the other Children, just watching the comms from *Oobii.*

"Yeah, we really had them trapped, and if we didn't stop them, they could lose us in the storm." Jo swatted her pillow again. "We should have captured a lot more of them, though. Damn that Gannon Jorkenrud. He just charged on through, whacking Tropicals. I'm gonna complain about that."

Ravna nodded. In fact, Johanna had already complained loudly and publicly, and her complaints had been heard by almost one hundred Children on *Oobii.* Jorkenrud's attack had been ineffectual, except as it forced a complete loss of coherence among the Tropicals. "Yes," said Ravna, "we saw." Via the camera carried by Woodcarver. "The Tropicals were hunkered down around their sleighs, almost clumped into rational groups. Then Gannon and company came in—"

"Yeah! And *poof,* the Tropicals ran off in all directions, *as singletons.*" Johanna glared at nowhere in particular for a moment. "No way could we catch many of them in the storm." A shadow passed across her face. "Tropical singletons in a northern blizzard. I'll bet they're dead now."

"Jefri and Amdi brought nets," said Pilgrim. "They managed to snag a few." He shook a head wonderingly. "What an unlikely team they make. Jefri is almost as good in the woods as a pack—and Amdiranifani is a pudgy, overly nice genius who doesn't even like to eat live food. I'll bet the nets were Amdi's idea. Between them, they caught more Tropicals than Woodcarver's troops and Nevil's idiots."

"What did you find in the sleighs?"

Johanna shook her head. "We're gonna have to wait for Nevil's big meeting to learn that. We were still in the air, and Amdi and Jefri were busy with their nets. It was mainly Gannon and company on the wagons. . . . I swear, even after ten years Down Here, they still seem to think that the world is built just for them. If objects don't have intentional response, or at least voice command obedience, they figure they're broken. These bozos ended up using axes to make kindling of the sleighs and cargo boxes."

"I saw some of what they spilled out on the ground. It was a jumble, but here and there I saw rainbows."

"Big deal," said Johanna. "For years, the Tropicals have been stealing tech items, mostly glittering garbage. I want some real clues. Where are Geri and Edvi and Timor? How can we get them back . . ." her voice became soft and sad, ". . . or can we ever get them back?" She looked up at Ravna. "I think Jefri is as upset as I've ever seen him, even when he was little. This takes us back to Murder Meadows."

CHAPTER 17

A tenday passed. There had been no sign of Geri or Edvi or Timor, but something new happened up at the cemetery—hundreds of packs and all the remaining Children showed up and stood in snowy, windy twilight for the funeral of Belle and parts of Dumpster and almost all of Beasly. For better or worse, this looked like a new tradition among the packs. Nevil said just a few words, thanking the fallen Best Friends, and promising that the stolen Children would be found. Then various packs and humans spoke to remember the dead. They even found nice things to say about the ever-churlish Belle Ornrikak. The last of Beasly stood quietly beside his pack's grave, looking sad and puzzled.

The murders and kidnappings brought the Children together as nothing had before. The growing complaints died, and everyone pulled together. Though there were no signs of the missing Children, there were clues. Along with the pilfered trinkets and toys, the Tropicals' sleighs had contained food supplies, including syrup-grain bars that only humans could stomach. Someone had planned to take the stolen Children far away. Nevil confessed that his leadership had been terribly unprepared and that their best rescue efforts had been a botch.

So the Domain had an external enemy, someone who evidently was interested in learning more about two-legs. The names Vendacious and Tycoon were high on everyone's suspect list. There was something very dangerous out beyond the Domain. This time it had used its puppets—but next time?

Nevil and Woodcarver were forced into closer cooperation. Both Tines and humans volunteered their time for special watches. The youngest Children were never without double guards. Jefri and Amdi stayed in town, working to devise a sustainable town patrol. Nevil appointed special committees to recommend new policies.

At twice-a-tenday meetings, Nevil summarized the results of the planning committees. The unsuccessful bioscience projects were swept away by the necessities of immediate safety.

It was such a perfect fit for Pilgrim's warning of what a regime might do to stay in power. But now Pilgrim was less the cynic: "Events have worked in Nevil's political favor, but I don't see how he could have engineered this."

"Not by himself," said Johanna, "but if Nevil has fallen into Vendacious' schemes, this is exactly the sort of thing that could happen." She glanced at Ravna. "You told me Nevil looked overwhelmed in the embassy."

"Yes."

Jo nodded. "I think Nevil did a deal with the devil and now he can't get out." She was silent for a moment. "Or maybe he is totally innocent. I talked to Jefri again today. If he stays in town long enough, I really think I may learn what's going on in his head. Jef and Amdi are desperate to keep this from happening again—but I'll tell you, they're whole-heartedly behind Nevil's security schemes.

Jefri says we really need those handcannons that Nevil mentioned at yesterday's meeting. Jefri would never put up with the kind of dark-hearted alliance Flenser was claiming. And yet . . . Jef's holding something back. Has Flenser had anything more to say to you?"

Ravna shook her head. "No. You know that." They had had this conversation before. Flenser had shown up at the meetings, generally backing Nevil, and without his usual sly innuendo. The help he had promised Ravna was not forthcoming.

The Mad Bad Girl crossed her arms truculently. "I say Woodcarver should grab Flenser and put the bastards to the question." She glared at Pilgrim. "How about it? You saw the Queen just this afternoon, right?"

Pilgrim looked around at himself. *Embarrassed?* "As a matter of fact, our latest chat was a bit more, um, intimate than any we've had in some time. I got some real insight. I fear she is going to become even more erratic than before."

"It's that puppy, isn't it?"

"Yes. Sht is older now, but the situation hasn't stabilized. Woodcarver knows he's a problem, but he's such a part of her now that she can't deal with it. She's bouncing around between some very different states of mind. I caught her in an affectionate mood."

"Hmmph. You should tell her to ditch little Sht," said Johanna, quite out of keeping with her normal soft-hearted attitude toward individual pack members.

"Heh, even in the midst of our loving, I suspect *that* suggestion would have provoked a very negative reaction. The Old Woodcarver would have never drifted this far. She knew she was giving up the stability of centuries when she started fooling around with me—but we never thought she'd lose it like this. The good news is, she knows she has a problem and she's trying to cope with it. I think she'll eventually be successful. In the meantime—well, there are several very different places her opinions dwell: She fully supports Nevil's plans for tightening up security. Some of the time she sees Nevil as a proper ally in those plans. Sometimes she is as suspicious of him as we are, regarding him as a puppet of Vendacious—or Flenser. Of course, she can't get her claws on Vendacious, but she's toying with exactly your suggestion: putting Flenser to the question!"

———

Fifteen days passed. Flenser-Tyrathect was holed up in the Old Castle down on Hidden Island, under unacknowledged house arrest. Ravna wondered if—considering all the secret exits—Flenser was really there at all. One thing was certain: he still wasn't talking to Ravna!

She continued her covert surveillance of Nevil's online activity. Nevil and Bili were as clumsy and cautious as ever. Their attempts to spy on *her* would be laughable even if she didn't have Command Privileges. On the other hand, Nevil had true control of the orbiter and the commsets he had appropriated. There were data links she couldn't snoop on.

Despite the tragedy and paranoia, Ravna found minor good news: the maiden flight of *Eyes Above 2*. The behemoth had the size and appearance of a small interplanetary freighter, and even though it was limited to the lower atmosphere and could hoist less mass than the agrav skiff, it was still a safe and relatively fast transport. Nevil was right when he said that *EA2* would revolutionize the Domain's rescue capability.

Meantime she worked on her Cold Valley project and did the gun designing that was officially assigned her. Both projects involved working with Scrupilo. When he demanded she visit him down on the North End, it was almost like the good old days before the Disaster Study Group and Nevil and the murders.

Ravna's town house was less than five thousand meters from the North End, but to get there, she'd had to walk to the funicular and trundle down it to the Inner Channel. The channel was still mostly frozen, but rain had covered it with centimeters of freezing water. Getting across was an ugly combination of boating and sleigh ride. The rest of the trip hadn't been much better, though Flenser's packs had cut drainage channels in the icy piles along the streets. So an hour and a half after leaving home, here she was in Scrupilo's office at the North End quarry. She was still drying out from the trip when Scrupilo trooped out from his glassware and electronics.

"Hei, Scrupilo, so why did you need to see me in person? Is it the guns or the Cold Valley project?" *And I so hope it's Cold Valley.* If not for the present dangers, that's where all her attention would be.

"Both and neither," said the pack grumpily. "Let's start with the fun things. Are you quite dried out? I don't want you dripping on this."

"I'm dry."

"Okay, then." He led her to a test stand at the side of the room. There were connectors and cables, locally made batteries and voltage regulators—prehistoric tech that had taken Ravna and Scrupilo years to make. Almost hidden in the middle of the equipment was a one-centimeter-wide smudge of carbon on glass. Scrupilo and his helpers had carefully cut it out of the ten thousand array, then connected power and data leads appropriately. "We just finished the setup this morning," said Scrupilo. "I've already done some testing, but I wanted you to see it." He clustered around the equipment, tapping switches with his noses, then correcting his own mistakes. Parts of Scrup were getting very old. His White Head member was nearly deaf in the lower frequencies, and Ravna figured from the way it was always closely surrounded by its peers that it also had problems with the ultrasonic frequencies of mindsounds. Scrupilo claimed that if he messed around getting younger members, he'd just lose his dedication. Considering what had happened to Woodcarver, maybe he was right. "There! I got it right. See? Binary of twelve coded on the top leads, binary of seventeen on the bottom." He waggled a nose at pattern of tiny lights, and then pointed at a third row of lights below the other two: the outputs. "Twelve plus seventeen is twenty-nine!"

"You did it, Scrupilo." Ravna almost whispered the words.

Scrupilo preened, but then some honest core of him replied, "*We* did it. Me and you and *Oobii*'s design programs. We three and the teams up north and down here." His heads were bobbing almost maniacally. "I've spent all day playing with this. I had *Oobii* sending down test settings at variable speeds, checking the results. Our little adder can reliably do one hundred thousand operations per second, second after second, for *hours!*" He looked up at her. "And the design we're making at Cold Valley now," —the one Johanna and Pilgrim had delivered just before the kidnappings— "that's a giant step up from this, but I bet it'll work too; it's the same hundred-micron feature size. Imagine, we'll have clock, and memory, and an instruction set all *together*."

Now Ravna was nodding back. That next step was the distillation of a thousand civilizations' processor designs, optimized for their grotesquely primitive situation at Cold Valley. "Of course," she said, "that will be even more tedious to wire up."

"Yup, like tying good rug knots. Thousands of hours. But in a year we'll have ten or twenty of our own processors. By then we'll be making vision chips. There will be even more tedious work for paws and hands—"

"But in ten years, we'll have local automation." The machines would be doing the wire-ups. It was the beginning she'd promised the Children. It would stink, but it would be enough: "Then we can start shrinking the feature size." That was the transition point that had always marked the beginning of technological civilization.

"Yup, yup," said Scrupilo; he had long ago brought into the histories he'd read in *Oobii*'s archives. For a moment they just stood grinning at each other like idiots. Very happy idiots. She would so much like to play with these connectors, set up her own automatic addition. It was the sort of thing that by itself would not impress any of the Children, except maybe Timor. He—

Timor would have loved this. The thought brought her back to their current awful situation. *Play with the gear later.* She stepped back from the miracle, her smile leaking away. "You seemed to have other things you wanted to talk about, Scrupilo?"

The pack's heads continued to bob for a moment, but Scrupilo eventually came down to earth too. He wandered to the window, looked down into the quarry, maybe at the actinic flashes coming from the shed where his crews were forging ribs and spars. Work had begun on a second huge airship, apparently to be called *Eyes Above 3*; Scrupilo had no imagination when it came to names.

But when Scrup turned back from the window, it wasn't to talk about *EA3*. "You know Nevil's miniature cannon idea is really stupid."

That was Nevil's main technological response to the kidnappings, an even higher priority than another airship. "Personal protection for all," was his slogan for the project. Most of the Children were very much in favor of the idea. Of course, Ravna had always known that very small cannon could be made; such were a commonplace in early civilizations. The trouble was, they were so easy to make and copy, and the Domain already had military superiority in this part of the world; better not to give other nations a clue before it was necessary. Besides, *Oobii* had ideas for making much more effective personal weapons once the Domain became a little more technically advanced. "But Scrupilo, you know

Woodcarver favors the notion of personal cannons." As of the most recent twice-a-tenday meeting.

The pack made an irritated noise. "You and I have discussed such weapons before. In principle, they are a moderately foolish idea, perhaps necessary in the current emergency. What is *stupid* is the actual design." He sent a member across the room to fetch an engineering drawing and thrust it into Ravna's hands.

The graphic was done by Ravna, from Nevil's overall description. She stared at it for a moment. "Um, I did include a flash and noise suppressor," which hadn't been on Nevil's wish list. "Did you want a longer barrel?"

"Well, yes! Would you want this going off in *your* face?" Scrupilo had damaged his White Head's hearing in experiments with the first field artillery. "But that's the least of it. Look at the, what do you call it, the stock."

That part was also Nevil's idea, but it had seemed rather clever to Ravna. "That's modeled after the handle on a Tinish jaw-axe, Scrupilo." But turned sideways, the lower half looked much like the handgrip of Pham's long-gone pistol.

"Foolishness!" All but one of Scrupilo came over and grabbed the paper out of her hands. "For a human with arms and hands, this would be easy to hold and fire and reload. But for a pack—look, helper members have to come around on the sides and stick snouts *forward* of the gunner. The idea of cartridges and cartridge boxes is nice enough, but I can't imagine scrambling around beneath the muzzle to insert a reload."

Ravna stared at the picture; she really should have fed Nevil's suggestion through *Oobii*'s multi-species designer. This was a weapon for humans. "Do you have some changes to suggest?"

"I could put my mind to it." Again, he glanced down through the windows. "If we have to waste time, at least we can do it right." He pulled blank paper from one of his panniers and began sketching. "Hmm, a longer barrel would improve accuracy *and* make the gun easier to shoot and hold and service. . . ."

Over the next ten minutes the two of them—mainly Scrupilo, since Ravna was a dunce at design without *Oobii*—worked out a number of features. Not surprisingly, what they came up with looked a lot more like a crew-served weapon than a hand gun. "But I'm sure a single human would be quite proficient with it. Then—" He looked up, as if listening. All Ravna heard was the continuing bang of the drop forge—but the one of Scrupilo still by the window was scrunched against the glass, trying to look straight down.

Okay, he was waiting for someone. Ravna crossed the room and leaned close to the glass, blocking the reflected room lighting with her hands. The flashes from the forge shone through the rain. Freezing water glittered as it fell from the lab's eaves. Looking down in the direction of Scrupilo's gaze, she could see the flight of rickety wooden stairs that zigzagged up the quarry wall to Scrupilo's office. Twilight showed dark shapes ascending single-file. It looked like three packs. A flash of light from the forge revealed that the middle pack was a sevensome, all in heavy raincloaks, including one wee member who rode the shoulders of the largest. Queen Woodcarver.

Woodcarver's first bodyguard emerged on the landing just outside Scrupilo's door. Ravna didn't recognize the pack. After a moment it spread around the outside of the building, watching in all directions. Then, one at a time, Woodcarver popped up. She stood for a moment under the portico, removing her raincloaks and shaking off the water that had made it through to her pelts. She gave Ravna a sharp look, then came indoors, bringing a frigid bloom of air with her.

"Spring is the worst season," she said. "It shouldn't visit us in winter." Two of her were looking directly at Ravna. The Puppy from Hell was staring at Scrupilo's labware, a destructive gleam in its eye. "But you have much more extreme environments aspace, don't you, Ravna?"

"Yes, though they're so extreme that adequate protection generally means visitors don't suffer the way we do here." *We're actually having a civil conversation!*

Scrupilo had moved to stand at the far end of the lab, behind quilted screens that were thick enough to allow him to remain in the conversation without getting in the way of Woodcarver's thoughts.

Woodcarver nodded in his direction. "Are we in private?"

"Yes, my Queen. And anything that could hear us is temporarily disabled."

The puppy hopped onto a lab bench and sniffed around at the connectors and charge holders. The rest of Woodcarver spread out around Ravna. "You were so much simpler to deal with than Nevil."

Ravna nodded.

Woodcarver thought a second. "Sorry, I meant that as a compliment. Even an apology. I know *I* have become difficult to deal with. Surely, my—Pilgrim— has gossiped enough about my state of mind?"

How to respond to that? Ravna tried for something like honesty: "Pilgrim said that your new addition was . . . distracting."

Woodcarver chuckled. "What delightful understatement." Her six adult members were all looking at little Sht. The Puppy from Hell looked back with innocent, what's-the-fuss body language. Surely that was just Ravna's human interpretation. After a moment, Woodcarver continued: "A century ago, I would not have gone this road. I certainly wouldn't have accepted Harmony Redjackets' crackpot broodkennery. But that was before dear Pilgrim made me adventurous. Now I'm in a bigger mess than I have any clear memory of in my entire existence. Sht came close to undoing me, all before I realized the danger. I'm still searching for balance. Pilgrim has made suggestions, but in the meantime . . ."

Woodcarver was mostly looking at Ravna now. "Just so you know, even when we disagree, I will trust you and Johanna and Pilgrim more than anyone."

Ravna nodded. *Powers above!* "Thank you."

"Meantime, we have a dangerous situation to deal with." She stopped, seemed to be thinking.

From across the room, Scrupilo said, "You mean Nevil and all the scheming he's up to."

Two of Woodcarver looked up. "Yes. I've watched Nevil carefully since he disposed of Ravna. He intends to take over the Domain, but he's not as clever as he thinks he is. The question is . . ." Woodcarver's voice faded into thoughtfulness.

Scrupilo helpfully put in, "The question is, is Nevil someone's puppet, some pack much cleverer than he is."

This time all of Woodcarver's heads came up. "Scrupilo! Will you please stop interrupting! It's bad enough having your obsessive mindsound rattling around the room."

"Sorry! Sorry."

Her heads turned back toward Ravna, the puppy's last of all. "The murders and the kidnappings have played perfectly into Nevil's claws. Was that accidental? If it is, we—you and I together, Ravna—should have no trouble with Nevil's grand ambitions. But you know Flenser hints around that this is Vendacious' work. If it is that—or worse, if this is Flenser in some double treason, then we may have been outplayed." She thought quietly for a moment. "Nevil would have us believe that the Tropicals were behind the attack. I've watched that embassy mob for almost ten years. It's very hard to believe that they could organize this attack."

"Godsgift was smart enough," said Ravna, "in an erratic way. Johanna thinks that maybe our trade over the last ten years has made some difference in the Tropics."

Woodcarver made a little hooting sound. "What difference could it make to a Choir of a hundred million Tines?"

Ravna smiled. "That's more or less Pilgrim's reaction to the idea."

"I know. I talked to both of them earlier this afternoon. Today is my day to grovel apologies and attempt reconciliation. But if Nevil is somebody's puppet, Godsgift and his mob were key to the operation. For at least five years, we've been sniffing around the East Coast, trying to learn more about Tycoon or Vendacious or whoever. Have we been looking in the wrong place? If there is anybody behind Godsgift, *that* would explain a lot. I think we should actively test the possibility."

Scrupilo said, "Send Jo and Pilgrim to the Tropics! Oops, sorry."

Woodcarver waved a head in Scrupilo's direction. "Just as he says. It's something we should have done long ago. Even now, Jo and Pilgrim are overflying the mouth of the River Fell."

Ravna knew how enormous the continental tropics were, even not counting the Great Sandy. "Negative results wouldn't really prove anything," she said.

Little Sht snapped at the empty air, but the pack's tone of voice remained reasonable. "That's true. But it's a start. Given what's happened, we should be paying as much attention to the Tropics as we do the Long Lakes and East Home."

"Yes."

"And I wanted some reconnaissance undertaken before Nevil and his friends know that we are about it. Johanna and Pilgrim felt the same way. Nevil thinks they're headed to Smeltertop today—instead they're going much much farther."

One trip was about sixty kilometers and the other was several thousand—but to the agrav, they were about equally difficult. Nevertheless, "I—I wish all of us had had a chance to talk about this. Woodcarver."

"Why? Both of them wanted to take a look. This first trip will just be a day or two, not like some of the East Coast missions. They'll stay silent until they're on the way back."

"I think there's a good chance Nevil will know of the mission in any case."

"So?" said Woodcarver. "That would also argue for us acting quickly. I was completely outmaneuvered by the murders and the kidnappings. And since then, Nevil's been pushing and shoving. I want to know who we're up against before they surprise us all again." She looked around. "And that's another reason we had to talk. You really must stop acting like a fool. Nevil needs your technical advice, but once he realizes we're working together, that might not protect you. If he is the tool of Vendacious, then expect the reaction to be violent. I want you to start using bodyguards. I've got four packs here who will take you home—that's in addition to ones you apparently have not even noticed." She smiled at the look on Ravna's face. "And as of tonight, I'm increasing the coverage." All her heads were bobbing, including little Sht's.

Three hours later, Ravna was finally back at her town house on Starship Hill. More had happened this day than any day since the Battle on Starship Hill—and not a single person harmed in the process! Her mind was working overtime, a combination of triumph and planning and worries: Very shortly, there would be thousands of processor and video components available from the Cold Valley lab—far more than could be immediately wired up to the devices that Scrupilo was building. There would be several years of hard manual labor before the combination of integrated devices and *Oobii*'s software designs would make a difference, but then life for the Children and the Domain would be transformed. It would be such an enormous win for everyone. So maybe the question was: Just how evil was Nevil? If he was not a partner in the murders and the kidnappings, surely some real compromises would be possible, compromises that would not humiliate him but would still allow the projects Ravna wanted.

And if Nevil was a puppet of Vendacious or whoever? Maybe he could be persuaded to renounce the association. If not . . . perhaps it all came down to what Jo and Pilgrim discovered once they started looking in the right places. *I wish I could talk to them now.* That would have to wait, probably for a day or two, to keep this mission secret. But what could they really find in one overflight, even if that was of the heart of the Choir? Mostly likely, this was the beginning of a number of flights—and no way could those be kept secret.

Ravna roamed the town house as she cycled through the possibilities. Outside, she could see the new guards that Woodcarver had assigned. Nothing covert about these fellows. The Queen's change of heart—or her success in controlling her heart—was almost as big a triumph as anything else that had happened this day. It was also one of the worries that nibbled around the edges of the day's optimism. So much depended on Woodcarver's favor and her stability. The Queen still had flashes of anger, failures of attention and memory. The battle to control Woodcarver's paranoia wasn't really over.

Ravna's own thoughts were skittering off in all directions: new insights, new worries. If only she had access to *Oobii* from here. *I should have gone there tonight.* There were things that she was missing.

An hour passed. Two. Beyond her second-story windows, she could see that the drizzle had frozen to glassy ice, a veneer that glittered and gleamed beneath the occasional streetlight. *Get some sleep.* Tomorrow she'd chat with *Oobii*, maybe find a way to talk with Johanna and Pilgrim. Ravna finally dragged herself off to bed.

She lay in the darkness, listening to the house settle into the subfreezing cold of the night. All these houses were so noisy. In Ravna's childhood, the indoors and outdoors had been indistinctly separated, and the only sounds one heard were deliberately engineered into the environment. Normally those were the sounds of living things, bats and birds and kittens prowling. Of course, you could make the sounds and the environment whatever you wanted. Her sister Lynne had been big on Silence, just another of the endlessly annoying things about Lynne as a youngster. The two had engaged in sound wars all the time.

Here in the wilderness—Ravna counted all of Tines World as wilderness—sound was the sometime domain of the Tines with their preternatural acoustics. Where the Tines were not involved, sound was a feral thing. Her first few tendays in this town house, before Pilgrim and Johanna arrived as housemates, Ravna could scarcely sleep. There were these thumps in the night. There were clicks and groans, and no matter how she rationalized them they seemed very threatening. Night after night they repeated. Some of them had come to be almost comforting.

Maybe she slept for a time. . . .

There was a new creaking. It almost sounded like someone was on the front stairs.

She quietly moved into the living room. Quietly? If it was a pack coming up the stairs, she would surely be heard! On the other hand, if she cried out, the guards on the street would be in here in a moment. She slipped close to the windows, being careful not to stand in silhouette. Outside was still and glittering—

—and no sign of even a single guard pack.

No more creaking on the front stairs. She turned her head a fraction; from here she could see partway down the stairwell. A pack might keep itself quiet to her ears—but human eyes could make up for human ears:

The walls were not utterly dark, and . . . she saw shadows that looked very much like the heads of two Tines. A pack was sneaking up the stairs.

Surely it can hear that I moved my head, hear the flat of my face. She turned and dove for the backstairs door.

There was a muted screech and the sound of paws pounding up the front stairs. Ravna pulled open the door, leaped through, and slammed it shut. Now the intruder's hissing was loud. An instant later its bodies slammed into the door. She leaned against the panel; the door couldn't be locked from this side. It was just her weight and strength that was keeping it shut. Somehow, she had to jam it closed. She flailed around, found the light switch. The stairs were just shoulder wide, and even though this was a house-for-humans, the ceiling was only one meter fifty high. The steps were piled deep with camping equipment and junk that Pilgrim and Johanna had brought back from their expeditions. They bragged about how they traveled light, but they always seemed to have souvenirs.

Just beyond her reach was a bundle of staves, each tipped with a short, wicked blade. She kicked at it, taking some of her weight off the door. The pack was ramming in unison now. The door sprang ajar and a paw full of claws extended through the opening. Ravna slammed back at the door. Something crunched. The member gave a sharp whistle of pain and the paw was withdrawn. There was an instant of peace, presumably while the other side had an "*ow ow ow*" moment. Ravna swiveled the staves around, jamming their butt ends into the stair railing. She stabbed two or three of the blades into the door. The rest of the bundle came loose in her hands. Okay! She sank all but one of the other staves into various points on the door. Now, when the pounding resumed, the door was jammed shut more securely than all her pushing had accomplished.

Then she scrambled down over the boxes and bags, sliding the remaining stave ahead of her. The pole was an awkward thing for a human to maneuver. The shoulder clasps were useless for a human, and the shaft had an awkward curve in its lower half. Still, it was long and there was something sharp at the end.

Her housemates' junk was deepest at the bottom of the stairs: tents, equipment, harnesses, boots. *Boots.* Ravna slipped on Jo's old boots and peeked out the tiny window on the outside door. She was looking into the field behind the house. Far away up the hill, she could see the scattered lights of Newcastle town. Deep shadows stood nearby, but she saw no sign of the rest of the gang.

Maybe they were *all* in the house. There was noise enough at the top of the stairs. Someone had axes. Woodchips flew from the shuddering topside door. She saw the glint of a metal blade breaking through.

Ravna turned back to the outside door. It was only one member wide, secured by a cross-timber. She lifted the bar and pushed. Jammed! She crouched down and pushed harder. The door creaked open. Ravna scrambled into the frigid cold. Behind her, the pack had broken through the upper door. Boxes and bags tumbled down ahead of the intruder, all but jamming the doorway.

Precious seconds. She stabbed the shoulder stave into the ice, using the staff to steady herself as she stepped off the stoop. The fresh-frozen ice felt as smooth as glass under Jo's boots. She poled herself along, skiing more than running. Loud gobbling came from within the house.

If she could get to the road before they did, there might be witnesses, even defenders. Ravna bent her knees and pushed off with her staff. She coasted almost five meters on each push, keeping her balance by lightly raking the ice with her blade. She pushed again, sliding onwards. *Should I be screaming for help?* She was out of sight of her back door and the windows above. Maybe they didn't even know where she was!

The Queen's Road was directly below, empty beneath the glow of a street lamp. She pushed off—and discovered that the water hadn't frozen into glassy smoothness on the slope. Pain blazed where her hip smashed into the ice. She slid, spinning, down the washboard surface.

Then she was out in the light, right under the streetlamp. She rolled over, came to her knees. Somehow, she had managed to hang on to the bladed staff. Up the road, lights were coming on in the nearest houses. Coming toward her from the other direction—it was Jefri and Amdi! They were actually running. Amdi's claws glittered with ice, and two of him were steadying Jefri from below. The gang of nine slid to a stop all around her. Jefri reached down for her hand.

"C'mon," he said. Around her, she felt Amdi helping her up, bracing against Jefri. For just an instant she was aware of the warmth of his arms around her and the penetrating cold everywhere else.

Then she saw at least one pack come tumbling down the front steps of her town house. Another skittered, sprawling, down the alleyway. Amdi squeaked something unintelligible to Jef. Suddenly Jefri's arms tightened around her, swinging her up and off her feet. "I've got her!" he called to them.

The other packs swirled surrounded them, steel tines and crossbows everywhere. She had a glimpse of an enclosed fodder wagon sliding into the lamplight.

"Stop her wiggling!"

Someone grabbed the back of Ravna's neck and whipped her head against the side of the wagon.

CHAPTER 18

Johanna loved to fly in the anti-gravity skiff, but sometimes, such as right now, it could be a bit *too* thrilling. She swallowed her heart and glared across the tiny cabin at Pilgrim. "How much altitude do we have left?"

"Not to worry," was his cheery response. "We still have plenty of clearance."

Johanna leaned out into the rainy dark. They had flown—or, more accurately, fluttered and flailed—across hundreds of kilometers of Tropicals' territory. Just before this rain, she'd spotted fires below—for cooking? sacrifices? She hadn't seen any details, or smelled the fires, so she guessed the skiff was at least a thousand meters up. Maybe it was still jungle down there, but Pilgrim claimed he could hear unending Tinish chatter. If this was a city they were flying over, it must be as big as the urban terranes of Straumli Realm.

The skiff flipped forward, nearly tumbling over. It was doing that a lot on this trip. Pilgrim struggled to right the craft. If he failed, they'd be stuck once again with flying upside down. That got old very fast. This time, he succeeded in bringing them back to a normal attitude. They coasted serenely through the dark for several seconds, almost as if this was a proper aircraft.

"Actually," Pilgrim said, "We're at 750 meters." All his eyes were on the flickering displays. Just looking at them gave Johanna a headache, and on this trip they were a constant reminder of larger problems. Over the years, most of the skiff's onboard sensors had malfunctioned toward silence and arbitrary errors. About the only ground imaging left to them was their own eyeballs looking out open windows and through those parts of the hull that weren't blocked by agrav repairs.

They should be less than ten kilometers from a more or less safe landing area, where the river swampland faded into the ocean. Normally, their best navigation information came from the orbiter, hanging out at synchronous altitude—and tonight they weren't using that.

"Are you making up numbers again?" she asked.

A doggy head turned in her direction and a muzzle patted her on the hand. "Hei," he said, "only the less significant digits." And of course, when they got really low, Pilgrim could *hear* the ground. "A little imprecision is worth it," he continued. "I'll bet Nevil and Company haven't even noticed we're not going to Smeltertop tonight."

"Yeah." Tomorrow they'd take just a quick look and then skedaddle back home.

"Not to worry," said Pilgrim. "We should have done this a long time ago."

The rain was a steady torrent, but the air was virtually windless, and the skiff was smoothly sliding along at several meters per second. Pilgrim claimed that the controls were benefitting from the water pooling at the bottom of their little cabin.

They were really low. The air stank faintly of sewage and animals. Those particular smells were not surprising; mariners and Tropical fragments told of cities larger and more crowded than anything else in this world, a mindless urbanization that destroyed coherent thought. It wasn't called the Choir of Choirs for nothing.

"They're louder than ever," said Pilgrim. "A mob all singing together. Sounds like they're having a good time, though. . . . Heh, maybe there really is nonstop sex."

They were so low that Johanna could see firelight again, but it was mostly shielded from sight, glints here and there and an occasional suffocating wall of hot smoke. She glanced off to her right and *up*. "Pilgrim! Is that something flying?"

The skiff fluttered as two of Pilgrim turned to look in the direction she was pointing. "I don't see anything. There are some really strange noises though."

Since the orbiter had been revived, there had been attempts at maintaining surveillance over the continent—including the tropical lands, where no packs had ever explored. The problem was that the orbiter's optics were barely more than light sensors, with something like thousand-meter ground resolution—much worse than *Oobii*'s on-approach imaging from ten years ago. Right now, their agrav skiff should be overflying the mouth of the River Fell. That was the location of the densest settlements—both in *Oobii*'s imagery and maritime legend.

The mystery light was gone, but now she realized that, flickering and very faint, there was a constellation of lights on her left. It was something huge and motionless, its shape lost in the steady rain.

"We're at four hundred meters, right on track for our swampy overnight hideaway. Hei, did I tell you how I—or something almost-I—spent a tenday there a couple hundred years ago? It's the closest I ever got to the Choir." He was silent again, listening. "The mob noise has faded. I'll bet the swamp has spread further inland than we thought. We could probably land right here."

"But don't, okay?" said Johanna.

"Heh, okay. But tomorrow is going to be fun. Even if Tycoon hasn't been messing around here, there is so much I've been dying to see for years and years—"

There was a loud noise. The skiff did a somersault and headed groundward. "Pilgrim!"

"Not my fault!" the fivesome shouted back, obviously struggling with the controls. This was worse than anything she remembered, except for times— like his long-ago "accidental" trip to the moon—when Pilgrim was creating the problem himself. "Left side lift is—"

The craft flipped over and was swinging back and forth from a single support point on the right side. That was the good and the bad thing about agrav. The fabric could be like a lawyer, negotiating with the laws of physics. It was even possible that now they had more lift than before.

Or maybe not: something snapped and they were falling again. Pilgrim scrambled around her. Two of him leaned out, jaws snapping, into the rain. Somehow he didn't lose anyone. A moment later he was back, gripping taut fabric. "Here!" he said. "Don't let go!"

She was holding the edge of the remaining agrav fabric. It wriggled in her hands, like something alive, trying to pull free. Pilgrim grabbed the rest of it with all his jaws. He jerked it this way and that, trying to keep them airborne, but now without any automatic control whatsoever.

"We're not going to make it!" he shouted. But they weren't really falling anymore, just going *down* much faster than was healthy.

Something whacked them from the right, then the left and the right . . . down to a stunning impact from below. Maybe she blacked out. She remembered Pilgrim's voice right by her ear: "You sound alive. True?"

Oh, not a memory after all. "Yes," she finally replied.

"Ha. Another perfect landing."

"Are *you* okay, Pilgrim?"

The pack didn't answer instantly. Members could take more bouncing around than adult humans, but a whole pack had more opportunity for individual bad luck. "Mostly," he finally answered. "I think my Llr banged a foreleg." Another hesitation. "Never mind that. We are safely down and well away from Choir sound."

"But we didn't make it to the swamps."

"True." He chuckled. "Even you could probably hear the difference. We've come down between rocky obstacles. We gotta get out and look around." Some of him was already on the ground outside.

"Yeah." Something was still holding her down. She thought muzzily for a second. *Oh.* She unclipped her restraints and crawled out into the rain. Pilgrim was right, they'd come down on something hard. Her hands felt around. There were shallow puddles, no mud. This might have been glacier-scoured rock or— her fingers found regular cracks—or flagstones. She stood up, the blood-warm rain soaking her.

She felt the pack clustering close around her shins. Pilgrim's big one, Scar-butt, leaned comfortingly against her.

"Let's see what's left of the skiff." A light came on, faintly silhouetting one of Pilgrim's heads. The lamp was turned down and he held it in his jaws so the gleam was in one direction. Pilgrim swept the glow across the skiff while two of him nosed around in the wreckage, doubtless probing with sound. "Oh my," he said, "flying this will be a challenge."

The skiff had never been a beautiful thing, and over the years, Pilgrim's repairs had made it motley. But now, the hull itself was cracked. The remaining agrav fabric strained upwards in ragged shreds.

Pilgrim abruptly doused his light. "I hear packs talking." His voice was a focused whisper in her ear. She felt him press the light into her hand. "Use it just bright enough for your eyes."

Johanna nodded. She made the light violet and so dim that she could barely see the ground below it. It should be invisible to whatever packs were out there. All of Pilgrim except Scar had crawled back into the skiff and was bringing out the emergency supply panniers. They had lived off that gear for tendays in the past.

Pilgrim's voice again: "I think the packs I hear are searching for us. We must have made quite a racket coming down."

Johanna replied with a nearly subvocal whisper. Scar, with his head at the level of her waist, would pick it up fine. "Are these normal packs?"

"Yes, indeedy. We should be in the middle of mindless Choir chaos, but what I'm hearing is East Coast Interpack." So even if they discovered nothing more, they had answered the big question behind this trip. Now the problem was how to get the news back to Ravna and Woodcarver. It might be nice to survive the mission, too.

"You have the commset?" she asked.

"Got it." Pilgrim was urging her along, away from the crash site. Her pale violet light hinted that they were walking between high walls of stone. Walls of brick actually, with nice right angles and waterfalls every few meters. This was an alley, and somewhere above them were roofs with rainspouts.

"The end of this path is open—and there are no voices beyond that. There are some real advantages to this situation, you know."

Pilgrim was jollying her along. He did that when things were . . . tense. Well, he had a couple of centuries of fairly successful survival experience. She played along: "You mean because we're still breathing?"

"That, and I'm still thinking. No Choir-driven mental destruction. If we can find a hiding place, we can operate almost like on our other trips. Except for the flying, I mean."

"Yeah, okay. And we can report back."

"Right. This may be the best possible place to go snooping. We may actually be able to learn if these guys are manipulating your boyfriend."

"He's not my boyfriend!" she almost said that in full voice.

"Whatever," said Pilgrim. "In any case—" The voice in her ear hesitated. "Wait up a second."

Johanna swung her lamp around. Llr had fallen behind. The member had a clear limp and her pannier had slipped partway off her back. Johanna reached down and unclipped the pannier.

"Thanks—"

But Jo wasn't done. She slipped her hands behind Llr's forelegs and raised the creature into her own arms.

"Hei wait!" said Pilgrim. "I don't need that much help."

Johanna didn't reply, just proceeded along with the pannier slung over her shoulder and Llr struggling in her arms like a big, fussy baby. After a moment, she heard Pilgrim give a resigned sigh. Llr relaxed in her arms, then reached up and nipped Johanna's ear—but only with the soft tips of her mouth.

They followed the alley for another thirty meters, moving at a better pace than before. That was good, since now even Johanna could hear Interpack gobbling somewhere behind them. Pilgrim said there was also a "spiky hissing" noise, probably not part of their speech. Directly ahead something hulked a little brighter than the violet backglow of the rain. A stone wall.

"I thought you said this end of the alley was open?" said Johanna.

"There's a turn," came Pilgrim's whisper, "to the right."

Now Johanna could hear the strange noise Pilgrim had reported. Something bright lit up behind them. "Come on!" she said to Pilgrim. They ran for the end of the alley. Just as they made the turn, the noise sharpened and a brilliant light shone through the veil of rain, lighting up the walls behind them.

They had escaped the light, but—there was a chord that meant "After them!" and she heard the clatter of metal tines.

Johanna and Pilgrim kept running, with Llr passing Jo directions about which way to go.

High ahead of her, she saw occasional flashes of light as the pursuers swept their hissing spotlight back and forth. It must be some kind of electric arc. Scrupilo had wanted to make such things, till Ravna found a low-power design that was actually easier to make. Such arcs were *bright*, surely bright enough for Tines—if they pointed them accurately and didn't blind themselves.

Pilgrim was leading her in a flat run along a stone way just a little higher than the puddles. By the light reflected from the enemy's crazy arc lamp, she glimpsed brickwork and half-timbered walls—very much like northern buildings except for the mossy fungus that grew all over them. Maybe the northern style didn't last long here. They ducked behind wooden sheds, out of sight of the probing light.

Jo felt Llr's claws tighten, cautioning. *Slow down.* Now that they couldn't be spotted, it was best to be as quiet as possible.

"But we need to get further away," said Johanna.

Pilgrim's Llr gave her a little pat on the shoulder, agreeing. But now their progress consisted of the pack moving a meter or two, testing for things that might cause noise, then signalling Jo how to bring herself and Llr forward. Behind them, the noise of the chase was slightly diminished. It sounded like several packs were pacing around, talking quietly to one another, almost as though they were embarrassed by all the noise they had made.

Meter by meter, Pilgrim edged away from the Easterners. Then light flared on a wall ahead of them, right where they would be in another minute or so. The light swept away, came back briefly a second later, then was gone again.

Johanna sat on the stone way, putting some of Llr's weight on her knees. "Maybe we should just hide here for a while."

She only mouthed the words, but that was enough sound for Pilgrim. He shook a head or two, then said: "See how tumbled down everything is in that direction?" Some of the structures were barely more than mounds of rotting timber. "I can hear Choir noise ahead. We seem to be moving out of whatever safety zone is protecting these East Coast bozos. Maybe we can go far enough to lose them, but not so far that the Choir destroys my mind."

"Okay." What else could she say?

Pilgrim's Scar had crawled forward, edging his snout out to look at their pursuers. He froze, and Jo felt Llr tense. "Heh. You gotta see this, Jo."

She set Llr down and crawled out behind Scar, all but hugging the slimy stone. She saw four packs about fifty meters away. One of them managed the electric arc light. It was a miracle that the contraption had not electrocuted anybody. The pack was swinging the arc around. Jo got a good view of the others. Two of the packs bristled with strange-looking pikes, all pointed at the ground. Huh! Those looked like miniature cannons, though nothing like Nevil's design. A numerous pack stood in a commanding posture in the middle of all this. Its speech was almost inaudible, but clipped and demanding. What was so familiar about that one? *Can it be?* . . . The arc light swept carelessly across the packs. The leader was wearing lightweight cloaks, barely more than pockets on harnesses. One member was turned so she could see its complete right side, the white streak that extended from haunch to snout.

Ten years ago, that one's teeth had hissed along Jo's throat, while another poked a knife into her side, and its pack gloated at the prospect of torturing her to death.

Pilgrim must have noticed the recognition startle through her. His secret voice said. "That looks like Vendacious, doesn't it?"

Johanna nodded. She had absolutely no doubt. So it really was Vendacious, pulling the strings. *Whose strings exactly?*

Pilgrim gave her a tap on the shoulder. "They're dazzled. Let's sneak across." He pointed at the gap in the timbers ahead.

It might not have worked with human pursuers, but the light was turned away from Jo and Pilgrim, and the Tines probably were bedazzled. Vendacious seemed to be complaining about something, maybe that very abuse of the arc light.

Jo slithered across the flagstones. Pilgrim was all around her. He was probably generating sound-damping noise; Pilgrim was more clever than most packs at such synthesis. In a matter of seconds they were out of eyeshot of the searchers. "Quiet and slow," said Pilgrim. Quietly, slowly, they crawled forward. Llr had no trouble keeping up. The buildings around them were still of the northern style, but the wood was rotted and buckled. In the pale violet light of her handlamp, she could see that some timbers were almost consumed by mossy fungus. Now the water carried a miasma of smells: food, sewage, rot, the body odor of myriad Tines. Was it her imagination or was that chanting ahead?

Pilgrim seemed to sense her unease.

"You can hear something, too," he said. "They're making noise all the way down."

"How can you stand it?"

"The rain and mist is damping mindsound to almost nothing, but we're moving toward something . . . enormous." Johanna had seen Pilgrim react to a starship coming down from the sky. Even that he had taken on with enthusiastic curiosity, but tonight there might be fear in his words. Then he urged her forward and seemed to recover some of his usual spirit: "I can get a lot closer. Closer, I bet, than Vendacious and company can come."

In fact, their pursuers seemed to have lost them. Johanna saw an occasional flash from the arc light but that was way to her left. She also heard quiet conversations, but those seemed to be on the right. The searchers were moving forward, but not straight toward her and Pilgrim. Were they scared of triggering a response from the Choir? Maybe the biggest mystery was how Vendacious and his pals could survive in this environment at all. What kept the Choir from sweeping across this area and destroying all coherent packs?

Jo swept her violet light across the rubble ahead. This wasn't the decay of Northern-style buildings. The soaking mess looked like garbage, organized here and there into structures that might have been nests. She had seen a weasel nest once, briefly, when its inhabitants were trying to kill her. "Weasels" were about the size and appearance of gerbils. She quailed at the thought of what such monsters would be like if they were as big as Tines.

She angled her light upwards. The violet drowned in the falling rain, showing nothing but misty backglow beyond a few meters. Right at the limit of her vision, there was something—it looked almost like a long, low spider web.

It was a fence! The "spider threads" were cords hung between wooden posts. Vertical strands dropped from the top cord to tie to each of the cords below. How could this stop anything? Were the cords poisoned? As they got closer, Johanna could see how frayed and ripped the network was, especially near the ground, where it was clear that critters at least the size of small Tines had broken through.

Pilgrim tugged at her sleeves, drawing her down to the ground. A moment later, the arc light swept along the fence.

"Sorry," she said softly. Then, "Are you okay?"

"Yeah. Let's see if Vendacious and company dare follow us beyond that fence."

The ground immediately beyond the fence was flat and open. Even if Vendacious wouldn't chase them, he could still see—and shoot—them. At the limit of her vision she saw piles of . . . something, maybe the true form of Tropical buildings. The thrum of Choir voices murmured loudly and yet she saw no Tines.

She and Pilgrim reached the fence. The cords were just woven plant fiber. Tearing a hole would be easy. They crawled along the fence line. . . .

Their pursuers had spread out. They must know that Pilgrim and Jo were at the fence, even if they didn't know precisely where.

"They're going to find us," she whispered.

"Yeah, yeah," was all Pilgrim said. He was still searching for the perfect breakthrough point. At least here, the open area beyond the fence was not as wide as before. They skulked another three meters. Abruptly, Pilgrim jabbed a snout upwards, pointing. A sign medallion hung from the top fence rope. The patterned ceramic disks were a style of announcement that dated from long before the humans landed. Day or night, a pack would hear the echoes from it. By the pale light of her handlamp, Johanna could see the design that was painted on the surface: the death symbol, a pentagram of skulls. Someone thought it was a really bad idea to go beyond this fence.

———

"And I don't want any *shooting*." Vendacious glared around at his trigger-happy minions. "We're not in my territory anymore."

The crowd of packs straightened and looked properly obedient. They might be trigger happy, but they weren't crazy enough to cross him. Normally, these fellows patrolled the west side of the Reservation, making sure that no one crossed the boundary. Of course, no pack would voluntarily walk *off* the Reservation, but there was a constant dribble of Tropicals coming in. The creatures were dumb singletons. That was the thing about the Choir: it wasn't a proper tyranny. Its behavior was describable only in the mean. There was always a tiny fraction of outliers who were confused enough or ornery enough do almost anything. Guards like these working for him tonight were supposed to pick up such and take them to the convocation bourse. That was a pain. It was much easier just to shoot disobedient intruders. On the far side of the Reservation, that was easy to do. It was good sport, Vendacious thought. On *this* side, such shooting would be heard by Tycoon people who would loyally report the behavior, raising all sort of problems for Vendacious. *Tonight of all nights*, thought Vendacious, *I don't want Tycoon's guns out here, nosing around.*

Having made his point, Vendacious eased off on the homicidal glare. He wanted his people to be at the top of their form this evening. "The two I want are somewhere between us and the fence. Don't worry about exactly where. Push forward along a broad front. Eventually we'll flush them out." Two of the gunpacks broke into uneasy smiles. They had been on similar outings before. Killing dumb singletons was one thing. Forcing a thinking pack into Choir territory was a different matter entirely. "Go quietly. Listen for my signals." They would have to stay quiet till the next density of the Choir swept through. When that happened, they could probably make as much noise as they wanted.

Vendacious watched as the packs spread out in a ragged skirmish line and started toward the fence. The lamp manager stayed somewhat back, sweeping its light toward likely shapes and sounds.

Vendacious followed his people forward, unlimbering his own small rifle as he did so. At the same time, he reached into one of his pockets and unmuted the commset hidden there, but at such a low volume that even he could scarcely hear it.

He complained into his pocket: "They didn't come down where you said." And they survived the crash.

There was the half-second delay and then Nevil's voice came back. As usual, the human was full of cocky rejoinders: "You're just lucky I noticed them sneaking down your way. You're even more lucky I'd prepped their aircraft. I crashed them right where you said."

Vendacious didn't reply immediately. He found that silence often provoked Nevil Storherte into informative elaboration. And after a moment Nevil came up with something interesting: "You know the, um, targets took a commset with them when they escaped from the skiff."

What! Can they hear us talking then? Vendacious stifled the question. He had come to know that the starfolks' "commsets" were nothing like radio cloaks. Unless Nevil reprogrammed the devices, each would have a separate "channel" through his orbital relay. So aloud, he just said, "That's interesting. I assume you're blocking their calls."

"Of course, though at the moment they're just carrying the device. The *interesting* fact is that I can tell you where they are."

Vendacious' current plans depended on two incredibly powerful, incredibly infuriating tools. One was Nevil Storherte. *I'm so glad Nevil is far away. I don't think I could keep from killing him otherwise.* Nevertheless, Vendacious was pleased at his own mild response: "And where is that?"

"Thirty-one meters from you—your commset—on a bearing of forty-seven degrees." You could hear the smirk in the two-legs' techno-speak. Nevil was supposedly a master of guile, but that was with other humans. His contempt for Tines was strong and obvious.

Fortunately, Vendacious had spent much of the last ten years learning everything he could about humans and the Beyond. There was vast power in their knowledge, even though the religious nuttery sometimes made it hard to tell what was real. In any case, Vendacious could reason with numbers better than any unaided "Child of the Sky." He looked out at where the Reservation fence stood in his spotlight. Johanna and Pilgrim would be at the fence now, near the right end of his searchers. He squeaked pointedly at the various packs, shifting them to converge on the pile of rubble where his quarry must be hiding.

Tonight should still be a major triumph, but it had turned out riskier than the original plan. He'd expected to find his two greatest enemies crushed and dead in their aircraft. Instead he was skulking through the dark after them, hoping that neither his light nor his noise would attract Tycoon's interest. And yet, there was a thoroughly delicious side to this. At this very moment, Pilgrim and Johanna were squeezed up against the fence. To cross that fence would mean certain death, torn apart physically or mentally or both. But if they stayed where they were, Johanna would be back in his claws. This time she would not be rescued by Pilgrim's clever, humiliating lies, for Pilgrim himself would be just as helpless as the human. *Either way, I win.*

Vendacious maneuvered himself closer to his searchers. Normally he loathed every second here in the Tropics, even more when he had to work in the filthy outdoors. Tonight . . . tonight he was truly enjoying himself.

"I think they know where we are," said Pilgrim.

Johanna nodded. Even though he was looking into the spaces beyond the fence, she knew he was talking about their pursuers. Looking over her shoulder, she could see occasional members of the searcher packs. They seemed closer, and now the search light was spending most of its time centered almost exactly over her head. The light glittered off the death-heads medallion. "Most of them are on the side we came from. Maybe we could sneak back the other way . . . flank them." It was a forlorn suggestion.

"No," said Pilgrim. "You know, you might not have any trouble with the Choir, mindless as you are." That was a bit of Pilgrim humor. Johanna doubted the serious point behind his statement. There were stories about what happened to animals in the Tropical cities. Everything here was consumed, in mind or flesh.

Nevertheless she tried to match him. "You might be okay, too, *near* mindless as you are." He didn't reply, and after a moment Johanna was reduced to miserable reality. "I can't see looking for mercy from Vendacious." *He will never get his claws on me again.*

"Me neither." Pilgrim's voice was no longer bantering, but it didn't have the miserable tone that Johanna had heard in her own. But then Pilgrim was a pilgrim and such as he bragged about their fearlessness. "You know," the pack continued, "all my life, even back to the myths of earlier me's, the stories about the Tropics have been the same, that the place is deadly to mind, that you only go there if you want to dissolve in joy. But look at what we're not seeing." He pointed a snout into the rain that glittered in Vendacious' spotlight. "Scarcely a single Tropical member. We hear chanting, but this rain and this humidity damps the real sounds of thought down to nothing. Look at how hunched together each of Vendacious' packs are. I'll bet this rain is having even more effect on the Choir, and the chanting we hear is the Choir cooped up, out of the wet! I could probably run right across this street and find us a hidey-hole on the other side."

"If you don't get shot by Vendacious' goons—"

"Piffle." Pilgrim waved dismissively. Johanna guessed that Wicky didn't believe any of what he was saying, and was dying to get her out of harm's way. On the other hand, his voice had that intrigued, calculating tone he used when he was planning something over-the-top. "Honestly, Johanna, this doesn't look as crazy as when Scriber and I rescued you on Murder Meadows. And . . . I've always wondered what the Choir was like. Imagine getting in, and returning alive." His Scarbutt member was pulling at a tear in the fence, making it large enough so the pack could sprint through.

"Oh, Pilgrim!" Her whisper was loud enough that even she could hear it. Not that that really mattered any more. She reached out, trying to hold him back. This was way too much like being a little orphan girl again.

"Hei, don't worry. We've gotten through worse." He wriggled loose from her, but did not immediately rush off. Maybe he was waiting for the arc light to drift away from their part of the fence. "Use your invisible light. Try to see where I end up on the other side. I'll find some place safe, and wave."

"Okay." She gave him a pat. Wicky was right, even if he was blowing smoke. She pulled the commset and other gear close and then shone her violet light out into the space beyond the fence.

A moment passed. The glare of the arc light shifted away, leaving blinding afterimages. That didn't stop Pilgrim. He sprinted out through the widened hole in the fence. She squinted into the afterimages and—the big light came back, shining right on the running foursome. Pilgrim zigged and zagged. Apparently the gun packs couldn't get a bead on him, for no one fired.

The chanting of the Choir was growing. Hopefully, the mind sounds were still attenuated by the wetness, but what Johanna could hear sounded like a mob at close quarters. An ambush on top of Vendacious' ambush? She swung her pale light to the right. There was a trickle of shapes in the rainglow. They were moving past her position, in the general direction of Pilgrim. The trickle became a crowd, a mob, members shoulder to shoulder as she had never seen before among the Tines.

Pilgrim turned, was running away, but all along the far edge of the open space, Tropicals were pushing into the open. They weren't running. The Tines strolled along almost parallel to the fence. Their numbers grew. Somehow Pilgrim Wickllrrackscar kept his mind. He was running all together, but Llr's limp kept him from full speed. It didn't matter. The Tropicals were a mob now, sweeping along the fence like the edge of some giant scissor blade, the cutting point of contact moving faster than any pack could run. Rac fell to slashing claws. The last Jo saw of Pilgrim was little Llr's body tossed into the air, like a tidbit for some vast carnivore.

"Pilgrim!" Maybe she screamed the name aloud.

Pilgrim was gone, but the mob did not overrun the fence. As a whole, they were sweeping parallel to the barrier. Avoidance wasn't perfect; the crowd was too jammed together for that. Here and there, Tropical members were rammed through the barrier. Most of them wriggled back; some wandered aimlessly further inward.

The Choir racket was a roar, even to her ears. The higher frequencies would be tearing at Vendacious' goons, but when she looked behind her: There was a pack with guns on one side. The arc light lit the rain on the other.

A human-sounding voice spoke conversationally. "Run, Johanna, run. Into the Choir. I want to see this." *Vendacious*.

It seemed like good advice, even considering the source. Johanna tore through the fence and ran into the Choir.

———

Well damn! So much for reverse psychology. The two-legs was running. Without thinking, Vendacious whipped up his rifle and aimed at her back. At the same time he was shouting to his troops "Don't shoot!"

His lips tightened on the trigger just as sense finally percolated all the way through him. There was a *reason* why he had threatened the others with death if they started shooting on this side of the Reservation. The work of eight years would be in jeopardy . . . *but oh, I could figure out a lie to cover it; Tycoon believes so many bigger lies.* He stifled the thought. He had taken enough chances tonight. He must be content to enjoy this from a distance.

It was her good fortune that Johanna Olsndot had sprinted through the fence just as the passing mob became slightly thinner. She made it twenty feet into Choir territory, forty feet. Now the mob came thick again, the mindsounds even louder than when they had destroyed Pilgrim. Vendacious and his comrades hugged the ground, each pack holding all its own heads together. If not for the rain, some of them might have been destroyed, even on this side of the Reservation boundary.

Somehow Vendacious managed to keep some eyes and ears tracking the fleeing human. The mindsounds wouldn't stop the mantis, but now she was battered by dozens of Tines, the brute force of the Choir. She was knocked to her knees, and now some of the members had wakened to her otherness and the biting began. Joy spread through every one of Vendacious' own members. Oh, how long he had waited for this. And he knew just what to expect, thanks to his special diligence. He'd always wondered what the Choir would make of humans, since mental destruction would be impossible. So when one of the first humans he had kidnapped ceased to be useful, he'd arranged that it would "escape" from the Reservation. Just as now, there had been an initial hesitation. And then just as it did with non-Tinish animals of all sizes, the Choir had torn the creature apart, playing with the parts much as they seemed to play with the parts of dismembered packs. But unlike member sacrifices, the Choir valued animal intruders only for their food value. The hapless two-legs had served the eaters well—and served Vendacious far better than it had as a prisoner.

Now he watched as the same pattern played out. Johanna was back on her feet. The noise was so great he couldn't hear her breath, the whimpering, but the arc light showed blood streaming down one side of her face. She staggered away from the fence, swinging her gear at the mob and shouting, as if she thought the flow would go around her. She got another ten feet, almost to the burrows that edged this side of the Reservation. He knew from observation that there would be no salvation there. Jaws waited. She fell again, and this time didn't get up. The mob piled upon her, a wave on a lump of flesh. He saw bits and pieces bobbing to the surface, mostly the equipment she'd been carrying.

It took fifteen minutes before the density passed into full rarefaction, an unusually long time. The feeding clump boiled in the arc light, eventually rolling what was left into the burrows. As the mob swept out of the area, there was only the rain and humidity to keep him from hearing the outcome. And even the rain had diminished. He could hear no one moving around in the wreckage. Listening very carefully . . . no, there was not even the sound of human breathing, just the moaning respiration of a thousand mindless Tines.

"So what happened?" That was Nevil's voice, from Vendacious' commset. There was ill-concealed uneasiness in his voice.

Vendacious didn't answer immediately. He stared out at the piles of soaked, stinking garbage. Somewhere under all that, just fifty feet beyond the fence, lay the corpse of the creature that had ruined his past life and threatened his future. Fifty feet. So near, and yet he could not safely cross that distance to crunch the marrow with his own jaws. He looked slyly at his loyal troops. It would take the threat of painful death to force them across. After watching the Choir, no normal pack could believe the stories about the Choir's endless joy. The chances of coming back from a fifty-foot sortie—even during a rarefaction—were close to zero. Besides, Vendacious operated this close to the House of Tycoon only when there was the deadliest necessity.

Vendacious thought a moment and realized there was something more he could do. He spoke into his commset, replying to his own pet human: "Where is Johanna's commset?" *Is it still functioning at all?*

"It's been stuck about twenty meters from you ever since she started screaming. There's no motion now. I—I could try to flush her out for you."

"Yes." *Let's be sure.*

There was silence from Vendacious' commset, and then Nevil's voice came from across the open area. Nevil seemed to be whispering, but the volume was easily loud enough to hear. "*Sst.* Johanna? Are you okay? Telemetry showed a problem with the skiff. Johanna?" This went on for several seconds. Vendacious thought it was quite artfully plaintive. Considering all the other evidence, it was wasted effort, but Vendacious admired the craft.

CHAPTER 19

The second time she went down, Johanna knew she would not be getting up. The first bites had been tasting nibbles. She'd seen that behavior in the members of coherent packs—just before they went into a feeding frenzy with unusual meat. Now her face and arms were slick with blood. Swinging her equipment as a flail only seemed to excite the mob. They butted her behind her knees in a coordinated way that sent her down again. She covered her face with her arms and rolled onto her front, leaving her knapsack covering part of her body. Paws and jaws rolled her over, again and again. They were tearing at her clothes, pulling her gear out of the knapsack.

And yet, the feeding frenzy never came, though the crowd was a crushing mass upon her. It was almost as if they were battling each other just to get a snout down and take a nibble. She tried to keep an airgap between her face and forearm as she wriggled in the direction she guessed would take her out of sight of Vendacious and company. The crushing weight seemed to ease; the nips and jabs were distant pain, like memories.

Huh? She was lying flat on her back, dizzy even so. Everything was dark. She wiggled her hands and felt about her. There was the commset and what was left of her knapsack. The ground was like slick mucous. Nowhere did she touch Tinish fur or skin. Somehow, suddenly, she seemed to be alone. Or maybe she had died. *Okay. So what's my next move?*

"*Sst.* Johanna? Are you okay? Telemetry showed a problem with the skiff. Johanna?" It was Nevil's voice, a loud whisper.

She reached for the commset—then froze and tried to be very very quiet. There are betrayals and Betrayals. Until this moment, her worst suspicion was that Nevil had been used by Vendacious. Until this moment, she had not believed that Nevil was capable of Betrayal. She stared into the dark, in the direction of the commset. *I don't have proof even now . . . only certainty.*

Nevil's voice came back on Vendacious' commset. "No reply," said the two-legs. "What about Pilgrim?"

"Both Pilgrim and the maggot are very dead," Vendacious replied. In fact, there might still be one or two members of Pilgrim alive, but past experience showed that such did not come back.

Nevil was silent for a moment, and then he sighed. "Well, that simplifies things, at least."

Vendacious smiled to himself. Though they had rarely met, Vendacious had studied Nevil Storherte thoroughly. Storherte was a young predator. Until recently he had never killed *anything*. The creature thought he was moved by virtuous necessity. He was still growing into his true nature.

Aloud, Vendacious said. "Indeed, it does simplify things." *All revenge aside, my most dangerous lie is now much more secure.* "And now it should be possible to deal with our other great enemy."

"Yeah. I'm going to enjoy giving you Ravna Bergsndot."

————

Johanna lay still for some minutes, but Nevil had nothing more to say.

All things considered, playing dead was easy. The mob had departed, but their warbling chant was still out there. Maybe that was enough to keep Vendacious' crew from searching for her corpse. The rain continued its windless heavy fall. Water dripped through the pile above her; what trickled down to her felt oily.

After a time, the Choir noise grew loud again. She could hear ten thousand paws scuffing in her direction. She could hear individual voices that made no sense, but just added to the grand susurrus. Now there were members snuffling all around, so close that their mindsounds, even though far kilohertz above human hearing, still made a buzzing through her body. They crowded over her, much as before, snouts pushing, but this time there were no painful bites, just gentle mouthing with soft forelips. The smells and sounds were overpowering, but after a moment, the swarm was flowing past her and almost no one was touching her.

Okay, so she was not to be eaten. And the mob's noise would be ideal cover, if only they would let her move. Johanna thought a moment, made sure she was taking nothing with her that might betray her to Nevil. *My Knife?* For sure. *My light?* She took a chance, kept that too. Then she rolled to her knees, tucked her head down, and crawled deliberately against the flow of the Choir, testing.

The mob was a tide of plush and flesh—but the Tines who rammed into her weren't biting. In fact, they seemed to be struggling to get out of her way. It was the pressure of the myriad bodies behind them that made that impossible. Then suddenly, as if some traffic information had been transmitted upstream, the pressure eased and the mob slid around her. Johanna crawled slowly through the roaring, warbling flow. She held the lamp in her mouth, the faint violet light splashing over the mob. The corridor's beslimed walls turned this way and that. In places there were forks or merges. Tines were coming from all but the lowest openings—maybe those were under water tonight. Johanna found that when she came to a fork, there were moments when the crowd was impassable, and then they would spread apart for her once more.

She must have spent an hour in the soggy catacombs. When she finally emerged, the rain had become drizzle and mist. Behind her, she could see lights, faint in the murk. She stared at them for a moment, noting the flickering, the occasional dark curling shadows that must be smoke. She was seeing torches in sconces. When the drizzle faltered she could see the straight edges of stone-and-timber walls, standard architecture from northern lands. Vendacious' landholding. The rest of the horizon was the unrelieved moaning darkness of the Choir.

She limped quietly away from Vendacious' lights, into the dark of the Choir. *Oh Pilgrim!*

Johanna wandered numbly for a time, vaguely aware of her slowly bleeding wounds, mostly remembering Pilgrim's dying. Her violet lamp was just bright enough to see her feet, to keep from walking into walls or water-filled pits. She'd kept the lamp so dim because some Tines could sense that violet color, if only as a nebulous patch at the edge of their vision. That fact had gotten her and Pilgrim into trouble on one mission to East Home. It really didn't matter anymore; she brightened the lamp, saw a few Tropicals ambling along their separate ways. None showed much interest in her. If anything, they were avoiding her. Where she was walking was almost like the middle of a city street. A city conceived in a mad and contradictory delirium, rebuilt and rebuilt on its own muddy ruins.

She proceeded along the gently descending street. In some places, the surface was rain-slick fungimoss over stone; in others, it looked like matted leaves. Where would downwards lead?

Silly question, when there was nothing more to lose.

And yet, just as she continued to walk, Johanna continued to think. *Why am I still alive?* Vendacious had seemed in mortal fear of crossing into Choir territory. He seemed to think the Choir would destroy Johanna as surely as it had Pilgrim. Vendacious was not stupid. He must have had precedent and observation to back up his belief.

On her left, the Choir noise was increasing. The simple solution to the mystery was that her survival was to be very temporary. The mob was thickening, oozing out from the vague walls. Their progress was the same slanting, scissors advance that had caught Pilgrim. There was a narrow cleft on the right, ahead. Maybe she should try to hide there.

Too late. The crowd was already upon her. But its touch was only occasional, and as she slowly walked onward, her private space moved with her. She still had no explanation for her survival, but it was clear that after the initial attack, something about *her* had been discovered, and communicated outwards from that contact.

After a time, the mob passed, and again she was almost alone on the street.

The lights of Vendacious' "safe" area were lost behind the muddle of the Choir's city. Johanna continued downslope, plans beginning to poke at her despair. If she *could* survive, could somehow tell Ravna and Woodcarver . . . This path would eventually lead to the River Fell. The maps had shown it flowing south, just west of the agrav's ground path.

Around her feet, the mud was ankle deep. As she continued into the swampy mess, she heard creaking sounds. They were noises that Tines could make easily enough, but . . . *the buildings were moving.* It was a gentle, repetitive motion, up and down just a centimeter or two. She went to the side of the street, and put her hand against the sodden mass of a wall. Yes, up and down, but with small horizontal motions too. She walked along the wall, still touching it. She crossed some irregularity in the street surface—and now the street had joined in the same mild motion. If she hadn't had the wall to lean against, the surprise would have sent her sprawling.

The edge of the street was floating in the River Fell.

Though she couldn't quite tell where rooted buildings gave way to floating rafts, the sound of quietly bobbing real estate grew louder as she walked on. Her street was more than a sandbar and less than a pier, and it extended into the slowly flowing Fell. In places, her light reflected off dark, rippling water. Whatever had been moored there had sailed away or simply broken off. In other places, the buildings were canted, piled two or three deep, perhaps the careless result of incoming rafts running onto occupied frontage. After heavy rains or a typhoon, all this might be swept away and even this roadway destroyed.

Tonight she had seen thousands of the Choir, but not a single froghen, not a single edible plant. However inefficiently, cargo must move into and out of here. The road ahead narrowed, but the rafts were larger. A crazy idea floated up; she knew where some of these rafts voyaged.

She walked onward, occasionally sending a violet light behind her, watching for the mob she heard coming. Ahead of her was a dead end: the tip of a peninsula. She could hear the Fell sweeping along like slow syrup. Her light gave a clear view of "buildings" festooned with rigging and jagged masts. Here and there, Tinish heads popped up from the jumble. A half dozen came off the rafts, running toward her, hissing displeasure. They circled close, nipping at her legs.

Meantime the main mob had returned from up the street. Okay, now she was truly trapped. But as these hundreds arrived, surrounding her, the Tines who had been hissing and nipping gave her space, merging with the rest. The crowd jostled and swirled, the space around Johanna disappearing as the hundreds behind came flowing into this bounded area. She heard splashing sounds that must be the occasional Choirmember squeezed off into the river.

The open space around Johanna was gone. Tines pressed upon her from all sides, even as they resisted the force behind them. Then, almost like a spring bouncing back, there was an easing of pressure and space opened up.

And yet, this wave of the mob did not ebb—perhaps because there was only one obvious way out. She watched the creatures mill around her. Their gaze seemed mutely curious, as if they were waiting for some insight.

Me too, thought Jo.

Around her, the empty spaces widened. The critters drew together in little clumps and clots. From their posture, they looked almost like . . . packs. An *ad hoc* fivesome approached her. Its members were almost naked, though a couple carried ragged panniers. Four were balding, but they looked healthier than the one with a full coat of fur. That fifth member came very near Johanna. It was missing an ear, and an interrupted scar ran across one shoulder. The scar could be evidence of an ax attack, balked by an armored jacket.

It spoke Samnorsk: "Hei, Johanna. Some of me remembers you."

There were less intelligible comments from the other transient packs. In the mob beyond, Johanna saw occasional bobbing heads—singletons who remembered the Domain and the Fragmentarium?

She looked at the masts in the moorage behind her, and then turned back to the godsgift who had just spoken. "I think I remember some of you, too." The idea that had been percolating up as she walked down this muddy path suddenly seemed quite reasonable . . . at least imaginable. She adjusted her light so that it would be dimly visible to those around her. "Do you suppose I could get a ride back to the Domain?"

By the time the mob finished wreaking enthusiastic havoc on the riverfront, at least eight rafts had been pushed into the river. The operation had not been entirely peaceful, as the small number of Tines who'd been living in the rafts (squatters? caretakers?) were completely taken by surprise by the sudden departure of their housing. Some of these were chased away; others merged with the mob. As far as Johanna could tell, nobody got seriously hurt.

She was thousands of kilometers from rescue, adrift on rafts that were scarcely more than flotsam, crewed by accident. In cold fact, her situation was as desperate as before she pushed off. But now remembering Pilgrim did not jam all other thought.

The vague gray light of morning showed in the east, maybe her first and last light on the grand landscape of the Choir. The city's low, jumbled silhouette still stretched across three-quarters of her horizon. A few lights marked taller buildings in Vendacious' safe area. She sensed something huge and dark looming over them. *It must be a cloud, but it doesn't move.*

Her motley crews had raised sails on at least three of the rafts—though at the moment there was scarcely a breeze and the Fell's slow current was steadily moving them along. They were drifting through the area where she and Pilgrim had intended to hide. That plan would have worked, too; there were stumpy trees and a canopy of leaves.

Johanna gave a little wave at the mystery disappearing behind her. *I will be back, Pilgrim. I promise I will find what became of you.*

CHAPTER 20

For Ravna, time was shattered, cause and effect broken into rubble enough for days. The smaller pieces were isolated snatches of sound and sight and smell: Pain. A bumpy ride. Suffocating in offal-smelling darkness. Gentle hands. Jefri's voice, angry and loud.

Other fragments were twilight bright. In one small shard, she was surrounded by warm, furry bodies. Amdi. He was talking to her, quiet, urgent words. In another—maybe the same one—a pack with ragged low-sound ears beat Amdi aside and nipped at Ravna the way a carnivore might tease its food.

Shattered days and shattered nights. A pack sat with her in most of these longer pieces of time. It had perfectly matched blazes on two of its snouts. Screwfloss? The pack fed her, turned her head when she choked on vomit, cleaned her as she soiled herself. He was not always nice. Many times, he hurt her face with a wet cloth. And he fell into jaw-snapping rages. "I'm just the prisoner's asswipe!" he once said. That was funny, but he also complained that she was delirious. "You're repeating what I say," he hissed at her, a head close by her throat. "'Prisoner's asswipe, prisoner's asswipe.' Can't you just *shut up*?"

The longest pieces of time were in bright daylight. She was wrapped in warm blankets, trussed to the top of a slowly moving wagon. When her eyes were open, she saw variously: snowbound forest, Screwfloss driving the wagon, Gannon Jorkenrud. Jefri, walking behind the wagon behind hers. Jefri looked so gaunt.

There were other packs. Sometimes they paced along with her wagon, and more than one shard began: "So. Will she die soon?" This from the pack with the ragged ears. The creature was a sixsome, each member as heavy as Amdi's biggest, but more muscular-looking. Its Samnorsk was crude, a patchwork of several human voices.

And Screwfloss replying: "Quite soon, my lord Chitiratifor. You can see the injury to her snout. Day by day, she weakens."

The two packs spoke softly. No human but Ravna could hear them. "Don't take shortcuts, Screwfloss." Parts of the creature were looking beyond where Ravna could see. "This must be a natural death."

Maybe Amdi came to chat, but Ravna only remembered Screwfloss chasing him off.

One other pack visited Screwfloss. This was a lean, small-bodied fivesome. It spoke no Samnorsk, but it seemed to be interrogating Screwfloss about Ravna's upcoming death. The parts she could see up close had pale, unfriendly eyes. There was deadly anger in its Tinish gobbling.

Then came the longest single fragment of time. It began with another visit from Raggedy Ears. The pack walked quietly along with the wagon for some minutes, just watching Ravna. "She is not dead yet, Screwfloss."

"Sigh. Quite so, my lord Chitiratifor."

"Her breathing is different. Her eyes move. She is not weakening day by day, like you say." The raggedy-eared pack emitted an angry hiss. "Humans should be *easy* to kill, Screwfloss!"

"But you said no shortcuts, my lord. Yes, the two-legs may survive after all—but take a look at her crushed-in snout. She will never have more mind than a singleton."

"That may not be dead enough." Chitiratifor looked away, watching something—someone?—beyond the front wagon. Finally he said, "I'll get back to you, Screwfloss." And he walked on ahead.

They rolled on for another minute or two, then Screwfloss gave her a little jab in the back. "Getting better, are you?" he said.

Ravna didn't reply. She remained still and lifeless throughout the rest of the afternoon, watching all that she could without moving her head. They were in a deep valley, and she had occasional glimpses of a white-foaming river paralleling their course. She could hear a wagon ahead of her. She could see a wagon behind her; it was the enclosed fodder carrier that figured in some of her most incoherent memories. Behind the fodder wagon walked Amdi and Jefri and Gannon. In times past, Jef and Gannon had been—perhaps not friends—but at least fellow delinquents. Now they scarcely spoke. When Gannon wasn't watching him, sometimes Jefri's hands tightened into fists.

Sunlight had left the forest canopy. She caught glimpses of brilliant snows on valley walls above that. This was far sunnier than . . . before. As the afternoon slid toward twilight, she heard the low hooting of a Tinish alarm. The wagons drove off the path, through the snow into the deepest shade. Chitiratifor came racing back along the path, unlimbering telescopes as he ran. He settled in the snow, angling the telescopes through a break in the tree cover. The wagoneers hustled 'round to their kherhogs and tried to quiet the animals. For several moments, everyone was silent, watchful. The only motion was the slow rising of Chitiratifor's telescopes. He was tracking something, and it was coming this way.

And then, finally, Ravna heard it: the purring buzz of steam induction engines. Scrupilo and *Eyes Above 2*. The airship's sound grew over the next minute . . . and then faded to silence in the minute after. Chitiratifor set down his telescopes and started to get up. Some pack outside of Ravna's view emitted a preemptory hiss, and Chitiratifor dropped back to a prone position. Everyone remained quiet for several minutes more. Then Chitiratifor came to his feet and irritably waved for the wagoneers to get back on the road.

As they drove into the deepening twilight, Ravna thought back over the afternoon. She could remember it all as a continuous stream of time, logically binding cause with effect.

It might be too late, but her life had resumed.

———

Pretending to be comatose might have been the safest plan, but Ravna soon realized that was flatly impossible. The smell that drenched her memories—that smell was her clothes, her *self*. Without Screwfloss, she would surely have oozing sores. For all his apparent anger at her, he had done miracles with a few damp rags and perhaps one change of clothes. But now that she was coherent, she couldn't go on like that. *So be a broken singleton, and hope that that is dead enough.*

When they stopped for the night, she let Screwfloss set her on the ground by the wagon. She let him rewrap her blankets. But when he brought food and tried to tease it into her mouth, she wriggled her hands out from the blankets, reached for the bowl. Screwfloss held back for a moment, then he let her take the bowl. He watched her with almost ferocious intensity as she sipped from it, but he didn't say a word.

This evening was Ravna's first good look at her captors. She counted at least four packs spread out around a banked fire. Amdi and Jefri and Gannon seemed to be doing most of the scutwork. They had their own small campfire, whence Screwfloss had brought her food. Even in the dim light, Jef looked as awful as she remembered. He was doing his best not to glance in her direction. Amdi was less successful at that, but he had more heads to account for. And Gannon? Gannon Jorkenrud did not look like a happy camper, but he was eating heartily.

These three might not be prisoners, but they were very junior members of the kidnap gang. Now that she had recovered her mind, Ravna had a million theories. Jefri had betrayed her in the past . . . but this *had* to be different. And Gannon? Another covert ally? That was much harder to believe.

The syrup-grain didn't quite make her sick, but now . . . Ravna struggled to get her feet under her. "Gotta go," she said to Screwfloss. The pack hesitated, but this time *very* briefly. Then he brought over Jo's old boots and helped her put them on. As she stood up and he chivvied her into the bushes, she heard Gannon laugh.

It wasn't hard to act like a brain-damaged singleton. Even her staggering progress would have been impossible without Screwfloss' support. When they finally stopped, she collapsed into a squat. Screwfloss steadied her for a moment, then all of him stepped back. It might be too dark for any pack to see, but Ravna noticed a wave of palpable joy spread across Screwfloss. He was no longer the prisoner's asswipe. And maybe his joy was for more than that:

"You've finally got your mind back, haven't you?" Screwfloss' voice was the faintest whisper, seeming to come from inside her ears. It was the sort of focused audio that a coordinated pack could do. Ravna made a nondescript affirmative noise. "Good," continued Screwfloss' whisper. "The less mouth talk you make, the better . . . we have a lot to catch up on." But then he said nothing more.

As they lurched back to camp, Ravna noticed that Screwfloss had a small limp of his own. He was the pack who had chased her out of her house, the one whose leg she had smashed.

She was aware of numerous heads watching as Screwfloss settled her down by their wagon. After a moment, the second-scariest kidnapper came over and waved Screwfloss away. This was the lean, pale-eyed pack. It poked around at her, talking Samnorsk that mainly showed it had no real understanding of human language. Ravna moaned and swayed and hoped she looked mindless. After several minutes of this, the fivesome stood back. It seemed as irritated by her progress as Chitiratifor had been. It turned, said something imperative to Screwfloss, and walked away. *So,* thought Ravna, *am I dead enough?*

Most of the camp settled down for the night; the dimly glowing embers were not bright enough for Tinish vision. That didn't stop the two chief kidnappers: a greenish light appeared atop the front wagon. Ah, they had one of the tunable lamps from *Oobii.* Chitiratifor had spread something across the flat of the wagon top. Maps? He seemed to be consulting with the lean fivesome.

After a time, they put out the light, but at least one pack was still moving around. She saw shadows sliding off into the undergrowth. A sentry being posted? Time passed. There were little animal noises, and then even that quieted. No doubt parts of the sleeping packs were still awake, but they made no humanly audible sound. Far away, she heard the river she had noticed this afternoon. She turned in the direction of the sound, and saw a tiny flicker of greenish light, surely too faint for any pack in the campsite to notice. So some pack had business down by the river, *technical* business they wanted done away from their fellow-kidnappers.

Ravna saw the light a couple more times, in the same direction, faint and vagrant through the underbrush. Eventually, one of Screwfloss shifted in its sleep, blocking her view. The pack had made no more secret talk.

It was getting hard to stay awake. She resisted sleep for a time, inanely. Consciousness was fun; what if she woke up without her mind again? As she drifted off, she played with possibilities. She'd heard Screwfloss conspiring about her murder, but since the abduction, his every *action* had protected her. Jefri, Amdi, Screwfloss. What if they were trying to save her? They hadn't explained themselves, first because she was out of her head, and now because they were in the midst of enemies with the sharpest natural hearing of any race Ravna knew. Never mind that these three had chased her from her house and grabbed her once she got outside. Ah, what Flenseresque ambiguity! But if she had to bet her life on a theory about friends and enemies, she knew what it would be.

———

The next day, Ravna *sat* among Screwfloss atop the middle wagon. He made a big deal of bracing her with supplies and tie-downs, but in fact she was suffering only occasional dizziness. She did her best to stay slumped and motionless—and *not* touch her face! Her nose and cheek still hurt, but it was touching the crushed bone and cartilage that that made her cry out in pain.

Pretty obviously, they were south of the Icefang Mountains, and following one of the long geological rifts that scarred this side of the continent. Nothing like these rifts had been active during humanity's time on Old Earth (or Nyjora), but such structures were common on terrestrial planets. On a time scale of centuries, these valleys suffered enormous ground shifts and killing lava floods. Even more commonly, carbon dioxide or methane would surge the length of a valley, killing everything that needed oxygen, or causing tornadoes of fire. The result was a turbulent patchwork of ecologies, full of paradoxes—at least to *Oobii*'s simple-minded analysis.

Her kidnappers were either crazy or they had an expert guide, some pack who knew the transient escape routes and understood the treacherous peculiarities of whatever life currently survived.

The wagons stopped near midday. The packs spread out, hunting lunch. Some of the results were humanly edible. Ravna was kept well away from other humans and Amdi. Screwfloss risked a few more words of focused whispering: "I think Chitiratifor has decided about you. I dunno quite what to do."

Late in the afternoon they crossed the boundary of some recent cataclysm. In the space of two hundred meters, the dense undergrowth and bushy trees were replaced by an open forest of tall, slim trees. The direct sunlight had melted the snow down to isolated drifts. This might have been a different world, except that the same river continued to roar along just a few meters downslope of their path. The other wagoneers looked around nervously. Chitiratifor paced the wagons, emitting blustery encouragement that didn't sound credible even to Ravna. She, on the other hand, was cheered by the change. If *Eyes Above 2* flew over today, it would be much harder for these guys to hide. Pilgrim's agrav skiff would do even better; Chitiratifor would have no audible warning at all.

That thought was the most exciting event of the afternoon.

As twilight deepened, Chitiratifor went on ahead; Ravna saw him consulting with the lean-bodied fivesome. When Chitiratifor returned, he waved the wagoneers forward another hundred meters and then off the road, into a relative dense stand of trees—tonight's campground.

Dinner went much like the night before, though now she got a little meat—and she was enormously hungry. She did her best to disguise her appetite. Screwfloss helped with her act, but in an enormously irritating way, cutting her meat into tiny chunks and pushing one piece at a time at her. He made preemptory gobbling noises, as if encouraging an animal to eat. Okay. Ravna played dumb, and did her best not to look across the gloom to where Jefri and Amdi sat with Gannon.

This night, no pack came around to inquire about her medical status. Yes, something had been Decided. Raggedy Ears and the fivesome had another map conference and then it was lights out. The packs spread out a bit, each hiding itself as few human campers would do. It was hard to tell just where they all were, or who might be on sentry duty, but somebody was moving around. She saw shadows departing in the direction of the river. Chitiratifor.

Ravna gave it about ten minutes, then leaned toward the nearest of Screwfloss. "Gotta go. Gotta go!" she said.

Screwfloss emitted complaining noises, but came to his feet quickly enough. Even better, he didn't object when Ravna started off in the direction of the river sounds.

Between the tree tops, the stars provided just enough light to avoid lowhanging branches. Ahead, the rushing river was loud, hiding whatever other sounds there might be. She saw no gleams of greenish lamp light. Finally Screwfloss drew her down. "Stay!" he said, in a focused whisper. So he wasn't willing to risk serious snooping. She should probably be glad. But as she squatted down, she noticed Screwfloss slinking off downslope on his own snooping expedition.

She had crouched down about as long as seemed reasonable, when she heard soft gobbling. This was like Tinish Interpack speech, but with most of the chords unstacked, the squeaks and hisses spaced out. If it had been a little louder, she might have understood it. Someone was using one of Scrupilo's voiceband radios, speaking very carefully to compensate for some kind of transmission problem. Even so, who could be in range? Now the words were Samnorsk . . . Nevil speaking. *Nevil was giving them relay service via the orbiter!* She stood, took a step or two in the direction of the muttered conversation.

A hand abruptly covered her mouth. An arm went around her waist. She was lifted off her feet and lowered gently to the ground. It was Jefri. They lay for a moment on the chill moist earth, both silent. Amdi's voice came in her ear. "We have to go back now."

Ravna nodded. Amdi was all around them. She and Jefri stood up and—

From downslope, there was an explosion of caterwauling, the sounds of monsters tearing each other apart. Jefri dived for cover, drawing her down with him. The night erupted with the cries of packs running from the campsite toward the river. Screaming rage was all around them. They huddled under something bushy as pack members hurtled past.

All the action was down by the river now. The fighting was louder, punctuated by whistling screams of mouth noise. Somebody was being murdered.

Jefri came to his feet and reached down to help Ravna out from the bush.

Her legs were tangled in the branches. Somehow she had wriggled in too far! She twisted around, looking toward the battle noises. That was louder now, but saner sounding too. Someone was shouting real language, orders. There were lights. A search—but still down by the river.

"I'm stuck!" she whispered.

Jefri braced his back against the lower branches and pushed up. She heard his knife slashing. Amdi had been at the edges of the undergrowth. Now he pulled as Jefri lifted, and Ravna slid out.

Someone had come running up from the direction of the river. Screwfloss, all five of him. "Get back to camp!" he said. With Jefri supporting her, the walk took only moments. As they reached the wagons, Jefri paused, let Screwfloss help Ravna the rest of the way. Then he walked around the wagons into the campsite.

"What the fuck!" came Gannon's voice, but this was no brave challenge. When Ravna staggered in with Screwfloss, she noticed that Gannon seemed alone. Even the kherhogs were clustered together as far as they could get from the sounds of the fighting. The draft animals were making their own frightened sounds, probably with as much sense as Gannon. Now bright lamplight was visible downslope, but the noise consisted of solitary screams and Tinish laughter.

A cold nose butted into Ravna's hand. She stifled a squeak and slid her hand around the head. It was one of Amdi, but his whisper came from all of him, audible only in its sum. "I'm so scared, Ravna."

"Amdi, get over here!" That was Jefri, already back by his bedroll.

Screwfloss settled Ravna down on her bedding and they both sat looking downslope. The survivors were already coming back, dark shadows that moved with the enthusiasm of hunters returning. She could smell blood on them, but their triumphant gobbling was edged with unease. Minutes later, six more shadows quietly moved into camp: Chitiratifor. She felt sure that some of his heads were turned in her direction, but he did not approach. All the surviving packs settled down and soon the night was quieter than it had been before the deadly fuss. There were no whuffling snores and less of the nighttime noise of small animals.

Ravna's stark panic gradually eased, even as her mind raced around the possibilities. She was sure that Screwfloss was entirely awake, apparently re-solved to keep silent. After a while, Ravna realized something else. Now she re-ally did need a potty break.

It was a very long night.

CHAPTER 21

Mere mayhem didn't slow down Chitiratifor. By the time the sun peeked above the valley walls, their little caravan had been on the road four hours. At their first rest break, the ragged-eared pack paraded around in the sunlight, as if to proclaim he was not skulking—or perhaps to show everyone that he was totally uninjured.

Ravna took a count: both wagoneers had torn jackets and wounds on vari-ous members. One of them had been a sixsome; now it was five. Amdi was crouched by Jef; the two were talking in the semi-private language they had used since they were little. Screwfloss stood all around the seated Ravna, as if keeping guard on the prisoner. Gannon Jorkenrud sat on the drivers' bench of one of the wagons. He was unscathed, but at least for the moment his cockiness had disappeared. He didn't even look sullen. Gannon was frightened.

The pale-eyed fivesome and one other pack were missing.

Chitiratifor swept close to each of the survivors; his gobbling sounded like a combination of boast and harangue. The two wagoneers shrank from his mind-sound even as they cast nervous glances at each another. When Raggedy Ears stuck a snout in among Amdi, the eight gave a frank wail of terror and tried to hide behind Jefri.

And Jefri . . . Jefri did not flinch from the snapping jaws. He stared back at the nearest of Chitiratifor and his tone was level and stony. "I have no idea what you're saying or what you want."

That was probably an exaggeration. Jef had as much knowledge of Tinish as any human. Nevertheless, Chitiratifor's verbal momentum faltered. He goggled at Jefri for a second and then emitted a very human-sounding laugh. "I was talking to the coward." He gave one of Amdi a rough poke in the ribs. "I laugh to see one of us who thinks a two-legs—a piece of lonely meat!—can be pro-tection."

Chitiratifor's laughter morphed into the natural Tinish equivalent. But he backed away from Amdi and Jefri. "And I forget my good manners. We are al-lies." Two of him looked in Gannon's direction. That worthy perked up, recap-turing some of his usual arrogance. "That we are, Chitiratifor, sir. Nevil told us to give you full cooperation. Just tell us what you want. Sorry we don't under-stand better."

"Ah." Chitiratifor rolled his heads with patronizing good humor. "Yes in-deed." He paused, giving all three humans a calculating glance. "So then," he continued, "in words of simple Samnorsk, I say I found traitors last night. They both are dead now, totally dead." He jabbed a snout at Screwfloss. "You. You speak Samnorsk."

Screwfloss dribbled around Ravna to stand respectfully before Raggedy Ears. "Oh, yes indeed," he said, "better than some humans do, as a matter of fact."

"Whatever. I want you to explain things to the two-legs when they cannot understand me." *I can't be bothered with dumb animals* was the message.

Screwfloss made a grovelling smile. He was the picture of an intimidated pack, but his Samnorsk was spoken with a sly, Flenser voice. "Yes, my lord. I can be useful in other ways. I may be the only one left who can advise you about the country ahead."

Chitiratifor emitted a cheerful Tinish laugh, but his patchwork of human voices said: "I'll cut your throats if you say that to the others. Do you understand?"

"Oh yes, your worship. This is just between you and me and some humans who don't really matter."

"Very good," said Chitiratifor, then added something jovial in Tinish. Amdi remained silent, still hiding his heads behind Jefri, but the wagoneers both chuckled back—surely as ignorant as rocks.

———

They were still following the river. The path was often steep, bordering rapids and waterfalls. The valley walls climbed high above them. To the west, the snow-covered heights were sun-bedazzled. Jefri was driving the last wagon now; Chitiratifor had given the usual driver some kind of scouting assignment. Raggedy Ears himself drifted up and down the length of the caravan but made no attempt to hustle them past open areas. Maybe Nevil had gotten control of the airship.

Several times that morning, Raggedy Ears consulted with Screwfloss—in Samnorsk. He was totally ignorant of this territory, and just as clearly, he didn't care if Ravna knew it.

Perhaps the most striking change in the new order was that now Screwfloss chatted quite openly with her. "I wasn't in on the kill, but I talked to the front wagon driver. The two traitor packs were killed. Chitiratifor hunted down the last of them and dispatched them himself. The pack called—" he warbled a chord or two "—the best you could pronounce it would be 'Remasritlfeer,' he was one of Tycoon's top lieutenants. The other was his assistant. Apparently they both were experts on this rift valley." At the moment, Chitiratifor was some distance up ahead. He might not be able to make out what Screwfloss was saying, but he could surely hear conversation noise.

Screwfloss must have noticed the surprise on Ravna's face. "Why am I talking to you now?" he said. He shrugged. "Now that your small human mind has recovered, you're just someone to listen. What you know doesn't matter."

Screwfloss was silent for a moment as he negotiated the wagon's way across a dip in the trail that at this time of the year was filled with fast-moving water. Some of Amdi braved the cold directly, while about half of him hopped on the back of the wagon and came across dry. They kept their heads down so as not to mix mindsounds with Screwfloss, but nevertheless that pack said severely, "None of your tricks! Understand?"

Among Ravna's disconnected memories was the vision of Screwfloss chasing Amdi away from her. What had that been all about? A moment later she found out, when Amdi's focused voice came in her ears: "Screwfloss doesn't believe I'm smart enough to talk secretly to someone as hard of hearing as a human, not when there is *any* chance of detection. But you have to know: With Remasritlfeer gone, Chitiratifor is just looking for—I'm sorry—some fun way to kill you, maybe kill Jefri and even Gannon."

Screwfloss emitted a screeching hiss.

Amdi hunkered down at the blast, but his secret voice continued: "Heh. He's just guessing." But then aloud Amdi said, "I'll be good. No more tricks. I promise."

Anyone who really knew Amdi would know that he kept his freely given promises. Apparently, Screwfloss was such a person. He gave Amdi a long look, then replied. "Very well, Little Ones."

In any case, that was the most informative, and frightening, moment of the morning. Screwfloss quit talking. Maybe he was sullen, or thinking—or listening to discover if Amdi would break his promise. They stopped briefly for midday meal, but Amdi was away with Jef and Gannon, and Screwfloss went with Chitiratifor to get a view of the way ahead. Back on the wagons, it was well into the afternoon before Screwfloss got into a talkative mood.

"It's really too bad that we killed the traitors when we did. We're entering an especially dangerous area," he said. "It's like I told Lord Chitiratifor at lunch. Little mistakes can be fatal here."

Three of Amdi were sitting at the back of the wagon, but faithfully honoring his promise. Aloud he said, "So has Chitiratifor told the wagoneer packs?"

"Oh yes. Those packs are just city thugs. Till now, this job has been a fun adventure—real hunting, live meat almost every day. But now they need all the help Lord Chitiratifor can give them." Screwfloss gestured expansively at the forest all around them. "It looks so peaceful, doesn't it? But why do you think it's mostly unknown to Tines? Because so few get through it whole—or at all. The Old Flenser studied the rift valleys. So did Steel. They got some of their most diabolical insights here." Screwfloss turned a couple heads Ravna's way. "Yes, I know you starfolk can be much deadlier, but we primitive folk, we do the best we can."

Gannon Jorkenrud had been behind them, between wagons. Maybe he had caught some of the conversation, because now he trotted forward and jumped onto Screwfloss' wagon, kicking Amdi's members overboard in the process. "You assholes have no business riding," he said. He settled down beside Ravna and gave her a big smile. "For that matter, we're being generous to let *you* have a free ride."

Amdi followed along the left side of the wagon, objecting: "Ravna's not well enough to walk along. Chitiratifor wants her kept on the wagon."

"Like I said, we're generous." He gestured Amdi away. "Why don't you go back to your great protector?"

On the wagon behind them, Jefri had risen from his driver's bench. Ravna knew that Jefri had some special recent hatred for Gannon; right now, Jef's expression was deadly. Then his wagon began to drift, and he sat down and guided his kherhog back into line.

Fortunately Jorkenrud wasn't really trying to start a fight. He was more interested in chatting with Screwfloss. "You're spilling Chitiratifor's secrets, eh Screwfloss?"

The pack shrugged. "It won't do her any good."

"So you've told her about the radio link to the orbiter?"

"No, but you've done that now."

". . . Oh." Gannon thought about that for a second and then laughed. "Like you said, it doesn't matter what she knows now. I bet it's fun to see her reaction." He gave Ravna a big grin. "The radio is just one of lots of toys Nevil has given our little friends. Giving you to the dogs is a similar gesture, and it removes a real inconvenience. It was a win all around. Nevil knew that word of the snatch on you would bring Woodcarver's troops racing down from the castle. That would give us a chance to disappear various gear we've been wanting."

Ravna couldn't help baring her teeth at this, "So now Nevil is unmasked."

"Not at all! I don't know the details, how they got rid of Woodcarver's guards, but the rumor is going to be that you weren't kidnapped. You defected because you'd been kicked out of your cushy place on the Starship—and it was your agents who stole the equipment, maybe to set up your own operation. When I'm officially rescued, I'll confirm whatever story Nevil decides on." Gannon looked at the wagon behind them. "Jef will too, if he knows what's good for him."

"That—" Ravna started to say, and was temporarily out of words. "That can't possibly convince anyone."

"Oh? We did something almost as complicated when we snatched the Children."

"Those stupid Tropicals played into our claws on that one," said Screwfloss. He didn't sound critical, more like he was stating a small correction.

Gannon started laughing. "True. But Nevil says that's the reward for good planning. He tricked them into running like the guilty. Who'd have guessed Godsgift would leave part of himself behind? He thought he could get a hearing from Woodcarver and damn us all. Fortunately, we got to him first."

Ravna looked at Gannon and felt sick. "And you grabbed those Children and killed their Best Friends?"

Some remnant of decency tugged at Gannon's face. "Not me personally. . . . Bad things happen, little lady. You should never have been put in charge. Now fixing things is a mess."

Amdi's voice came up from beside the wagon. "We didn't know, Ravna."

Gannon gave a wave in Amdi's direction. "The fatso pack is probably telling the truth. He and Jefri have been very useful, but not for the rough things. I know they weren't supposed to be in on this current operation."

Ravna closed her eyes for a moment and leaned back against the top of the wagon. It wasn't hard to see why Jefri hated this boy so much, but, "Why, Gannon?"

Gannon looked back at her. It was clear he understood what she was really asking. For a moment she thought he would make some sadistic retort, but then something seemed to crumple inside him and desolation stared out at her. "Once upon a time, I was smart. Back in Straumli Realm, back in the High Lab. It was easy to understand what was going on. Then I woke up here, where I understand nothing and all my mind tools are gone. It's like somebody cut my hands off, poked out my eyes."

"All the Children have that problem, Gannon."

"Yes, some more and some less, even the ones who don't realize it. And you know what, little lady? Countermeasure took our home from us, exiled us here. You want to make that permanent. Well, it won't work. You're going down. If you cooperate, help our little Tinish friends, maybe Chitiratifor's boss will let you live."

Gannon stared at her for a moment, his face full of pain, for once free of sadism. Then his gaze flicked away, and after a moment he relaxed into his usual lazy bluster. He waved at the forest all around them and said to Screwfloss, "So what makes you think these woods are dangerous? I've been on expeditions before. I can spot weasel nests and weasel-made rockfalls. Chitiratifor has a pack scouting around us all the time. We've spotted one or two cotters' cabins, but no organized settlements. So what's coming down on us?"

"There's the bloodsucking gnats. They make arctic midges look like friendly puppies. We'll see them as soon as the weather gets a little warmer."

"Gnats? I've heard of those." Gannon's voice was full of jolly contempt. Then an uncomfortable look came to his face. "Or do you mean these ones carry some kind of disease?"

Out of Gannon's line of sight, Ravna noticed Screwfloss exchanging looks with himself, as if wondering how big a whopper he could put over on the idiot human. Then he appeared to pass up the opportunity: "Oh, no. Well, not that I know of, and you humans are mostly immune to our diseases anyway—at least that's what *Oobii* tells you, right?"

"Er, right."

"Anyway, the really bad diseases are in the Tropics," continued Screwfloss. "The biting insects we'll see are just extremely annoying. What makes this here variety of forest dangerous is the—I guess the simplest translation is 'killer trees.' Or maybe 'arrow trees.'"

"Oh, I've heard of those," said Ravna. Amdi made an agreeing sound. Killer trees had been part of some of Pilgrim's stories.

Gannon made a rude noise. "Bullshit. Where are you getting the know-it-all?"

Screwfloss gave him a haughty look. "I was woods-runner before I entered Flenser's employ. I'm a renowned expert on the rift valleys."

Ravna remembered Woodcarver describing this pack as one of Flenser's whack jobs. Whatever else, Screwfloss was an expert at telling tall tales.

Gannon had a narrower skepticism: "This patch of forest looks like bannerwood. It's rare stuff, but I've seen it before. I hear it makes great building timber. Or are you saying these arrow killers are something rare, hiding, ha ha, like in ambush?"

"You have my point, sir—but not quite the way you may think. Bannerwood doesn't like to be cut or chewed on—oh sorry, my lady Ravna, I don't mean to be an ignorant medieval. I know that trees can't think. I just don't have the patience to dance with jargon. I leave that to Flenser and Scrupilo. In any case, only a certain percentage of this type of bannerwood has deadly capabilities."

"What percentage?" said Amdi.

"It varies. It's a very small percentage, though the killers are more common in these rift valley crazy patches. I imagine it depends on the nature of local herbivores and such." He glanced at Amdi. "You, genius little ones, could probably figure a good estimate."

"Probably," said Amdi. He seemed unperturbed that Screwfloss constantly mocked him as "little ones."

In any case, the gibe gave Jorkenrud a rather distracted chuckle. "I was supposed to be rescued before we got this far," he said. "How long can it take Nevil to pry the dirigible loose from Woodcarver's dogs?" He seemed to be looking at the forest with a more personal interest now; it might not be someone *else's* amusing doom. The trees appeared to be of a single type, tall and graceful evergreens whose needles ranged from short and slender to long and thick. "Okay," he said, "some of those needles could make arrows—if you cut them down and had a proper bow for them."

"Ah, but there's no need if you're the killer kind of arrow tree. Next time we stop, climb up to the lowest branches on one these trees—one I say is safe. You'll still be able to see the tensioning knot at the base of the longer needles."

"Maybe I'll do that," said Gannon. "You've told Chitiratifor about this?"

"Oh, yes. He's spreading the word to the others. See?" Up ahead, Raggedy Ears was indeed lecturing the front wagoneer, waving emphatically at the trees. "Hei, but don't worry. Very few of the trees are deadly, and if we follow a few simple rules, we should get through fine." Screwfloss didn't say anything more for a while; he definitely had Flenser's talent for teasing his listeners. They crossed over two more of the spring freshets, chilly snowmelt spilling down to the river. In places the beautiful, sometimes deadly trees came close to the trail, forcing those on foot to walk behind or in front of the wagons. Amdi was looking in all directions, but he seemed more curious than fearful. In this new forest, there was scarcely any undergrowth, just the great, vaguely fungal bushes that popped up around some of the trees. Ravna could almost imagine Amdi estimating the cover they might provide, figuring the fields of fire, generating a million questions that would break into the open if Screwfloss let him dangle long enough.

Gannon was also looking all around, and it was he who finally broke the silence, "Okay, you bastard, what are those 'few simple rules'?"

Screwfloss chuckled, but he dropped his teasing game. He had lots of definite advice: "Notice all the open space? Those spaces are deadly. You can't run far when you are full of arrows. If there was even one of the killer variety within bowshot, and if it got triggered, that would be enough to kill a two-legs. If there's a cluster of the killer variety, then once one gets triggered, the whole mob goes—arrows coming from dozens of trees. You spacers would have lots of explanations once you studied them. Maybe there's pollen that gets released and that's a signal to others. Anyway, they all go off."

"Are they aimed?" said Amdi.

"Not really. There's a ripple of shooting that sweeps away from the beginning tree. The point is, there could be *thousands* of arrows. They can cut down whole packs, right to the last member. So rule one is, don't stay in the open. See those bushes at the base of the trees? Those are the tree's flowers—ha, the equivalent of a pack's crown jewels. Very few arrows will strike there. So the best strategy whenever we're stopped for any length of time is to stay near the bushes. Be ready to dive into them if arrows start flying." Screwfloss shrugged. "That may be too late if you're a two-legs, but it should be a life saver for us packs."

When Screwfloss finished his advice, Gannon was thoughtful and silent. Amdi scouted ahead and around, sniffed at some of the bushes. Now he was in question mode. Amdi wanted to know everything Screwfloss could tell him about what would trigger a shooter attack and about how clusters of shooters might be arranged. Screwfloss was full of details, a weird combination of technical analysis and medieval folktales.

Amdi ate it all up and had even more questions. By the time Chitiratifor signaled that they were stopping to make camp, Jorkenrud's interest in safety procedures had been satisfied in mind-numbing detail.

Apparently, Chitiratifor had absorbed some brief form of this advice at lunch time. Ravna could tell by Raggedy Ears' nervous uncertainty in setting up the night's campsite.

As Ravna climbed down from the wagon, Amdi was standing all around her. "You know," he said, his voice quiet and casual but not really secretive, "this really doesn't make any sense."

Then he trailed off in the direction of Jefri.

———

Half an hour after they had stopped, Gannon and Jefri were at work with the evening housekeeping. Chitiratifor had decided on where the campfires should be but he was still ordering the wagons and draft animals moved around, trying to find the safest formation. Screwfloss accompanied Chitiratifor, providing his expert advice. Every time the two packs came within earshot Ravna listened with interest. One thing about Screwfloss' story, it might distract Raggedy Ears from planning the murderous entertainment Amdi feared.

"Yes," the ever-informative Screwfloss was saying, "you have to distract the trees. The things they react to are vibrations and physical attack."

Raggedy Ears objected: "But we don't eat these plants; we're not even loggers. We won't hurt the trees."

"I'm afraid that doesn't matter, my lord. The killer trees are more common here than I've ever seen, and I suspect that the way ahead will be even worse. Tonight we have some good luck, an opportunity to practice proper technique. On this side of the road we've found a small area that's free of the killers, but our sounds will eventually cause a cook-off—that's a human technical term, my lord, for when weapons spontaneously discharge. We'll need to provoke a partial cook-off just to protect ourselves."

"The troops aren't going to like that."

"Present it as a perfectly safe test, my lord—which is exactly what it will be. We're camping on the west side of the trail, near the protection of the root bushes. I suggest you cause some small trauma to the trees on the east side."

"Trauma?"

"I mean, cause some wound to the trees. You can have a single member do the job, using a wagon to provide it with safe cover. The rest of us can take shelter by the root bushes on this side of the road. We'll get a good idea of what to expect on the road ahead."

Raggedy Ears emitted a thoughtful noise, but the two packs were walking away and she couldn't hear the rest of the conversation. The wagons eventually were parked, and the kherhogs sheltered a little behind the wagons. Jefri and Amdi were out of sight when Gannon and Chitiratifor came strolling in her direction. He was carrying a utility axe in one pair of jaws. Ravna suddenly realized that Raggedy Ears had figured out how an entertaining murder could help solve his other problems.

The pack dropped the axe on the ground in front of her. "You!" he said. "Go across the road and make cuts on the middle tree."

———

"You'll do what Chitiratifor told you!" Gannon waved her back to the east side of the path and away from the wagons. "Now take the axe, damn it." He lobbed the utility axe across the trail. The spinning blade sank deep into the ground two meters from Ravna's feet.

At the sound of Gannon's voice, Amdi and Jefri came around the fodder wagon. They must have been feeding the kherhogs. The weather was so warm now that there was no need for ferment-warming, but feeding the hungry animals was still a messy job—the kind of work that even Gannon managed to avoid.

"What are you doing with Ravna?" Jefri shouted. There was a good ten meters separating Gannon from herself, so this was evidently no ordinary form of harassment.

"He wants me to chop a tree," Ravna shouted back.

"*What?*"

As Amdi and Jefri ran toward her, Chitiratifor moved casually into their path. He'd pulled battle axes from his panniers and idly swung them back and forth. Ravna noticed that the wagoneers had unlimbered their crossbows.

Gannon waved Jefri back. "Hei, Jef. Keep cool."

Jefri looked across the trail at where Ravna stood, alone. His gaze swept up, across the trees. Abruptly, he turned on the nearest of Chitiratifor. "You *need* her! That's the whole point of this expedition."

There was a lazy smile in Raggedy Ears' aspect. He flipped a battle axe adroitly. "You're wrong. I don't need the Ravna two-legs alive. I have a good use for her now. More use than I have for most two-legs."

Gannon gave a nervous laugh and said to Jefri. "Just go along with it, Jef."

Jefri glared at him and then around at the packs. The air was still for a moment, and Ravna saw that Amdi had been absolutely right. With Remasritlfeer gone, Chitiratifor was free to complete *his* mission. *Please don't try to fight them, Jefri.* Amdi seemed to feel the same. He uttered a loud screech and tried to hold Jefri back by grabbing at the cuffs of his pants.

"Fine," said Jefri—and reached toward the nearest of Chitiratifor. "Then give me an axe, too."

"You craphead!" said Gannon.

For an instant, Ravna thought Raggedy Ears might slash at Jefri's hand. Then the pack gave a rattling laugh and flipped one of the axes out of its mouth.

Jefri snatched the axe from the air. He kicked loose of Amdi's grasp and stomped across the path to stand by Ravna. Amdiranifani followed all around.

Chitiratifor's laughter swelled into full honking, and he said something to Screwfloss and the wagoneers. They were all having a good time. Their leader was going to show them just what all the killer tree fuss was about—without putting anyone worthwhile at risk. He gobbled something imperative at Amdi.

Amdi replied in human talk. "No, I won't leave Jefri." The words were brave, but there was white around his eyes.

Chitiratifor boomed angrily. Then he said in Samnorsk, "You are of interest, but you can still be punished. Would you like to be seven? or six?"

Screwfloss put in: "Oh, let him stay, my lord. He can stand over by the tree with the root bush. That should be relatively safe."

Amdi cowered back, shuffling toward the tree that Screwfloss was pointing to. Ravna noticed that the campsite had been very carefully chosen. No tree near hers had a root bush.

Chitiratifor watched Amdi move; a smile spread across his aspect. "You are a coward clown." His attention returned to Ravna and Jefri, but he had good humor for them too. "Now you, the female. Pick up the axe. Cut the tree behind you. Is that the one, Screwfloss?"

"Quite so, my lord. That's almost certainly a true killer, and the lowest arrows look well-tensioned."

"Are the kherhogs safely away?"

Screwfloss glanced at the carts and animals. "Oh yes." The kherhogs were milling around as if they realized that something extreme was in the offing. "You've positioned them perfectly."

Chitiratifor gobbled to the others. He sounded like he was putting on a show. Ravna recognized the word for "wager" in his chords. "And you, the male, stand by the second tree on the left."

"But don't chop anything yet," said Screwfloss. "We want to see if one attack can provoke the other trees."

Raggedy Ears elaborated for his Tinish audience.

"I *said*, pick up the axe!" Chitiratifor boomed at her. "You have a good chance at living if you do." He said something to his audience. They gobbled back at him, and he added. "Four to one odds in your favor. But you're sure dead if you don't *move*." His wagoneers had both cranked back their bows.

Ravna grabbed the axe's jaw handle and pulled it free of the sod. Flecks of needles fell from it and the edge glittered in the late afternoon light. It might be a utility blade, but it looked freshly sharpened.

On the other side of the trail, the wagoneers and Chitiratifor were watching her in the intense, still way that always bothered her about Tines. This wasn't all a matter of entertainment. Except for the bow-holding members, they had wiggled most of themselves into the protective cover of the root bushes. Only Chitiratifor, Screwfloss, and Gannon were still standing in the open. Gannon looked around, seemed to realize his exposure. He turned and headed for the nearest unoccupied bush.

And now the wagoneers were making noise again. They were chanting, a blend of harmonics that made Ravna's ears hurt. She knew the meaning: *Do it, do it, do it*. There were packs who chanted just that at the kids' ballgames.

Ravna turned to the tree behind her. On her right, Amdi danced around in frightened excitement, edging nearer to the root bush that could protect him. He had no secret messages, at least nothing he would chance on human hearing. On her left, Jefri was looking at Amdi and then at her . . . and suddenly she realized that he and Amdi were playing a *game*, just as when they were very little, but now as a matter of life and death.

Do it, do it, do it.

"All right!" She walked toward the tree, gave the axe a little swing. An ancient human might have described the thing as double axe head fixed on a bale hook handle. There was no way she could get the full leverage a human would have with a real, made-for-human axe.

But the blade was sharp.

This particular tree was about eighty centimeters across, the bark almost as smooth as a baby's skin, but a pale buff color such as you rarely saw on modern Homo Sapiens. The tree seemed no different from the thousands of bannerwoods she'd seen the last few days. Its straight trunk extended some forty meters up, a beautiful slim tower. The lowest branches grew straight out. The nearest were some thirty centimeters above her head, their needles growing in great sheaves from the lumps that Screwfloss called "tensioning knots."

Do it, do it, do it.

She raised the axe and gave the smooth pillar a blow that was more a tentative tap. The blade sank a centimeter into the wood. When she eased the blade out, there was a film of clear sap on the steel and a little more oozing down the side of the tree. The smell of the sap was a dry, complex thing, somehow familiar. *Oh.* It was simply a sharp version of this forest's pervasive smell.

Most important, the scent seemed to have no effect on the peaceful drowse of this late afternoon. Above and around her, the needle leaves hung in greenish silence, unmoving.

On the other side of trail, the audience was not happy. The chant had stilled, but the wagoneers gobbled irritably to each other. Screwfloss had nothing to say, but there was an ironic smile in his aspect, as if he were waiting for someone to say the obvious.

Chitiratifor's voice boomed out, in Tinish and Samnorsk all at once: "*Cut the tree, human! Chop up and down. We will see its insides, or we will see yours.*"

The wagoneers laughed and swung their bows back toward her.

She turned back to the tree and began whacking. Her blows were still weak, but she did as she was told, hitting upwards and then down, at something like the same target line. At this pace, it might take her an hour to cut the tree down, but she was gouging a deep notch in the wood, revealing the growth ring pattern that was near-ubiquitous in the trees of Tines World.

She paused, partly because she was out of breath, partly because she heard Amdi make an anxious *wheep* sound. She noticed that Chitiratifor had edged closer to the safety of a large bush.

The forest was no longer silent. She heard a clattering sound in the branches above her. The nearest branches trembled, clusters of needles shivering faintly, jerked about by the tensioning knots that anchored them in place. The knots themselves, were . . . *smoking*? No, not smoke. It was a heavy haze of pollen, drifting slowly on the faint currents of the cooling afternoon. Where it floated through the brightest light, the reflection of the sun from the peaks above, it shone golden green.

On the other side of the path, some of the sporting humor had evaporated. The packs watched the drifting haze with wide eyes. As it floated outwards from Ravna's tree, the rattling of branches spread to the trees around her and then across the wagon trail, creating a growing, golden green alarm. The wagoneers squeezed back beneath their root bushes; not even their bow carriers stood in the open now.

When the rattling reached the trees around Chitiratifor, he finally gave up his brave stance and wiggled himself deep into his own bush. Only screwloose Screwfloss was left unprepared. He hadn't picked a big enough bush and now he was mostly unable to get adequate cover.

For the rest: the kherhogs were staring at them in uneasy wonder. Depending on how far the alarm spread, the wagons might not provide sufficient cover.

A dozen seconds passed. The rattling had spread beyond hearing, but no arrows had been triggered.

Screwfloss spoke up, sounding a bit nervous with his explanation: "When it comes, it could be an avalanche of arrows, my lord. Perhaps we have, um, over-extended ourselves."

Chitiratifor gave him an amused look. "Perhaps *you* have overexposed yourself, you silly asses. I see a small bush behind this tree. It may be enough for you. Burrow deep!" Then his attention finally returned to Ravna. "Chop us more wood, human."

She turned back to her tree. Out of the corner of her eye, she noticed that Amdi was all hunkered down, stubbornly refusing to take cover. *What's the game, Jefri?*

Do it. Do it. Do it.

She held the axe by the handle and the haft and took out all her fear on the poor dumb wood. Whack. Whack. *Whack.*

The arrow needles clattered louder than ever, and the alarm pollen grew chokingly thick. When she triggered the cascade, the pain was like arrows piercing her ears. She dived for the ground, trying to find cover in even the most shallow troughs of the earth. But the pain was not from real arrows. The pain was in the sheer power of Tinish screams.

"Get up! Run!" Some of Amdi was around her, trying to pull her to her knees. She came up, saw the rest of him racing toward Jefri.

It was chaos that didn't make much sense at the time. She staggered to her feet, still crouching against the ambuscade. But there were no arrows flying. Anywhere. And yet across the trail, the screaming grew louder, backed up by the fainter, whistling mouth noises of Tines in terrible pain. She couldn't see either of the wagoneers. The bushes they had been hiding under seemed lower and wider than before, and they trembled as if something struggled beneath. . . .

Amdi pushed and pulled her. "Back to the wagons!"

As she stumbled along, she saw that not all the other Tines had disappeared. Most of Screwfloss was standing just at the edge of a root bush, hacking at its branches. His limper hadn't been fast enough to jump away; it was tangled at the edge.

Some of Chitiratifor was clear of the bush that was munching on him. He was fighting back with all his remaining hand axes. He almost had his bow carrier free of the trap. Then he noticed Ravna and Amdi. He gave a roar of anger, and his three free members raced after her.

Ravna ran. Ordinarily, that would have been a futile gesture. On open ground, pack members could outrun any two-legs, and packs with military training could give up consciousness for a brief killing charge. But the part of Chitiratifor that couldn't follow must be in terrible pain. The three that raced after Ravna seemed to be on an invisible leash. Never slowing, they circled wide around, heading back to the rest of their pack, where they resumed hacking at the bush that trapped them.

Screwfloss was doing much better. He had freed his one trapped member. It staggered along with a three-legged walk, but the pack was making progress in their direction.

"I've got him," shouted Jefri. He was closer to the wagons than she, but now he rushed back, scooped up Screwfloss' limping member in his arms.

"Help me, *help me!*" It was Gannon. The boy was on his elbows, his lower body hidden by the bush that had flattened itself upon him. Stark terror was on his face and his hands were reaching out to her.

She had not known Gannon Jorkenrud when he was a small child. At best, he'd been a snotty teenager, growing more malevolent with each passing year. But in the beginning she had seen him as she had all the Children, as someone she could help. There had been a time when he had not seemed evil.

By some miracle, she still had that axe in her hand. And now she was running across the trail, toward Gannon's beseeching hands.

Amdi was still pulling at her. "No! No! Please—"

Someone else just sounded angry: "Well, *damn!* Okay." That was the able-bodied part of Screwfloss, running back from where Jefri had set down the wounded part. Jefri came right behind him. They circled around in front of Ravna, blocking her from Gannon.

But they were doing what she wanted done. Jefri got to the tree, used his reach to attack the bush near its base, where there was no danger of striking Gannon. The four of Screwfloss used knives to cut the branches, then grabbed at Jorkenrud's jacket and began pulling him out.

Ravna was in the midst of Screwfloss now, pulling with him. She had Gannon around the shoulders. Every blow that Jefri struck with his battle axe sent a spasm through the bush and won another centimeter of freedom for Gannon.

Screwfloss shrieked and staggered back, losing his grip on Jorkenrud. Ravna looked up in time to dodge the metal tines. Raggedy Ears' loose members were among them, slashing. At least one part of a wagoneer had freed itself and joined the attack.

Jorkenrud slipped from her fingers, the relentless pull of the bush winning at last. As his body disappeared from view, there might have been one last scream, silenced with a crunching sound.

Bodies tumbled all around, bleeding.

She was on her feet, staggering back. She had never been in a fight before, but Johanna had regaled her with stories. Against even one pack, an unarmed human would be the loser. *Stay on your feet. Climb some place where packs can't follow.*

Something slammed into her from behind, sweeping her off her feet. *Jefri!* Then she was looking down, from over his shoulder. He was quickly backing away from the battle, of which she could now see nothing! Parts of Amdi swirled around them, bloodied. Amdi was unarmed, but Jefri still had his axe. She could feel him swing it, hear the screaming. He staggered, turned, and she had a glimpse of Screwfloss. *That* pack was armed in every jaw and forepaw, even the limper. Between them, Screwfloss and Jefri were making a controlled retreat from—not so much a pack as a killing mob, three from Raggedy Ears, two from the wagoneers.

They'd reached the nearest of the wagons. They had all of Screwfloss; if she wasn't counting anybody twice, Amdi was still eight. He had split into three groups and raced ahead, heading for the kherhogs

Jefri shrugged Ravna to the ground. "Help Amdi. We're getting out of here."

In this, Ravna really could contribute. One two-legs was worth at least four pack members when it came to dealing with kherhogs. She got her animal hooked up to the front wagon before Amdi was done with the other animals. Her own kherhog was cooperative—maybe too much so; the wagon was already moving forward. The kherhog didn't want to be near the screaming carnivores.

"Don't let it run away!" shouted Amdi, even as he scrambled to guide the second and third wagons. There was blood all over him, but he was eight for sure.

Behind them, Jefri and Screwfloss were continuing the defense. The enemy mob ran back and forth across the trail behind them, darting forward repeatedly. Jefri held the center of the line, but Screwfloss—all but the limper—was rushing back and forth, cutting and slashing, matching the desperation of the attackers with his own brand of mad rage, chasing any who tried to flank the rear wagon and go after Ravna and Amdi.

Meter by meter, their three wagons proceeded away from the campsite. Ravna walked beside the lead kherhog. It wasn't pulling so nervously now. She had no trouble keeping up and staying on her feet. She glanced back. From somewhere under her own mortal panic, a tiny horrified vision rose . . . of the nightmare that faced their enemy: The two from the wagoneers, the three from Chitiratifor, they were now about fifty meters from the trees that held the rest of themselves. They were beyond the reach of their mindsounds. Pursuit would be mindless and would give up any chance of pack survival.

The two wagoneer members broke first, turning and heading back toward the campsite. The three of Chitiratifor shrieked rage at this desertion, then shrieked rage at the escapees. The fragment took one more wild charge at Jefri and Screwfloss, and then turned back, desperate to save itself.

———

"The ones in the bushes, they're all dead, or they will be soon, either suffocated or crushed." That's what Screwfloss said when she asked him about Gannon and the others. His words were flippant, even more than usual. "Heh. What we gotta hope is Chitiratifor dies slowly, so what's left doesn't come after us till we are well gone."

They were pushing on as fast as they could go. It had been light when they escaped, but now twilight was deepening into night and the wagons' progress had slowed. For that matter, how do you do first aid when you can't see the injuries? The stolen lamps were somewhere on the wagons, but they couldn't stop and dig them out. When there had still been light, she had seen the general size of the problem. *Everyone* was cut up to some extent. Over the last ten years, Ravna had done her best to learn about first aid. Jefri's forearm needed a pressure bandage. She had managed that, and he understood how to maintain it. Amdi had looked ghastly, blood oozing now from three of his heads—and yet he seemed to be thinking as clearly as ever. Okay, maybe they were just scalp wounds, not near his tympana. She had wrapped his heads in strips torn from their cloaks. *That* made it harder for Amdi to hear himself think, but the bleeding stopped. "I'm fine," he said, "I just gotta pay more attention to where I'm at. Please. Check on Screwfloss."

Now it was really dark. One of Screwfloss was aboard the rear wagon, driving it along. The rest of him was sprawled in an exhausted jumble atop the second wagon with Ravna.

"We should stop, get you properly bandaged up," said Ravna.

"Naeh," said Screwfloss. "We gotta keep moving. How is Amdijefri?"

Ravna looked around. Jefri was walking by the lead kherhog, guiding it along. All eight of Amdi was trotting beside the middle wagon and its kherhog, keeping them on the road. "I'm good," said Amdi, but he was looking up at Screwfloss anxiously. "Are you all right?"

Screwfloss replied, "You did great tonight, Little Ones."

Ravna brushed her hand across the nearest of Screwfloss. "But are *you* okay, Screwfloss?"

"Am I okay? Am I okay? What kind of an idiot are you? I still have the broken leg you gave me; it hurts like hell. Then tonight you screwed us into trying to rescue Jorkenrud. He was more of a dirtbag than either of the wagoneers, you know that?"

Ravna was taken aback, remembering the moment when all she could think of was saving Gannon. She'd never thought of herself as a racist. That was a Straumer vice. She bowed her head. "I'm sorry, Screwfloss. It's just that I knew Gannon, I knew all the kids, when they were younger. I felt responsible."

Screwfloss emitted a soft laugh. "Would you have done the same if you'd known he was the one who smashed your face into the side of the fodder wagon? Never mind, I'm afraid you would have. You and Woodcarver are both so soft-hearted."

Woodcarver soft-hearted? Compared to what?

Screwfloss shifted uneasily under her hands, but let her touch and probe. She could see so little now, but there was blood all over, like Amdi. Keep him talking. "You were on our side from the beginning, Screwfloss. But you were part of Nevil's conspiracy, too."

"Of course I was! Didn't Flenser tell you he had tunneled into the conspiracy? You can't do that without being pretty damn credible."

"You had me fooled about the trees, right up to when the arrows didn't start flying."

"Heh, I had a good time with that. There really are arrow trees, you know. Just not anywhere near here. The crusherbushes are much rarer, a transient stage in the way these forests sometimes regrow. I couldn't believe our luck the other night when I saw that crusher grab you. My lies practically told themselves, though Chitiratifor was the perfect ignoramus. I don't know why Vendacious put up with him all these years. Remasritlfeer wouldn't have been fooled. But then he wanted you for Tycoon. We should be glad that's not gonna happen. We have a chance. We just gotta avoid Vendacious and Tycoon, and wiggle our asses back to the Domain."

It suddenly occurred to Ravna that she was in the middle of someone who could explain most of the deadly mysteries, and who surely must be a friend.

Twilight was past, but now the moon stood low in the south, its light chopping the forest floor into silver and shadow.

She used an open stretch of road to peer down between Screwfloss' huddled members. He wasn't talking so much now, though the one on the other wagon was peering alertly into the gloom, taking advantage of the moonlight just as she was. Then she realized that except for the outlier driving the rear wagon, Screwfloss was *huddling*, the dazed reaction of a pack that doesn't consciously understand how badly it is injured.

"Talk to me, Screwfloss."

The pack gave its human chuckle. "Yeah, yeah. I bet you have a million questions. And I have lots of answers, though if we knew exactly what was going on we'd never have wound up in this mess." He mumbled to himself for a moment. "We didn't realize how important Vendacious was. We didn't realize he might double-cross Tycoon. We didn't realize they would grab so *much* and all at once."

The words weren't slurred. The actual sounds were coming from all the pack. But there was a singsong cadence to the delivery; *some member* was not pulling its mental weight. Ravna slipped her hands gently between him, trying to encourage the pack to get out of its huddle. Here and there a jaw snapped at her distractedly, but the four slid apart. There was *so much blood*.

The one protected by the huddle was in a pool of it. The critter was humming to itself, not really in pain. In the reflected moonlight she could see it turn its head toward her, the faint glitter in its open eyes. She ran her hand up its shoulder, felt a faintly pulsing gash just short of its neck, the blood flowing past her fingers.

"*Jefri!*" she shouted.

―――――

Ravna and Jefri and Amdi did what they could, but it wasn't nearly enough. She'd stopped the bleeding. They'd found a clearing, coaxed Screwfloss down to lie in the moonlight, where they could find all his injuries. By then the one member was silent and unconscious, and it was too late to save it. The death was a peaceful, painless ending. It might not have happened if there had been pain and whistling screams. Instead, the member had quietly bled and bled, its pack just dazed enough to miss the mortal peril. . . .

CHAPTER 22

After that one stop, they rolled on through the night and into the next day, till fatigue stopped humans and packs and kherhogs.

Ravna took another look at everyone's wounds. Jefri and Amdi were keeping a nervous lookout all around, but mainly back along the way they had come. "I don't think any of the surviving fragments could have chased us this far," said Jefri.

"So what does Screwfloss think of this theory?" asked Ravna.

What remained of Screwfloss looked more lively than Jef and Amdi. After they stopped the wagons, it had slid off into the woods, a self-appointed scouting party. Yet now the remnant hissed when she tried to tend its wounds. The four were snouting around in the front wagon. After a moment, it pulled emergency rations out of the depths of a cabinet and began eating. It chewed grumpily, looking speculatively at the surrounding trees.

Amdi said, "I'm afraid he can't talk anymore." Amdi detoured around Screwfloss and brought both human and pack rations to where Ravna and Jefri had settled. She ate as much as she could. She was so tired. Everything was a bit of a blur. Today was actually *warm*. There was a faint, keening whine all around, gnats rising from every pond and river stillness.

Finally what Amdi had said percolated through her muzziness. "I've seen many packs of four," she said. "They can talk well enough."

"If that's how they've made themselves," said Jefri. He was sitting at the edge of Amdi, still a couple of meters from Ravna. She noticed that he still avoided her eyes, but there was an occasional flickering glance, challenging as often as not. He continued, "It should be obvious: the one that died was a principal speech center. So no more Samnorsk. It looks like his Interpack speech has gone, too."

"We should keep trying," said Amdi. "What's left has some speech capacity, I know it." Amdi was shaking his heads this way and that, but not as fierce negation; he was just trying to wave the gnats away.

Jefri brushed helpfully at Amdi's nearest faces. "Could be. It'll be a while before we know what's left of his mind."

"So he's a little like I was," said Ravna. *But he won't let anyone help him.*

Jefri nodded. "A little. But in many ways, he's an able-bodied pack. He drove his wagon well. His other wounds are minor."

The subject of their conversation didn't seem to be paying attention. He came to his feet and ambled over to the middle wagon. Being only four, his limping member seemed to affect the gait of the other three. Two of him flipped up the door on the wagon and searched around inside. When they hopped back to earth, they were holding a leather satchel and what looked like soap and clean cloaks. He swatted at the swirling gnats with his new cloaks, then turned and shambled off in the direction of the river.

Ravna gave a surprised laugh. "He's going to wash up. I guess he isn't too concerned!"

Jefri came to his feet. "Yeah, but none of us should do that alone." He started after the foursome, but it directed a warning hiss back in his direction.

Jefri settled back down. "Okay. I never understood Screwfloss, even when he was whole." He glanced sidelong at Amdi.

"Yes," said Amdi. "Sneaky, funny, Flenser-renser." He looked at Jefri and Jefri looked back and Ravna wondered if the two were having one of their cryptic conversations. It always seemed that there was more going on between these two than she knew. It had been cute when they were little. . . .

A gnat scored on her neck, another on her hand. She swatted them, but there were clouds of replacements. The Old Screwfloss' predictions about bloodsuckers had really come true. If only he could say "I told you so."

She looked at Amdi and Jefri and saw that they were looking back at her. In fact, *all* of Amdi was looking at her. "We have a lot to talk about," she finally said.

Amdi scrunched down into the moldering needles of the forest floor. Some of him looked at each other, some looked at Ravna. "We are so sorry, Ravna," he finally said.

Jefri was silent for a moment, then slapped the ground angrily. "But we did what I thought was right!" he said. His glance flickered back to her face. "I couldn't believe Nevil was behind the murders and kidnappings, but then Screwfloss told us you were being snatched. We figured that we might be able to get you out of your house first. And you *did* escape—"

Ravna nodded. "Screwfloss got me down the stairs and out-of-doors." *And probably quicker than any civilized explaining would have.*

"Y-yes. It almost worked, but Chitiratifor was too fast. He had a crossbow pointed at your back once you got into the street."

Ravna leaned back against a wagon wheel. Chitiratifor would have welcomed a fatal "accident." So Jef and Amdi had made a big deal of grabbing her and then coming along. She could believe that. "Okay, Jefri. But why earlier? Why at Nevil's big meeting . . ." *Why did you betray me?*

Jefri the teenage lout might have shrugged angrily, or thrown up some counterattack. This Jefri let the pain and anger come into his face, but his voice was level. He was making an honest attempt to explain: "I thought— Powers help me, I still think—that you and Johanna have the most important things exactly backwards. Something very bad happened at the High Lab, but I know our scientists were the best of Straumli Realm. They would not have been as *stupid* as you think."

"I've never said they were stupid."

"Never those precise words, but oh, we kids know you, Ravna. In the early years you were as close as a Best Friend. We could tell by your silences, by what you didn't say about our folks and the High Lab—we could tell what you think of them."

Ravna couldn't deny his accusation.

Jefri gave a little nod and continued. "Nevil brought all the facts together. He convinced me to speak unforgivable lies about you. But Ravna, I remember the High Lab. We Straumers had things going our way. We were becoming something . . . awesome. It was *Countermeasure* that was the poison."

"Johanna doesn't believe that."

"I love Johanna, but she's never been tech-oriented. She saw less of the High Lab than some of the Children. Now she's a lot like the Larsndots, turning away from our destiny."

"You're a Denier."

"*Don't call me that!* Most of the Children, if you really talk to them about their memories of the High Lab, would agree about this. They're just very shy of correcting someone they . . . respect . . . as much as they do you."

"Even so, Jefri. You recognize that Nevil is evil?"

Jefri looked away from her, as if refusing to answer. After a moment, Amdi said, "You know he's evil, Jefri."

Finally, Jef said, "I tried so hard to believe otherwise. Maybe there were sensible explanations for the strange things Amdi and I noticed when we were chasing the Tropicals. Or maybe even, Nevil had been duped by some monster like Vendacious . . . but when I saw Gannon smash your face into the side of the fodder wagon . . ." His gaze flickered back to Ravna. "Every day afterwards, I had to listen to his detailed bragging. And you know what? Almost all the mayhem Gannon committed was at Nevil's explicit instruction. So yes, Nevil is evil."

Amdi was nodding, *yes, yes, yes.*

Jefri wasn't finished: "And now, I'll do whatever it takes to get you safely back to the Domain, and to . . . deal with . . . Nevil. But when that is done"—his gaze was defiant and desperate all at once—"there are still the Greater Threats, and I'm afraid they'll leave us as absolute enemies."

Oh, Powers. These last ten years, Ravna had imagined the future as a long climb to a faraway confrontation. What deadly foothills stood in the way of that! "Okay, Jefri. One step at a time. Don't worry about being enemies someday."

Blessed Amdi. He brightened instantly. "Yes! Let the future take care of itself." He bounced to his feet and flowed around Jefri to sit in snuggly closeness with both humans. Clouds of gnats followed him along. The bugs really did like Tines more than humans. "We have serious problems in the here and now."

Ravna leaned forward, counting noses. "Where's the rest of you, Amdi?"

"Oh! I'm strung out into bushes that way,"—he jabbed a nose—"making sure that Screwfloss is okay. He won't let me come close, but I can hear him splashing around. If he has a problem, we can come running. Meantime, we've got to decide what to do next." He wriggled against her and patted her hand. "We should take inventory . . ."

———

Amdi was right. Thinking about the problems of the next day and tenday was almost a comfort. They might be caught, they might be killed, but at least they weren't busy betraying each other.

They didn't go any farther the first day. Ravna was nervous about that; parts of several packs might still be following them. But the kherhogs were exhausted and the day remained clear and bright. What they could see of the forest ahead provided very little cover, at least where they could drive the wagons. A few days ago she would have prayed to be spotted by one of the Domain's aircraft. Now she was terribly afraid that Nevil had control of the air.

When Screwfloss came back from his bath, Amdi asked him about the safety of camping here. The remnant gave every impression of understanding.

It looked almost as cocky as when it had been five, emitting a Tinish laugh at Amdi's question. Okay, then.

Amdi gobbled some more at the remnant, asking it to stand guard while they went down to the stream. The pack wandered off, hopefully to do as it was asked.

The day was much too cold for real bathing, but washing off the blood and the sweat suddenly was about the most important thing that Ravna could think of. Jefri insisted on going first, with Amdi making a watch line between the stream and the wagons. "You just stay with this end of Amdi, okay, Ravna?"

She shrugged. "Sure." She had known these two since they were little kids. Modesty was an absurd notion here.

But when Jef returned, all of Amdi went down to the stream with her and kept watch. She knelt, drinking from the edge of the fast-moving water, away from the standing water and the gnats. She stared for a long moment at her reflection. This was the first time she had seen her face since Gannon smashed her. It was even worse than her touch had promised. Well, the blow had practically killed her. She shouldn't be surprised that her face was a disaster area.

She took off her awful, stinky clothes. The pants and shirt were padded canvas, oversized and misshapen—what Tines might create based on a description of human form. Clearly, *some* of the kidnappers had intended to take her alive. What nice fellows. She soaked the fabric and soaped it, then soaked it again. Cleaning her own skin was easy by comparison, though that was like scrubbing with ice cubes. Amdi had brought unfilthy cloaks as towels and temporary wraps. They felt so good. Funny how much this improved her outlook.

When she returned to the campsite, she discovered Jefri pacing about impatiently. Amdi looked back and forth between them and said, "So, I thought we were going to start an inventory?"

"Of course," said Jef, a bit abruptly. "I was just keeping watch." He walked off toward the wagons, Ravna and Amdi trailing behind. Maybe Jef had been afraid she'd accuse him of hiding things if he started the inventory without her. Ravna realized she had still not figured out Jefri Olsndot.

The two cargo wagons were big enough for gear and supplies. And for hiding places—such as for those maps that Chitiratifor and Remasritlfeer had been using. Jefri broke into the locked cabinets. There were no maps, but one of the boxes held clean blankets and two more changes of crude human clothes! The main supply bays were more familiar territory. The food was mostly gone, especially the kind that humans could eat. There had been one unexpected human on this expedition, but even so, maybe Chitiratifor had expected an end to this trip—or to the humans—relatively soon.

Ravna had seen most of the camping hardware before, but rarely in good light. Some of this equipment was not the sort that Scrupilo's factories made, but neither was it medieval. Jefri held up two canteens. They looked identical, stamped from tin or pewter. "You noticed the logo, right?" Both canteens bore the same impression, a godlike pack surrounding the world.

"That's the mark of Tycoon," said Ravna. Johanna had shown the design at an Executive Council meeting. At the time it had seemed a very poor payoff for three tendays scouting Tycoon's East Coast headquarters.

"A twelvesome," said Amdi. "He's a confident fellow." God was usually shown as twelve. Any more and there were comical implications of a choir. "I'll bet no one has ever seen Tycoon because he's really just a wimpy four."

The middle wagon contained Nevil's technological gifts. Nevil had not been overly generous: there was a camera and the lamps, all originally from *Oobii*. The radio was locally made, one of Scrupilo's creations. It was as dumb as a rock, but still the Domain didn't have enough of them. "The radio we're going to have to dump," she said regretfully. It was something that Nevil could track via the orbiter. If he was clever, he could probably pulse the orbiter's transmitters hard enough to get an echo even if the radio's charge had leaked away.

"Yes," said Jefri, looking nervously at all the equipment. "We should get rid of all this gear." To him, a child of the High Beyond, machines were capable of unfathomed sneakiness.

Ravna gathered up the camera, and poked around under the lamps. "The cam will have to go." She was no High Beyonder, but anyone from a tech civilization had default assumptions about such machines. "On the other hand, I've used these lamps. They've got a security local mode. I'll set that. If we're careful when we use them, they should be fine."

"Okay," said Jefri, looking dubious.

Amdi was still snouting around in the cabinet. "I want to know where the maps were. This should be where Chitiratifor and Remasritlfeer kept them."

Their hour or so of direct sunlight had passed. Even the snow dazzle from high peaks was fading. "What in hell are we going to do?" said Jefri, sounding very tired.

"One way or another," said Ravna, "we have to get back to the Domain, on our own, without getting 'rescued.' If we can get close to *Oobii*, I can—" It hurt that she was afraid to tell them all that she could do.

Jef didn't seem to notice the hesitation. "Well, I don't want to go back the way we came. Parts of various nasty packs may still be alive. And I don't want to go forward. I'll bet there are some *complete* nasty packs waiting for us ahead."

Amdi emitted annoyed squeaking sounds. "So help me find the maps!"

"Okay." Jefri walked forward to where Amdi had climbed up on himself to rummage in the wagon. "Though maybe Chitiratifor had them in-pack."

"No! Not yesterday. They're in this wagon."

Jefri leaned over the pack and looked down into the compartment. "There really is nothing more there, Amdi. Trust my human vision on this."

"Well then, it must be above or below. I watched Chitiratifor almost every time he got the maps."

"A secret compartment then." Jefri walked along the side of wagon, tapping it above and below. "It must be small and well shielded. I could get one of the axes and open this thing up a little."

Some of Amdi was trailing along behind him. "Maybe there's no need. I'll hear it eventually. You keep tapping on the wood, and I'll . . ." He built a little pyramid of himself and snuggled close to the hull of the wagon. The rest of him had climbed up on the wagon and hunkered down in various places. ". . . and I'll listen."

Now the snow in the higher hills was just a lighter shade of gray against the sky. Ravna heard something behind her. She looked around with a start, saw four dark shadows gliding toward the wagons. It was Screwfloss, returning from sentry duty. She gave him a little wave, and wondered at the remnant's on-again off-again diligence. Screwfloss lolled about, watching Amdi and the two humans. If this had been the entire Screwfloss, she would have been sure that he was amused by their searching. He had his old personality, less the cheeky repartee.

She cocked her head at him and asked, "So you can do better?"

Screwfloss emitted a burbling sound, probably a chuckle. Then he got to his feet and shambled past her. He nosed around under the wagon.

She heard a metallic click, but from the top of the wagon.

"Nice camouflage sound!" said Amdi.

"He did something down here," said Ravna, and she ducked under the wagon. Screwfloss was standing around, his aspect smug. One of him was pointing at a narrow wooden platform that had swung down from the belly of the wagon. Ravna reached up, felt a narrow ledge. She felt silken paper within.

"Aha!" She drew a heavy, flat object into the open. "Huh?"

Yes, she was holding oilskin paper, but it was just a bag. Jefri helped her open it. Inside was . . . the most opulent suite of Tinish clothing she had ever seen, clean and new as if never worn.

Jefri thumbed through the thin wooden holders. "Six sets," he said. "What was crazy-asses Chitiratifor thinking?"

"This is for when he returned to his boss in triumph."

"Maybe, but—" Jefri felt further into the bag, pulled out a small, bejewelled disk. It glittered even in the dim light, showing Tycoon's logo in tiny gems. "Packs use this kind of badge the way we would a comm token, to establish authority. I wonder—"

Amdi had swept around them. "Never mind. Where are the maps?" He stuck a couple of snouts deep into the secret space, sweeping back and forth as a human might search with hands. "I found them!"

Ravna and Jefri set the fancy clothes on the top of the wagon, then helped Amdi bring his finds into the open. They stepped aside so Amdi could unscroll them. Ravna had a glimpse of suspiciously fine graphic artwork. Okay, it was Nevil's data, but who did the print job?

"Wow!" said Amdi, then after a second, "But it's so dark now, I can't see the details; we need those lamps."

"I don't want to use the lamps when the night is clear," said Ravna— though maybe it didn't matter, if Nevil was tracking the radio.

Jefri reached past Amdi and lifted the maps up to a flat surface on the back of the wagon, where the last light of day was brightest. In a moment, Amdi was topside, heads weaving about to get the best view.

"Ha!" he said. "This is *really* detailed."

"Now if we only knew where *we* were," said Jefri.

Amdi glanced up into the twilight. "With maps this good, we should be able to match to landmarks. Meantime"—three of him were still peering near-sightedly at the map—"I know we're about here." He tapped the paper with a nose.

Jefri was standing by the wagon; he was tall enough to see the map. He looked at the spot Amdi had indicated and said, "Oh-oh."

"What?" asked Ravna. She should get up there with Amdi.

As she climbed up top, Jefri enlightened her. "There's a snout-drawn 'X', just a few kilometers ahead. I bet we're almost to Chitiratifor's welcoming committee."

"Yup," said Amdi.

She settled down with Amdi and looked where Jef was pointing. The 'X' was in a widening of the valley one to three days' drive ahead, depending on their own precise location. "They have a fort this near the Domain?"

"I don't think there's a fort there," said Jefri. "That looks like a wide place in the valley, not a choke point. And the 'X' mark is in the middle of the open area. I'll bet Chitiratifor—or Remasritlfeer—intended to meet some larger party there."

"Ha, yes," said Amdi. "They may even think Chitiratifor is doing fine, on schedule . . . except he won't be checking in with them tonight."

Ravna shrugged. "So we can't go forward. And we can't stay here. We haven't seen anything of Chitiratifor. Surely it can't be that dangerous to go back?"

"Okay," said Jefri, but he was shaking his head. "You realize that once the bad guys realize we're free, that's just the route they all will be searching."

Amdi was still snuffling at the map, oblivious to their dilemma. "This valley doesn't stay steep and cliffy forever," he said. "See, right before the 'X', there's all sorts of paths up the eastern wall. We could wriggle out sideways. Who'd ever think?"

CHAPTER 23

Johanna Olsndot roamed the strange raft, and watched her fellow-travelers. She had no sailing skills herself, but she had been aboard seacraft of the Domain. A common design was the multiboat, a meshwork of pack-sized boats; individual packs could retain their identity. Multiboats might have a central structure for larger cargo items and be big enough so a number of packs might comfortably meet.

Even the largest Northern multiboats were smaller than the rafts in this flotilla of ten. Johanna wondered how the mess managed to sail together. Every raft had masts and sails, but nothing like packs to manage them. On her raft, the mob wandered here and there, collecting in little groups that might tug on a tiller, while others climbed in the rigging (and sometimes fell off into the sea!). The squeaks and chirrups from above might have been directions, though very few of those below paid any attention.

One by one, these rafts must surely founder, perhaps the last ending up on some faraway shore, like the shipwrecks that used to wash up on the rocks below Starship Hill.

On the second day, she sought out one of those temporary almost-packs that gathered near the booms and was tentatively pulling the sheets this way or that. Not all of these Tines were sparse-haired Tropicals. Some had deep fur pelts, scruffy and ragged and surely uncomfortable in the heat, but very Northern-looking.

"Hei, Johanna. Hei, hei." A clot of five was all looking at her and the Samnorsk words were very clear. When Johanna sat down by them, the almost-pack surrounded her, the heads bobbing with friendly regard.

"We sailing north, I think," it said. That might be nonsense blather, since actually they were sailing west, and the coast of the continent was just few thousand meters to the north. But if they sailed west far enough to round the Southwest Horn of the continent, then it would be north to the Domain. She took a closer look at the five heads. The nearest had a white star splash on the back of its head. It was hard to remember all the fragments she'd known over the years, but this one . . . she reached out her hand. "Cheepers?"

"Hei, some maybe, some," it said. Wow. Cheepers would count as a failure by broodkenner standards, but he had survived his flight from Harmony's Fragmentarium, and made it all the way to the Choir. Over the years, others had too, but there were still only hundreds spread through all the millions of the Choir. When Vendacious chased Johanna into the Choir, when the killing swarm knocked her down, the image and the strangeness of her must have spread at near-soundspeed across the city. Here and there, the sight had reached some few who remembered, and mercy percolated back. Just in time.

The almost-pack stayed with her a moment longer, then was joined by others and reassorted. Some of them wandered off to another mast while others merged with the larger mob that was tricking seabirds to come down for lunch.

By now all the Tines on her raft seemed to recognize her. She had no more aborted, hostile encounters. And yet, the mob did have moods. Five nights out to sea, there was a deadly riot. Johanna hunkered down, listened to mouth-screams of mortal pain. The next day, she saw dark stains smeared across timbers near the edge of the raft. *I hope they weren't fighting over me.* Maybe not. Even milder fights were rare, but she eventually saw one or two in daylight, sub-mobs of Tines facing off. She couldn't see any motive, nothing like food or sex—and there didn't seem to be enduring fighter cliques. Singletons were scarcely smarter than dogs, but something like memes must battle around in this choir. After a while she learned to recognize the crowd's most harmful moods and craziest rules. For instance, she always got in trouble if she tried to open any of the storage boxes that were stacked everywhere, highest at the middle of the raft. Maybe that reaction was some vagrant meme left over from the raft squatters; maybe it was something kinkier. The wooden sides of each box were marked with circular burn marks, a little like Northerner hex signs. For whatever reason, nobody messed with cargo.

Perforce, Johanna spent hours each day studying her mob. This wasn't like the Fragmentarium; random sex and mindsound was perversity to coherent packs, and the broodkenners did their best to suppress it. Here, perversity was the name of the game. But these singletons rarely did really stupid things like pissing in the raft's rain cistern. In fact, they had some sailor skills, and they were quite coordinated in their diving for fish. That last was good for Jo, though raw fish could not sustain her indefinitely.

Most coherent packs didn't like to swim, couldn't stand the way the water interfered with their mindsounds. The members of the mob were not so squeamish. In the water, they zoomed around like they were born of the sea. Parts of her crew were in the water almost all the time—except when something black-and-white and larger than any Tines swept through the area. The Children called those animals whales; they spooked the Tropicals as thoroughly as they did Northern packs.

The whales must have been loud and relatively stupid, because the Tines seemed to know when it was safe to go back in the water. By the fourth day, Johanna was swimming with the Tines. Over the next tenday, she visited all the other rafts. The mobs on each were similar to those on her own. In the end, she became familiar with all the "crews."

On every raft, she eventually communicated the same question: "Where are we going?" The answers were mostly variations on "we go north," "we go with you," and "this big river is fun!"

She eventually returned to the first raft, partly because Cheepers was there, but partly because she had decided that this raft had been intended as the primary vessel of the fleet. It was the largest, certainly. It also had an open area near the masts: the space was bounded by drawered cabinets—*not* subject to the cargo taboo, though the drawers were mostly empty. If she hadn't hijacked the fleet, perhaps these drawers would have held equipment for the proper crew.

The first couple of tendays were all cloudy and rainy, with open sea on one side, and coastal jungle on the other. They were going generally west and at a fair average speed. She did some arithmetic—not for the first time she thanked goodness that Ravna had forced them to learn that manual skill—and concluded that soon they would round the Southwest Horn. Truly, this fleet might be headed for the Domain. *Was I really that persuasive? Or was this flotilla supposed to go north, and I just forced a premature departure?*

Johanna had a lot of time to think, perhaps more time than ever before in her life. Most of that time was useless circling; some of it might save her life.

Nevil had turned out to be evil beyond anyone's imagination. She saw so much in a different light now that she understood that. Since well before he had betrayed Ravna, he had been spreading lies. She thought of all the times he had persuaded Pilgrim and herself to steer clear of the Tropics. For *years* they had searched for Tycoon, everywhere but where he was. Now, perhaps, Nevil had overreached himself. Woodcarver and surely Ravna had known of this flight to the Tropics. Not even Nevil's marvelous persuasiveness could cover things up for long now.

The first time Johanna looped through that logic, her spirits had risen—for about three seconds, until the implications came crashing down upon her. Who *else* did Nevil murder the night he crashed Pilgrim and Johanna? If she ever got home, what allies might still live?

There will be allies. I must be smart enough to get home and find them. So she spent a lot of time thinking about everything Nevil had ever said, assuming every word a lie. There was a world of consequences. Nevil said the orbiter's vision was barely a horizon sensor, with only one-thousand-meter resolution. What if it was better? She remembered the orbiter; she and Jef were the only Children who had seen the inside of it. She remembered her mom saying that there was nothing useful left aboard. So Nevil's claim had been plausible—but wouldn't one-centimeter resolution be equally plausible? Unfortunately, just assuming Nevil lied about everything did not give her definite numbers!

The first time she'd run through this reasoning was only a day out to sea; up until then, there'd been very little clear sky, and *that* had been at night. She'd looked up into the rain and overcast and concluded that probably Nevil's "horizon sensor" could not see through clouds—else she would not be around to think about the issue. And even in clear weather, the orbiter's surveillance could not be much better than one-meter resolution and/or not effective at night.

Two tendays into the voyage, the sky was often clear, and stars were visible at night. The rafts were truly headed north; Johanna was all but certain that they had rounded the Horn. By day, she kept under the sails, or hunkered down in a little cubbyhole she'd made for herself in the jumble at the center of the raft. At night, she would carefully peek out. The orbiter was a bright star, always high in the southeastern sky, further east than it had ever been since Nevil took control. *How does he explain this to Woodcarver? Does he have to explain anything anymore? What service does this do Vendacious and Tycoon?* She had lots of such questions and no way to get answers. The good news was that if Nevil was searching for *her*, he was looking in the wrong place! She became a little less paranoid about exposure to the sky.

Perhaps another thirty days would bring the rafts to Woodcarver's old capital. Then the life and death of Johanna and her friends might depend on how quickly she could discover just what was going on in the Domain.

For a while she stewed on possible scenarios. A few more days passed. There was only so much she could do with scenarios. She needed some clues about where this fleet had originally been headed. She needed to break into the cargo.

How could she persuade the mob to let her do that?

By now, Johanna had been all over the surface of all the rafts. Every one of them was Tropic chaos, and yet they were nothing like the wrecks she had seen in the Domain. Somebody coherent had suggested specific design tricks. The masts and spars and rigging were much like Woodcarvers'. The cargo boxes were regular and uniform, quite unlike everything she associated with a choir. Now that she'd had time to study them, she realized that the burn marks on the sides were a version of Tycoon's Pack of Packs logo.

Those boxes aside, the mob was quite happy to have Jo around. She was often a real help, with her clever hands, and with her very sharp and durable knife. In many ways the mob was more fun than coherent packs. These creatures were all among themselves, playing and fighting like young children—leaving aside their occasional fits of madness and their rule about cargo tampering.

Sometimes, they would break apart in the middle of some serious job and start playing with the elastic balls that seemed to have no other function than mob amusement. (The balls floated in water, but every day a few more were lost overboard. They would not be an unending source of fun.)

Other times, especially at night, the Tines would gather in a mass on the highest part of the raft. Across the water, the same would happen on the other rafts. All together, they roared and hissed, and sometimes sang pieces of Straumer music overheard years ago in the Domain. At dawn, most would come down and fool around in quieter ways. Some would dribble off the edges of the raft to fish. Johanna had plenty of opportunity to try little experiments. She had almost ten years of experience with packs and singletons and pieces of packs—but that was under broodkenner rules, and Northern notions of acceptable behavior.

She'd found lots that was new and bizarre here. Choirs were almost as strange compared to coherent packs as the packs were, compared to humans. She found a shaded spot high on the raft. She could stand there and be seen by almost everyone on board. When she shouted to them, some heads would turn in her direction. The few who understood Samnorsk were enough so that *all* the mob had some idea of her meaning. Of course, this wasn't a super-intelligence, but it was a different-intelligence. In some ways dumb as a dog, yet a choir could do local search-and-optimization better than any pack or natural human. She could ask it questions—"Where are the play balls?"—and within seconds, all the balls on the raft seemed to be bouncing in the air, even ones that she had carefully hidden the day before. She looked across the hundred meters of sea to the two nearest rafts. Yellow balls were bouncing into the air there, too!

Hmm. Choirs could do miracles of local optimization, but they couldn't see the big picture, they couldn't see across the vastness of the search space to connect results. They were like a spreadthink toy without an aggregator. That limitation applied to everything from the space of ideas to the space of . . . fishing.

Once she had the idea, making it work took almost a tenday of preaching to the choir—and the choirs on the other rafts. Often, they didn't want to play. Since the fleet had turned north, the sea and the air had gotten steadily colder, the storms deadlier. The water was too cold for even the Tines to comfortably fish.

The mobs' mood was grumpy and sullen. But day by day, she achieved more complex results. Finally there were temporary godsgifts who would climb the masts and shout out fragments of Interpack or Samnorsk about the schools of fish they were seeing. Eventually, the coordination included the part-time sail masters, and the fleet managed to catch enough fish with just a fraction of the swim time.

Credit assignment was a near-incomprehensible idea for a choir, but Johanna liked to think that the Tines trusted her more after this success. They certainly tried harder to understand what she asked of them—and were quicker to do what they thought she wanted. Maybe it was safe for her to break into Tycoon's cargo boxes.

From furtive experiments, she had learned that the boxes were tough, not designed for easy in-and-out privileges. Her knife was not up to the job. Okay. But she'd found a steel prybar in one of those drawered cabinets by the masts. It looked a lot like the leveraging tools used by packs up north. Given the prybar and some time, she could break into a cargo box.

After a morning storm—the sort of meatgrinder that had killed several Tines before her riverboat sailors got serious about safety tiedowns—Johanna noticed that one of the cargo boxes had slipped partway off the central mound. As usual, the mob tried to prevent more slippage. As usual, the result was a mishmash of ropes, fastened with variously effective knots. She noticed a crack in the box's wood panelling, black tar oozing out—waterproofing?

She watched the crowd swirl around the box, Tines bobbing and bouncing, somewhat more incompetent than usual. Another time, they might have noticed the crack, but not today. Johanna waited till the crowd drifted away, mostly to huddle together under a "stolen" sail on the lee side of the raft. The cold weather affected the Tropicals the most, but everybody was suffering. *Sorry guys. If I hadn't persuaded you to hijack this fleet . . .*

This side of the raft was about as Tines-free as it ever got; Johanna grabbed her prybar and scrambled across to the damaged cargo box. "Just doing repairs," she said. Her words should be audible to everyone on the raft, and they might give her some protection via the Tines who understood Samnorsk. She slipped the prybar into the cracked panel—and hesitated an instant. The sound of breaking wood could bring all hell down her.

She didn't get a chance to test this possibility, for even as she hesitated there came a bass honking behind her. She glanced over her shoulder. *Powers!* It was Tines on another raft, up in the rigging. Maybe it was a crazy-diligent fish watcher, but now it was watching *her*—and raising the alarm!

Within seconds her own mob came surging back, hissing all around her. Johanna dropped to her knees, tilted her head to the side and turned her hands outward. That was about as nonthreatening as a human could get with Tines.

Jaws snapped close, lunging, tipping toward a killing flood. But the crowd coming up behind the first wave wasn't pushing inward. Here and there, thoughtful clusters tried to form. Just now there was too much anger and chaos for that to work: the almost-packs lasted for bare seconds before they were shouted down, before they shouted each other down.

Johanna leaned back against the cracked cargo box. She hoped the gesture might seem protective of it. In fact, some of the most threatening heads moved back a bit, and the roar of humanly audible sound diminished. She looked around, trying to spot any grouping she might use as an intermediary. No, they were still all mobbed together. Okay. She had talked to the whole mob before: "Please listen to my words," Johanna said. "We go North. True?"

The mob's effort to comprehend was so strong she could feel the buzz. Finally a single word of Samnorsk sounded. "Yes," and then a dribble of other words, like echoes: "To Domain." "To home." "To old home."

Johanna bobbed her head, a singleton form of a nod. "I can help. But I need to know more."

The mob continued to dither, the buzz of mindsound growing stronger and stronger. This was a situation where a godsgift would really be one. But the mob didn't make the space. Instead it swayed back and forth, its Tines shuffling about. After some seconds, another bit of Samnorsk floated in the air: "Trusting you."

So Johanna got a peek into the damaged cargo box, maybe a big insight into Vendacious' master plan. As the mob watched, all quiet and nervous looking, she split open the wood covering, pulled back the tarry waterproofing goo . . . and a cascade of yellow play balls bounced onto the deck. The crowd forgot itself as it variously grabbed and bounced the balls, sending most of them right back in Jo's direction.

Okay! A fix for the incipient shortage of play balls! Behind the yellow balls was a wall of tidy bricks. But they were soft to her touch. She used her prybar to lever the tightly wedged objects free, then pushed the loose mass out into the open. When she recognized the cargo, she stepped quickly out of the way and gave a loud whistle. The crowd continued to play with the balls for a few seconds, but Jo could see a ripple of understanding pass around it. The cargo box was mostly full of heavy jacket-cloaks. In another second, the yellow balls were forgotten as the mob swarmed down on the promise of warmth.

The box didn't contain enough cloaks for everybody. There was much pushing and shoving all around the crate, but nobody got killed. Very quickly, the notion of breaking into more of Tycoon's cargo outweighed the taboo against such activity. Johanna led the way with her steel prybar. They found many more cloaks, another box that was mostly play balls, and a very well-sealed store of smoked meat. At this point, the mob was totally preoccupied with the plunder. Johanna decided not to risk spoilage with more exploration. She wrapped herself in a couple of cloaks and retreated to her usual cubbyhole to think about what had been discovered: So the top layers of cargo were just supplies, set by planners who expected this to be a long voyage. Was Tycoon's deliverable cargo further down? Or maybe she'd stolen the fleet before both its proper crew and main cargo had been put aboard.

All over the raft, Tines were playing with their new clothes, trying them on, making little tents out of them. At the same time, they were passing around the smoked meat. She'd never seen such Tinish enthusiasm for cold, dead flesh; well, it wasn't fish.

Very loud gangs of Tines had gathered at the edges of the raft, flaunting their warm cloaks at the rest of the fleet. Their shouting was mainly Interpack but she heard her name in it.

Johanna watched the Tines on the other rafts. At first, they responded with bogus counter-brags, but there was also much clueless cocking of heads.

Finally the mob on the nearest raft—the one with the snoopy Tine who had ratted on Johanna—seemed to get the idea. The mob swarmed their top cargo boxes, slashing at them with claws and jaws, pounding them with weighted ropes. This went on for five or ten minutes with no success; the Tycoon boxes were proof against unaided Tines. What the mob needed was Johanna's prybar—or someone of human or pack intelligence.

The futile assault subsided as the mob backed off and hunkered down. Any second now, its unity of purpose would dribble away. . . . But no: The mob spread out, creating a kind of belly-down mesh across their raft. They were chanting, rhythmic whoops that swept up through Johanna's hearing into silence, and then started low again. After several minutes, the chanting ended; the Tines hesitated, silent. Abruptly, they scrambled to their feet and began *dancing*. Well, hopping up and down, anyway. They danced on and on, a beat that circled their raft in time with the sea waves, and in time with the movements of their cargo. Almost impercepibly, the whole platform began to tip and sway. The oscillations grew. The cargo boxes at the top of the raft's pile were free to move since the mob's initial assault had cut them loose. First one crashed down and then another and another. The effect was worse—or more effective—than storm damage. The avalanche of shattering wood swept half the pile into the sea. So much for Tycoon's cargo taboo!

Now the sea around the raft was crowded with boxes and pieces of boxes. She could see heads in the water and Tines hanging on to the main wreck. It was much like the raft disasters she remembered in the Domain—except that in this case no one was being smashed into a rocky shore. Tines paddled out from what remained of their raft in some kind of salvage and rescue operation. As the sun slid down to the sea, it looked like most everybody had managed to return to the surviving part of their raft.

That evening, the sounds from the other rafts seemed generally happy. Each had succeeded with its own "shakedown" demolition—though the Choir on the half-wrecked raft sounded more boastful than any. The gobbling and honking only got louder as the wind picked up. Johanna sat in her usual place, but well-fed and wrapped up toasty warm. What wonderful things were Tinish storm jackets—even if they were narrow and short, and the tympana cutouts so terribly drafty.

She watched as the moon rose higher and the festivities became wilder. It was the usual mix of chanting and orgy and mad rushing around. And yet, tonight there was a difference. Every few minutes a singleton or a duo or trio would shyly approach her. Almost every group brought her some gift, an extra cloak, a block of smoked meat. In some ways, this reminded Johanna of the Fragmentarium. There, too, she had wistful, friendly relations with creatures who could not quite understand what was going on—but who were grateful for her help. For all the hard times of this voyage, the rafts were a happier place than the Fragmentarium. Here her friends weren't haunted by the fear that they would never become people again. Choirs didn't look at these issues the way broodkenners did!

The celebration peaked around midnight with a serious attempt at synchrony between all the rafts. The screeching pounded a rhythm that beat against similar sounds from across the water. For a brief time, the combination warbled like a single voice, a huge, slow, coherence.

Johanna drowsed. She was vaguely aware that even though the celebration had quieted, individual Tines were still snouting around. They weren't going to get into any more cargo boxes without her prybar. *Hmmm*, unless they tried to shake the whole raft apart; that was something she'd have to discourage . . . tomorrow. She burrowed deeper into the warm cloaks and gave in to sleep.

Some unknown time later: "What's this? What's this? What's this?" A snout was poking her shoulder.

"Whuh?" Johanna struggled back to wakefulness. It wasn't morning. Not at all. The moon was only halfway down the sky. By its light she could see the crowd surrounding her. A trio that included Cheepers stood closest.

"What's this?" Cheepers said again, and another of the trio stepped toward her, giving her a small box that glittered like dark glass in the moonlight.

"Powers!" she swore softly. What glittered in the moonlight was the solar-electric side of a torsion antenna. This was one of the analog radios Scrupilo had built. Each had taken significant effort. Pride aside, Scrupilo had had important uses for each of them. She remembered him complaining every time one was missing.

"What's this?" Cheepers—the whole crowd, really—continued to ask.

Johanna looked up. "It's a radio." At best, its peer-to-peer range would be a few kilometers, but with the orbiter relaying, it could reach across the world— all the way to Vendacious and Nevil.

"Where did you find it?" she said.

The Cheepers trio gestured toward the pile of junk around the masts. Ah, up where she had found the prybar, maybe. This radio must have been intended for the proper crew.

From somewhere in the crowd, someone else said, "Heard it."

Heard it? She held the box close to her ear. If it hadn't been in the sun, its charge should be down and—she heard faint sounds! The orbiter's signal must be *strong*. The message was Tinish, a simple chord repeated again and again: "Answer if you hear."

"It's not dead," Cheepers said helpfully.

". . . Yes," said Johanna, thinking fast. She noticed that the send button was in the off position. "But it's dying, right?" she said.

Heads drooped, a wave of despondency that spread beyond her vision. "Maybe. We shout louder and louder, but it not hear."

The trio thought a second more, maybe listening to advice from the larger group. Then it added, "Voice sound dead."

Yeah, it wasn't surprising the transmission sounded strange. No doubt it was an audio loop. Tines could repeat sounds with great fidelity, but doing so again and again bored them.

"We bring to you, right? You fix?"

Sure. Fixing it would amount to waiting for sunrise and then pressing the send button. Then her friends could chat with Vendacious and innocently report that Johanna would arrive in the Domain some tenday soon.

She looked around at Cheepers and all the rest. She had to lie to them. Closer to the Domain, this gadget might be very useful, but for now she should just disable the snout-friendly send button. *That* could be tricky. She had seen how this mob played with objects that interested them. They'd bounce the radio around, maybe even break it—but they'd also tweak and push at things in ways she hadn't imagined. Watching the mob play with puzzles reminded Johanna of little Wenda Larsndot. That girl's naive fumbling was a constant source of surprise. Once she'd even bypassed a cabinet lock to play inside the gear train of her parents' loom; Wenda, Jr. was lucky she hadn't killed herself. These Tines would eventually either break the radio or get it into send mode.

Johanna turned the box this way and that, pretending to inspect it. Finally she said, "It's almost dead, but I can help it." A happy movement swept across the Tines. "But it may take days."

The Cheepers trio drooped, and as Jo's meaning spread, wider distress was evident. But the choir trusted her now more than ever, and over the next few minutes the crowd dispersed. Johanna made a big deal of taking extra cloaks and making a nest for the sacred object. Then she wrapped her own cloaks around herself and the nest.

Cheepers and his trio were all that remained nearby. They looked at her hesitantly.

"I will care for the radio every minute," Johanna promised.

They dithered a moment more, maybe wondering if they should break apart or stay the night with her. Then they bobbed their heads and turned to leave. *Whew.*

"We go," said Cheepers and his friends. "Listen to the other radios."

"What?"

"In boxes. Fours of fours of fours of radios."

CHAPTER 24

Bili Yngva was the number two player in Nevil Storherte's Disaster Study Group. Privately, Bili considered himself the brains of the operation and Nevil the smooth-talking mouth. Thus Bili was always amazed at how much scutwork he ended up with. For instance, somebody had to do maintenance aboard *Oobii*. The starship was the center of power on this world and the highest system technology for lightyears around. Lose control of *Oobii* and the DSG would fall in a matter of days. The traitors, the know-nothings, and the dog-lovers would take over. More likely, the local warlord would kill all the humans, dog-lovers or not. Woodcarver was a deadly threat even when she was at the mercy of *Oobii*.

Whoever did maintenance had to have admin authority over the starship. Very rightly, Nevil didn't trust anyone but himself and Bili Yngva with that power. So, natch, Bili ended up here most nights, "master of the world."

Bili switched from camera to camera, snooping around through places that Woodcarver and Scrupilo thought were their private territory. It might have been fun if it weren't so tedious. Without a doubt, *Oobii* was the dumbest piece of automation Bili had ever encountered. In the High Beyond, there were ribosome plugins smarter than this starship. Sitting here at the local Pinnacle of Everything just reminded Bili of how low they were in the pits of hell. He could almost see why the dog-lovers had gone native. If you wanted to do *anything* with the *Oobii*, it had to be done manually. The ship couldn't think tactically, much less do strategic planning. All that must be done by Nevil and—mostly—Bili. The starship was simply too dumb for a real genius like Gannon Jorkenrud to use. And if you let the ship putter forward on its own defaults, all sorts of terrible crap would start to happen.

This was where Bili really missed Ravna Bergsndot. Powers, what a slope-skulled Neanderthal that Sjandran was. Yes, she looked like a human, but just talk to her for a few minutes and you realized you were trying to make points with a monkey. On the other hand, her limitations had made her a perfect match for *Oobii*. Bili remembered the thousands of hours she had spent here, working out the tedious details that made this little settlement possible. Hell, it was what he was trying to adapt for his own project. It was a shame she'd been so bloody dangerous.

Bili pulled up the notes he had compiled for his Best Hope planning: they just sat there, drawing only the simplest conclusions from the latest spy camera surveillance. Both Johanna Olsndot and the pack Pilgrim were definitely out of the picture. That had weakened Woodcarver as much as the disappearance of the Bergsndot woman, but there were a lot of loose ends.

Gannon must be retrieved. Unfortunately, *Eyes Above 2* was proving hellishly difficult to operate; after all, it was a machine from before the dawn of technology. For that matter, *Oobii* had lost track of Gannon's expedition! Bili had shifted the orbiter some degrees eastwards, trying to get a better view of the search area. So far he had found nothing.

Nevil's contacts with Woodcarver's enemies claimed Ravna Bergsndot was dead, or soon would be. Okay, if that's the way it had to be. But even with her gone, Woodcarver had managed to co-opt more of the Children. If they demanded another election and if Nevil couldn't smooth-talk his way to another victory—well, then Nevil said (very privately, just to Bili) that maybe they should use *Oobii* against their own classmates. Nevil figured it would just be a few deaths, a temporary tyranny. Besides, he said, tyranny was the natural organizational form Down Here. Maybe so, but Nevil had gotten way too bloody-minded; now he'd upgraded the ship's beam gun with an amplifier stage. *We should be protecting humanity. We need everyone if we're going to climb back to the Transcend.* Bili was working on an alternative plan to cope with a Woodcarver attack, something that wouldn't harm any more Children, whatever their loyalties—and would leave the Disaster Study Group in a position to counter-move at its leisure. He just had to model the thing clearly enough to convince Nevil.

Bili forced his mind to plod through the endless detail that was necessary to work with *Oobii*. How had humankind ever survived the dark ages of Slow Zone programming . . . ?

When next he noticed the time, it was nearing morning. This was going to turn into an all-nighter. He must have been at it for another hour or so, when *Oobii* began acting strangely. That wasn't unusual, of course. Any time you asked *Oobii* for something novel, however simple, you were also asking for new stupidity. At first, this latest weirdness just looked like more bugs: three million lines of intermediate code had just collapsed into a few squiggles of script that Bili didn't recognize. The so-called "results window" started scrolling sentences in simple Samnorsk. At first he thought it was another of those infinitely useless stack tracebacks that happened every time the system claimed that *Bili* had made a mistake.

Something was flashing a friendly shade of green at him. It was a warning from the resource monitor. He'd set that up to watch for secret grabs by players such as the Bergsndot woman. With both her and Ristling gone, this would be somebody else messing around. Øvin Verring? Øvin was more and more a pain in the neck, but he wasn't the kind who conspired. Wait. Resource use was, huh, *over* one hundred percent. For a moment Bili couldn't make sense of the representation—and of course *Oobii* made no effort to enlighten him. Now usage was at 100% *times ten thousand*! Maybe *Oobii* had found a new way to go wrong. Over the next five seconds, usage increased to 100% times seven million. And then he noticed that the user was listed as . . . Bili Yngva.

Somebody is jerking me around. And this was not some school-chum jape. He searched wildly for options. Could he shut this down? That *green* resource alarm—he'd never seen that before. He queried help, and for once got a relevant reply:

The resource monitor notes that the ship has upgraded to standard processing components. The ship is now handling your planning job in state—0
which is only ten million times greater than the capacity of the Slow Zone
emergency processors. For more reasonable performance, you should
consider asking for non-deterministic extensions.

"Holy shit," he said softly. This could mean only one thing. The great darkness had ebbed; Tines World was no longer in the Slow Zone. The walls around
him shimmered, jobs wakening. Some of these tasks must be ten years old, suspended when Pham Nuwen had done his killing. Most of the jobs flickered into
termination, the ship recognizing that they were no longer relevant. A few jobs
grew across Bili's vision. His painfully constructed planning program was being rewritten, being merged with the *Oobii*'s tech archive, which was now running with something like internal motivation.

Bili watched the process for several seconds, shocked into immobility. The
displays were mostly unintelligible, but he recognized the inference patterns.
This was mid-Beyond automation, perhaps the best *Oobii* had ever been capable
of. Bili was surprised to feel tears come to his eyes, that something so simple-
minded could bring such a surge of joy. *I can work with this.* He waved for an
interface, but felt no increased understanding. *Shit.* Maybe all the salvage
wrecking they'd done on *Oobii* had destroyed the capability. Or maybe the ship
had never been that capable. He leaned forward, watching the patterns. It
didn't really matter. He could see that the basic patterns were Beyonder. Reality graphics should be possible, even if they had to bootstrap from natural matter. He looked from process to process, probing with questions, thinking about
the answers and the consequences. Most of the thinking still had to go on inside his head, but after ten years he'd gotten pretty good at that.

Then he hit the most important insight of all. And apparently it was a gift
from Ravna Bergsndot: a set of simple windows that pointed him where he should
have been looking all along. The bitch had known something like this could
happen! She'd set the *Oobii* to run a zonograph, to monitor the relevant physical
laws. But what had just happened was orders of magnitude greater than that
program's detection threshold. It was so great that *Oobii* had restarted its standard automation.

He pushed the other projects aside, waved for more detail and explanation. . . .
Okay, Bergsndot had used a seismic metaphor for shifts in the zone boundary.
Bili's lips twisted into a smile. That made sense, depending on your model's
probability distribution. In this case, hah! Maybe the better metaphor was the
ending of sleep state. The shift had begun one hundred seconds earlier, but
had risen so fast that *Oobii* could go to its standard mode automation less than
ten seconds later. Improvement had leveled off over the next minute, but now
the physics was mid-Beyonder. A reasonable starship—even the *Out of Band
II*, if they hadn't gutted it—could fly at dozens of lightyears per hour. For this
region of space, that was better than *status quo ante* Pham Nuwen. And that
meant . . .

Rescue was not centuries in the future, the remote promise that Bergsndot's twisted mind considered a threat. She had always claimed that the rescue fleet was just thirty lightyears away. Now on Tines World, the Zone physics was still improving. What was it like thirty lightyears higher?

Bili turned the zonograph program this way and that, trying to see the state of near interstellar space. *Oobii* was smart enough that it should be helping. Oh. Explanations hung all around his various demands. The only accessible zone probes were onboard. If the ship had slightly more distant stations—even a lightyear away—a reasonable extrapolation might be made.

Bili waved down the objections and forced an extrapolation, presumably based on historical gradients. The result came back in the pale violet of extreme uncertainty. Bili was warned. Nevertheless . . . the windows showed a fleet of dozens of starships, translating under ultradrive. The rescuers were thirty lightyears zone-higher, and the violet estimate showed a pseudo-velocity of fifty lightyears per hour. Rescue was not centuries or even years away. It would arrive within the hour.

The hard numbers from the ship's instruments showed that the Zone improvements had leveled off. It didn't matter! After today, this exile would just be a very bad memory. With working ultradrive, the rescuers could take them higher and higher, finally reaching the Transcend. There, borkners like Gannon and Jefri (at least if this world had not completely destroyed Jef's potential) could rebuild the High Lab, complete what their parents and all of Straumli Realm had dreamed of.

In less than an hour they could say good-bye to this soul-sucking trap.

Huh? In the violet display, the estimated fleet velocity had fallen to thirty lightyears per hour. Yeah, but that was vaporous conjecture. *Oobii*'s zonograph still showed—Bili's eyes flickered around the displays; data fusion was next to impossible Down Here. *The ship's zonograph showed local conditions degrading.* Maximum possible ultradrive velocity right here, right now, was fifteen lightyears per hour. Twelve.

So what does it matter? Rescue might be an hour away, or a day. Or a tenday. But a sickening chill spread up from Bili's gut. Maybe Pham Nuwen's Zone Shift was not a diseased sleep. Maybe Ravna Bergsndot had had the right metaphor.

Conditions still degrading. The hard local estimate: five lightyears per . . . year. *No, no, no!* The violet fleet was just twenty lightyears out, broadjump distance if you were at the Top of the Beyond.

Two lightyears per year. Operation alarms were flickering all over. *Oobii* couldn't maintain standard computation in this deadly environment. Bili waved for it to try.

Afterwards, Bili realized that it was unwise to make demands of Beyonder automation when it was near its operational limits; you might win the argument. The zonograph estimate hit 1.0 lightyears per year—and all around him the displays reformatted, or simply crashed. The ship's lighting brightened, but Bili knew that it and he and all of Tines World had fallen back into stygian darkness.

He sat in the programmatic ruins for a moment, too shocked to move. For just—193 seconds according to a surviving clock display—salvation had been at hand. Now it was jerked away. He just wanted to start bawling. Instead he forced himself to survey the damage. During those three minutes, the *Oobii* had probably done more solid computation than it had in the last ten years. There were the results of his planning project—now reinforced with technical details for using their surviving equipment, and political options for Nevil. There was the record of the Zone surge itself. Maybe they could learn from that what more progress might be expected. There was . . . there was ongoing data loss! The ship had run on its standard processors right till the Slow Zone crashed down on it. The transition to backup computation had been successful, but translating data to passive/dumb formats had been interrupted. Absent intelligent refresh, the physical memories themselves were fading. What was left, even the passives, needed manual backup immediately.

Bili hunched forward, waving commands. *Don't panic.* He had lots of practice getting things done in this environment. Don't skip any steps, don't make *any* mistakes. *Don't panic.* If Nevil and Øvin or Merto had been online, all working together, they could have saved almost everything. Yeah, but what did the dogs say? "If wishes were froghens we'd never go hungry?" The dogs knew the limits of their world, even though they didn't recognize them as limits.

Bili managed to capture almost all the data from his planning program. From the headers, it looked like good stuff, insight that would help him persuade Nevil that Best Hope was doable. Unfortunately, he couldn't tell how much detail had survived reformatting. And partway through his rescue of the Best Hope data, a burning smell rose from the zonograph displays, the classic diagnostic for lost data. *Damn it, I can't be everywhere at once!* He riffled through Bergsndot's notes. The program itself was a simple sequential, something that would have made sense to the earliest humans. *That* kind of recipe did not easily get lost. But the violet analysis and the raw zonograph session, those were gone.

He ran a quick heal on the zonograph spew and restarted the program. Meantime, he finished an oh-so-gentle foldup of his Best Hope output. And finally, he did what Nevil would complain that he should have done first thing:

"Ship, give me a secure link to Nevil." Bili was firmly back in caveman mode now. He even remembered to specify that the link be secure. Among other things, that meant the comm would go to Nevil's head-up display, or by direct line of sight to Nevil's town house.

Unfortunately, there was only one HUD left, and Nevil was just as careful as Ravna Bergsndot had been about using it. Nearly ten seconds passed, and then a woman replied: "Yeah?"

"Um, hei Tami. May I speak to Nevil, please?"

"Hei Bili. Nevil went up to Newcastle—you know, getting ready for the big protest against Woodcarver's conspiracy. He made me stay behind to be his answering machine. So what's your message?" There was a pouting tone to her voice. Tami was no Johanna Olsndot, but she could be trouble in other ways. Bili wasn't quite sure what Nevil saw in her.

"No, that's okay, I'll catch him at the meeting. Thanks, Tam."

———

Bili stared at the zonograph display for a moment more. It was showing low levels of random noise. Most likely, the Slow Zone was again lightyears deep above them. *But that could change in seconds . . . or years.* And Nevil had to be told immediately. Nevertheless, Bili took a few minutes to make sure nothing open-ended was running, nothing that would fry its own output if there were another surge/crash.

He hustled off the command deck, down to the great meeting hall. For a wonder, the place was empty. Somehow, Nevil had persuaded *everybody*, even the die-hard dog-lovers to attend the rally. Maybe folks were finally getting the message: with Bergsndot and Johanna gone, they had only one hope for salvation and that was Nevil and the DSG.

He stepped out of doors, into a solid wall of cold. Fortunately, the air was still and he didn't freeze anything. He stepped back into the relative warmth of the entranceway and buttoned up his jacket. Even as he stood there, the first rays of the morning sun lit the hillside above him, showing the town houses along Queen's Road all the way to the roofs of Newcastle town. Beyond that stood the castle's marble dome—the Dome of the Lander.

It was another perfectly normal morning at the nether end of nowhere, all thanks to Pham Nuwen and the fungus that came down with the Lander. Bili knew the stories about the day Pham Nuwen raised the Slow Zone high, how the sun had gone dark and the packs had danced in madness. The surge this morning—Bili couldn't see any evidence of it. Most likely he was the only person on this world who had noticed a thing. It had not been a grand change in the universe. It had been just a tiny slip back toward the natural equilibrium.

As Bili started the long walk to Newcastle, some of his frustration slipped away. Salvation had been snatched away at the last second, but this was a message. Rescue was on the way, and it would arrive sooner rather than later.

CHAPTER 25

"Escape by wriggling out sideways." Amdi's suggestion was much easier said than done. The wriggling began with a midnight sneak several kilometers closer to the sinister 'X' on Chitiratifor's map. They forded the river at a fast-moving shallows, under a merciless rain. Once safely across, Ravna decided to be heartened by the weather. The storm might mask them from any enemy scouts. The clouds (probably) meant that Nevil's orbiter could not see them. And the rain had swatted down the armies of gnats that had so enjoyed yesterday's sunny warmth.

The path Amdi had found on the maps should eventually take them over mountain passes into another rift valley. The "Wild Principates" was one of the less geologically active rifts, but its name was a confession of ignorance. Its last valley-long blowup had occurred perhaps a thousand years earlier. Afterwards, settlers had trickled into the region, risking merely local catastrophes. Two hundred years ago, such an eruption in the northern part of the valley had suffocated every last member of Woodcarver's colony there. Queen Woodcarver had a long memory for such things; she had not been back.

Compared to the alternatives, the geological risks were entirely acceptable to Ravna and company.

As they climbed out of the valley, the wind picked up and lightning slammed into the cliffs above them. Nothing came falling down, but their path was narrow and the racket made the kherhogs nervous.

After about half an hour of this, she noticed that the lightning had somehow triggered the tamper alarm on the lamps in the middle wagon. The alarm pattern flickered from cracks in the cabinetry. This didn't further upset the kherhogs, but it was very distracting to Ravna—and to Amdi, some of whom were driving the wagon behind her.

"It's all the lamps," he said to her. "Um, um, They're coordinating in phase! See the rainbows along the side of your wagon?"

"I know. Don't worry, Amdi. It should stop after the storm," unless Nevil was smart enough to be probing from the orbiter—but even that would be a useful bit of information. "Just keep your eyes on the road." It was better advice for her than for him, considering how many eyes he had available.

The alarm display lasted only another minute or two. Eventually the winds calmed and the lightning retreated. The rain continued, sometimes in icy sheets so dense she couldn't see beyond her kherhog's ears. Then there would be a minute or two during which she could see partway across the valley, to where the storm looked more like drifting fog. They were far above the valley forest. Good-bye crusherbushes and arrow trees and stately bannerwood. Up here, the trees were thick and twisted, guarding snowbanks slowly melting in the rain.

The one of Amdi beside her had hunkered down, looking miserable; the rain was a powerful damper on his mindsound. She just hoped the ones on the rear wagon were enough to keep it on the road. In places, the path was defined by cliff rock on one side and vague mist on the other. When the downpour eased, she had scary views of how far she would fall if her kherhog strayed off the path.

Screwfloss kept close together, mostly ahead of Jefri's wagon. Last night, after revealing the maps, the remnant had been no help at all. When Amdi explained to him about cutting east and asked about the risk of detection, the remnant just stood around cocking its heads in all directions, a kind of sarcastic shrug. But today the pack was really helping. When the path disappeared or appeared to fork, Screwfloss would scramble above and below them. Then he'd come back into sight and lead them forward. Several times they'd had to dismount and lever rocks clear of their way, but they'd always made progress, more eastward and upwards than not.

Just now, Screwfloss was heading toward the last wagon. The Amdi member beside her twisted around to watch. "I think he's checking on the spare kherhog," he said. The extra draft animal followed the third wagon, on a short tether.

As the remnant passed she glanced down. As usual, the limper affected the pack's collective gait, but . . . She had gotten very used to the pack's appearance. There were two members with white blazes across their heads, so perfectly symmetrical they had to be littermates. One was the poor fellow whose leg she'd broken. The limp made the critter impossible to miss, but now the border of its white blaze was smeared like . . . like a cheap dye job.

Huh? Aren't there enough mysteries? The thought flitted through her mind, and then her kherhog slipped a half-meter downslope—and all her attention was back where it should be, on surviving the day.

The rain continued into the afternoon twilight, but now they were past the worst of the climbing. Their little caravan trundled along the edge of alpine meadows. If not for the overcast, the orbiter's cameras could probably have spotted them. Jefri cajoled additional kilometers out of the kherhogs, finally stopping where Amdi judged a cliff side would keep them out of sight of the orbiter even in sunny daytime.

"Unless Nevil maneuvers it again," said Ravna.

"Yes." The eightsome looked skyward nervously. "I gotta think. I spread myself too thin today."

Screwfloss did some climbing, maybe looking for rockfall threats. When he came back, he circled forward, indicating where they should put the wagons.

By now, everyone but Ravna had plenty of practice with the scutwork. Despite the rain, they soon had the fodder set out for the kherhogs. Screwfloss started a campfire and they sat down to eat.

"Even cooked, this stuff still tastes like crap," said Jefri.

"The salted meat is worse," said Amdi.

"Ah," said Ravna. "Then the good news is that we're almost out of food."

Screwfloss did not add to the chitchat, but he was chewing unenthusiastically. Being crippled and only four, maybe he wasn't up for normal Tinish hunting. She noticed that he kept a speculative eye on one of the kherhogs, the nearly lame animal they'd been keeping behind Amdi's wagon. Screwfloss and Jefri had worked on the kherhog's front paw, removing a jammed rock. The creature might do some work tomorrow, but it was smart enough to realize that the implicit contract with its meat-eating masters was in jeopardy. Now, it uneasily returned Screwfloss' gaze.

"Well, I figure we're at the midpoint of the cut across," said Amdi.

Ravna remembered what they had seen on the maps, in the valley that lay ahead. There had been scattered settlements. "We'll find some place we can stop and trade for food."

Amdi said, "The Tines we'll meet down there, very likely they've never seen humans before."

Ravna looked from Amdi to Jef. "You think they might attack us out of hand, the way Steel's troops killed your parents?"

Jefri looked around thoughtfully, then shook his head. "Steel was Old Flenser's madpack, conditioned for over-the-top treachery."

"It won't be like Steel," said Amdi. "There are still a lot of unpleasant possibilities. I'm sure that people in the Principates have heard of humans, but—"

"Okay," said Ravna. "Maybe Jefri and I could stay out of sight at first. You and Screwfloss could pose as lone travellers. If we have to, we could trade them our lamps, maybe other things. We can get past the initial encounter, guys. The question is, what then? We have to get home fast, and without anyone noticing— until we want to be noticed."

Jefri hunched forward, his hands making a thatchy mess of his hair. Abruptly he sat back. "I'll bet we'd be rescued by now if Jo and Pilgrim were still around. Nevil must have acted against more than just you, Ravna. *We* may end up having to rescue everyone else."

"I can do it, Jefri," said Ravna. "Just get me to *Oobii*."

He gave her a strange look. "You can take control so easily? And yet you let Nevil just push you aside?"

Ravna felt her face warm. "You think I was a fool for that?"

Jef looked away. She couldn't tell if he was angry, or contemptuous—but when he continued, his voice was mild: "Counting Nevil, we have three enemies looking for us. We have evidence that none of them is above betraying the others, but we don't know exactly what each wants. Maybe Tycoon really wants us for some kind of zoo. Vendacious' goon was mainly interested in quietly killing us—you, anyway—while pretending to take us to Tycoon. I think Nevil just wants you out of the way. With you gone, he'll have *Oobii* all to himself." He looked back at her. "In any case, by now all three factions must know that we've slipped loose. If we try to signal for help, one of them will get us. We have no place to hide out. The best we can do is what you're saying: get over these hills, hike home through the Wild Principates, and . . . and then get you to *Oobii*."

Amdi made a whining noise, not objecting, just very unhappy. "And I'll be the one who has to do all the talking, to strangers!"

Jefri: "You know Screwfloss may recover some of his Interpack speech, Amdi."

"Maybe," said Amdi, hope creeping into his voice. "He was always—"

"Where is Screwfloss, anyway?" Ravna said. Somewhere during the conversation, the remnant had wandered off.

Jefri gave a disappointed sigh, belying his optimistic comment of the moment before. "He got bored, I suppose. I'm not sure how much he understands about strategy. Hopefully, he's settling in for sentry duty."

That reminded Ravna of what she had noticed earlier in the day. She described the remnant's smudged pelt coloring. "So what is he *hiding*? How many layers of secrets are there?"

Amdi gave a tentative laugh. "Oh, that Screwfloss. Being murdered has

hurt his self-image. His grooming has gotten so careless . . ." His voice dribbled off. Some of his heads tilted as he exchanged a look with Jefri. They were
deciding whether to clue her in.

Finally Jefri said, "It's your story to tell, Amdi."

The pack gestured them nearer, until she was sitting shoulder to shoulder
with Jefri, and two of Amdi were leaning onto their laps. This had worked more
comfortably when Amdi had been little. "It's two secrets really. Please don't
blame me, Ravna, but . . . I've been 'prenticing with Flenser since, well, for a
long time."

The one by her lap twisted its neck to look up at her. Its eyes were big and
dark. "It wasn't a Nevilish thing. We weren't betraying anyone, though you and
especially Woodcarver might not see it that way."

"Yeah, don't ride Amdi about this, Ravna. We all have our issues."

Ravna nodded, suppressing a smile. "Amdi, I know a little about what
Flenser was up to. He promised you some kind of medical help, right?"

Amdi emitted a squeak and all his heads came up. "How did you know
that?"

"Later," said Ravna. "It's about the only secret I knew, and I didn't believe it
at the time."

"Okay, but you're right." Amdi's heads dipped. "I know my problem is cow-
ardice. You humans are brave; you lived with death for so long. Like you, I was
born all together and I am so . . . *afraid* of dying."

Ravna petted the one that leaned onto her lap. "I don't think it's cowardly."
She wondered just what Flenser had promised Amdi. "But you were going to
tell me about Screwfloss," she said.

"Oh, yes. About his disguise!" Some of the perkiness came back to Amdi's
delivery. "Helping with Screwfloss was a more successful project. I'm proud of
what I did, even if Woodcarver might call it treason. I knew Flenser-Tyrathect
is mainly good."

Jefri gave the one on his lap a light tap. "Are you deliberately tantalizing
Ravna? Get to the point!"

"No, no! I'm circling in on the truth." He huddled in even closer, took a
sweeping look at the darkness. The rain had started up again, but it was gentle
in the windless night. "It's not a figure of speech to say that Flenser-Tyrathect
is mainly good. Three of him is from the schoolteacher he murdered. She's running the show, even though the pack doesn't consciously interpret events that
way."

"I know," said Ravna. "Flenser even jokes about it, but in a sly way that
implies it's all a lie."

"Well, it's not a lie." This was asserted with un-Amdian truculence.
"The one with the white-tipped ears is the critical connector, but all three
contribute."

"I knew that, too," said Ravna.

Mischief crept into Amdi's voice: "I'll bet you didn't know that all three have
had puppies within the pack."

"What?" Even her broken surveillance system should have noticed that. Unless, "Was this when Flenser went missing up north?"

"Yup."

That had been five years ago. Woodcarver had pitched a fit, coming close to making war on what was left of the Flenserist movement. "So Flenser-Tyrathect was trying to recruit from within himself for when the Tyrathect members die?"

"Yes, but that part of it didn't work out. Flenser had all sorts of broodkennerish explanations, but it came down to the fact that what was left of the Old Flenser was capable of rejecting the puppies . . . *So*, he gave one to Wretchly and I helped him place the other two."

Ravna looked out into the rainy dark. If this story was going somewhere, she could guess what became of the other two puppies. "Then who is the rest of Screwfloss, Amdi?"

"Jefri and me, we smuggled the two puppies into the veterans' Fragmentarium— where the remains of Steel were being held prisoner."

"Ah. I suppose that was right before Steel's 'suicide.'"

"Yes," said Amdi. "Somehow, Flenser persuaded Carenfret to fool everyone, Woodcarver included."

"Yeah," said Jefri, "I've always wondered what Flenser had on Carenfret."

"I don't care," said Amdi. "Mr. Steel was a monster, but when I was very little, he was—I thought he was—my first friend. Anyway, the whole thing worked out the way Flenser and Carenfret planned. What was left of Mr. Steel was crazy, but part of the insanity was because Steel had always wanted to prove himself to the Old Flenser, to become something truly worthy. After he stopped trying to kill the two Tyrathect puppies, they fit with him perfectly. Some of the result still *looked* like the original Steel, so he needed the pelt painting for disguise."

Screwfloss' sneakiness and killing rage had saved them all, but it was his patient caring that had brought her through the days she lay mindless. Could he really be from the pack that got Murder Meadows its name? It wasn't a form of redemption available to humans, at least not Down Here.

No one said anything for a moment. There was just the rain and the tiny fire dying down to embers. Finally, Ravna said, "So which of him got murdered last night? Is Steel half, or three-quarters, of what's left?"

"Ah, um." Amdi's voice was a little too cheery. "Don't worry. You know personality doesn't go by percentages. Three quarters of the remnant is from Steel, but the four is still a reformed soul."

——————

The object of their discussion did not show up for several hours, though Amdi said he could hear him patrolling around the camp. "He figures none of us make good sentries," said Amdi. "I bet he's going to sleep a perimeter."

They'd made the kherhogs as comfortable as possible in the lee of the steep hillside where it was about as dry as anywhere. As for their own sleeping arrangements: there were some waterproof cloaks in one of the cabinets as well as the clothes that Jefri and Ravna had worn the day before.

They changed and Amdi and Jefri laid out the waterproofs. The two huddled together as they had on the cold nights of the trip south.

"You can lie with us, Ravna," said Amdi, making space.

Jefri hesitated, then said, "It makes sense. We need the warmth."

The issue hadn't arisen the night before, when their sleep consisted of brief catnaps on top of the wagons.

"Right." She lay down behind Jefri and let Amdi cluster all around. She hadn't cuddled these two since they were small. Now . . . when she slipped her arms around Jefri, it was very different.

CHAPTER 26

The highlands were easier going than the climb up, even where rain had left centimeters of loose muck. The kherhogs could graze on tender meadow grass—though water lay just below the green, disguising deep holes. It wasn't raining anymore, but the sky was densely overcast—ideal weather for making unobserved progress. Remnant Screwfloss (Remnant Steel?) behaved as he had the day before, scouting ahead of the three wagons, pointing out usable paths. His limp slowed him down, but it didn't seriously affect his agility.

The maps were stowed, but Amdi had memorized them: "These mountains dribble off to the west more gently than to the east. There's a steep descent up ahead."

Ravna remembered that; "steep descent" was too kind a description. The map's contour lines had merged into a single curve, a sheer cliff. Amdi didn't deny that, but at the moment he was worrying about something else: "In a few more hours—two days at most—we'll run into a village, or an inn, or just farmer packs. What are we going to *say* to them?"

"It depends on the situation, Amdi," said Ravna. Poor guy. He was trying to plan for an *ad lib* performance. Of course, while he was doing that, he didn't have to think about the coming descent, or the fact that they were out of food (for all values of edible that Ravna wished to consider), and were being hunted by as many as three different gangs. And now, a wind was sweeping across the meadows. Maybe it wasn't arctic cold, but it jammed icily against her sodden jacket. And they were all tired and filthy and cold and. . . . Think about something else:

Screwfloss had moved to the rear and was snooping around huge boulders that were scattered in the meadow. His alertness was a comfort, though with every passing day, it seemed more likely that Chitiratifor's gang was safely lost behind them. Amdi was not comforted. His heads snapped around to follow the foursome. "*Wah!* We could run into local packs even before we get to the dropoff!"

Ravna noticed that Jefri had slowed the lead wagon, and was watching Screwfloss' investigation, too. In fact, these meadows didn't look much different from old-style farms of the Domain. Before genetically modified fodder crops, the packs' idea of farming was much like the human notion of a game preserve. Traditional Tinish farmers simply made the land more hospitable for prey, keeping their animals fed and protecting them against *other* predators. Sometimes farm "fences" could be mistaken for natural tree lines and rockfalls— though she had seen nothing really likely hereabouts.

Caterwauling erupted from behind the boulders. *Something* member-sized came racing out, heading away from the meadow. Three of Screwfloss outflanked it. The creature made a turn so tight it was a flip and headed into the meadow— but Screwfloss' limper was waiting for it there. The thing had no choice. It made another hairpin turn and was sprinting along the path, straight at the wagons. Three of Screwfloss were closing fast.

It was far too big to be a weasel—and if you saw one of those, you saw a hundred, and then you were probably the weasels' lunch. Besides, this thing had two extra limbs at its midsection! As it raced past her wagon, she realized that its "extra legs" were the torn and muddy remnants of a travel cloak.

Then lots of things happened at once. She almost lost her reins as her kherhog spooked away from the runner. Up ahead, Jefri and one of Amdi had jumped down from the front wagon.

"Gotta go!" said the one of Amdi beside her. He bailed out, just as Screwfloss stampeded through, followed by the rest of Amdi.

Jefri moved back and forth to block the creature's escape.

Ravna rose from her bench. "Be careful—" was all she got out before the runner skittered around Jef. But the faster of Screwfloss had caught up. They circled, forcing the singleton back. And now all of Amdi was ranged in front of Ravna's wagon. Corralling the thing was probably an accident, but it looked like a masterpiece of teamwork. The fugitive had stopped running. It was crouched low, still shrieking monstrously loud.

Nobody moved for a second. Three seconds. The hissing stopped. The creature looked back and forth at its antagonists, then focused on the least numerous: Jefri. A pack could be deadly. What about a singleton? Jefri looked very calm. He kept his eyes on the runaway, but his words were directed elsewhere.

"Ravna, sit back down. Don't let your kherhog overrun us." His own wagon had run forward almost fifty meters, then off a little ways into the meadow. "Amdi, you're doing fine. Just stand up a little straighter."

She suddenly noticed that Amdi was trembling. His members were large and there were eight of them, but he'd spent most of his life thinking like a human child, with none of the internal role models of normal Tines. But Amdi did his best, all eight rising to alert poses. And he was talking, both to the singleton and to Screwfloss behind Jefri. That pack had been edging around the human, as if planning a sudden rush on the singleton. Now it backed up a little and settled for blocking the singleton's exit.

"You're carrying some snacks, right, Amdi?" Jefri asked.

"Yech, if you can call them that." He reached into one of his panniers and pulled out a big sausage, green with mold. "Not even all of me can still eat these things." He held it gingerly in the soft tips of a muzzle.

"Why don't you toss it to our new friend here."

"Ah! Okay." Amdi said something to the singleton, then lobbed the sausage toward the creature. It landed just beyond the animal's reach.

The singleton didn't move toward it immediately. Its head swept across Amdi, then quickly turned to check out Jefri and Screwfloss, and then sharply looked back at Amdi. It was strange to see a member working so hard just to see what was around it.

After a second more of warning watchfulness, the singleton leaped upon the sausage, flipping it into the air and biting. Big surprise: this food was rock hard. It dropped the sausage to the ground, held it in place while gnawing vigorously. As it ground away, it shuffled around, trying to keep an eye on all the threats.

Suddenly the singleton was gobbling Tinish. The sounds boomed loud from its shoulders. Ravna recognised the chord for "afraid." Or maybe there was a negation there: "*not* afraid." That repeated, became a stream of sounds that was much more complicated.

"It's a talker, isn't it," said Jefri.

Everyone relaxed a little. Ravna let her kherhog turn from the path, just far enough to munch on the attractive grass. "Who is it from, I wonder," said Ravna. "One of the wagoneers?" Surely this wasn't part of Chitiratifor. The singleton looked starved, its ribs marking high ridges in its ragged pelt. Chitiratifor's had all been too fat to be so transformed in just three days.

Jefri went down on one knee for a closer look. The singleton raised its head, and its babbling turned into one of those ear-piercing hisses. When Jefri made no further move, it gave a look all around. Then it set the sausage back on the ground and resumed struggling with it.

After a moment, Jefri said, "I don't think it's from either of the wagoneers. What's left of that cloak doesn't look like what they were wearing."

"I recognize her markings," said Amdi. "She's one of Remasritlfeer." He threw a second sausage in the direction of the singleton. "But Chitiratifor claimed he killed him all."

Jefri grinned. "Well, Chitiratifor was a bragging liar . . . and this is one tough animal."

———

They called the singleton "Ritl" even though Amdi wasn't certain that had been its given name.

Ritl ate both sausages and then threw up, all the while making threatening noises. Then it drank of the meadow water and more or less collapsed in the middle of the road. She was silent except for occasional hisses, mainly directed at Remnant Screwfloss.

Amdi circled around and persuaded Screwfloss to back off. Then he and Jefri sat down and chatted gently at the critter.

"I'll bet that was the last of her strength," said Jefri.

Ravna had climbed down from her wagon and walked forward until Ritl started hissing at her. "You figure she was a speech center?"

"We won't know for sure till she's rested." Jef shrugged. "Sometimes language ability isn't concentrated in one member."

"I'm like that with math," said Amdi. "All of me is mathematical."

"Yeah, but you're one of kind, pal, a genius in every part. Lord Steel . . ." Jefri hesitated, possibly because much of Lord Steel was right behind them, grumpily climbing aboard the middle wagon. And Jefri had his own terrible history with the original. ". . . Lord Steel made you of puppies from the greatest geniuses he could kill, gull, or kidnap from."

Jefri reached out tentatively in the direction of Ritl. The singleton responded with another hiss, but it seemed to be running out of energy. "I don't think Remasritlfeer was ever a great linguist."

"If Ritl were friendly, could she tell us much about Tycoon?"

"A singleton? Probably not."

Amdi gave a sad little laugh. "She probably remembers useful things, but they would come out as nonsense riddling."

Ravna thought a second. "You know, there is the obvious thing. It would solve two of our problems at once." She glanced over her shoulder. All of Screwfloss was sitting atop the middle wagon, looking down at them.

"Can you understand Samnorsk?" she said to it.

Screwfloss' gaze continued intent and calculating, but the pack didn't respond.

"I don't think Screwfloss understands human language," said Amdi. "I'm not even sure how clear he is on Tinish."

"Okay. I was just wondering . . . maybe if what's left of Screwfloss could get together with Ritl . . ."

Jefri grinned. "That would be a win, but I'll bet it doesn't happen. Ritl is so emphatically hostile."

"Maybe she's just frightened," said Amdi. The singleton was babbling again. The noise was less painful than her hissing, but it didn't sound friendly.

"Yes, but Screwfloss doesn't look interested either. Accepting Ritl would probably mean a flip in pack gender, and that's usually an issue." Jefri gave an impatient shrug. "If Ritl doesn't run away then this will be something to think about. Meantime," he glanced at the sky, "we really want to be on our way."

"She'll just run if I back off," said Amdi.

"Naeh. I'll bet she's been chasing us; you know how singletons are."

"Well, okay." Amdi said something comforting to Ritl, and retreated from the confrontation. At the same time, he was talking to Screwfloss, maybe asking him to look less threatening. Jefri walked back toward the front wagon.

The critter watched all this from its hunkered-down position. It was still blabbering.

Jefri translated: "Mainly it's threatening what will happen to us if we misbehave."

Abruptly, Ritl came to its feet and sprinted off—but stopped when it figured it was out of sight in the meadow grasses.

Jefri and Amdi walked forward to where the first kherhog was grazing. In a few minutes, they had persuaded the animal to drag its wagon back onto the path. Amdi came back to drive the rear wagon and they were on their way once more.

As usual, one of Amdi sat with Ravna on the middle wagon. As the afternoon passed the humidity fell, and Amdi seemed to be thinking faster. That was not necessarily a good thing. "This is the last day when things will be easy," he said. "Can't you hear the waterfall? We're almost to the big dropoff." He had escalated the "steep descent" to something more realistic. "We're gonna meet strangers real soon."

She guessed he was saying similar things to Jefri up ahead. Amdi was like a worrywart on ultradrive. She took one hand from the reins to pat his shoulder. "We can't do anything about that till we get there. Meantime, you should be paying attention to that wagon you're driving, and keeping watch on Screwfloss and Ritl."

"Oh, I am, I am." He glanced up at her, wriggling under her hand. "If you could see me all at once, you'd know I'm looking every which way. Screwfloss must have understood what I told him. He's staying behind us. And from Jefri's wagon, I can see that Ritl is just a little ahead of the wagons. She hasn't run off, though she's trying to stay out of sight."

As a matter of fact, Ravna had no trouble tracking the singleton. It never strayed more than thirty meters beyond Jefri's wagon, sneaking from hiding place to hiding place. At the same time, the critter was trying to keep track of the wagons and Screwfloss. Sometimes Ritl would stop in plain view, twisting her neck back and forth—then see them watching her, and abruptly run for cover.

Amdi gave a human-sounding sigh. "I feel so sorry for Ritl. You're right. If only she and Remnant Screwfloss could accept each other, they would be so much better off. Do you read romance novels, Ravna?"

"Huh? Tinish romance novels? Where—?"

"Pilgrim lets me into Woodcarver's library."

She had no idea Amdi researched such topics. "Have you read any of the romance stories in *Oobii*?" she asked. When Ravna worked for Vrinimi Org, she'd noticed customer interest in romance literature. It was probably the most idiosyncratic of all written art forms. No surprise there; when it was intelligible, romance lit gave more insight into an alien culture and psyche than anything this side of Transcendence.

"Our romances are nothing like as weird as in *Oobii*, but we Tines have more *kinds* of romance than other races! See, there's pack-level romance, like Pilgrim and Woodcarver. Then there are romances about injured packs looking to become whole, either from within or without. And one type of story is about packs romancing singletons and vice versa."

"From what Jefri says, that's a long shot in our case."

Amdi said, "Yup. Maybe that's why people like to read stories where it works out well." Amdi rode along for a minute or two without saying anything more. He lowered his long neck and rested his head on his forepaws. When she glanced down, she noticed that his eyes were closed. For a wonder, the worry-wart was taking a break! Or maybe he was worrying about his larger problems, what had driven him to Flenser in the first place. After a time, he raised his head and continued: "Romance is such a weird thing. It's how we Tines sneak past death. I think it's like that with other races, only more metaphorical. I read your human romances especially. This kidnapping is just like in some of your stories, bringing people together, showing them how much they need each other. Don't you see how good you and Jefri would be for each other?"

"*Amdi!*"

"What? What? I just want you to be happy."

―――――――

Events intervened before Amdi could make further unsettling comments.

They were descending into scrub forest, and the mud was now a serious problem. Streams cut across the path, and water was coursing through the meadow on their right. As best as they could tell from the maps, they were within a few hundred meters of the "steep descent." The sound of falling water was loud even to Ravna's ears. Jefri and Amdi hiked forward to take a look, while Ravna slayed with the wagons. Ritl was nowhere to be seen, but Screwfloss was patrolling some kind of perimeter.

Ravna got down and walked around the wagons, checking that the kherhogs were secured. She was surely the wimp of this expedition. She could barely keep standing, but right now she was too sore to sit down. She leaned against the middle wagon and struggled to stay alert. Since her delirium, she'd been irrationally afraid of the sleepiness that crept over her in the middle of the day. *What if my mind comes undone once more?*

Perhaps twenty minutes passed. Jefri and Amdi emerged from the scrub. Amdi was huffing and puffing to keep up.

"The maps lied," said Jefri. He was speaking in a lowered voice, almost a whisper.

A few seconds later, Amdi arrived. "No," he said, also speaking softly, "the maps were made from orbiter data. They can't show what's out of sight."

Jefri shrugged. Like most of the Children, he tended to attribute motivation to artifacts. "The point is," he continued in the same soft tones, "there are buildings on the valley floor. It looks like a caravanserai."

"Yes," said Amdi, "and there's a winch station up here, at the edge of the dropoff."

She noticed Screwfloss walking around the wagons, rousting the kherhogs as if to continue the drive. He was making no effort to be quiet about it. "Screwfloss seems to know what he wants to do."

Jefri glanced over his shoulder. "I get his point. He figures we've already been spotted. We might as well go forward. Now, about our cover story . . ."

"Our cover story?" Ravna's words came out in a kind of incredulous squeak.

Two aliens and a jumble of Tines come strolling in, with the most amusing story. "Sorry. Right. We two-legs should keep out of sight to begin with, let Amdi do the talking. . . ." Both she and Jefri were looking at the eightsome.

Poor Amdi was beside himself, each member trying to stay out of sight behind the others. "I can't! You can't do this to me!"

"You're the only one who can even speak the language, Amdi."

"*Wah!*" wailed Amdi. "This isn't *fair!*" He hesitated briefly, then launched into a string of mostly illogical objections. "Those could be the bad guys up ahead, Vendacious and Tycoon waiting to pick us off."

Jefri shook his head. "I think Screwfloss would suspect if that were the case—and look at him." The remnant had mounted the front wagon and was looking back at them expectantly.

"We could go back. We could hunt and trap! I know Screwfloss could. You could. I caught a fish the other day!"

Ravna went to her knees among Amdi. It was not entirely a controlled gesture. Amdi seemed to realize this; she felt him close in, steadying her. She slipped her arms around his nearest necks, and after a moment the dizziness passed. She could feel the cold soaking her knees, and Amdi's fur against her face. What to say? "You're the smartest pack in the world, Amdi."

"That's . . . probably true. Mr. Steel made me that way. He got a very, *very* smart coward."

"Okay, that's probably what Old Steel expected. I don't think what's left of him believes it." She looked up, gave a nod in Screwfloss' direction.

"Maybe, but—"

"Steel made something smarter than himself. I can tell you—personal experience of a Mid-Beyonder—that means the rest of what he expected is vapor. You have a power tool, and no one knows what you can do with it." Her point applied to peer intellects as well, but Ravna was too tired for full disclosure.

Amdi didn't say anything for a moment, but she felt a buzzing through his fur.

"We'll come with you," said Jefri, "openly. There's no pointing in hiding us two-legs if we've already been seen."

"We could advise you," said Ravna.

That might be an empty offer, considering how much fast talking was needed. And yet, Amdi eased back from Ravna and angled his heads together, thinking intensely. "Advise, yes. With the right cover story . . . hmm. I'll bet the local packs only have rumors about humans, stories of a supernatural race so intelligent that even their singletons are as smart as a Tinish pack. Maybe I could claim to represent the two-legged godlings."

Ritl had crept into sight. It sat down near the edge of Amdi's mindsounds. Amdi gobbled at it, and it responded with a long ramble.

Amdi laughed. "Ritl likes the idea—even if she doesn't understand a word we're saying." And now he was full of supporting ideas: "With you as gods, then *I'm* just the middleman, the interpreter! We'll have plenty of time to get our lies right, even if there are surprises. And then . . ."

They decided to take just the first wagon and three kherhogs. If this meeting worked out, they could hire someone at the winch station to bring down the other two wagons and the lame kherhog. Meantime, they wanted to put on a good show.

They moved the stash of lamps—their most exotic tradables—to the front wagon. The maps got moved, too, though they were emphatically not for trade. There were no clean human clothes, though Jef's *Oobii* weaves were presentable.

And they finally had a use for Chitiratifor's flashy outfits. They carefully removed one set from the oilskins. The cloth was so clean it fairly glowed, and the fine stitching was almost machine precise. There was a cape and matching jacket—even leggings. Chitiratifor had been big-bodied, but nowadays Amdi was big, too. There were enough outfits for six of him. Amdi immediately slipped into the clothes, adjusting the various belts and clasps.

Amdi strode around the wagons, admiring himself and making final tweaks to the outfit. He was on a roll, his anxiety either forgotten or forcibly suppressed. Ravna studied the beaded designs on the jackets. They probably represented something, though it might not be evident if you couldn't get your eyeballs more than ten centimeters apart. "Any chance this outfit is a uniform of some kind, Amdi? Maybe now you're a colonel in the Vendacious Bastards Army."

"Oh, no," said Amdi. "This is just a super-nice rich-pack thing." He looked away from himself. "Now we have to decide where to put you two-legged gods." He wanted Jefri and Ravna to keep apart so the locals would know they were sufficient even as singletons. "Later, when you are together—then they can tremble in fear of you!"

Jefri was nodding, but he looked seriously at Ravna. "Are you up to walking?"

"Yes." She did not want to get back on a driver's bench.

"Okay, then. I'll walk forward with Amdi. Ravna, you stay near the rear of the wagon."

"Something I can duck behind, eh?" She noticed that he didn't smile fast enough at her joke. "Why should you take the greater risk?"

"Don't go Age of Princesses on me, Ravna. It's . . . it's one of your most irritating habits."

Okay. She *was* the weak one here. In fact, she might need the wagon to steady herself.

When they finally rolled forward, the overcast had lowered to a foggy gloom and it was deep twilight.

They'd set the best-charged lamps to cast long, narrow beams past the three kherhogs pulling the wagon. The exhausted animals were doing their part for the show, making it look as though the wagon held awesomely massive cargo.

The two of Amdi that had no costumes were driving the team. Screwfloss walked at the front, behaving like a bodyguard. He was followed by most of Amdi, his beaded cloaks sparkling in the spotlights. After Amdi's six came Jefri, not so gaudy, though the lamps did strange interference-fringy things with his clothing. Ravna, no doubt invisible in the glare, walked near the back of the wagon. Everybody but her was a fine target.

Amdi was bumptiously loud now, piping the equivalent of cheerful humming. "Just wanna make sure they don't start shooting out of surprise."

"Not much chance of surprise," said Jefri, looking up into the trees around them. The wide, low-set limbs should be easy to climb, even for Tines. "I'll bet they're tracking us with nocked arrows."

As if to prove the point, something member-sized dropped from a low branch and ran forward around the rightmost of Amdi, and then out in front of Screwfloss. That pack started to give chase, then brought itself back.

The newcomer was Ritl. Maybe it *was* her employer who was lying in ambush.

But the singleton did not keep running. About ten meters beyond Screwfloss, it settled into a sedate promenade and started to blabber on its own. It sounded like doors crashing shut.

"*Powers!* What is that animal doing?" said Jefri.

"I think she's trying to announce us." Amdi dithered a moment, stopping the wagon. "She's playing something like royal pomp, but with her own nonsense lyrics." On the ground, Amdi spread out a little, and Ravna guessed he was focusing audio on Ritl. The singleton stumbled, and briefly looked back at Amdiranifani. Then the creature executed an indignant flounce and pranced on, its cacophony louder than ever.

The lights on their wagon showed trees thick on both sides of the path, the remaining twilight a dim patch of gray overhead. The sound of the waterfall was clear and loud ahead. They were truly committed. Forcibly retrieving Ritl and starting over was not an option.

Amdi must have concluded the same. The six resumed their walk, while the two on the wagon cautiously eased the kherhogs into the descent. Ravna caught her first glimpse of what Amdi called the "winch station." It looked like a small ferry mooring—except that it hung from the side of a cliff. Next to it was what seemed to be a large waterwheel, an arc of shadow biting into the river. Their own path led down to a building close by the waterwheel.

"See the arrow slits?" said Jefri, but he wasn't talking about the view below. He pointed to the side of the road just ahead, to pitch-dark slots cut in a timber barricade. "We didn't see that this afternoon."

The wagon's lights would be blinding to anyone that close. "Amdi," said Ravna, "dim the lights." Sometimes, intimidating the other side just got you killed.

"Okay." One of him on the wagon glanced back at her. Amdi's sound effects ceased, leaving just Ritl's flourishes banging away up ahead. The lights stayed bright.

"Well?" said Ravna.

"Urk. I'm thinking what to do!" Then he was speaking Tinish, fast and unintelligible.

Maybe there was a sound behind her; maybe it was Amdi's sudden weirdness. Ravna looked behind her. She was not alone. The closest pack held a crossbow with an enormous quarrel—the point of which was less than ten centimeters from her nose.

CHAPTER 27

Humans and kherhogs were forced down the hill, into a large shed that was smelly and filled with hay. A few tendays ago, Ravna Bergsndot would have thought this was serious mistreatment. But indoors, with the kherhogs, it was warm enough. And the hay had no fermenter stench.

"Maybe we still have a chance with the godling scam," said Jefri. He was tied to a pillar at the far side of the barn from Ravna.

"Yes, and we rate heavy weapons." Two packs, each with a huge crossbow.

"Yeah, what foolish—"

The pack nearest to him hissed loudly and crashed its weapon against the side of Jefri's head. He went down without a sound.

"Jefri!" Ravna pulled against her tether. The pack guarding her pushed its weapon into her midsection, knocking her back. She lay quiet for a moment, then rolled slightly forward and looked across the floor. A small mantle lamp hung from a rafter above Jefri. It must have been very dim to Tinish eyes, but for her it was more than adequate. She saw Jefri's hand move in an "I'm okay" gesture. She signalled "okay" back. The guards didn't react. Jefri's hand moved slowly into other gestures.

It was the sign language the Children had invented in their first few years on Tines World. By nature, Tines had an enormous advantage when it came to covert communication. The Children used their signing as a counter strategy. Some of their Tinish friends had learned to understand the signing, but in semidarkness, the packs couldn't even see it. Ravna remembered the kids chortling over their secret "message channel." It had been endearing and silly . . . and Ravna had never bothered to learn much of it.

After a moment, Jefri seemed to realize she couldn't understand. He gave her another "okay" sign and settled back. She watched him for a long while. There were different degrees of "okay."

———————

Remnant Screwfloss showed up an hour later, herded in by another guard. Screwfloss didn't rate a permanent guard, but he was a prisoner. He paced around at the limits of his tethers, more talkative than she had seen him since his partial death. He seemed to be arguing with the guards. They didn't beat him up, though after a bit of chitchat, one guard flicked a long whip at him. The remnant retreated, looking more surly than intimidated. He settled down in apparent silence, peering around at Jefri and Ravna. Jef had rolled onto his side to look back, but didn't try to communicate.

Ravna drifted uncomfortably in and out of sleep, vaguely aware of the kherhogs shuffling around their big manger. She had dreams, and thought she heard Tinish music. What had become of poor Amdi?

The new day was leaking gray light under the eaves when someone pounded on the barn door. Two members from one guard slid the door open. Ravna squinted into the brightness, which in fact was no more than drizzly morning twilight. Something—Ritl—came bounding in, loud and argumentative. Behind the singleton came Amdi, and a sociable distance behind him there was another pack. Amdi looked in all directions. "Jefri? Ravna?"

"Over here." Jefri's voice was a groan.

"And here," said Ravna.

"You're hurt!" Amdi surrounded Jefri, patting him, touching his face.

"Hei, not there! It's just a bruise, Amdi."

"Okay. But they were supposed to treat you well." Two of him looked back at the stranger, hissing at him in Tinish. Ravna had never seen Amdi complain to another so firmly.

Maybe . . . "So what about the god scam?" she asked.

"I—I blew it. The locals are nervous about humans, but many of them don't believe you can think at all. Even so, I might have had a chance except that this stupid, *blabbering* singleton kept—"

Ritl was circling Amdi, crowding into his personal space and chording all the while. Amdiranifani turned all his heads on Ritl and blasted her with a focused hiss of annoyance. The singleton gave a whistle of pain and retreated to a far corner of the barn.

"Sorry, sorry. I don't mean to hurt anyone, not even that silly idiot, but she came close to getting us all killed—" He said something Tinish to the guards and the third pack, and they all honked raucous laughter. Evidently, he was carrying on two very different conversations.

Jefri came to his knees. His eyes were on the nearest guard and its crossbow-cum-club. "So what is the deal, Amdi? It looks like you have something going with these guys."

"I do, I do. At least it's better than nothing. Look, I'll explain on the way down okay? The Winchmaster wants us on our way while the storm runoff is still manageable. If we hustle, there's time for you to get some hot food first. I negotiated—"

Now Ravna could smell it. One of the guard packs was rolling in two steaming wheelbarrows of . . . slop? No, not quite. The wheelbarrows themselves looked like they had hauled their share of slop, but just now they contained piles of boiled yams. There were also tankards of broth, the sort of thing that the Tines themselves liked to use to garnish cooked meat. It was mouthwatering if you were hungry enough, and even under normal conditions it would have been tolerable, a rare example of Tinish cuisine that worked for humans.

There were no utensils, not even Tinish jaw-knives. The filthy barrows were simply shoved close to their faces. It was more the treatment of farm animals than gods. They were given a few moments to feed and then the guards marched them outside, still keeping the two humans well apart.

Their wagon was up ahead, parked next to the odd-looking wooden structure that was the winch station.

"Potty stop once we reach the valley floor," said Amdi. "I'll see you all in a minute." He started off ahead of them.

"What did you have to trade them, Amdi?" shouted Jefri. "Do we still have any lamps?"

"And the maps?"

"Yup. And the wagon and the two best kherhogs."

"Wow," said Jefri.

"So what *did* we give up?" said Ravna. The other wagons and kherhogs?

Amdi had crossed the yard to talk to a couple of packs standing near the winch station. Behind Ravna, Screwfloss was driving two of the kherhogs out of the barn. The remnant seemed to have a better idea of what was going on than did Ravna or Jefri. As the beasts plodded past, Screwfloss stayed mainly on the downhill side of the path, keeping the beasts away from the tasty grasses that edged the stream-grown-to-flooded-river. Ritl brought up the rear, nipping at the kherhogs and emitting skirling chords that might have been commands directed at Screwfloss.

The morning was both chilly and humid, with little droplets of water forming on every exposed edge. They were in a rain cloud just before it burst. Ravna squished through the mud, struggling to keep her balance.

The river showed little crescents of white water as it raced past the winch station, almost swamping the big waterwheel. Beyond that, the flow met an unnaturally near horizon. The sound of falling water was a roar. The winch station looked quite different today. For one thing, last night, the place where their wagon was parked had been off the edge of the cliff. Now that space was occupied by a gated platform, almost like a gazebo. The top of the structure was hidden by a squat wooden tower.

Jefri reached the platform first. His guard pushed him to the far end and tied him to the railing there. Screwfloss drove the two kherhogs aboard and tied them down. Then it was Ravna's turn.

The kherhogs shifted uneasily about on the platform—which moved perceptibly in response. A local pack came aboard; it checked Screwfloss' knotwork and then shouted to the packs who remained on solid ground. It retreated, heads together, as Amdi came aboard.

Most of Amdi strutted around the kherhogs to be with Jefri. The rest stood at the railing near Ravna. His splendid outfits were mostly in good repair, and his posture was pompously self-important. But at the same time he was hooting cheerfully with the Winchmaster, his human little-boy voice was tentative and fearful. "I'm sorry, I'm sorry. Every story I've told these guys has got us into worse trouble."

From other side of the kherhogs, she heard Jefri laugh. "It sounds like you're their great chum, Amdi."

"Oh, I guess I am, but I just know they'll see through me. I can't keep this act going much longer."

"So what *is* the act, Amdi? If we aren't gods then what—"

Whoa! At that instant, the platform was cut loose from its moorings. It swung through at least five degrees. Timbers creaked loudly as the kherhogs staggered against their ties, lowing their startlement.

Even their crew pack looked a little nervous at that. Somebody shouted an apology from the tower above them.

Amdi shouted something back. Ravna recognized the chord as good-natured forgiveness. Then in human talk he said, "The Winchmaster says he's sorry. The waterwheel is overpowered by the river surge. The clutch system is very tricky . . . I got a tour. The gears are all wood. I could make it a lot safer with a few days' work, but—"

The platform lurched downwards in jolts of a centimeter or two. Ravna could imagine what Amdi was talking about. In her early days on Tines World, she'd seen similar devices in Scrupilo's factories. The use of wooden gears didn't bother her as much as the manual control. Even after ten years, she still got the shakes when she realized there were no software controls monitoring and protecting against the whims of gears, fools, and nature.

The jolts became smaller and swifter, and soon their descent was almost stately. The air was full of spume and waterfall noise, but they seemed to be descending a protected notch in the cliff face. Just beyond her arm's reach stood naked rock. Here and there, straggly trees and vines scrabbled for purchase.

Fifteen seconds passed, smooth as silk. "This looks like a couple of meters per second," said Jefri.

The platform emerged from the cloud layer. Suddenly she could hear the sounds of faraway birds, and to her left—Powers! They must be a thousand meters up. The cliff wall marched off toward a misty horizon. She turned away from the view. Funny, vertigo had never been a problem for her in the Beyond.

Their crew pack looked calm enough. He clambered around the railings, all without using any safety lines. On top of the wagon, Remnant Screwfloss seemed positively relaxed, enjoying the view.

"Well, I guess this must be safer than it looks," said Ravna. "This local guy doesn't seem worried. How many years has this been operating?" She turned back to look at the view.

"Um, they started last summer," said Amdi. "It's a leasehold that Tycoon bought, trying to encourage traffic among the wilderness valley chains."

Since last summer? Tycoon? What a variety of scary news to cram into just a few syllables. Ravna stared at the rock wall . . . and realized that she was looking at the splintered pieces of a platform not too different from what was transporting them today. *Okay.*

Amdi saw the same thing and his voice took on a forced chipperness. "But really, today should be an easy ride. The Winchmaster told me this carriage is a madhouse when it's doing pure third-class passengers and no freight. Before they had all the risks figured out, they squeezed ten packs into this space. There was a choir and a panic and the platform crashed into the rock . . . um, like you see us passing now."

They were all silent for a moment. Ravna noticed that Ritl was perched on the railing halfway between two clumps of Amdi. The singleton would stare into the abyss, then quickly look up to check on Amdi's position, then stare back into the abyss. Its claws were extended deep into the wood, and it seemed to be muttering to itself.

"Okay, Amdi," said Jefri. "Consider us all comforted. Now, while we have a few minutes of peace and quiet—what story are you peddling to the locals?"

Amdiranifani's human voice made a whimpering sound. "I did the best I could, Jefri."

Ravna remembered how hard it had been for Amdi to undertake even the smallest part of this. "You got us this far, Amdi. Whatever you're pretending to be—" she waved to indicate his costume and grandiose manner "—it looks marvelous."

"Yes, but what is the scam?" There was laughter hiding behind Jefri's annoyed tone.

"Okay. Things will be busy once we hit—I mean, touch—the ground, so now is probably the best time to tell you. The 'humans-as-gods' story was in trouble from the start. They ambushed us too easily for us to have super-Tinish powers. Things got worse when I claimed you two were only weak because you were apart. *That* almost got you killed."

Ravna nodded. "And it's why we're kept apart."

"Yes. I'm sorry."

Jefri said, "Never mind. We all thought it was a good idea."

"Yeah, well, the current plan is something I had to make up on the spot." He turned all his heads to glare at Ritl. "Even before the ambush, the singleton was messing us up. She screwed us into this."

"I don't think she's smart enough to scheme, Amdi."

"She's a trouble-making *animal*. Didn't you understand what she was saying last night?"

"When she was marching on ahead of us? I got some of it. It sounded like royal flourishes, something Remasritlfeer must have picked up around East Home. Coming from just one member it sounded a bit silly."

"Yes! She never makes sense and she always gets in the way—like right now she's squatting in the middle of me, making it hard to think." Amdi darted a member angrily at the singleton. It hunkered down on the railing and hissed back. "Last night her background chatter just made me look like a fool. More of a fool."

"We're still here, alive and breathing, Amdi. And we held on to all our important things. You must have done something right."

"We lost the other wagons. But yes, I got us through the night. I'm not sure I can get us through this day. We are in such deep trouble. These packs are all employed by Tycoon, at least indirectly. The inn at the bottom of this winch drop is owned by Tycoon. That pack is spreading his influence all through the Wild Principates, not conquering anybody, just making money."

Jefri was silent, so Ravna said the obvious: "But Tycoon is hunting us."

"Yup. The temporary good news is that Tycoon's schemes are so spread out that he can't keep track of them. Heh," Amdi emitted a Flenserish chuckle. "The Winchmaster knows humans are important, but he doesn't know we're fugitives. Same for the Innmaster below. For the moment, they think that helping us will get them Tycoon's good will and make them some money in the process."

The platform shuddered, its smooth descent shifting back to jerk-at-a-time mode.

Amdi said something to the crew pack, and at the same time stuck a head over the railing. "Looks like we're less than a hundred meters up. Our pilot says we'll be slowing soon." He fell back from the railing and hissed at Ritl. "I can't stand it. This *monster* is feeding me pictures!" Some of him staggered around for a moment, then settled securely on the decking. ". . . Okay, where was I?"

"Explaining how you persuaded these folks to cooperate."

"Yes. Once I realized they were Tycoonists and that they were ignorant of *us*, I thought maybe we could pretend to be almost what we are. I showed them Chitiratifor's badge of introduction." Amdi stuck a snout into one of his pockets and pulled out the edge of the jeweled badge. "I told them we were on a special mission from the North, how you were an embassy from the humans, and to be protected."

"That's good, Amdi!"

Amdi brightened at the praise. "It might have worked, too. I doubt if there are any of our stolen radios in these parts. It might be tendays before Tycoon hears about us." He slumped a little lower. "The problem was that everybody was laughing too hard to take my story seriously." He glared at Ritl. "The animal just kept blabbering around, making everything I said into a stupid joke. The Winchmaster finally congratulated me on my *act!*"

"Huh?" came Jefri's voice. "He thinks you're acting about what?"

Their platform jerked to a full stop. The crew pack—their pilot?—scrambled up a ladder to the roof. She could hear him spread out across the lightweight planking. His shouts were very loud, and seemed to be directed upwards. Faint shouting came back in response. Ravna leaned out, looked up. Their cable disappeared into drizzle and cloud deck. It occurred to her that shouting back and forth was the only feedback system available. This made flying in Scrupilo's first *Eyes Above* seem like a happy holiday.

But now they were almost even with the gables of a half-timbered structure, the ground just a few meters below. She saw packs there, peeking out from beneath heavy awnings.

Their pilot spoke an imperative chord.

Amdi translated: "Stay back from the railing!"

The platform edged downward, five centimeters to a jerk. The kherhogs were getting wild-eyed, but Screwfloss' intimidating hisses kept them knees-down on the platform. There was a prolonged crunching sound from beneath the platform. They fell another couple centimeters, and then Jefri's side tilted down a couple of centimeters more. Chorded yodeling sounded from beyond the railing, something Ravna recognized as "Well done, well done!" Their pilot came hustling down the ladder, looking all casual and professional. Ravna noticed, however, that he flinched as much as anyone at the extended crashing noise on the roof he'd just left. Falling cable slack? In any case, the crashing stopped; the Winch-master, somewhere up beyond the clouds, must realize that the job was done.

As the pilot lifted the railing gate, Screwfloss was all over the kherhogs. Out in the rain, a pack was adjusting a ramp next to the tilted edge of the plat-form. Yeah, just another routine sky-ferry touchdown. It seemed very appropri-ate that Ritl chose that moment to clamber atop the wagon and start shouting orders at everyone.

Amdi gathered himself together, adjusting his cloaks and leggings. The hu-man little boy voice gave an occasional whimper, but in a few seconds he looked as imposing as he had when first she saw him this morning. As the winch-pilot came back and undid the ties on the livestock—kherhog and human—Amdi strolled over to the gate and waved a gracious snout or two at the packs who were coming out from the inn. "I'll go ahead. If you come down right after me . . . well, I've got my speech planned, the story I finally had to settle on: See, the Innmaster thinks we're a travelling entertainment troupe. 'The Magnificent Am-diranifani, Master of Fragments and Zombies from Lands of Mystery.' And"—*wail*—"our first big show is tonight!"

CHAPTER 28

Jefri and Ravna were housed in a stable again. Otherwise, things were much improved. Amdi had persuaded these people that the humans could not form godlike packs. True, they were amazing creatures, naturally clever singletons. Jefri and Ravna recognized the word for "walking corpses" when they were pa-raded from the winch carriage. The notion predated the arrival of humans: imag-ine thought without sound. Apparently, this added enormously to the interest in Amdi's upcoming show.

The inn's stable was high-ceilinged, dark, and only moderately smelly. Like the rest of the inn, it stood well away from the deadly jumble of boulders at the base of the cliff.

"After last night, I don't even mind these," Jefri said, shaking the kherhog fetters that bound his wrists. Since Amdi and the innsfolk had left, Jef had scouted out the loft and the various wagons parked on the main floor. "And for the moment, I think we're as safe as we've been since before Chitiratifor."

"Yes." Ravna munched on the last of the yams—served on wooden platters, the kind the local Tines themselves ate from. "It helps to have a friendly guard."

"Guard" was how Amdi had identified Screwfloss to their new hosts. The term was at least an overstatement. Remnant Screwfloss was content to sit by the main door and watch the outside through various knotholes. He hadn't been at all bothered by Jefri's explorations. And yet, when the locals were around, he was surprisingly guardlike, flicking a whip threateningly at Jefri and Ravna.

Jefri walked back from the kherhog stalls and squatted down just a meter from the remnant pack. "You're more together, aren't you?"

The pack's whip didn't twitch. After a moment, his heads bobbed and he gobbled a few chords.

"Wow. That sounds as though he understood your Samnorsk!"

"Yes. He didn't say much more than 'I'm okay,' but it matched my question." Jefri reached out to pat the nearest shoulder. "That happens sometimes, you know. A member with a critical talent gets killed, and the other parts slowly learn to fill in the function. He may never be really smart, but . . ."

Ravna eyed the pack's smudged disguise. "But we know he was a mix of very clever parts."

"Um. Yes."

———

Throughout the afternoon, they heard wagons and packs outside. Through the knotholes, they could see two packs just beyond the walls. Were those to keep the curious out, or the zombies in? In any case, Jefri and Ravna had time to clean up and speculate on what kind of show a two-legs circus act could put on. Ritl came down from the loft and blabbered and blabbered, despite obvious threats from Screwfloss. Most of her complaints seemed to be about being locked up here, but when the real guards opened the door in mid-afternoon to bring in water, Ravna noticed that the singleton stayed clear of the doorway. Maybe she was saving her serious troublemaking for Amdi—or maybe she had a certain animal caution: In some Tinish cultures, loose singletons were fair game for murder, rape, or impressment into transient slave packs.

About an hour after the water delivery, Screwfloss abruptly came to his feet. Ritl gave a startled yelp and made a quick retreat toward the loft, but Screwfloss' attention was on the knot holes in the stable wall. He gestured Jefri and Ravna to back away.

Now Ravna could hear the gobbling of multiple packs approaching. Riding above that noise was a little boy's voice: "Hei Jefri. Hei Ravna. Look harmless!"

Then the stable door was slid to the side. Besides the two fellows who had been there all day, there were three other packs, one of them Amdi. They strolled in, each clumped together—the normal comportment of strangers. One of the visitors was a swaggering sixsome, with members as big as Amdi's.

Amdi waved for Screwfloss to back off and give the visitors space. He was talking to the strangers, saying something grandiloquent. At the same time, he said in Samnorsk: "The six-pack is the Innmaster. He wanted to see you before the show. He's fascinated by the whole concept of two-legs, but I think he's a little frightened of you, too. If we can convince him you're no danger, things could go a lot smoother."

Jefri said, "You could order me forward, Amdi. Then let this guy get close."

"Okay. But you gotta look meek."

There was gobbling back and forth between Amdi and the other packs. Everybody was speaking more slowly than packs usually did. Ha. Ravna suddenly realized that Amdi had his own language issues with these fellows. The result was a substantial simplification in everybody's speech. The words weren't stacked quite as deep and there was some repetition. Amdi was assuring them there was no need to restrain the humans. Abruptly, he waved at Jefri. Jef came out of the shadows to stand just centimeters from the nearest of Amdi. Then he dropped to his knees. Now his face was just about at eye level with the largest pack members. "That meek enough?"

Amdi cocked a head in the direction the Innmaster. "I don't see how we could do better." He said something encouraging to the Innmaster—and then all of him stepped back and waved encouragingly for the sixsome to approach.

Ravna realized that she was holding her breath. She rarely saw any Tines who were unfamiliar with humans, and when she did, they were in no position to do harm. Here, now, Jefri was meeting a dangerous stranger.

The Innmaster had lost his swagger. His eyes had widened and some of him fidgeted with the jaw hatchets in his panniers. The prospect of getting closer to Jefri was clearly unnerving. But after a moment, the pack seemed to remember he had witnesses. He stood a little taller and—thank the Powers—stopped fiddling with the hatchets. He boomed something confident at the other packs and sidled around Jefri. Now he was making the sort of placating sounds that packs (some packs—not Screwfloss) made when they were trying to gentle a kherhog.

Jefri sat back on his heels and made no effort to track the members who were circling him.

The nearest of the Innmaster was well inside Jefri's reach—and suddenly the critter seemed to realize as much. It stopped, licked its lips. Then it jabbed out a nose, tapping Jefri on the shoulder. Jefri just smiled back, not showing any teeth. The sixsome hesitated a moment more, then closed in all around, slapping Jefri on the back, almost as hard as one would pat a kherhog. At the same time, most of him turned to face the doorway and made loud conversation with the other packs.

Amdi provided some translation: "'See,' he's saying, 'it's every bit as docile as I knew it would be.'"

The critter was grinning from one end to the other. If these people had had cameras, he surely would have been demanding the others take video of his triumph.

"Now he wants me to prove that you're clever like a pack." Amdi gabbled something at the Innmaster. "I told him that would have to wait for our big show tonight."

The sixsome huffed impatiently. Two of him were pulling Jefri's shirt out of his pants, examining the fabric. For a moment, Ravna thought the fellow was going to argue. But then the Magnificent Amdiranifani moved a little closer and delivered some kind of bombast. If Ravna hadn't known him for ten years, she would have been intimidated. Certainly, the Innmaster was impressed. He gave Jefri a couple more patronizing thumps, at the same time surreptitiously trying to tear off some of his shirt—but then he stepped back.

Innmaster and maestro chatted amiably for a few moments. It wasn't quite casual, since the Innmaster was still mostly watching Jefri, and two heads were aimed at Ravna; she'd finally been noticed lurking in the shadows. But he was no longer insistent. In fact, he looked downright thoughtful. He asked if Amdiranifani needed anything more. Amdi's reply was something about privacy and . . . huh, toys?

In the brightness beyond the doorway, a crowd of locals had gathered, standing so close to one another that there was some actual pushing and shoving. They were so close and dense that Ravna could feel the buzzing. The Innmaster stepped out of the stable and jabbered rapidly at the crowd. Ravna heard the "big show tonight" chord several times.

As the crowd dispersed, the Innmaster's assistant returned with a wheelbarrow piled high with colored balls and cloaks. He brought two more loads of mysterious gear. Then he and Amdi cooperated in sliding the door shut.

And they were alone, their guards presumably keeping the curious away from the stable. The secret preparations of the Magnificent Amdiranifani could begin.

Amdi unlocked the fetters that bound Jefri and Ravna. He and Jefri lit a couple mantle lamps and hung them above the wheelbarrows. Ravna was already digging through the "toys." There were colored balls, four whips, cloaks, and wooden tines. All that was just in the first wheelbarrow. She looked up from the junk, at Amdi. "Jefri and I have been trying to imagine what this big show is going to be."

The Magnificent Amdiranifani drooped. "Yes. Me too!"

———

As usual, Amdi was very short on confidence. However, he did have the beginnings of a plan. There was a purpose for the gear the Innmaster had left them. "It's from the last circus that came through here," said Amdi.

Jefri picked up one of the colored balls, tossed it at a nearby pillar. The rebound was lively; this must be Tropical latex. Such items should not be cheap in the local economy.

"Why would a circus just leave these things?" asked Ravna.

"Well, um, they went bankrupt. That's what the Innmaster told me. He foreclosed on them." Amdi looked nervously at Ravna and Jefri. "Maybe this gear couldn't help a troupe of performing packs, but *anything* you do will be new and magical. I thought we could be something like those circuses that come through the Domain. I-I would introduce you and you'd come out and juggle, maybe tie knots . . ." His voice dribbled off into anxious silence.

Jefri gave the ball another bounce, then glanced at Amdi. "Your idea is lightyears ahead of anything I've come up with . . . but no matter what we do, do you think the Innmaster will let us leave afterwards?"

"I—maybe. I can see how much he'd like to steal you and Ravna. If he guessed Tycoon is looking for you, he'd grab you in an instant. But I think I've convinced him that we have Tycoon's protection. If we do well, I really think he'll make good on his promises. He'll give us the circus wagon, these supplies, and half the admission fees."

Ravna had a different problem: "Is this show going to be out of doors, Amdi?"

"Yes, there's an arena behind the inn. You couldn't see it from your side of the winch platform. Why—"

"I know this place isn't on Chitiratifor's maps, but since Nevil has moved the orbiter eastwards—"

"Oh yeah!" said Amdi. "I thought about that. The new position still doesn't have a line of sight on us. I mean, unless he's moved it *again*."

Ravna pondered the foolishness of this chitchat. They didn't really have a choice. Aloud, she said, "So let's give this Innmaster a show. It sounds easier than playing with arrow trees and crusherbushes."

That brought a weak smile to Jefri's face. She could almost see him summon the appearance of confidence. "For sure. And when I was twelve years old, I was a really good juggler."

Ravna smiled back. She remembered. For several tendays, little Jefri had been a frustrated and frustrating nuisance, bouncing beanbags and sticks in all directions. It had even strained his relationship with Amdi, since the pack of puppies had learned to juggle with ease.

"Okay," she said. "We've cleaned up our outfits. Your costume is still in good shape, Amdi. You just have to come on strong. You're the Magnificent. What else can you introduce besides the juggling?"

"Knot tying? Can you do that, Ravna?" Amdi was pulling cordage from one of the wheelbarrows.

"Sure." Better than a Tinish singleton, anyway. "And what about the comic relief?" That was a big part of circus performances in Woodcarver's Domain.

A glint came into Amdi's eyes. "I've been *thinking* about that." Three of him were fiddling with a leash, making idle loops of it. "There's a certain singleton that has been has been making me look the fool. Maybe now I can turn that around—"

As they'd been talking, Ritl had circled in on Amdi and was blabbering more and more loudly. She was now well within Amdi's personal space. Five of him turned abruptly on Ritl, throwing the leash in a coordinated attack so that the singleton's neck, forelegs and hindlegs were simultaneously caught in three separate loops. Ritl exploded in shrieking fury as Amdi flipped the creature onto her side. From the loft, Screwfloss hooted laughter.

Amdi stepped back, keeping tension on the various loops of leash. "Where was I?" he said. "Oh, yes. Ritl still needs her costume." Two of him walked to the far wheelbarrow and took out a conical leather collar. He passed it from member to member, and those standing by Ritl's head fastened the cone around the critter's neck.

Ritl twisted about, jaws snapping on empty air. Her hissing spiked painfully loud. The conical collar stuck forward all around her head, drastically reducing her field of view. Her screeching quieted as she seemed to realize her total helplessness.

Amdi noticed the look on Ravna's face. "I haven't hurt her, honestly. This is a standard costume for clown singletons. Isn't that right, Jefri?"

"Um, true." But Jefri had a surprised expression on his face too. Amdiranifani was so rarely aggressive. More than most packs, the eightsome had sympathy for the oppressed.

"Right! Now it's time to put on the clown paint." He passed a couple of dye sticks to Ravna. "I'll tell you what to draw. Just don't touch her eyes or tympani and she'll be fine."

Ravna looked uncertainly at the two sticks. The handles were especially broadened for easy jaw handling. Amdi had plenty of free members to do the job himself.

"Go ahead, Ravna. The mindsound is awful, even from a singleton. I don't want any more of me to stand near Ritl."

"Okay." Ravna knelt beside the animal, drew her hand in a gentle petting stroke along its back, much as the Children did with their Best Friends. Ritl shrieked and tried to scratch at her, but gradually settled back.

"Now start with big pink circles around the shoulder and haunch tympana . . ."

It took about fifteen minutes, and Jefri helping with the other colors, but in the end Ritl was dolled up more than any member Ravna had ever seen, including Godsgift.

When they were done, Amdi refastened the leash to a clasp that hung from Ritl's collar. Then he let it go loose. Ritl was quiet for a second, then raced across the stable to where the brightest bit of sky light shone on the straw. The singleton spun around and around, futilely trying to get a look at what they had done to its body. Finally, the poor thing got tangled up in the leash again and tipped over.

"See?" said Amdi, though not quite with perfect enthusiasm. "The audience will think it's hilarious." He pointed a snout upwards. "Screwfloss thinks it's hilarious."

In fact, Screwfloss' heads were rippling up and down in amusement. That cut short when Amdi sang out a sequence of chords that meant something like "now it's your turn," and gestured at the remnant to come down to ground level.

All heads but one jerked back, out of sight. Ravna heard sullen gobbling. Amdi replied with something cheerful. Three of him gathered up the dye sticks, the others looking up and gesturing to Screwfloss.

One by one, the remnant came down the ladder, the limper last of all. The four grouped at the bottom, glowering at Amdi.

Ravna and Jefri exchanged glances, and Jefri said, "Be careful, Amdi. Remember who that is."

"I . . . I remember. I'm not going to force anything on him." Amdi started toward the far end of the stable, where the harness gear was hung. It was cozy, but with enough room for two packs to have a private chat. After a moment, Screwfloss followed suspiciously. The two disappeared behind the harness racks. There was the sound of quiet discussion. "I can't tell what they're saying," said Jefri. Half a minute passed and still no battle sounds. The loudest sounds in the stable were the kherhogs fidgeting in their stalls and Ritl hissing to herself.

———

It was getting noisy outside. Ravna recognized the wheezy music that announced entertainment events.

Screwfloss and Amdi broke off their rehearsing. Amdi hustled around the stable, getting everyone together, making sure the necessary props were all in a single wheelbarrow. Screwfloss moved close to the door. His smudged disguise had been wiped away—not that a disguise made sense this far from Woodcarver's Domain. Now his pelts were decorated with a black and white checkered pattern. He held Ritl on a leash. Screwfloss didn't look happy, but that might have been Ritl's fault. Ravna walked over to give the pack some encouragement. Screwfloss looked up at her and spoke the first Samnorsk she'd heard from him since the night that part of him died: "We make big laugh. You see." One of him gave her a gentle bump.

Outside, a pack thumped on the door and gobbled loudly.

"They're ready, guys!" said Amdi. "Ravna, please get on my general left." Jefri was already standing on the other side of the eightsome. "Don't worry. Don't worry. I'll give you plenty of cues. We'll be okay!" *Wail.*

The door was already sliding open, the music shifting to a fast tempo. Screwfloss lurched into the daylight, Ritl perforce accompanying him. Beyond the musicians (one or both of their guards were making all the wheeze), Ravna could see a well-spaced crowd, nothing like the mob of earlier in the day.

Screwfloss still had his limp, but now he was faking another limp on the other side of himself. The two of him who were holding the leash walked close together as if they were suffering from lateral hearing impairment. It was the gait he'd been practicing since he'd finished putting on the checkered makeup. Ritl might not be acting a part, but her dogged efforts to inconvenience her "master" were a perfect foil for Screwfloss' performance: the fool and the fool's pet. It was cruel medieval humor, and the crowd's laughter drowned out the music.

Then Amdi stepped out into the daylight, flanked by the two humans. The crowd's laughter faltered, and there were wondering hoots. The two guards walked forward, clearing the way. One of them was dragging the barrow like a small cart.

"Just stroll along after the guards," said Amdi. "The Innmaster told me these are paying customers, charged double to see us both here and then again for our performance."

The guards followed a flagstoned path leading to the inn. There were wagons parked everywhere, even near where the winch platform sat like a cockeyed gazebo in the roar and the mist of the waterfall.

More packs were watching from the portico of the inn, but now the guards swung wide around that building, leading both the performers and the high-paying customers on a long parade that ended at the largest amphi-theater Ravna had yet seen on Tines World.

Amdi's troupe paused under awnings at the edge of the arena, hidden from the view of the crowd.

The Innmaster walked to the center of the arena. The flagstones were fitted in an intricate design, but here and there were dark splatter marks that were not part of the design. *Ugh*. Animal sacrifice?

The Innmaster was giving some sort of speech. That went on for only a few seconds before there were shouts from above, and a then a steady chanting from all sides. Amdi had a couple of heads in public view, but the rest of him was crouched down. "Hei! They're shouting 'We paid our money and we don't have to listen to you!'"

Out on the arena, the Innmaster tossed his heads in a disgusted gesture, and stomped off to his box in the grandstands.

"Does that mean we're on?" said Ravna.

The eightsome huddled down lower.

"Amdi?" said Jefri, cajoling from the pack's other side. "You've done fine so far. Go!"

"I, I, I haven't had enough time to plan. I—"

The crowd chanted louder and louder. A very rotten yam splashed across the awning, sending little splatters down on Screwfloss. He made a disgusted noise and lost his close hold on Ritl's leash. The singleton bounded into the open, her caution of earlier in the day forgotten. She ran in a wide arc, all the while gobbling loudly. She stopped, pranced about on her rear legs for a moment, then lost sight of the ground behind her collar/blinder and tipped over. She bounced up, still shouting. She was bragging about something, almost certainly nonsensical. But the eerie thing was how much she sounded like the Innmaster giving *his* spiel.

The crowd's chanting turned to laughter.

Ritl hesitated, nonplussed. She hopped back and forth, demanding serious attention. When the laughter just came louder, she charged the nearest of the tiered stands—and was hauled up short by Screwfloss' leash. She darted off to the side, pulling on the leather. Meanwhile, Ravna noticed Screwfloss' heads bobbing in surprised amusement. He slid a glance in Amdi's direction, and then—still out of sight of the audience—very deliberately dropped the leash.

In the arena, poor Ritl almost fell over again. Then she recovered and ran along the edge of the stands, trailing her very long leash.

Screwfloss bumbled out into public view, his members covered with that checkered design, limping on two sides. He chased after the singleton's leash, remarkably missing it again and again. Finally he did a four-way body flop on the stone flags, trapping the leather somewhere under himself. He rose, the leash grasped firmly in four pairs of jaws. He bowed triumphantly, and started making his own speech. But the fool's pet was not cooperating: Ritl ran round and round the foursome, faster and closer as the length of free leash diminished.

Finally, Screwfloss tripped on the leash. He staggered around, squawking indignation. The crowd thought this was still funnier. More rotten vegetables splattered down, but this was crude applause. One caught Screwfloss on a shoulder, splashing color across his checkered design. Ritl seemed to be laughing about this, but she had her own missiles to avoid, and without success.

Screwfloss dithered in apparent panic, then all of him turned toward where Amdi and company were hidden. Even Ravna could see the melodrama in his pose. His Tinish plea meant something like: "Master. *Master!* Come out!"

And so Amdi was forced into action. He gave a low, heartfelt wail . . . and bounded into the arena.

The laughter changed to cheers, and the rain of rotten vegetables ebbed. Amdi was walking more proudly than Ravna had ever seen him, with the ones in the middle pointing their heads straight up. If this were a human, it would be a guy holding his arms up for the audience's acclaim.

Jefri slid across the space Amdi had vacated. He had a huge, wondering grin on his face.

"What's he saying?" asked Ravna.

"It's too fast for me. He's promising them things—"

Consider the local dialect differences, Amdi was probably talking too fast for much of his audience—but maybe that just added to the glamour. Amdi waved grandly to Screwfloss and Ritl. The two left the arena, still very much in character—though Ravna was convinced their behavior was only an act for one of them. Screwfloss slid under the awning and tied Ritl to one of the wood pillars. He was grinning and grumbling—and taking turns trying to swab the juice off his pelt. He glanced across at Ravna and Jefri and there was something wicked in his smile, something that seemed to say "your turn is next!"

"Jefri! Ravna!" Amdi's human voice spoke as he continued his showman gobbling. "I'm just about ready to invite you out. Jefri comes to me and Ravna stays back out of mindsound range. Okay?" It was essentially what they had discussed back in the stable.

"Okay!" Jefri shouted back.

But then the clouds briefly parted and Amdi was standing in late afternoon sunlight, his cloaks' beadwork aglitter, his painted footgear shining like real silver tines. Somewhere in the midst of him were the two members that didn't have fancy costumes, but Ravna couldn't see them.

Amdi glanced up at the sunlight, startled. Then: "Very good!" he boomed, now making a simultaneous translation. "I give you the wonders of the northern world, the creatures from beyond the sky, the creatures who can think without sound, who can think each by itself. I give you . . . the two-legs!" Four of him jammed their heads straight up, and the other four swung around to point where Ravna and Jefri were hidden beneath the awnings. By golly, there was even a musical fanfare coming from the eight.

"Do you suppose that's our cue?" said Jefri.

"Unh," said Ravna, finally feeling stage fright herself.

They walked out from under the awnings, and stood at their full height, visible to all. Just as when they emerged from the stable, the audience fell nearly silent. Jefri and Ravna turned in opposite directions, raising their arms to show off their hands. Ravna was scanning the crowd, watching for yam throwers. These stands were similar to Woodcarver's meeting place at her old capital, but even larger. Each tier was built almost directly above the one below, and the "seating" was delimited mainly by quilted sound absorbers and premium boxes. Amdi's moment of sunlight was past and the grandstands were in deepening gloom. It was hard to say how many packs were up there; they were crammed together closer than she had ever seen. There were heads everywhere, almost all focused downwards, on the two humans.

And then she and Jefri were face to face again. She reached out, brushed his sleeve with her hand. "I never guessed we'd end up here."

Jef's tense expression broke into a smile. "And I'll bet you never guessed that my juggling was a survival skill." He caught her hand for an instant and then they parted, Ravna retreating to the edge of the arena.

Amdi surrounded Jefri, continuing his showman's spiel. He wasn't translating anymore, but Ravna recognized the chord "five-tentacle paws." He walked to the wheelbarrow that was set near center of the arena, and tossed three colored balls to Jefri.

Jefri began cautiously, with just the three balls in a simple up and across. Then he launched them higher and higher, brought them down low, bounced the cycle of tosses off the ground. Amdi threw him a fourth ball. That had worked well enough when they were practicing in the stable—but now Jefri lost control. It took him several tries to keep all four in the air. Ravna looked across the stands. Still no rotten yams, and the storm of clicking sounds was applause. To these packs, the impressive thing was that this monstrous, teetering singleton could juggle anything at all.

The most popular part of Jefri's act was a bit of luck right at the end: A persistently rowdy pack in the second tier tossed a single yam down at Jefri. Jefri snagged it without getting splattered—and now he was juggling five!

"Toss it *back*," said Amdi, and shouted some kind of warning into the stands. Jefri brought the other balls down to earth, then stood eyeing the stands. No pack could have seen much in the beclouded twilight, but after a moment, Jefri stepped back and threw a high, slow lob—that plinked exactly the member of the pack who had tossed it.

Ravna held her breath. She had no idea what such an insult might mean to these creatures. But everyone was laughing. The fellow looked around, even its own heads bobbing with amusement. It had other veggies, and after a few tries—and a sturdier yam—the pack and the two-legs were playing catch.

Before there could be more audience participation, the Magnificent Amdi waved Jefri out of the arena—and gestured to Ravna. Her show business debut was at hand.

———

Alas, the knot-tying made a limp finale. Even with the heavy ropes the Innmaster supplied, there wasn't much for the audience to see, especially in the fading light. On the other hand, it didn't challenge her sense of balance—and no one tossed rotten yams at her. As she held up her latest creation, she looked across the stands. The applause wasn't wild, but she sensed a kind of somber speculation looking back at her. Perhaps she had not proved her super-singleton intelligence, but she had demonstrated that, for close work, a two-legs was defter than any full-bodied pack.

In any case, her act did not go on as long as Jefri's. Amdi began to wind things down, waving at Screwfloss to do one more comedy go-around. But as the remnant untied Ritl, the Innmaster came strolling out from his private box in the grandstands. His gobbling carried liquid overtones. He was asking for something, all very politely. Whatever he was saying met with loud approval from the audience.

Amdi dithered in surprise. Jefri was walking out onto the arena.

"What? What?" said Ravna.

Jefri gave her an odd smile. "I think our host wants permission for a select few of the audience to come down and . . . um . . . pet us."

Amdi had turned his attention to Ravna and Jefri, and for the first time his posture slumped out of magnificence. "That's exactly right. None of these packs have met humans before; if even a few are hostile . . . what do you want to do?" Now all of him was looking at Ravna. And so was Jefri.

"I—" she looked up at the crowd. At this moment the vast majority were actively friendly. *And we may need that tomorrow, when we try to leave.* It was the story of her life on this world, making scary near-term bets. "Tell them 'yes,' Amdi."

"Okay." Amdi boomed his agreement, for a change speaking very slowly and simply. Then to Ravna and Jefri he said, "I told them only one at a time. The Innmaster's guards will stay near enough to make sure no one plays rough."

The packs in the first tier surged onto the field, maneuvering for the privilege of a close encounter with the zombies. The Innmaster set his guards to regulating the customers' approach—incidentally collecting still more coinage.

Amdi arranged himself generally behind the two humans while Screwfloss brought Ritl out and settled on Ravna's right. Ritl blabbered away self-importantly—but she toned it down when the remnant drew her near and began snapping at her.

The first of the "select few" of customers had gotten past the guards. The fivesome approached at an enthusiastic trot, then slowed, even backed up a little. All five of its heads were craned upwards, intimidated by Jefri's height. The customer right behind squawked at the delay—but it didn't try to circle around.

Jefri went to one knee and extended a hand, gesturing the pack forward.

Amdi shifted nervously. "This isn't the Innmaster; you don't have to take chances."

"It's okay, Amdi. This is just like our first expedition to the Long Lakes." Jef's body language was relaxed enough, but his voice was tense.

The five spent almost a minute variously inspecting Jef's clothing, mouthing his fingers with the soft tips of its own muzzles, and chatting with Amdi. "He complimented me on how well I've trained you, Jef," Amdi reported, as he passed the customer on to Ravna.

Some of the strangers were like that first one. Others mugged around for friends who lurked at a distance, as if to say "Look at me, up close to a monster!" Many tried to talk to Jefri and Amdi, echoing the humans' own words and watching for a response.

As twilight deepened, fire circles were lit at the corners of the arena. The flames climbed bright and high—adequate light even for Tines. And the customers kept coming. A few of them even took time to compliment Screwfloss on *his* act. Ravna wondered if the Steel inside had ever been the object of honest praise; in any case, the remnant seemed pleased. Ritl didn't know quite what to make of the chitchat, but she clearly considered herself a co-equal entity in the receiving line.

And there were a few, a very few, who came close to doing what Amdi had been worried about. One pack jostled Jefri. When Amdi complained, the creature seemed to apologize, easing past Amdi to get close to Ravna. The pack was seven, but scrawny and misshapen. Put some checkered makeup on this fellow and it could play a mean version of Screwfloss' character. It swirled close around her, all yellowish eyes and Tinish bad breath. Amdi was watching it closely and he translated the creature's gobbling: "He's saying to everybody that even up close, you are making no mindsound." When Ravna remained silent, it squealed something that might have meant "alive" (or "not alive")—and slammed into her knees.

Ravna fell, but before the creature could do anything more, Jef and Amdi jumped in on her left and Screwfloss on her right, all grabbing at the stranger. For a moment, bodies were flying in all directions. Ravna struggled back to her feet. The attacker was scattered, out of easy thinking range of itself. Its members looked around dazedly, then skedaddled to the edge of the arena, ran back together, and disappeared through one of the openings between the stands.

"That's it!" shouted Jefri. "Time to close down!" He reached out to Ravna and said more softly, "You okay?"

"Yes, I—" She hadn't been hurt at all, just reminded of the risks.

Amdi was talking over the crowd, at the Innmaster. That worthy was standing near his money collectors. Amdi's words sent him into a frantic dance. The crowd of packs started protesting, too. Nightmare visions came to Ravna's mind.

Amdi reported, "The Innmaster is promising us the sun and the moon, if we'll just stay in place a little longer."

"We've got to stay," said Ravna.

Amdi raised four of his heads high, and gobbled loudly across all the voices. "I'm repeating what the Innmaster is promising us," he said. "I'm saying we'd love to cooperate, but we want everyone to make sure that all promises get kept."

The Innmaster was bobbing heads in agreement. Ravna could see the reason for *his* enthusiasm: The panniers on his guard packs were swinging heavy with the loot. This was jackpot night for the guy.

Jefri was nodding too, but not with enthusiasm. "Okay, you're right; we've got to see this through." He returned to the pack he'd been chatting with right before the blowup. Interactions were strained for a few moments, but now in fact everyone was watching for troublemakers. The flow of customers and cash resumed.

Afterwards, Ravna wasn't clear how late into the night they stayed. The packs just kept coming. She noticed an occasional pack give her an aggressive stare, but none of them misbehaved. As for the rest . . . she came to see why Johanna and Jefri and the other explorer kids had loved their dangerous jaunts beyond the Domain. Most Tinish strangers, once they got over their initial un-ease with humans, seemed to revel in their ability to get close, to deal with apparently intelligent singletons. As the evening progressed, and the fires were renewed and renewed, more of the packs were trying to echo talk with her and Jefri. Some packs, who had been through the line and saw that they would not make it back for a second turn, hung around at the edge of the arena, shouting suggestions at the customers who were closer.

Here might be enemies and monsters, but also potential Best Friends for future generations of the Children.

CHAPTER 29

Things were very different after their show at Winch Bottom. They had a real circus wagon now (the one lost to default by its unfortunate original owners). The wagon had a passenger cabin and was so large that it really needed its four-kherhog team. Under the watchful eyes of customers who had stayed over-night, the Innmaster had also given them food supplies and crossbows. Perhaps as important, he'd given them an official-looking letter, advising that as Ty-coon's manager at Winch Bottom, he and Tycoon were pledging safe conduct to these marvelous entertainers. That, combined with the Tycoonist badge that Amdi had found in Chitiratifor's gear, could count for a lot. Ravna hoped the fellow wouldn't be in too much trouble when real word from Tycoon finally reached these parts.

When they left Winch Bottom, there were at least a dozen packs who wanted to sign on with the circus, to guard them and guide them in the journey northwards. Chances were good they were all sincere, but Amdi turned them down. The more famous they became, the easier it would be for Tycoon and Vendacious and Nevil to find them. The moment word of the search overtook them, even honest packs might turn them in.

So when they departed Winch Bottom, only a few fans had followed, fur-tively straggling along some hundred meters behind the circus wagon.

Amdi passed up the first villages to the north, picking his way around them on paths he'd discovered on the maps. As they rolled past each successive vil-lage, they lost more of their retinue. These were ordinary packs of the Wild

Principates, peasants and small landowners. No matter how intrigued they might be by the two-legs, they did not have the leisure time of fans in a more technological society.

On the third day, Screwfloss scouted all around and reported they had lost the last of their followers. Now it was time to change the course from what Amdi had advertised back at Winch Bottom. "There are plenty of alternative paths on these maps," said Amdi. "The problem is, whichever we choose, we're going to run out of food before we get back to the Domain." They'd have to engage in some skilled woodcraft . . . or stage more shows.

When this stark choice was presented to Amdi, he'd dithered a moment and then a shy smile spread across him. "I—I guess I could take another turn at being Magnificent."

Over the next few days they looked at each little village they came across, with Screwfloss scouting for threats and friendliness, balancing the risks with the current state of their supplies. Most places they still avoided, but eventually they performed three times, once indoors at a farmers' meeting hall and twice in open fields under cloudy skies. The days stayed mild, with cold rains and muddy roads, but altogether more pleasant than what had gone before.

Their shows improved. Ravna's own act was still a loser, but she had tweaked their lighting system into being a major part of the event. Even Ritl seemed to enjoy performing; she tried to upstage Amdi in more and more hilarious ways. Amdi was now completely fluent in the local dialect. His presentation had become positively polished, except that he seemed genuinely to be angered by the singleton's antics. The high point of the show was always the petting zoo routine, and they had that worked out so well that it felt almost safe. Already, their fame had gotten ahead of them: when they tried to bypass a town, there were often packs on the side paths, begging them to stop and perform.

"These lands are just too civilized," Jefri said one evening, after they had set up camp for the night. Moonlight trickled down through the trees, but hopefully they were out of sight of the primitive optics on the orbiter. "Once upon a time, they really were wild, too dangerous for most explorers. Now there's trade everywhere. The arena at Winch Bottom was huge, and *new*."

"And the towns are growing," said Amdi. "They're even bigger than what's on Nevil's maps." Those maps might have been honest information for Chitiratifor, but they were already out-of-date.

"Yeah," said Jefri. "Tycoon's finished goods are everywhere. I'm getting sick of seeing that Pack of Packs logo. It'll be a miracle if we get to the Domain before news of us gets back to him."

Ravna gave a gloomy nod. "And I'll bet Nevil is waiting ahead, probably with *Eyes Above 2*."

Amdi was humming, which was often the sound of good ideas being born: "But Woodcarver will be there, too," he said. It was almost a question. Both Jef and Amdi were getting more and more afraid for Johanna and Pilgrim. And what about Woodcarver?

Ravna thought back to that strange final conversation she'd had with Woodcarver. "I'll bet she's still running the Domain, Amdi. And she's not fooled by Nevil."

"Well then. She'll have loyal troops looking for us all along the frontier. If we can get to her people, we can get you back to *Oobii*."

"If you can get me back to *Oobii*, it's show over for Nevil." It's what Ravna told them every night.

"*Hmmm*," emitted Amdi. "So what can we do that will—"

Ritl interrupted Amdi's thinking with a loud suggestion of her own. When it could, the creature would creep near them, quiet and innocent until she was unseemly close—and then insert herself into the conversation.

This time she got a laugh out of Jefri: "That almost makes sense, Amdi, at least if kherhogs had wings."

Amdi was not amused. He bounced to his feet. "She's just a damned trouble-maker! Can't you see that?" The eight flounced off into the moonlight-spattered dark.

"He's getting even more sensitive about Ritl," said Ravna. "I wonder whether the Magnificent Amdiranifani is really acquiring a showman's ego."

"I heard that!" Amdi shot back at them. "If I can't think, I might as well do guard duty."

Remnant Screwfloss had returned from ranging around the camp. He was over by the kherhogs, setting down fodder for them. Now one of his heads turned to follow Amdi's departure. When he was done with the kherhogs, he settled down beneath the wagon and commented, "Ritl make him a fool." The remnant was speaking a fair amount of Samnorsk these days, though not with the teasing sarcasm of when he'd been whole.

Ravna looked around the wagon. Normally, Screwfloss staked down the singleton on the other side of the kherhogs. It was more peaceful that way. "Hei, Screwfloss. Didn't you have Ritl tethered?"

The pack cocked its heads, looked out from under the wagon in the opposite direction. Maybe he wasn't going to answer. But then he said, "She get loose."

Jefri gave a little laugh. "Ritl must be learning from your rope tricks, Ravna."

Ravna smiled back. "She's just a good wriggler." Ritl had slipped loose once or twice before; no one but Amdi seemed to get very excited about it. She looked across the dimly glowing embers at Jefri. "Could Ritl be a threat? Remasritlfeer was an enemy—maybe not as bad as Chitiratifor—but still one of Tycoon's henchpacks. Given the opportunity, won't she betray us?"

Even in the dimness, she could see the grin on Jefri's face. "Ah, paranoia speaks." He scooched around the dying fire in her direction. As usual, they had set their pallets out of arm's reach. With Amdi's eight filling the gap between them, there were plenty of warm bodies. Besides, the last few nights had ended in the usual unpleasant arguments. Last night was the first time Ravna ever heard the Blighter fleet called a *rescue party*. In a way, hearing Jefri say that had been more terrifying than all the rest of this ordeal.

Jefri warmed his hands above the glowing embers. "If and when we run into Tycoon, what Ritl would do is hard to say. Old Screwfloss said Remasritlfeer was one of Tycoon's top lieutenants. Depending on just who comes after us, it's quite possible Ritl would betray us—though I'll bet she's not smart enough to do much more than shout 'Hei, Boss, look here!'"

"Okay. I guess it is silly to worry about that here." She watched Jefri silently for few moments. She'd known him for ten years, had watched the loving child grow up to be their best explorer—and a man who believed the most terrible lies she could imagine.

Jefri looked up at her silence. "What?" he said. There was still a smile on his face, but she could see the wariness in his eyes.

If she said one wrong word, they would slip into another night of argument. *But I have to try.* "Jefri, we have this terrible disagreement about the Blight and Countermeasure. You know what I think; you know the sacrifices your parents made to escape the Blight. On the other side, there's—"

"There's Nevil, right, a certified monster." Jef's agreement was angry. "But so what? *I* remember the High Lab. And Down Here, *I* saw how Countermeasure murdered Pham. Even you admit that Countermeasure raised the Slowness, and probably destroyed civilization as far as we can see the stars on a clear night. What counts is not who's nice and who's not, Ravna; what counts is the *truth*."

"I'm not talking about being nice, Jefri! I'm talking about trustable observations. You were just a—"

"Just a young child? That's what you said last night!"

But that's what you were! And she would never forget how Jefri and Amdi had tried to comfort her after seeing Pham die. She hesitated, trying to think of something to say, something sensible, something that would make this go right. "Jef, have you ever thought that there might be existing facts, things to be discovered or tested, that might change your opinion?"

"You want me to put my beliefs under review? How very nice. Are you willing to do the same?"

"I—"

"Never mind. At this stage, what undiscovered evidence could there be?" Jefri turned back to the fire. He sat hunched forward, hands extended over the embers. He was silent for a long moment, then: "We're going to get you past Tycoon and Vendacious, safely back to *Oobii*. Then you'll do what you think is right. If you can't stop Nevil, I will get rid of him *myself*." His gaze returned to her face. "But you know what? There will still be a Disaster Study Group. And its new leader won't be Bili Yngva."

Ravna drowsed. The moon set and the fire's embers cooled to darkness. She heard an occasional snarfling snore from the kherhogs, but none of Ritl's irritating chatter. Eventually, she heard someone entering the campsite; that would be Amdi, come to wake the next sentry. The thought brought her almost fully awake. She usually took the second watch—though she was sure that neither Amdi nor Screwfloss trusted a human sentry. Some of them would be listening all through the night.

Faint and far away, she heard what might have been Ritl, but not quite as querulous as usual. Then the night exploded into hissing and squealing. Some number of creatures chased each other through the surrounding brush, fighting as they ran.

"*Amdi!*" shouted Jef. There was no answer, but Ravna heard somepack— Screwfloss?—scramble over the startled kherhogs and bound to the top of the circus wagon.

The shrieking continued, the noise coming together on the far side of the wagon.

Ravna kept one of the lamps with her at night. Now she shook it into surveillance mode. The light flickered in pseudo-random hops, scanning into the underbrush in a pattern that should confuse anyone trying to spot the source.

The sounds of the monster cat fight continued, but she saw no sign of attacking packs. If Ritl had betrayed them, it wasn't to a simple ambush.

"Let me point light." That was Screwfloss from atop the wagon, where the second lamp was stored. He swept the illumination onto something beyond the wagon. Looking beneath the wagon, Ravna saw Tinish legs scrambling around.

"That's part of Amdi!" Jefri started around the wagon. He had his crossbow up and cocked.

Two packs of four came racing round the wagon, one on each side. They ran towards each other, jaws snapping. All were dressed in plain workcloaks just like Amdi wore when they were on the road.

"Huh!" Jefri said. "Amdi?"

All eight collapsed in a heap. The lamplight swung in to spotlight the crowd. Indeed, this was exactly Amdi.

"Are you okay, Amdi?" Ravna knelt beside the pack, looking at each of him. There were cuts and scrapes. One of his ears was torn. "Who did this?" *And is it still out there?* But she could see that up on the wagon, all of Screwfloss was watching Amdi; he wasn't worried about an attack.

Amdi was hissing and sputtering, but she heard a high, keening whistle behind all his sounds. The pack was in terrible pain. Finally, he slipped into Samnorsk: "No attack. There was no attack. No one's sneaking up on us, though Screwfloss should take sentry duty." He emitted two or three chords. Screwfloss sang something back. The remnant dropped off the far side of the wagon and walked into the bushes.

Amdi wriggled miserably in the bright lamp light, exchanging looks with himself, darting glances at Jefri and Ravna. "Turn off the light, okay?"

Ravna did, and Amdi's voice continued in the darkness. "It was Ritl."

"I don't understand," said Ravna. "If there's no one else out there, how could she do so much harm?"

Ravna heard a muffled click, Jefri safing his crossbow. "I think it's more complicated than that," Jef said, and she heard him go to his knees beside the pack.

Amdi was making a strange medley of sounds. There was the whimpering, almost the sound of a human child. There were chords that she didn't understand, and there was the pack's little boy voice speaking in tones that were full of self-loathing: "The Ritl animal has been a troublemaker from the beginning.

She is *not* smart, but she is always saying the wrong thing when I try to perform. You saw that too, right? She almost got us killed at Winch Top. At the same time, she is in my personal space every chance she gets."

Jefri's voice was soft: "She's a singleton, Amdi. She can't live apart."

The whimpering got a little louder. Ravna had a sense of quick motion within the pack, heard a pair of jaws snapping on air. Jefri made soothing sounds. "Don't be so hard on yourself, Amdi."

After a moment, the little boy voice continued, "Sigh. I knew Ritl was an issue the moment she turned up, but I thought—I hoped it would be like in the romances. Ritl would make Screwfloss whole again! It would have solved both their problems. Instead, that stupid remnant has no interest in her. And Ritl doesn't like Screwfloss either. Then she made, um, advances towards me. But so what, I thought. I am so perfectly matched. There is nothing that having another member could cause me except harm."

Amdi didn't say anything for a moment, though the whimpering continued. ". . . Tonight I was strung out all the way around the campsite. It's really kind of an interesting way to be. I get very stupid, but I can see so much and the thoughts rattle around one step at a time, each of me adding a little insight." The whimpering got louder. It wasn't a group sound; it was coming from the three members hunched down closest to the ground. "Ritl came in among me. She didn't sneak up exactly; I knew she was there. She started bothering the parts of me . . ." Amdi's voice rose into keening: "the parts who *like* her." He twisted around, jaws snapping. Jefri reached down, risking some nasty cuts to caress a head here and there. After a moment, coherence returned to the eightsome. "Ritl is tearing me apart!"

CHAPTER 30

The maps showed a town thirty kilometers up the road. There were nearer ones on other roads, but this was their best bet for a full provisioning. From there, they could sneak forward, scouting Woodcarver's border forts for the safest one to approach.

This would be their last show, and then the real climax would be ahead. Meanwhile . . .

Ravna rode atop the wagon. Nominally, she was driving, though she suspected that all by herself, Ravna-from-the-stars could not have managed a team of four kherhogs. Their cooperation was more likely due to Remnant Screwfloss, who was almost always here and there around the animals, bullying them along.

Jefri and Amdi walked together, dropping further back than usual, their forms almost lost in the morning fog. The eightsome was clustered tight, the posture a pack normally used when in a crowd or coping with bad acoustics or needing to do hard thinking. The fog alone couldn't account for that posture.

Since his midnight collapse, the pack had been like this, cheerless and quiet, talking in low tones to his Best Friend.

Ravna gave the reins a tentative slap, just to let the kherhogs know that she wasn't asleep. She glanced at her companion atop the wagon. "So is that what you are, Ritl? A pack wrecker?"

Ritl cocked her head toward Ravna. It was hard to see any expression in a singleton's posture, but the animal seemed to have some understanding. *Is she laughing at me?* This morning, Ritl's leash was tied short to the cargo railing behind the driver's bench. Getting her up here had been a struggle. She seemed to think that after last night's shenanigans she had achieved privileged status. Her hissing complaints had continued some minutes after they got on the road. Then she had settled into near silence, staring back along the road in Amdi's direction. Every so often Ravna felt a buzzing sensation through the wood of the driver's bench, probably a side effect of Ritl's shouting ultrasonic endearments.

Ravna continued her one-sided conversation with the creature: "You know, among humans, it's considered very bad form to break up another's relationship, even if you're needy yourself."

"Very bad form, very bad form," Ritl looped on the phrase a few times. Then her gaze returned to the object of her immoral advances.

Calling Ritl a "pack wrecker" was not just a figure of speech. Poor Amdiranifani was simply too big to take on another member. That's what he claimed, anyway, and Jefri agreed. Amdi probably couldn't even retain a puppy born of his own pack. Accepting an unrelated adult member would surely split the eightsome. The three male members who were enamored of Ritl would break away. Amdi said that one female was wavering. Either possibility would be the end of Amdi.

Screwfloss shouted something at her, and abruptly Ravna was brought back to the present. The kherhogs were making frightened noises and pulling the wagon to the side, into the undergrowth. Screwfloss had abandoned the animals and circled behind the wagon. Whatever he was saying had brought Jefri and Amdi running forward.

Ravna struggled with the reins. The roadside brush hid a gully and deep mud. She rose from the bench, bracing her legs and pulling as hard as she could at the reins. "Need some help here!" Then she heard the sound. It came out of the fog ahead, the buzz of steam induction engines. Scrupilo's airship! The aircraft was still hidden in the mists, but it was getting closer.

Amdi and Jefri ran past the wagon. "We should get off the road, Ravna," Jef called to her, but softly. Ritl piped up with complaints. Amdi hissed a "be quiet!" at the singleton, and for a wonder, it fell silent.

So now it was Ravna on the reins, and Screwfloss and Jefri and Amdi up ahead guiding the kherhogs into the brush. Fortunately, this was the general direction the animals wanted to go. They just needed help negotiating the roadside gully.

Meantime, the sound of Scrupilo's steam engines had grown louder. Was this salvation, or Nevil's gang? She put the question on hold as the wagon tilted sideways. She didn't quite lose the reins, but now she was aware how easily she might be dumped and crushed.

Then the front wheels were climbing over the far edge of the gully, and she was back in her seat. Leafy branches swept the top of the wagon. Without thinking, she reached up to rescue Ritl from her perch at the top. They huddled together beneath the scraping branches.

"Sorry," came Jef's voice. "I didn't realize the fit was so tight."

"We're fine." Ravna pushed at the heavy, wet foliage. They were well protected against eyeball detection from above. She started down the ladder-stairs from the driver's seat. Behind her, Ritl was complaining. The singleton's voice was still soft, but growing toward loudness. "Okay, you can come, too." Ravna unlatched the leash from the wagon. Ritl immediately scrambled across her shoulders and leaped to the ground.

A moment later, Ravna was standing ankle-deep in the mud. She backed away from the wagon, staring upwards. The buzz of the airship's steam engines was still growing, but with the fog and forest cover she couldn't see anything.

"Amdi!" Jefri's voice was scarcely more than a whisper. "Spread out and get a look-listen."

But Amdi stayed heads together, hissing softly at Ritl. "I can't move with that *animal* so close," the pack said. "She'd come between me."

Okay . . . Ravna went back along the way the wagon had come. If the airship had real surveillance gear, then hiding the wagon was a waste of time. If not, well, she might be able to learn more about them without revealing herself. She moved along the gully, staying under the thickest of the brush, but looking for a view of the sky.

Something scuttled through the brush around her: three, no, all four of Screwfloss. One of him nipped at her pants leg, drawing her down to an opening the pack had found. She went to her hands and knees and followed him up to the edge of the road. Yeah. Ahead was the perfect spy hole.

Zzzzzzzzzzzzzzzzzzzzzzzzzzz, the sound of steam induction engines flying just a few meters overhead, moving south but no faster than a human could run. She reached the break in the bushes and cautiously looked out, just in time to see . . . the form of the *Eyes Above 2* disappearing into the murk, spinning out a helix of foggy spume behind it. *Powers take it!* A second earlier and she might have seen recognizable faces! Around her, Screwfloss poked a couple heads into the opening. She held her breath for a long moment, listening for any sign that the airship might be turning back; their wagon's maneuvers would have left signs that might be visible from above.

For better or worse, the engine sounds became steadily fainter, vanishing into the south. They stayed low in the dripping foliage for some minutes, but finally even Screwfloss seemed to give up on the possibility of a return. They stumped back to the wagon, where everyone was full of questions.

"We were too far away to see or hear anything," said Amdi. "Did you?"

"You didn't hail them," said Jefri. "Was it Nevil's people?"

"I couldn't see. Sorry. Maybe I was too cautious." *Maybe I should have just run out into the road.* Very few Deniers could be bothered with primitive gadgetry; surely, Scrupilo would have had a crew aboard.

Amdi and Screwfloss were gobbling back and forth. Ritl stood unseemly close to the eightsome, injecting noise into the conversation. Abruptly, Amdi turned on the interloper, screeching and snapping at it. "*Tie it up!* I don't have to be nice to it anymore!"

The singleton danced back out of everyone's reach, making sounds that seemed mocking even to Ravna. *Catch me if you can!*

Jefri leaned down and snatched the singleton's leash where it lay near his feet. He gave it a wiggle, catching Ritl's attention. The animal shot him a wide-eyed glare, then raced around Amdi, trying to trap the pack's legs in the leash. This not being a circus act, Jefri and Amdi managed to outwit the creature, and in a few moments it was bundled—clawing and biting and squawking—up the ladder-stairs to its tie-down point atop the wagon.

"Okay then," said Amdi, ignoring the continuing complaints. "Screwfloss was listening to the flier while Ravna was watching it. He says there were Tines aboard."

Jefri was partway down the ladder. He stopped, considering. "He heard mindsounds?"

"No, it was too far away and humid for that. But he heard Interpack speech."

"I didn't hear any voices," said Ravna. "But that's not surprising. Did he recognize anyone? What were they saying?"

Screwfloss had been following, heads cocking back and forth. Now he answered in Samnorsk: "No sense. No words. But the sound is like two-legs can't make."

Ravna squatted down by the remnant. "Did you hear any humans?"

Screwfloss thought a moment. "No." He gobbled some elaboration.

"He says that if there were any humans aboard, they didn't say anything during the time he had good hearing, and that was at least two minutes."

Ravna stifled an unhappy laugh. "I should have waved them down."

"They'll be back, Rav."

"Maybe. Or maybe they'll just keep searching south. Either way . . . I don't see how it changes things now.

———

Twice that morning, Amdi and Screwfloss claimed they heard the sound of the airship. Both packs spread out from the sides of the road, trying to get a baseline on the sound. All they could be sure of was that the aircraft was far to the south.

Meantime, they had their final show to prep for. As the fog gave way to a misty rain, Jefri and Ravna climbed into the wagon and worked on the costumes and props. Screwfloss drove the kherhogs, and he and Amdi alternated riding on the top of the wagon—except that when Amdi was up there, Ritl was exiled to walk on a leash behind the carriage.

Mostly Amdi seemed to be worrying about what they'd do *after* this show, how to get out of town and thence to the border with the Domain.

Ravna smiled as she polished the lamp emitters. "Hei Amdi, if this were a tenday ago, your stage fright is all we'd be hearing about."

Amdi's little boy voice drifted through the open window of the cab: "Oh, I still have stage fright, but now it's a *solvable* problem, like math of tractable complexity." He was silent for a second or two. "Ritl is a different sort of problem. If I can just keep away from her, I think I can stay together. And as long as I can stay together, I can manage easy problems like stage fright." He was silent for a longer time, and then, "I want to thank you for giving me courage, Ravna. I was ready to give up back at Winch Top."

What did I say at Winch Top? Oh yeah. "I, I just told you the truth, Amdi. Steel created you for his purposes. At Winch Bottom you discovered you were something more."

"No, I don't mean what you *said*. It's what you did, what you do. You're just a single person and you've been so terribly banged around. Back at Winch Top you could barely stand, but you just kept going. . . . I'm going to see this through, too."

Jefri had look up sharply at Amdi's words. Was he irritated? Surprised? "Just be careful, Amdi."

As they neared their destination, they realized that a discreet reconnoiter was not possible. Even far south of the town, the farm lanes were crowded with wagons and packs.

"They say they're here to see the two-legs perform," Amdi reported after chatting up the strangers.

Jefri looked out from the curtains they had drawn across the cab's windows. "This welcome is bigger than anything we've run into before. Somebody's organized it."

Ravna pushed curtain aide and leaned out. The wagon ahead of them was painted in lively colors. Beneath a rain tarp, she could see canvas bales imprinted with the ubiquitous twelve-pack logo. A little sign advertised the contents as "fine cloaks." Two of the driver were looking back in her direction. The fellow gave out a little whoop and waved at her. She waved back. "Maybe we're just famous. What do you think, Amdi?"

The eightsome's voice sounded from beneath the window. "They say the local prince sent messengers out early this morning, proclaiming a special festival day, complete with 'real mythical two-legs.' They think it has something do with the big creature in the sky—they've heard the airship. Look, I should go on ahead and talk to somebody who can make us a deal."

Ravna and Jefri exchanged glances. Usually, they would stop just outside of town, and wait for some local landowner to make them a deal; often that could take a day. Amdi's plan would save time, but it would leave them with the dubious diplomatic skills of Remnant Screwfloss. Just now, that worthy was atop the wagon and apparently following the conversation: "Amdi go ahead."

Jefri looked out at the traffic jam around them. "Okay, Amdi. But keep it simple."

"I will. One show, stipulated payment. And then we're gone in the early morning."

"Be careful," said Ravna. Maybe she *had* encouraged him too much.

"Hei, I'll be fine without Ritl!" Amdi was already running on ahead of their wagon, and shouting something to one of the few official-looking packs in sight.

———

This might be a frontier village, but it was not small. Amdi eventually returned with directions, guiding them to a pavilion by the town square. "The local boss calls this place 'The Northernmost End of Civilization.'" Amdi laughed. "Woodcarver would not be amused!"

Ravna walked around their wagon, taking in the view of downtown. Woodcarver had her sculpture, but this was the first place on Tines World where Ravna had seen heroic statuary. Each work depicted a single pack in some grandiose pose, climbing tall on itself to wave around swords and shields. According to Amdi, they all represented the local boss, "Prince Purity." The pack was no Innmaster; Purity ruled from a huge castle of whitewashed stone. The structure sat on a rise north of town. It was impressive, until you noticed that most of the whitewash covered naked bedrock with a relatively small building at the top. Amdi shrugged. "Except for the wealth that Tycoon's trade has brought, I figure this guy is phony. Most of the construction I see is new. I'll bet that ten years ago, Northernmost was a tiny village."

Jefri was looking around, nodding. "And we know that fifty years ago, this was uninhabited badlands."

"Purity claims to be a continuous hereditary ruler, back to times of legend."

"Hmm," said Jefri. "We've seen that sort of lie in some downcoast kingdoms. Woodcarver wannabes."

Nevertheless, modern-day Northernmost was a bustling place. Across the square, carpenters were putting up wooden stands for tonight's show—but every other wide-open place was occupied by street vendors. The guy with the "fine cloaks" was selling to packs who were already climbing onto the finished benches. Lots of heads were looking at the shadowed pavilion where the humans were standing.

The parts of Amdi that were in the open gave this audience a grand wave, but his voice stayed local: "This looks like a small version of the South End marketplace, doesn't it?" He came all back into the pavilion and began putting on Chitiratifor's glitzy uniform. "Nevertheless, this is the first place we've visited where the people actually seem to be intimidated by who's in charge." Despite his somewhat ominous words, Amdi sounded chipper. Maybe that was because Screwfloss had tethered Ritl by the kherhogs, well beyond the range of mindsound.

"Do you think he might renege on paying us?" said Ravna.

"Ah," Amdi said as he fiddled with his last cloak. He hadn't yet donned the fake tines; that would be the final touch, just before showtime. "He's more villainous than anyone we've run into since we escaped Chitiratifor. On the other hand, I showed him our safe passage from Tycoon. And you know how the airship was flying around here last night? Well, I told him we had Woodcarver's protection, too."

"What did he say to that?"

"He tried to laugh it off, but I could tell he was taken aback." Amdi looked up at Ravna and Jefri. He seemed to notice their anxious looks for the first time. "If he knew Tycoon was after us, we'd be locked up already. I figure if we can keep him wondering, we'll be okay."

———

The show was their best yet. Part of it was the enthusiastic audience. The rumors of the wondrous two-leg circus had had longer to ferment here than anywhere else. And part of it—the strangely pleasurable part—was that all the performers, in some sense even Ritl, had truly gotten their act together.

Ritl started things off, chased by a comically inept Screwfloss. Every time Screwfloss' leash-carrying member got close, Ritl would skitter away, sometimes to stand mockingly near one of Screwfloss' others, sometimes to run along the stands and carry on nonsense conversations with the nearest of the audience. The second time around, Ritl found the member-wide servant steps that led to the ruler's personal seats. Ritl danced along the ledge of the royal box, orating.

Jefri leaned close to Ravna. They were still both hidden from the crowd. "Those are statesmanlike noises," he said, grinning. "Ritl is coming on like a visiting monarch. I think she's promising the sun and the moon if the prince will meet her . . . requests? demands?"

Ravna wasn't quite so amused. "I just hope she doesn't get us executed."

"Well, there is that."

The crowd was hooting laughter. Maybe nervous laughter. The prince's private box was draped in deep acoustic quilting that might double as a form of armor. Guard and servant packs stood all around the box, but the interior was as dark as a cave. Pure this prince might be, but he did not project amiable lightness. Ritl didn't seem to notice, and her boldness was rewarded. Ravna saw three bejeweled heads move into the fading daylight. There were other heads too, but still in the shadows. The prince boomed a response to Ritl, who preened and blathered some reply. Now the crowd's laughter seemed more natural; Prince Purity too was playing to the audience. Ravna recognized the rippling of his heads as a mocking bow. Everyone but Ritl could see Screwfloss' leash-carrier sneaking up the steps behind her.

The crowd hooted even louder when Screwfloss pounced and then dragged the arrogant singleton back down the steps. Screwfloss shambled once more around the square, bowing this way and that. Ritl was dragged part of the way, complaining loudly. Ravna made a note to check the beast for cuts and bruises. This was conventional local humor, but Ravna Bergsndot wouldn't use such excuses.

Then Screwfloss was running back toward the circus pavilion, Ritl racing ahead of him. As she passed into the shadows, the singleton let out an impudent squeak and dived toward Amdi. The eightsome shrank away, and she honked singleton laughter.

"Damned animal!" Amdi said *sotto voce*. He slid the last of the wooden tines onto his paws, and pranced into the open. The sky was heavily overcast, so there was no risk in using the lamps: the spotlight tracked the Magnificent's progress toward center stage. The light sparkled and coalesced, synthesized from emitters that Jefri and Amdi had mounted along the top edges of the pavilion. For pre-tech creatures such as this audience, the dissociation of lightsource from light was magical. Amdi was always careful to claim that without special knowledge, the gadgets were useless. That was close to the truth, though the control interface was pretty intuitive. So far no one besides Screwfloss-as-Idiot had tried to steal the lights, and Screwfloss' attempt was a gag routine in which he made off with pseudo-sources that turned out to be kherhog patties.

The high point of the show was still the performance of the "clever singletons." That was Jefri and his juggling, then Ravna and her rope tricks, and finally some bogus spelling tests intended to impress those who insisted that intelligence meant more than juggling and knot tying. As usual, Jefri got the most attention, though Ravna's act now included a simple lasso trick. She walked around the square, followed by the spotlights and a sound show from Amdi. She got near enough to the front row packs that they could hear the silence of her mind, and see the awesome flexibility of her hands. As always, there was the goggling surprise of such first encounters, the combination of amazement and uneasiness and interest.

Then Ravna came to Prince Purity's box. The guards below it were a sharp-eyed bunch. When they looked up at her teetering height, jaws twitched crossbows. No lasso flicking at these fellows. Ravna stepped back and played to the prince in his box. The three crowned heads came forward, and after a moment, another appeared with a puppy on its shoulders. The pack was saying something, complimenting her? Maybe not. One of him was looking back, into the darkness of the box. It was almost as if there was some other pack in there. Who could be so close?

She rose up on the balls of her feet, trying to get a better view into the dark. *What if it's a human back there?* With that thought, she lost her balance and control of the lasso. She hopped around, trying to make it all look like part of the act.

"You okay?" Jefri's voice was a shout from across the square.

"Yes!" She didn't dare say the truth. Maybe there'd been no humans on that airship because Nevil's gang had already landed here—and they were here, now!

Ravna danced away from the prince's box, but now she was seriously distracted. She stumbled on her rope a couple more times, and even botched some of Amdi's spelling questions.

Finally, thank the Powers, Amdi segued into the finale, the pseudo-impromptu invitation for the audience to come down and be introduced "paws-to-tentacles" to the marvelous creatures from beyond the sky. Prince Purity said something from his box, and the packs queued up for the privilege. These people were more orderly than any they had run into before. Maybe it was the armed guards that materialized from the side streets. There were more of *those* than they had seen before, too. Prince Purity's operation looked more like tax collection than salesmanship.

Jefri cut across the square to be next to Ravna. For the petting zoo part of the performance, they were always together. Tonight . . . Ravna grabbed his arm. He stepped close, put his head close to hers: "What happened?" he said, almost whispering, somehow guessing that they mustn't be overheard.

Ravna put her lips by his ear and spoke as quietly as she could. "Keep watch on the prince's box. What do you see in the back?"

"Ah." Jefri didn't look up immediately. Arm in arm, they strolled back to the center of the square, to Amdi and the beginning of the "reception line." Partway there, Jefri casually looked back over the stands, at the prince's box. "The prince is still up there," he said in conversational tones. "I'd hoped he would come down for the petting zoo." And then very quietly: "I don't see anything else."

And then they were overwhelmed by the meeting and greeting. More than ever before, there were packs who wanted to faux chat, repeating Ravna's Samnorsk back at her. This far north, maybe they had heard rumors about the Domain; if Prince Purity wasn't already dealing with humans, he soon would be. Ravna looked out at the crowd, and suppressed a groan; even if second visits weren't allowed, this could last as long as the show at Winch Bottom.

Or maybe not: the prince's guards were bugling.

Amdi looked up at the royal box. "Prince Purity has announced the end of the public performance. He's going to bless us with a personal audience." The packs who had already paid were allowed through, but the guards encouraged them to trot quickly past the humans; there was no more extended chitchat. Ravna noticed more than one head looking nervously at the prince's box.

Ravna noticed Jefri signing to Amdi, out of sight of the royal box. Amdi's eyes widened in surprise. He waved to Screwfloss to take Ritl further away. "She's not going to mess me up with the prince." Amdi spread himself out into the newly vacated space, and looked very attentive as Prince Purity came down his private staircase one by one.

Jefri stood tensely beside her; he was looking at the prince, actually looking *over* his members. From here, they could see further into the royal box than had been possible standing right in front of it. And when the last of Purity came down the steps, there was no one standing between them and whatever mystery lurked within.

"Nothing as tall as a human is standing there," came Jefri's whisper.

No, but there was *something*, and now it moved partway out of the shadows. She still didn't have a clear view, but this looked like a singleton. Unlike the prince's members, this one's cloak was very dark. The creature didn't follow the prince down the stairs.

Ravna glanced at Jefri and he gave her a little shrug. If that singleton had been up in the box the whole time, it should have been difficult for the prince to keep his mind on the show. "Different customs?" he said softly. "Or maybe this prince is just personally kinky."

As the prince came across the square, the last of the commoners were cleared away. None were left in the stands either, but a number of packs still clustered on the streets that led into the square, standing as close to one another as packs could comfortably come. Others looked down from tiny windows that faced the square. Their audience was still large, but somewhat subdued, almost as if trying to pretend that it did not exist. Ravna noticed Amdi surreptitiously playing with the lamps, making sure the spotlight followed the prince across the plaza. Hopefully, this looked like an honor—but one that would also remind the fellow of powers beyond his ken.

No commoner clothing for Prince Purity. His capes and jackets were sewn from the pelts of hundreds of weasels. Ravna had seen such pieces in the Domain, but only for leggings and singlecapes. The fur-dressing process created a white that Tines prized for its purity—though to human eyes it was more a pale and grubby puce.

As the prince advanced, two guard packs circled wide around Amdi and the humans. Amdi was forced to close in on himself, but the guards didn't approach Jefri and Ravna. That privilege was reserved to the autocrat. Purity walked to within a few meters of them, visibly squinting in the spotlight. The creature was a fivesome, mostly overweight except for one puppy that stayed behind the others, its beady eyes just visible over their rumps. The four adults sat for a moment, heads bobbing in a pattern that Ravna took for a cocky smile. Unlike some in their audience tonight, the prince could not fully overcome his uneasiness about two-legs. Instead, he sent a couple of his members to walk close to Jefri and then Ravna. The two brushed around the humans' legs, tasted at the fabric of their clothes. Then as they retreated, the two gave Ravna a co-ordinated shove. Jef's hand kept her upright.

Amdi squawked a "Hei now!" chord.

The prince gobbled something back. Amdi started translating even as the autocrat spoke. The voice he chose for the prince was smarmy and sly: "No harm intended, Circus Master. I must say, these tottering creatures can scarcely keep on their feet." The prince's forward members continued to circle Ravna and Jefri, but just out of arm's reach.

Amdi puffed up, managed to look indignant despite the armed guard packs standing around them. His Tinish reply was overlaid with a Samnorsk translation: "We are honest performers, Sir. Have we not provided you with profitable entertainment?" Amdi poked a head meaningfully at the bags of loot that the prince's fee collectors were now counting into strongbox wheelbarrows.

Prince Purity hooted softly, a chuckle that Amdi didn't bother to recast into human mouth noise. He gobbled on. Amdi's overlay was: "Of course. My people enjoyed every minute of it and they've paid handsomely. But you held my center square here for hours. No traffic could pass. We are a trading town, my circus-minded friend. We can't ignore the damage that loss has caused to the market folk displaced."

Amdi gave an indignant squeak, dropping out of Magnificence for an instant. Meantime, the prince rattled on. Amdi's voice-over hurried to catch up: "You shouldn't be surprised that there are additional fees involved here."

"Um, perhaps we could contribute part of our agreed-upon payment to cover these expenses."

"Good, good!" Amdi's Purity voice got even more snotty. Somewhere under all the deadly tension, Amdi was having a good time mocking this villain. "I'm sure we can work something out. These laws after all—I make them. We will talk more on the problem tomorrow."

"Tomorrow? But milord, if you will recall, the whole point of performing tonight was to pay for supplies and be on our way before morning."

"Oh, I'm afraid that will be impossible. You are far too valuable to simply disappear into the night."

Amdi dithered a moment. What could he do? From under the pavilion, Ritl started squawking. It wasn't the focused sonic mayhem of a pack, but she was screeching louder than any human could shout. She bounced out to the end of her leash, blasting imperatives. Was that support for her fellow circus members or something more like "Stop thief!" and "Seize them!"

Amdi was looking off in all directions. The commoners had moved back from the wide streets. Some of them were bumping into each other, competing for space under awnings and doorways. Heads pointed upwards, and to the south.

Amdi spread out, actually invading the space of the two guard packs. After a silent moment, a knowing smile spread across his aspect. "I showed you my letter of safe passage, my lord."

Prince Purity emitted a dismissive noise. If he knew they were fugitives, that safe passage would count for nothing.

But Amdi continued, "I also mentioned to you that I had the protection of the Domain of Woodcarver. That nation may have seemed far away before now—but the sounds you heard over your principate just last night, that was the magic flier of Queen Woodcarver. You laughed when I mentioned our protection. You laughed when I suggested that her airship might come back to find us. Now please reconsider." And then Amdi shut up, as if he had made some stunning, winning play.

In fact, Purity didn't have any zippy reply. He was grinning much the same masterful smile as Amdi. He too had spread out, almost doubling his area on the ground. For a moment they looked like two frauds trying to out-bluff each other. Then Ravna noticed that both packs were looking off into the night, all in the same direction as the packs around the square. Amdi and Purity had spread out because they were *listening*.

Ravna and Jefri turned and looked up with the others. Full night was an hour old. The dark was starless, the cloud cover complete. Now . . . even to nearly deaf human ears . . . there was the sound of the airship's steam engines.

Powers above, don't let this be Nevil.

Amdi and the prince continued their proud poses, still grinning at each other. Purity's guards were buckling up their armor; maybe they weren't as confident as their boss.

Zzzzzzzzzzzzzzzzzzz. It sounded as close as this morning, but there was an undertone that had been missing then. "There's two of them out there," Amdi said in his little boy voice.

Sound became substance, looming out of the dark. The aircraft coasted toward them above the south road, descending gently into the plaza. There was plenty of room for Scrupilo's airships to land here, but the packs on board had extended poles to push the craft sideways to the edge of the open space. Eight members—two packs—tumbled out, carrying mooring lines in their jaws. They raced around, tying the airship to Purity's heroic statuary.

Amdi was playing with the lamps: multiple spotlights splashed along the airship's hull. They were looking at it head-on, but what she could see was *Oobii*'s design, adapted from aircraft of myriad terrestrial worlds, optimized for Tines World.

"That's too small to be—" Amdi started to say, but he was interrupted by the prince's laughter. A singleton was racing along the edge of the square, toward the airship. For an instant, Ravna thought Ritl had escaped. But this creature was larger than Ritl, and wore a dark cape. It came from the prince's box. Amdi brought down a spotlight, tracked the running creature till it disappeared among the crewpacks who had dismounted from the flyer. That moment of light was enough for Ravna to notice the golden highlights in the glossy blackness of the cape.

There was only one cloth in the world like that. So the stolen radio cloaks had not been lost, and—

The engines on the grounded flyer hummed down to silence while the buzz of the other continued to grow. She stared into the darkness above the southern road: the second craft was slightly bigger than the first. Its circular cross-section almost filled the space between the buildings. Amdi brought the lamplight to bear on it, diffused to reveal the expanse of what they faced.

Ravna saw that Screwfloss had probably been right this morning, claiming that there were no humans flying above them. Nevil's gang was most likely two hundred kilometers away, still at Newcastle on Starship Hill. But so was Woodcarver and anyone who could save them. The wash of light from Amdi's lamp revealed the design painted around the bow windows of the second airship. It was the disk of the world, surrounded by a godlike pack of twelve.

CHAPTER 31

The face-off between Purity and Amdiranifani didn't end quite as the prince might have wished. Some minutes passed while the airship crews made sure of the tiedowns; the prince's statues were more fragile than they looked. The radio-cloaked singleton went from one ground crew to the other. The creature didn't behave like any singleton Ravna had ever seen, not with the bombastic nonsense of Ritl nor the plaintive silence of a less articulate fragment. It seemed to be talking to the packs in a sensible way.

Finally a stairway was dropped from the second airship and one pack, a small-bodied foursome, emerged. Each member carried a pair of sticks that looked like the stocks of crossbows. They were strapped along the back, the metallic tubes extending to just short of the shoulder. They looked a bit silly to Ravna, until she realized they were lightweight guns—very much like the firearms she and Scrupilo had designed. The gun-toting pack approached Prince Purity, the radio-cloaked singleton walking almost shoulder to shoulder with it.

Pack and singleton stopped a few courteous meters away from the prince. When the singleton spoke, Amdi's voice-over translation sounded in Ravna's ears: "Well done, my good pack. You delayed the fugitives a fine amount of time."

Prince Purity gobbled back, Amdi's voiceover as snotty as ever: "It was at great expense, my lord. We all suffered, setting aside the Great Square for so many hours, pretending to enjoy this monstrous performance. Surely there will be some additional consideration for the unexpected unpleasantness of it all."

Ravna looked sharply at Amdi. "Quit exaggerating."

"I swear," said Amdi, "Purity really said that."

"Oh yes, Purity is as s-silly as your eightsome says." The new voice sounded like a frightened little girl, though the sense of the words was sardonic. It was the singleton, speaking Samnorsk.

Amdi rocked back on his haunches, all his eyes on the singleton. "Who are you?"

Now the singleton sounded like an adult human, vaguely familiar: "You'll find out soon enough, my fat friend."

The radio cloak covered most of the singleton's pelt pattern, but in any case, it was hard to identify a pack from a single member. Somewhere out there, each wearing its own cloak, was the rest of this pack. *But where did the little-girl voice come from?*

Prince Purity was staring at them all, perhaps realizing he was out of his depth. He repeated his demand for money, but more tentatively. The radio-cloaked singleton laughed and pointed its snout at the wheelbarrows of coin already collected.

The humiliation! Purity rose in heroic anger, his puce cloaks fluffed wide. All around the square, his soldiers unlimbered their crossbows. Two more gun-packs descended from the airships, and the local thugs wilted. Apparently they had seen what these firearms could do. Purity's gaze swept the guards, the crowd. He came down from himself and walked with stiff dignity from the square. No doubt tonight's story would be recast in his later speeches—but only when the contradicting facts were far away. His packs dragged the loot from the plaza. The crowds were gone, though Ravna could still see commoners, hiding in the shadows, watching with fearful fascination.

Tycoon's packs left Jef and Amdi and Ravna alone in the center of the square while the radio-cloaked singleton directed a search of the pavilion and the circus wagon. They grabbed both lamp interfaces and all the emitters, even the ones placed on the far side of the plaza. Then they took jaw axes to the beautiful circus wagon. *Strange*, thought Ravna, *I never really thought of the tinted wood and worn filigree as beautiful till now when it's being hacked apart.* The radio singleton showed no care for the folk art, but it directed the operation with great caution, evidently thinking there might be more magic toys to be found. All they found were the maps.

Meantime, Ritl had been released from the pavilion. She wandered around the demolition of the wagon. She looked mystified and maybe even sad, but soon she was giving advice to the ax-wielding packs. When her blathering was recognized as non-informative, the radio-cloak singleton took her aside. There was a short conversation. Then Ritl gave out a whoop and danced across the square, heading toward the airship with the Tycoon logo. She ran through the center of the square, gobbling even louder than usual. She dodged into Amdi's personal space and warbled something questioning. Amdi lunged out at her, jaws snapping.

Across the plaza, the radio singleton said something imperative. Ritl backed off, looking at Amdi with her head cocked, very doglike. Then she turned and resumed her run to the airship.

"What did Ritl say, Amdi?"

Amdi had piled into a defensive bunch, glaring in the direction of the departing Ritl. "I don't want to discuss it," he said.

The tech trinkets, including the maps, were all put aboard the ship that bore the sign of Tycoon. The radio-cloaked singleton walked back to the center of the square. One of the gunpacks followed, with Screwfloss. The remnant was complaining about something. The chord for "loyalty understanding" kept popping up. The singleton just ignored the remnant. He looked at the two humans and spoke in the adult human voice it had used before. "Such a long chase, but now it has ended happily. Come along." It started off for the airship that had landed first. Then it stumbled and turned. Its little girl voice spoke: "Correction. The humans go aboard Tycoon's ship . . . *squeak rattle gobble*—" That last was some command to the gunpacks.

As one of the gunpacks herded Ravna and Jefri across the square, another moved to stop Amdi and Screwfloss from following. The singleton turned to Amdi: "Not you, my fat friend. You go on *my* airship."

Jefri wheeled. "Now wait a minute! We all stay together or—" He closed in on the singleton, towering over him. The creature staggered back, its butt striking the cobblestones. One of the gunpack's members shifted its shoulders and its twin barrels slid forward till the muzzle silencers were well past its head. Another member stepped behind it, sighting between the barrels at Jefri. Ravna noticed that the other member of the gunpack was watching *her* attentively.

The singleton came awkwardly to its feet, but its adult human voice sounded amused. "I think in this case, you will *not* stay together. Fatso and the remnant are coming with me."

Jefri glanced at the twin barrels facing him. His hands were in fists.

Amdi came around his friend, pulling him back from the confrontation. "We have to, Jefri. Please. I'll be okay." But Ravna noticed that Amdi was trembling.

The singleton chuckled, started to say something, and then its voice shifted to the tones of the little girl: "Don't be s-scared. You'll like m-my ship."

Jefri unclenched his fists and stepped back. The anger in his face was replaced by wonder. "This thing"—he gestured at the singleton— "isn't anybody. It's just a comms network!"

Amdi was nodding. "What a dumb use for radio cloaks. We never guessed they'd be so—"

"Enough!" said the singleton, and the gunpacks pushed and prodded the captives toward their respective flying jails.

At the base of the ship, the air stank of fuel oil. It smelled exactly like Scrupilo's concoction. But Tycoon's industrial plagiarism was not complete; the dropdown stairs were pack-wide, grandiose compared to Scrupilo's design. *I wonder if they got the trick of stabilizing the hydrogen in the lift bags?*

Partway up the steps, she turned and looked across the square. There was no sign of Prince Purity, but she could see townsfolk and peasants still watching from the shadows. *We had a great show tonight.* The thought flitted inanely through her mind. Over by the other airship, the radio-cloaked singleton was still on the ground; Screwfloss and most of Amdi had already gone aboard. Two of Amdi's heads looked their way, and he chirped something encouraging.

Jefri stooped to look out from under the curve of the hull. He waved back at Amdi. Then the pack beside Ravna waggled its gun barrels and Jef continued up the steps, Ravna close behind. To aft, the steam induction engines were buzzing up to speed.

———

Tycoon's airship was the collision of Tinish imagination with the engineering realities of *Oobii*'s original design. The passenger carriage had been crudely split into two levels, the resulting interior decorated in a grand East Coast style. The main corridor was polished softwood veneer (easy on the hearing, you know), with frequent padded turnouts; packs could walk past each other with only moderate mental discomfort. The ceilings were mostly one meter thirty high— airy for Tines, but not high enough for a human to stand.

"I wonder what Nevil thinks when he comes visiting?" said Jefri. The two humans had been stuffed in a—well, to be fair, it might be a stateroom. The distance from the door to the outer hull was about two meters. The walls were heavily padded, probably thick enough to make a pack comfortable even though there might be other passengers within centimeters, in the rooms on either side.

"I guess Nevil's allies have about the same respect for him as he has for Tines," said Ravna.

A pair of fifteen-centimeter portholes were mounted in the hull, far enough apart to give a pack a good parallax view. The ship had turned and moonlight splashed across the cabin. "There's some kind of metal lid here in the corner." She lifted the cover. There was a faint whiff of potty smell, and the engine noise came louder. Ravna laughed. "A stateroom with its own toilet." The sanitary facilities aboard Tycoon's flying palace might be adequate—as long as you didn't care about the folks living in the lands below.

Jefri crawled to the hull and looked out one of the portholes. His face was a pale blur in the moonlight. "We seem to be heading south. I don't see the other airship." He stared out for a long moment. "Nothing!" He turned away from the port and continued more quietly, "I'm so afraid for Amdi."

"I don't know, Jef. Tycoon seems to be treating us decently." Her optimism sounded weak even to Ravna herself.

Jefri shook his head. "Only for the moment. There were two packs speaking through the radio cloak. The one who took Amdi had a voice like in Oliphaunt's tutor programs. I'm betting that was Vendacious."

Ravna bowed her head. "And the other voice, the little girl—"

"That *was* Tycoon. The monster said as much. And he dared to use the voice of one of his victims to speak the words."

Tines often favored a human voice based on their first language tutor, but the little girl's voice had been frightened and shrill, almost unrecognizable. *How long do you have to torture someone to learn their language?* "Geri Latterby," Ravna said softly.

———

In the end, their speculation and futile planning fell into uneasy drowsing. Jefri shifted uncomfortably on the cabin's mat. Of course, neither of them could stand up in the tiny space, but at least it was wide enough for Ravna to lie flat. Jefri was not so fortunate. Even with his feet propped up on the toilet lid, he was still cramped.

The sound of the airship's engines was a steady buzz, making the floor and walls hum in sympathy. Sleep eventually came.

———

Dawn was brilliantly bright. Ravna awoke thoroughly disoriented. Where could she be to see sunlight on embroidered pillows? Then she felt the buzz of the engines. She looked around. Jefri was watching her silently from the other side of their tiny cabin. The sunlight was from the twin portholes. The "pillows" were the room's acoustic quilting; their soft fabric was decorated with elegant landscapes. . . . And somehow she had annexed most of the floor space.

"Oops, sorry," she said, moving back to her side. "I didn't mean to thrash around."

Jefri just shrugged, but she noticed that he was quick to use the freed space to get close to a porthole. After a moment, he spoke: "It's all clouds down there, but we're still heading south. So much for the theory that Tycoon's headquarters is on the East Coast. I think—"

He was interrupted by the sound of something rolling down the main corridor. A moment later the door bolt lifted—but the door itself remained shut. Whoever was in the corridor tapped politely, emitting chords that Ravna recognized as a cheerful request to enter.

Jefri turned on his knees, crawled to the door, and slid it open. Outside stood a small-bodied foursome, dressed all in blue capes, surely a uniform. The creature stepped back a little fearfully, but then—perhaps because Jefri's eyes were at its own level, or perhaps because it was putting on a brave front—two of it pushed forward with a tray of food. "Twenty-three minutes. Twenty-three minutes, okay?" The words were spoken with Geri Latterby's voice, but they sounded like rote repetition. This creature scarcely seemed a torturer.

The food came in soft wooden bowls and consisted of overcooked vegetables and curd soup. Ravna guessed that it had been carefully chosen by someone with a secondhand knowledge of human diet. It tasted *so* good. Strange that in the clutches of Tycoon she was eating better than in all the time since the kidnapping. She lost herself in the food for a moment. When she looked up she noticed the Jefri had already finished and was watching her intently. Had he said something to her?

"Um. So what do you think is going to happen in twenty-three minutes?" said Ravna. *They take us off to interrogation? They come back for the dirty plates?*

"Dunno. But till then, let's check out the view." He returned to his porthole. Ravna downed the rest of her breakfast, then went to the other window. The sun was out of her face now. She could see clear sky above unending, brilliant clouds. Many kilometers away, a thunderhead broke the horizon. Details were lost in the distorted window glass, another example of what happened when Tycoon customized *Oobii*'s design.

Abruptly, the engine noise increased and she felt a chilly breeze.

"Jefri!" Somehow he had managed to *open* his port! Now she noticed the metal clasps and hinges.

"Hei, the benefits of low tech," he said.

"Um." Of course, it should be safe. They weren't more than three thousand meters up, with an airspeed of only a few dozen meters per second. She popped the other tiny hatch and pulled the glass inwards. The engine sound became a buzzing roar, and eddies of frigid air blasted around the cabin. But the view was utterly clear. She stared into the cloud deck, seeing detail within detail.

Jefri looked down as steeply as he could. "I figure they're taking us to the Choir!"

For a moment, Ravna's mind looked out much farther than the physical windows. So Nevil had been conspiring with just about every one of the Domain's antagonists. Who was villain-in-chief?

"Wow." Jefri's voice was muffled by the wind, but it brought her back to the physical view. The thunderhead was closer now, its tower a maze of light on dark, its anvil climbing out of sight above them. Flying with Pilgrim on the antigravity skiff, Ravna had come much too near such things. Pilgrim loved to fly right into the vertical drafts of great storms.

The pitch of the engines changed. The ship was angling away from the storm, but losing altitude at the same time. Soon the cloud deck had become fog, curling up to them. The turbulence grew.

"I hope these people know what they're doing," said Ravna.

"Maybe that was what the steward pack meant when it said 'twenty-three minutes.'"

Yes, a courteous warning.

The clouds closed darkly around them. They motored along for some minutes. Still descending? The clouds had come into their cabin. She felt tiny droplets of moisture condensing on her face and eyelashes. Outside, lightning flashed electric blue, diffused by the dense mist. The deck tilted as thunder crashed. Their breakfast bowls were scattered all over the cabin.

The lightning gradually diminished and after some minutes the airship broke through the bottom of the clouds. There were still more clouds below, but they were scattered flotsam in the grayish-green depths. A steady rain ricocheted off the hull. The turn and descent had brought the other airship into view. It was pacing them, perhaps a thousand meters away, but it was almost invisible except when silhouetted by the glow of distant lightning. Jefri was silent for some time, just watching the other craft.

In the hours that followed, the thunder and lightning were more distant, but the airship was not the stable platform of before. It rode up and down like a boat on ocean swells, except that this motion was much more arbitrary and abrupt.

They spent most of the time at the portholes, watching their progress from forest to jungle and swamp. They were flying so low that when the rain lessened, they could see flowers in the treetops and wader birds in the open swamps. This was very much like the environment of equatorial Nyjora, when the Techie had battled both the exploiters and the plague that was killing the last of their men. She glanced at Jefri; how little of that history made any sense here.

Jef didn't seem to notice her look. He was staring downward more intently than ever. "I still don't understand what Vendacious and Tycoon are doing here. We seem to be as far south as coherent packs can survive."

"How can you tell?"

"I can see a bit under the trees when we pass over rivers. There are Choir settlements—at least that's what I think they are. When these settlements begin to connect together, there's no way that packs can penetrate and still keep their minds. Look down there. Around the trees. That mottling, I think that's floating shacks."

". . . Yes." She could see a change in the texture of the river shore. And here and there, she saw polygonal shapes that might have been real buildings. Within an hour, they were flying over settlements in open clearings. As the day darkened into true twilight, the settlements merged and the forest was replaced by an unending, chaotic jumble of vegetation, swamp, and artifact.

By the time their little steward showed up, it was night outside—and pitch black in their cabin. The cabin had a small mantle lamp but it had seemed to be disabled. Besides delivering dinner, the steward showed them how to light the lamp. The foursome was a cheerful creature, not at all the jailer Ravna would have expected.

After dinner, the rain slackened and—strangely—the air became steadily warmer. They doused the cabin lamp and returned to the portholes. There was no more lightning, but no stars or moonlight either. Here and there, what looked like campfires shone below. The air coming in the ports smelled faintly of compost and sewage.

"We're descending," said Jefri. "We'll come down in the middle of that." But an hour passed. Two. They fell asleep as the rain increased and the air grew choppy.

The door bolt clicked, lifting open. Someone was scratching at the cabin door. Ravna struggled to wakefulness, confused. The steward would have tapped politely on the door and sung out for them to rouse themselves.

Jefri was up on his elbows. "What—?" he said, but very softly.

"Maybe we're finally landing?" Ravna noticed that she was whispering too. Pointlessly. Any Tines on the other side of that door could hear them fine.

The furtive scratching continued.

She put out a warning hand, but Jefri was already at the door. The hall beyond was lit by a single gaslamp. Two members were visible, but only in silhouette. One stuck a snout into the room, peering about. Then it wriggled past Jefri.

Powers above, it was Ritl! And quieter than Ravna had ever seen her. The singleton looked over her shoulder and gestured at the—pack?—beyond.

Not a pack, a piece of Mr. Radio; in the lamplight, Ravna could see an occasional glint off its cloak. The creature hesitated, perhaps communing with far off employers. Then it squeezed past Ritl and blundered around in the dark, evidently not much good at echo location. It flinched back every time it stepped on their legs, but there wasn't very much human-free floorspace. It ended up scrunched against the wall.

Ritl slid the door almost shut, then sprawled across Ravna's shins and pressed her head close to the narrow door opening, as if listening out into the hall. The light from the hall lamp made it easy for Ravna to see, though for the Tines, the room must seem very dark. The radio-singleton looked seriously nervous. And Ritl? Well, maybe she was scared quiet, but more likely she was just being animal crafty.

After a moment, Jefri said dryly—but softly!—"Well, who do we have here?"

The radio singleton looked up at the sound and seemed to relax. "Jefri, is it just you and Ravna there?" The words were barely the breath of whisper . . . but the voice belonged to Amdi.

Jef gave a stifled whoop. "Amdi! Are you okay? How—?"

"*Shh shh!* Gotta be very quiet. If you get discovered, it'll be almost as bad as if I do. But I'm fine, specially now that I'm talking to you. Part of our good luck is that Vendacious is indisposed, some kind of upchuck bug. That's why you didn't see him in person; he's still talking snooty, but he's barfing from half his mouths. Anyway, two of me are jammed in Ut's off-duty compartment. Ut and Il are the radio-cloak members on this ship. Your guy is Zek. Anyway, we have the door cracked open and the rest of me is next door. There's just enough of a sound path that I can think straight."

Jefri was silent for a moment, seemingly stunned by the turn of events.

On the other side of the tiny cabin, Ritl gobbled softly. It wasn't an alarm, just a variant of her usual scolding. Amdi's voice was resigned: "That Ritl. Even when she's helping, she's a pain." Then he continued, "We had to try and talk, Jefri. There are things you have to know, things we have to plan." To Ravna these assertions had a rushed, questioning quality.

Certainly, Jefri heard that too. His tone was reassuring: "It's okay, Amdi. How did you manage this? Who—what—is Mr. Radio Cloaks?"

"Utzekfyrforfurtariil is a Vendacious creation—though Tycoon doesn't know that. Vendacious figures that by controlling the Mr. Radio network, he's the puppetmaster of everybody."

Ravna looked at Zek suspiciously. "So what went wrong?"

Zek relayed Amdi's very human, little-boy laughter. "What do you think? Vendacious himself. He's smart, but he's the craziest, meanest of Woodcarver's offspring. And he's still all-male."

"Still?" said Jefri. "Any other pack with that makeup would have self-destructed years ago. That's Vendacious' miracle and a disaster for everyone else."

"*Not* necessarily," said Amdi, "Even his minions hate him. In any case, Vendacious isn't as smart as Old Flenser. And he's nowhere near as smart as *me*." Amdi's voice filled with confidence. "It's been scarcely a day, and I've already figured how to talk along paths Vendacious can't hear. That's how I contacted Ut, right under Vendacious' snouts. That's how we smuggled out Ut's cloak during his off-duty time. Of course, it helped that most of Vendacious was barfing sick at the time." His voice trailed off. "Vendacious has already figured out who Screwfloss really is. Vendacious, he *capered* when he learned the truth. Poor Screwfloss. Oh *Jefri*—" His voice collapsed into weeping, all confidence fled. "Oh, Jefri, this isn't like my show in the circus." The sounds of weeping abruptly stopped, and his voice continued: "Th-this is something I have to do. I'll do my best; I promise."

Jefri started to say something comforting, but was interrupted by another voice: "I help."

"Who spoke?" said Ravna. There was a moment of silence, long enough to be aware of oppressive meat breath and animal body heat. Finally:

"I'm sure that was some part of Utzekfyrforfurtariil," said Amdi. "Every one of him hates Vendacious."

"But I thought Mr. Radio was being used like a line? How smart can it be?"

Amdi said, "As a line or a ring or a star, he's as dumb as you'd expect, just good enough for Vendacious' purpose. I think if he were all in range of himself, he'd be smarter than most packs. But he hasn't been together much since Vendacious' broodkenners first assembled him."

Jefri took a closer look at Zek. "But even partially connected, he's still smart enough to learn some Samnorsk. Or is he just a blabber like Ritl?"

Amdi emitted a snort (via Zek): "He's much smarter than that idiot singleton. In fact—and this is something Vendacious doesn't know—big parts of Mr. Radio sometimes have mutual radio communication. Right now, there's three of him on these two ships—not enough to be very smart. But depending on atmospherics, he can reach several others and be almost a complete person. That doesn't happen very often, and so far, Mr. Radio has kept it a secret from all the packs who are using him."

"Hmm," said Ravna. "I wonder if he's smart enough to play Princess Pretending."

"Huh?" The word came from both Amdi and Jefri. After a moment Ritl chimed in with a mimic interrogative of her own.

"Sorry." She had violated her personal ban on Princesses. "Straumers call it a 'Man in the Middle' attack."

"Oh yeah," said Amdi, "I thought of that. The problem is Vendacious has conditioned all the members to follow certain forwarding protocols. At best Mr. Radio is variably intelligent. From moment to moment, he may be smart enough for simultaneous lying. In between, he'll drop the ball."

Jefri nodded. "And if he fluffs even once, the game is over."

"Right."

Zek's own voice spoke over Amdi's: "Besides, I still not good to be a person, even when I can think with all of me."

Amdi's voice: "His whole life has been torture, but if he ever gets himself together, I'll envy him. That's our radio future! And *I've* never even gotten to use radio cloaks!"

Ravna smiled. Amdi had never given up on having his own radio cloaks. Even at the edge of a torture pit, that annoyance could still distract him. "Amdi, when we get out of this, I promise we'll get you your own cloaks. You, you *all* have worked a miracle here." Even Ritl.

"Yeah," Jefri was nodding. "Can we meet again, Amdi? Safely?"

"I'll figure something out. We've talked too long this time. One last thing. Vendacious and Tycoon are both scary, but they're very different, and Vendacious is lying to Tycoon about lots of things. Vendacious doesn't want you talking to Tycoon. Your greatest near-term danger is that Vendacious will assassinate you. He would have killed you back at Prince Puce's, except it would have been too hard to disguise from Tycoon. He was very angry that you got put on Tycoon's airship."

There must be a bright side to this. "Could Tycoon be turned into an ally?" said Ravna.

There was a moment of silence. Then: "Maybe. But see, Tycoon really, really hates humans. And one in particular."

Ravna thought of what Tycoon must have done to little Geri. If this was what the creature did to lesser enemies—

"So who is his number-one enemy?" asked Jefri.

"Johanna."

"What!"

"Why?"

"I don't *know*!" Amdi's voice was plaintive. "Johanna has always been the most beloved human in the Domain—sorry, Ravna, but you know what Jo did for the veterans. You'd be second, though!"

"Ah, thank you." She glanced at Jefri. "We've got to figure this out."

"And not get killed." That was probably Mr. Radio, but the point was valid, whoever made it.

"Yes," said Amdi. "Now we gotta go. I . . ."

Amdi seemed to hesitate, then Zek gave a squeak and collapsed across Ravna's middle. He remained silent as Ritl gobbled softly at him.

Jefri bent to stroke Zek with his own forehead, much the way a pack will try to rouse an injured member. Ravna was surprised that any good could come from a human making the gesture, but after a moment, Zek struggled back against the wall. He swayed, still disoriented.

"He must have lost comm very abruptly," said Jefri.

Ravna heard no alarms from the hallway. Without Radio, their activity here might remain unnoticed for some time. "Amdi's side could be fine," she said.

Jefri nodded. "But we have to get these two back to wherever they're supposed to be." He said something to Zek. It sounded like he was humming and whistling at the same time, but different tunes. Ravna had never figured out how some of the Children could manage such coordination. But Zek waved his head uncomprehendingly. Next to Johanna, Jefri Olsndot might be the most Tinishly-fluent human, but it still took practice for a pack to make sense of humans attempting Tinish. "Okay," said Jefri, speaking Samnorsk now, "can you understand me?"

"I hear," Zek said.

"Amdi?"

"No."

"He's making sense," said Ravna. "He may still have a link to some other members."

Jefri nodded. "You alone now?"

Zek gave another uncomprehending shake of the head.

Jefri glanced at Ritl. "Together, these two could probably get back where they came from . . . at least if they don't run into somebody who wants explanations."

"They got here okay," said Ravna.

"Yeah, but that was when Radio had most of his mind and Amdi was along for the ride." He paused. "Well, if Zek is nearly single now, there is something that might work. After all, Ritl is already a desperate singleton and Mr. Radio Cloaks must be a loosely-held soul." Jef reached out and softly patted Zek's shoulder. Then he slipped his hand under the creature's cloak, pushing it away from where it covered Zek's shoulder tympana.

Zek flinched back with a whistling sound. Lots of needle-sharp teeth were just centimeters from Jef's face.

"Not to worry," Jefri spoke the words gently, calmingly . . . to whom? "If this is like Flenser and his cloaks, Zek has sores all around his tympana. I just have to be very gentle. And Zek has to trust me." He lifted the cloak free of Zek's left side. The creature was trembling, but it didn't bite.

Jef folded the left side of the cloak over Zek's back. "You're really out of contact, aren't you, kiddo?" He looked at Ravna. "This is a long shot, but I can't think of anything else." He waved for Ritl to come close. The singleton hesitated, maybe taking one more close listen on the hallway, then it crawled close to Jefri. Ritl's eyes were on Zek, her head shifting uneasily back and forth. Jefri scooched himself out of the way, then tugged at both creatures, urging them close together. Now they were both sitting mostly on Ravna.

Ritl made a Tinish "yech" sound, then gobbled on, softly complaining. Now that Zek was out from under his cloak, his mindsounds would be loud to any nearby member. This close to each other, the two creatures were in a fight, flight, or merge situation. For normal pack members, "merge" would have been by far the least likely outcome. Even in this desperate situation, the two acted like debutantes confronting sexual perversion.

"Well, crap." The human words seem to come from the space between the Tines.

"They synched up!" Jefri's voice was full of wonder. "Can you understand me?"

"Yesss." The voice sounded more annoyed than frightened. Ritl plus Zek might be smarter than either was separately, but it wasn't a happy camper.

Jef said, "You lost contact with the rest of yourself, right?"

"Hurt noise, lost all radio."

Ravna said, "Zekritl? Can you make it back to your cabins?"

Puzzled head-weaving was the reply.

Jefri rephrased: "Go back? Safe and quiet?"

The duo looked at each other. "Okay. Will try." The two climbed over Jefri and Ravna, an elaborate dance that endeavored to keep Zek's exposed side available to Ritl's hearing. Ritl lowered her head and slid the door open. A moment later she was out in the hall, turned so that mutual thought was still possible.

Zek followed, but the top of his cloak caught on the door. Jefri helped undo the snag and guided him out. Jef peeked out into the hall, blocking Ravna's view. She heard someone say softly, "Bye bye."

Jefri watched them for a few seconds more. Then he slid the door shut and jiggled its bolt into position. He was shaking his head. "By the Powers, they look like Tami and Wilm staggering home from the pub."

He lay back, silent. . . . "You know, it could have been a low charge problem. Scrupilo's radios fail like that. When they've been away from sunlight too long—*bam*, no error message, no bit-rate backoff, just silence."

"Right," said Ravna. "I'll bet these cloaks were at the end of a long-use period." She thought about it for a second, imagining innocuous explanations for the apparently global failure. They were possible.

After a moment, Jefri said, "Oh, Amdi. You didn't have to be a hero."

CHAPTER 32

The next morning, it was the friendly steward, not the gunpack, who was at their door. "Amdi must be okay, too, Jef," said Ravna. Believe it.

The airships were cruising lower than ever, but the cloud cover was incomplete. Sunlight slanted down in misty shafts, shining in fragments of rainbows where it found patches of rainfall in the greenish dark.

The city extended to the limits of their vision. It was still chaotic; you could see it was a slum. But now Ravna sensed patterns lurking in the landscape. If you ignored its constituent junk, this place had a claim to beauty, a clash of fungus and forest pretending to be a great city. And even the details were not all unpleasant. She could smell cooking fires. The food smells were *good*, almost covering the sewage taint that also hung in the air.

"Powers. Look, Ravna, the Tines just swarm!"

Most of the streets were hidden by surrounding structures, but she saw . . . plazas? Most were just five or six meters across, but they were connected to occasional larger open spaces. In the distance she could see what might have been a hectare of stony open space. Tines were everywhere—on rooftops, in the streets, in the plazas. Myriads of Tines, but crowded so close together there surely could be no packs at all.

"Ten years ago, this looked different," said Ravna. "*Oobii* took pictures as it approached Tines World." The Tropics had been in the whole disk images only, and there had been only a few breaks in the jungle cloud cover, but, "What we saw back then was not so crowded and somehow—well, it looked *simpler*." She watched silently for a moment, wondering. Down Here there was no possibility that the Choir itself was super-intelligent. For that matter, there wasn't even the communication technology to support wide-area cognition: Mindsounds would take minutes to percolate across the megacity. And yet, there was some form of group activity. The mob seemed to have greater and lesser densities, and not just where Tines gathered around the piles of rotting vegetation that filled many of the smaller plazas. There were places where she could see the ground, where members were separated by meters of empty space. Such open areas couldn't be for coherent thought, though, since there was no pack-like clustering. It was almost as if. . . . She focused on one particular empty area, watching until the airship had passed it by. *Ah!* "Those empty areas? They're moving."

"What?"

"Just look—" Given that they each had their own tiny porthole, it was impossible for her to point. "Look down that street," zigzagging into the distance, mostly unobscured by surrounding structures, there was only one thing she could mean.

"Right . . . okay, I see a couple thin spots in the crowd." He watched for the minute or so that they could keep the path in view. "Yes," he finally said. "I think the uncrowded areas were slowly moving further away. Huh. I suppose you would see that in pre-tech cities. Didn't they have special policemen to order the traffic around?"

"I don't think it's traffic control. The sparse areas also shrink and expand. Look at that plaza."

For a moment the view was nearly perfect for Ravna's purpose. Thinning swept in from a side path. Then the plaza *and* the main street became a little less crowded, Tines moving slightly to the sides of the street. As they drifted back to the middle of the street, it became as packed as ever—but the thinning continued to propagate down the side path.

"Yeah," Jefri said slowly, amazement in his voice. "These are density waves moving across the city, but we can only see them in the streets and plazas."

"It's like the Tines are swaying to music." Truly a Choir.

The airship executed one of its long, slow turns and their view swept across territory that had been directly ahead. Now the nearest lands were hidden by low clouds, but pillars of sunlight shone into the far distance . . . upon the largest structure Ravna had ever seen on Tines World. "Powers," she said softly. "There was nothing like this in the approach photography."

They were too far away to see details, but the main structure was tetrahedral. Its edges were slumped and irregular, but on *average*, the pyramid's lines were perfectly straight. Parts of the surface gleamed golden even in the haze. Secondary pyramids sat at the base of the huge one, each quite possibly larger than Newcastle—and at the corners of *those* were still smaller pyramids. Smaller and smaller, Ravna followed the progression down to the limits of her vision.

Their airship was turning again. The pyramid slid out of sight. "There's the other airship," said Jefri. The craft was well below them, descending into the lower cloud deck. It swirled the cloud surface like a fish diving through sea foam. Then it was gone, and a moment after that they, too, were in the clouds. They broke through into a drizzly gray morning. The ground below looked nothing like the jumbled slums or the great pyramid. She caught sight of spires and domes very like the palaces of East Coast royalty. *I'll bet that's where Vendacious and Tycoon lord it over the locals.* Directly ahead of the other airship, the ground was as open and flat as a tabletop. The landing field would have been recognized by any low-tech inhabitant of an earthlike planet, though this one was marred by floodways and several large ponds.

Five structures hulked at the end of the field. They were small by comparison with the pyramid, but each was large enough to shelter an airship. The clamshell doors on two of them had been slid open.

———

Vendacious stood by his ship's landing pylon and watched the ground crews work to lash down Tycoon's airship.

How I hate the Tropics! The thought surfaced every time he returned here.

The heat and humidity were as bad as any he'd known in his well-remembered life; this morning's drizzle counted as comfort by the standards of this place! Then there were the parasites, the gut worms and flesh burrowers, and all the diseases—themselves caused by microscopic predators, according to the ever-cheery Dataset. He never used to get the vomits, and now that happened regularly. In the early years of his time here, Vendacious had lost two members to disease. Finding appropriate replacements had been no small challenge, even with an endless stream of raw material to choose from.

And yet . . . part of Vendacious was gazing to the left, at the magnificent palace Tycoon had built for him. Vendacious couldn't have risked such magnificence up north, not with Woodcarver's death sentence hanging over him. Now that two of Vendacious were Tropical, sometimes he actually felt an insane fondness for the place. In Dataset, Vendacious had read about natural selection. The notion was quaint and obvious, but no fun when you were doing it to yourself! It was frightening to realize that if his triumph were delayed long enough, he might *prefer* this hellhole to the north.

Meantime, he'd have to put up with both the climate and Tycoon. The local fragment of Radio stood just a few meters away, providing a link to the great Tycoon. Ut looked even more miserable than Vendacious felt. Part of that was the heavy, muffling cloak the creature had to wear. Part of it was the fear in the creature's eyes. Ut had been taught to fear and obey and keep secrets. The lessons necessarily had been delivered in covert ways, unseen by those outside Vendacious' inner court. After last night, Ut had even more to fear. *What had the animal been up to, playing with the cabin keys?* The guards said he hadn't been wearing his cloak, so whatever it was had been mindless and confined to the ship. That was the only thing that had saved Ut from a proper and final punishment—no matter how suspicious the death might look to Tycoon. Nevertheless Ut faced some strict discipline; no more deviations would be tolerated.

Ut fearfully came closer. When it spoke, it was to relay Tycoon's confident and demanding voice: "Recall, Vendacious, I want both two-legs delivered to me. What's left of Remasritlfeer, too."

No doubt Tycoon was lounging about in the comfort of his palace. The fat bastards' notion of "surviving in style" was to have Vendacious do all the hard work. Eight years of practice had not made it any easier to suck up to the fool, but Vendacious managed a respectful response: "I understand, sir. Their airship is just now being moored."

"What about the two packs who were captured with the humans?"

Vendacious had been expecting this question. With the right strategy, he wouldn't have to release them. "They're loyal dupes, but eventually I should be able to undo the humans' influence."

Ut relayed a sigh. "That's the way it has so often been with these two-legged monsters. One wonders how they can fool anyone."

"Their *technology* gives them an overwhelming advantage, sir."

"Of course. But in the end, that will not protect them from me."

Vendacious grimaced. You couldn't talk to Tycoon for more than a minute without his ego slopping out. Of course, that was half the reason he was so easy to manipulate. "Your time will come, sir. . . . I see the ship's hatch has opened. I'll have a wagon deliver the humans directly to you."

Mercifully, Tycoon wasn't interested in further conversation; there was no need for more groveling. Vendacious stayed near the landing pylon but spread out to watch the prisoners coming down from the other ship:

Ritl. All that was left of Remasritlfeer. He watched the singleton as it pranced regally across the concrete, a bit of flotsam that could still cause trouble.

Ravna and Jefri. With Johanna gone, these were the two most dangerous humans alive. They could destroy everything he had created. From interrogating Amdiranifani and the Steel remnant, he knew how Chitiratifor had botched his mission.

Still, a clean solution might have been possible if Tycoon had not meddled in the follow-up search. And now? Perhaps it was just as well these two weren't in his clutches. The temptation to end them would have been irresistible and alas, he'd already spent far too much of his credibility by murdering others he'd held for Tycoon.

He watched the rickshaw wagon pull away with the two humans and the singleton. Tycoon's guard padded along after.

What then was the good news in this debacle? Amdiranifani. He was perhaps the ideal hostage and certainly an entertaining victim. Breaking down a genius was often the most fun, especially in this case, in which the victim still thought it could outsmart the interrogator.

————

When the airships landed, Timor Ristling was up in his dungeon. The early morning had brought the usual rain, but also a good breeze. Maybe it wouldn't get too terribly hot today. He sat in the westside window, enjoying the rainy breeze, doing his best to ignore all the old aches and pains. They were still there, but if he gave in to them, he would not have a life.

Timor's dungeon was in one of the four spires that surrounded Tycoon's palace. This was the highest point anywhere in the Reservation—though the Choir's pyramid was so much taller that on sunny mornings most of the palace was in its shade. From his west-side window, Timor could look down on the airfield and the cuttlefish ponds, as well as the factories beyond. He kept his ankles wrapped around the nearest window pillar and leaned back firmly against the wall. Just sitting on a ledge so high up was deliciously scary.

The lead airship was audible now. It slanted down toward the pylon in front of Vendacious' hangar. Okay, so nothing *officially* belonged to Vendacious—but he controlled that area and the palace annex, and all who lived there. It was a miracle that Geri had survived her tendays in the annex.

He watched the landing crew tie down the first airship. The airships reminded him of insystem freighters floating on agrav; the similarity always made

Timor sad. *Someday, someday, if Ravna can only win . . . we'll make it back to the Beyond.*

Several packs got off the first ship—and now the second aircraft was coming down. Tycoon had been unusually secretive about what to expect. In principle that should mean Timor was almost clueless, since very few packs in Tycoon's palace spoke Samnorsk. On the other hand, the cuttlefish gave him occasional clues in their scatterbrained way, and Timor had become adept at building speculations out of Tycoon's silences and complaints and brags and favors. Five days ago, these two ships had abruptly left. Tycoon had let slip that Vendacious was aboard, so action against humans was probably planned. If no humans were aboard this second ship . . . well, that might be a very bad sign.

Someone was coming out of the second ship! It was a singleton or maybe a small human child. Timor's eyesight was almost as bad as the average pack member's; all he was sure of was that this passenger was not a pack. Timor climbed down from the windowsill and grabbed the binoculars Tycoon had given him. The gear was heavy and—of course—without a bit of stabilization or enhancement. Timor had had to wheedle a connecting frame out of Tycoon; the guy had complained about the inconvenience of dealing with human limitations, but Timor could tell that he was secretly proud to show off. Tycoon claimed that telescopes were the invention of his own pack brother, more than ten years ago. "We really don't need you humans, you know." Tycoon said that a lot.

Timor rested the device on the window ledge and looked through it, seeing nothing but a lot of rain-wet concrete. No sign of that small first passenger. Ah, now he was looking at some part of the airship. The main hatch was hidden beneath the curve of the hull, but he could see a pack near the entrance. It was watching something that it thought was important. Timor looked for a second more, holding the optics as steady as he could. . . . A gunpack came smartly down the stairs, its gun muzzles down, but watching in all directions. It looked like Mr. Skeetshooter, the fellow who usually guarded Timor.

And then there was a human. A guy, tall. From this angle, it was hard to . . . that was Jefri Olsndot! *But I thought he was one of Nevil's toadies?* The thought flitted out of his mind because a second human had appeared.

Ravna!

Timor hunched forward, losing the view for a moment. When he found her again, Ravna had descended the stairs. She seemed to be leaning against Jefri. Seeing her here was the best thing he could imagine . . . or was it the worst? He'd know when he saw which direction they were taking her. Mr. Skeets herded Ravna and Jefri to a little rickshaw wagon. There was the singleton, already aboard.

After a moment the rickshaw driver pulled them away, followed by Mr. Skeets. They were headed here, to the House of Tycoon! The rickshaw disappeared beneath his tower's view. He watched the airships a few moments more, but saw only crew and maintenance packs.

Timor slid down to the floor, the binoculars now unnoticed in his lap. Maybe he should keep watching, but he was too busy thinking about what this could mean and what he should do: Tell Geri. Decide how to approach Tycoon on this. Timor had gotten better at guessing how the big guy would react to developments— even if the *reasons* for the reaction were not always clear. In the beginning, Timor had tried to explain that Ravna was a good person who should be an ally. That had not worked very well, though Timor was sure—*almost* sure—that Tycoon would not kill her out of hand the way Vendacious wanted.

Suddenly he was overcome by the need to move; he'd plan on the way. He climbed to his feet and set the binoculars in their velvet box. Geri's cell was above his. Getting up the stairs was always a pain, though Tinish steps were easier for him to climb than steps the size most humans preferred. He'd considered complaining about the problem—but there was no way to make the stairs more convenient for his bad legs. If the Big Guy took him seriously, he might just move Timor out of the tower entirely.

The tiny stairwell was cool, the walls and steps slick with condensation. The door at the top was metal, edged with a rubber sealing ring. He tapped politely on its surface, then popped it open.

"Hei, Geri. It's me, Timor." Actually, it couldn't be anyone else, not through this door. "Can I come in?"

There was no answer, but Geri replied only on her really good days. Timor eased the door open and stepped into the cold semidarkness. Actually the room was pretty warm by Domain standards, but it was at least ten degrees cooler than outdoors, and unlike in the stairwell, the air was relatively dry. Timor himself had lived in this room for a few tendays—till the lack of windows and the hassle of moving in and out of the heat had gotten to him. Geri would have that problem too if—*when* she felt well enough to leave the room.

"Geri?"

Shadows shifted and a head poked up. "She here. She say no visit." That was the jailer, a not very bright foursome—but one of the few packs who spoke some Samnorsk.

"Hei, Jailer," and he tried to gobble-whistle the Jailer's given name.

As usual Jailer bobbed a smile, but whether she was amused or pleased, Timor had never been able to figure out. The pack was gathered together all on one side of the bed. Geri became visibly upset when a pack surrounded her. As Timor settled down on the other side, Geri shifted uneasily under her blankets, shrinking away from him. She stared determinedly away from both Timor and Jailer. This must be one of her bad days, when she couldn't bear to be touched, much less hugged.

Darn the luck, but he had to tell someone. Timor rested his hand on the edge of the five-year-old's blankets. Geri was years younger than Timor now, but he was still only a little taller than she was. Once upon a time, Geri surely had understood that Timor was older, just stunted down to her size. Now she often seemed to confuse him with her Academy playmates. Since her time with Vendacious, there was a lot she was confused about, and lots more she refused to think about. "Geri, I have good news. Ravna is here! I saw her myself!"

Her violet eyes shifted in his direction; some distant emotion passed across her small, dark face. Timor took any expression that wasn't fear as a positive thing. The little girl seemed to consider him for a second. "What did she say?"

Um. What a smart and deflating question. Geri could do that. He remembered the four-year-old he'd known back in the Domain. Back then, she'd been inquisitive all the time! "I haven't actually talked to her yet. I'm going down to Tycoon right now. Maybe I can help her."

Another pause, but Geri didn't look away. "Can I come? Can Edvi come? We can help too."

She liked Tycoon, but this was the first time she'd ever talked of going to see him. Unfortunately, Edvi was almost certainly dead. "Not this time, Geri. I have to get down to Tycoon right away. But I'll tell him that you need Ravna."

Interest dimmed, but after a moment Geri replied, "Okay."

———

The stairs extended downwards only as far as the veranda at mid-tower. When Timor got there and emerged into the heat, it was like diving into a pool of very warm water.

The veranda was the only way in or out of the tower—and that only if you could convince two gun-toting guards to let you pass. One of those packs stood around the door now, watching Timor impassively. Timor gave him a wave and limped a few meters around the curve of the tower to where the other pack—it was Mr. Sharpshooter this morning—sat by the elevator dock. "Hei, Sharpsie. I want to go down. Must see Tycoon."

Sharpsie rolled his heads in an officious, irritated way. He exchanged some hooting and gobbling with the pack by the door. The gunpacks really didn't like to leave just the one guard here. On the other hand, it was Tycoon's rule that Timor was not to be allowed to run around by himself. In the end—no big surprise—Sharpsie caved in. The four of him came to their feet. One of him slid open the elevator gate, while two others grabbed Timor's shirt and pants to make sure he didn't fall through the space between the veranda and the elevator carriage. These guys thought Timor's tremor was much more dangerous than it really was. He had only fallen that once, and that was on the stairs. . . .

The elevator cable extended from the tower dock, diagonally down to a point on the palace dome. The ride was always exciting, the carriage slightly swaying, nothing but thirty meters of empty air between them and the dome below. Tycoon claimed that elevators were just another of his long-lost brother's inventions. Maybe, but the thin little cable was made by char-burning woven reeds in just the right way—surely *that* was another trick stolen from Ravna's starship.

Five minutes later, he was safely at the dock on Tycoon's own residential level. Mr. Sharps didn't object when Timor took the shortcut through the aquarium room, though he insisted on walking both in front and behind.

They weren't more than five steps into the room before the cuttlefish spotted him. "Hei Timor! Timor! Hei Ti'Timor! Hei—hei—h'h'h'hei!" The squeaky voices started nearby, sweeping away from the door he had just come through, along the walls of the aquarium, all the way to the far end of the hall—where the little squeakers could not even have seen him yet.

Timor moved as fast as he could down the aisle between the leaky glass tanks. Any other time he would have stopped in wonder, and stayed to chat. The aquarium had a water ladder down to the pools and streams of the airfield, so there was often news here from very far away. The cuttlefish were such marvelous creatures. The torpedo-shaped bodies were just thirty centimeters long. Their eyes covered one end; their tentacles extended the rest of their body length. Hundreds of them tumbled and turned as they swarmed to follow his progress. *I don't have time, little ones!* Their greetings had shifted into questions. The cuttlefish were not mindless, but they were differently minded. The cuttlefish were scatterbrained and careless of their own lives. But they spoke Interpack. Tycoon claimed that they had spoken a Southseas version of pack talk when they were first discovered. They had learned a little Samnorsk just since he had started talking to them.

Two of Sharps ran a little way ahead. One looked around the corner in the direction of Tycoon's audience hall—and suddenly the whole pack seemed to go on parade, all its steel claws clacking on the floor in unison. Something strange was going on ahead. Timor slowed down, provoking an irritated hiss from Sharps' two behind him.

He reached the corner, and peeked around. The audience room doors were shut! Tycoon hardly ever did that. He liked to wander back and forth and schmooze with the cuttlefish. Not today. He must be running the air-conditioning a lot, like he did when he really wanted to impress someone. Okay, that was good.

Unfortunately, there was a pack standing by the doors, glaring in their direction. That was Sharps' boss, what would have been the royal chamberlain back in Woodcarver's palace. Timor straightened up as much as he could and approached him. Mr. Sharps' two walked in formation with him, then merged with its two members that had gone on ahead. All four stopped and came to attention. Sharps' maneuver was supposed to be fierce and impressive, but to Timor he just looked like doggies with toy guns strapped to their backs.

Timor walked on forward, right up to the boss pack. He really needed to get through these doors. If Tycoon would give Ravna a fair hearing, they were all home free. The problem was, sometimes the Big Guy would go running with his preconceptions. Vendacious was always trying to take advantage of that. *What if Vendacious is in there too?* Timor stifled the thought.

"Hei, Boss." He waved at the doors. "Tycoon want me now. I help with words."

The boss pack stared back impassively. This one had no sense of humor, and today he seemed even less jolly than usual. Several of him looked past Timor at Sharps. There was a warbling exchange of views. Timor could only pick out a few of the chords, but he made up the rest with this imagination:

Boss pack: "Hei, Sharpsie. Did this two-legged clown really get an order from the Big Guy to come down here?"

Sharps, doing his best to stay at full attention: "No way, Sir. Jailer is the only one who's been to the tower today."

The Boss turned all his attention back to Timor, and what he actually said in Samnorsk came as a surprise even to Timor's imagination: "You no go here. Tycoon make that real order. To me, about you."

CHAPTER 33

Tycoon's great palace might not have been *where* Ravna had expected, but it was every bit the grandiose thing she had imagined: huge, domed, and spired. Unfortunately, she and Jefri spent the rest of the morning stuck in the lowly outskirts of the place, even as the rickshaw whisked Ritl merrily off to some more honored destination. The gunpack guided Ravna and Jefri toward magnificent twenty-meter-wide stairs—then off to the side, where there was an awning-shaded area. Packs brought them food (yams!) and some kind of weak beer. So they sat and looked across the airfield at the airships and the long barracks-like structures beyond. Eventually the airships were wheeled into their hangars, but there was no end to mysterious comings and goings near those barracks. The clouds scudded away and the sun beat down and things got *really* hot, even here under the awnings. Jefri paced to the limits that the gunpack would allow, looking at everything, arguing with gunpack and the occasional servant, even though nobody seemed to speak Samnorsk. Finally, he came back, looking as wilted as Ravna felt. "You okay?" he said.

"Yeah." This was very much the setting of the Age of Princesses, and yet another blow to her childhood fancies.

"I think this is some kind of psychological warfare," Jefri said.

"They're softening us up?"

"Maybe." He looked around. "You know, a lot of this doesn't look so regal up close. I see mildew, water stains. Choir aside, there are good reasons why Northerners never settled here. Maybe Vendacious and Tycoon came here out of *weakness*. Maybe they're moving the furniture around right now," he jerked a thumb at the palace's main entrance, "polishing up the part we're going to see."

Hmm. Ravna looked across the airfield. The hangar doors had been slid shut, and there was no further activity around them. This side of the mysterious barracks, there were hectares of open space with just a pack or two, perhaps fishing at one of the ornamental water pools. This emptiness was in the middle of the most densely populated place on the planet. Somebody had some clout. Rather than fraud and façade, maybe this was Tropical reality.

The sun had slid into afternoon before they were finally ushered into Tycoon's grand palace. Yes, it was grand inside, too. Everywhere she looked, packs hustled this way and that; most of their members had the plush pelts of Northerners. Ravna and Jefri were led through vast carpeted rooms, up more stairs to only slightly smaller rooms, their walls draped with acoustic quilting. She noticed the kinds of imperfections that Jefri had mentioned. There was a faint odor of mildew, an occasional squishiness in the carpet. But the walls soared, and the dome overhead almost seemed to float. Tycoon and company had been cribbing a lot of tricks from Domain designs and, at least indirectly, from *Oobii*.

After the fourth set of stairs, Ravna would have been just as happy to be back under the outside awnings.

Up here the rooms were not large. Their guide opened doors to reveal a short hallway. At the far end, a pack stood by another set of doors. This pack was dressed in full cloaks that would have made sense on a summer day up North—but which looked a bit silly here. Gunpack waggled its rifles, urging them forward as the doors behind them swung shut.

The shutting of those doors seemed to be a signal to open the inner doors. *Almost like an airlock.* The thought flitted by at almost the same instant as a breath of cool air swept through the opening. They walked forward, into a room in which the air temperature couldn't have been more than 25C. She stumbled at the surprise; the sudden change was both a relief and discomfort. Jefri helped her across the room to benches set before a cluster of Tinish thrones. This was some kind of audience chamber.

Sunlight spilled through muddy glass. It was their first view to the east since they had left the airship. A second-degree pyramid towered high, but the second-degrees were like foothills before the immensity of the first-degree pyramid. Ravna had to look up through the ceiling windows to see the top of that.

It was an odd thing to see in a throne room. Ravna had to forcibly yank her attention back from the windows. Directly ahead were elevated throne seats. A smaller perch—for a singleton?—was set close by. All of those were unoccupied, but the room was not: To the right, a sevensome spread across a set of lesser thrones. Some meters to the right of him was a second pack. At first she thought it was Godsgift—but no, it wasn't, though it was dressed with the same harlequin gaudiness as the Godsgift she had known in the Domain.

The first pack gobbled something at the gunpack and then spoke in Samnorsk: "You don't recognize me, do you?" Two of the pack had patchy Tropical pelts. "Not even the voice I'm using?"

Vendacious. At least it was the voice they'd heard via Zek, doing business with Prince Puce.

Jefri gave him a stony look. "Where are Amdi and Screwfloss?"

A smile rippled across the pack. "They are guests in my annex. They are cooperating with my investigation. They have nothing to fear. You have nothing to fear if you cooperate equally." He jabbed snouts at them as he spoke. Now he paused and sat back in a dignified posture. "In a few moments you will have the honor of meeting the great Tycoon."

The Tropical pack popped into the conversation with, "I'm sure we'll get along famously if we all cooperate." The speech was chipper and unthreatening—*and where did this fellow learn to speak Samnorsk so well?*

The question was forgotten as the gunpack came to attention and bugled out royal flourishes. An instant later, the pack-wide doors behind the thrones were pulled open. A single member came strolling through, wearing a radio cloak. It looked well-fed and rested and almost certainly wasn't Zek. The critter headed for the low seat by the thrones. Immediately after the singleton was seated, a heavyset eightsome came through the doorway.

Ravna had seen packs as numerous—Amdi was eight, too—but several of this fellow's members were hulks, bigger than Pilgrim's Scar, even if not as tough-looking. The pack wore plain silk cloaks that would have been understated elegance, except that one or two had drag stains. Ravna watched the eight settle themselves on the thrones, their gaze focusing implacably on Ravna and Jefri. So this was the pack at the center of all their problems the last few years. What sort of creature could conspire with Vendacious—and still be alive after all those years?

The gunpack's bugling stopped, but now Vendacious took over with, "Bow to the great—"

There was an angry squeak from behind the thrones. One more figure came into the room. Could a pack as numerous as Tycoon be raising a puppy? No, this was Ritl—and as loud as ever. She was dragging a large stool, and Ravna guessed her squawking meant something like, "I could use a little help here!" Ritl dragged the stool across the carpet, toward Tycoon's thrones. She tipped it down unseemly close to Tycoon, then scrambled aboard and looked around. You really couldn't see much expression in a single Tines, but somehow Ritl looked . . . smug.

Ravna glanced back at Tycoon; he was still all staring at her and Jef. The pack waited a moment for Vendacious and Ritl to pipe down. When he finally spoke, it was with that totally inappropriate and self-damning Geri voice they had already heard via Mr. Radio: "I have waited far too long for this." He switched to Interpack for a moment, then back to Samnorsk: "Vendacious, which is the leader, the one your puppet deposed?"

"That's the smaller of the two, sir. Ravna Bergsndot. She managed the Domain's invention development program."

Tycoon hooted gently, a Tinish chuckle. "Ah yes. The machine operator." He pointed at Jefri. "And the big fellow? Is that really . . . ?"

Vendacious replied in Interpack. Ravna only recognized the name "Johanna," superposed on a connection marker.

Jefri must have understood: "Yes, I'm Johanna's brother," he said.

Tycoon leaned forward, all of his eyes on Jefri. He stared for a full ten seconds while Vendacious gobbled on, urging Tycoon to do . . . something. Finally, Tycoon shook his heads, an irritable negation. Some of him looked at Ravna; one of him was watching Ritl. "You two humans should have been here seven tendays ago. Instead you murdered Vendacious' best assistant. You murdered most of Remasritlfeer. Then you managed to trek almost all the way back to your precious starship. Was this magic technology, or are you simply much deadlier than even my friend Vendacious has always claimed?"

Jefri's face clouded. "Neither, and you are full of lies. We—"

Ravna interrupted: "What does Ritl say happened?"

The singleton in question was glaring at Vendacious, a low-level faceoff. A strangely large percentage of Vendacious was glaring right back. It occurred to Ravna that Ritl might be one of the few creatures with whom Vendacious had no leverage.

Tycoon reached down and focused a soft hooting sound on the singleton. As Ritl twisted to look up at him, he said, "Poor Ritl. I tried to question her before this meeting. She is a talker, but not very smart. It's quite possible that she doesn't remember exactly how the rest of her pack died."

Vendacious gobbled something.

"Speak human," said Tycoon. "I want these two to understand what we're saying."

"Yes sir. I just said, we'll eventually figure out what these two humans did. After all, I still have their servants to question."

The eightsome waved dismissively. "However you humans escaped, you only hurt your cause by doing so. Events have passed you by."

Jefri: "We'd be dead now if we hadn't escaped."

"Nonsense!" said Vendacious. "My lord Tycoon's purpose in this expedition was to show Ravna that cooperation was her only choice."

Ravna had the feeling that murder and conspiracy were piled in very deep layers here. She touched Jefri's arm. *Put the Olsndot temper in a bottle, okay?* After a moment, he settled back on the bench, seeming to get the unspoken message.

She looked up at Tycoon. "You say events have passed us by. What is it that you want from us now?"

"I want nothing from the Johanna sibling." Perhaps Tycoon didn't notice that he was clawing the thrones as he said that. "But from you . . . I want to convince you that opposing my wishes and those of"—he glanced at Vendacious—"what's the stooge's name?"

"Nevil Storherte, my lord."

"Yes. Opposing me and Nevil is suicide. You and Woodcarver must accept the coming alliance—ah, but you don't know about that either, do you?"

Ravna tried to smile. "As you say, we've been out of touch. Why would my opposition matter?"

"You still have the loyalty of many of the two-legs. You may have technical knowledge that will help us manage two-legs machines. And you may have influence with Woodcarver."

I bet Woodcarver is still the Queen, and Nevil has his back to the wall. Nevil is so desperate he's finally gone public with his foreign allies. She tried sit up a little straighter, act like she had some kind of power in the world. "I mean no disrespect, sir, but how did you intend to convince me?"

Tycoon looked back and forth at himself, nonplussed. "Didn't you look out the windows as you flew here?"

"Yes. We saw hundreds of kilometers of chaos, and then this reservation you've built in the middle of it all. Is there some secret weapon that we missed?"

"I suppose *I'm* the secret weapon." The voice came from the other side of room, from the harlequin-cloaked Tropical. "Or in proper terminology, I should say that I represent the secret weapon. I am the Choir's gift."

"Godsgift?" said Ravna. "We ran into another of you up North."

"You murdered another of him up North," said Tycoon.

Next to her, Jefri was all but shaking with outrage. *Lies and truth, how to untangle them?*

The local version of Godsgift was watching them intently. "Don't bother to deny the murder," it said smoothly. "Some of that godsgift escaped, enough to tell us how it left part of itself behind to attempt negotiating. We know what happened." It waved the issue away. "It's not a great matter. We gifts come and go, rather like a feeding clump in a city square, though we are rarer and globally significant." The pack slid off its seats and strolled around the other packs to come closer to the humans. The gunpack had to retreat to make room.

The Tropical walked up to them with the ease of a pack who knew humans—or who didn't fear losing its mind in others. In either case, it had none of the aggressive posture of Tycoon or Vendacious. "Our secret weapon has been all around you. The Choir." It gestured through the high windows at the mountain range of pyramids.

"And your god is speaking through you?" Sarcasm edged Jefri's voice.

The godsgift cocked a head. "Oh no. Or only indirectly. But by this evening the Choir will know everything that is being said here now." The creature pointed again at the pyramids. "Surely you see the gathering?"

Ravna looked through the crudely made plate glass. Sunlight was coming almost straight down, mottling the golden surface of the grand pyramid.

Jefri's voice was soft and wondering: "Those shadows, Ravna—I think they're mobs of Tines." Individual members were visible as dots on the closest of the second-degree pyramids. On the great pyramid, the thousands were a finely mottled discoloration, creeping higher and higher. This surpassed Pilgrim's most extreme Choir tales.

"Are you impressed?" said Tycoon. "*I'm* impressed, and that is not easy to do."

Ravna looked way from the windows. ". . . Yes," she said. "But just how does this make a secret weapon? I know the Tropical Choir has existed at least as long as the northern civilizations, but it has never mattered except as a barrier to land travel between the north and the south. There's no way that the Choir could be any smarter than an individual pack or human." *Not down here in the Slow Zone.* There were group minds in the Beyond, but even they were never more than witless hedonists. You had to go into the Transcend to do better—and *there* large group minds were just one of a number of paths to real Power.

"Ha ha!" said Tycoon, his high-pitched voice like a child teasing. "They doubt your Choir's godhood."

Godsgift had settled itself on the carpet around the humans. Now it laughed. "*You* doubt the Choir's godhood, too, O Tycoon." The pack shifted around in its harlequin cloaks. Its mangy pelt had big bare patches, altogether consistent with the ragamuffin clothing. Ravna wondered how uncomfortable the fellow was with Tycoon's air conditioning.

Godsgift continued with a kind of sly diffidence: "In truth, all *I* remember from the Choir is an enormous feeling of well-being. I pity you Northern packs who won't give yourself to it. I pity the humans even more that they can never become part of it, even if they wished. Both you and they are so upset about the murders the humans committed. How little you have to lose that you squabble over a member here, a pack there." But now it paused. "I suspect that as a matter of cold fact, Ravna Bergsndot is right about us. The Choir is *not* smarter than a unitary pack. But there are places and times—millions of places and times every day—where it is almost as smart. And sometimes, the Choir's gifts—those such as myself—last longer. It is a sacrifice, since for a time I am left as limited as you.

"So yes, the Choir as a whole may not have what you call intelligence, but it *is* a happier way to know reality than is your stunted existence." Godsgift was silent for a moment, most of the fellow staring out at the pyramid—doing a good imitation of thoughtful yearning. Abruptly the pack gave a start. "It just occurs to me that you two humans could satisfy your curiosity about the Choir in a way that no unitary pack ever could."

Tycoon leaned forward. "What can they do that *I* cannot?"

"Well, sir," replied the godsgift, "you *could* experience the Choir, but it's unlikely your parts would ever reassemble into that unitary self you value so much. On the other, um, hand," he waved a paw in an artificial flourish, "these two humans could ascend with the crowds. They could witness the highest pinnacle of the Choir, where myriads stand within the diameter of a single song, where even such as I would dissolve. Their minds would survive—by the fact that, alas, they can never be more—and they could report back on the experience!"

Vendacious perked up. "I think that is a capital idea!"

Tycoon had his heads together, apparently giving the suggestion serious thought. "I don't think it is as simple as you say. A few years ago, I had Remasritlfeer build a closed and padded rickshaw wagon, one that he could propel from the inside. The idea was similar to what you're suggesting but without the humans—and of course the rickshaw couldn't have climbed any pyramids. Even so, the project was a failure. Remasritlfeer wasn't more than twenty meters outside the Reservation when the mobs attacked his rickshaw and tipped it over." Tycoon was watching Ritl, but the singleton just continued grooming its claws, oblivious. "He would have died in the experiment, except that we had a cable attached to the wagon and were able to drag it back before the mob could get to him."

"Ah, but consider the ecstasy lost!" said the godsgift, carried away by an ecstasy of its own salesmanship. "I think it's likely the Choir was simply trying to free what it regarded as imprisoned members. I know you Northerners have all sorts of terrible myths about the Choir, but in fact, except for boundary fights and occasional pyramid sacrifices, individual foreign Tines are rarely killed by the Choir. For humans it should be even safer, since the creatures have no mindsounds to provoke aggression."

"Hmm," said Tycoon. His technical curiosity reminded Ravna a little of Scrupilo: nothing was too gross if it had an experiment in it somewhere. "But wouldn't the two-legs be dealt with as corpses or invading animals?"

"Oh, no, I doubt that would happen." The godsgift waved breezily. "In fact, I'd wager that no human would ever be harmed at the heart of the Choir."

Ravna glanced at Vendacious. She saw a smile flicker across the members Tycoon couldn't see. So Vendacious knew this claim was false. The godsgift and Vendacious were doing a good job of maneuvering herself and Jefri into a front row seat at the Tropical sacrifices. The godsgift didn't have Vendacious' air of palpable menace, but maybe that just meant that he was the more dangerous of the two.

The godsgift rattled on enthusiastically, ignorant of or ignoring Vendacious' sly smile. "I tell you, I almost wish I could be human. You could go to the very top. You could see everything there is to see—and still exist afterwards to remember it! Maybe there is something beyond the sounds of mind there. Either way, you would *know*!"

Ravna raised a hand. "No. I think we'll pass." She noticed Jefri nod emphatically. "Perhaps another time." *When we're not being held prisoners under threats of torture and death.* "In any case, I thought your point was that the Choir was Tycoon's secret weapon."

"Oh! You want the crass details." The pack sounded hurt that it had failed to sell them on a hike up sacrifice hill.

"Enough of this religious talk," said Tycoon. "The crass details are the important part. Here we're sitting cool and comfortable in the middle of endless mind death. From the safety of the Reservation, I *do business* with the Choir. The combination of their multitudes and my genius makes me the greatest power in the world." He waved at the radio-cloaked Tines that sat silently on a nearby stool. "With my radio network, I am watching across a market domain that is ten times wider than your royal Domain. My factories create more goods than all the other businesses in the world put together. I'll wager you've seen some of them yourselves. My presence simply can't be disguised anymore. My inventions are changing the entire—"

Ritl had been uncharacteristically quiet. Now she let loose a chittering complaint.

Jefri leaned close to Ravna's ear. "Ritl says Tycoon brags too much!"

Tycoon gave the singleton a couple of heads of attention, and gobbled a rather mellow form of "Keep quiet." Ritl grumbled almost the way she used to around the campfire, but settled back on her seat.

For a brief moment, Tycoon looked a little embarrassed. "The whole of that one was a good employee," he said. He looked back and forth at himself, as if recovering his train of thought "Nevil Storherte understands the situation. In less than a tenday, he and I will reveal our alliance. But even now, if I can convince you of my power, there could be a place for you in the new order of things."

"I'm eager to be convinced, sir," said Ravna. *Can it be? I actually have some leverage with this guy? Okay, then*: "We've always been impressed by your successes, even though we had no idea how you managed them."

The pack actually preened. "Heh. Be prepared to learn then. This afternoon I'll show you one of my factories. Multiply that by a thousand and you'll know what you're up against Today. Multiply by a million and you'll know for Tomorrow. You could be a valued junior partner."

"I'm grateful." She wondered who had provided the job recommendation. "There is a matter of trust, however—"

"You are not in a position to set conditions, human."

"Nevertheless, there is the matter of the three young humans that you took."

From across the room, Vendacious said, "Both humans will be returned unharmed."

Jefri burst out with, "*Both?* You fucking murderer! And what about the Tines killed in the kidnappings?"

"There were no killings," Vendacious replied flatly, "not by our packs. Of course, we can't know all that Nevil Storherte may have done."

Tycoon's heads were turning unnecessarily back and forth between Jefri and Vendacious. "Yes," he said, "humans don't really care about the lives of packs. Despicable maggots. . . . Understand: I dislike you two-legs as a race, but I've found that business can bring cooperation between anyone." Heads flicked in Jefri's direction. "Almost anyone."

Jef shook his head. "Hei! At least tell us the names of the surviving—"

Tycoon shifted forward, all heads weaving in Jefri's direction. "You dare make demands of me, Jefri-brother-of-Johanna?" His Geri voice climbed in pitch, stretching into an inhuman hiss. "Jefri-brother-of-Johanna-who-killed-my-brother."

Jefri came up off the bench, but his anger seemed swept away by shocked understanding. "Brother? Powers above, you're Scriber Jaqueramaphan's brother?"

Tycoon swarmed down upon Jefri. Maybe what saved Jef was the fact that godsgift was still sitting close around him. That pack emitted a surprised squeal and exploded in all directions, incidentally getting in the attackers' way and knocking Jef backwards over his bench.

Ravna dove sideways along the bench, trying to block the surge. She felt two of Tycoon slam into her, then had a glimpse of his members lunging under the bench, claws reaching. At the edge of the fray the gunpack was maneuvering around in confusion—trying for a safe shot?

"Wait! Stop it! Stop!" she shouted, but in fact the madness had ended. It couldn't have lasted more than a second or two or she wouldn't have been around to shout. Tycoon was all around her, but his jaws weren't snapping. Four of him were on the other side of the bench now. They dragged Jefri Olsndot off the floor, set him on the bench behind Ravna's. Their claws made little spots of blood where their grip sank through his clothes, and two of them had jaws right by Jef's throat.

For his part, Jefri was sitting very still. Ravna remembered when he was little, how Jef and Amdi would mock fight. Sometimes that would get out of hand, and Jefri had learned the safest thing to do was just become still and submissive. It was certainly the right strategy now.

Tycoon held him tightly for several seconds. The eightsome's voice boomed around the room, hissing and screaming that certainly wasn't Samnorsk, and wasn't Interpack either. Finally he gave Jef a hard push and backed away from him. All eight stared at Jefri for a moment more, then dabbed at the froth that dribbled from various jaws. Finally, he turned a couple of heads toward the uncertain gunpack and gobbled at him. Ravna recognized an imperative and the word "dungeon."

So maybe no factory tour today.

CHAPTER 34

The "dungeon" was actually a suite of rooms near the audience chamber. It had running water and air conditioning. Was there any closed area in this palace that *wasn't* air conditioned? Dinner was delivered—more yams and beer.

Once they were alone, Ravna walked around the high-class accommodations. "I assume these walls have ears pressed against them," she said.

Jefri shrugged. "The truth is one thing that jackass really needs to hear." Jefri had a long bloody slash on his face where one of Tycoon's claws had grazed him. He thought a second and then shouted: "Jo didn't kill your brother, damn it!"

"But do you think he really is Scriber Jaqueramaphan's brother?"

Jefri sat back on his chair. The seat actually had a back to it, though not quite what would suit a human. "Once upon a time, I think he was. Now, I think the pack is a rebuild."

"A what?"

"That's a word Johanna came up with for something she saw occasionally at the Fragmentarium. Sometimes a pack—usually a rich, foolish pack—tries to recover a prior form of its personality by incorporating several new members."

"Wouldn't that just be a merge pack?" These creatures had more reproductive modes than any dozen races she had known in the Beyond.

"Not exactly. Rebuilds are much rarer; the broodkenners find puppies that are likely to contribute such skills and mind styles as were in their client's former personality. Then the client tries to mold itself and the puppies into what it was before. You noticed that four of Tycoon are a lot younger than the others?"

Ravna shook her head. "They all looked grown to me."

"They're all adults, but—my theory is that the four older ones really were a fission sibling of Johanna's Scriber. The pack is trying to recover what it was before the split." Jef's face twisted into an unhappy smile. "Scriber and Pilgrim were Jo's first friends here. You know how she always talked about him:

Scriber Jaqueramaphan, the mad inventor. He was a fairly recent fission product, and he always seemed a bit unhappy about it—like a human regretting a broken marriage."

"And it looks like the other half of the fission felt the same way." Ravna was quiet for a moment; now here was a story for Amdi's collection of romance novels!

Jefri was nodding. "This would explain a lot: the commercial empire building—that's from the old entrepreneurial half; the wild inventiveness—that's what the pack imagines of Scriber; and even the murderous hatred of humans—somehow Vendacious has convinced him that Johanna killed Scriber."

So perhaps Tycoon was not a villain . . . not naturally a villain. They sat for a moment in silence. "Okay, then," said Ravna. "We know what we're up against. That has to be an improvement. We've got to convince this fellow of the truth—"

"—without triggering more violence." He gave another smile, this one not despairing. "I'll be my very nicest, no provocations."

"I'll be properly respectful, too. We've got to find out which children are still alive."

Jef nodded. "Yeah. I'm afraid for Geri. Tycoon's Samnorsk vocabulary is adult; he's obviously been reading. But Geri's voice, when Tycoon uses it, that's like a confession of—"

Of torture at least, thought Ravna. She raised a finger to her lips. If there were ears pressed to the walls, there was much that should not be spoken. "Another thing: somehow we have to learn more about Johanna."

Jefri gave a little nod, and seemed to be choosing his words carefully. "Yes. Tycoon wants her dead—which means he thinks she's still alive. But he doesn't seem to know where she is. And no one mentioned Pilgrim, either."

They stared at each other for a moment. When Pilgrim and Johanna were missing together they were generally off snooping in the agrav skiff. She had told Jefri about their mission to the mouth of the Fell. In the past, Johanna and Pilgrim had hidden for tendays at a time near foreign cities. Hiding within Tycoon's operation would be much more difficult than any of that, but it was possible that right now the two were—she leaned toward Jefri and traced a circle with a dot on the arm of his chair—right here.

He gave another little nod. "It could be. It's another thing to watch for."

The next morning, they were wakened by a pack bringing breakfast. It waited impatiently for them to dress and eat and then hustled them out of their cool "dungeon" and down all the stairs they'd had to climb the day before.

It had been raining, but now the sky above was brilliant blue. Thunderheads still hid both the great pyramid and the sunrise. The air was sopping wet, but this was probably the nicest moment of a tropical day. Considering how much cooler and drier it had been back in the dungeon, Ravna could not fully savor the moment.

She and Jef were piled into one of the rickshaw wagons and rolled across the landing field, accompanied by the usual gunpack. On the north side of the field, two of the hangars were open. Packs were working around the airships, but at this distance it was impossible to tell what they were doing.

Maybe it didn't matter, because their driver was not taking them toward the hangars. This might be the factory tour Tycoon had advertised. Their course angled to the south, occasionally crossing bridges over the floodways they had seen from above. The morning air was much clearer than on their flight in. What had been lost in cloudy mists was now visible . . . dozens of the long, barracks-like buildings. But even now, she could not see the most distant of them.

As they neared the first structure, she realized it was at least fifteen meters from floor to ridge and almost forty meters wide. The ground around it was littered with huge piles—of what? Refuse? No. Up close she saw lumber and finished metal stampings, all more or less neatly set on pallets. Lines of Tropicals dragged carriers back and forth, moving the . . . factory inputs, that's what they had to be . . . into the main entrance. Their rickshaw had to angle even further south to avoid that traffic.

They turned again and rolled straight toward one corner of the entrance, out of the way of the haulers. An eightsome was standing under the portico: Tycoon, here to greet them in person. And there was his radio singleton and the godsgift pack. There might have been another gunpack back in the shadows.

"Powers be praised," Jefri said dryly, "I don't see Vendacious." There was only one other pack in the apparent entourage, a small-bodied foursome.

As Ravna climbed down from the rickshaw, she heard a childlike human voice. At first she thought it was Tycoon, but the voice was shouting, "Ravna! Ravna!"

She turned and saw—*"Timor!"*

The boy had come through Tycoon and was limping toward her as fast as he could go, his arms outstretched. Ravna ran across the concrete toward him, Jefri right behind her. They met just a few meters short of the waiting packs. Ravna knelt, hugging him as she might a child as young as Timor looked. Today, he didn't object. "I am so glad to see you!"

"I'm so glad to see *you!*"

When she set him down and let go, Ravna saw the tears streaming down Timor's face. He was laughing or crying, maybe both. After a moment, he looked away from Ravna and took a step toward Jefri.

"Hei, Timor," Jefri said solemnly and stretched out his hand. "How are you?"

Timor reached out, shook his hand. "I'm fine. Are you helping Ravna now?"

"I—" Jef glanced at Ravna. "Yes, Timor, I am." He hesitated, then nodded. "I really am."

"Have you seen Geri and Edvi, Timor?" said Ravna. "Are they okay?"

"Geri is getting better. We're both in dungeons up on the main spire." He gave a little wave toward the palace. "Edvi, I'm afraid Edvi is—"

"Edvi Verring succumbed to one of the bloating diseases. I did my best for him, but alas—"

Ravna looked up at the interruption and saw that all of Tycoon was watching them intently. But the voice, that had been the one Vendacious normally used, and a radio-cloaked singleton was standing near Tycoon. She couldn't help but glare at the poor innocent. "So then, Vendacious," she said. "You had custody of Edvi? Has anyone looked at the body, verified your diagnosis?"

As she spoke, Timor slipped his hand around her fingers. She felt a warning squeeze.

But Vendacious did not seem upset by the question. His voice came breezily, "The diagnosis was obvious. I've preserved the remains, however. You are welcome to inspect."

Timor's hold was still tight.

"There's no immediate need," she replied.

Tycoon made an impatient noise. "That's good." He said, "You are not the boss of us, Ravna Bergsndot. I've brought you here to discover if *you* can work for *me*." Some of him was staring over her shoulder at Jefri.

————

It was a bumpy start to their factory tour, but Tycoon's mood seemed to shift as often and as fast as sunlight and clouds. They went into the hall and climbed up to a long platform that ran the length of a production line. Tycoon insisted that Ravna walk with him, at the front of the group. Now the eightsome sounded very much like Scrupilo, the proud engineer, pointing out this detail and that, full of opinions about everything. His snouts swept the length of the hall. "This is twelve hundred meters long, with two thousand Tines working at full shift. This is one of the older halls, so it is not wired for electricity. All the main power still comes from steam engines. And yet, I'll wager you have nothing so grand as this single factory up in your Domain."

Okay, he was even more a braggart than Scrupilo. Still, this was preferable to some of Tycoon's other moods. "You're quite right, sir," she said, and that was the truth. The far end of the hall was almost lost to sight. All of Scrupilo's North End operation would have fit in this one building. She could see no coherent packs on the floor below, but Tines were crowded almost shoulder to shoulder at work points long the line. The activity was rapid and intricate, unceasing, like the sweatshops that the Princesses had overturned. She tried to think of something nicer than that to say—perhaps an admiring question. *Wait.* There was one part of this picture that didn't fit any of the ancient file images. A water stream flowed just this side of the production line, almost directly under the elevated walkway. This channel was like the ones out on the airfield, and seemed to run the length of the hall. Where the skylights let the sun fall upon the water, she could see tiny squid-like beasties flitting about. "What are those creatures in the water, sir?" she asked.

From behind them, Timor piped up, "They're cuttlefish!"

Tycoon shrugged. "In Interpack they're called—" and he gobbled a simple chord. "It means small swimmers with eyes on the sides and grabbers streaming from one end. This particular variety can remember and repeat simple phrases. I use them to carry short messages, when no packs are at the destination."

Ravna leaned a little further out and looked straight down. Yes, the critters had enormous glassy eyes. Their tentacles were long and moving all the time. And Tycoon didn't seem to have anything more to brag about them! Interesting. She brought her gaze back to the assembly line itself. "What are you making in this factory?"

"Today? Today, this line is set up for rain gutterage gardenware. Hmmph." He was making little annoyed sounds at himself, as if realizing that this did not fit his grand image. He turned a head and rattled Interpack at his radio singleton. A question, it sounded like to Ravna. The singleton was silent for several seconds, but when it replied, its gobbling was much more musical than normal Interpack. Ravna realized that it was chanting numbers stacked into chords. Tabular data. Tycoon summarized in Samnorsk: "Ta reports two hundred tonnes of product per day, five thousand rain gutters per hour. Still to run four more days on this lot." Somewhere Tycoon must have a radio singleton stationed with an army of clerks. "The rain gutters are mainly for use within the Choir region. Nowadays internal sales are my greatest source of income, certainly of raw materials. But in four days, we'll be making something else here. Productivity. Flexible productivity!"

"Yes, sir," said Ravna. "We saw all manner of your goods while we were in the Wild Principates." That was flattery, but again the absolute truth—and another mystery resolved. "But how do you design the actual steps to be performed, the—" Workflow was the term she would have used if she were dealing with *Oobii*.

Tycoon waved airily. "That is where my genius for detail work comes into play. There is the high-flying inventor part of me and then there is my interest in the smallest detail"—Two of him had been looking back as he spoke, and now suddenly he was off on a new topic.—"Timor! You are delaying me!"

Tycoon had separated Timor from Ravna when they entered the hall. Since then, the boy had been limping along behind the Ta singleton. "Sorry," he said, hustling forward.

"Where is your rickshaw?" said the eightsome.

"Um, back at—oh, there's another one." Timor pointed at a small utility wagon by the outer wall.

Tycoon reached out a member and snagged the little red wagon, dragging it back to Timor. "Get in. I won't have you holding things up." Two of him glanced at Ravna, "Normally I have a servant to take care of this, but there isn't room for one with this crowd." He waved at the various packs accompanying them—and then seemed to notice Jefri. "You!" he said. "Come over here and pull this wagon."

"Yes, sir." Jefri gave a Tinish bow and came forward. Ravna thought she saw a smile hiding just below his solemn manner.

"Now, where was I?" Tycoon said, proceeding along the walkway. "Yes. Details! In fact, I've discovered an assistant for that. Timor is quite good at detail planning, better than any pack besides myself. He's even devised methods for planning the planning. Quite remarkable."

Ravna glanced at Timor, now riding along in the little wagon. Timor looked back, smiling hesitantly. "I hope it's okay, Ravna. It's the sort of thing you do, but you do it so much better."

She grinned. "That's only when I have *Oobii*. Good for you, Timor." And now she knew who had given Tycoon the glowing job recommendation for her.

As Jef pulled Timor along, the boy pointed out features of the factory floor, where intermediate parts were brought through side doors, how the racks on the steam-powered main line held the parts so that simple Tinish actions could complete each assembly step. For a wonder, Tycoon kept quiet, letting someone else do the bragging.

Jefri nodded, looking down into the mob. Finally, he glanced at Tycoon. "Everyone is working so closely. I don't see a single pack."

The question and tone were very polite, but Ravna held her breath.

Tycoon walked along for several seconds, not replying, maybe waiting for Timor to answer. When the eightsome finally spoke, he seemed to ignore the question: "You know, I pioneered the factory line. I had the original idea back in the Long Lakes even before I fissioned. Then I actually implemented the invention when I moved to East Home. The easterners are open-minded; they even had a primitive form of the idea. You see, most work doesn't need a full mind. In fact, if you really had to think about what you're doing, you'd go mad with boredom. So I thought to myself, why not take the idea of a sentry line and make it a just a little more complicated, having each member do some simple, repetitive task?"

Ravna nodded. "We have something similar in the Domain. Street diggers work as a large team, then when they're done with their shift they revert to separate packs, and collect their pay—and enjoy the rest of the day."

Tycoon made an irritated noise. "As I said, primitive forms of the idea have always been around. I raised it to a high art at East Home. I'm sure you in the Domain heard of me there. The problem was, there were those bothersome labor guilds, and the local aristocracies had to be bought off—"

"And your other inventions were becoming too grand for a place so small as East Home." That was Vendacious' voice coming out of Ta.

"Yes, yes. I'm not forgetting you, Vendacious. Your, um, advice about my other inventions was indispensable even then. I had to find larger pools of labor, without petty squabbling—and out of the view of Woodcarver's Domain."

Ahead, the walkway opened into a kind of terrace, wide enough so that—if the two gunpacks stayed at the ends of it—all the rest of their party could stand together. Tycoon stopped there, and some of him walked to the edge of the terrace, waving for Ravna to follow. "Here in the Tropics is the place for my ideas. The workers can be molded into whatever form fits my purpose. No northern factory could function with this perfection. . . . " His heads tilted slyly at her. "You really can't hear it, can you?"

There was a *lot* to hear: the distant pounding of steam engines, the steady crash, crash, crash of the assembly line, wheels on supply lines clattering across the factory floor. In an open-topped room directly below, several Tines had their heads together, almost like a coherent pack. Maybe in fact, they were:

A steep stairway led from there up to where she now stood. But she heard no Interpack gobbling. "Hear what?" she said.

"Mindsounds! From all up and down the row. The factory is a-roar with them." He jabbed a snout in the direction of the silent little foursome who had accompanied them along the walkway. "Have you wondered who this fellow is?"

"Well . . ." The question seemed a complete non-sequitur.

The foursome squeaked something in Interpack, but almost inaudibly high-pitched.

From the radio singleton, Vendacious gave out a sigh, "Yes, my lord, I'm told you are pointing at Aritarmo. I admit my weakness. I've never been able to come to the factories in person. The radio provides me voice and ears to ac-company my lord Tycoon. My assistant Aritarmo sends descriptions of what it sees, what the radio might have missed noticing." He gobbled something more in Interpack.

Tycoon laughed. "Quite right, Vendacious. But my point was simply that this factory hall *is* a mild form of the Choir. Not all packs can tolerate it."

Godsgift had been silent to this point—at least where humans could hear. The pack had crowded close the railing and all of it was looking down. "In fact, my lord Tycoon," it said, "this is Choir territory, not part of your Reservation."

"Ah, um. Quite so." Then almost to himself: "It's beyond me how a mob of millions can remember fine print that some godsgift saw seven years ago."

More of Tycoon came to the railing, stuck some heads over, then re-treated. "It takes real strength of character to face that roar. A bracing test of discipline. . . . My point is that these factories are fundamentally different from those of the north. These are factories that know their goals, and can man-age the flow of raw material coming in and finished product rolling out. There are waves of attention and decision crashing back and forth the length of the hall. My assistants provide the overall design, the basic product models, but it is the mob that makes the details work. See down there, that room with five Choir members all heads together? I'll wager there's some local bottleneck in production, something that requires coherent attention. Those five are a form of godsgift."

"A very temporary form," said the godsgift standing by the railing.

"How flexible can they be?" asked Ravna. "You say this factory's current run goes only four more days, but how long does it take for a factory to retarget on something entirely different?"

"Entirely different? That depends," said Tycoon. "What the Choir can't do is the original design and invention, however much a godsgift may brag. It's been my genius that has lifted the Choir out of its eternal misery."

Where is Ritl when we need her? thought Ravna.

"The Choir was not miserable," objected the godsgift.

"We could argue about that, my friend. I remember how you lived when I first negotiated the Reservation. Physically at least, what you have now is a paradise."

"Well, *physically*, of course." The godsgift waved dismissively. "The Choir would never cooperate with you if that much were not true."

"Whatever," said Tycoon and gave his heads a little roll of exasperation. "The hardest part of any new product is convincing the Choir that the effort is needed. That takes a combination of market research and animal handling. I've become very, very good at it. Once I have a new invention properly working and a factory and shipping plan, it takes one to ten tendays for the Choir to build and start a new factory. Do you understand now why I couldn't hide from the Domain anymore, even if I wanted to?"

All of Tycoon was staring at Ravna now, as if he thought what he said had impressed her. *And it certainly does,* she thought. Tycoon's bragging amounted to massive understatement. Without a shred of real automation, he had recapitulated the power of an early technological civilization. . . . And done almost everything she'd been attempting the last ten years.

————

That night, back in their air-conditioned, perhaps snooped-upon dungeon:

"In fact, Tycoon *does* have automation," said Jefri. "He's persuaded the Choir to be his personal automation. Powers! This is more than the Old Flenser ever dreamed of doing."

"This pack is no Flenser. Tycoon is a . . ." Ravna looked around at the walls, thought better of saying *naive buffoon.*

Jefri laughed. "You don't have to spell that one out. Yeah, Tycoon isn't Flenser, either Old or New. But he's accomplished far more." He glanced at Ravna. "What I'd like to know is how he wedged a snout into the Choir in the first place. Packs have been trying to penetrate the Tropics for—well, for centuries. Explorers went in, frags and singletons and small mobs dribbled out. Their stories were full of madness and member sacrifice and ecstasy—but never a hint of reason. The closest thing to trade was the occasional wreckage that drifted into the Domain. Maybe we shouldn't be surprised that the Choir can manage complex procedures when it is convinced of future payoffs—but how did Tycoon get close enough to do the convincing in the first place?"

"A human could have done it."

"Hah. No human we know, not if this operation is as old as Tycoon claims."

Ravna hesitated, wondering whether to voice her suspicions about the "cuttlefish." Finally she gave a shrug. "Okay, there are still mysteries. I may just ask him straight out. I think that despite all his"—*bragging*—"all his pride and confidence, Tycoon really does value human technical knowledge."

"Yes! And your expertise in particular!" Jef grinned. "You can thank Timor for some of that."

Ravna sighed. "Timor has done better than any of us. You talked to him more today than I did." The boy had been whisked away at the end of the afternoon, an ugly finish to a very strange day. "Do you think he's okay?"

"Yeah, I really do. He was less upset than you when Tycoon dragged him off. I think he wanted to get back to Geri. . . . I don't think she is doing nearly so well."

"We have to see her," said Ravna. She hesitated, did her best *not* to look at the walls. *I hope this doesn't sound like a planned statement*: "You know Jefri, after what I've seen today, I think I could work with Tycoon. What he's achieved here—well, if we could use it to assemble the output of Scrupilo's Cold Valley lab, the combination would give us one hundred years of progress in ten. On the other hand, if we can't see Geri, if we can't return all the stolen kids, then I'm not sure that it makes sense to hire on with Tycoon and, um,"—a tip of the hat to the main monster, in case he was listening too—"Vendacious."

The terrifying thing about her little speech was that it was mostly true.

The factory they visited the next day was almost ten kilometers away. This time their wagon was drawn by kherhogs, the first large animals they had seen in the Tropics. They rolled past the airfield, past the south end of dozens of factory halls, and through one morning rainstorm. Immediately to the left of their path, the ground was an urban marsh, much like what they'd seen on their flight in. In the east, behind them, the palaces and hangars were lost to sight. The great pyramid stood above the mists like a distant mountain.

When they finally disembarked, they found Tycoon and company already waiting for them. The eightsome was talking even while Ravna was still greeting Timor: "You think this was a far ride, do you? Maybe a year or two ago it was, but the factory count is still doubling. I have smaller reservations a hundred kilometers from here. We'd have to take an airship to get them. Come along now, stop fussing with Timor. I have so much to show you."

He dragged them through another rain shower to look at a coal-fired power plant. This rank of factory halls needed no steam engines. The equipment inside was entirely driven by electrical gear of various sorts. The factory next to where they had stopped seemed to be running some sort of drop forge. Tycoon claimed the one on the other side was for electroplating. Ravna thought all this must be the reason for the long trip—until she got indoors and discovered what this particular factory made:

Radios.

The devices were stacked at the output end of the factory. Tycoon snagged one from a departing pallet, then stood on his shoulders to put it in Ravna's hands. Ravna turned the boxy contraption around, not immediately recognizing it. Perhaps that was because it seemed to be gold plated, a mirror-perfect job. She turned it over, saw the dark glossiness of an ordinary solar cell, the same as on radios built up north. Okay. Leaving aside the useless gold plating, this was the analog radio design she had created from *Oobii*'s archives. Scrupilo must have made dozens of the devices over the last few years. Ah. She looked past Tycoon. The bin he was standing in front of could easily contain a thousand radios.

All she could think to say was, "So why the gold plating?"

Tycoon suddenly was looking lots of places besides at her. "Yes, well, my local market likes them gold plated."

Ravna raised an eyebrow. "The Choir?"

Godsgift was watching; it seemed amused: "Who but the Choir can know what is truly valuable?"

Tycoon made an irritated noise and snatched the radio out of Ravna's hands. "They like shiny things," he said. "It doesn't matter. We've made many more of the usual kind. Come along and I'll show you the production steps."

Inside was much cleaner and—to Ravna's ears—quieter than yesterday's factory hall. That was not really a surprise considering this place produced a form of tech gear, and the power was electric. Tycoon was full of detailed explanations. This building was the final assembly point for the radios. More than the making of rain gutters, making the radios showed that production depended on physical *networks* of factories, going from raw materials, to components, to intermediate assembly, to a factory like this. No doubt each step was plagiarized from *Oobii* and Scrupilo, but the networking was a separate design achievement. Though Tycoon never said so, Ravna guessed that planning those networks was also his greatest limitation.

"And I have improvement plans," said Tycoon, "not just for silly things like gold plating. I'm working on re-creating the design of full radio cloaks. Consider the use I have made of the single set of cloaks that Nevil, um, acquired for us. If radio cloaks were common and if we could use them safely, it would revolutionize my operations!"

Ravna almost laughed at this. *You have improvement plans? So Nevil has not been able to dig up the original design for the cloaks, has he?* They walked some meters further, Ravna silent and Tycoon blathering on. On the other side of the pack, Jefri was pulling Timor's wagon. Close behind came the Ta singleton and, almost as close, Aritarmo and the godsgift. A gunpack or two drifted around behind *them*.

"Isn't it so?" said Tycoon. *Oops.* His latest bit of bragging had ended with a question.

"I'm sorry sir, what—?"

"Isn't it so, that my inventions surpass your own achievements?"

Perhaps it was time to approximate reality: "Sir, you and the Choir have accomplished miracles of production—"

Tycoon preened.

"—but the basic inventions, those are from the Domain."

"Nonsense!" Tycoon was all glowering at her. But his heads weren't weaving around; this was not the killing rage of their first meeting. After a moment, some of him looked away. "You are a little bit right. Much of my success, I owe to Vendacious and his superb espionage service."

"Thank you, sir, thank you." That was Vendacious, via Ta. The monster must think this tour was important, to be listening to every word.

Tycoon gave a gracious wave, where Aritarmo could see. "That said," he continued, "when I was whole, I was an inventive genius. Over the last seven years, I've recovered that genius. I have ideas all the time. Inventions for flying, inventions for swimming beneath the sea. I keep notebooks full of them. But I am just one pack, and I've learned there are myriad details that must be resolved in order to go from insight to accomplishment. In fact, that's what caused the breakup of the first me. My current success is based on three things: my genius and drive, the Choir, and the hints and details that Vendacious' espionage service provides."

"From us humans," said Ravna.

Tycoon shrugged. "From the archives you stole. I doubt if you humans have ever invented anything for yourselves."

Jefri was listening with an expression of unguarded surprise. *Be cool, Jef!* But no: "Humans have invented some form of every single thing you've made! We did it thousands of years ago! Every civilized race does as much—and then goes on to do the *hard* things!"

Tycoon was silent for a moment. "The . . . hard things?" He seemed more intrigued than offended.

"There's always something more, sir," put in Ravna, and gave Jef a look that she hoped would shut him down.

"Yes," said Tycoon. "Spaceships. Starships."

"Yes, sir."

"But I've had ideas for those, too." They walked on a few paces, and perhaps honesty or sanity forced him to say, "Of course, I know those may take some years more work. Is that what the Johanna-brother means by 'hard' problems?"

Jefri replied, "Of course not."

"What then?"

Vendacious popped up with the answer: "We've talked about this before, my lord. The sky maggots were trying to become god."

Tycoon hooted, "Yes! The god thing." He tilted a glance at Ravna. "That was our original wedge into human affairs, the religious warfare between your two factions."

Vendacious gobbled enthusiastic agreement, then reverted to Samnorsk, "In fact, their superstitious beliefs are the best argument that they are fools."

As usual, the godsgift had been drifting along at the edge of the walkway, mainly looking down at the assembly line. Now his heads looked up and he said mildly, "I object to this deprecation of religion. *My* god is real enough. If you doubt that, I invite you to take a walk on the factory floor."

———

Tycoon mellowed as they proceeded down the production line, and Ravna managed to avoid any further criticism of his originality. It really wasn't difficult; there was so much that could be honestly praised. By the time they reached the midpoint of the hall, it was raining again. The sound came as a distant drumming on the metal roof, and even the skylights were dark, except for occasional lightning. Electric arc lamps had come on over critical stations on the production line, rather like an automatic system responding to the environment.

Just as in yesterday's factory, there was a terrace at the walkway's midpoint. Today, Tycoon waved at the others to stay back, and took Ravna out onto the terrace as if to have a private conversation. She glanced back at the entourage.

Private conversation? Certainly Timor or Jefri couldn't hear what she and Tycoon might say—but the rest? Thunder crashed, and the sound of rain intensified. Okay. If Tycoon focused his voice properly, the others might not be able to hear his words.

On the other hand, maybe it didn't matter: "You know," he said, "You could do very well working for me."

"I'm honored, sir, but I'm not sure I—"

"Oh, I think you understand; I'm really very good at taking the measure of potential employees. You've pointed out weakness in my operation, and quite frankly, I agree with you." He paused, as if to let his high praise sink in. Then: "You know that I'm at the point of an alliance with Nevil Storherte and the Domain?"

"You mentioned something about that, yes. But what about Woodcarver?"

He waved dismissively. "A detail. I'm flying to the Domain in the next day or two, to make it official. My landing is timed to match the arrival of a shipment of 1024 radios, a gift demonstrating the power of my operation. Vendacious assures me that Woodcarver will be impressed by the implications. Cooperating with Nevil and with me will benefit her enormously. And for myself—well, finally coming out of the shadows will be as important as my original entente with Nevil. Now he can provide me with full and direct access to the archives that came with the starship *Oobii*."

"Ah." Tycoon mispronounced "entente" but his point was all too clear.

"Yes. And *you* could benefit immensely from this, as my employee. You would have protection from Nevil. You would have access to the *Oobii* archives. You would have access to Choir production for your own religious projects—though that would require separate trades with the Choir. There are two main things that I would ask in return. First, you would persuade your faction among the two-legs to stop opposing Nevil. And second, you would, um, hm, you would use *Oobii* to help me with my various production problems. As you've remarked, I need significant assistance in translating my inventive genius into deliverable products. Nevil has been of some help with that, but I've come to believe that *you* are the master when it comes to the *Oobii* archives." He paused, perhaps to let the flattery sink in. "So, what do you say?"

I could repeat the little speech I made to Jefri—but you've probably already heard that. Outside the factory, the thunder and lightning was building up to a real storm. Above that, the air would be cold and dry and thinning into the vacuum of interplanetary space. Somewhere thirty lightyears beyond that . . . the Blight was coming their way, the end for this world and everyone on it, perhaps the end of much more. *And today, at this moment, I am closer to stopping it than ever before.*

She brought her attention back to the here and now, to the eightsome who waited on her reply. "What of Nevil?"

"Nevil stays in overall charge of the two-legs. I will not betray a current ally to get a new one." Tycoon bobbed a grin. "Be happy. Vendacious tells me that Nevil will be as unhappy about this deal as you are."

Hmm. She looked across the terrace to where Jef stood by Timor. They were in the shadows, but then the lightning shone stark blue-white across them all. Both were looking in her direction. Just in front of them, Aritarmo had spread out, no doubt straining to hear.

She turned back, looked at Tycoon, every one. "I want the Children you stole."

"Timor and Geri. Certainly. I'm . . . I'm sorry about the third human, even though its death was an accident." He seemed about say something more, to offer some excuse perhaps. One thing she was learning about Tycoon: he could not abide being in the wrong.

"And no more killing," she said.

"Of course." But then a startle rippled through the pack. "No more killing—except to serve justice. Johanna Olsndot murdered my brother. There must be justice for that, no excuses, no compromise."

Again, lightning flashed. Ravna waited for the thunder to pass and then replied in a quiet, hard voice. "Then deal with Vendacious. He is the one who killed your brother."

Tycoon hooted softly, but all his eyes were on her now. "You lie, or you repeat lies. I have years of evidence, and not just from Vendacious. Nevil Storherte—was he not like a pack lover to Johanna?—he himself reports Johanna's confession. I've sometimes wondered if that was what turned him against her. Maybe he does have some respect for pack life. . . . I notice your mouth is open, but you aren't saying anything. Are you surprised?"

"N-no." For a moment she thought she was going to throw up all over Tycoon. Instead, she swallowed hard and said, "What Nevil said is a lie. What Vendacious says are lies."

"Ah, so I'm surrounded by liars?" Tycoon gave a shrug. Two of him were looking back at Jefri and the others. "Do you know where Johanna Olsndot is now?"

"No," Ravna replied shortly, which was not a lie since she had only guesses.

"Well, neither do I. Neither does Vendacious. Neither she nor her friend Pilgrim—nor their flier—has been seen since the night we abducted you. I suspect she's in hiding back in the Domain, protected by Woodcarver. Vendacious thinks she may be dead, finally crashing that crazy flying machine. *If she is never found, I will never be done with this!*" He gave a little shriek that might have meant despair. "But Vendacious has offered a solution. He tells me that the Johanna-brother may well know what has become of the brother-murderer—and that if he does know, a few days of professional interrogation will retrieve the facts."

"Don't you—"

"Vendacious tells me the Johanna-brother would likely survive the questioning, but he makes no guarantees." All his eyes swiveled back to Ravna.

Ravna stepped into the middle of the pack, all but treading on claws to do so. Now most of Tycoon had to look straight up to see her face. "No more killing!"

Tycoon swarmed up, forming a packish pyramid that put two of his heads above Ravna's eye-level. He leaned forward, all teeth and bad breath, and rapped a glancing blow to her face. "Make no mistake, human. I will find Johanna Olsndot. If her brother dies in the process, it would be a form of justice. A brother for a brother."

CHAPTER 35

Two days later, Tycoon's much-bragged-about expedition to the Domain was ready to depart. Nothing had changed in the standoff between Ravna and the eightsome. The good news was that Jefri was still unharmed and still out of Vendacious' claws. The bad news . . . wasn't entirely clear yet, and probably depended on what Tycoon planned for this trip.

Just after sunrise, a rickshaw took them out onto the airfield. The usual gunpack trotted along behind them. Puddles left by recent rain covered wide stretches of the concrete, but the top of the sky was clear, the air wet and still and almost cool. At the north end of the field, two hangars had opened, and their airships were being dragged out.

They stopped near a rain pool in the middle of nowhere. The gunpack made no objection when Jefri scrambled down from the rickshaw. After a moment, Ravna followed, even though the view standing on the ground must surely be worse than the one from the rickshaw. Jef walked around the wagon.

Ravna shaded her eyes and stared at the airships for a moment. At this distance, details were lost, but "This really looks like takeoff preparations," she said. "And we're standing nowhere close."

Jefri came to stand beside her. "I figure this is just more psychological warfare. Tycoon won't leave you behind. He really needs you."

Ravna didn't say anything for a moment. Jef could be right. The last four days had given her some feeling for Tycoon's bragging and bluffing—and occasional murderous tantrums. She guessed there would be one more confrontation before Tycoon flew off, and even success could come in dark degrees. *Which airship would they put Jefri on? And where are—*

"Where are Timor and Geri and Amdi and Screwfloss?" said Jefri, as if reading her mind. "We haven't seen Timor since you told Tycoon to go to hell." Jef had ragged on her mercilessly about that recent confrontation. At the same time, he had seemed to admire her "lack of restraint" more than anything she had done in a long time.

They stood for some moments observing the activity around the hangars, watching for more wagons to appear from the palace and Vendacious' almost-as-grand annex. The expanse of damp concrete had an eerie, open silence to it, a kind of vast obeisance to the pyramids beyond. Pillars of sunlight punched through the eastern clouds, glittering from the gilded surface of the great pyramid. As the sun rose above the thunderheads, an avalanche of light spilled across the field, bright and cheering . . . and searingly hot once it arrived.

"Tycoon is trying to melt us down," said Jefri. "We should get back in the wagon." There was shade there. Their driver had retreated under some of it.

"Yes—" Ravna took one more look around. The sunlight had put everything into sharp contrast. The shallow rain pool she had noticed earlier was further away than she'd thought. And it wasn't shallow. "Hei, Jefri. We're only about forty meters from one of the cuttlefish ponds."

She started walking toward it, and after a moment Jefri followed. The gunpack made a spiky sound of surprise. He trotted around and ahead of them as if to turn them back—but he kept his gun muzzles down and seemed more irritated than imperative.

As they reached the pool, Jefri commented, "A wagon just left the palace. Want to bet that's Tycoon?"

She looked up. The wagon hardly seemed to be moving at all. Ah, it was headed *here*, not across to the hangars. Yes, one last confrontation. She wasn't afraid to argue with Tycoon, but she was very afraid of the consequences of losing the argument. This time, things could not end in a draw.

She knelt by the pool, hoping she looked unconcerned to whomever might be watching. Despite the open water, the swarms of bloodsucking insects were no thicker here than anywhere else. Maybe they didn't have a water larval stage. Or maybe . . . Here and there across the water, there were flickers of motion, tentacles snapping up through the water's surface. So in addition to their other virtues, the cuttlefish liked to eat insects.

She leaned over the edge of the pool, looking straight down. The concrete wall was steep; even here, the bottom looked to be a meter or two under water. There was one of the squidlike critters. And another. After a few seconds they seemed to swarming below her.

"We seem to be attracting them," said Jefri.

"Yeah." She reached her hand into the warm water.

"Hei, careful!" Jef grabbed her arm, holding her back.

"It's okay. They get along well enough with the Tines." Besides, she had a theory she wanted to test.

"But you don't know what *else* is in the pond."

The tiny bodies tumbled around her hand, the huge glossy eyes peering curiously up through the water at her. She felt tendrils tugging gently on her fingers. She waggled her hand, lifting the creature up for a better view. It was a small thing to be intelligent, but—

"Hei, hei, hei!" piped a small voice. All around it other voices chimed. "Hei human. Hei humans!" The one who had touched her let go. The crowd darted off, then a moment later was back in even greater numbers. Dozens of little voices were shouting simple Samnorsk greetings.

Jefri's grip on her arm loosened and he dropped to his knees beside her. "So they really do talk! I wonder how they compare to singletons."

"Oh, I think they're considerably smarter." It was still a theory, but—she glanced across the airfield. The approaching wagon was much nearer, trailed by another gunpack. She recognized the elaborate ornamentation on the wagon; this was Tycoon. Maybe it was time to try to *use* her little theory.

She and Jefri stood, but remained near the pool. Tycoon's wagon slowed and came to a stop by the other wagon. When Ravna and Jefri did not move, there was some irritated gobbling. After a moment, Tycoon's driver brought him over to the cuttlefish pool.

The eightsome came streaming out of the wagon, followed by a radio singleton—hei, it looked like Zek! Behind him was a more expected companion, Ritl. She was in her usual fine form, bitching loudly about something or everything. When Tycoon sent a *be quiet* in her direction, Ritl shifted to sporadic muttering. She walked along with Zek for a few paces—and then seemed to notice the pond. She ran off around it, and for a time the air was free of her complaints.

Tycoon ambled over to them with the air of a great leader slumming around without his entourage. *Well, I'm just as glad not to see Vendacious or even Aritarmo,* thought Ravna.

"It's g-going to be a very warm day," said Tycoon, his Geri voice as incongruous as ever.

"I'm sure it will be, sir," replied Ravna.

The eight bobbed a smile. "Not that it matters. This afternoon I will be flying away. You know, the air is quite cool even a few hundred meters up. It's nature's own air conditioning. I expect *I* will be quite comfortable."

"You're not taking us then?" said Ravna, still trying make it sound like casual chitchat.

"The passenger list and ship assignment isn't entirely decided," he said. Two of him were staring pointedly at Jefri.

Ravna continued to play along. "Vendacious is going?"

"Of course. In the second airship." He waved a snout in the direction of the hangars. "No room for Aritarmo, but we'll still have the network. I'll continue to supervise my worldwide operations."

"And Ritl?" said Jefri, as if just passing the time of day.

Tycoon made an irritated noise. "Not Ritl. In close quarters, that little monster—I mean, that remnant of a loyal employee—is too difficult to deal with." All his heads turned toward Ravna. "But that's not the important question as far as you two are concerned."

Ravna returned the look as best she could, having only one head. "Of course. There's myself and Jefri, but also the Children you stole, Geri and Timor and—"

"No." It was flat negation, even if spoken in his high-pitched, little girl voice. "They will stay here."

"But—"

"I don't want them getting in the way. I—" There was a subtle shifting around within the pack. Ravna could almost imagine that some faction was embarrassed and desired a bit of frankness. "Timor is a good worker, as honorable as a pack. He will be safe here. Geri will be safe as well. Protecting both of them is important to me, even if they are human. You should know, Vendacious dislikes humans even more than I, and sometimes I wonder if he realizes how fragile you are. Even I find it hard to understand what it means to be a truly new mind; it is not a natural state. Eventually, I promise to return them. In the meantime, they will be kept far from Vendacious." He jabbed a snout at Ravna. "My inclination is to take you with me. The packs we captured with you will go north with Vendacious. They will provide a good cross check on assertions that you make."

"And Jefri?" Ravna asked.

"That depends on you and him. I want to locate Johanna Olsndot. You two are hiding something; we could hear you all yesterday conspiring in your dungeon. Confess the truth, and you can both travel on my airship."

"We have told the truth," said Jef, "and we weren't conspiring!" But they had spent hours trying to decide what to say if it all came to this. Much of that conversation had been silent spelling and cloaked allusions.

Tycoon's words rolled on right over Jef's: "Otherwise—it will be as I told you two days ago. Jefri will go north with Vendacious."

"I'm sure I can make the Johanna-brother talk, my lord." That was Vendacious' voice, via Zek.

Ravna glanced at Jefri, saw his impatient look. The result of all their "conspiring" had been simple: You can't win if you have nothing to confess and that fact is not accepted. Okay, you might postpone the nightmare simply by making a faux confession. Jef would have already started lying, except that she'd persuaded him to let her make the first move. *There must be some other way. I just need a little more time.* As if all of yesterday hadn't been enough to find a way out, if one existed. She turned away from Tycoon and Jefri and Zek, and stared across the pond. There was something near the middle that she hadn't noticed before. Here and there tentacles poked into the air, slowly moving. They weren't jabbing at insects. They were larger and more frondlike than the cuttlefish limbs she had seen. *They were hard proof for her theory about the cuttlefish.* She felt a smile come to her lips; in other circumstances it would have been a joyous shout.

She looked back at Tycoon. She had nothing but the lies she and Jefri had agreed on, but damned if she was going to say them while she could still stall. "Out of the whole airfield, you had us brought here. You wanted us to see this pond, didn't you? Why?"

An indignant chord came from Zek. That must be Vendacious, impatient with the change of topic. Tycoon, bless his various parts, was more easily distracted. He sidled around, some of him tilting a glance at the water. When he finally spoke, his geekiness seemed ascendant. "I noticed that you never asked hard questions about the cuttlefish, never said much about them even when you were alone with the Johanna-brother. I wondered if you would ever figure out how important they are to my program."

Ravna nodded. "I had a theory. Now I think I know much more about the cuttlefish than you do."

"Oh *really?*" Tycoon stepped closer, challenging. He didn't seem angry, but she had the feeling that the pack's enormous ego, both as businesscritter and inventor, was engaged. "And what is it that you think you know?"

"The cuttlefish are more than mindless repeaters. They've learned your language and more recently mine. They can speak both sensibly."

"Yes. So?"

"The cuttlefish were how you originally made contact with the Choir, how you were able to communicate with the Choir when all packs before had failed."

Tycoon emitted a string of clicks, mild applause. "Very good. You are absolutely right." He settled down, continued almost chummily. "See Ritl playing with them?" On the other side of the pond, Ritl was racing back and forth, gobbling fiercely at the water. Tiny voices answered her. "It was Remasritlfeer who brought the creatures from the South Seas. It was my idea to use them here with the Choir. Remasritlfeer tried and failed, tried and failed. I don't know how many of the creatures were eaten—though they don't really seem to care about their own lives. Finally Remasritlfeer gave up—but I demanded he go back and try again. And as usual, my diligence and initiative paid off." He looked up smugly. "It was a small start, but we found a few things to trade and were able to negotiate the first, tiny reservation here." He waved expansively at the airfield, the palaces, the factories. "The rest is history."

"It never puzzled you that something so strange could talk, that it could have a mind?"

"Um, yes of course. I'm always thinking on deeper meanings. Early on, I had the theory that perhaps these were a baby form of whales. It's well known that whales are smarter than weasels, almost as smart as singletons—and they swim in pods that may be even more intelligent."

Over the last ten years, an occasional "whale" carcass had washed ashore in the Domain. Ravna had overseen the dissection of two of them. They were like seamals. She'd run simple phylogenetic programs on the results and concluded that the animals were a distant cousin of the Tines, one that had never returned to a life on the land. "No way are the cuttlefish young whales," she said.

"*Grmp.* I know that. After a time it became evident that the creatures eventually lose their intelligence. The few who survive more than a year root themselves like plants and become mindless egg generators—making a new generation of cuttlefish. We almost lost the whole operation here before we figured that out. I sent an expedition back to the South Seas, found that single atoll where they spawn, uprooted all the mature egg-layers we could find. You can see the tops of them sticking out of the water."

"I saw them." Now the fronds were a little higher out of the water, and more of them were turned broadside towards the humans and packs at the edge of the pool. The sight was so familiar, so welcome . . . *okay, Pham, so unnerving, too.* In the bright sunlight, she could even see the eyespots on the fronds. Mindless they were, more or less—but evidence that children of a friend had survived. She walked slowly along the edge of the pond toward the side that was closest to the forest of fronds. "You uprooted them? Brought them here? You're lucky they survived. They much prefer the surf by the open sea, not this silty, brackish water."

"What? How would you know?" There was both anger and curiosity in Tycoon's words. His sitting members scrambled up and he followed along behind her.

Jefri's were wide with unbelieving surprise. "It can't be, Ravna! The cuttlefish look completely different. The eyes, the—"

"They're Rider larvae, Jef. I'd never seen riderlets before, so I wasn't sure, but look what they grow up to be." She waved at the fronds.

Tycoon came out around her. "What can you know? You guess that because they come from mid-ocean, that's their ideal. I'll have you know, since I brought them to the Fell estuary, their breeding has increased a hundredfold."

Vendacious (via Zek, who was following along uncertainly): "My lord, *what is going on?*" His speech morphed into plaintive gobbling. *Poor Vendacious,* thought Ravna. *He had his next round of torture all set up, and now it's been delayed.* The question was how to turn the diversion into something more lasting. She was still clueless about that.

All she could do was let the geekiness in her speak to the geekiness in Tycoon. She looked down at the eight around her and said, "Tell me, Tycoon, do you have any idea how rare it is that two intelligent races arise naturally on one world, and coexist there?"

"Of course I do! Vendacious' spies have told us much about the other worlds. Multiple intelligent races are common everywhere."

Ravna shook her head. "That's on worlds of the Beyond, sir, where there is fast interstellar travel and decent technology. Down Here—where evolution runs at biological speeds, in its old bloody way—Down Here new intelligence does not tolerate competition. If two intelligent races arise naturally, one competes the other into extinction, usually before either begins its recorded history."

"Nonsense!" But he brought himself together, thinking hard with all his heads close to one another. "So then this is a marvelous bit of good luck, or—"

"Or your cuttlefish are like us humans, recent arrivals from space. In fact, these are the children and grandchildren of two of my own shipmates."

Tycoon dithered. "Implausible, but I don't see how you would gain from lying. In any case, what difference does it make? The creatures have no technology. The adults—the egg-layers—have never spoken. They are vegetables." He hooted. "What grand shipmates they must have been. Did you keep them as ornamental plants? Did you—" He paused, then gobbled something in Interpack, a question. The two gunpacks responded in the negative, but then they spread out . . . watching? listening?

Ravna wasn't paying much attention. She looked out at the sessile-stage Riders, planted forever where the fate named Tycoon had stuck them. These would be the generation after Greenstalk. Without skrode devices, not even the do-it-yourself model that served Greenstalk, they would have almost no ability to form new memories. They'd be innocent, as nearly mindless as before their race was ever uplifted. *But I'm glad your children survived, Greenstalk.*

"What *is* that sound?"

"Huh?" Ravna looked back from the water, noticed that Tycoon was spread out along the edge of the pool, an alert listening posture. "I don't hear anything," she said.

Tycoon made an irritated noise "Some of this is pitched where even you can hear. And it's getting louder."

"I hear something," said Jefri.

"What's going on?" That was Vendacious, more confused than anyone.

Now Ravna could hear the . . . buzzing. Such a familiar sound. Such an impossible sound. She looked across the pond, at the fronds that marked the immobile adults. Several of those slender blades had risen higher, just in the last few seconds. Impossible, impossible. But testable. She gave a little wave and took several quick steps along the edge, almost bumping into one of Tycoon. The tall fronds turned to follow her motion. They made a rattling noise against one another, a kind of language of its own, one that Ravna did not know. That didn't matter; the buzzing became recognizable voder speech, though muffled by the water: "Ravna, oh *Ravna!*"

"Greenstalk?"

"What's this? The egg-layers don't talk!" Tycoon scrambled up all around her. Some of his paws were on her shoulders, giving him a view down into the water from as high as possible. On either side of her, the gunpacks were closing on the edge of the pool. Ravna was only vaguely aware of Tycoon waving them back.

Maybe there are limits to miracles. Greenstalk said Ravna's name again, but now the voder was scaling up and down, the syllables almost unintelligible. Was that disuse or disrepair? If Tycoon had not noticed the skrode perhaps it had been cut apart in the transplanting. Ravna reached out her arms, waving back to her friend.

"The egg-layers can't move, either!" shrieked Tycoon. The part of him that was teetering on Ravna's shoulders lost its balance and tumbled into the pond. The rest of the pack collapsed around her and dragged the fallen member out of the water—but all of him and all of Ravna had their eyes on the tall, blade-like fronds in the pool. Those *were* moving, a lurching progress, a meter forward then a half-meter back. As the Rider rolled closer, Ravna could see its body below the waterline. There was the swelling of Greenstalk's stem, the lower fronds. The flat platform of the skrode was . . . not gone, but hidden. No wonder Tycoon's employees had not seen the machinery. Now Ravna saw smooth composite surfaces where Greenstalk's current efforts were cracking away the coral that had grown upon her during years of sitting alone by her little atoll.

Even before Greenstalk got to the edge of the pool, her fronds had slipped across Ravna's arms, seeing and touching all in one motion. "I have been dreaming long," buzzing obliterated a word or two as the voder glitched, "and now I'm not where I started. I always wondered what became of you." More buzzing. "I've had so many children, and now children's children. I'm sorry, Ravna. One thing I do remember is your kindness and my promise about limiting myself. I'm sorry."

Ravna smiled. "I remember the promise too. But here you've been invited. By friends." She waved at Tycoon standing all around her. "And your children have been protected and lived in greater numbers than you might ever expect." Ravna looked at Tycoon. "Isn't that so, sir?"

Tycoon was all crouched down, every eye on this magical, mobile apparition. It was the first time he'd seemed intimidated. Two of him looked up at her. "I'm sorry, what's the question again?"

"I said that you are a friend, that you've invited Greenstalk and her children to live here in their numbers. Isn't that correct?"

"I, hmm, never thought of it that way. But then I never thought that this, hmm . . ."

"Greenstalk," Ravna supplied.

"—that Greenstalk was a person to talk to." His gaze was equally split between Ravna and Greenstalk. Finally he boomed out with, "Of course! You state the obvious. I am Greenstalk's friend. I'm delighted she is here, doing as she is doing."

Greenstalk wisped a frond across Tycoon's nearest head. "Thank you, sir. I think slowly and dream a lot. My skrode doesn't make memories easily, but I and mine will be good servants? citizens?"

"Employees," Tycoon said firmly.

"I am so glad to see Ravna again. It has been—?"

"Years," said Ravna. "I couldn't find you."

"That time doesn't matter so much to me. These are friends you are among now?"

Ravna looked at Tycoon, at Zek who was surely relaying this conversation back to Vendacious. The truth, right now, could not be spoken and would not be understood. It would have taken tendays for Ravna to explain the situation to Greenstalk, repeating and repeating until the memories sat firm. She turned back to Greenstalk and said, "Tycoon here is my friend." She gestured around to the eight.

The voder buzzed. It might have been cheerful laughter if the device weren't so old and under water. "Good. Good. I am glad. Sit and repeat it to me some times."

Ravna looked to the north, far past Greenstalk's pond. While they had been talking, Tycoon's great airship had been dragged clear of the hangar. It floated just clear of the ground, tethered by its landing pylon and dozens of tie-down cables. She glanced at Tycoon. "This will take a little time," she said.

Tycoon look around at himself and then back at Greenstalk. Finally he said, "So Greenstalk, this Ravna Bergsndot is your friend?"

"She is my dearest friend in all the world."

The Great Tycoon's expedition to the Domain was delayed by one day. During much of that time, Ravna and Jefri and Tycoon sat around the cuttlefish pool— the *riderlet* pool—and explained that they were going away for a brief time, but that they would be back, with interesting news and projects. One day of repetition was probably enough. Greenstalk would remember, and would cooperate in ways that already seemed to have Tycoon—both as inventor and businesscritter— vastly intrigued.

At no time did Tycoon state any concessions, even when Ravna spoke to him alone. But when the two airships finally departed, Jefri and Ravna were both aboard Tycoon's airship.

CHAPTER 36

As a child in the Beyond, Ravna Bergsndot had lumped everything before spaceflight and automatic computation into an amorphous romantic haze of "pre-technology." Ravna's years among the Tines were a never-ending discovery of how much the simplest advances could change one's life. Tycoon's airship was such a primitive machine, but Ravna had *walked* much of the ground they were now overflying. Land that had taken tendays of painful effort to traverse now passed below her in just a few hours. It would have been glorious, except that they spent the first day and night locked up in that familiar tiny cabin.

On the morning of the second day, their progress slowed. The air was bumpy, and the shadows in the clouds below were pointing in the wrong direction. Sometime in the night, Tycoon had changed the ship's bearing. In the distance, they could see Vendacious' craft. It had been behind them, out of sight for most of yesterday.

The steward foursome came tapping at their door, but not with breakfast. "This way, this way," it said. Ravna crawled through the hatch. To her right, the steward was already a meter or two forward, walking along with only an occasional look back in her direction. Their gunpack was to Ravna's left. Aboard the airship, it carried short-barreled weapons, all the barrels tucked downwards.

"Beware the guns," she said back to Jefri.

"Hei, guy," Jef gave the gunpack a little wave as he came into the corridor.

Sandwiched between the steward ahead and the gunpack behind, the humans' progress was slow. There were hatches at regular intervals along the corridor: more staterooms. The mantle lamp by each turnout was lit. Not for the first time, she gave a little prayer: *I really hope these guys also stole the tech to stabilize hydrogen.*

The corridor extended the length of the carriage, gently curving along the belly of the ship. They were heading for the bow. Where else would Tycoon hold court?

The ship's passenger carriage did finally come to an end. The passageway opened onto a cross-corridor that ran the width of the carriage. There were the usual fifteen-centimeter portholes on either side, the sunlight trumping the light from the mantle lamps. In the middle of the open space was a Tinish version of spiral stairs, a fan-like helix of rungs, quite suitable for Tines ascending single file. The steward pack sent a member up the steps. Ravna heard it gobbling, announcing the humans' arrival. After a moment it came scooting back down. "Go up now, please to go."

Ravna started up, winding herself around like some comedian in a cross-habitat comedy, but she didn't quite get stuck. Finally she climbed out onto the carpet of the upper level and looked into bright daylight.

Powers. With the most primitive technology, Tycoon had achieved a visual effect that would have done credit to a designer in the Low Beyond. *This guy is a megalomaniac, but he has an imagination to match.*

Tycoon's bowpoint audience chamber extended almost ten meters from port to starboard. Its ceiling followed the dirigible's hull, curving upward so that parts of it were high enough for a human to stand upright. No portholes of dirty glass here. Tycoon hadn't yet plagiarized the making of large sheets of clean glass, but he'd used the very best of his tiny portholes. Hundreds of them. The glass was fitted in a fine metallic mesh that surrounded the bow side of the room. Not surprisingly, Tycoon was perched on thrones, giving him the best view. Two of him might be looking in her direction. The rest were looking outward, into daylight so bright that they were just stark silhouettes.

She was distracted from awe by Jefri's unhappy swearing. Jef was halfway up the stairs, fully wound around the first turn, and just a little too big to get through.

She reached down, grabbed both Jefri's hands, and braced her feet on the far side of the stairwell. She pulled and Jefri pushed, rocking him upwards a centimeter at a time. With the sound of snapping metal, Jefri was freed. He sprawled onto the upper deck's carpet and rolled into a sitting position.

Someone spoke, with Vendacious' voice. "Is that the big human tearing up your stairs? When I told you these humans would wreck whatever they touch, I didn't expect such literal proof."

Someone else gobbled something dismissive. Ravna looked around. Ah, there was Zek, on a separate perch, draped in his radio cloak. So there were others listening in, offering advice. Was there anyone else physically present? Behind her, she noticed a head or two of the gunpack, sticking up from the stairwell. Wait. There was one more, not a pack or a Radio Cloak member: It was Ritl. The singleton was sitting in the sunlight, on the bow side of Tycoon's thrones. There was something self-satisfied about her; she had gotten away with something.

Ravna gestured at the singleton. "I thought you were leaving Ritl back in the Tropics?" she said to Tycoon.

Tycoon made an irritated noise. "Yes. The creature popped out of a storage cabinet last night. Remasritlfeer was an excellent employee, but perhaps I'm honoring his memory too much." He gave his employee's remnant a speculative glare. Ritl wriggled insouciantly on her velvet perch and let loose with chords that sounded sassy even to Ravna.

Tycoon ignored the comments. He waved grandly ahead. "We're approaching the Domain."

From where she was sitting, all Ravna could see was sky. She came to her knees, and looked down over the edge of the bow windows. She saw painfully bright snow, patches of shade and dark stone. The glaciers and peaks of the Icefang Mountains spread out before them. She remembered the maps, Amdi planning their final run over these mountains. The valley below led to one of the Domain's southern border posts.

"I see you still have some hills to climb," said Jefri.

Vendacious said via Zek: "Enjoy the delay, humans. Nevil will take you soon enough."

Tycoon said something peremptory, and then in Samnorsk: "*I* will decide that, not Nevil."

"Sorry, sir," said Vendacious. "Of course, Nevil has no authority in this."

Some of the eight were looking at Jefri. Even against the glare of the day, you could see that it was not a friendly stare. "We'll get over these mountains by tomorrow at latest. The winds can change much faster than the tides."

The great Tycoon was silent for a moment. All eight of him resumed their contemplation of the gleaming snowfields and jagged black rock. Knowing Tycoon, this was an heroic pose, mainly for their benefit. Maybe Ritl thought so, too: She emitted some belittling remark. Tycoon laughed and shrugged it off.

From way aft, the muffled buzz of the engines came slightly louder. Tycoon's flight crew—presumably in the airship's control gondola—was changing direction again. Ravna wondered what starting a day late would do to Tycoon's plans and Nevil's. *And I wonder how often his crews have been over these mountains?* It hadn't happened before she was kidnapped; *Oobii* would have spotted the intruders instantly.

Partway through the long, slow turn, the deck dropped from beneath Ravna, then bounced back, knocking her across the deck. Jefri grabbed her under the shoulders, and they managed to ride out about thirty seconds of turbulence.

The Tines had it easier. They didn't use tiedowns here, but those perches had rows of wooden bars, and every paw she could see had its claws securely wrapped around a grab hold.

Tycoon gobbled something at Zek.

Jefri translated: "He's talking to Vendacious about the turbulence."

Zek squawked something back. His radio cloak had slipped sideways, off-center from his tympana. The poor guy shrugged this way and that, finally got the cloak on properly. He slowly spoke seven separate sounds; they sounded like member names. *Checking connectivity with the rest of himself?*

Then Vendacious was back on line: "We're fine, but the air is still bumpy. Tell the humans that their pack of puppies is feeling a bit under the weather . . ."

Okay, a threat. Maybe Vendacious thought there were things she might say that could turn Tycoon.

Tycoon nodded soberly—missing the meaning that Ravna heard. "We must track back and forth across the front of these mountains. I am sure there are passes in the air, just like there are mountain passes for travellers on the ground. The difference is that the air passageways must be guessed at and they change from hour to hour. I say again, we'll be over these mountains in the morning." He spoke with the assurance of someone who is never contradicted.

They reversed course twice more, a long slow scan across the Icefangs. Except for fast and contrary windflows, they found nothing, certainly no airway over the mountains. Tycoon passed the time by unleashing his geeky side to pick Ravna's brains about the "high spaces."

"I used to wonder about the spaces beyond the sky," he said, "but it never brought an ounce of profit and then I expelled that unproductive part of my imagination. Now I wish I had been more understanding. You humans give us new insights at the same time you do monstrous things. Someday we will visit the highest spaces, and not just scrabble over mountains."

"Yes, sir," said Ravna, "the stars are not too high."

Talking about what that meant got them through another turn. He regarded her claims about the Zones and speed-of-light limitations as naive negativism—and he had even less interest when she tried to explain the Blight.

"No more religious nuttery!" he said. "I want humans of a practical mind, who are open to new concepts. We could do so much with my ideas, and your machine skills, and Nevil's whatever—"

"And without Woodcarver's interference," put in Vendacious.

"Yes, of course," said Tycoon. A head or two looked out at the mountains. The afternoon shadows were stretching deep across rock and glaciers. "This is insufferable!" he said. "There will be moonlight tonight, but I can't risk as close flying as during the day."

Ritl gobbled something.

"You be quiet!" Tycoon replied. The eight were not nearly so tolerant of Ritl as earlier in the day. He jabbed a snout in Zek's direction. "What are the consequences of another day's delay?"

Vendacious replied, but sounding more tentative than usual. "I'm afraid that Nevil Storherte is rather, um, insistent. He says that he's set up a public meeting, and used various intrigues and coercion to persuade Woodcarver to attend. If we don't arrive by tomorrow afternoon he's afraid there'll be catastrophe."

"Damn that two-legs. I should talk to him directly!"

"That might not help, my lord. I think Nevil is being truthful in this. I know that Woodcarver can be very difficult to get the advantage of."

"Is it just Woodcarver? Has Johanna surfaced? Or Pilgrim?"

"No, my lord."

"Keep watch for surprises," said Tycoon. He was silent for a moment. "Nevil aside, we need to arrive by afternoon. There's our sea fleet to consider. That's some tonnes of cargo, including 1024 radios, a *gift* that will surely impress both the humans and Woodcarver's supporters. Heh, after all, it could just as well have been a thousand guns on the backs of gunpacks. You're sure the fleet is to arrive by midday?"

"Yes, my lord. Its progress has been very steady. Nevil has been tracking it, and my own agents have now spotted it too."

"Right," Tycoon was nodding emphatically. "One thing I've learned about marketing. You have to have the pitch and the move and product all coordinated. I—"

Zek interrupted him, but the voice did not belong to Vendacious: "What I don't understand, is why we haven't heard directly from the fleet? They have radios; we should simply request that they delay landing till it fits the overall schedule."

Vendacious replied to the unknown speaker: "It's true, we haven't had direct word. After all, the Choir is more a thing than an ally, and these rafts are only a small fragment of that. The fleet should never have left as early as it did, but it had the full merchant cargo on board."

"Who is Vendacious replying to?" asked Ravna, the words just popping out. Whoever this was, it spoke pretty good Samnorsk, and sounded strangely familiar.

Tycoon said, "That's partly the godsgift you knew in the Domain, relayed from the south via Zek/Ut/Ta/Fur/Ri. I asked him to replace the usual Tropical counselor. Even now, he understands the North better than most of us."

"Oh!" Jefri looked as surprised as Ravna felt. "I'm glad, I'm glad he made it home."

Zek shook himself and gobbled briefly. Then in Samnorsk: "I mostly survive, not the best talkers. No thanks to you murderous humans. If it had been Johanna—"

Zek was interrupting himself even before he finished, Tinish chords overlaying the Samnorsk. Poor Zek twisted this way and that. It seemed to Ravna as though he was shrinking from invisible blows. After a moment, Zek recovered and spoke with Vendacious' voice. "Sorry, we hit a spot of turbulence here. My lord, I have various suggestions about how we might accommodate late arrival— but if you intend your two humans to be present at the landing, I suggest we carry on this conversation in private."

There was a back-and-forth between Tycoon and the remote advisors, entirely in Interpack. At least four of Tycoon was looking out at the sunset colors that were deepening across the icefields. He gobbled something at the gunpack and Ravna and Jefri were led down the twisty stairs.

As they crawled along the main corridor toward their cell, Jefri said, "I wish we were even half as clever as Vendacious says."

———

By now, Johanna had been at sea for six tendays. Since the crates of radios had revealed themselves, it had been a never-ending struggle to keep the mob away from the devices. Thank goodness, only this primary raft carried radios. (But why so *many*? She still hadn't figured that out.) She'd persuaded her people to repair the crack in the crate that had split open, so the only loose radio was the one that had fallen out of it, the one she still "protected."

You'd think that fooling a choir would either be impossible or trivial. In fact, Cheepers' various associations truly did believe her every word. They had defended her again and again from the complaints and the little nips, and in one case from a screeching crowd of the incredulous.

For a time, Johanna had been tempted to throw her own radio overboard: just wait for a stormy night and hope that no Tines heard her commit the act. But then she noticed the occasional Tines sniffing around the radio crates. Such random contrarians were a major source of choir creativity. When their foolishness didn't kill them, these fragments discovered things no one else had imagined. Even if the mob stayed generally loyal, eventually someone would break into those crates—and the fleet's radio silence would fail in a big way.

So she might as well hold on to her own radio. It took some nights of work, messing around under the blankets, but she'd managed to get the gadget open and remove the spring on the send switch. She was a little unclear about mechanical springs, what would make them push or pull when you pushed and pulled on them—so she took out all the little moving parts. She bet herself that even the mob's distributed intellect couldn't make that button work.

After that, she put the radio out in the sun. The mob immediately swirled around her, amazingly quiet. They were listening intently as only Tines can. After a time, they relaxed a bit. Cheepers reported to her, "It sounds like this." He played back his amplified interpretation, a clicking and stuttering that sounded like random impulsive noise to Johanna. Maybe Nevil had given up on his robot query—but then loud noises came from the box, interrupting Cheepers' rendition. It was that Tinish voice, asking for a reply again and again. The mob went wild trying to answer—with no success, of course.

The transmission ceased after about five minutes. An hour later, the voice loop ran again, and again an hour after that. Vendacious and Nevil were just poking them desultorily on the off chance that comms could be established. Johanna smiled to herself. *That* wasn't going to happen, but she would find some use for this gadget.

———

They were past Woodcarver's old downcoast capital. To the east, Johanna recognized the cliffs and glacier-reamed valleys of the Domain, of . . . of home. The west was no longer open sea. The islands of the North began as little mounds. Gradually, she saw more and more of them, half-drowned mountains that turned this part of the sea into a network of straits. Very soon they would run into Hidden Island or Cliffside and things would get really exciting. One way or another she wouldn't have to drink fetid water and choose between smoked meat and raw fish anymore.

One afternoon, multiboats flying Domain colors came into view. The vessels cruised along on the mainland side of her path, but at a distance, never coming close. When Johanna first saw them, she almost raced to the top of her raft to wave and shout. Surely Nevil and Vendacious hadn't taken over Woodcarver's Domain? Surely?

In fact, she didn't know, so she hunkered down, out of sight.

The next day, her radio was still receiving hourly pokes from Nevil or Vendacious, but now there were more interesting sounds. Many of these were lost in noise, but Cheepers and his friends repeated them to her clearly. They were human voices; they belonged to Nevil's special pals.

The conversations were fragmented and one-sided. Nevil was using *Oobii* or the orbiter to reach individual radios—as well as sense their weak emissions. Johanna couldn't hear Nevil except when he aimed his silly automatic message at her, but as the rafts got closer to the heart of the Domain, she was in range of the nearest of the other senders:

"Yeah, Nevil, there's ten barges, just where you said. What? . . . How should I know? They look like junk to me." That was Tami Ansndot, as argumentative as ever. "One is only halfsize, like it got split down the middle. . . . So why don't you have Scrupilo fly over in that gasbag of his, and take a look?"

Scrupilo lives! Consequences, consequences . . .

There was a pause, probably for Nevil's explanation of why Scrupilo couldn't help. Johanna bit her lip, trying to imagine just what lie was being peddled, and what it covered up. *If I hadn't busted my send button, I'd give Tami a piece of my mind!* It was bad enough that Tam was a Denier, but worse that she believed the rest of Nevil's lies.

She recognized all the voices, Deniers with some forest experience. Nevil must think these rafts were important. So where was her brother's voice?

Throughout the afternoon, Johanna continued to listen. Here and there, she picked up useful information. Her flotilla was indeed important; somehow it would reveal Woodcarver as the "obstructionist fool we've always suspected"— that tidbit from some idiot obviously parroting Nevil's current propaganda. A great treaty was about to be consummated; these ten rafts would seal the bargain and show the way to the new future. *Yeah, but only if they can get control of my mobs!*

At one point Tami said something like, "Too bad about Jo and Ravna. If only they could be here, to see how wrong they were about everything."

Johanna was just as glad she couldn't hear the choked up, false grief coming back from Nevil.

"The last raft just passed my position." This was a new voice. It sounded like Bili Yngva. No, it was his little brother. Merto probably knew all about the murders and betrayal, but he wasn't quite as smooth as Bili or Nevil. Right now, he sounded furtive. "No. Like I told you, there's no sign of a human on any of the boats. Why don't you just send someone out to check on them before they land? . . . Yeah, yeah. Well after today, that's all gonna change."

CHAPTER 37

For the next twenty hours, Tycoon's airship buzzed back and forth, knocking at the door of the mountain airs, hoping to finally find the winds asleep or at least flowing in the proper direction. Somewhere before dawn, Tycoon's strategy paid off—or maybe Nevil figured out how to coordinate the orbiter's observations with *Oobii*'s programs, and guided the airships to the right mountain pass at the right time.

In any case, by late the next morning both airships had made it over the top of the Icefangs and were descending. On this side of the mountains, the day was a gloom of towering clouds, clouds above and below. The chop and the buffeting was not clear air turbulence, but the violence of thundering squalls.

When the ship's steward came for Ravna and Jefri, the light was still as dim as dawn—except for an occasional flash of lightning. The three of them, with gunpack trailing behind, made their way along the main corridor, which was swaying far more than usual.

Ravna wriggled up the spiral stairs into Tycoon's bow chamber. Behind her, Jefri climbed up almost as easily. Apparently, Tycoon had removed some of the railings, widening the stairway just enough for him.

As usual, the view from the bow was spectacular, but there were no sun-dazzled glaciers this morning. Tycoon's airship was scudding through the bottoms of clouds. From moment to moment there was zero visibility—then they would see forested valleys, and meadows that were impossibly green beneath deep clouds and rain.

Most of Tycoon was gazing out at the sky, as usual pretending to ignore such trivia as the arrival of his prisoners. Stretching off to port and starboard were ranked kilometer after kilometer of clouds. Lightning played between them and the ground below. Every few seconds, the bow was lit by a blinding flash, and thunder shook the grid of the windshield. Tycoon flinched, then turned a head or two back in the direction of Ravna and Jefri. "There is nothing to be alarmed about. Vendacious tells me that we'll come out of the storm area in less than half an hour."

Fifteen minutes of very bumpy ride followed this assurance. Tycoon and his various remote advisors exchanged occasional remarks, but it was all Interpack gobble. There were at least four packs talking through Zek. One of them was clearly Vendacious; another seemed to be the godsgift who had been on the network the day before. She heard Nevil's name popping up now and then.

"Tycoon is sounding less and less pleased with Nevil's advice," Jefri whispered to her. Two of Tycoon looked up at Jef's words, but otherwise the pack continued to ignore them.

Twenty minutes passed. They had lost sight of the ground. Who knew what mountain height lurked just ahead? Then, in the space of ten seconds, the ship broke through the edge of the squall line, emerging from bright cliffs of cloud. They were well within the Domain, past the hardscrabble farms of cotters and peasants, approaching the highest of the rich steadings. The land was splotched with snow and muddy waterfalls.

Spring in Woodcarver's Domain was tendays of mud and rain. The land was not yet to the middle of that season, but this was one of those miracle days, when the storms briefly called truce and endless blue skies appeared, a tantalizing promise of summer. Mixed with the mud and avalanches and melting snow, the first flowers had turned meadows all the colors a human could see (including tints to which the poor Tines were blind). They could see all the way to the horizon through air swept clean by wind and rain. The horizon was a glistening line of silver, broken here and there by dark serrations.

The conversation between Tycoon and his various advisors had become mutually congratulatory. Tycoon gave a hoot of triumph and spoke to Ravna: "You're surprised? Vendacious has radio contact with Nevil, so we have all the power of the starship in our support. No more do we have to skulk around, afraid that you would see us."

"Indeed," said Vendacious. "Your decision to abduct Ravna Bergsndot was a brilliant move, my lord. It has revolutionized our operations."

"Ah, but it was truly your suggestion, Vendacious." He made a noses-up gesture that was probably lost in Zek's relaying. "I commend you."

Jefri rolled his eyes, but remained blessedly silent as Vendacious continued with his analysis: "Things are sunny and clear in all ways now. We're on schedule for the alliance show we've planned with Nevil. The raft fleet is even now at Hidden Island."

"There's still the Ravna faction to deal with," said Tycoon.

"Trust me, sir. You recall our discussions about that. We and Nevil must simply make the proper show of our landing. And frankly, Ravna never had any powerful support, bar the absent Johanna and Pilgrim. Woodcarver has discovered her own reasons for disliking Ravna. If we play things aright, Woodcarver will have to accommodate the new order of things."

"There will still be Flenser," said Tycoon. "He may be our ally, and I have always admired him, but I fear he plays his own game."

"Yes," Vendacious' voice trailed off in a thoughtful hiss. "Flenser will always be a problem . . ." For once, sincerity?

Through this, Jefri had been staring intently at the horizon. "There! I can see Whale Island!" Ravna followed his gesture. They were just two tiny blips on the edge the world, but she recognized the Notch and the Arch.

"Just follow right half a degree," Jef continued, "and that should be Starship Hill." The directions were clear, but all she could see were blotches of green and gray and white.

"Finally, a proper use for humans!" said Tycoon. "As lookouts . . . if only they could be believed." Tycoon dragged up two long brass cylinders and set them in pintle mounts beside his outermost members. Four other members, still facing Ravna, were gazing down at a map set before their thrones. The two on the ends swept the telescopes back and forth in concert. "Vendacious! I see the starship! It's exactly the magical glassy green you've always said." He admired his telescopic view a few seconds more, then seemed to worry about further dangers: "Here's where we bet we've found a human we can trust." One of Tycoon was still looking at Ravna. "It's true, is it not, that your ship could destroy us in an instant, even from this range?"

". . . Yes," said Ravna. If Nevil had installed the amplifier stage, the beam gun could burn anything in its line of sight. And in Ravna's absence, Nevil's sysadmin authority was probably sufficient to use it as a weapon.

Vendacious had his own ideas about the matter: "That's still another reason to keep Ravna captive. Yes, Nevil is another two-legs, but he really needs us."

———

Johanna's flotilla was strung out along the direction of their course. As usual, her raft had ended up at the front. She looked back along the line of rafts. They stretched in a slight arc across two thousand meters. Hah. Blur your vision enough and they might be great sea battleships of the sort that Ravna had shown them back when she still thought Nyjoran history might mean something to Straumers. (Johanna, of course, had cherished the Princess tales since she was five.)

Altogether, there were over two thousand Tines aboard the flotilla. Once ashore, they would be the kind of trouble Tropical shipwrecks always were—times ten. Or maybe not. These Tines were her allies.

Now they were past the south tip of Whale Island. Ahead was Hidden Island to the west and the inland cliffs to the east. Her sailors had become quite the experts. Right now, all that skill seemed to be dedicated to a perfect "threading of the needle," heading right up the middle of the Straits.

The radio abruptly came to life. This was not the barely audible mumbling of overheard conversations. This was Tinish sent directly from *Oobii* or the orbiter: "Come land. Come land east. East." Even Johanna could understood the chords.

"There there there!" Cheepers' association shouted in Samnorsk, pointing toward the inland cliffs, but north of the piers at Cliffside. She saw a narrow beach, backed by rugged talus. Humans were standing there, waving colored squares of cloth.

Around Johanna, heads perked up. Tines shifted about on the various masts. Members on the deck were pulling at the multiple tillers. The whole craft began drifting toward the makeshift semaphores.

Merto again: "Hei, that worked! They're turning toward Rock Harbor."

To the south of Johanna's raft, the rest of the formation was drifting right, all toward the narrow strip of Rock Harbor. She squinted for a better view. She hadn't been down to Rock Harbor since the year two shipwreck, before the Tropical Embassy. The place was not so deadly anymore. The worst of the jaggedness had silted over and Woodcarver's packs had used gunpowder to break the most dangerous rocks—but despite the name, it was not a proper harbor.

Ah! Of course. That was the reason Nevil wanted the Tropicals to land there. Innocent observers could be kept at a distance. The Tropicals and their freight would be completely in the control of whoever Nevil and Vendacious had positioned there.

And I will be caught before anyone knows I'm alive.

The rocky shore was less than a thousand meters away. Johanna froze for a second or two. Then she grabbed the radio and raced up the familiar path to the top of the cargo jumble, the base of the tallest mast. After all these tendays, she had that worked out so the move was safe and fast—and every step was shielded from the orbiter's lookdown.

She would not be shielded from observers on the shore.

"Hei, hei, listen up!" Johanna's human voice was such a frail thing, but it was all she had. The Tines were looking toward Rock Harbor, or pulling on the sails to guide them eastwards. Johanna jumped up and down, waving. Cheepers and scattered heads turned in her direction; attention spread across the choir.

"Go west. Go west!" She pointed first at Rock Harbor and then swept her arm around the horizon, jabbing at Hidden Island. It was her best imitation of the sort of gesturing that a singleton might do with its snout and neck. *"Go west!"*, and she repeated the gesture.

The radio at her feet remained silent. Her luck was holding; she hadn't been noticed by Nevil's observers.

The mob milled around for a moment. They'd gotten clear directions from the radio. This was the sort of situation where they might not play ball with her. By now she could even recognize their rippling dance as factions of mind dithered. But the radio remained silent, and more and more little clots of awareness were appearing in the mob, amplifying Johanna's point.

Then she saw coordinated unanimity. All around the raft, jaws tightened on ropes and tillers, pulling just so, responding to the result to correct and maintain the maneuver. The raft turned again, ponderously drifting westward across the straits.

That got noticed. The radio came alive with two or three human voices:

"Holy shit, the lead raft has lost control!" At Rock Harbor the hand-waved semaphores bounced frantically. Johanna could hear faint shouting coming from the shore, human voices all. Nevil might be consorting with Vendacious, but he remained a racist.

"What's gone wrong?" That was Tami's voice. "Powers! Nevil, there's something strange on that lead barge. There's a bundle of rags flapping around by the main mast." *Thanks for the fashion comment, Tam.* Johanna couldn't resist: she stopped cheerleading the Choir long enough to face the cliffs. She could only guess where Tami was watching from, but she gave the rocks a cheery wave.

Tami's voice came immediately. "Uk! It's *alive*, Nevil! There's a human on that barge. It's *Johanna!* . . . What do you mean? I know what I see. We can finally learn why she did all those terrible things." Then the radio went silent. Jo waved again, but that didn't provoke anything more from Tami. Johanna looked to the south. The raft behind them was copying her maneuver—and the one behind that! Maybe all ten would elude the cozy rendezvous Nevil had planned.

Johanna's raft was less than fifteen hundred meters from the piers of the South End of Hidden Island. She could see packs and humans there, a crowd forming.

The radio at her feet came to life, gobbling Tinish. Here and there, Tinish heads came up. The chords sounded like the same demand as before. Hah! It was exactly the same, just a recording of the demand that the raft head for Rock Harbor. That was dumb, Nevil. The exact repeat would be recognized as unmindful. Sure enough, not more than a dozen of her mob paid any attention. And when the message repeated again, there was no visible response whatsoever.

There were more people on the South End piers than a minute before. It was still too far away for her to recognize anyone, but there were lots of Children and lots of Tines. She stood tall and waved. Even if they didn't have binoculars, they would know that some human was out here among the Tropicals.

Johanna watched the perspective change as the raft slid toward Hidden Island. The tide was with them, and as the channel narrowed, the winds had picked up. The raft must be making three meters per second. All the rafts were following her. To the east, the semaphores by Rock Harbor waved desperately, ignored by all. Ahead of her on the mainland side, she could see the funicular's steep path up the cliffs. Springtime waterfalls made little rainbows all along the sheer drop and at the top she could see the tiny silhouettes of houses against the sky. Starship Hill and Newcastle town were out of sight, but in another few seconds she would see *Oobii*.

And vice versa!

Even as she crouched low, Johanna caught a glimpse of iridescent green, one of *Oobii*'s ultradrive spines. She grabbed the radio and slid down the west side of the cargo pile, out of sight of the cliffs and the starship. She and Jef were the only Children who had seen the beam gun used for much more than warming residential hot-water tanks. Johanna remembered what it could do with its amplifier stage, the slagged metal, the exploded bodies. Surely, Nevil wouldn't dare commit murder in front of so many witnesses? Maybe not. But how much had those on the South End really seen? He might chance it. He would make some slick, crazy explanation. After all, didn't Tami say that the "something on the barge" looked like a rag mannikin?

So play it safe, stay out of sight till she was ashore and everyone could see the undeniable truth. She tossed her radio into the water, just another red herring for Nevil.

Johanna crawled around to the west side of the raft, taking little detours to keep out of the way of Tines who were busily managing the sheets and rudders. The mob's attention was fixed on making a safe landing; the fact that she was no longer cheerleading had become irrelevant. She crawled onto one of the forward containers that she'd torn open in the search for heavy cloaks. From here, she had a clear view of the approaching piers.

There was Ben Larsndot! He was part of the mixed crowd, humans providing just enough buffering that the packs didn't get in each other's space. They were armed with all manner of ad hoc weapons: timbers, cargo hooks, staves. Johanna waved as broadly as she could. "Hei, Ben! All of you. These Tines are friendly. Don't hurt them."

Her voice was lost in the sea breeze. She felt a snout poking at her shoulder. It was Cheepers. Johanna swept her hand across his shoulders. "Say what I just said, okay?"

A second later, her voice boomed across the water, the same words she had shouted the moment before. Other Tines on the raft picked up on it. The chant grew louder. She stuck her fingers in her ears to blunt the pain of it. The chant was mercifully brief, but as they swept closer, the echo of her voice came back from the inland cliffs. Denying her arrival had just gotten a lot harder!

She didn't say anything more. Her ears couldn't take the reshouting. Instead she crawled forward along the "deck" of freight containers.

They were thirty meters from the pier. This close to shore normal packs would bring down the sails and use ground lines and mooring poles to ease the raft to a soft stop. The mob wasn't into that. They were used to the crushable middens along the River Fell. The sails stayed up, but her crew was doing miracles with the breeze, slowing the craft as they slid closer and closer. Ashore, packs and humans were backing away, shouting at the mob to drop their sails.

Johanna looked up and down the pier. She'd have no trouble getting off, and there were plenty of humans around. Once ashore, Nevil would have to kill lots of others to get at her. *But he just might do even that.* Somehow she had to get off the pier and hidden in town.

How about going *under* the pier just ahead of the oncoming crash? This was getting crazier and crazier, but. . . . She looked into the shaded spaces below the pier. *Maybe.*

"Cheepers!"

Cheepers and several others moved closer. "You stay here. You all stay on the raft, okay? Everyone is friends here."

Then Johanna slipped down from the level of the top freight boxes, down below the line of sight of those on the pier. No one was going to see exactly where she was headed. Surely no one would think she was crazy enough to . . . she dove headfirst from under the overhang of cargo, aiming for a gap in the timber strutwork of the pier.

Numbing agony. She floated back to the surface, all but paralyzed by the cold. This was springtime in the arctic. As she sank back down, scarcely able to wiggle, Johanna had a very clear recollection of when all the Children had been young and Ravna and Pilgrim had lectured them on how quickly humans could die swimming in this water.

She forced her arms out, bumped into something solid. A diagonal timber. She hit another one with her foot, pushed herself up, grabbing at a horizontal beam. For a moment she just hung there, out of the water from her thighs up. Her legs were numb, and she was too weak to climb anywhere hand over hand. She bent her head against her arm, wiping hair out of her eyes. The barnacled strutwork was a zigzag pattern all around her. She had no place to stand and no way to move down the pier toward solid ground. Her grip slipped a centimeter or two. Where were the walkways!

Yeah, there were walkways, and just now the nearest one was a meter to her left—flooded by the rising tide. She swung herself from side to side. Her good fortune was to lose her grip at just the right instant. She splashed down on hands and knees—onto something solid and flat. The walkway was under only ten centimeters of water.

As Johanna struggled to her feet, her raft slid into the pier. The mob had slowed it down to under a meter per second, but the raft was so massive that that didn't matter. Wood against wood, the front edge of the strutwork creaked and then snapped apart.

She staggered along the walkway, holding onto the struts for balance.

The raft had finally come to rest. The pier was still shaking, but the twist and tilt had stopped short of collapsing the entire structure. She heard shouts and even a few cheers from the Children. She picked up her pace. Shore was somewhere in the shadowed timbers ahead. Jefri and Amdi used to play on these piers; she'd had to come down here and apprehend them. There would be stairs at the far end of the pier, a covered passageway into the warehouses. What then? Maybe she should stay hidden for a few days until she could figure out what was going on, contact Woodcarver, Scrupilo, Jefri—if Jef had come to his senses.

As she stumbled along, she heard human and packs running the length of the pier. There were shouts, some in Samnorsk, but too loud to be human. "Johanna! Where are you?" . . . "You say she dove into the water?"

"So where is she now?"

She reached the stairs and discovered an unexpected challenge. Normally, you took Tinish stairs three at time, but now Johanna had to lift her numbed legs with her hands, and carefully watch that she set her nerveless feet down. It was like climbing on stilts. Fortunately, the stairs were only member-wide, so she could lean against the walls as she lifted first one foot and then the other.

She shrugged off the last of her icy cloaks. Sometime really really soon she needed to get dry and warm. For a few moments she forgot everything else as she negotiated the last few steps.

Then she was at the top, in a covered passage. She saw a dirty glass window mounted in an external door. She got close and looked back—just to see how everybody was doing, she told herself. Never mind that she was too weak to do much else.

Nowadays Scrupilo's glassworks could turn out clear glass by the square meter. This little window was from the early years; for Johanna's purposes, it was good enough. She could see humans and packs clustered around the raft. The second and third rafts were pulling in behind it. When the entire fleet arrived, the South End harbor would look like that jumble on the River Fell.

She could step outside and wave to the kids on the pier. She'd still be out of *Oobii*'s sight. The hell with further paranoia. As she reached for the door handle, she noticed several Tropicals climbing onto the pier, approaching the Children. They had recovered the radio!

No!

The side blast from the beam gun sent shards of glass ripping past her face. The shuddering wall bounced her off her feet. She rolled to her knees, her ears ringing with the thunder. No need for a door or a window now. In places the wood panels had been blown away from the wall studs. Thirty meters down the pier a cloud of steam was rising from a hole punched through the pier itself.

As Johanna struggled to her feet she tried to wipe the blood from her face, but the stuff kept dribbling. There were survivors, lots of wounded. She tottered a step or two toward the open pier. *I should help! Yeah, and give crazy Nevil reason to shoot again.*

She turned the other way and staggered up the passage, into the warehouse.

CHAPTER 38

Vendacious' airship was slightly smaller than Tycoon's. Tycoon could believe that he was the star of this operation. Inside, of course . . . that was a different story. Tycoon did not come here; Vendacious could do as he pleased. Tycoon had staterooms and crew quarters. Vendacious had room for cargo and cages and weapons. Crew could sleep at their posts. Tycoon had his command deck high in the bow, unbalancing his ship and isolating him from his servants. Vendacious ruled from his ship's control gondola with just enough quilting so the crew didn't interfere with his thinking. Instant discipline could be exercised. None of those silly speaking tubes for Vendacious. He often thought that Tycoon's command deck was what the eight imagined of human automation. Though Tycoon would have fiercely denied it, he was a slavish admirer of almost all things human. That was just one more reason to keep humans and Tycoon from getting friendly.

"M'lord, the *Pack of Packs* is pulling away from us." This news came from Vendacious' ship's captain, the sound focused so that only the nearest member of Vendacious could hear.

"Very good," Vendacious replied. As he'd directed, his airship was lagging behind, keeping relatively close to the ground. Vendacious was watching with binocular telescopes, following as Tycoon flew blissfully on into the jaws of the mantises. Vendacious really didn't want to follow, but soon he would have to expose himself to those same jaws.

He suppressed his trembling fear and concentrated on the audio from Ut. The singleton had its own perch, well away from the crew. Ut's purpose in life had been very simple for some years now. He wore his prison around his shoulders, the radio cloak glistening black with hints of gold. Ut should be happy, though. He was treated better than most crew.

Tycoon bragged endlessly about the Radio Cloaks network. In fact, it was Vendacious who had persuaded Nevil to supply the cloaks. It was Vendacious who had winnowed hundreds of singletons to find the few who could wear the cloaks and still survive. It was Vendacious who controlled the network. All eight lived in proper fear of him. Vendacious had trained them to speak only along the paths he directed, when he directed. And he was just as careful to keep them from ever getting all their heads together. Now they were his ears across the empire: Earlier this day, he had spoken via the Ut/Ta/Fur/Il relay to Aritarmo down on the Tropical Reservation. An hour later he talked via Ut/For/Fyr to Dekutomon, on the mainland south of Hidden Island. Now he was simply listening via Ut/Zek as Tycoon used the network to make final preparations for the landing on Starship Hill.

Tycoon's various pronouncements and directions were mainly directed at his crew. Vendacious paid a small amount of attention to that; mainly he was interested in any trouble the Ravna maggot might stir up. Abruptly, he realized that Tycoon was talking to *him*: "Where in hell are you, Vendacious? My lookouts have lost sight of you."

Damn you, I'm not being a perfect target in the sky. But aloud, Vendacious said, "Sorry, my lord, sorry. We've had a bit of mechanical trouble, unable to make much altitude." In fact, mountain walls loomed on either side of their path, thousands of feet of rock between his precious members and the maggots' beam gun.

"Are you going to crash then?" said Tycoon. "I've told you to be more careful about repairs. It's stupid to have your own maintenance crews."

"Not to worry, sir. My people have a solution. You'll be seeing us soon." Vendacious glanced at the dataset display in front of him. The position map showed that he was running out of mountains to hide behind. He must soon decide between trusting Nevil Storherte and dropping out of the game.

"Very good then!" Their conversation was in Interpack and thus free of maggoty smart remarks. "Another thing," continued Tycoon. "I need to talk to Nevil directly. There's final planning—"

"I believe I've covered everything, my lord." Vendacious did his best to be the middlepack in all contacts between Tycoon and humans, even—and especially—Nevil Storherte. Fortunately, Storherte really didn't like to talk to packs. Keeping Tycoon from chatting with Nevil had been much easier than keeping the eightsome from talking to the various surviving prisoners.

Not today: "I'm sure you've done your best, Vendacious, but now you're lagging and I'm less than an hour from landing. I want to ask Nevil some questions about just who is present, and the current status of the likes of Woodcarver and Flenser and—" Tycoon's voice scaled up a couple of octaves as he spoke.

"Yes, my lord! Have you used your ordinary radio? Nevil is listening all the time via the orbiter. Now—"

"I've tried that! The two-legs is not replying."

"I'll look into it, my lord. I have agents on the ground." *And other means of communication.*

"I need results on this quickly, Vendacious. As you know, the Ravna two-legs has been saying many harsh things about Nevil. Now is not the time to have her proven right."

"I agree, sir. I'll get back to you directly." In this, he was utterly sincere. "I'll be out of communication with you for a few minutes."

"I understand. Use the cloaks network and whatever else is needed."

Vendacious waved at Ut to stop relaying with Tycoon's ship. *Damnation.* Too many problems were suddenly piling up. He should prepare for one of those problems immediately. Vendacious glanced down from his platforms, "Cargomaster!"

"Sir!"

"Bring up our special prisoners. The four goes in its usual cage, but I want Amdiranifani shackled around the bow hatch."

The Cargomaster cowered slightly, then it hustled immediately off for the prison cells. The pack had been through this procedure before.

As for the more difficult problems: How to get in touch with Nevil? Was that maggot playing some new game? He thought he had Nevil figured out, but the prospect of facing the beam gun made him want to rethink everything. *Dekutomon is close to* Oobii. *I could have him take Fyr and visit the maggot.* If there'd been more time, that would've been the best approach; let Nevil know that Vendacious' agents were everywhere, even on Nevil's doorstep.

Or, he could use an ordinary radio to try to reach Nevil through his heavenly high orbiter. No, that was grovelling, and it hadn't worked for Tycoon. Besides, ordinary radio might be overheard by the radio sets Tycoon had aboard *Pack of Packs.*

Vendacious glanced at his dataset. Right now it was displaying a map of his ground track, the ridges on either side of his ship marked with altitudes and proximity. In the early years of his exile, this dataset—Oliphaunt, Johanna had called it—had been his most precious possession, the true reason why he was so esteemed by Tycoon. Since his alliance with Nevil, the dataset had not been nearly so important an informational tool, and at the same time he had come to worry about the possibility that Nevil might be able to corrupt the device. Nevertheless, like his commset, the dataset was galactic technology, putting him on a par with the maggots. And now that Nevil controlled the starship, it was by far the most secret communication path between them.

Vendacious reached out a couple of noses and tapped the sequence of instructions that should change Oliphaunt from an atlas to a commset. Johanna had always been more adept at this than he, but then she had used it all her human life; Vendacious took considerable pride in how adept *he* had become with the device. There, he was in commset mode and . . . He noticed the red light blinking at the bottom of the display. That was the special signal he had installed; Nevil was trying to call *him!*

Vendacious startled into action. The parts of him nearest Ut pulled on cords that dropped heavy quilts on every side of the singleton's perch. He checked it above and below. Now, properly pitched sounds would not be heard by Ut. Not that the Radio pack would dare to deliberately betray Vendacious, but stretched out as it was across the continent, the individual parts were scarcely more than relays. Vendacious had used that fact to snoop across hundreds of leagues—but he lived in horror that his innermost secrets might inadvertently be revealed to others.

He tapped a snout at the dataset, initiating a call, but with the sounds shifted way up into frequencies so high that they came close to interfering with thought. Such squeaking would never penetrate the quilts that surrounded Ut; no chance that dear Tycoon would be bothered by inadvertent relays.

"Vendacious here," he said, squeaking soft and super-high himself. Oliphaunt dataset had Tinishly good hearing. Somewhere inside, it transformed Vendacious' voice into *digital* (whatever that was) and boosted it out to Nevil. Vendacious' heads hurt when he tried to imagine all the things the dataset did automatically. *Somewhere* out among the stars, there were things worth fearing.

Some seconds passed. Was he going to have to leave a message?

Then Nevil's upshifted voice came from the dataset: "Why in hell are you flying so low, man?"

Vendacious suppressed a snarl. Aloud, he made a noncommittal human noise.

"Never mind," the maggot continued. "We've got a problem. You told me Johanna was out of the picture."

"Of course. Torn to pieces." But suddenly Vendacious had a very bad feeling. *"She was on your frigging fleet!"*

"But I saw her die. *You* were listening yourself."

"Well, I just saw her alive through trusted video. Now we know why we haven't had contact with the rafts. Powers on High, Vendacious! How could you?"

Vendacious' jaws snapped. If the maggot had been physically present, he would have lost his one and only throat. "You think I arranged this complication?" he said.

"I, no." Nevil's voice was choppy, as if he were trotting or climbing stairs; humans were such simple animals that they couldn't disguise that sort of thing. "Look, things are a bit dicey here. If we bring this off, Woodcarver will be so discredited that she won't dare grab power. My sisters and brothers will be safe. We can make something of this miserable exile—with your help of course. You can have all this damn world when we are done with it, but—"

Vendacious' spies often reported that Nevil was wonderfully persuasive with his fellow larvae. That was very difficult to believe. The maggot had *never* sounded like anything but a crude manipulator to Vendacious.

In a way, that was comforting. Vendacious let Nevil rattle on for a moment more. When the maggot came to a natural pause, Vendacious had something reasonable and constructive to say: "All agreed, of course. The question is, what should we do about this unpleasant surprise?"

"Well, I've already done what was necessary. That's one reason I'm so pissed." Nevil explained how he had blasted Johanna and a crowd of maggots into superheated steam. "The beam killed six of my brothers and sisters. We Children count, Vendacious! I need every one of them to work with me." He was silent for a moment.

Was he inviting a reply? Vendacious couldn't think of anything non-sarcastic; finally, he responded, "So this has damaged your credibility."

Nevil gave a sour laugh. "I'm not an idiot. Used this way, beam gun targets just explode. You know, like a bomb. I've made a big deal of the terrorist factions within the Tropicals—it's what today's 'peace treaty' meeting is all about. So the story is, Tinish dissidents on the barge fleet tried to sabotage Tycoon's generous gift. There are rough edges, but I can make it work. If anything, this will strengthen our current position—but that's not the point!"

"Indeed not," said Vendacious. "So you actually *saw* Johanna die?"

"Ah . . ." the human had the grace to acknowledge the irony. "Okay, not exactly. It looked like the guys on the pier were walking someone toward shore. And the instant I fired, *Oobii* lost contact with that broken radio we'd been tracking."

"That sounds even less certain than what I managed in the Tropics." Vendacious had hated Johanna Olsndot for so long. In a very real sense, she was responsible for the debacle of ten years ago. Tycoon might be surprised to learn that Vendacious hated Johanna even more than Tycoon did—and for much better reason. "Nevil, I think our problem may be more serious than explaining a little gunfire. At least we should plan for the possibility that Johanna is still out there, actively seeking allies."

Nevil was silent for a moment. It sounded like he had just moved out of doors or turned up one of his mechanical sound-dampers. Then: "Yeah . . . Bili made pretty much the same point. He thinks we should switch over to my backup plan."

Vendacious shrugged angrily and put a certain bluff irritation into his voice: "Nonsense. That's defeatism." Without Ravna's technical support, and now with Woodcarver's active opposition, Nevil's position in the Domain had become steadily more difficult. In some ways that was good; it made the maggot easier to manipulate. Unfortunately, it also meant he had increasing interest in his "backup plan." That scheme might make sense in the long run—for Nevil— but it would render him almost useless to Vendacious.

"Nevil, I, um, beg you to stick with our grand plan. Let's think on other options we can exercise if problems arise."

"Okay, suppose Tycoon lands and behaves even more the fool than usual. Suppose he insists that Bergsndot and Jo's little brother accompany him on stage, in front of all the Children. And then—"

"Yes, that would be bad, but—"

Nevil's voice rode over his words: "—and then suppose Johanna has miraculously survived and teamed up with Woodcarver? She could upstage us all—and I can't kill *everybody!*"

Vendacious gave a derisive hoot. "Johanna couldn't speak a single syllable before Tycoon would rip her throat out." Nevil simply didn't understand Tycoon's hatred for that particular two-legs.

"Worst case, Vendacious, I'm talking worst case. I know the Ravna bitch is an idiot; she couldn't convince a friendly audience that the sun is going to rise tomorrow. And Jefri Olsndot is just a follower. But they've had several days to chat up *your* idiot, right?"

Vendacious ground his teeth as he replied, "I've been following that; I'm in control of the situation."

"You're betting a lot on that assessment, my friend. What are we going to do if Tycoon gets turned?"

Vendacious didn't have to think too hard on that. "Ultimately, Tycoon is simply a tool, a very very valuable tool. If he ever figures out the full truth of things, then he must be immediately destroyed. . . . Um." And what would that mean in the present situation? "If you and I coordinate on this . . . we could cover all the possibilities. If I determine that Tycoon has gone bad, I will immediately tell you. So if your 'worst case' materializes—"

"Then I would fry them both? . . . Okay. I could say I was trying to protect Johanna but that *Oobii* glitched. The weapons Down Here are so crude I might be able to make that story work."

"Fine. But remember, killing Tycoon is truly a last resort. We need him more than I think you know. Even if Johanna pops out in front of him, don't just kill Tycoon. I'm confident he will quickly destroy her, but I'll signal you otherwise."

"Ah. So you're going to come out of hiding then?"

Sigh. "Indeed. I'll circle overhead in honor of this historic meeting of our races."

They briefly chatted about details, and Vendacious mentioned Tycoon's demand to speak with Nevil.

"Yeah, I noticed he was pinging me." Nevil was silent for a moment. There were human-sounding voices in the background. Nevil continued: "I don't want to talk to that shithead now. I've got to get on stage myself. What does he want to talk about anyway?"

"I think he wants some kind of last-minute reassurance about the situation with Woodcarver and Flenser."

"The idiot! There is no last-minute reassurance; that's why getting this meeting right is so important. Okay. I'll talk to him when I get to the stage area." And then Nevil signed off. At least that was what the symbol on the dataset's display indicated. As far as Vendacious could tell, the dataset did not covertly transmit to the two-legs. Given that Oliphaunt was Johanna's toy and it had never been in Nevil's hands, Vendacious was inclined to think it was not corrupted by him. With the two-legs' gadgets, you never knew for sure. When Vendacious did things Nevil must not know, he locked the dataset away and used the Radio Cloak network. He had ten years of evidence that the starship could not snoop on mindsounds.

Speaking of which, he should talk to Tycoon to claim credit for Nevil's upcoming call—

The thought was interrupted by whistling cries of anticipated pain. The Cargomaster dragged Amdiranifani into the space below Vendacious, then fastened the pack's neck collars to the garrote stands that ringed the bow hatch. As the Cargomaster left the area to bring in the other prisoner, Vendacious leaned down a head to inspect Amdiranifani. The eight heard him and shrank back.

Vendacious smiled. Intelligent victims were always entertaining. They thought they could outwit their torturer—and after you broke them, their own imagination became your best ally. Without a doubt, Amdiranifani was the most brilliant victim Vendacious had ever had. This eightsome had come a long way down. In the first day or two, it had actually tried to suborn crew and radio with covert speech, echoing threads of sound that evaded Vendacious' hearing. The arrogance of the eight, to think it could bring off such a scheme. Vendacious had let Amdiranifani hope for three full days. Apprehension had been sweet, the punishment tuned to the victim: Vendacious had gouged out two of Amdiranifani's eyes. Just two, just eyes—and then he had called on his victim to *imagine* how much worse the punishment could be. For this pack, with its imagination, the effect was as devastating as cracking half its tympana, or killing a member outright. And the mild punishment left so much more for Vendacious to work with. . . .

Amdiranifani was making little squeaking noises, fighting within himself for the courage to speak.

Vendacious raised the tip of one nose, a gesture that normally preceded harsh punishment during interrogation. Amdiranifani froze into terrified silence.

"Ah, my dear Amdiranifani. So sorry for the poor view you have down there. Don't worry, you may yet *hear* some interesting things. Here's something very important: Think quietly. Remain speech silent, except where I give you leave to speak." He raised a second nose, also a signal he had used during interrogations, when an absolute order was given. There was nothing this creature could say that would make any difference, but Vendacious wanted any screams of pain that leaked across the radio net to be under his own control. "If you disobey— well, I think you know where you're standing." Vendacious gestured at the bow hatch in the middle of Amdiranifani. "Take that as your suspended sentence. I would just as soon have you be seven or six or even five. It would be a pleasure to throw some of you to the winds, and I could tell Tycoon you were trying to escape and overreached yourself. You have no doubt of me, do you?"

Here and there, Amdiranifani's heads dipped in trembling acknowledgment. Just last night, Vendacious had thrown one of his own crew's members out that hatch—and made sure that Amdiranifani had witnessed the discipline. Whether dealing with a single member or a whole pack, Vendacious always enjoyed such punishment. Usually the victim was a prisoner, but killing an occasional malingering bit of crew did wonders to encourage good performance from the rest.

Cargomaster was bringing in the foursome, all that was left of my lord Steel. *This* prisoner was not so manageable. It was enraged beyond fear, and not very intelligent—ordinarily not an entertaining combination. This remnant of Steel had become steadily more killing crazy as the days passed, perhaps recalling its old hatreds. Its insanity exploded whenever it came within ear- or eyeshot of Amdiranifani. The four bounced off the walls of its cage, searching for some way out, shrieking murder at the eightsome. Remnant Steel and Amdiranifani's own imagination kept Amdiranifani forever at the edge of collapse.

If only I had this strong a hold on the humans with Tycoon. Vendacious eyed Amdiranifani speculatively. Avoiding Nevil's "worst case" might come down to whether maggots Jefri and Ravna would keep silent if the alternative was to see pieces of their dear friend raining from the sky.

Now Ravna could see Newcastle town and *Oobii*. Both Tycoon (with his telescopes) and Jefri claimed there were crowds on the heather southeast of town.

"I have them in sight, too," came Vendacious' voice. His airship was rapidly catching up. "That's where the great meeting is to be, my lord. Nevil has constructed a stage there and cleared a landing field, just as we agreed."

"And he'll call the moment he arrives?" said Tycoon.

"Yes, my lord, direct to your ordinary radio. Do you have—"

"Hello? Hello?" That was Nevil's voice, coming from an analog radio by Tycoon's thrones. In the background there were human voices, and the sound of whipping wind.

Tycoon leaned toward the radio box and said, "Greetings, Lord Nevil." The portentous words sounded incongruous in his frightened little girl voice.

"Yes. Well . . . Greetings to you, too." Nevil's voice clipped in and out. She heard snippets of confident-sounding advice he was giving to someone near him. Ah. Nevil must be wearing the single remaining HUD, using it to maintain two conversation streams. "Okay, I'm back. Everybody can see your airships now. They're waving. I'm about to go up on stage, give everybody a pep talk. Woodcarver is already up there, but she's cooperating. Too many other people really want this alliance. Everything is under control and per our previous discussions." Ravna almost smiled. She had never heard Nevil Storherte sound, well, frazzled. "So, um, are you ready for our meeting, sir?"

"We are on schedule as well," said Tycoon, "but I have several questions."

"Yes, sir?"

"First, are you hiding Johanna Olsndot?" The whole pack was watching Ravna and Jefri.

"What? No!" Nevil's voice clipped out for a second. "Why in heaven's name would you ask me that? Haven't I—"

"You've been very helpful on this issue in the past. I thank you for that." Tycoon was still watching Ravna and Jef. "But at the same time I know you were—mutually promised? sex-involved?—with Johanna. Even humans must have some forms of loyalty, so I wanted to ask."

"Mister, I assure you that after what Johanna did, I have no loyalty towards her!"

"Very well then. I just wanted to ask."

"Are your other questions as interesting?"

"You can be the judge of that," said Tycoon, and proceeded into the fine points of who would be seated where onstage, and where Woodcarver might have security packs, and how they were armed. Vendacious would circle overhead while Lord Tycoon was on the ground. Finally, Tycoon said, "This all sounds very good, my lord Nevil. Thank you. I will see you on the ground in a few minutes."

"Yes, sir," said Nevil, "I look forward to making our alliance official." He was sounding something like his normal diplomatic self. "Ah, one other thing, my lord Tycoon. For best effect, I recommend that you not speak with your human voice. Use Tinish. More dignified, don't you think?"

Tycoon cocked his heads. "My use of your language is poor?"

"Not at all!" protested Nevil. In fact, Tycoon spoke better Samnorsk than most Starship Hill packs. Nevil must be worried about the Geri voice; *that* by itself would betray Nevil's lies. "It's just that . . . um . . . speaking Tinish will seem so much more dignified. More powerful, too."

Vendacious put in, "I'll be happy to translate, anonymously of course."

Tycoon admired himself for a moment. "Yes . . . I see your point. Very well."

"Excellent. I must go onstage now. Talk to you in person soon."

After a moment, the little analog radio emitted background static; no one was transmitting to it. Two of Tycoon picked up the device and a third head punched a button in the side; even the static ceased.

Tycoon set down the device and looked around the command deck. "Of course, he's lying about Johanna."

"*Huh?*" said Jefri. Vendacious gobbled similar surprise, and some kind of question.

"Yes, Vendacious. Well you might ask." Tycoon's stare returned to Ravna and Jefri. "You see, since we've had specimens, I have become a great student of human nature. In fact, understanding them is not that difficult; they are such simple creatures, with such simple motivations. While I was talking to Nevil, I was watching these two here. Both realized that Nevil is lying." He spoke with the confidence of a real expert—or a revenge-obsessed nutcase.

"See?" He waved at Jefri. "The Johanna-brother is speechless. I have found him out yet again. And you, Ravna. Can you honestly say that Nevil was telling the truth?"

How would I know? I'm not sure I've ever heard Nevil telling the truth. Hope and fear chased around in her head, and she was as silent as Jefri.

Vendacious was not so shy. "My lord, I would never have guessed, but it . . . it could be so. These next few hours, I will watch for signs of other lies."

———

They were about ten kilometers from Starship Hill. Ravna had flown over this area often enough—both with Pilgrim, and in recent times on Scrupilo's little airboat. Below were the merged farms of the Margrum River Valley. To the west, the edge of the sea cliffs was obvious now. Just on this side of the edge, the town houses stood along the Queen's Road. Newcastle town sprawled to the north, climbing right up to the marble dome of the castle itself.

Tycoon's attention was spread across several tasks, talking on the speaking tubes with his pilots, watching ahead, occasionally chatting with his advisors. Vendacious claimed to have Amdi on his ship's command deck, and had persuaded him to cooperate in providing information. "I'll trust the pack for nothing critical of course," said Vendacious, "but he's lived near Starship Hill all his life. And he knows that lying will be strictly punished."

"I don't know," Tycoon replied, even as he continued to talk to his own crew via speaking tubes. "I wouldn't trust a prisoner's word at a moment like this."

"Ah, but I also have agents on the ground."

"Dekutomon?"

"He's the most important, my lord. He's near the landing spot and he is with the radio cloak Fyr."

"Good! I had wondered what you did with Fyr! So Nevil can't hear what Dekutomon is telling us?"

"Indeed, my lord."

Tycoon gobbled something that meant *oops*, and made some hasty correction to what he was saying to his crew of pilots. In Samnorsk he said, "Very good, Vendacious. Now I should concentrate on this landing." Tycoon looked mainly forward, with two of himself on the binoculars. Apparently he intended to manage the landing directly, using the speaking tubes to specify every smallest detail to the real crew. It was typical Tycoon foolishness.

Mercifully, Vendacious and the other various advisors were silent for a time. There was just Zek, every fifteen seconds or so, calling out range information in precise Samnorsk units:

"Altitude 750 meters, range to touchdown 3300 meters."

"Altitude 735 meters, range to touchdown 3150 meters."

"Altitude 720 meters, range to touchdown 3005 meters."

None of Tycoon looked around, but he made an approving sound. "Very good, Vendacious! Your ranging information is making this much easier."

Ravna had seen no evidence that Tycoon's operation had any location technology beyond the natural sonar Tines were born with. Where were those numbers coming from?

Jefri gave her a little nudge and nodded in the direction of Zek. The singleton was looking back at them. It turned, stared for a moment at the landscape ahead—

"Altitude 705 meters, range to touchdown 2850 meters."

Then its eyes were back on Ravna and Jefri. The creature was all but quivering with tension, as if to *will* them to understand something more than the numbers. *What was behind those eyes?* The two airships must be less than a kilometer apart, so Zek and Ut were essentially together. Dekutomon's Fyr was probably closer than it had ever been before. That meant that Mr. Radio was at least a threesome. There were likely two others fairly close, one that had been used for long-range relay to Fyr and one at the head of the chain to the Tropics. Right now the radio pack could easily be a fully-connected fivesome, perhaps even smarter than the night it had linked them with Amdi.

Maybe such a pack couldn't run a full Man-in-the-Middle, but all it had to do was *not* relay all it heard from here. If it was willing to risk its life. . . . She glanced at Jefri. He was as pale as he could be, stricken. He gave her a nod, understanding.

Meantime, Zek still looked at them, intent. The creature had made a brave offer. Okay. Ravna nodded at him, and quietly asked something that might be innocuous even if it were relayed to listeners up and down Mr. Radio's network: "How many are you?"

"I'm between five and eight," Radio replied. "depending on sky bounce reception. We must be quick."

Tycoon was preoccupied with his speaking tubes and binoculars, but now one of him glanced up, curious at the strange conversation. He gobbled a query wrapped around the Tinish for "Vendacious."

Zek shrank back on his perch, but his reply was Samnorsk: "Not Vendacious at the moment, sir. This is myself, Radio."

Another head came up. "So you're really all of one mind? Remarkable. What does Vendacious think of this?"

Zek cringed a bit lower. "Vendacious doesn't know, sir. I'm not relaying this conversation."

Tycoon made a surprised noise. He angled some heads at the speaking tubes and emitted a single chord that meant "carry on." Then all his attention returned to Zek: "Why not?"

"I . . . I'm his victim, sir. I beg you to keep this conversation secret."

Tycoon shrugged. "Perhaps. So you must be passing lies on to Vendacious then?"

"No! I used your voice, but only to elaborate on what you said, that you need to concentrate on your landing."

"And the numbers you were saying to me? They are lies too?"

"No, they come from combining the view from my Ut and Zek and Fyr. Just as I began the deception, I lost part of myself, and was afraid to say anything to you at all. Amdiranifani thought—"

"Ah. Amdiranifani." Tycoon nodded. "So he's been operating right under Vendacious' snouts. Amazing."

Zek's voiced gained a little confidence. "Yes, sir. I couldn't do this without him and the crazy soundpaths he dances around the control gondola. When my radio mind weakens, he makes suggestions."

Half of Tycoon was looking at Jef and Ravna now. The pack's whole aspect was a ferocious smile. "I understand. Amdiranifani is even more remarkable than Vendacious claims. He has made a *puppet* out of my radio network."

"No, please! I am not a puppet—"

Tycoon voice rolled over the protest: "Just listen to this, Amdiranifani!" He grabbed up his voice-band radio and waved it at Zek. The two airships were so close that this device would surely work.

"No, no, no. Please don't betray me—" Zek's Samnorsk dissolved into Tinish, and then not even that. A bubbling noise emerged from the singleton's mouth, a sound that Ravna had never heard from Tines before.

Jefri was on his feet, shouting. Behind him, the gunpack had surged out of the stairwell.

And they were both trumped by the squall of outrage that came from the other side of the chamber: Ritl bounced off her perch, blathering as loud as she had when Ravna first met her. She ran across the deck to Tycoon's thrones, shrieking at him one and all. Then she danced sideways till she was standing in front of Zek. She turned, snapping belligerently.

Tycoon waved the gunpack back. Then he shifted position slightly and focused a roar down upon Ritl. This level of sound was a weapon. The singleton was knocked off her feet. Even outside of the focus, the noise was a spike of pain in Ravna's ears.

Ritl lay on her back, twitching. Finally she rolled over and belly-crawled back toward her perch, Tycoon's gaze following her centimeter by centimeter. When she was under the partial cover of the perch, she emitted a defiant little squawk.

Tycoon stared at Ritt for a long moment. Then he put down the analog radio and said to Zek, "Have your say."

Zek didn't reply immediately. He looked dazed, maybe by the splash of Tycoon's roar, maybe by the terror of the moment before. "Thank you, sir," The creature hesitated. "There will be interruptions. I wasn't able to entirely disguise—" Abruptly he was gobbling Interpack, some kind of question.

Tycoon answered in Samnorsk, "Give me a moment, Vendacious! This landing is tricky." He gestured for Zek to relay his words.

And Vendacious replied, "Indeed, my lord! Sorry for interrupting!"

In fact, it looked to Ravna as though the *Pack of Packs* crew was doing just fine without any micro-managing from Tycoon. The ship wasn't more than a thousand meters from touchdown. Ahead was familiar ground, Murder Meadows. It was the nearest open ground to the city. Today the heather was festive with crowds and banners.

But Tycoon continued, "In fact, we may still be too high. I'm going to circle the landing area and try again. It will give me more time to be sure of the ground."

"As you say, my lord." Then Vendacious' voice brightened. "I imagine the maneuver will impress Woodcarver's subjects."

"Follow me, then." Tycoon didn't say anything for a moment, but he was watching Zek.

"I've resumed faking the relay, sir," Mr. Radio Cloaks said.

"Good. We'll have few minutes to chat then." Tycoon looked almost gleeful; the geeky side of him must find this deception fascinating. He said something into a speaking tube. Almost immediately the engines buzzed louder. The airship turned and they could see Newcastle town spread out below them.

Tycoon sobered and he gave Zek a sharp look. "Well? You have your time. Speak!"

Zek sat a little straighter: "Thank you sir. I've rarely been a person, and never for very long. But at this moment, I am eight. Vendacious can't keep his secrets from me, not all of them. He is the king of lies, sir, and the king of death. He kills and kills—his own people!"

"So? Overthrow him."

"You don't know much about killing, do you, sir? If you kill often enough, and cleverly enough, you can build a palace of terror. Someday it may fall, but just the thought of that is enough to be murdered for."

"Until Amdiranifani came along?"

Zek gave a one-headed nod. "Until Amdiranifani and the good radio conditions that my parts have been wishing for the last tenday. A word from you, sir, just a word of hope. It could make the difference. It could bring Vendacious down."

Tycoon made a disbelieving sound. "I know Vendacious treats his prisoners harshly, sometimes his employees too. I've curbed the worst excesses. And his spies gets results. *He* gets results. Can you gainsay that?"

"Yes!" But now Zek seemed to lose track of the conversation. His eyes became unfocused. "Sorry. I'm down to three. A moment—"

Murder Meadows slid beneath the airship. Now they could see downslope to Hidden Island and beyond, but the real spectacle was *Oobii*. They would be flying along the starship's length. *Oobii*'s drive spines drooped around her and the ones underneath were crushed, but the ship still gleamed greenfly bright. Even packs who didn't know what that ship had been were overcome by its beauty. Ravna noticed that Tycoon's members were all staring at the ship, almost as distracted as Zek, but for different reasons.

Mr. Radio resumed, "Vendacious murdered *gobble* and *gobble*"—these were names Ravna didn't recognize—"when they gained too much favor with you. He murdered the human, Edvi Verring, ran him into the Choir land, then told you that he died of the bloat."

Tycoon turned a head back to Zek and commented, "Vendacious offered to let us see the remains."

"A ploy, sir. Recall, he made the offer to Ravna and Timor. He's convinced Timor that Edvi might still live. Vendacious uses hostages for everything. Even when the hostages are *dead*, he still uses them."

"That's far-fetched. *I* could have asked to see the remains."

Mr. Radio replied abruptly: "You *could* have, but you didn't. Even if you had, Vendacious would have had some explanation *you* would accept. In the year that I can remember, your gullibility has shown no bounds." He hesitated and Zek shrank back from his standing posture. "I'm sorry, I'm sorry."

Tycoon didn't react except to raise one snout ironically, "You plead a little radio interference, do you?"

"No, sir," the words came softly, "that was from all of me." Maybe, but Zek looked confused now. "In the time I have, I don't know quite what more to say . . ." He glanced across at Jefri and then continued, "There is the murder and the lie that made all the rest possible. Vendacious killed Scriber Jaqueramaphan. Then he lied to say that Johanna—"

"Yes, yes, you don't have to repeat that claim." Tycoon nodded at Jefri. "I hear your friend Amdiranifani behind these pleadings." But Tycoon did not really sound enraged. Most of him was still staring outwards. *Oobii* filled the view, its stately curves sweeping past, its drive spines arching so close you might think to reach out and touch them. There was a kind of awed distraction in Tycoon's posture. "Scriber would have loved you humans," he said. "He was such an innocent and *impractical* person. Before we seperated, I—we—were more creative than any sane businesspack. We were so successful we couldn't keep up with all our ventures. So we decided to become two, one pack to specialize in practice and the other in farthest imagination. One was to be the steady businesspack, one the flying imagination. Scriber kept notebooks of his inventions. I worked to expand our businesses while he created.

"In his notebooks, he had flying machines and tunnelers and submersible boats. There's only one problem with going from a notebook idea to a salable product. Well, no. There are ten thousand thousand problems. Most of his inventions depended on materials that didn't exist, on engines more powerful than any we could make, on precision of manufacture that he barely had words for. He diverted our company into debacle after debacle. We had been so beautiful before . . ." All Tycoon's heads were drooping. "In the end, I—the creature of business and common sense—couldn't tolerate Scriber's endless, brilliant failures. I forced him out of the business. He was agreeable enough. I . . . think . . . he understood why we had come to an end. He cashed out and left for the West." Tycoon jabbed a snout at Jef and Ravna. "I know Scriber befriended you people. I know he was both too clever and too naive to survive the meeting. What did he discover about you two-legs? Why would this Johanna murder him in pieces, till all of him was dead?"

Poor Jefri was beyond indignation, perhaps beyond rage. He sat back, his mouth opening and closing in silent shock. Ravna put her arm across his shoulders. *Let me try, one more time.* She looked at Tycoon. "I never met Scriber Jaqueramaphan," Ravna said. "But I know him through Johanna. She loved him. Her greatest shame is that she didn't respect him enough. He died because he was trying to protect her, but it was Vendacious who murdered him. Won't you even consider that possibility? Even after an, an employee has risked his life to tell you?"

Tycoon hesitated. "If that really is my employee and not just Amdiranifani's speaking tube. . . . You and I have talked about this before. I have always taken these matters seriously. I have interviewed witnesses. Nevil himself—"

Zek interrupted with a long gobble, complaining about something or other.

Tycoon visibly pulled himself together. Then two of him leaned out from their thrones, looking almost straight down from the vertex of the bow. "Yes, Vendacious. I see it."

There was more gobbling from Zek.

"Oh?" said Tycoon. "Woodcarver thinks that, does she? Well you tell Nevil to tell her that—" and then he was speaking Interpack, too.

Ravna glanced at Jefri. He gave his head a little shake, but kept silent. A moment later, she saw what was under discussion. There was a third aircraft, below and ahead of them. It was Scrupilo's little airboat, the original *Eyes Above*. The boat was flying in its own circle over the field.

As the *Pack of Packs* continued on its course, the two craft came closer, but now the airboat was turning away, heading over the Inland Straits, perhaps to Scrupilo's labs on Hidden Island. She glimpsed a pack in the gondola; it flipped a member impudently at them. *I'll bet that's Scrupilo himself.* She could imagine him and Woodcarver desperately trying to put the brakes on Nevil's "Alliance for Peace."

Zek was making genial laughing noises. Then he spoke in Samnorsk, with Vendacious' voice. "Woodcarver's balloon has run away, my lord. One little threat from Nevil was all it took."

"Indeed," said Tycoon, though he watched the departing airboat with only a single pair of eyes. The rest of him was looking ahead. "In less than half a turn we'll be back in landing position, Vendacious."

"We are still tracking directly behind you, my lord. We'll continue on our course as you land. Please keep in touch via the network."

Tycoon turned a couple of heads to look at Zek. The poor creature had collapsed on his perch. He looked very tired, past coherent fear. Ravna guessed that relaying was all he could manage now. More of Tycoon looked around, glancing at Jefri and Ravna. He cocked his heads as if indecisive. Would he betray Zek and his peers? But then all he said was, "Very good. I'll keep Zek close."

———

Airships might look like some flyers of the Beyond, but the only real similarity was that both could float in the air. Airships were fragile balloons, slaves to the atmosphere. Landing an airship was an enormously awkward exercise, at least if you didn't have reasonable automation, or trained ground crews.

As they descended upon the meadow, Tycoon had six heads forward, staring down and forward. This time, he wasn't bothering his pilot. Every meter of descent was a balance of ballast and fine maneuver. They were now so low that most of Newcastle town was above them. Nevil's open-air stage was at far end of the field, but dozens of humans and even more packs were running along below the airship. Ahead were clusters of younger Children let out of their Academy classes. The colors were festival cheerful, as if the crowds were welcoming back far explorers.

Suddenly the ship's engines buzzed louder, and the deck shivered beneath her. She could see the tiny heather flowers just beyond the bow window. Still under power, the ship was motionless. Depending on how much lift gas the pilot had vented, they might be floating like thistledown. Then the engines died. She heard crunching noises as the airship was drawn down to the vegetation.

Humans and Tines rolled tie-down weights across the ground just in front of the bow. She recognized faces. These were people from Scrupilo's ground crew. Tycoon watched with nervous twitches.

Zek was relaying assurances in Tinish, presumably from Vendacious circling above, but Tycoon seemed more interested in what he could see and what he was hearing via the speaking tubes from his own crew. Now he hopped down from his thrones and padded past Ravna and Jefri to the spiral stairs. He was giving orders in all directions, though Ravna could understand only a little.

Jefri looked surprised by something the pack was saying. "Hei, I think Tycoon wants *us* to accompany him."

Zek got down from his perch and almost tripped on his cloak. Ritl ran to him and made encouraging noises. Zek didn't seem especially frightened; he rearranged his cloak and walked over to Ravna and Jefri. When he spoke, it was Vendacious: "Ah, the humans. What to do with you? M'lord Tycoon says it's safe to take you outside, that your presence will disarm the likes of Woodcarver."

The gunpack had two heads stuck up from the stairwell. It waggled a snout in Zek's direction, evidently telling him to get a move on. Zek started toward the stairs, but he seemed to be getting conflicting orders. He stopped to relay one more piece of advice from Vendacious: "I hope my lord Tycoon is right in this—but keep in mind that *I* am watching from above. I will use Amdiranifani to assure that you do not make trouble." Then he followed the gunpack down the stairs.

CHAPTER 39

That afternoon, Johanna Olsndot discovered some true friends. The surprise and the life-saving miracle was that they were exactly everyone she met. Within ten minutes of Nevil's attack on the pier, she was in the Larsndots' apartment above the tailor shop on Wee Alley. Ben Larsndot had found her tottering down back alleys.

"I was just at the front of the crowd. I saw you peeping out of the stormwalk and then the world blew up." He was half-carrying her. "Did those Tropicals bring a bomb ashore?"

"No. It was . . . beam gun." She could barely gasp the words that should have been screamed.

Even so, Ben stopped in surprise. "But—even Nevil wouldn't do something like that!"

"But it's the truth," she said. This conversation was the story of Nevil's life.

Ben didn't say too much after that, but she sensed his rage. When they got to the apartment, he stayed just long enough to tell his wife what had happened, and then he departed to go back to the pier. Wenda went tight-lipped when she heard the story, but she let him go. She looked at Johanna, "Ben has to help out. On the other hand, I'm the one with political savvy in the family."

Johanna was lying limply on a sofa, under a nice warm cloak. She was vaguely aware of Wenda, Jr., and Sika hovering about. They didn't seem frightened, just generally awed by all the sudden activity. "Political savvy is what I need. I want to get the word out about what's really happened—without any more innocents getting killed."

Wenda gave her clean clothes, warm and good for hiking. Over the next two hours, Johanna learned what the tailor family could really do. Indeed, the Larsndots had spent these years going native. Wenda and her kids knew the backstreets of the South End. They were merely being properly paranoid, not using the telephone system, but not worrying about automatic surveillance. The kids, especially Wenda, Jr., seemed to know just where Deniers might be looking, and more than once took Johanna on little detours to avoid revealing encounters. "We play these games every day now," said Wenda, Sr. "We don't like Deniers down here on the South End. Since you disappeared and Ravna was kidnapped, things have been . . ."

Johanna was still limping, but she had no trouble keeping up with the three. "Jefri. What about him and Amdi?"

Wenda, Sr., looked away. "Both gone. The same night Ravna was grabbed. We . . . we don't know about them, Jo. You know those two had dealings with Nevil and Gannon Jorkenrud. Gannon's gone too."

They were walking in deep shadow now, down a narrow alley between Tinish-style half-frame buildings. These had been built since the Children landed—most of the South End dated from then, but the style was medieval. Out of the shadows, ahead and behind, a couple of packs materialized. Johanna recognized Benky ahead and Wretchly behind.

Jo faltered. Benky was Woodcarver's most reliable lieutenant, but—"Hei, Wretchly is—"

Wenda nodded, waved at her to keep walking.

From behind, Wretchly's voice wafted forward. "Heh, yup. Now that Screwfloss is gone, I'm Flenser's number-one flunky and hatchetman."

There was quiet giggling from Junior and Sika. Junior slipped forward to be with Benky. Sika dropped back and walked among the Wretchly foursome. They took several sharp turns, skirting the Ferryside market and heading downslope. Around them was the faint scent of garbage. Now Sika wanted her mother to carry her. The timber-frame dwellings gave way to stone slab buildings, two and three stories tall. Here and there, packs crossed their path, but Jo didn't see any humans. In fact, the market sounds were sparse. Maybe that was no surprise.

After one last turn, the alley opened out onto a view of the ferry docks. They were just a meter or two above the water. The Straits was a flat silver line across their view. Ordinarily, there would be a ferry or two in the moorage. Another ferry might be out in the Straits, and a couple more would be parked on the mainland side. Today, not a single ferry was pulled up on the Hidden Island side. Jo looked across the water at Cliffside, just a couple thousand meters away. She counted five ferries there.

Benky settled one of himself beside her. "That's where everybody went. Most all are up on Starship Hill where Nevil's gonna bring us all peace." Benky was a fluent Samnorsk speaker. He did sarcasm very well.

"But if we can get you up there, maybe we'll have a chance against his lies." That was Wretchly, crouched around the Larsndots on Johanna's left.

Jo looked back and forth at the two. "Woodcarver and Flenser are *allies* now?"

Benky nodded, but the gesture was also a ripple of suspicion. "That's the theory."

Wretchly was more emphatic: "Of course we're allies! Always have been, even if your Queen Woodcarver never trusted us."

Benky emitted a sniffing noise. "You're also allied with Tycoon and Vendacious."

"Falsely so, but yes. And where would you be now, Benky, without all the inside information we've supplied?"

It was Flenser's justly famous slippery nature. Johanna gave Benky a look: "Has Woodcarver decided to trust Flenser?"

Benky rolled his heads in a kind of embarrassed shrug. "Yeah. Woodcarver has always been too soft with her misbegotten offspring; it may be her fatal flaw. I'd oppose this alliance, except that"—he sent a glance in Wretchly's direction—"we're really desperate." He gave Johanna all of his gaze. "In any case, there's no way *I* can get you safely across the Straits."

"Ah." If Johanna couldn't get across to the mainland and up the cliffs to Starship Hill, her great confrontation would have to wait for some other day. Like after the bad guys had won. She looked back at the Ferryside docks. There were utility twinhulls tied up there. She could use one of those to get to the mainland—all out of sight of the beam gun. The ferry crossing was one of the few blind spots in its coverage; that had always bothered Ravna Bergsndot.

Wretchly followed her gaze. "Don't think for a minute that makes you safe, Johanna."

"What?" but she guessed what he meant.

Wretchly elaborated anyway: "There are other ways of killing folks besides beam guns. And they don't need *Oobii*'s super telescopes to spot you. If Nevil knows you're here on Hidden Island, he'll expect you to try to get across. That's more than a kilometer of open water. Even if we take you across in a box, he'll see the boat and we'll be stopped the moment we land."

Johanna glared at the pack. Even Flenser's flunkies had their boss's talent for causing irritation. There were lots of little moorages along the eastern side of Hidden Island, but none were any less exposed than this. The alternative was to hike across town to the west side, then island hop around the north— maybe thirty kilometers of skulking. A two-day trip. "Okay then, do you have a better way?" She saw the gloating smile hiding in Wretchly's aspect. "Oh, of course you do."

The smile bloomed. "Oh yes. My lord Flenser has not been idle these ten years. Woodcarver penned him in with her various unjustified attempts at house arrest. What was he to do with such restrictions? Well, in fact, he dug some tunnels." Wretchly pointed a snout in the direction of the ferry crossing. "I can get you right across, *under* the Straits."

Wenda Larsndot gave a little squeak of surprise. "So that's where all the cheap fill dirt came from," she said.

Johanna looked at Benky. "Woodcarver knew about this?"

"Not . . . until very recently. Flenser fessed up after Ravna was kidnapped and you and Pilgrim disappeared."

Wretchly nodded. "He did it to finally win Woodcarver's trust."

"That and save his own necks," said Benky. He pointed across the Straits, zigzagging a path upwards. "See, it's not just the understraits tunnel, though I'll bet that was the hardest piece of work. Flenser also dug a stairway inside the cliffs, up to a warehouse in Newcastle. . . . We should have guessed. Flenser was out of sight much too often."

"Yeah." So those mainland tunnels had been just *part* of Flenser's construction. The guy was as sneaky as Woodcarver always claimed.

"But now we're all trusting buddies," said Wretchly. "I can get you up to Newcastle. In fact, if you want, I can probably sneak you right on stage with Nevil himself."

"You have Flenser's okay to do all that?"

"Um, well, this morning he'd only heard a rumor you were down here. I'm . . . interpolating a bit, but we'll know more once we're up there, won't we?"

Benky looked mostly glowerful, but he didn't speak. Johanna glanced at Wenda. The woman shrugged. "This is Hidden Island, Jo. Flenser has been a decent landlord. The last of his monsters died several years ago."

Jo had never been sure of Flenser, but: "Okay, take me up to Newcastle town." There, at least, she might be able to figure out the right thing to do.

————

Jo left the Larsndots at Ferryside. Junior had been outraged, but fortunately Wenda Senior was around to rein her in. It was Benky who was the biggest problem. "I'm coming too."

But what could Benky do if things went bad, in particular if Wretchly went bad? "Stay here, and be around to tell the truth," said Johanna.

"I'm coming. If—once we get atop Starship Hill, I'll get Woodcarver." He glared at Wretchly.

The neo-Flenserist just smiled. "That's okay with me."

Wenda, Sr., took her two youngsters back along the alley. When they were out of sight, Wretchly led Johanna and Benky along a winding path behind garbage bins and down passages that were barely more than cracks between buildings. They passed through a well-concealed door and down steep stairs. The darkness was total.

"Keep bent down, Johanna. This isn't made for two-legs."

"I guessed that," said Johanna. Her fingers traced along the stone just ahead. In Tinish structures, you never trusted for headroom. "How come no lights?"

Wretchly said, "Oh, you want a light? I brought one." A glow appeared ahead, silhouetting a couple of members. Wretchly didn't try to turn around. He just set the lamp on the ground and continued on.

"Thanks." Johanna picked it up. The glow made it a little easier to avoid the irregular ceiling, though now her main view was the hindmost of Wretchly's rear member.

They walked for some minutes, long enough that the inconvenience of being bent over grew toward intolerable soreness. Wretchly merrily chatted away, claiming that he could hear the water shushing by overhead. He seemed totally confident that no intruders were lurking ahead. "Hei, I can hear all the way to the other side." By the time they reached the mainland stairway, Benky was talking too, curious as to how Flenser and company managed to keep the tunnel from getting flooded. Johanna ached too much to pay much attention.

"Ta da!" Wretchly's voice came back to her. "The front of me has reached the mainland. Another few steps and: "See? You can stand up straight now."

Glory! Johanna stretched tall, reaching as far as she could into the empty air.

"Now we just have a little climb up the nice stairs." That would be more than five hundred meters.

The stairs zigzagged irregularly, following natural drainage faults. Some flights were thirty or forty meters, with the spring runoff almost a waterfall down the side gutters. She did better on the stairs than either of the packs. Both Benky and Wretchly had to accommodate ageing members. Very soon, those were huffing and puffing.

It took almost an hour to reach the top. In that time, Johanna got a rather complete summary of all the crap that had happened in her absence. And she had the information from what were probably the top lieutenants of Woodcarver and Flenser.

"Woodcarver and Nevil have been teetering on the edge of a civil war for more than a tenday," said Benky, speaking over the wheezing of his members.

"There have been rumors of your fleet, sightings when you passed the old capital."

"The Tropicals are just bringing trade goods."

"That's what Nevil claims . . . officially. Unofficially, the Deniers are saying, 'what if it's all guns?' They're claiming that Tycoon has boosted our world into the bottom end of technology, that if we don't make peace with him, we'll be swept away."

"It's Vendacious, not Tycoon! I *saw* Vendacious down South. Pilgrim and I searched for years for Tycoon and never found him. I'm thinking he's just another Vendacious lie."

"Yeah," said Benky.

"*Someone* has made a miracle out of the Tropics," said Wretchly. "You really think that's Vendacious? My boss doesn't."

"So has Flenser ever met Tycoon?"

"Well, um, no." Wretchly seemed a little embarrassed that his boss, the great Traitor-to-All, might not be totally in the know. "He should be waiting for us at the top, though. You can ask him yourself."

There was a four-kherhog carriage parked in the warehouse at the top of the climb. Flenser-Tyrathect was inside, dressed for a party. The crippled one's wheelbarrow was gilded.

Johanna climbed in among him. Outside, Wretchly latched the door and ran forward to look after the kherhogs. Jo leaned close to the open window and gave Benky a wave. He was mostly still lying on his bellies and panting from the climb. He gave her a little wave back and then staggered to his feet.

"I'll tell Woodcarver you're here," he said, and stiffly walked out of Johanna's view.

Flenser stuck a head out the window to watch Benky's departure. The pack spoke musingly: "I can't tell you how nervous it makes me that outsiders—Woodcarver's top agent, for heaven's sake—have been inside my secret tunnels. I worked so long to make those passages, and keep them out of her view. Ah, well."

Flenser latched a quilted shutter across the window. All of him settled back as the carriage lurched into motion. Johanna heard various gobbling outside and then the sound of heavy doors being slid aside. As they rolled out of the warehouse, the interior of the carriage was lit via baffles mounted in the roof and sides. Flenser's voice continued, but soft, "We can talk for now, but be very quiet. Vendacious trusts me about as much as Woodcarver used to. If he or Nevil finds you, there's nothing I can do to save you. Hm. I might not even be able to save myself. Perhaps I could say you have kidnapped me."

Johanna felt a laugh burbling up. She stifled it. "I doubt that even you could make that lie stick. Look, I got quite a briefing from Benky and Wretchly. I know about the big meeting this afternoon. You look so pretty, I figure you're an honored guest. All I need is for you to get me to where I can jump onstage.

Outside of Nevil's inner circle, the Deniers are good kids. Most of them are my friends. In front of everyone, Nevil won't dare kill me. I can finally say the truth."

Flenser's heads were bobbing in a smile. "Say your truth and not be Denied, eh?"

"Yes."

The carriage bumped across badly-kept cobblestones. They must be near the edge of town, maybe at the edge of Murder Meadows. This might be a short trip.

"I could do what you suggest, Johanna, but there is a problem. Tycoon himself will be on that stage."

"So he exists? Okay, but why should that be a problem?"

Flenser waved for Johanna to keep her voice down.

"You see, even if Nevil doesn't dare act, Tycoon . . . well I very much fear he will tear you apart the moment he understands who you are."

"*What?* Sorry." She brought her voice down to a whisper. "Even Vendacious wouldn't be that stupid."

There were many voices all around them now, both the gobbling of packs and the speech of humans. Flenser raised a head the way a human might lift his hand, meaning to wait a moment on the answer. Outside, Johanna could hear somebody up above—Wretchly in the driver seats?—arguing. Something about whether kherhogs were allowed to proceed under the something-or-other. Under the stage?

The wagon turned and edged slowly up a slope. All of Flenser turned toward Johanna and his voice came soft and focused: "You're right. Vendacious wouldn't be that stupid. . . ." He paused again, listening to muttering from the top of the carriage. "You see, there's something we didn't know about Tycoon. He's Scriber Jaqueramaphan's brother."

For a moment, Johanna couldn't make sense of the statement; it connected such unrelated parts of her life. *Scriber?* . . . She knew he had a fission brother. Estranged. Scriber had told her the story the last night she saw him all alive. When she beat the crap out of that poor, innocent pack. She opened her mouth a couple of times. No need to worry about making sound, she couldn't find her voice. She was just mouthing the words, "But, but . . ."

Flenser continued, his voice the tiniest butterfly touch on her ears, the sense of it pounding like hammers: "Honestly, I didn't know until Tycoon was on his way here. Vendacious has worked very hard to keep me away from Tycoon. I do know that Tycoon is exactly the genius at organization we thought. He's turned the Tropics into a magical surprise and given Vendacious the lever to overturn the world."

Johanna remembered. Scriber had said his fission sibling was a dour business type. What had changed? And why did Tycoon want to kill *her?* "Why—?" she spoke the word too softly to hear her own voice.

Of course Flenser heard her—and more—he understood her real question.

"Why do you think? Vendacious told him that *you* killed Scriber. Vendacious is at center of all this, and he's sneakier than I was, even at my best. He has to be, because sneakiness is all he has going for him. He's based his plan on Tycoon, and on making Tycoon hate humans, you in particular." He sounded almost admiring.

Yeah, that was perfect Vendacious. Flenser might admire such perfection.

The carriage stopped, jerked forward a few centimeters, stopped again. She heard the scrabble of Wretchly bouncing down from the driver's seats. There was an irregular tapping on the door, and when Flenser slid it open, one of Wretchly was looking in. "Here we are, Boss, right under the platform. Heh! Inside all Nevil's fabulous security."

Flenser was already streaming out the door. "You can be sure that if Vendacious was in charge, things would not be so easy. Nevil is so new to our primitive villainy." Now all of him struggled to help his crippled member exit. White Tips was watching Johanna alertly, but as usual made no detectable contribution to the speech sounds.

"I'm supposed to be up onstage," said Flenser. "This parking spot is to give me easier access. My handicapped condition, you see. I'm leaving Wretchly with you. If you don't scream or shout, you should be safe." Flenser wiggled a snout, gesturing Johanna to come to the opening.

Sunlight splattered down through cracks in the construction. She smelled fresh-cut lumber. They were parked somewhere on the heather of Murder Meadows. Crisscrossed timber reinforcement beams were all around the wagon. Flenser was on the ground below her, turning White Tips' little cart toward a path that led off into the dimness. "Hear the racket, Johanna?" he said.

In fact, she could. Tinish trumpeting. Flenser continued, "Somebody just landed their airship. They'll be up top on the platform in another minute—and I'm late to greet them." The slower parts of Flenser were already heading off. "If that's Tycoon, it's your death to go up there. You should stay down here where you're safe."

"If I decide to risk it, how can I get directly on stage?"

"Ah," Flenser's heads twisted around, searching for something in the cracks of light above. "Wretchly?"

Part of the henchpack looked up, studying the strutwork. "Okay. We had the contract on putting this thing together. It was all very hastily done, with lots of screwups. See over there," Wretchly pointed to where reinforcement struts tilted together. "It may not look it, but that's the start of an easy climb"—he gestured back and forth, upwards—"to a knockout panel that's at the center of the main stage."

Flenser was grinning, that joy-in-shadows posture that annoyed Woodcarver so much. "You could make a very dramatic entrance, very very short-lived, at least if Tycoon is nearby. Part of me would truly like to see . . ." He brought himself up short. Literally: The parts of him that were furthest along the path stopped, began pulling the wheelbarrow back. "Ahem. Seriously, Johanna. Don't go up there unless you—and Wretchly—can hear that it's safe.

Even if it's just Nevil, you should think twice. I took a chance once, going public in the Long Lakes—and look what became of me."

Johanna brought her gaze down from the ceiling. "Yes. I understand." In fact, Flenser's advice was completely sensible—at least if you edited out the maniacal asides.

"Okay, then! I'd best be on my way." He caught up with himself and soon all five were lost in the gloom.

The rest of Wretchly came over to the carriage steps. "No one's near. You can come down from the carriage if you want. Be ready to hop back in if I say."

Johanna descended the little steps, stood in the moist, ankle-deep sod. It was all very stamped down and shaded, but here and there the sunlight caught the color of a wilted flower. Murder Meadows. She seemed to end up here every time things got really really tough.

———

"So that's Tycoon up there. Pack of Packs, it sounds like there's eight of him, and they're all big bruisers!" Wretchly was circled widely around their carriage, watching and listening in all directions. One of him stayed close to Johanna even now, as she walked over to the jumble of strutwork he had pointed out earlier.

Johanna looked up into the shadows and bright cracks above. "So what is he saying, Wretchly?"

"It's still Nevil talking. What a noisemaker that guy is. 'Peace, prosperity, our new friends, no more terrible attacks, . . . blah blah.'"

"You know he can talk for hours, Wretchly."

"Yeah. Well, that would be stupid today. The audience doesn't sound as patient as usual." He waved a snout at the unseen fields. "And one particular guy is not patient at all."

"Me," said Johanna.

"Somebody else. The eight that I think are Tycoon is shifting around like he has bugs up his rears." Wretchly paused. Looking around, Johanna could see several of Wretchly shifting, angling their shoulders and heads, building up a sonic image of what was going on above. "That's strange," said Wretchly. "I think Tycoon has humans with him. Ravna and Jefri it sounds like."

Johanna restrained her desire to shout. "What? Then it must be safe!"

". . . Not if they're prisoners."

"But Woodcarver and Flenser are up there."

"Yes," Wretchly pointed into the shadows in the direction that Flenser had departed minutes before. That would be stage left, if she was visualizing things properly. "They haven't gone to meet Ravna. It sounds like Tycoon has a pack or two with him. Flunkies with weapons, I bet."

A minute later, it sounded like a human child had shouted something.

Wretchly pulled back in startlement. "Huh! That's Tycoon. He wants to talk."

Various thumping-around noises came from above. Johanna might have laughed in other circumstances. She didn't think Nevil had ever been upstaged at a public event.

The little girl voice from above was loud, but Johanna still couldn't make out the words. The tones sounded frightened and lost and . . . angry?

Wretchly had grabbed her sleeve, was pulling her back to the carriage. "What?" said Johanna. "What is Tycoon saying?"

"He's talking about peace, but he doesn't sound happy about it. That's not the point, Johanna. I hear packs coming back under the stands, some humans too."

"Woodcarver's?"

"No, they're Deniers and the lowlife Tines that Nevil hires. We got a couple of minutes. I can get you out of here."

As he spoke, the rest of Wretchly had come rushing in from their listening posts. Now they were clustered around her, silently pushing and pulling her toward the carriage. When she still resisted, Wretchly stepped back, his heads cocking indecisively. "Cripes. My boss knew this would happen. Can't you see? He set you up."

Maybe, and so what? Jo looked up one more time. From here she could see the top of the path Wretchly had pointed to. It ended at a panel, quite thin and weak-looking compared to the walls around it. *Scriber's brother is up there.* In the early years, she had wondered about that nameless brother, wondered if he ever knew what became of Scriber, or if that estranged pack would even care to know. If Flenser was right, Tycoon had really really cared. The lie Vendacious had told him had propelled a decade of history. Vendacious had murdered Scriber and turned that into a monstrous coup. The old rage rose up in Johanna, what she had felt ever since Vendacious had escaped execution and then escaped imprisonment. *This must not stand.*

"Get to someplace safe, Wretchly."

"Good. C'mon!" said Wretchly. Then as she started up the ladder: "Aw, cripes."

She glanced down, saw him clustered around the base of the ladder, one of him starting up toward her, the rest all looking at something out of sight behind her. Three looked up, waving their heads, but not daring to call aloud. Then the one on the ladder tumbled back to the heather, and she heard all of him rushing away.

From above, the little-girl voice continued on, wailing with words Jo couldn't quite make out. Surely the distress was an illusion. And yet, Tycoon deserved to learn how close his brother had come to greatness, how his special crazy goodness had gotten him killed.

She was at the top of the ladder. She swung to the side, reached out to touch the wood panel. It was tacked on with temporary pegs. She could smash right through. She hesitated, let the rage give her strength. Somewhere there was a voice in her head, but it wasn't the voice of caution; that was still tied and gagged. The Mad Bad Girl of Starship Hill was in charge.

CHAPTER 40

Ravna climbed down the stairs and stood in the soaking heather. The airship's carriage was seated thirty centimeters into the heath. The main hull was only a few centimeters above their heads. They were in the ship's shadow, mostly out of sight of the welcoming crowds. Even here the daylight was awesomely bright and cheerful and familiar.

The gunpack urged them to follow Zek and Tycoon. Ravna took a step or two, unsteady after all the low ceilings. As she stepped out into direct sunlight she stumbled and would have been crawling again if Jef hadn't had an arm around her. Together they staggered a few steps more, then stood straight for a moment, reveling in having the space to do so.

Cheers came on the wind. Ravna turned. The ground crew had retreated. Except for Tycoon's entourage, the nearest people were thirty meters away. The cheering was coming from the Children and Best Friends. And Ravna suddenly realized they were cheering Jefri and herself.

She gave them a wave back and then gunpack pushed at their legs, urging her and Jefri to catch up with Tycoon. Their progress across the field was slow, partly because of Ravna's unsteadiness, partly because the hummocky heath was an ankle-twisting obstacle course.

None of the Children came running out to meet them. They were staying behind low barricades. Several older Children—Nevil's people—were keeping the more enthusiastic from rushing onto the field. All for the safety of the public, no doubt. A lot had changed since she was kidnapped.

Tycoon's party turned across the bow of his airship and walked in stately splendor toward the midpoint of the stage. Ravna and Jefri hobbled along behind. Nevil's voice was audible even from here. Of course, he was using his power with *Oobii* to advantage: ". . . and the attack this morning must not get in the way of our meeting here. Peace is finally within our reach. . . ." she heard him say. But his voice was mainly focused on the crowd, and she lost the rest of the words.

Nevil was standing behind a high lectern at one end of the stage. Three humans were with him, and two packs, one wearing crowns. Downhill, beyond the stage, Ravna had a view of *Out of Band II* in all its iridescent splendor. Nevil had positioned his stage so that all the participants were within the field of fire of the ship's beam gun. With his admin authority, Nevil figured he could kill anyone here, pack or human. He could burn the meadow clean if he wished. Was Nevil really capable of such monstering? *I better assume so.* In any case, it was his top threat against anyone who truly knew him.

Except perhaps for me, thought Ravna. *Oobii* was smart enough to recognize a human face. And Nevil, by putting this scene in its line of sight, had guaranteed that *Oobii* could see *her*. If it recognized her . . . She leaned against

Jefri, letting him steady her. She looked at the ship and said softly, "Ship! Give me a milliwatt of red if you hear me." Her voice was whipped away in the breeze. Jefri himself didn't seem to hear her.

As they walked on, Ravna stole an occasional glance at the ship. There was no sign, no red glint. Okay, that had been a long shot.

Tycoon had reached the edge of the crowd. Nevil's guards made way for them, keeping humans and packs away from Tycoon and Zek and Ritl. Ritl? The singleton trotted along like an official part of the delegation.

Now that Tycoon was past the barricades, some of the younger Children pushed forward, eluding both Nevil's guards and other older kids who tried to stop them. Tycoon shied back slightly, then walked forward, not showing the loathing he must feel. He actually acknowledged the greetings with something like cordiality. He was doing better than most of the first-timers she'd encountered in the circus.

Zek lagged back from Tycoon and spoke to Ravna and Jefri with Vendacious' voice. "Remember remember, up in the sky." *Yes, Vendacious and Amdi up in the sky.* The other airship drove along, heading into another turn.

Then she and Jef were in the crowds. The kids closed in, arms outstretched to both of them. Some shied back when they saw her face, others kept coming. She hugged one or two, even as the gunpack's snouts were pushing at her knees.

Closer to the stage, she noticed something new. On one side, she saw people like Wilm and Poul Linden, who had never approved of Nevil and company. On the other, were those who had avoided her after the vote. The human world had split into camps, a civil war waiting to happen. They all looked uneasy, shying away from Tycoon. Some flinched when they saw Ravna's face.

"What did they *do* to her?" she heard one of the Children say.

Ravna continued forward, trying to smile, biting back the things she wanted to shout to everyone. Today she wore an invisible muzzle.

Timbered steps led to the top of the stage. The risers were high, more for humans than Tines. That would be Nevil making a statement about human superiority, obliging Tycoon and his Tinish company to scramble up the steps.

The stairs reached a platform, still twelve steps short of the main stage. Three older Children stood at the top of the stairs, all Nevil's pals. Strange, none of them was Bili Yngva; had there been a falling out? The three stepped back a little nervously as Tycoon clambered heavily toward them. Ravna heard a little of the indignant hiss that Tycoon cast their way. Zek and Ritl climbed up after him, followed by Ravna and Jefri.

She gave Nevil a hard glance, then noticed that he was wearing the remaining head-up display—a link to *Oobii*. For a moment her gaze caught on the device's crystal facets. Then she forced herself to look away.

Flenser was sitting nearby, looking indolent and relaxed. He gave Ravna a friendly, ambiguous nod. To the right of Flenser, past a sound baffle, was Woodcarver. All her heads were turned to look at Jefri and Ravna. The pack was a picture of tense alertness. And anger. There was the Puppy from Hell, perched on one member's shoulders. But wait . . . a *second* puppy was shyly looking up from between the legs of another member. The Queen had become eight!

Ravna stepped out onto the platform, moved a little way around Tycoon. Woodcarver shifted slightly apart, and Ravna heard her whisper: "*What of Pilgrim?*"

Ravna gave her head a little shake.

Nevil's voice boomed over the crowd. "Let us welcome Tycoon, come all the way from the East Coast. Unwise policies of the past set us against people who would be our friends. Today we unite against those who bring violence upon both our peoples. Today—"

The words were misleading nonsense, but his frank openness was almost what Ravna remembered. Almost. Even though Nevil hadn't been kidnapped and chased through wilds, the guy had lost some weight. The time since he had grabbed power had not been kind to him. That had been true even before Ravna's kidnapping. Apparently things had not improved since. And what was this about an attack earlier *today?*

Nevil carried on for a while longer. In the crowd below the stands, there was some milling around, especially among the opposition, but no one walked away and no one shouted objections. Nevil had control such as Ravna had never dreamed. "So the agreements Tycoon and I sign today will return those who have been taken from us"—he waved graciously at Jefri and Ravna—"and begin a technological alliance for prosperity."

As he spoke these last few words, Nevil edged back from the lectern. Tycoon was eight, and each of him was a heavy critter. He could project implacable purpose better than anyone Ravna had met on this world—and now he was gliding toward the lectern. The only thing that saved Nevil's dignity was that Tycoon's approach was out of sight of most of the audience below.

Nevil cut his loud voice and leaned down as if to speak courteously to the pack. He jerked a hand at Ravna and Jefri. "Why was it necessary for you to bring *them* here?"

"As proof of my goodwill," said Tycoon.

"Then you should have brought the young ones." Another quick glance at Ravna. "This—this Ravna, is just trouble."

Tycoon's heads bobbed in a grim smile. "She can be useful."

Nevil's mouth turned down. He stared blankly for a moment. He might be speaking to someone, but the words were inaudible to Ravna.

Zek had followed close behind Tycoon. Now he pushed awkwardly through the eight and spoke softly to Nevil. It was Vendacious' voice. The tone was placating: "It's okay. Deal as before. My colleague here is too forward."

Tycoon gave Zek a hard bump. "I am not forward and you do not speak for me." Then he advanced, forcing Nevil away from the lectern. He hopped up on himself, leaning against the lectern. Now the pack was in pyramid posture, visible to all. And even without mechanical aid, his words boomed: "I am Tycoon!"

So much for Tycoon's promise to avoid human speechifying. The voice that sounded across the meadows belonged to a frightened little girl. It was Geri Latterby's voice, but transformed by the force and arrogance of Tycoon's personality. "Nevil Storherte says we all want peace. He wants peace. I want peace. We will have war if you do not make things right!"

People reacted very differently than they had to Nevil's smiling nonsense. There was shouting. A woman—it was Elspa Latterby—screamed: "Geri? Geri! Give her back . . ."

Tycoon had their attention. "We can't make up for all the bad things, but you and I *will* make up for what we can. Or we will have war." He gobbled something at Zek. A moment later, Vendacious' airship spun up its engines and coasted across the sky to hang just west of the stage. Nevil watched the ship's progress with an unbelieving expression. He was talking to someone again. *Oobii?* Vendacious? But the starship held its fire.

Tycoon waited for the shouting to die away. Then he said, "I will give you back what can be returned. We bring you wealth, now, and in future trade. In exchange, you will give me access to *Oobii*. And most important, you give me the human who murdered half of me! I want Johanna Olsndot. I want her here. I want her *now!*" As he spoke, Tycoon's heads turned this way and that, jaws snapping.

Everyone on the platform seemed frozen in horror. Well, everyone except Flenser. He had hunkered down, but his heads were weaving and bobbing. He was enjoying this with the sort of shameful joy that mayhem brought out in him.

Nevil eased around Tycoon, back to the lectern. He must be truly rattled, because for the first time Ravna could actually see him figuring up the odds, deciding what to do to stay on top. When he spoke, his voice was somber and tense. "My friends, we've known of this demand for several days. Tycoon has cause for making the demand."

"Tycoon kidnapped our children!" came a voice from the crowd, but wind-whipped and faint. Nevil didn't quite have the audio control he had aboard ship, but the wind and the open air was almost as effective.

"Tycoon is reasonable to ask for a human wrongdoer no matter how much she was beloved by me, by us." Nevil seemed to choke up. Beside her, Ravna could feel Jefri trembling, his gaze alternating between Nevil and the airship above. There were limits, and Jef was being pushed well beyond his.

After a moment, Nevil found his voice again and continued, as if struggling against tears. "I was very close to Johanna all my life. Infatuated, I see now. But I loved her, and as much as she was capable of it, I think she loved me. Now . . . well, the proof that Tycoon has provided and her own unguarded words to me . . . It means I was wrong in my love and my trust. I'm sorry." He paused, turned toward Tycoon, whose pyramid still topped his own height. When Nevil continued, his voice was firm and statesmanlike. "Sir, however just your demands, they stand moot. Johanna Olsndot has been missing for some tendays."

"You lie! Give her over!" roared the eightsome.

Nevil damped his audio so low that Ravna could barely hear it: "Are you crazy?" he hissed. "Look, she's dead. I can get you the body. Just—"

Jefri lunged at Nevil. "You murdering—" Nevil's friends tackled him before he could do Storherte harm. Tycoon dropped down and lumbered around the fray, gobbling at the gunpack. That pack backed off, shifting its firearms so they weren't pointing at Jefri.

As Jefri was bundled off down the stairs, there was a momentary clear area around Ravna, and an unrecognizable voice whispered in her ear: "Watch the wall beside me." Ravna's head jerked up. *Woodcarver? Maybe. Flenser!*

Tycoon's heads came up too. He walked across the stage, heads questing toward Flenser and Woodcarver. Had he heard Flenser?

Now what Ravna heard was the sound of splintering wood. Part of the wall popped a centimeter out. There was a *crash* and another and another.

Tycoon flinched back. The wooden panel fell to the stage and . . . Johanna stepped into the sunlight, carrying a sturdy timber. She was out of breath, her violet eyes wild—and she was very much alive. She dropped the timber and spoke to the eightsome, who stood jaws agape before her. "Hei, sir. I am Johanna Olsndot."

Now that he had his hate's desire, Tycoon hesitated. He stepped back, milled around almost like some of the newbies Ravna had met in the circus. Or a killer savoring the moment.

Jo dropped to the deck before him and tilted her head back, imitating a submissive singleton about as well as a human could.

Jaws snapped on either side of her throat. Tycoon jostled himself as members at the rear tried to get at her. Two of him grabbed Johanna's arms and began dragging her toward the vacant right end of the stage. "We *talk* before you die," he said.

"But—" Nevil started after them, then stopped, apparently realizing that unless he wanted to start shooting, things were totally beyond his control.

As Johanna was dragged across the stage, Woodcarver's puppies jumped down and pushed something across the deck to Flenser. Two of Flenser slid it toward Tycoon.

Maybe it was reflex, maybe it was curiosity, but Tycoon grabbed the object. It was some kind of book, the style that Tines had "hand" printed before the Children landed. It was very old, or it had been through a fire. The pages were black and curling, held together by metal hoops. Ravna got just a glimpse before Tycoon surged around the book. He was completely motionless for a moment, then resumed his march to the far end of the stage.

Zek had watched all this silently, nervously moving out of the way when necessary. Now he stood still for a second, as if listening. Then he gobbled something desperate and negative and ran across the stage toward Tycoon. Ritl followed a second later.

Tycoon was having none of it. He swiped claws at Ritl and hissed at Zek, "Back! This is my vengeance."

No matter how determined Vendacious might be to spy on Jo's last words, poor Zek was in no position to enforce that will. Both singletons backed off.

The confrontation between Johanna and her would-be executioner might be short, but it was not going to be private. The two were in full daylight at the far end of the stage, visible to most of the audience and everyone on the stage. Øvin Verring and the Linden boys rushed the front stairs, backed by several others. Nevil's friends had been drilling; they used their staffs to knock the kids down the stairs. Wilm was helped up by his brother; their group tried again. Now the crowd was mixing together, fighting in places. Others just stood, watching in horror.

Nevil was watching in horrified fascination, too. But he was also mumbling to . . . *Oobii?* Ravna edged closer to him. Nevil's audio was not fully damped. He glanced at Vendacious' airship and his voice raised a fraction, though still barely audible. "So is this worst case or not?"

His eyes flickered sideways, noticed Ravna's approach.

Nevil's goons were over by the stairs; there *was* something she could do! "It's coming apart, Nevil," she said. "Tell Vendacious that—"

Nevil's mouth twisted in contempt. "Shut up. I have ship's admin authority, remember? I can burn you down where you stand."

Maybe. Ravna found the presence of mind not to correct him—at least, not with the truth. Instead: "Burn me in front of all these people? I think not."

Nevil glared back, but after a moment gave an angry shrug. He looked around, probably for some thug to drag her off. Alas for Nevil, they were all still busy. If she could just get a little closer to him. . . . *Concentrate on Nevil.* She turned away from the nightmare at the other end of the stage and walked casually toward him.

"Stay back!" Nevil hissed at her. His gaze swiveled back and forth between Tycoon and Ravna. He was waiting for some kind of signal; till then— well, it was fortunate for him that the crowd couldn't hear him now. Nevil was rattled. "You bitch. You suppressed everything Straumer. Even the fools who love you puke at what you believe." He nodded in the direction of Tycoon. "If you hadn't kept dividing us kids, I wouldn't be allied with these *barbarians.* Because of you, even more people may have to die. Now stay back or I *will* burn you down!"

Across the stage, Johanna had risen to her knees. Blood stained her sleeves; four pairs of jaws hovered near her throat. The charred book lay on the ground right ahead of her knees. Two of Tycoon had opened it and a third was reading the text—a classic Tinish posture. A fourth snout tapped at the text while the rest beat questions down upon her.

What is that book anyway? thought Ravna.

Johanna seemed to know. Her head came down and she pointed into the manuscript, then gently raised a page and pointed at something beneath. The ones holding the book looked up at her, and the rest of the creature's heads came together around Jo's face.

Flenser and Woodcarver had crept off their perches, but Tycoon hissed them into silence. Zek paced anxiously just outside that same threat zone. Shrouded in his radio cloak, Zek must be hearing even less than Woodcarver and Flenser. He turned away from Tycoon and ran—staggered—back toward Nevil and Ravna. He cringed as if from invisible blows and collapsed at Nevil's feet. "I can't hear what Tycoon is saying," he said. This was Vendacious talking, but the communication channel was in such pain that the voice stretched across several octaves, almost unintelligible. "*You* tell me what they are saying!"

"Huh? I can't get near enough to hear." Apparently Nevil didn't know how to use the HUD for such snooping.

Maybe Vendacious realized that; his voice became a fraction calmer, but full of crazy surmise: "You. Ravna animal. You always were the smarter. Show Nevil how. Tell me what they are saying. Stop this or I'll kill Amdi, first one piece then all the rest—where you can see."

Zek writhed in pain on the deck before them, one small singleton relaying terrible threats. Nevil stepped back from the creature, uncertain.

It was the best chance Ravna was going to get. She took three paces toward Nevil and launched herself at him. As a physical attack, the collision was pitiful, but she held on, shouting into his face: "Ship! Usurp, usurp!"

Nevil's fists punched into her, sending her flying back. The crash hurt as much as the fists, and for a moment she couldn't breathe. She looked up. Nevil was pointing at her, mumbling to himself. Nothing happened. Nevil jabbed his hand again.

And still Ravna lived. *Oobii* would be paying close attention now. She struggled for breath, finally gasped out, "Ship! Delete all Nevil authority. Delete—"

As she spoke, Nevil's eyes went wide. Now *he* was ground zero. He scrambled back, then turned and ran down a backstage stairway, out of Ravna's sight—and *Oobii*'s.

She crawled over to Zek. Ritl was nosing around him, licking his face. Zek rolled onto his belly; he was trying to arrange his cloak properly. Words popped into Ravna's mouth, anything to satisfy the monster: "Okay, Vendacious. Tell me what you want to hear—"

She heard a strange sound, a low, broad moan. *From the crowd.* Ravna looked out, saw human and Tinish heads looking in a single direction. Not at Ravna. Not at the jumble that was Johanna and Tycoon. They were looking into the sky.

She swung around to stare at the airship. Something small and dark was falling from it. A living thing, flailing. A pack member, perhaps slightly overweight. The member fell and fell and fell, surely still alive. It disappeared from view behind the top of the stage.

Ravna looked down at Zek. "Why?" she said. "You didn't give me a chance!"

Zek looked up, his head weaving almost blindly. His whole body was twitching. He gobbled chords she could not understand.

"Hei!" Ravna cried. "I'm doing what you want. Don't kill any more of Amdi!"

She ran across the stage toward Tycoon. Amdi was eight—had been eight. He could still be mostly the same person at seven.

There were scattered shouts. In the sky above, she saw a second body, dressed like the first, drop away from the airship. Its legs pumped as it fell, as if it was fighting for traction.

Johanna had risen above Tycoon to look at the sky. The pack surged around her, dragging her down. He pulled Jo across the stage toward the main stairway. The gunpack spread out in front of him, its rifles aiming at Flenser and Woodcarver, and then at Ravna.

Tycoon stopped by Zek, gobbled a fierce interrogative. The singleton made some reply, but he was still twitching. Tycoon seemed to think a moment—he could still *think* in the middle of all this!—and then he grabbed Zek by the collar of his cloak and continued toward the stairs. As the eightsome passed her, Ravna reached out to Johanna. Jaws snapped at her, driving her back. "Now you will see what I do to liars and murderers," said Tycoon. Then he was down the stairs with Zek and Johanna, his gunpack clearing the way.

More screams, maybe for Johanna, maybe—Ravna turned back to the west. Parts of Amdi were still falling from the sky. Three bodies, tumbling. Or maybe it was four, since one of them might be two members holding tight to each other. Then another . . . and another. Now that Amdi was mostly dead, Vendacious was just flushing the rest.

Ravna slumped to the deck. *But I am not injured. Not at all. Why not?* The bad guys had won and all the good intentions in the world had not made a bit of difference.

"Ravna? Ravna?" snouts poked gently at her. Woodcarver. Ravna turned and embraced the nearest of her. It was a gesture she had never dared with the Queen before, but just now she had to hold on to someone. A puppy—*the Puppy from Hell?*—crawled across another member's back and nuzzled Ravna's cheek. Woodcarver's voice was a purring vibration from all her members: "Do your best now. Please, Ravna. There are still so many things to do."

CHAPTER 41

Vendacious' airship was flying off into the east even as the last of Tycoon's gang loaded themselves onto the larger craft. Nevil's people were the only ones helping, but the great airship made it into the air without problems. The craft was perhaps forty meters up as it passed over the stage—heading westward toward the Straits. These ships couldn't turn in place; no doubt Tycoon would swing around to follow Vendacious.

She ignored the airship and looked around. Nevil's buddies looked back uncertainly. They and the mass of the Denier children were drifting off the field. Most were heading uphill, toward Newcastle town. No one was stopping them, but Ravna noticed that suddenly there were lots of Woodcarver's troops in evidence. Nevil himself was nowhere to be seen.

She turned towards *Oobii* and shouted several commands into the air. Nothing. "I need comm with *Oobii*," she said to Woodcarver.

"I know. I have a runner bringing a radio."

"You don't have one with you?" asked Ravna.

"No." Three of Woodcarver's turned their gaze on Ravna. An angry hiss was the background of her words: "Nevil demanded we come without them. He used *Oobii* to destroy any radio that wasn't used according to his desire. I still had most of the people on my side. He thought to change that with today's meeting. You and Johanna made things come out a little differently."

They watched as Tycoon's airship made a broad turn over the Inner Straits. Children and packs swept around them, shouting and crying and pointing, imagining another body falling, this one human. No. Tycoon was a different kind of villain. Pray he was different.

Poul Linden came through the crowd, pushing even through Woodcarver. "Ravna!" He was gasping, so out of breath that the words wouldn't come at once. "I'm sorry, I wasn't able to stop him."

"What? Who?"

"Nevil! I found him coming out backstage, but he was too much for me."

"Show her what he dropped, Poul!" That was Wilm, flapping his arms impatiently.

"Oh, yeah." He held out the HUD. "This is yours."

Nevil had been dumb not to destroy it, but smart to let it go.

As she took crystal tiara, the Children around her grew silent. Awed? *I hope not*, thought Ravna. It was the sort of moment later times made paintings and Princess myths about. *And I've sworn off all that garbage.* She set the device on her head.

"Ship!" she said.

———

Having *Oobii*'s support was like stepping out of the dark. Tasks that would have otherwise taken Ravna hours or days could be done in minutes. Unfortunately, the most important things were still beyond her power.

The two enemy airships were heading steadily eastwards, not responding to the various radio methods that Nevil had been using. Both ships were at Ravna's mercy, a fact that was worth exactly nothing.

The orbiter was not responding either. Maybe no surprise there. That was still Nevil's special domain. Ravna did manage to talk with Scrupilo aboard *Eyes Above*, persuading him not to go chasing off after Tycoon.

Here on the ground the Children and their Best Friends swirled around her. They had shown remarkable patience with her these last few minutes, but now they were calling a thousand questions, crying—and crying for vengeance.

Ravna held her hands up. After a moment, the babble quieted. "Let the

Deniers go back to their homes in Newcastle. Those are still their homes. They are almost half of the human race. We need them."

Woodcarver boomed out: "I agree. No pack may harm them. But none of us should have to put up with Nevil anymore. Where is he, anyway?"

The question was put to everyone, but the answers were scattered and contradictory. Of course, this was one of the easier problems. Nevil might lurk out of *Oobii*'s direct sight, but his people were using radios. Sooner or later, Ravna would have a definite location for him. The current best guesses showed as a bright dot in Ravna's HUD. Strange. "It looks like Nevil is heading out of town—" going northeast, toward the valley forest.

"Follow him!"

"We are." *Oobii is.* Meantime—

────────

They found Jefri behind the stage. Alive. Nevil's people had left him hogtied in the mud. It was probably not deliberate that they had provided him with a forced view to the west. When Ravna showed up, Jef had been untied. He sat on the ground with his back to the timbers, staring into space. The front of his shirt was splattered with vomit. He didn't seem to notice.

Several Children were on their knees, talking softly at him.

Ravna walked around in front of Jef, blocking his view downslope. "Jefri?" she said. "We think Johanna is still alive. We'll get her back."

Jef's gaze came up to her face. She had never seen him so bleak, even in his deepest shame. After a moment his voice came low and hoarse. "We'll do whatever we can? Yes, but . . ." *but what good has that been so far?* He staggered to his feet, helped by the kids around him. "The best I can do now is find what's left of Amdi." He would have stumbled away across the meadow if the others had not held him back.

There was no way they could keep Jefri from this search. *There's no way they can keep me away either.* "We'll all search," she said.

────────

It turned out that some Children and Best Friends had already taken the funicular partway to the water, then climbed down pilings to reach the cliff face. Now they were close to being stranded, their rescue operation in need of rescuing. Ravna and Woodcarver sent some of the older kids after them, with instructions not to get anybody killed.

There were safer ways down the cliff, and that was a proper reason for Ravna to come along. *Oobii* did not have a line of sight on the cliff face, but over the years, the area had been carefully surveyed. With her HUD, Ravna was probably a better scout leader than anyone.

Now they were moving from ledge to ledge, back and forth across the rock face. Before the funicular train, the trip from Hidden Island up to Newcastle had taken a good part of a day. The cliffs were a deadly attraction that over the years had maimed adventuresome packs and killed two Children. Today, the leaves of spring rose all around them, clothing the evergreens with extra softness, obscuring the teeth of stone.

"Here, take this," said Woodcarver, passing a safety rope forward. The pack was mainly behind Ravna, but staying close. Nowadays, the Queen was young—maybe too young for this, with the two puppies—but she seemed to be having no problems. As she walked along, she was calling loudly to packs above her. In her own way, Woodcarver was coordinating operations, too.

Ravna took the safety line, passing the remaining loops forward to Øvin, the only human ahead of her in the party.

"Do you think there's any chance that—" said Ravna, her voice low, for Woodcarver. Thank the Powers she had persuaded Jefri to stay with Magda and Elspa in the middle of the troop.

"—that any of Amdi survived?" Woodcarver finished the question. "I don't see how. These springtime leaves are gossamer, and the evergreens beneath are like steel bars. But this . . . recovery is going to happen anyway."

Ravna nodded. "We can make it safer." For the next few minutes, she had no time for chitchat. Her head-up display was synched with her position. She could see through the trees to *Oobii*'s topo map—and guide Øvin Verring along the safest paths. At the same time, she had windows opened on other problems. Nevil's people were making no attempt to mess with *Oobii*, but there was a plume of hot air rising from the Dome of First Landing. Ravna even had video from inside the castle! Apparently Nevil had diverted all the cameras into his spying—that was why she had only low-resolution information on the bodies' trajectories. But she could snoop all around the castle. Bili or whoever had stuffed the Lander with flammables and lit it off. Woodcarver's firefighters had already doused the fire, and she could see that the coldsleep caskets were unharmed.

Ravna pulled her attention back to the rocks ahead of her. "Øvin, don't go down that way." The higher ledge was narrow, but it became a real path a few meters further into the greenery.

"Okay."

As Ravna sidled onto the ledge after him, a little red alert flag popped up in her HUD. Behind her, Woodcarver was talking loudly with unseen packs at the top of the cliffs. She translated for Ravna: "They say something's happening at Newcastle town."

"Yeah." That red alert flag. As she followed along after Øvin, she accepted the alert: It was a view of the north road out of town. The Denier Children had returned to their houses after the debacle on the Meadows. Now they were on the move again—but not back to Murder Meadows or to *Oobii*. The ship counted seventy Children, including Bili and Merto, but not Nevil. The older ones had knapsacks or sling bags. There were a few wagons, but most were walking—out of town, toward the northeast. "You know, I think some of them are carrying guns," exactly the human-style weapons Ravna had pictured for Nevil.

"My troops have many *more* guns," said Woodcarver. "I could stop them. Does this look like a mass kidnapping?"

Ravna watched the scene for several seconds. ". . . No."

"Then I suggest we let these people go. No civil war today."

Ravna suddenly realized that while her attention had been on the other side of Starship Hill, she had walked along a ledge that had narrowed to thirty centimeters. Woodcarver was gently pulling her back from the edge. She came to a full stop and leaned against the sheer wall of the cliff face.

"You're almost there, Ravna. Give me your hand." She looked up and saw Øvin. He had reached the wider path that the topo map had promised. A second later she was standing beside him. She sat down for a moment and waited until the rest of their party came up. Woodcarver settled close around her. The new puppy was barely old enough to be a constructive member. It peeped out of a puppy pannier, whereas little Sht rode on an older member's shoulders.

The Queen must have noticed her gaze. "The new puppy? It's to balance Sht's paranoid nature, a very old-fashioned bit of broodkennery. It was Pilgrim's suggestion . . . and his last gift to me." Woodcarver was silent for a moment, and then she spoke publicly loud: "I hear Scrupilo's airboat."

Ravna nodded. She had been following his progress via *Oobii*. "What's become of his air*ship*?" she asked.

"That's a bit of history," said Woodcarver, rolling her heads. "Nevil's all-human crew crashed *EA2*—on their very first solo flight. There were no casualties, but that put an end to long-range searching for you. Opinion is divided on whether the crash was a real accident or a Nevil accident."

"Ah."

Now the boat's little electric motor was audible to human ears. It wasn't visible through the spring leaves until it flew directly overhead. Then she had a naked-eye glimpse of it—and two of Scrupilo's heads stuck over the gunwales, peering down. *A year ago I was up there with Scrup, looking down, trying to track Nevil's thieves—only we thought we were chasing Tropicals.*

She relayed through *Oobii*: "Scrupilo, we're at—" she sent her map position. "Poul Linden and the other team are on another path about fifty meters below us." The other path was a safer walk, but it didn't extend as far into the region where *Oobii* figured most of bodies had come down.

"I see Linden, but not you," Scrupilo's voice boomed down from the sky. He wasn't bothering with radio.

"Okay. Do you see any sign of, of the bodies?"

Scrupilo was as grumpy blunt as ever. "The birds know. They've found three places to swarm. I've got a crappy little camera here; I'll send *Oobii* pictures of what I'm seeing." The video was already showing in Ravna's windows.

Two of Woodcarver's foresters came up from the ledge below, and then— Jefri wobbled along the path, staring upward and ignoring all of them. "Scrupilo!" Jef shouted. "How many bodies are we looking for?"

The pack responded: "Most people say eight, but some of the younger Children say seven with one holding onto a member-sized object."

Jefri stood silent for a moment, still staring up. Then he started up the path, walking past Ravna. She came to her feet, reached out to stop him. For an instant, she thought Jef would shrug away. Then he was trembling in her arms.

"I can lead us there, Jefri. You'll see all we see, but stay in the middle for now. Please?"

Magda and Elspa caught up with Jefri and softly encouraged him to let Ravna and Woodcarver go ahead.

As Ravna turned to follow Woodcarver, she heard a burst of angry Tinish. A single member came scrambling up from the lower ledge. "Ritl! What the devil . . . ?"

The critter gave Ravna an imperious nod, emitting a chord that meant something like "You again" as it swept past.

Heida Øysler was next up from the ledge. She seemed to take Ravna's question as directed at her. "Yeah, yeah. I'm sorry. We thought this was part of Tycoon. Hei, it was member-close to the guy, and wearing the same insignia. It even talks like a boss. So we grabbed it." The kids coming up behind her looked a little shamefaced, too; maybe this had been a group effort. "Now it looks like we got someone's ugly pet."

Oh my, I don't have time for this. "But why did you bring her *here*?"

Heida glared at the singleton. "Well, it wasn't our choice."

Scrupilo's video was so low-resolution that it must have come from his own locally-made camera. However much he might call it crappy, Ravna bet the guy was vastly proud of the device. And when she had *Oobii* mesh them with the survey imagery . . . they were everything the recovery parties needed.

There were three towering swarms of birds. The pictures didn't reveal what was on the ground beneath them, but Ravna's topo map showed one of the sites was just ahead of Poul Linden's group. Woodcarver shouted guidance down to Poul as Ravna's group closed in on the highest projected impact point, one that the birds had not yet discovered. This spot might take some hard climbing, but for now Ravna and Øvin walked almost abreast of each other, with Woodcarver occasionally extending herself out between them.

As they walked, Ravna cycled through her task list: Nevil's radios were motionless on the other side of Newcastle, under forest cover. Either he had discarded the devices, or he was waiting for "his people" to catch up with him. The Denier Children were visible on the north road, heading toward the valley forest, shadowed by Woodcarver troops. More wagons had joined the group. Several packs seemed to be guiding the caravan. Dekutomon and company? There was no avoiding the conclusion that this was a planned exodus. Nevil was either nuts or still playing a turn ahead of Ravna and Woodcarver.

Whatever Nevil's strategy, it didn't look like he would be rendezvousing with his main Tinish allies any time soon: Vendacious and Tycoon were still driving into the eastern sky, rising steadily as they approached the Icefangs. If they thought they were out of beam gun range, they were dead wrong. They would be visible to *Oobii* for hours more, unless they decided to play a risky game of hide-and-seek in the mountain valleys. Even now, Ravna could count the fasteners on Tycoon's steam engine gondolas. A word from her and *Oobii* could flash-fry both airships.

Øvin interrupted her impotent daydreaming: "Hei! Where did this come from?" He was kneeling at the side of the path. Now he held up something bright and yellow.

Two of Woodcarver eeled forward for a close look. "A gold coin. Long Lakes mintage."

Øvin turned it over a couple of times, hefting it. Like a number of Children, he had gone native to the extent of valuing heavy metals; gold and silver could be exchanged for things the starfolk couldn't yet make. "When I was little, we used to hike around here a lot," he said, glancing up at Ravna.

"All forgiven," she said. *Rascal.*

Øvin smiled fleetingly. "The point is, we never saw anything like this. And if we had, we'd have snarfed it up."

Woodcarver said, "Sigh. Maybe it's not such a mystery. I'll bet that after we got you and your friends off the cliffs, Vendacious and Nevil turned this into their private highway."

Jefri walked past them, oblivious. Magda and Elspa tagged along behind him, scarcely pausing to glance at Øvin's coin. These three knew what was important.

"C'mon," Ravna said to the others.

"Hei up there! Are you seeing lots of gold coins?" The question came from some pack on Linden's team.

"Just one," Woodcarver boomed in reply.

"We just found a dozen, some on open rock, some wedged into the trees."

The words set Jefri moving at a trot, barely slowed by Magda and Elspa's cautions.

"I see yellow, too!" Scrupilo chimed in. "Hei, you on the high path! It's just a little further on. The birds haven't found it yet, but there are holes punched in the spring leaves—"

Jefri and company had disappeared around a corner of naked rock. When Ravna and the rest caught up, they found the three stopped, staring: not at a handful of gold coins, but at hundreds of coins and gems, a splash of gold and glitter that swept across the path. It lay in bright, direct sunlight. Indeed the Spring forest canopy had two wide tears in it. Where the light fell, greenish gloom was replaced by uncompromising detail. *But Amdi, where are you?* Like in the fairy tales, where the dying friend is turned to treasure?

Jefri scrambled up the rock, bracing his feet against tree trunks to lean against the steepness. He swept wildly at the branches. Gold coins scattered from around his hands, unheeded. "Where is he?" Jefri shouted. "Where—" He paused, steadied himself, and *pulled.* Something large and angular broke loose from where it had been jammed between rocks.

The wreckage bounced and crashed down to the path. It was—had been—a strongbox. Where it hadn't splintered, the surface glistened with polish.

Ravna felt a touch on her shoulder. She turned. It was Øvin, grim and solemn. He jerked his head upwards. Ravna followed his gaze. Something dark and member-sized was caught in the higher branches. She noticed Ritl pacing beneath it, staring straight up. For once the critter was not spewing commentary.

Ravna swallowed. Then she looked at Jefri, still braced precariously between the cliff face and various tree trunks. "Please come down now, Jef." She kept her tone even and comforting.

"We have to find him, Rav."

"We will. I promise." It took a force of will not to look at the dark, still form that hid in the shadows just beyond Jef's reach. "But you shouldn't be way up there. It's not safe. I want you to come down now."

He stared back at her, his eyes wide. It was a look she hadn't seen in years, from long before he had grown and gotten mixed up with the Deniers and betrayed her and rescued her. It was the little boy that Pham had rescued on Murder Meadows.

Jefri gave a sigh. "Okay," he said and carefully came down to safety. No one spoke, but by the time Jefri reached the ground, almost everyone else had noticed the body in the trees.

The hardest part of getting the body down was keeping Jefri out of the way.

The body. *Think of it as the body, the creature, the member—not as part of Amdiranifani.* The *creature* was dead beyond doubt. The poor fellow had been impaled on one of the thornlike branches at the apex of the tree, where the evergreen needles didn't grow. The accidental spear had passed through the length of the body, ending where the branch was almost fifteen centimeters wide.

As they began cutting down the body, Woodcarver shouted news of the discovery to Linden's group.

"Okay!" came the reply. "We're fighting off a mob of stubborn—*yeowr!*—seabirds. They're swarming around something just ahead of us."

Magda and Elspa were sitting with Jefri on the ground. They finally had him calmed down. Ravna leaned against a large boulder and sent all sorts of surely unnecessary detail back to *Oobii*. From Scrupilo's video, the ship had already located seven bodies, all dead for a certainty, though this one and the one by Poul Linden might be the only members they could get to today. *So I'll be free to think on other things.* But now her attention was stuck on the impaled body, all the other windows ignored.

One forester sawed at the tree as the other sailed restraining ropes around the upper branches. Ritl circled underneath, acting more like a real dog than Ravna had ever seen among Tines, even singletons. Ritl wasn't saying much. She just looked curious and mystified and—for once—as stupid as she probably was. But the dogs Ravna remembered were plenty smart enough to realize when their betters were upset—and surely Ritl remembered Amdi. She had caused poor Amdiranifani enough problems. Ravna hoped the little beast couldn't be hurt as much as Jefri and Amdi's other friends.

As they lowered the body to the ground, Jefri shook himself free of Magda and Elspa. Everyone but Ritl stepped back at his approach. Fortunately, the corpse's head was turned away from view; it looked like the tree branch had burst through the face. The body was shrouded in a long cloak. As Jefri knelt beside it, Ritl slid forward, peering suspiciously at the body. Jefri waved the singleton away. He reached for the cloak—

Ritl emitted a piercing squawk and darted past him. She tore at the corpse's throat, screaming in rage.

Jefri didn't seem to notice. He had fallen to his knees and was staring in blank shock. Magda and Elspa rushed forward to grab Ritl, but the singleton rolled off the corpse and scuttled into the underbrush on the high side of the path. She was making a weird hooting noise. After a moment, Ravna recognized the sound. It was a small part of *laughter.*

Jefri didn't look up, but when he spoke, his voice was full of wonder. "This isn't any part of Amdi."

And finally, Ravna took a close look at the torn, dead thing. One paw extended beyond the cloak. The claws were painted; what might have been a fetter was made of silver. All else aside, the creature's grayed muzzle made it older than any of Amdi.

Woodcarver was mingled with the humans around the corpse. She pulled the cloak entirely aside and stared for a long moment at the corpse. Then she stepped away.

"Is this anyone you know?" asked Ravna, but Woodcarver didn't answer and now the other packs were crowding as close as they could get.

"No one I've ever seen," one said in Samnorsk.

"It could be a recent addition to someone we know."

"Unlikely. It's too old."

Øvin Verring put in: "We'll have to get to the other deaders before the birds strip them down." Now that this was simply a whopping mystery, such things were easier to say.

In her hidey-hole at the side of the path, Ritl was still chortling. Now she started gobbling loudly, more like the usual Ritl.

This time, no one ignored her. Heads came sharply around, then turned to stare at one another in consternation. After a moment, even Ravna understood the simple chords:

"*Vendacious dead. Vendacious dead. Vendacious dead!*"

CHAPTER 42

There was no word in Samnorsk for the quality of the next twenty-four hours. Woodcarver said there were chords for it in Tinish: a yodel that denoted wrenching change, a time filled with events that might lead to total catastrophe, or survivable disaster, or maybe grand victory. For Ravna it was a nonstop run of problems and decisions, punctuated by short catnaps, food, and Lisl Armin's help with *Oobii*'s sickbay equipment. "You're dehydrated, starved, with half-healed lacerations all over. Food and rest and the sickbay can easily make those things right. *Oobii* sees evidence of a concussion. That shouldn't be a problem as long as you don't get too stressed out, but I'm afraid sickbay isn't up to truly curing the problem." Lisl brightened: "On the other hand, I bet I can fix your broken nose and facial bones! I'll just need a few hours of your time, and then you'll have to be careful of yourself—"

Ravna shut her off there. There just wasn't time for cosmetic frills—

The ship woke her from a nap in the mid-afternoon of the next day. She actually felt pretty good! But the first full meeting with the remaining Children was downstairs in just fifteen minutes. As she left the command deck, she was reviewing her personal log and *Oobii*'s latest news. The starship had tracked Tycoon's airships to a landing at some outpost east of the Icefangs. For resupply? In any case, the ships rose again and headed south. Closer to home, Scrupilo had taken his little airboat—the Domain's only surviving aircraft—to overfly Nevil's caravan.

One of the first things Ravna had done was to sweep *Oobii* for lossage and vandalism. She had quietly removed the amplifier stage from Pham's beam gun; the thought of some software glitch slagging Newcastle town was just too scary. On the other hand, she hadn't wasted time on Nevil's interior decoration, so when she showed up in the "New Meeting Place," she found that a lot had changed. Gone was the friendly atmosphere that Nevil had set up when he was peddling democracy. There were none of the game environments, and only one or two computational access points. Nevil had mercilessly stripped the ship to set up the surveillance system that she had noticed the day before. The walls had a new theme, a starscape. The view was in the galactic plane, but very far out, at the edge of the abyss, perhaps in the Low Transcend. *The view from the Straumers' High Lab.*

There was a podium set against the intergalactic dark, with a seat for Nevil that was almost as impressive as the throne he had once built for Ravna. Ravna walked tentatively to the podium, but she did not sit down. She saw smiles and greetings, but no joy.

Today, the room held twenty packs and only about seventy Children. It was strange the way the kids would stare at her—and then look away. Repulsed? She knew what a ruin her face was; surely they would get used to it. The packs didn't seem so affected. She noticed Flenser and Woodcarver in the audience. Ah! And there was Jefri, too, sitting impassively a little apart from everyone else.

Ravna said, "We all need to be talking more than ever now. Given the state of the interfaces"—she waved around the room—"that may be a problem. I wanted to make sure you know what I've been doing, what *Oobii* is seeing. I—I also want to hear what you've been up to, what's worrying you most."

She noticed that Wenda Larsndot, Sr., was already standing, her hand raised. Giske Gisksndot bounced to her feet. "I want to talk about Nevil! We lost half the human race yesterday."

"They wanted to go. Good riddance." That was from someone hidden from Ravna's view, but the remark was not intended to be anonymous. Around the room, many of the Children were nodding agreement.

"Yes!" shouted Elspa Latterby. "Instead, we need to go after that Tycoon fellow. He *stole* my little sister!" *And Edvi and Timor and Amdi and Jo and Pilgrim and Screwfloss and. . . .* Agreement and argument swirled all around. Suddenly Ravna felt as incompetent as ever with the Children.

She raised her hand, a tentative request for order, and—

Everyone fell silent.

How did I do that? For a moment Ravna was speechless herself. "Look, everybody, I have various pieces of information about some of these problems. But please, let's take things a step at a time. Wenda, you seemed to be first?"

"Yes, uh, thanks. This is a little off-topic, but I think it's important. I talked to Johanna yesterday, before she went up to Starship Hill." Once more, the silence was total. "She told me some things she said we need to know and some other things we are honor-bound to do. First off, there were no 'Tropical terrorists' on those rafts. There was no bomb; the killing was done with the beam gun on *Oobii*."

"We've guessed that," said Øvin, his voice flat and deadly.

Wilm Linden waved at Ravna. "But you could prove it, right? *Oobii* must have logs."

"Yes." Short of an underlying software failure, she could uncover any attempt Nevil had made to hide his actions. "I'll get the logs, but I'm afraid Nevil will just say they're faked."

Wenda made a dismissive gesture. "Jo's main point was that we *owe* these Tropicals. They may not have minds like packs or humans, but she says it was their decision to rescue her and their sacrifice that saved her life. She asked—ah, actually the word she used was 'demand'—that we treat them well and help them return home if that's what they seem to want."

Woodcarver raised several heads, all looking in Ravna's direction. "If I may?" she said.

"Yes. Please."

"I've already moved most of this mob up to the old embassy. Ten raft crews is more than in any past shipwreck. It'll be very expensive to adequately enlarge the place. . . . but I'm willing to do so. That's partly because they're innocent parties"—a nod in Wenda's direction—"and partly because if we mistreat Tycoon's creatures, we increase the risk to my Pilgrim and all the other poor souls Tycoon is holding."

Ravna nodded. "Thank you, Woodcarver. Was there anything else, Wenda?"

"Oh! Yes. We have a little inventory problem down at the South End. One thing Nevil *wasn't* lying about was the rafts' main cargo."

"Oh yeah," someone said, "the *peace* offering from Tycoon."

"Well, whatever you call it, this cargo is not junk. There's about fifteen tonnes of fabric." Wenda rolled her eyes in distress. "It's as good as anything we currently make. There are other things; we're still going through the containers. So far we count nine hundred and five voice-band radios."

Tycoon would have been pleased by the stupefied expressions that Ravna saw around the room. Wenda shrugged. "Okay, that's all my news." And she sat down.

One by one, everyone had their say. Most of the kids seemed to realize that Tycoon was both out of reach and a new kind of problem. The concern about the Denier exodus was different. Giske said, "There have always been Deniers, but Nevil made the idiocy deadly. My Rolf was such a good person. I'd never have married him otherwise. But he bought into everything Nevil was peddling. We argued about it every night, especially after Ravna disappeared. Now he has my kids, and I want them back!"

There was a muttering of agreement, not just about Giske's family, but about everyone's experience.

Ravna glanced at Jefri. Jef was also a good person. That wasn't sufficient to solve the problem.

"In the end, they'll come crawling back," said Wenda Larsndot, sounding much less gentle-minded than usual. "Most Deniers never bothered to learn how to live *here*. The idea of them living in the wild is a joke!"

"That's not the point!" said Giske, her voice rising, "So far *no one* has overestimated Nevil's capacity for evil. Maybe he's one of those nutso-freakos who loses big time and then takes his followers into a corner and murders them! *I want my children back! Now!*"

———

The meeting went on for another half hour and then there were separate chats with Woodcarver and various Children. But not with Jefri; he left right at the end of the meeting.

Scrupilo's radio had failed, but *Oobii* could see that both the airboat and Scrupilo were well enough. He would be back in an hour. Maybe he could add something pro or con to Giske's unpleasant theory. Ravna straggled off for a short nap.

As she settled down in her old room by the command deck, she wondered again at her success in the meeting. Not since the Children were little—and rarely even then—had the kids deferred to her as they had this afternoon.

Maybe they saw her as a competent hero who had been to hell and back. Ha. If they only knew how little of that was her doing. It still bothered her the way the kids winced when they looked at her crushed nose and cheek. But what if that wasn't revulsion? What if the kids saw the injury as proof of tremendous sacrifice? Then sympathy and admiration all worked their magic in her favor. If it had been Nevil in her shoes, he'd squeeze that advantage as hard as he could, as long as he could. She thought about the notion for a moment, struggling to hold back sleep. Maybe she was a fool but, "Ship!"

"Yes, Ravna?"

"Please call Lisl Armin and tell her I'm a go for the face repair."

And then she slept.

———

Scrupilo's overflights didn't support Giske's worst-case theory. Ultimately, Nevil might be as crazy as Giske thought, but the Denier caravan was well equipped, and well prepared. Considering all the gear they had stolen, "well equipped" was no surprise. As for being well-prepared—Bili Yngva had something to do with that. The logs showed that Bili had spent a lot of time up here on the command deck, planning. He had recognized some of the gear in the Lander— what Ravna had mistaken for junk—and figured that it might still have limited functionality. That accounted for the strange thefts from the Newcastle catacombs. As for the fire they set in the Lander—Nevil and Bili really did believe in Countermeasure. The details were lost in a chaos of corrupted log files— what looked like a system failure, not encryption. Maybe she could unscramble the mess eventually, but for the moment she concentrated on trying to contact Tycoon and trying to break into the orbiter.

Meantime, Nevil was probing back at *Oobii*. The Chief Denier—that was her most polite term for him—had most of the commsets, and access to the orbiter. Ravna deliberately left the Denier user accounts in place, but in virtual cages. Nevil was all over them, probing for security holes, posting Nevilish propaganda. The incompetent hacking was very informative—to Ravna.

Woodcarver sent scouts with truce flags after the Deniers. They were peacefully received and allowed to talk to whomever they pleased. They even persuaded six from the caravan to return.

But when Ravna walked the streets of Newcastle town, the empty houses were everywhere, tears in the thin fabric of humanity. Denial had hijacked almost half of the human race, and there was yet a trickle of Children still departing, trying to catch up with the main group.

After five days, Nevil's exodus reached its destination, a warm-springs cave system more than one hundred kilometers to the northeast. Woodcarver recognized the place. She told Ravna that she'd known about it for about a century and always believed it too dangerous for long-term settlement.

The place was beyond the range of Scrupilo's little airboat. Three days passed, where the only word was Nevil's voice reporting and happy messages from various of his followers. He was promising pictures any day now. When it came down through the orbiter, Ravna put the video in the Meeting Place.

Ravna and Woodcarver were present at the first showing, along with almost all the remaining Children and their Friends.

Nevil's "Best Hope" settlement was near the edge of a hanging valley set in the wall of the Streamsdell river valley. It was in the Icefangs, just beyond Woodcarver's territorial claims in that direction. Those highlands were not much favored by Tinish hunter-farmers, but Nevil was optimistic. In fact, the first video showed him near the middle of the Streamsdell Valley. "This land is ideal for humans, for independence and growth. Come see this in a year. There will be the green buds of our new hardicore grass, a chartreuse carpet stretching all the way to the edge of the Nordhus glacier."

"Good luck, asshole!" someone in the audience shouted. "You guys never grew anything when you were *here*."

The viewpoint bumpily slewed around, away from the glacier, past the river and then up the north valley wall. Some of the Tines were making wondering noises. Øvin said, "Hei, look! That must be why they picked this place!"

From the camera's position, they could see something that was probably not visible to travelers taking the usual route along Streamsdell: a vertical slit in the dark rock of the side valley.

"That's what, twenty meters tall?" someone said.

Nevil's friendly voice rambled on behind their local commentary: "—apparently the Tines were never aware that the warm springs here supported a cave system. It is a truly human discovery." He walked back into the field of view. "Fortunately, the team that found it were loyal to the best human values. Jefri Olsndot reported this directly to me."

The hall erupted. "That son of a bitch!" "All that time he was the 'great explorer,' he was working for Nevil!"

Ravna had already checked: Jefri was not in the room.

On the display, Nevil had raised his hands, almost as if he knew the racket his announcement would cause. "I know, I know. It could not have been a purely human discovery. Jefri was accompanied by pack Amdiranifani. Friendship with the Tines will always be our policy. We seek friendship with Woodcarver. We have found friendship with Tycoon of the Tropics."

There was angry laughter. "Hei, don't forget your late good friend Vendacious!" and, "Ten days ago it was 'Tycoon of the East Coast.'"

Nevil continued, "But my friends, a time has come for moral decisions. For too long, we've accepted the advice of misguided humans and Tines. Humans who truly want peace have a place with our settlement here at Best Hope. There is no need for the endless preparation for apocalypse that Ravna Bergsndot has forced upon you and the Tines of Woodcarver's Domain. There was a time when we were too young and too desperate to know any better. Ravna and Woodcarver and Flenser saved the lives of all us young refugees who survived their initial massacre. We owe them so much. But at the same time, we owe our *parents*. They died at the High Lab in a noble effort, the highest striving that any humans have ever undertaken. We must not fall into the destructive hatred that Ravna preaches."

"Same old, same old!" Giske said. "We have records."

Ravna heard Øvin reply, "I'm sure Nevil will soon have his own records."

"Besides, no one knows what really happened at the High Lab," said someone else, that Ravna couldn't see.

"We don't even know what happened in near space, ten years ago!"

"Shut up!"

Nevil's voice swept on, leaving a wake of tiny dissensions. "I hope that as more of you take honest inventory of the facts, you'll see beyond the loyalties of the past, and that you and your friends—including any Tinish Best Friends!—will come to join us here at our redoubt of Straum. All who come with honest hearts will be welcome. But whether you agree with us or not—*please!* Whatever the disagreements, peace between our two human fragments is a desperate necessity. We may be all that is left of our race. In fact, after the galactic genocide of ten years ago, we may be all that is left from the High Beyond."

Now Nevil was walking up the hillside, toward the entrance of his "redoubt." His people were coming out, walking down to meet him, all smiles and laughter. Surrounded by familiar faces, Nevil turned and looked into the camera. "So even if we remain apart, even if we have profound disagreements . . . let us cooperate in surviving. You of the Domain have immense resources. You have *Oobii* and the treasures in Newcastle. These are the shared inheritance of our Beyonder origin. Let us cooperate in using them."

That first video left the kids arguing throughout the afternoon. The second and third videos were so similar that by the time the fourth one came in, Ravna just watched the kids' reaction from the bridge. There was no crowd in the Meeting Place; the message could be rewatched at any time. The live audience consisted mainly of sad Children hoping to see a few seconds of their lost loved ones.

———

But Nevil's fourth message was different.

The video started with pictures of the Deniers' new construction, inside the caves. They were building without the aid of *Oobii* technology, but now Ravna saw the use the Deniers had made of the gear stripped from the Straumer Lander. Indeed, it was not junk—she'd simply never figured out the user interface! Under sunny artificial lighting, the caves looked warm and dry. Three "participation homes"—that's what Nevil called them—were already in place. Fresh timber was stacked everywhere, sawn and measured, ready for the construction of more housing. The timber and carpentering must be from Tycoon via Dekutomon. Somehow Nevil had patched things up with his remaining ally.

The few Children down in *Oobii*'s Meeting Place were using their new radios to tell others about the pictures. By the time a crowd started to form in the Meeting Place, Nevil had finished his show-and-tell of Best Hope marvels and was moving on to the platitudes. As usual he was surrounded by smiling faces. But now, Ravna wasn't paying much attention; she could almost recite what the rest would be. Sure enough: "So even though we have profound disagreements . . .

let us cooperate in surviving. You of the Domain have immense resources. We at Best Hope have the goodwill of Tines from the Tropics all the way to the Long Lakes and the East Coast. We have made peace with what was once a fearsome Enemy: Tycoon. By winning his trust and goodwill, we have secured the release of everyone he is holding. The release"—

Ravna's eyes snapped up to the display. Downstairs, she heard gasps and then babble.

—"is without conditions. It's happening because we showed Tycoon that— unlike Ravna and Woodcarver—we of Best Hope mean him no harm." Nevil paused. Around him, his Deniers were cheering. Downstairs on the *Oobii*, the Children were cheering too, but more raggedly.

"We expect," continued Nevil, "that most of the newly freed will prefer to stay here at Best Hope." He paused, letting them all think on the consequences of *that*. "But we recognize that for the most extreme of Ravna's acolytes, that would destroy whatever goodwill our effort should bring." His expression darkened, one of the rare moments when the public Nevil looked angry. "Make no mistake. We won't trade the freedom of any of these Children. We won't force anyone to return to Ravna and Woodcarver and Flenser. But we welcome a peace party from the Domain. Any may come. Your party will have free access to all who are released. You can determine for yourself the desires of the freed Children and Tines."

Ravna saw that Elspa Latterby had collapsed in tears. She wasn't the only one weeping. Ravna ran out of the bridge, heading for the Meeting Place.

CHAPTER 43

Everyone wanted to go to the Great Prisoner Release. Woodcarver exercised some of her old authority and asked Ravna to come up to the New Castle for a private chat. They met in Woodcarver's throne room. Sht was big enough for its own little throne now. The other puppy nestled on the shoulders of another member.

"Nevil has stolen half the human race and almost all the equipment that wasn't nailed down. I don't want the rest of you in his claws."

Ravna nodded; she had spent the afternoon talking to the kids, and worrying about the same thing. "But you'll provide a military escort, right?"

"Of course! And unless Nevil has magic we don't know about, my troops totally outgun him. But consider. We have only Nevil's word of this agreement"— there was still no direct communication with Tycoon—"and if there *is* a deal between those two, we have no idea what it is. For all I know, Tycoon could field a force that would trump mine. There is *no* treachery that I put beyond these two."

That was something the remaining Children agreed on, too. "Okay. I think

I can persuade most of the Children to stay behind." Ravna no longer looked like the victim of a sadistic mugging, but the kids were still amazingly solicitous of her. She had to be careful in making casual statements lest they take them as imperatives. "I am going, however."

Woodcarver emitted a sigh. "That's what I was afraid of, and I fear it undoes all our other caution."

Ravna smiled. "I take it that you're not going?"

"I'm not crazy." Woodcarver's tone was sour. "On top of everything else, there's the possibility that all this is a feint, and Tycoon is set to attack us *here*."

Ravna nodded. What Woodcarver said made sense, but—"You know, I think there's still a chance for Pilgrim. From Wenda, I gather that Jo and Pilgrim crashed right in the middle of Tycoon's operation. I know Tycoon wasn't aware of that! It's possible that Pilgrim is still in hiding down there. And Tycoon is not the monster Vendacious was. Even if Tycoon has captured Pilgrim, I think he'd be safe."

Woodcarver sat back. All her eyes were on Ravna, except for the puppies, who were looking at each other. They did that just when the old Woodcarver would have said something really nasty. When she finally spoke, Woodcarver just sounded sad: "But Jo didn't tell Wenda what had become of Pilgrim. And when we were all on stage, we learned nothing more; Tycoon was too busy ripping at her. Face it, Ravna. Both Jo and Pilgrim are dead."

This was a dark outlook Woodcarver was not showing in public. Maybe the pessimism was entirely little Sht's influence, or maybe it had more history. "You also grieve for Vendacious, don't you, Woodcarver?"

Woodcarver's heads came up abruptly. "Yes. I grieve for a monstrous pack, who after a century shared virtually none of my blood. Even my own advisors call my sympathy 'the Queen's madness.'"

"Not . . . madness." But Ravna remembered her horror when Gannon was crushed; Woodcarver's grief was a different thing. "You packs—you in particular—have done something most civilizations can't do until they've externalized thought; you've taken biological selection by the throats and put it in service to ideas. Your offspring packs are your great experiments."

"And two of them were the greatest Tinish monsters of all time."

"True," said Ravna. "But consider. Old Flenser changed the Northwest almost as much as you have—and he created and recreated Steel, and Steel designed and assembled and guided Amdiranifani."

After a moment, Woodcarver replied, "Long ago, I imagined Vendacious as a weapon against Flenser. That weapon ran amok. It has killed so many. It probably killed the pack my members especially loved. And yet, however much I hate Vendacious, I can't share everyone's joy at his total death."

Ravna nodded, trying unsuccessfully to imagine a reformed Vendacious. "So now, listen more to your members. Hope for what still may be."

———

Of course, their wagon trip up the Streamsdell Valley was nothing like Ravna's days with Chitiratifor. This expedition had decent food and good tents to sleep in. Domain troops were spread out around them and scouting ahead. The travelers who suffered were the Children who were most desperate to come. Øvin refused to give up on Edvi. Elspa had more hope for her sister Geri, even though she had heard Tycoon's terrible voice. Jefri said he was optimistic about Amdi, but he didn't *look* optimistic. Giske Gisksndot didn't talk about her feelings at all, but anger radiated from her. Right after Nevil's big announcement, the Chief Denier had "generously" allowed her to speak with her husband. Giske *knew* that no hostages would come home with her, that Rolf was determined to keep their two sons. "Powers be damned, I just want to *see* them!" she had cried to Ravna, begging to be included in the expedition. In the end, Ravna couldn't refuse her, but she worried what Giske might do when she finally confronted Rolf and Nevil.

The only traveler who seemed unconcerned was Ritl, though she complained as much as ever, especially when she was around Ravna. The singleton had not been given a choice about coming, but then she hadn't been left in the Domain by her own choice either. Fate had bounced the animal from place to place, but within the limits of her intelligence, she seemed to be searching for something. Ravna hoped that Tycoon would be grateful for her return—or at least not hold that return against Ravna and company.

After five days on the road, their expedition came in sight of Nevil's hanging valley. Benky's troops set up a perimeter and the travelers made camp by the river. While everyone waited impatiently for some sign from above, Flenser-Tyrathect spread himself out on sun-warmed boulders by the river. Flenser had brought several telescopes. He idled away the time peering up at the lip of the hanging valley. He seemed to be enjoying himself. "I wager that Nevil won't invite us into his caves. I remember when I was a co-conspirator." His heads, except for the ones eyeballing the heights, all bobbed in a grin. "He never trusted me with the exact location, but it was clear that Vendacious and probably Tycoon knew about it. I predict that Tycoon will support 'Best Hope' just enough to be a problem."

Ravna had come over to sit nearby, beside the member with the white-tipped low-sound ears. Even at its best, this crippled creature couldn't have climbed the rocks, but the rest of Flenser still kept it close. Ravna stroked White Tips along the neck, almost as she would a dog. It always accepted such affection. That had been one of the things that had made her want to trust Flenser-Tyrathect. White Tips emitted a rumbling purr; all of Flenser might be less of a sarcastic twit for a few minutes now.

"So you think the prisoner release is going to be down here?" said Ravna. "I don't see signs of anyone but us here."

Jefri and others were walking toward them from the tents. Despite Jef's ambiguous reputation—some of the loyalist Children thought he was Ravna's secret agent and others were convinced he was a traitor—Jef had ended up being their chief human advisor on this outing. As long as he was clearly working from Ravna's game plan, everyone seemed willing to accept his expertise. The camp wouldn't have settled down so quickly and comfortably without Jefri and Benky.

Elspa was just a few feet behind Jef. She gestured to Flenser. "Still no sign of Deniers?"

"Nope, sorry." Flenser waggled his telescopes authoritatively. Today he had better eyesight than anyone.

Elspa plunked down near Ravna. "I pray . . . I pray they have my Geri."

Jefri came around to Ravna's right so he was standing by White Tips. He muttered just loud enough for Ravna's ears and the pack. "They better have Amdi. There's no excuse for not returning him."

Flenser's voice came even more softly, barely more than a hum that Ravna felt where her fingertips touched White Tips. "And they better have Screwfloss."

Their party sat by the river for a time, speculating, sometimes arguing. A meal broke up the discussion, but not the mood. Afterwards Jefri was gone for a time, checking with Benky that the soldiers and lookouts were in position. Ritl was occasionally visible, on some scouting mission of her own.

Ravna checked in with their hidden expedition participant: Scrup had parked his airboat on a mountain pass selected by *Oobii*. He was playing relay; ionospheric bounce was not good enough today. Ravna wanted reliable communication back to Woodcarver and *Oobii*. Scrupilo kibitzed on the link but wasn't supposed to mess with the main data stream. "Amazing," he said. "From this mountain top looking east, it's like being the Pack of Packs. I see glaciers and mountains going on forever, like a stony sea. Pilgrim used to brag about this."

"I still don't have imagery, Scrupilo." Ravna's data tiara was giving her audio, but she had no windows from *Oobii*.

"Sorry," said Scrupilo. "Maybe your tiara is finally busted? We're getting good pictures from Wilm Linden's camera."

"Okay." Audio plus Wilm's camera should be enough for today. She talked past Scrupilo: "Ship! What are you seeing?"

Oobii replied, "My radar shows mostly clear sky, a few bird swarms. I can't see all the way down into the valleys."

"Yes," interrupted Scrupilo. "Damn Nevil. If his idiots hadn't crashed *EA2*, we might have our own look-down radar." He ranted about Denier incompetence for some minutes; Scrupilo had his own geeky slant on what was wrong with Nevil.

The sun was well past noon when the packs farthest from the noise of the river sounded alarms. Their shouts were not quiet alerts. They were booming chords that announced, "Airship sounds! Airship sounds!"

Flenser was instantly scanning the ridgeline. "I don't see anything." He kept his scopes aimed at Nevil's side valley, but there was a subtle change in the rest of him. He was *listening* with most of his attention. "I'm too close to the river. It's not the best hearing . . . Yes! Airships, definitely."

Now other packs began shouting. They were racing around, not looking anywhere in particular. *Give me a clue, guys!* thought Ravna. *Where should I be looking?*

Benky came racing down from the tree line, jabbing snouts at the southeastern sky.

Ravna followed the gestures. Nothing. And she still couldn't hear a shred of engine sound . . . but now *Oobii* reported secondary radar echoes that might be aircraft following the curve of the Streamsdell Valley.

A minute passed. *There!* Just above where the glacial valley turned further south, she saw two dark spots floating against the snow glare.

Flenser was dancing around his telescope watchers. He had his own news: "Hei, hei! There are two-legs coming down from Nevil's little valley."

Eyes turned from the sky to the ridgeline. At least a dozen tiny figures were descending the valley wall. The abrupt, simultaneous emergence was as dramatic as Nevil and Tycoon had no doubt planned.

One of the airships might have been the one Ravna and Jefri had flown on; it had the Pack of Packs twelvesome painted on its nose. But the other airship was just as large. There was plenty of room for all the prisoners.

The ships didn't immediately land. They circled in a long elliptical path above Ravna's group, flying back and forth along the breeze that swept the valley.

Øvin made a rude gesture at the airships. "The crapheads aren't going to land until the Great Nevil gives the command."

Flenser's had one telescope on the descending humans and the other two on the airships. Øvin Verring's comment got his attention though: "Heh. That's certainly the claim Dear Nevil would make. But I remember *EA2* landings. It's tricky without a ground crew to help."

Magda Norasndot said, "Yes. Be nice, Øvin. We can't afford nastiness." She and Elspa Latterby were already talking about where the ships would land. They wanted to be at the front of the welcomers.

Benky had run back into the forest. Now he and some of his troops came into view, accompanying the Denier party. Ravna didn't need a telescope to spot Nevil Storherte. How did he keep his clothes so clean out here? The villain strode confidently toward them. As he came nearer, Ravna could see he was grinning as with general good nature.

"Greetings, greetings!" Nevil shouted as the loyalist Children ran out to meet him. He stopped well short of Ravna to talk with those most desperate for news.

There were fifteen Deniers in his party. Tami Ansndot and several others were carrying cams and comms. They looked like a news crew from some ancient time. It was interesting the added importance they seemed to give whomever they were pointing at.

Nevil had picked Elspa out of the crowd. Ravna strained to hear him; the tiara was no help today. "Yes," Nevil was saying, "communications have been awful. Getting better comms should be everyone's highest priority. But I know your Geri is one of those whom Tycoon found. I know for a fact she is on the first airship—" He turned as Magda touched his arm. He nodded, giving Magda a hug. "Yes, I hope the Norasndots will be here too. We'll know soon enough." Some of the Children were openly crying.

Oops. Where is Giske? She wouldn't be in the middle of all this unless she was carrying a knife. Ravna glanced quickly around. There—Giske was almost thirty meters away, arguing with Bili Yngva.

Now Nevil stepped back and his voice became more public: "Please. Give us a few minutes. We have to get the airships safely landed." He looked into the sky at the farther airship, just now making a turn at the far end of its circuit. "I'll land the one with our friends first. The other is just a backup flier." He delivered this disappointment so casually that people scarcely seemed to notice. Could you really get all the missing on one of these airships?

Nevil touched his ear, like some player in an ancient drama. In addition to what he had stolen, he must be getting radios from Tycoon. With the orbiter for a relay, he had better comms than the Domain. Nevil looked around, then gave a go-ahead wave. Most of the Denier Children ran out into the marshy flats by the river's outer curve. Ah, there was Del Ronsndot in the lead, waving an arm in a wide circle. The other Children spread out. One of the airships was coming toward them.

The ship's buzzing rose to a whine. Its bow dipped till the long airform hung foreshortened, descending to earth. All conversation stopped. This was a little like what you might see in civilization—only there, the ship would be a solid mass, perhaps one hundred thousand tonnes, a vehicle that could navigate solar systems.

By the time the first craft had dropped lines and Del's crew had pounded down anchor spikes, the second airship was descending to land a hundred meters behind. Ravna noticed that Benky was shifting his troops around, inconspicuously setting up fields of fire.

At that point, almost everyone surged forward onto the marshy ground. Benky looked outraged; some of his own troops had joined the crowd. Here in the middle of nowhere, a couple of dozen humans and some packs were doing a good job of imitating a mob. Jefri—who was already at the first airship—got some of the troops into a circle around the ship's main hatch. Wilm Linden had made it to the front with his camera.

Flenser scrambled down from the river rocks. He let Ravna help with White Tips and his wheelbarrow. They made slow progress across the marsh. Ritl hung back with them. Maybe she realized that she was likely to get trampled if she rushed into the crowd.

Everyone made way for Nevil. As he walked by Jefri, words passed between the two, but Ravna was too far away to hear. She glanced at Flenser, who was watching the exchange too. "Couldn't hear it," he said.

Maybe Nevil's expression had darkened at Jefri's words. But then he grinned at Jef, and seemed to say something encouraging. He turned back to crowd, all smiles. *Powers*, even improvising, he was doing as well as back at the New Meeting Place.

"Friends," he shouted, his voice thin in the breeze. "Friends. Please stay a little back. I'm not sure of the order our loved ones will come out—" but he was waving Elspa to come forward.

Ravna and Flenser had reached the back of the crowd. Ravna tried to see around or over those ahead of her. Ritl wasn't helping. She was running around between Ravna's legs, complaining, presumably because *she* couldn't see a thing. Except for the fact that she was making trouble, this was very unlike Ritl. Why wasn't she flanking the mob, or worming her through the Children to get a front row view?

Wilm Linden held the Domain camera high over his head, scanning across the crowd. Then he turned back to the sealed hatch. "You're getting Wilm's video?" Ravna said to her relay link.

"Yup," Scrup's voice came back, and a second later Woodcarver confirmed: "Ravna, I'm keeping your audio private to Scrupilo and myself. We've got Wilm's transmission showing in *Oobii*'s meeting place—as well as the video the Deniers are sending through the orbiter. We're hanging on Nevil's every word." She gobbled a mild obscenity.

Ravna grinned but didn't reply. Beside her, Flenser had made a Tinish pyramid of himself and now had a pair of eyes with a clear view. Benky stayed close to ground; she noticed he had three packs watching *away* from the main event.

Both airships had shut down their engines. Nevil was into a pregnant pause. The moment captured Ravna as much as anyone. Down by her ankles, even Ritl had fallen silent. The loudest sound was the breeze whistling up the valley.

Behind the port, there was a squeaking sound, the hatch wheel being turned. Ravna stepped to one side, finally got a sliver of a good view. The hull section swung out, dropping the main stairway down.

"So what's inside?" Flenser hissed at her.

"It's too dark for me to see," said Ravna. The entrance was in the shadow of the overhanging hull.

Woodcarver's voice came over the link. "*Oobii* did something with the image. There's at least a singleton crouched at the top of the stairs."

Somebody was pushing at Ravna's side, licking her hand. Ritl! "What? Are you crazy?" Ravna said to the animal. "Go run! See for yourself." Why was Ritl suddenly so shy? She was making desperate little whistling noises. In a way, that was more distracting than her usual bitching. "Okay," said Ravna, "but you better not slash me." She reached under Ritl's forelegs and hoisted the creature up the way the Children lifted their Best Friend's puppies. Of course there was a problem since Ritl was an average-sized female adult. Ravna staggered back a step, then recovered. At least the creature didn't try to hold on with her claws, but now Ravna was facing into lots of pointy teeth and the usual bad breath. Then Ritl twisted her head around to look at the airship.

For a moment Ritl was as quiet as everyone else, watching the space at the top of the stairs. Then the singleton that Woodcarver reported came sauntering out. No wonder it had been hard to see. It wore a cloak of midnight black. The radio cloak's golden highlights were mostly lost in the shade.

The singleton was Zek. He looked a lot better than the last time Ravna had seen him. Zek glanced around with an alertness and self-possession that must mean he had good connectivity. He nodded in Nevil's direction and boomed out the words, "I speak for Tycoon." His voice was not Tycoon's frightened little girl's voice. It actually sounded like one of Amdi's voices, the kind he used when he was pretending to be an adult human, someone serious and important.

Nevil gave a little start of surprise, but his response seemed as confident as ever: "As we agreed, sir, I have brought humans and packs from the Domain. Today we can settle many of the issues that poisoned their minds in the past. Have you brought those you rescued from the wild?"

"Indeed." Zek's head gave a jerky nod that might have been part of a cynical smile. "My employer has sent me with all the humans and Domainish Tines that we *rescued* on your behalf."

Zek stepped to the side, giving way to whatever was behind him. Ravna noticed that Nevil was urging Elspa forward so she would be at the foot of the stairs and visible to all his cameras.

A small human figure appeared at the top of the stairs. Elspa gave a cry and started forward. But this wasn't Geri Latterby. It was Timor Ristling, who even at fourteen was almost as short as Geri. He gave Elspa a little wave and smiled, maybe not understanding the disappointment in Elspa's face. He turned back into the darkened hallway and made coaxing gestures. After a moment, someone as small as he was took his hand. The face that peered out at them was as pale as any Straumer's face could ever be.

"*Geri!*" Elspa ran up the steps, sweeping her little sister into her arms. She teetered for an instant at the top, then came down a few steps to lean against the top rungs with her knee. For a moment, she just rocked the child in her arms and wept. Geri herself was much quieter. She seemed to be reaching back toward Timor, and after a moment Elspa brought the boy into her embrace.

As Elspa and the little ones came down the steps, the crowd jostled close, Nevil's camera crew at the fore. Ravna felt Ritl tense, buzzing. *She* was still looking at the top of the stairs. The only thing there was Zek—but now the creature was looking past the crowd, directly at Ravna. Or Ritl. The singleton exploded out of Ravna's arms and raced into the crowd. *Crazy animal!* Or maybe Ritl had somehow concluded that Amdi was here and about to be released.

Ravna had had enough of standing back here. She touched Flenser's White Tips and said, "I'm going to get closer."

None of Flenser looked her way, but the pack replied, "That's fine. Check out Geri. I don't think she qualifies as a propaganda coup for Nevil."

———

Three packs came out of the ship. Two were city guards who had been missing since before the first kidnappings. They were battered and scarred, though their injuries were mostly healed. The third was a fragment, all that remained of Edvi Verring's Best Friend Dumpster. There was angry muttering from Benky's troops on seeing all this evidence of mistreatment.

Some of Tycoon's packs had descended from the other airship. They looked like soldiers, but they kept their distance. Zek was the only crewmember who appeared from the first craft. He kept to his place at the top of the stairs; he wasn't saying much, mainly just ushering each prisoner out the door. Nevil did the talking. It took all his skill to spin this to his advantage.

Ravna worked her way through the crowd toward the little hillock where Elspa was sitting.

"Ravna!" Timor saw her and hobbled quickly in her direction. Ravna gave him a hug. Timor was talking fast and enthusiastically. "I was so worried about you, Ravna! We were mostly kept in our dungeons, but Tycoon said that—" He stopped himself as if he shouldn't be saying more, or perhaps he thought Ravna wasn't paying attention.

But I was paying attention. Ravna leaned away and brushed his hair into place. His face lit up with the smile she remembered.

Timor drew her over to where Elspa sat with Geri on her lap. Magda and Lisl were on their knees beside her, ignoring the continuing hubbub by the airship's stairs.

Elspa Latterby sat with her head bowed, almost curled around her baby sister. Kneeling beside her on the soaking grass, Ravna looked at the little girl. Geri Latterby had been such a happy kid, but ever since Ravna had heard her frightened voice coming out of Tycoon, Ravna's fears for the girl had grown.

Geri was not crying. Her expression was distant. She scarcely reacted to her sister's touch. But even though Geri didn't speak, Ravna could see. Two fingers were missing from Geri's right hand. Her left arm lay at a strange angle. She was dressed in a clean, warm robe . . . that didn't quite cover the scars on her neck.

"She's been tortured," said Magda. She looked like she was chewing on glass. "Tycoon must pay for this."

"No!" said Timor. "The big guy only helped her—" but the Children didn't seem to be listening, and he shut up.

———

Nevil Storherte was circulating, mainly among the Deniers. His camera gang was split between tracking him and watching the airship entrance. Giske was nowhere in sight, but Ravna noticed that Jefri and Øvin were closing in on the Chief Denier. If this was the end of the releases, there was going to be trouble.

"S'cuse me, s'cuse me," she said, working her way through the crowd around Nevil. Meantime, she muttered to her remote link: "Is this all the people we're getting?" The airship's hatch was still open, but Zek had disappeared from his post on the stairs.

Woodcarver's voice came back: "That could be . . . but hold off for now. The smart thing is to see how Nevil tries to explain the missing prisoners, *then* decide on the proper action."

"I don't think that's an option. Both Jefri and Øvin are going to start pounding on Nevil."

In any case, Nevil had noticed her approach. He waved in her direction. "Hei, folks, please let Ravna Bergsndot through."

Okay, for sure she was being set up. *So be it.* She nodded as casually as she could, and stepped into the open space in front of Nevil.

Nevil's smile was as gracious as the day when he ambushed her at the New Meeting Place—but this time Ravna was attacking: "Nevil, I've been talking to Elspa Latterby. That's her sister Geri who came down the ramp first and—"

Storherte blinked, but she'd given him enough warning that he actually managed to interrupt her: "Yes, I asked Tycoon to have Geri brought down the very first." His smile had morphed into sympathy and serious concern. "I'm afraid some Tines are insanely hostile toward humans. Some of them got to Geri before Tycoon could make a rescue."

There was muttered gobbling among the Best Friends and Benky's troops. Woodcarver's voice sounded privately in Ravna's ear: "I had to put up with a lot of this 'insane hater' talk while you were gone." But the Deniers were nodding sympathetically. Even some loyalist Children seemed to accept Nevil's point. And in fact, something like Nevil's claim was true, though apparently Nevil had decided never to mention Vendacious.

"Okay," said Ravna, "but we're still missing at least three packs and five humans. What about Pilgrim? What about Johanna? Remember her? The woman who loved you enough to propose marriage. Are we going to see any of these people today?"

Nevil's head rocked back a fraction and a certain "honest" indignation showed. "Whatever you may believe, I *don't* control Tycoon. He's my ally, and at least as honorable as your Woodcarver. You all know what that means." He let the words hang, creating lies out of pregnant silence. Just an instant before Ravna recovered from her own stunned indignation, Nevil continued, "I think we were all at the meeting on the Meadows. That did not turn out well. Sometimes a past wrong is so terrible that a person can't think straight. I think that's what happened to Tycoon that day. We're not going to get Johanna back today. Tycoon claims she's alive, but I'm not sure we'll ever get her back." He looked around imploringly. "And if we do get Jo back, then it would be up to *us* to judge her. I—I don't think I could do that."

Mr. Radio—the Zek end of him—was back at the top of the stairs, no doubt transmitting every syllable back to the Tropics. Zek's gaze flickered back and forth between Ravna and Nevil.

Ravna gave the singleton a glare, but her main attention stayed on Nevil: "Your lies are piled so deep, I don't know where to start shovelling. Woodcarver is *not* like Tycoon. Understand this, both you and Tycoon: Having peace with us means getting Johanna back. In the meantime, what about the others? Or do you claim they're criminals, too?"

"Yeah! What about Edvi?" That from Øvin Verring.

Magda Norasndot shouted, "And what about my sister's family?"

Nevil raised his hands. "Look, we didn't receive a good accounting till just after today's landing. Tycoon understands your point as well as anyone. He wants justice, too—but not all our missing friends were ever held by him. He knows nothing of Pilgrim. He has searched the wilderness and the Tropics, used all his contacts. Tycoon found Øvin's cousin, but too late to rescue him. Edvi's remains are aboard the airship. As for Jana and Basl Norasndot and their baby Kim—no sign of them was found anywhere. I'm so sorry, Magda." There were no glib condolences for Øvin. Maybe Nevil realized that any such might cause an explosion.

Magda had turned away as Nevil spoke. She was staring into the distance, maybe believing. The Norasndots had been missing well before the kidnappings. The two young parents had chosen to travel with a small trading group all the way to Woodcarver's old capital, through wilderness that was known to contain weasel nests. Their party had never arrived. Rescuers had found the remains of a weasel ambush, but no human bodies.

"So then, what about the *packs* that we *know* Tycoon is holding?" That was Jefri! Somehow he had slipped past the Deniers to stand next to Nevil. Jef had his left arm draped across Nevil's shoulders. It might have been a gesture of bonhomie—Jef was smiling—but Ravna could see that his hand was dug into Nevil's shoulder, and Jefri's other hand was holding something under his jacket.

Merto Yngva and his friends started forward, their hands slipping into the sling bags they carried. Every faction here was armed, but so far no one had been waving around their guns. Nevil gave Merto and company a strangled grin. "It's okay, guys." His smile stabilized as he looked at Jefri. "Hei, Jef. I think you've had firsthand experience with Tycoon. He can be obsessive, true?"

Jefri must have tightened his grip, because Nevil gave a little gasp. Now *that* was the properly eloquent way to respond to Nevil! Storherte continued, his voice strained. "Tycoon has been releasing folks in approximately the reverse order of captivity, the most needy first. Okay?"

Jefri shrugged. "I'm still waiting for results," he said.

"Well, this chitchat is just delaying the final releases." Nevil turned his head toward Zek. "Bring us the two remaining packs."

Zek disappeared from sight. A moment later, a pack member poked its snout into view. It came bouncing down the stairs, followed by three of its fellows. The pack's cloaks covered most its body, but she recognized Remnant Screwfloss—even down to the bodypaint disguise.

Certainly Flenser-Tyrathect did too. From his place behind the crowd, he bellowed something painfully loud. "*COMING THROUGH!*" was what the sound meant, and even a naive human would get out of the way. With two of him pulling White Tips' wheelbarrow, the pack really couldn't run. It didn't matter. Screwfloss came bouncing across the boggy grass, meeting his creator more than halfway. The two packs stopped a couple of meters apart, so close that coherent thought might be a problem. One of the remnant snuffled closer. It twisted its cape to lie down on the grass. Flenser came partway around it, almost reaching the others—and grooming the one it could touch.

"Are you getting this?" Ravna said to her remote link.

Woodcarver's voice came back: "Yes. I don't know what to think. I'm still pissed at Flenser for resurrecting Steel." But Woodcarver sounded more sad than annoyed.

Jefri had eased up on Nevil. Jef's smile didn't have quite the deadliness of seconds before. "One more now," he said.

Zek had disappeared again. So Amdi must be next. All eyes were on the stairway, but something made Ravna looked back at the crowd, especially around their ankles. The last six tendays had taught her to watch for low-flying surprises. Yes. There was a single snout poking out from between a couple of Children. Ritl was waiting in ambush.

Zek came back into view. He scanned the crowd, maybe pausing at the sight of Ritl. Then he arched his neck and waved at whoever was behind him.

The members that came to the top of the stairs were not as heavy as Ravna remembered, and one of the heads was slightly misshapen. "*Amdi!*" Jef shouted, turning away from Nevil. The rest of Amdi came out in rush, almost knocking Zek off the platform. They were all looking at Jefri. Amdi was saying something in Samnorsk, about Johanna, but it was so focused on Jef that Ravna couldn't make sense of it.

The stairs were wide but not eight-wide, and Amdi came down like an avalanche.

Ritl streaked out of the crowd, babbling loud abuse. She swung around in front of Jefri and turned toward Amdi. For a moment she had both Jefri and Amdi balked. She was chastising Amdi, or perhaps mocking him.

Amdiranifani drew in on himself, not responding.

After a moment more, Ritl made a spiky, dismissive noise—and ran directly *through* Amdi. The Amdi pack didn't scatter, but milled around, disconcerted by this foreign fragment of mind and fur and gender that was pushing and shoving past its members. Jaws were snapping and heads were turning, and when Ritl emerged on the other side, some of Amdi started after her. But Ritl didn't stop, and all of him were left behind, watching her departure. Ritl continued on her way, but more slowly. She was still emitting abusive noises, but now her head was stuck snootily in the air. She climbed the airship's steps, then turned to stand close to Zek.

All the packs were gobbling. Most of the Children looked puzzled, but Ravna suddenly imagined a human analogy. Amdi was like the teenage boy who long has been rejecting the advances of an aggressive girl. Then one day, she gives him a big smile and brushes close by him, running her hand through his hair as she walks—out of his life. And the boy is left looking around, relieved and suddenly wistful for what he's missed.

Jefri must have noticed the same thing. He was laughing even as he ran to Amdi, even as Amdi recovered and surrounded him.

———

So these were all the prisoners they were going to get.

Jefri came out of his huddle with Amdi and strode angrily back toward

Nevil. Ravna could guess the reason. Two of Amdi wore dark bandages on their heads. More torture. Amdi ran along after Jef, pulling at his trouser cuffs as if to restrain him.

"Hei, Nevil!" The shout came from uphill, at the edge of the forest. It was Bili Yngva. Giske was right behind him. She had both her sons! The older one was holding her hand, while she carried the other on her hip. Rolf walked just behind the trio. As she came closer, everyone could see that she and Rolf were smiling. Giske was clearly overjoyed; she couldn't keep her eyes off her two boys.

Giske and company walked to the edge of where the river grass turned marshy. Nevil and most of the Children ran to greet her. "What's this?" asked Nevil, his voice full of surprise.

Bili grinned back. "Giske has made a decision." He gave Giske an encouraging nod.

"Ah, yes," said Giske, looking back and forth across her audience. "Bili showed me what you've done up there in the caves. It truly is as comfortable as what we have on, on the coast. It was so good to see my husband again." Rolf gave her a pat on the shoulder. "And it's *so* wonderful to be with my sons!" She looked down at her kids and her smile blossomed. "I think that Best Hope is truly humankind's best hope. Please let me join you."

Ravna heard scattered gasps. Nevil looked as surprised as anyone. "Giske, you are *welcome* to join us." He stepped forward as if to embrace her, then turned to face the crowd. "All persons of goodwill are welcome to be a part of Best Hope!"

It might only have been Ravna's imagination, but in that instant she saw a flicker of revulsion cross Giske's face. Giske had given up a lot to be with her sons; she had not given up what she believed. But she answered the crowd's questions, still smiling, seeming to convince even her closest friends that she was happy in her decision.

Afterwards, Nevil looked well-satisfied with himself. Giske's apparent change of heart gave him the ideal platform for his Best Hope sales pitch and distracted from everything else. "We have a good relationship with Tycoon, my friends. If we all—those living under Woodcarver and Ravna and those of us here at Best Hope—if we all can cooperate, I think we can convince Tycoon that villains are rare among the humans. Someday, hopefully someday soon, even Johanna Olsndot can be returned to us." It was all a bit illogical, but he brought it off; some of the loyalist Children were giving him a serious listen.

Pray Nevil shuts down soon, thought Ravna. She wasn't up to listening to the monster. She had get out of here, chat with Flenser and Woodcarver, decide how to deal with Tycoon's failure to release Johanna.

Then Nevil looked her way, and she realized she should have walked away sooner. "So I'm pleading with you, Ravna. Will you and Woodcarver cooperate with us here at Best Hope?"

Ravna opened her mouth. *No peace! Not without Johanna. Not without word about Pilgrim.* For better or worse, she was preempted by words that boomed from the airship's hatch: "I think the question is, will Ravna cooperate with the Tines of Tycoon?" It was Zek. At least, Zek was making the sounds.

Nevil turned toward the airship, a stupefied expression flickering across his face. "Um, yes. Of course, I meant—" Nevil was actually floundering! It was heartwarming, even if it took a crazypack like Tycoon to make it happen.

Zek's voice rode over Nevil's: "However much we are allies, we have independent interests. I want to know Ravna and Woodcarver's intentions—"

"Yes, certainly—"

"—and I think a private meeting is in order."

Nevil's expression was fixed and blank. He turned and had a short, emphatic conversation with Bili. When he turned back to the crowd he was smiling again, literally putting the best face on the inevitable. "I agree, sir." He gestured in Ravna's direction. "I can only hope that Ravna has sufficient trust to meet with you."

And now Ravna was the center of attention. "I'd be happy to chat with Mr. Radio. As, as for privacy, he's welcome in one of our tents."

In her ear, Woodcarver said, "Good."

"That's not really private." Zek's voice was uncompromising. "Please come aboard. My employer guarantees your safety. You may leave as soon as you wish."

"No!" hissed Woodcarver. "Tycoon already has Johanna, and he's clearly nuts."

Across the field, Flenser was still visible, though beyond the range of focused sound. He was looking back at Ravna, and now gave her a surreptitious, encouraging wave. So this world's deepest student of treachery thought she should trust Tycoon—but wanted that advice kept secret?

Ravna slowly walked to the base of the airship's steps. Those seconds gave her no insight, but Scrupilo and Woodcarver were full of anxious objections. Benky and Øvin came running over. "You're not going in alone," Øvin said. Where was Jefri?

From the top of the steps, Zek gazed down at her. "I said private, Ravna. Leave these others behind you."

Nevil was looking less puzzled and more satisfied. This was outside his game plan, but he seemed to figure that no matter what, it would work to his benefit.

Woodcarver: "*Ssst!* What does Amdi say?"

Jefri and Amdi were still with the other rescuees, also beyond the range of focused sound. Like everyone else, they were just . . . watching. Jefri was on his knees, close to Amdi, his gaze fixed on Ravna. So was Amdi's. They looked very much as they had that day by the arrow trees.

"It'll be okay, Øvin," she said softly. And then more loudly: "I'm going aboard."

The inside of the airship smelled of packs and humans all crammed together. In fact, this was the ship she and Jefri had flown in; she recognized the dings and scratches. Funny that she hadn't noticed the smell then. Behind her, somepack ominously slammed the hatch closed. Ah. It was the innocuous steward, *not* a gunpack.

Zek turned left and led her along the main corridor, toward the bow. Ritl stuck close to Zek. She was making a singsong racket that probably didn't amount to anything. Every so often, Zek emitted a chord that meant roughly "please be quiet already."

Zek's new human voice said, "We'll talk on the command deck. It's been properly muffled against eavesdropping."

Woodcarver's voice came faintly in her ear, maybe inaudible to Zek: "Except for me and Scrupilo! Just pretend we're not here."

"That's fine," said Ravna. Her words might have been a reply to Zek's comment. She glanced down at the singleton. "So, Zek, who are you speaking for right now?"

Zek emitted a very natural-sounding human chuckle. "This is really just me, Mr. Radio. It's good to see you, Ravna."

Ah?

They had reached the end of the corridor. Zek scooted up the spiral stairs with Ritl close behind. Ravna had the usual problems winding around the spiral. Up top—

Up top, Johanna sat on one of Tycoon's perches. She had a huge grin on her face.

Ravna must have let out a shriek, for Johanna put a finger to her lips. "We're shielded, but there are limits—and we don't want people to think you're being tortured." She bounced to her feet and they had a big hug, not saying anything for a moment.

Then Ravna stepped back, speechless. She'd had surprises this big in the past—but rarely pleasant ones. Now she could only wave her hands inarticulately. On her private link, Woodcarver and Scrupilo sounded even more confused than Ravna.

"It's Johanna," Ravna finally said.

"Yup. It's really me. I'm really alive, unharmed, and happy to see you."

"And you're not a prisoner?"

"No . . . I could walk off this ship right this minute. But I'm not going to." Jo wasn't smiling anymore. She turned and looked through the gauzy quilting that covered the bow windows. Outside, the sun was so bright that you could see the landscape ahead of the ship. "I'm sorry to mislead my friends, though I'm sure Jefri already knows the truth." She waved at Ravna's tiara. "And I'll bet Woodcarver does too."

Ravna nodded and touched the tiara. Now Woodcarver's voice was audible in the room: "Yes, I'm here. Scrupilo, too. I think I've figured out what's going on. This is all to set up secret cooperation with Tycoon?"

"That's pretty much it. And *I'm* here to convince you of Tycoon's good will."

Ravna put in, "She looks fine to me, Woodcarver."

Woodcarver: "And what of Pilgrim?"

Johanna brashness disappeared. Suddenly, she looked like she'd walked into a wall. "I . . . I think Pilgrim is dead, at least dismembered. Vendacious chased him into the Choir. Woodcarver, can we talk about this, just you and me?"

Woodcarver's voice came back after the briefest of pauses: "Certainly, but later."

"O-Okay." Johanna turned back to the bow windows and didn't say anything more for a long moment. A couple of Benky's troopers were visible, patrolling back and forth. "I think this maneuver has fooled Nevil." Some of the sass crept back into her voice. "Tyco! Are you listening?"

Zek emitted a different voice now. It sounded like Timor, but grumpier. "Of course I'm listening. You want me to explain my change of hearts, right?"

"Yes. You spent years trying to find and kill me. What happened to change that? Keep it short since we have people outside waiting for Ravna."

"Very well, but I don't want anyone to think that I change my mind lightly. My resolve is nearly infinite. I would never have succeeded in the Tropics otherwise. And yet, part of me was always suspicious of Vendacious—even as he was enormously helpful to me. I noticed that the humans I met were not monsters. When Mr. Radio spoke up for the humans, that made me just curious enough not to kill Johanna the instant I saw her."

"Yes, thank you for that," said Jo.

"But it put me in a difficult position," Tycoon continued. "Fortunately, I'm a very quick thinker. I had to get away from Nevil and his beam gun. That weapon supposedly has a range of hundreds of kilometers and I needed hours of safe passage. So I grabbed Johanna and took off, all the time giving Nevil hope that I was still willing to deal with him."

Jo nodded. "Tyco and I had a very . . . tense afternoon. It was like what you saw on Nevil's stage, but spread out over hours. I think Scriber's invention notebook made the difference."

Tycoon: "Scriber used to bore me so much with his notebooks. Talking to Johanna, I could see Scriber had irritated her the same way. She hadn't murdered him, she'd just wanted to. We both had rejected him . . . and we both had spent years regretting the act. And I had been wrong about Johanna. I don't often make mistakes, but when I do, they can be of awesome proportions. I've used the tendays since to revise my strategies."

Scrupilo sounded skeptical, but in a geeky, nitpicking way: "If it took you hours to decide about Johanna, wasn't it a bit impulsive to toss Vendacious when you did? You hadn't even taken off."

"Well, um, as I said, I can be very quick thinking. In this case—"

Zek's voice changed in mid-sentence as Mr. Radio interrupted his boss: "In this case, it was Tycoon's employees who anticipated his wishes. You see, Vendacious died as the result of . . . a mutiny. Ravna, you know that Amdiranifani had been helping Ut and those other parts of myself he could contact. That wasn't all. Vendacious' operation was always on the verge of mutiny. Vendacious reveled in that; he had years of experience playing the game. Amdiranifani undertook to win through the crew. He lost two eyes in his first attempt—and that just made him come back smarter. Bits of me have seen Vendacious' victims before. I don't think he was *ever* outsmarted by someone he tortured—until Amdiranifani."

Amdi? Amdi the shy? Ravna almost said the words aloud.

Mr. Radio continued, "That day over Starship Hill, when we opened the drop hatch, Vendacious was going to toss out pieces of somebody—probably Amdiranifani. Amdiranifani was channeling sound all around the control gondola, never quite detected by Vendacious. He had nearly constant communication with Remnant St—Remnant Screwfloss, as those four were always moving in their cage, never giving Vendacious a chance to add up the sounds. Then Vendacious sent one of himself down to the open hatch and had the Cargomaster unshackle part of Amdiranifani. I—Ut—did just what Amdiranifani had planned for us. I slipped off my perch, got the keys from Cargomaster, and opened Screwfloss' cage. Those four are a bloody killer pack, do you know that? They turned the gondola into mayhem, hacking at Vendacious and anyone who was still loyal to Vendacious. Cargomaster tossed one of Vendacious out the hatch. Then Vendacious caught me from behind and cut my throat. About all I remember after that was lying on the deck, bleeding to death."

Mr. Radio's voice had remained steady throughout his story, but Zek's eyes were wide and he was trembling. Ravna reached out to him. "That's okay," she said softly. "We know the rest."

When Tycoon spoke again, he didn't sound quite so full of brag. "They did the right thing. I am grateful."

"Yes," said Johanna, grim and satisfied. "In the end, Vendacious got something like what he gave poor Scriber." She was silent for a moment. "So that's what happened. It's best if we keep it from Nevil as long as possible."

Scrupilo said, "Oh? Much as I like to mess up Nevil, what's the point? If Tycoon is *our* ally now, it doesn't really matter what Nevil thinks—at least as soon as Ravna's expedition gets back to Newcastle."

Zek emitted a negative, and then Tycoon's voice continued: "You misunderstand. Johanna Olsndot is my advisor—and also she's fun to have around—but I am *not* your ally. If you must, you may consider Johanna your ambassador to me. I regard the Domain as a business competitor, and though I . . . dislike Nevil, I will trade with him too."

Scrupilo was outraged. "That's absurd! You have no business opposing Woodcarver now. *I* say—" but then his voice faded off as he heard no support from Woodcarver.

Ravna looked at Johanna searchingly. "Are you really free to leave, Jo?"

"Of course she is!" said Tycoon.

Johanna smiled. "I've scouted things out, Rav. I figure I could shoot my way out of this ship, if I really wanted to."

"You could?" Tycoon sound a little abashed.

"Yup."

"Well then," said Ravna. *To hell with being diplomatically oblique.* "Is it really safe for you to go back to the Tropics, to live in this fellow's power?" Ravna had her own experience with *that.*

"Hmm," Johanna sounded thoughtful . . . and happy. Sometimes she had sounded this way when she was sitting with Pilgrim, petting him like a pack of friendly dogs. "Do I feel safe going back to House of Tycoon? Not entirely. Tycoon can be bastards if he's convinced *you're* a bastard. But he rescued both Timor and Geri, and he learned from them. Facts *can* eventually pound their way through his thick skulls. He hated me more than is easily imagined. Now? Well, I feel safer with Tycoon than I do, say, with Flenser. The reformed Flenser is a good guy. He probably saved my life by getting Woodcarver to bring that notebook—but he's sneaky to the point of being unpredictable." She hesitated. "Tycoon is the most successful rebuild I have ever met. He's spent ten years trying to reconstitute what he lost. Talking to him is almost like I've found a lost friend."

Tycoon: "I'm only partway there."

Johanna said softly, "Tyco, you'll never get all the way there. But I think Scriber would be proud if you make something even better from his memories. That's exactly the grand leap he would admire."

"Heh. . . . You're right!"

"Okay, then," said Ravna. "We're not allies, but trade partners and competitors. But I still question Tycoon's continued support for Nevil." This was really a point she'd expect Woodcarver to make, but there was only silence from that quarter.

Both Johanna and Tycoon started talking at the same time. "Let me take this one," said Johanna after they got sorted out. "*Nevil* thinks he has an alliance, but Nevil is lucky that Tycoon doesn't hate him quite enough to kill him. Of course, Nevil is no real friend of any Tines; I'm sure he figures *he's* using Tycoon. The longer he is fooled about the Domain's relationship with Tycoon, the better. In the end, Tycoon intends to build Nevil's operation into a credible human counterweight to the Domain, but one that owes its existence to playing ball with Tycoon."

"That's even less diplomatic than I would have been," grumbled Tycoon.

"Of course it was. As long as I'm your advisor, expect quite a bit of frankness with my friends back in the Domain."

Scrupilo made a spluttering noise. "If this scheme were a machine, it would fall apart." He gobbled a few more complaints, then returned to speaking Samnorsk: "If we are to be secret friends, then I demand a show of good faith. Tycoon must return what Vendacious stole, in particular, the computer Oliphaunt." That was Scrupilo's favorite piece of automation outside of *Oobii.*

"Sorry, Scrup," Jo replied. "That ain't going to happen. Tycoon is as much in love with my old plush toy as you are."

Scrupilo made more irritated noises. "We are giving up a lot, and being asked to tolerate Nevil, even enrich him. In return we get the promise of fearsome competition. And that's only if we can believe this aggressive crackpot from the Tropics. Can this possibly work?"

Ravna thought back on what she had seen down south, the factories that stretched for kilometers, that could save this world. "Oh, it can work." But at what price? She looked at Johanna. "You're also our friend to the Choir, Jo."

"I—of course."

"You know about exploitation, right?"

"Like on Nyjora, in the Age of Princesses?" She smiled.

Ravna didn't return the smile. "I don't want that to happen here, Jo."

The girl looked puzzled for a moment, but then she nodded very seriously. "I promise, Ravna. The Choir will not be exploited."

———

After Ravna left the *Pack of Packs*, Johanna remained on the bridge. It was late afternoon. The sun would be setting soon, but there was still enough light to see through the gauze quilting that she and the ship's steward had hung behind the bow ports. If she leaned forward and looked to the side, she could see most of Ravna's expedition. There was Jefri and Amdi. By now Jef knew she was okay. But there was Giske and Magda and Øvin. As long as Johanna continued this scam on Nevil, most of her friends must think her lost. That was a price Johanna was willing to pay, but she hadn't counted the cost to others, the pain of waiting and waiting to learn the terrible truth. . . . She could see Øvin sitting beside Edvi's little coffin. *We should have risked sneaking word back to those who were really hurting.* Instead, she and Tyco had only thought how to stick it to Nevil. That was a success, but now Johanna just wanted to flee this place.

Her thoughts were interrupted by Tycoon's new voice: "I say we take off for home." Johanna turned, saw Zek sitting on a throne right behind her.

Hooray! Aloud she said, "Ah. I thought you wanted to get a few more hours of intimidation out of this trip."

"I did, but I don't hear anything happening. Better to return my flagship to profit-making."

"You're leaving the troopship, right?" she said.

"Of course. Nevil can claim me as his ally, but never again is anybody going to murder people and then claim they were doing me a favor."

"Okay. Let's go." *Please!*

Zek departed for the ship's main hatch. A moment later Ta came up the spiral stairs, probably from the pilots' gondola. There were two members of Mr. Radio aboard *Pack of Packs*. Ta used the bridge's speaking tubes for some final directions to the crew; apparently he'd come up here in case Tycoon had something to say to her.

She heard the faint buzz of the steam induction engines, and a moment later—somewhat louder—Zek's voice booming out from the main hatch. The official spokescritter for Tycoon was announcing their departure and asking for help from Nevil's ground crews.

Ten minutes later, Johanna felt the last of the ties slip loose. *Pack of Packs* bobbed free, rising slowly from the valley floor. She had a last glimpse of Ravna's expedition and Nevil's group. The Deniers were waving solemn farewell. Most of Ravna's people were just staring. Everyone was out of sight before she could spot Jefri and Amdi.

The ship turned after it was above the walls of the Streamsdell. They flew back along the north side of the great river valley. Ravna pulled down the quilting so Ta and Zek could get a good view.

"That slit in the side valley. Is that the entrance to Nevil's cave system?" The voice belonged to Mr. Radio.

"Yup. If Woodcarver already knows about it, we should be able to get some maps."

Tycoon's voice grumbled: "I'm putting video senders at the top of my to-make list."

In less than a minute, Nevil's rat hole had slid beneath their view. The horizon ahead was an endless stretch of rock and snow and glaciers, lit by the setting sun. Flying at altitude, they had enough fuel for a nonstop return, but the trip would take all night and into the next day.

More than enough time to do one thing right. Johanna looked at Zek. "So where did you stow the commset?" she said.

Ta and Zek jabbed snouts at one of the low cabinets that lined the walls. It wasn't locked. She pulled out the commset, one of just two that had finally fallen into Tycoon's claws.

"What's that you're doing?" said Tycoon.

"I'm going to have a chat with Woodcarver."

Mr. Radio emitted spluttering noises, no doubt from Tycoon. "Nevil will overhear!"

"Nope," said Johanna. "Commset traffic is encrypted, and we're so high that I can send direct to the coast. Nevil will not even know we're talking."

Tycoon was silent for a moment. Then: "Very well. Sooner or later we do need a detailed discussion with this Woodcarver."

"That's true." Johanna put down the commset and looked at Ta and Zek. "But Tycoon, that's not what I'm looking for in this chat. Woodcarver and I—we need to talk about personal things. If you refuse me, I won't be mad, but . . . will you leave me alone for this, not even eavesdrop?"

It was a test Johanna had never intended to set. Truly, she didn't expect Tycoon to trust her this much.

Tycoon was silent for a moment. "This is about the Pilgrim pack, isn't it?"

"Yes."

Another silence. "Very well." Ta and Zek started toward the stairs. "But I want a full report on everything else!"

In just a few seconds, they were gone from the stairwell and the anteroom below. Johanna fiddled with the commset, trying to set up a session. Since the device didn't know where it was, and she didn't want it to ask the orbiter for a position, this was not entirely easy. But after a few minutes, she had clear green, and shortly after that—

"Woodcarver here. Johanna?"

"Yes. I said we should talk. Is now—?"

"Yes, now is fine. I'm alone in the thrones room."

"I'm alone as well. I—I wanted to tell you about Pilgrim. . . . "

Johanna described the agrav's last flight, the crash. Then there were the memories she tried not to think about. Maybe it was nuts to talk about each death now, to say all the things she had seen, but she did and Woodcarver listened. She wasn't sure how anyone could make sense of her voice by the time that she finished. Woodcarver did. She asked questions, wanted to know everything.

When everything was said, and Johanna's voice guttered to a stop, Woodcarver said, "He was dismembered, without a doubt." Her own human voice sounded almost normal, maybe speaking a little slower than usual: "And is he totally dead? Probably. But this is Pilgrim. When you get back to Tycoon's hideout in the Tropics—"

"I'll keep watch, Woodcarver. I won't give up."

They talked of Pilgrim for some time more. They had other memories of him. Johanna's went back ten years. Woodcarver's were a patchwork of encounters that extended far longer.

They must have talked for two hours. Outside, the Icefangs had faded to dark and stars ruled the horizon. The *Pack of Packs* continued to climb as it approached the mountain passes. The air was steady and smooth, quite unlike Jo's earlier passages over these peaks.

Reminiscence had turned into imagining how Pilgrim would have handled the present situation, and a general discussion of strategy. Johanna would definitely have things to report to Tycoon.

But strategy included discussing Tycoon himself: "Are you sure Tycoon is not snooping on this conversation?" said Woodcarver.

"I—" Johanna glanced at the speaking tubes. They were all capped. Where she was sitting, she had a good view of the stairs and the empty anteroom below. "Woodcarver, I truly believe he's not eavesdropping, but that's more a matter of trust than anything else—"

Woodcarver said, "In this case, what you believe may be the important thing. I've wondered for so long: what kind of creature is this crazypack?"

Oh! Johanna thought for a second. "He is weird. Numerous and weird. Sometimes he reminds me of Scriber, but he can be just as grumpy as Scrupilo. And then there's the businesscritter side of him. Imagine what Flenser would be like if his goal in life was to sell you trinkets and used wagon parts."

Woodcarver emitted a multi-hum that was surprised laughter. "Do you suppose I might have a chat with him?"

CHAPTER 44

Seven tendays passed.

The scam against Nevil continued successfully, so Johanna remained stuck here in the Tropics. It was the most fascinating time of her life. Each time she went into the Choir, she found something new. She'd returned to the River Fell, watched the rafts come and go. (Cheepers and company returned just sixty days after she did!) She'd walked the floor of a wild factory. Someday, she would pole a twinhull up the Fell to the North One Reservation—but when she'd suggested that to Tycoon, the Big Guy had completely lost his bluff brutality. He'd begged her not to be so stupid. Okay, he might be right about that expedition . . . Ha, she'd make the trip with Cheepers' riverboat sailors! Meanwhile, there was always the Great Pyramid of the Choir. Johanna loved to hike on the Pyramid. She had lots of reasons, including the whiff of danger.

On this day, she sneaked out of the House of Tycoon near sunrise, the coolest time of day. Heck, it wasn't more than 38 degrees Celsius and the rains had magically cleared away. Of course, the main reason for getting out so early was that this was before Tycoon roused himself. Half of him was much too nervous about the danger in her jaunts off the reservation—and the other half was too envious of them. Better to simply avoid the inevitable arguments that caused.

Zek and Ritl ambushed her just as she thought she'd made a clean getaway. Mr. Radio was hard to fool when he had good connectivity . . . and when the perverse Ritl was onboard.

"Going up on the hill again, aren't you?" said the twosome, speaking nearly perfect Samnorsk. Most of the pack must be participating.

"Yes. Don't tell," said Johanna. They walked through one of the myriad staff entrances and stood in the almost-cool morning. She waved at the sky, now mostly blue, but with cloud tops catching the first rays of the sun. "I think it's a perfect day for a walk in the Choir."

"For you, maybe."

The twosome strolled companionably along with Johanna toward the edge of the reservation, for once not relaying complaints about her possibly unhealthful hobbies. "Actually, I wanted to ask you a favor," said Mr. Radio. "We lost the video from the northern-looking camera last night."

"Yes, I know. It got knocked over. I'm pretty sure that was an accident. I'll reset it while I'm up there."

"Thanks." Mr. Radio seemed to realize better than Tycoon how important Johanna's hobbies might become. He also had his own ideas. This morning, those were about what to do with the coming glut of analog cameras, and how they might process the output without shipping it via Nevil. She looked down at the twosome and tried to hide her smile. Mr. Radio Cloaks was unique. Here, physically, it was just a twosome, what should have been a mental cripple. But Mr. Radio's real mind was spread across hundreds of kilometers, managing an enterprise as complex as major business ventures in early civilizations. She had no trouble dealing with that; there would be several more such packs if Scrupilo could build safer cloaks. There could be *millions* more once they had digital versions with user multiplexing. But Ritl gave this creature a special strangeness; Ritl was not wearing a radio cloak. To be part of this pack, she had to keep her head very close to Zek's, or better, Zek had to let her under his cloak. The result was a kind of fragmented communication. It was a small miracle that the pack could tolerate such a frail and sometime marriage. No wonder Ritl was training so hard to use Ut's cloak.

They were almost to the reservation's main gate. Like the fence, the gate was a flimsy thing, essentially a symbol. Sometimes the Choir would swarm across the boundary in what looked like a mad attack, an animal tsunami that would end all Tycoon's grand plans—but the swarmings weren't really attacks; the Choir had simply forgotten itself, and a wave of its excitement had brushed across the edge of the reservation. Afterwards, Tycoon's folks would repair the tattered cords and timbers, and all was as before.

Today, the mob looked placid, with only a few Tines coming nearer than five meters to the boundary. Beyond ten meters, the mob surged as thick as ever, but there were no stampedes in sight.

"The Choir is watching us," said Mr. Radio.

Johanna shrugged and waved to Tycoon's guards to slide open the gate.

Mr. Radio continued, "This isn't like when I come down here with Tycoon. This morning, the mob is watching intentionally, almost like a pack." The twosome stood a little apart from itself; Ritl had slipped partway out from under the cloak. Her tympana were free to listen to the mindsounds from beyond the fence. Mr. Radio continued, "I—I can hear the Choir. It's making more sense than usual. It's watching *you*."

"It's really okay," said Johanna. The sounds she could hear were just a cacophony of gobbling and hissing, sounds that animals might make—but she could tell that Mr. Radio was right. This happened whenever she approached the gate. Her gaze swept across the foothills of the fractal pyramid. What looked to the inexperienced eye like disorganized jostle, was repeated on different scales. She had learned to recognize mood and sometimes even intention in those patterns. What she was seeing here was a vast . . . anticipation.

She walked toward the opening gate, ignoring the way Tycoon's guard packs hunkered down on themselves. They were always nervous when the gate was open, choosing to imagine that when closed it gave them some protection.

Behind her, Mr. Radio Cloaks emitted an imperative squeak that meant something like "You come back here!"

She turned to see that Ritl had broken free of Zek and was walking purposefully toward Johanna and the gateway. Except in bloody hospitals, Johanna had rarely seen such impudence in a singleton aspiring to membership. Ritl was one tough customer. Normally that endeared her to Johanna; just now, it made her fear for Ritl. Johanna stopped in the middle of the gateway, ignoring the myriads watching her. She jabbed her hand at the critter, doing her best to imitate a Tinish warning wave. "Stop! You can't go out there, Ritl. It's safe for me, but not for you." At the very least Ritl would never return from the adventure.

The singleton kept coming, ignoring Radio's gobbling and Johanna's Samnorsk. Jo would have never thought this particular singleton would be susceptible to the Choir's siren call. No, Ritl seemed to be forcing herself forward. Mr. Radio hadn't moved but he sounded very worried. Ritl ignored them both. All her attention was forward, staring into the Choir. She moved slower and slower, as if the mob's mindsound were physical opposition. Finally she stopped, standing right on the boundary of the reservation. She'd lift a paw as if to take another step, then hesitate, then try again. The creature was shivering with the effort.

Finally Ritl said in very loud, very clear Samnorsk, "Well, crap! Double crap!" She lunged forward and tapped her snout on the ground beyond the gate, very clearly in the territory of the Choir. It reminded Johanna of a human child counting coup. And now that she had her claim to triumph, she scuttled back into the reservation.

Johanna gave the duo a little wave. Then she turned and walked into the open space beyond. Behind her, the guards quickly closed the gate.

———

Normally it took most of an hour to get to the top of the central peak. The way was a zigzag across the west face, more of a walk than a climb. The pyramid's surface was everything from undressed granite to cut quartz and jade. There was a hectare of copper and silver and gold plating, but that was scattered across the greater and lesser mounds. Tycoon had studied the pyramid for seven years now (from the air and from his palace below). Except for the recursive nature of the thing, he had not discovered much pattern to it—though it had grown steadily more durable and huge. The original that Remasritlfeer surveyed had been a muddy midden by comparison.

There was much to see as she walked back and forth and up and up. The House of Tycoon and what had been the Vendacious Annex were larger than any palaces of the North, but they were dwarfed by the foothills of the Pyramid. The airfield stretched westward from the palaces. She could see riderlet ponds there, though the full network of ponds did not respect the reservation boundary. The modern Choir was very tolerant of the "talking cuttlefish." That was fair, considering that the riderlets were the link that had made all this possible.

One of Tycoon's airships had just taken off, heading north. That was the personnel shuttle that touched down at every one of the far reservations. At the same time, she could see the daily flight from the Wild Principates coming in for landing. Most freight went by sea and river and caravan, but it was radio communications and those airships that kept Tycoon's markets in synchrony.

Beyond the airstrip stood the long gray rows of Tycoon's first Tropical factories. Nowadays they covered practically every square meter of the West Side. And beyond the western edge of the reservation she could see the Choir's wild factories. Those ramshackle structures were continually being ruined and rebuilt. Tendays would go by with no output. Then just when you concluded that the copycat effort had failed, suddenly product would spew out, misshapen or miswoven and barely recognizable. Mostly, such items were junk . . . but sometimes, as with their mirrors and glasswork, there were real improvements.

Jo was on the third switchback now, more than one hundred meters above the reservation. The crowds here were as thick as ever, Tines swarming over the network of smaller paths that branched from the main path she was on. They kept an open space around her, but it wasn't a well-respected boundary. Tines brushed against her, going this way and that. The sounds of the Choir pounded her, gobbling and hissing and honking, scraps of Interpack speech mixed with imitations of thunder and rain. Behind all this noise, there was the feeling of something louder, a buzzing in her chest and head—all a human could ever sense of mindsound.

Most of the creatures ignored her, but some gave Jo a squeak or a honk. There were little swirls of coherence, a godsgift that might last just for seconds. "Hei, Johanna!" was all those might say, but sometimes there was more, words that might have been relayed Tine to Tine from far away, even reminiscence of their time on the fleet of rafts. Perhaps one in five of these Tines was a full-pelted Northerner, but as often as not it was a hairless Tropical who claimed to remember Woodcarver's Fragmentarium.

Sometimes she'd see an unusually large, full-pelted Tines, or a pattern of black and white that reminded her of Pilgrim. Twice she had chased into the mob, careless of whether she bumped those who stood in her way, her only goal to get close to the familiar sight. And both times, when she got close she found only a stranger. Still, parts of Pilgrim could be out there, surviving in singleton form. She'd found little pieces of his attitudes in some Tines of the Choir.

The last switchback was only twenty meters long, but by now the sun and the clear sky had conspired to make the morning broiler hot. Sweat was streaming off her and those last twenty meters felt like a real climb. When she finally reached the summit, she was quite ready to stop and sip from her canteen. She leaned against one of the gilded spikes that bordered the tiny plaza at the top. If there was any logic to the pyramid, this open space would be the most holy of holies. To Johanna it was just a small muddy field—and the Tines on the summit usually avoided it.

The video camera was on the other side of the summit, and indeed it had been knocked over. She crossed the field and retrieved the box. The gadget was purely analog, *Oobii*'s design. It was so simple that Tycoon's factories could make it—by the millions, if the Choir was sufficiently enchanted by the gadget, or if somebody else was enchanted by video cameras and had something to trade for them.

She picked up the gadget, wiped the mud off the glass lens. Abruptly the box was talking Samnorsk at her:

"You took long enough." It was Tycoon's new voice. He still liked Geri's voice—said it sounded "pretty"—but he accepted that it tended to give human listeners the wrong impression. "Are you okay?" he continued. "I've had to slow some of the harbor operations. Even the Tropicals don't like these really clear days."

"I'll bet those were Tines with too much pale skin. We humans are dark-skinned all over, perfect for hot, sunny weather."

"Oh. Right. You know, sometimes the Choir isn't very careful of itself. I wonder . . ." Tycoon hummed to himself, no doubt coming up with something crazy. Then, slipping back into bossy mode, he said, "That's really neither here nor there. We need that camera you're holding. And *this* time, set it up so it doesn't get knocked down!"

"Hei, Tyco, if you want it perched at the top of everything, the mob is going to knock it down occasionally." Johanna reseated the camera and righted the tripod. Actually, the assembly was sturdy and bottom-heavy. It would have taken a bump from a large Tine—or the concerted effort of a group—to knock it over. *Well this is the heart of the Choir. Plenty of strange maybe-ceremonies happen here all the time.*

She struggled to shift the tripod and camera closer to the edge of the parapet, where it would have an unobstructed view. A dozen Tropicals moved in close to her, but they weren't objecting. Instead they bumped around among themselves. It was quite unlike the coordination of a real pack, but she could tell they were trying to help her move the equipment. Johanna and the moblet tipped the tripod this way and that, in effect walking the gear out onto the stony parapet.

She shooed them back and did the final placement herself, this time making sure that the tripod was wedged between the golden spikes of the parapet. Maybe Tycoon was watching her through his telescopes *and* the camera: "Be careful. If they think you're harming the pyramid—"

Johanna had been watching the Tines as she worked, with just that concern. "Nobody's complaining. You know I'm special to the Choir." That was probably true; in any case, she liked to tease Tycoon.

Tycoon made a grumbling response, but in Tinish. Then in Samnorsk: "I don't mind my employees risking their lives. I just want them to know that's what they're doing! Now, since you're up there, how about pointing the camera so we can get some useful information. I want coverage of the north road."

"Hei, I'm your advisor, not your employee," she replied, but she turned the camera toward the northwest horizon. The "road" was really a system of clearings that changed from tenday to tenday, but it extended nearly a thousand kilometers into the deepest jungle of the Fell Basin. At first glance, the Choir was the chaotic saturnalia that Northern packs always claimed, but something more complicated than nonstop joy was going on. The coast needed an enormous hinterland to support itself. With cameras like this—and the remote reservations—Tycoon was beginning to figure it out.

This pattern of Tropical life had existed in some form for centuries, but Tycoon's reservation had been a revolutionary upgrade—witness the Great Pyramid. Now that revolution was accelerating. Raw materials were flooding in and millions of manufactured items were streaming out. Woodcarver and the Domain saw this as a tidal wave of products. Ravna saw it as advancing her projects by decades in just a year or two. Johanna knew that what Northerners saw was just a fraction of what Tycoon's factories were producing. Most of that output—and all of the output from the new, far reservations—was being used *within* the Choir. Just stand at the output end of the factories. Watch the wagonloads of fabric and radios and solar cells being carted off along the North Road and the River Fell. On a really clear day—like today—this camera could follow the road traffic for many kilometers, see it split into tributaries, apparently reaching every nook and cranny of the Choir's domain.

Something had awakened here, the combination of the Choir and Tycoon and the shortcuts from *Oobii*. Jo knew it; Tycoon knew it. He never tired of bragging about the size of his "new markets"; sometimes the businesscritter in him literally rubbed its snouts together in glee. This camera and the reports that Mr. Radio made from the new reservations were all part of Tyco's ceaseless efforts to anticipate his customers.

"Okay," came the voice from the camera. "Point a little to south. That's good! Nevil may have his eye in the sky, but *I* know what's happening on the ground. And when I get better telescopes mounted on the video . . ." Tycoon's voice drifted off, his technical imagination taking over. When he resumed, he was back to worrying about her. "Now that you've got the camera set up, you should get yourself back down here. I have a godsgift on a dumb radio from North One. He says there's been some kinky moodshifting up there. If that propagates to us, there could be a sex riot on the Pyramid."

Johanna looked down at the House of Tycoon. Tycoon's audience hall was marked by a row of windows. The new ones were three meters high, but still tiny-looking at this distance. She'd bet Tyco was watching her from there. She gave a little wave. "Don't worry. I've seen that before. No big deal." That was a little bit of an exaggeration. "Besides," she continued, "I didn't come up here just to fix your silly camera. I want to sit and take in the scenery."

"*Grump. Mumble.*" The tiny speaker on the camera couldn't do justice to Tycoon's response, the mix of indignation and concern and envy.

Jo gave the palace another cheery wave and sat herself down on the parapet. In this swelter, her most extensive piece of clothing was her sunhat, and now she plunked it on her head. Black hair and dark skin were all very fine, but she still needed some protection against this sun.

Johanna looked out, but she wasn't watching the *physical* scenery. She liked to tell Tycoon that from here she had a clear view of the Choir's innermost thoughts. Tyco claimed she was spouting superstitious nonsense—but then he tracked the moods that swept across the Tropics like superfast weather fronts. *That* was marketing information.

Here at the City of the Choir, it all came together, a million times bigger than what Johanna had seen on the rafts. She leaned her elbows onto her knees, and stared off toward the northern horizon. This world was in the Slow Zone, not the Beyond, not the Transcend. Most intelligent life in the galaxy had originated in this primordial ooze. Nothing much smarter than human could survive Down Here. So no way was the Choir a superhuman intellect. Right? It was the sort of question that made Johanna wish she knew more about Slow-Zone limitations. The subject had never been big in the High Lab. The grownups were too busy becoming God to waste their time on the problems of lesser minds.

Very soon the charade with Nevil must be abandoned; the cooperation between Tycoon and Woodcarver was too blatant to disguise. *My friends will know I'm alive. I can visit them!* Ravna would be able to come down here and see Greenstalk, and see what the Choir was really like. Commset chats were not enough. There were things Ravna didn't understand—like that promise she'd asked of Johanna, to save the Choir from exploitation. In one sense that was an easy promise to keep. But at the level of individual Tines, of Cheepers—the problem was just the same as Johanna had argued with Harmony Redjackets and even with Pilgrim. . . .

Johanna drew herself a little further under the shade of her broad hat. It would be great when she could travel back to the Domain, but there were so few humans in the world; she couldn't imagine finding anyone now. Even Ravna was better off, *at least if my stupid little brother will get his act together.* From what Johanna could tell, Jef alternated between thinking Rav was too good for him and regarding her as the agent of ultimate evil.

Finally, the sun was too much. Johanna stood and started slowly down from the summit. She often hit an emotional low just as she retreated from the pyramid. Sometimes she thought the Choir's mood changed too. *Maybe the Tines are unhappy to see me go!* Hah, absurd of course. And yet, after losing the High Lab, losing her parents, losing the promise of Nevil . . . after losing it all, she had a fate that was kind of a marvelous thing. She knew that Nevil's gang had called her the "Dog Lady." Well, they were right. She had the fragments, the packs, and the Choir. It was a weird trade she had made, and maybe she didn't care about the rest.

CHAPTER 45

Today was the longest day of summer. For many Tinish nations, that was a big holiday. Here in Woodcarver's Domain, the holiday was celebrated, but it came in the middle of almost seven tendays when the sun never set. The dayaround tendays had always been a time for unending, often joyous, activity. There was an unrelenting enthusiasm about the sunlight, something that only total exhaustion could correct. Both Children and Tines worked almost nonstop, slowing down just a little when the sun got lowest, what would be the starry dark in any other season. Even then, there were often parties at low sun, exhausted kids *dancing*.

On this Longest Day, Ravna took a low-sun break of her own. Coming out from her private entrance to *Oobii*, she skirted the western edge of the Meadows. The path should have kept her out of sight of where the kids partied. But this time she ended up walking past Children and Tines playing with the gliders that Scrupilo had recently built. She stood in awe for a moment, forgetting why she was outside so late. Øvin Verring was running straight toward the cliff's edge. He leaped over the dropoff and popped his wings. Ravna felt an instant of stark fear. True, the glider rig was an *Oobii* synthesis of a thousand civilizations' history, optimized for exactly these conditions—but there was not a bit of automation aboard the contraption! It could tumble and fall, and she had already seen enough bodies rain from the sky. . . . But the wings did not tumble. The glider sank smoothly, flying straight. And then Øvin, the mind onboard, took the glider into a shallow bank, searching for updrafts, climbing across them until he was *above* his launch point, soaring almost as if he had agrav.

A sigh went up from the Children on the ground, maybe remembering heritage lost. Then everyone was cheering, and the packs among them were complaining because there was no way *they* could participate in the adventure. *This is so dangerous,* thought Ravna. Someone turned and saw her standing there. A year ago, Ravna would have had to stop this, and the kids would have known that and everybody would have been hurt and embarrassed and irritated. More recently, after her return, it would have been worse; they might have meekly obeyed her! Now when the Children saw her, they waved. And Ravna waved back . . . and few moments later, another glider sailed out over the abyss. Ravna stayed at the fringes of the crowd, watching the launches. She counted five of the craft in the air, circling back and forth along and above the cliff face. These vehicles would never be of use in real applications. *But the pilots may be.* It all depended on how fast other tech progressed.

Ravna watched for a few minutes more, then drifted back from the crowd and continued on her walk. The shouts of excitement faded behind her. Ahead, sunlight sparkled blindingly off the north end of the Hidden Island straits. The island itself was set in a kind of silhouette by the brilliance of the surrounding water. Her path led around the northwest face of Starship Hill, toward a very special place.

––––––––

The Cemetery for Children and Tines. She had been here only once since her return, a memorial for Edvi Verring and the Norasndots. She hadn't been here by herself since that rainy, treacherous night with Nevil. *You'd think that that night would have cured me of my attraction to this place.* Okay, the important lesson was that if she ran into anyone up here, she should question the coincidence very seriously.

And truly, this visit wasn't one of desperation. Things were going *well*. Come this winter, Scrupilo's Cold Valley lab would fabricate its first microprocessors. When those made it into Tycoon's production stream, tech would be everywhere. Something like civilization would be right around the corner.

Even Jefri seemed to be doing okay. He and Amdi were working with the reconstituted Screwfloss to build cargo highways. Both Woodcarver and Flenser were sure that Jef wasn't acting as Nevil's agent. More and more, it looked like he would stay with the Domain.

Ravna walked between rows of headstones set in a field of spongy moss. At the memorial, she'd noticed a few new stones, not just those for Edvi and the Norasndots. There'd been flowers on the graves of Belle Ornrikak and Dumpster Peli. The Children, at least some of those who remained with the Domain, were turning to older forms of remembrance. It was something they argued about among themselves.

Today—tonight—she had one particular person she wished to remember. Pham's rock, the huge irregularly shaped boulder that crowned the promontory, was at the far end of the field. She could sit on the north side for a time, leaning against the sun-warmed rock.

She came around the rock—and was confronted by eight Tinish heads looking back at her.

"Ah! Hello, Amdi."

"Hei, Ravna! What a coincidence."

The pack occupied almost every flattish niche on the north side of the rock. Amdi had regained most of his weight, and nowadays he wore rakish eyepatches on two of his heads. He didn't really seem surprised to see her. Of course, he probably had heard her coming from forty meters away.

Amdi shifted aside to make room for her on a human-butt-sized flat space.

As Ravna sat down, he said, "You up here to talk to Pham?" There was no sarcasm in his question.

Ravna nodded. *I was.* She looked down at Amdi's nearest heads. He was already snuggling close. "What are *you* doing here, Amdi?"

"Oh, I come up here a lot now. You know, to sit and think." *Amdi was into solitary contemplation? Could he be that changed?*

He settled a head in her lap and looked up at her. "Really! Well, today I had another reason. I was waiting for someone."

She brushed her hand across the plush fur. "Am I that predictable?" So not a coincidence at all.

Amdi shrugged. "You're somebody to depend on."

"And why were you waiting for me?"

"Well," he said mischievously, "I didn't say you were the person I was waiting for." But he didn't deny it.

They sat there for a time, warming in the sun, watching its glare reflected off the chop in the straits. There really was peace here, even if it didn't feel quite the same with Amdi above, below, and beside her. Amdi reached another head up to her. Petting it, she could feel a deep scar under the fur. It ran from the throat to just short of a fore-tympanum. So, more of Vendacious' work. "Don't worry," said Amdi. "It's all healed, good as new."

"Okay." But not his two eyes; those could not be fixed as easily as his other wounds or Ravna's broken face.

Just now there wasn't a single boat visible, and the country further north was lost in the glare. Ravna and Amdi might be the only human and pack in the world.

Correction. One of the kids' gliders had drifted into view from the south. It had caught some marvelous air current and climbed halfway up the sky, angling around the curve of Starship Hill. As it turned to loop back it seemed to hang, motionless, in the sky.

Amdi poked a snout in the direction of the aircraft: "You know, that's another reason why we need radio cloaks. A single pack member is way smaller than a human. It could fly fine, with all the rest on the ground—or on other gliders!"

Contemplative mood broken, Ravna grinned. "I remember my promise, Amdi; you'll get your own radio cloaks. Scrupilo is working on that second set, but you know the problems. Vendacious did some very brutal things to create a pack that could use the cloaks."

"But Flenser used the cloaks straight away," said Amdi. That had been eleven years ago, at the Battle on Starship Hill. Ever since Amdi had been puppies—even before Ravna had met him—he had been wild about radio cloaks. She remembered his endless whining to be allowed to wear radio. Today he was more mellow: "We'll figure it out. Just you wait, Ravna. Radio cloaks will make us packs be like *gods!*"

"Hmm." Amdi's problem was his limited experience with real gods.

Amdi was chortling to himself. "And if we don't do it, Tycoon will. You know, Mr. Radio is now his closest advisor—not counting Johanna."

"Hei, Johanna is on *our* side."

"'Advisor,' 'friend,' whatever. My point is, it's Radio who is his closest Tinish advisor. He's even more enthusiastic about cloaks than I am. He thinks that with clever broodkenning a tensome—maybe even a twelvesome—could have coherent intelligence."

Twelve. Like Tycoon's pack-of-packs logo. "Down Here there are other limits on mind, Amdi. You're not going to get much above the most brilliant human genius, except in the Transcend."

"Yes, okay, right. But the way radio packs can *use* their smarts will be amazing. Mr. Radio is already pretty smart. He's back to eight. You know he found a replacement for Ut?"

This question was delivered with shy, almost embarrassed, sidewise looks.

"Ritl?" said Ravna. "She's able to use Ut's cloak?"

Amdi gave a nod. He was smiling in a wobbly way.

"Well, good! I mean, I know she caused you problems, Amdi. But the critter was desperate. She didn't mean to do you harm."

"Oh, she meant to do me harm all right! She tried to break me up. I was terrified of her. But yes, she was in a desperate situation. Part of me misses her, but all of me is relieved she's gone. You know, she's turned out to be the keystone member of Mr. Radio. She makes him smarter and a lot more articulate. I talk to Mr. Radio when he reaches up here. Now that Ritl is not on the make . . . well, Mr. Radio is really a nice fellow. The story of Ritl and Radio would make a nice Tinish romance novel . . . if I were into writing romance fiction, I mean. Which of course I'm not."

Ravna looked around at him. Maybe he really had come up here to make peace with himself. "What about your own problems, Amdi?"

"I've . . . made progress. Being all puppies made me too human. I don't know how you two-legs can deal with death. The version that packs suffer is bad enough." Amdi was silent for a moment, mostly looking down. "Ritl made me see that I can't stay me forever." He look back up at her. "I learned from Vendacious, too. I learned that death can be the least of your problems. Fooling him wasn't that hard, but after he started poking out my eyes . . . finding the courage to continue with my scheme, that was harder than anything I had ever imagined."

He spoke the words softly, solemnly. Ravna noticed that every one of him was looking at her. It was as though a curtain had been drawn aside. Amdi had been to hell and back. That could happen to anyone with enough bad luck and then enough good luck—but Amdi had *engineered* his return. During his terrible time with Vendacious, the child in him had become something deep and quiet and strong.

Ravna nodded and gave him a pat. "So what's next for you, Amdiranifani?"

Amdi looked away, and she sensed that his moment of stark openness had passed. He squirmed around for a moment, then said, "You and me and Jef had some good times, didn't we?"

Okay, Amdi, and she replied in a like tone: "You mean when we weren't running for our lives, and when Jefri and I weren't playing at being enemies?"

"Yes. *I* would never be your enemy, and Jefri . . . well, you know Jefri loves you, don't you?"

"You both loved me when you were little, Amdi."

"I mean now, Ravna."

That was what I was afraid you meant. Now it was her turn to look down at the ground, embarrassed. "Oh, Amdi, I—"

Amdi tightened up all around her. The one of him closest to her face tapped her cheek gently. "*Shh,*" Amdi's voice whispered. "I hear someone coming."

Of course Ravna heard no such thing. No one was visible on the hillside below them. Even the glider had flown out of sight, leaving the sky to the birds and the low sun. She gave Amdi an acknowledging pat and leaned back against the rock.

Yes, there was someone coming up the south path, out of sight behind them. The squish-crunch of boots on moss sounded like a single human.

Ravna and Amdi sat silently for another thirty seconds. The footsteps came along the west side of Pham's rock—but the visitor wasn't headed here.

It was Jefri Olsndot; he took the path down to the two headstones that sat nearest the end of the promontory. He and Johanna had picked that place for their parents. As much as Pham Nuwen, Sjana and Arne Olsndot had fought the Blight. *So Jefri, what do you believe and what do you deny?*

Jefri knelt between the headstones. He put one hand on each, and stared out over the glittering sea. After a long moment, he shook himself, like a man waking or remembering an appointment. He stood and turned—and saw Amdi and Ravna watching him from Pham's rock.

"Hei there, Jefri!" said Amdi. He waggled some noses in a tentative wave.

Jefri approached with measured tread. He stopped three meters from the rock and glared at both human and pack. "What is she doing here, Amdi?" His words were flat and angry.

"Just a coincidence?" The pack looked at Ravna for confirmation.

"That's what you told me, Amdi." She glanced at heads that were looking everywhere else. Just now, Amdi reminded her of a way-too-smart teenager. Well, literally, he *was* a way-too-smart teenager.

There was no good humor in Jefri's reaction. He closed in on those of Amdi who were farthest from Ravna. "*You* suggested meeting here. *You* picked the time. I show up half an hour early, and I find you—and, and *her*—" a look in Ravna's direction, "waiting for me."

"I'm *sorry,* Jefri!" Amdi's voice rose, childlike. "I just couldn't stand the idea that you, I mean that we—" He dithered a second, then his voice took off on a new tangent. Now he sounded a little like the salesman he had learned to be in the circus. "We should talk about this. We really should." The one on the ledge above Ravna moved aside, and the one that had been resting its head on Ravna's lap climbed up to fill the gap. At the same time, another patted the space beside Ravna that had just been vacated. "Here, why don't you sit down and we can all explain this to each other."

This chatter lost some of its audio fidelity about at the word "explain," when Jefri grabbed the one who had been patting the open space and shoved him against Ravna.

"Oops, sorry," Amdi said in an aside to Ravna.

She had seen these two play this roughly, even since their return from the Tropics, but there was no playfulness in Jefri right now. He'd have been taking a chance with his life if he used this kind of force against a stranger pack as big and heavyset as Amdiranifani had become.

"Okay, we'll have our talk." Jefri sat down.

Now one of Amdi was sandwiched between him and Ravna. The rest of the pack surrounded them. Altogether, Amdi seemed a bit disconcerted. He looked back and forth at himself for a moment, then patted Jefri gingerly and crept in close to his old friend. When Jef didn't respond, Amdi continued in his showman voice, the volume turned down to an intimate purr: "Okay, I confess. Though this was a coincidence, I gave it some help. I was pretty sure Ravna would come up here at low sun. If she hadn't, I would have thought of something else to get us together. We three have been through so much, don't you know? I didn't want it to seem to Ravna that Jef and I were sneaking off—"

"What?" said Ravna.

"Amdi, I swear, you have no right—"

"You two are leaving, Jef? I thought, I thought you were staying with the Domain."

Jefri didn't look her in the eye. Maybe he was too busy glaring at first one of Amdi and then another. "We aren't sneaking off. Amdi is just jerking you around."

"I am not!"

Jefri finally looked at Ravna. "This may seem like another betrayal, but I've talked to Woodcarver and Flenser about it, ah, just this afternoon. You and Johanna would have learned soon enough, but I really didn't want to argue about it with either of you." And as an aside to Amdi he said, "How could you do this to me?"

"You're going to Best Hope?" she said. *Powers, how I hate that name.*

Jef nodded. "But it's not what you think. I'm not doing any good around here. No one really trusts me. You—"

"I trust you," said Ravna. *As long as you stayed, I could hope.* "Why are you going, Jefri?"

Jef hesitated, then: "Okay. You remember when we were on the road, you suggested I look for testable evidence about the Blight. But what could I find, Down Here, ten years later? Now . . . I think I have a chance. Bili stole equipment from the Lander, equipment that idiot-me never recognized. I know Bili. By now, I even know Nevil. Watching them, watching what they do with this gear—one way or another, I'll figure out what I have to do."

"That's—" *insane.* "That's not reasonable, Jefri. After you saved my life, Nevil has less reason to trust you than almost anyone."

"I've been working on that. Vendacious is gone. Chitiratifor and company are gone. No one on the other side knows what went on with you and me except Tycoon's people. And Tycoon is perfectly happy to feed Nevil a story that will suit me."

"Huh?"

"I had Amdi work out all the details the last time Mr. Radio was up here."

Amdi shrank down a fraction. Now he had Ravna glaring at him. "It'll be okay, Ravna," he said.

Jefri nodded, deeply into his crazy spy plan. "Nevil won't trust us, but we'll be good propaganda for his cause—I-I'll speak out in his favor. He'll want to keep us around. And we've got a snoop-proof way to report. Amdi has a set of Scrupilo's new prototype radio cloaks; he's been practicing with them. Amdi will be Woodcarver's ambassador to the Deniers."

Ha! She glanced around at Amdi. "What do you *really* think of Jefri's plan?"

Amdi's gaze—all his gaze—was steady. "I think it's the best we can do, and it's *our* plan," he said.

"Oh." She wasn't going to be able to stop this. She sat back, remembering their endless, futile arguments. Her suggestion had turned into an incredibly dangerous long shot or—her gaze snapped up to Jef's face as she remembered the promises he'd made about Nevil and the Disaster Study Group. "Oh, Jefri—"

Jefri shook his head. "You see why there was no point in this meeting?"

Amdi was watching them from all sides. The one between Ravna and Jefri had its snout stuck up toward them, its gaze twitching back and forth. Now it wriggled free and hopped to the ground. The ones behind Ravna were nudging her like a gentle hand, toward Jefri. One of those above gave Jef a sharp tap on the head. "Say what you never say!" demanded Amdi, his voice adult and imperative. And then suddenly, the pack was scarce.

Jef gave his head an angry shake; he looked as surprised as Ravna felt. He was silent for almost ten seconds, his eyes averted. Finally he turned back to Ravna. When he spoke, his voice was stiff: "You still think I'm eight years old, don't you?"

"Huh?"

"An incompetent little boy with deadly, false beliefs."

"Jefri! I—"

He gave her a jagged smile. "Well, I'm not little anymore, and my beliefs are under review, but"—The smile went away, and his gaze was direct and angry.—"I was a terrible fool, and my shitheadedness almost got you killed."

Ravna was too shocked to speak. She gave him a vague shake of her head.

Jefri rolled right on: "I watched you for seven tendays, up close, in terrible circumstances. I've learned things about you I never knew, things *you* don't know either. See, whether you're right or wrong about the Blight, you're every bit the kind of princess you used to talk about . . . and compared to that, I *am* an incompetent child."

Jefri paused and looked away. Somehow, Ravna didn't think that he was waiting to hear her response—which was good, because she couldn't think of a thing to say.

His gaze turned back upon her. "But you know, I am Sjana and Arne's son. And as Tycoon endlessly reminded us, I am Johanna's brother. There will come a time when you think more of me."

And then Jefri ended their discussion in a new way. His arms swept around her, drawing her into a thorough and uncompromising kiss.

————

Ravna remained on the rock after Jefri and Amdi departed. After all, she had come up here to consider the most important things: The next thousand years. And now, the last five minutes.

The sky gleamed too bright to see any star except the lowering sun. No matter. When Ravna was on *Oobii*'s bridge, she kept one special spot marked. Even here, even without her tiara, she could point toward that spot, just thirty lightyears out, the best estimate of the Blighter fleet's location. So far, there had been only that one Zone temblor, back in year two. *Pray I have Jefri and the Tines and the time to prepare. Down Here, we have the edge.*

The End

ABOUT THE AUTHOR

Vernor Vinge is the author of the Hugo Award–winning novels *A Fire Upon the Deep, A Deepness in the Sky,* and *Rainbows End.* His other novels include *The Peace War* and *Marooned in Realtime.* He also wrote the seminal short novel *True Names.* He has won two Hugo Awards for shorter works, and two Prometheus Awards for Best Libertarian Fiction. A mathematician and computer scientist noted as a visionary proponent of the Technological Singularity, he lives in San Diego, California.